Havoc

Visit Paul Henke on his website
for current titles and future novels at:

www.henke.co.uk

or e-mail Paul at

henke@sol.co.uk

Havoc

Paul Henke

GOOD READ PUBLISHING

First published in 2004 by Good Read Publishing
A Good Read Publishing paperback

10 9 8 7 6 5 4 3 2 1

ISBN 1-902483-06-5

Typeset by Palimpsest Book Production Limited,
Polmont, Stirlingshire
Printed and bound in Great Britain by
The Bath Press, Bath

Good Read Publishing Ltd
PO Box 1638
Glasgow
G63 OWJ

Acknowledgements

To Anne Buhrmann, Mary Young and Rosemary Bowe for
their editing, proof-reading and pertinent comments. To
Wendy and the staff at Palimpsest – as helpful as always. A
special thanks to Frank McClendon in Nevada for his support
and keeping me abreast of events on his side of the pond.

Havoc

Prologue

His passport described him as a reporter. When pressed, George C. Clarke *also* described himself as a reporter. The truth was, he hadn't reported much in over a year. In fact he had been sliding down the totem pole for nearly a decade now. And at fifty-five he had few places left to go. Which was why he'd accepted this latest assignment to Egypt. His editor back in New York had made it clear – either go to Africa or clear his desk. So he'd gone. Now here he was in a crummy bar in Cairo, drinking too much aquavit and beer chasers.

He could trace his slide from grace to exactly eight years ago. *Happy Anniversary*, he toasted himself in the dirty mirror lining the bar. Getting home from the Moscow trip early and finding his wife in bed with another man had been a shock. Breaking his jaw had been satisfying but expensive. She'd got the house, the kids, and the portfolio of stocks. He'd been lucky not to go to jail for assault.

Alcohol cured his despondency for a while. He'd started drinking. Only in the evenings at first. Within a year it had been lunchtime. Now lunchtime started around eleven o'clock and frequently finished twelve hours later. His hand shook as he raised the shot glass of clear liquid to his lips. He threw it down in one smooth gesture and followed it with a mouthful of beer. The shaking stopped.

He took stock of the dump he was in. The room held about fifty scarred and battered tables, arranged to face the small stage. A fat belly-dancer was lethargically going through her routine.

1

The place was half full or half empty, depending on your outlook. For him, like his glass, it was half empty. He knew he needed to get back to the conference centre to cover the afternoon's session, but what the hell. He'd get what he needed from one of the others. Hacks stuck together. Usually.

Fans turned slowly, re-distributing the smoke-filled and oppressive air. He signalled the barman for a refill and watched hungrily as the liquor was poured. To delay the moment of drinking, he turned his back on the bar and surveyed the room. The clientele consisted mainly of men, with a few prostitutes adding colour here and there. One table in the corner caught his interest. There was something vaguely familiar about the man sitting with his back to the door.

Clarke turned back to his drink. It would come to him if he gave it long enough. He stared at the drink like it was his enemy, before wrapping a clammy hand around the glass. His was the action of the practised drunk and he drank it greedily. Lighting a ciggarette, he leaned back against the bar and tried to stop thinking about the next shot. The gyrating woman did nothing for him and he lost interest as soon as he looked at her. The occupants of the other tables showed the same lack of interest. He glanced again at the corner table. Two Europeans and two Arabs, in deep discussion. His reporter's instincts twitched. It was a feeling he hadn't had for many years.

With beer glass in hand he moved to an empty table for a better look. He definitely knew the man. But who was he? His memory, befuddled by years of alcohol abuse, was working slowly. Even one of the ragheads appeared familiar.

What the hell, there was no harm in it. The thought had barely formed when he found himself at the table, looking at the four men.

'Say, don't I know you?' The reporter held his hand out to one of the Europeans, a silver-haired man about his own age.

'I don't think so. This is a private conversation. Please go.'

'Sure I do,' Clarke withdrew his hand, too drunk to notice the consternation he'd caused. 'It'll come to me in a moment.'

The man he had addressed said something to one of the Arabs. The man nodded and quickly rose.

2

'Hey,' Clarke protested as he was hustled towards the back door.

Another man crossed the room to help. Clarke found himself in a filthy alleyway at the back of the club. The Arab slipped a stiletto through the base of Clarke's skull and into his brain in a flash of agony. He didn't die for three seconds. Time enough to make the connection. *Charles Gustav.*

1

Know your enemy. Hunter had been studying his prey for several minutes. Watching the palm spider weave its delicate track across his arm. Tenacious, a survivor, it scurried into the bed of rotting leaves as soon as Hunter made a minuscule movement of his fingers. Hunter closed his eyes, allowing the sensations of the jungle to pour over him. Instinctively he filtered the noises. Directly above was the hiss of a tree-rat. The TIFAT operative hoped the rodent would stay until nightfall, when the other, larger mammals went marauding.

Hunter had been in the jungle on three previous occasions and had hated each one. His love was the sea, his passion was diving and sailing. Being in a hide in Suriname was not his idea of fun. He and his team had been there for four days. The smallest country in South America, Suriname in recent years had become a major route for the transhipment of drugs destined for Europe. According to intelligence reports, the heavily escorted mule train of cocaine that they were waiting to ambush was worth in the region of half a billion dollars. The sums of money involved were astronomical.

There were ten of them in the team and most of them lived on incomes of less than £32,000 per annum, which included special services pay . . . And here they were yet again putting their lives on the line. He grinned mirthlessly. Neither he nor the rest of the team would have it any other way.

Their ingress into the country had been secret. Official permission for the operation would never have been forthcoming. For eight of the last twenty-two years the military had been in power. Suriname was trying to strike a fine balancing act between the civilian and military rulers. No permission and no official recognition. It was too easy to be betrayed by a corrupt pen pusher. There were many hands greased by the huge bribes that oiled the trade.

They had parachuted in from a Hercules W2, normally used for weather reconnaissance and operated by the Meteorological Research Flight based at Boscombe Down, in England. The white and grey fuselage, with its long pointed nose sticking out far in front of the plane, operated mainly in the northern hemisphere. A special visit to Brazil had been arranged at short notice and the plane despatched. They had refuelled from Hercules C1K tankers twice before arriving in Suriname airspace. The team had bailed out high, at night, aiming for a clear spot in the jungle. Not long ago the jump would have been considered suicidal. But using satellites and mobile positioning gear they could leap out at 25,000ft with pin-point accuracy. They had landed safely with all their equipment, bivouacked for what was left of the night and at dawn began a forced route march through the interior. Two of their number had taken the opposite direction. They had the heaviest loads to carry but had only five kilometres to cover. They would make the journey four times ferrying the back-up equipment. Hunter hoped they wouldn't need it.

The remainder of the team had twenty klicks to travel. Thanks to up-to-date satellite mapping, they were steered along existing paths, past impressive waterfalls, to the track they wanted. The trip had taken under five hours. It had seldom been necessary to machete back the encroaching jungle. Each man carried 65lbs on his back, carefully packed into his bergen. The going was tough, with the temperature in the nineties and the humidity over eighty. Sweat poured out of them as if they were under a shower. They chewed salt tablets, sipping their specially prepared water – doctored with much needed chemicals – at regular intervals. Rests were taken five minutes every hour. No one complained. It was what they had signed up for.

The nine men and one woman in the TIFAT patrol were

hand-picked special services operatives from the world's best. Hunter would have trusted any of them with his life and often had. Their skills and tenacity had carried the team through countless disastrous situations. A mine and bomb-disposal diving specialist in the Royal Navy, Hunter led the team. His second-in-command was Joshua Clements, an American on secondment from Delta force. In the party were Jan Badonovitch, a Russian Spetsnaz, Claude Masson, a Frenchman from Commandos de Recherche et d'Action. Doug Tanner – the only African American, was a SEAL from Louisiana. Frank Hales – a New Yorker seconded from the Green Berets – was the other American on the team. All the others, REME sergeant Don Masters, a quietly spoken, tough Scotsman, David Hughes, a SAS sergeant from Wales, and Douglas Napier, a lieutenant with the British Special Boats Service, were British. The tenth person – Ruth Golightly, the only woman in the team – was on loan from the Israeli Mossad. Bringing her along on the mission had been a difficult decision for Hunter. They had been lovers for some time and his instinct was to protect her, not expose her to the vagaries of the South American jungle. But Ruth was as committed to the eradication of the drug runners as any member of the team and he had no justifiable reason to leave her out.

In recognition of her sex, Ruth's pack weighed merely 45lbs, the only concession offered or accepted. They had yomped in single file, with Hughes half a klick ahead, and Frank Hales the same behind. Intel updates were transmitted every hour, on the hour, from TIFAT HQ in Scotland.

They had set up the ambush along a well-worn path, wide enough to allow two donkeys to pass without touching. Hughes continued on point, ready to warn of the smugglers' arrival. Frank Hales went back half a klick along the path to mop up the advance guard they knew would be leading the donkey train.

When it wasn't raining it was steaming hot. On arrival, each of them had dug a hole waist deep and long enough to lay down in. The hides were carefully camouflaged. Nobody moved outside their hole to ensure that there was no disruption to the area. After only a few days it looked like a natural part of the landscape.

One give-away in these situations was the sense of smell. Rotting vegetation was one thing, cigarette smoke and the minty tang of toothpaste another. None of the team were smokers but they all missed brushing their teeth. Hunter used small pieces of twig to clean his, chewing fern tips he knew to be safe.

The other major problem of being in a hide had been taken care of. Prior to arriving in Suriname they had spent four days eating special rations. By the second day their systems had been cleansed. They would not need to go to the toilet until after the operation. Apart from urinating. Even that was an art form, as their urine passed through a personal purifier for re-use. They had tried a group purifier but the consensus of opinion was they would rather die of thirst than drink it.

Each of them heard the Intel updates on their personal sat-nav phone and were assured that the narco-traffickers were finally coming. Only their time of arrival was unknown. The smugglers were using a trail that was over a thousand kilometres long. A combination of dense rain forest and vast quantities of camouflage netting kept the smugglers hidden from the spy-satellites. Infra-red seekers were almost useless. The temperature difference between the surrounding jungle and the bodies walking the route was insufficient to register properly.

Three days they had been in situ. The hours had dragged slowly, sapping their energy. It was too dangerous to walk through the jungle at night and so there had been no fear that the smugglers would have arrived while it was dark. Day and night the jungle was never silent. Small animals and reptiles roamed freely amongst the ferns and spiky palms that made up the under-growth. The odourless insect repellent the team was using was a washout. They were tormented by mosquitoes at dawn and dusk.

They had two escape routes once the job was over. The one Hunter favoured was a helicopter ride into Brazil. The second meant a trip down the River Maroni, fifty klicks to the east. The two-man escape team was already there and waiting. Just in case.

The radios picked up a signal a few minutes before 3pm. No voice. Just three clicks then a pause, followed by three more clicks. There was a further delay while Hughes counted the advance patrol as they passed him. He sent five clicks. Five armed men in front. The team waited, nervous sweat mixing with the perspiration caused by the heat and humidity.

Five men came into sight, dressed in army fatigues and carrying rifles slung over their shoulders. They were speaking loudly in a Portuguese patois that was incomprehensible even to the two Portuguese speakers in the team.

More clicks. Two this time, as Hunter and his team watched the five men vanish around a corner in the trail. The main body of the caravan was half a klick behind. They waited with cold-eyed determination. Half a billion dollars worth of coke would cause untold suffering in the West. It had to be stopped.

'Boss,' Hughes broke radio silence with a whisper. 'I don't like it. I count eighteen armed guards and here's the bad news, they're all either European or American and highly alert.'

'Roger that,' whispered Hunter. 'Any tail-end Charlies?'

'Negative. There are twelve donkeys being led by one peasant with another bringing up the rear. The guards are either side.'

The team was using silenced Steyr Tactical Machine Pistol submachine guns. Constructed entirely in synthetic material, the TMP was so tough that steel inserts to guide the bolt were not required. It fired in single or automatic bursts and the magazine held up to twenty-five rounds of 9mm Parabellum cartridges. The sound suppressers they had fitted reduced the noise of the gun to a burp in a high wind. Yet their primary weapon remained surprise.

They could hear the caravan approaching. Two soldiers came into sight, unshaven, their wary eyes roaming back and forth. They spared only a glance for the positions where the team were hiding. The first soldier had already passed Hunter when a click in his ear piece told him that the last smuggler had reached Badonovitch at the furthest end. It was the signal to begin. Hunter aimed upwards from a distance of about three metres, firing through a slit in the foliage. He fired twice, aiming at the third man in the file. Both shots hit home – one through the heart, the other through the throat. His second target screamed as he smashed onto the track, struck by Hunter's bullets. The man in front spun around with an oath but he was far too late. Hunter's next two shots killed him instantly.

Pushing back the camouflage, Hunter leapt out of the hole. The jungle air was filled with yells and curses. The donkeys began to bray and kick as automatic gunfire rent the air. Hunter took a snap shot at one of the peasants but he was already vanishing into the jungle and the bullet missed. One guard lying on the ground brought his gun to bear and began pulling the trigger. It was on fully automatic and the bullets stitched a pattern across the track and into one of the foxholes. Hunter killed the man with a double tap, both shots to the body.

The other members of the team were climbing out and finishing off the job. Because they had been so well hidden none of the team were shot at directly. Most of the smugglers had died before they even knew what was happening. The peasant at the end of the donkey train had turned and fled. Hunter sent out a radio message which Hughes acknowledged. He would wait until the man arrived at his position.

Frank Hales reported in. 'All five down. No problems.'

'Roger that. Stay where you are in case of unexpected visitors.'

The team began cutting open the sacks tied across the donkeys' backs. They contained pure white cocaine, refined to the highest quality. They hacked the sacks to pieces, scattering the fortune in coke across the jungle floor. Already the slight breeze was dispersing it, wiping out half a billion dollars. The rain began again and helped the process. The donkeys had settled down and stood placidly, snorting, shifting a leg, unperturbed amongst the clouds of white dust.

Napier had been rifling the pockets of the dead men. 'Boss, you'd better take a look.'

Hunter took the offered document and recognised it as a French passport. He compared the picture. It was him all right.

The wounded smuggler groaned. Hunter knelt by his side. 'What's your name?'

The man looked at Hunter with hatred and spat out a mouthful of insults, his French vowels identifying him as a native of the

Midi. Hunter asked the question again, in the same language. He was given another mouthful of abuse.

The remainder of the team had been ready to move at a moment's notice and were already pulling their bergens from their holes and strapping them to their backs.

Hughes radioed in. 'Boss, we've got problems. A patrol has just rushed past me, moving fast. I counted twenty in all. They're on foot and heavily armed.'

'Roger that. Time to go.' Hunter was preparing to put a bullet in the head of the injured man when the Frenchman arched his back and exhaled for the last time.

Standing up Hunter grabbed his bergen, searching Ruth out automatically. 'Are you okay?' he asked her.

'Sure. No problems. You?'

He looked into her brown eyes and grinned. The shower had already passed and the sunlight filtering through the treetops reflected on her smooth, lightly tanned skin. The shadows from the leaves made geometric patterns across her beautiful face. 'Listen up,' he called. 'You heard Dave. We need to move fast. All set?'

They moved out at a rapid pace. Hunter had already prepared a number of booby-traps while he had been in the foxhole. He quickly set them.

'Dave, are you following?' Hunter transmitted.

'Affirmative. They're coming fast as they're travelling light. Between me and them are three donkeys, each with a minder, with packs. Another man has just joined them.'

'He was probably the one who ran up the track. They'll slow down now, if they know what's happened. Can you take out those four and ditch their supplies?'

'Will do. They've stopped. Some of them don't look too happy about following. They're arguing. Hang on.' The radio went silent for a few seconds. 'They're coming this way. They're heading back up the trail.'

'In that case leave them. As soon as they're out of sight follow us. Frank?'

'Here, boss.'

'Stay hidden. As soon as we're past, set the explosives. When Dave reaches you follow behind. We'll have whoever is chasing us between a rock and a hard place.'

'Roger that.'

Hunter surveyed his handiwork. The green thread was impossible to spot. He hurried after the others, opening out his stride. At six-foot two he had a long reach. The traps he had just set were, according to international agreements, illegal. Classed as an anti-personnel mine they were a variation on the Claymore. He had set four of them. Any of eight tripwires would set them off. When they did, C-4 plastic explosive would fire seven hundred steel balls in a forward sixty degrees pattern that grew to six feet and killed anybody within one hundred and seventy feet.

They passed Chief Petty Officer Frank Hales who had set a similar trap before dropping back into his hide.

The team had travelled nearly three klicks when they heard the explosions, remarkably faint in the distance. They continued on, moving fast, returning along the path they had followed three days earlier. It was twenty minutes before Hughes called in.

'The Clays took out three and wounded one. He was shot through the head by his own people. One of the men went berserk, screaming orders at the top of his voice. They radioed in somewhere but I've no idea where or to whom.'

'Roger that. I'll ask HQ. Isobel's listening to all frequencies in this area. When you reach Frank follow – fast and carefully.'

Hunter broke the connection. Like the others he was breathing heavily as they kept up their killing pace. Plan Alpha was the cushy option – a helicopter ride out. They were meant to return to the drop point and await the arrival of the helo. If they couldn't stop their pursuers there was no chance. They would have to use plan Bravo. They were nearly forty minutes from Hales when he radioed.

'The trap took two. They're well strung out now, taking fewer risks. I count fourteen.'

'Roger that. Follow with Dave but don't get seen.'

12

'He's here now. We're moving out.'

They had a lead of about forty-five minutes. Too small a margin to sit waiting for a helicopter to arrive, so there was no choice. The odds now were almost even. An ambush would turn the situation to their advantage. Hunter was already planning ahead, remembering the terrain they had crossed. One piece of ground sprung to mind. He knew the track passed through a defile, with walls as high as twenty or thirty metres in some places. At one time it had been the bed of a stream but the water had long since dried up.

Explosives each end and an ambush from above would soon settle matters.

Between gasps he briefed everyone over their personal radios. He had just finished when the sat-nav phone warbled.

'Nick? Isobel.' Hunter recognised the voice of TIFAT's IT expert. 'You've got a big problem. We intercepted a radio message from the scene of the ambush to somebody in the capital, Paramaribo. They called for helo backup. Three have been scrambled.'

'Hell! We've nothing to take out a helo. Are they attack 'copters or just bringing in reinforcements?'

'We don't know at this stage. But from the transmissions we've intercepted you've kicked over a hornets' nest. Somebody is going berserk over the loss of the shipment – over the half a billion profit, more like. The men chasing you have been told if they fail they needn't bother returning.'

'Any chance of back-up?'

'The General is working on that right now.'

Hunter was thinking furiously. They had about eight klicks to the ambush site. He was gasping when he asked, 'Are those enemy helos airborne yet?'

'Negative. I'll let you know as soon as they are. You can cross into French Guiana at the River Maroni.'

'What's the chance of hot pursuit?'

'Inevitable, I should think. They could scream murderers and thieves and demand free access.'

'That's what I figure. All right, I need to go.'

Breaking the connection, Hunter knew that if they were to survive they had to make the river.

Hunter checked the sat-nav picture and broadcast to the others. 'Three klicks. Let's step on it.'

They increased their speed, the pace murderous to all but the fittest. It became a brutal race. They needed cover, they needed time to prepare and they needed luck, and not necessarily in that order.

The team got to work as soon as they reached the narrow gorge. Each member knew what was required without being told. Hunter left them to get on with it while he climbed the steep slope to the top. From the jungle plain the hill he had climbed sprung up like a carbuncle. It had been cut in two by eons of water erosion, though the stream running through had dried leaving a rocky defile. Steep-sided, a hundred feet high in the middle, it was surrounded by impenetrable jungle on all sides. It was the only way through and a good place for an ambush. A fact their pursuers would surely recognise as well.

Staying low he crawled over the top and lay behind a boulder, focusing binoculars on the path they had just run. He called Hughes and Hales for a sitrep.

'Boss, we're about five klicks away. About half a klick behind the enemy.'

'Roger that. Close up when you're one klick away. When I give the word launch an all out attack.'

They broke the connection. The sat-nav phone warbled softly and Hunter answered it. General Malcolm Macnair, head of TIFAT, his gruff voice, slightly distorted by space and distance, coming all the way from Rosyth, still managed to instil Hunter with a sense of power and authority.

'Hullo, sir. Any good news?'

'Yes. The *Ark Royal* is on exercise in the Atlantic. She's steaming at full speed towards Suriname. According to the Captain, he can launch in five minutes.'

'What's he sending?'

'Harriers, Foxtrot Alpha Twos.'

Hunter knew the Sea Harrier named was used in the twin roles of combat air support and battlefield interdiction. They carried Sidewinders, AMRAAM missiles and cannons.

'How did you manage it, sir?'

'Friends in low places,' joked the General. 'They know the picture. They'll be coming up country following the river Maroni, staying on the border between Suriname and French Guiana.'

'How long will they stay?'

'No more than five minutes. The enemy helos have launched and we reckon they'll be on site in thirty to thirty-five minutes.'

'Roger that, sir. Thanks and thank the *Ark* for us.'

'Will do.' The General paused and then added, 'Good luck, Nick.'

The connection was broken and Hunter turned his attention back to surviving the next forty minutes.

The team had already deployed. If they were tired after their yomp through the jungle they didn't show it. Hunter shucked down by Ruth.

'You okay?' He respected her professionalism too much to compromise her with anything more.

Their eyes met, conveying emotions which could not be articulated just then.

'Sure, Nick, quit worrying.'

At that second, he wished fervently that they had told the General about their plans. Maybe Ruth could have gone home and told her parents. Her father had been the Deputy Prime Minister of Israel and was about to start fighting a general election. He was a man Hunter greatly respected.

As if reading his mind, Ruth smiled. 'Once this is over we can make the announcement and celebrate in style.' She eased her bergen and lifted out a couple of hand-grenades.

Hunter tapped her shoulder, smiled and moved to his position ten yards away. The team checked in. All preparations were complete. They lay silently in the baking heat. The sun was hidden by a thick layer of cloud and as they looked across the top of the jungle they could see isolated storms. Jagged flashes of lightning streaked across the sky. There was no rain as yet, just a heavy, hot and humid atmosphere.

Hughes radioed in. 'One klick and closing fast.'

'Okay. Close up and when I give the word hit them with everything you've got.'

It was another five minutes before Masters broke the silence. 'Here they come. They're at the edge of the jungle.'

'I see them,' replied Hunter.

One man was edging along the path, cautious now without the cover of the jungle. He stopped and spoke to another, who was still out of sight. There was more movement and the second man appeared. He put a pair of binoculars to his eyes and began to slowly scan the defile. Nobody in the team moved, hardly breathing. Another two men came equally cautiously into view.

Hunter spoke softly into his microphone. 'Dave, Frank, hit them . . . now.'

From inside the green jungle screen came the unmistakable sound of machine-guns opening fire followed by the loud bangs of detonating grenades. Hughes and Hales were certainly doing as they had been instructed. Across the two hundred metres of open ground came the yells and curses of soldiers being attacked.

The man with the binoculars pointed and bellowed an order. All his men came streaming out of the jungle and along the path towards the defile. Hunter and the team waited patiently. Twelve men in total, so the attack had whittled down another two of their number.

The lead man was already at the gorge and turning to give covering fire to his colleagues. They quickly entered what they considered to be the relative safety of the defile and fanned out, ready to fend off whoever was behind them. They could afford to wait. With attack helos and reinforcements arriving soon they had nothing to lose and everything to gain.

Masters set off the first explosion.

The plastic had been carefully laid at the entrance to the defile. When it detonated tons of rock were dislodged, raining down on the men in the gorge. Two were killed outright and three were seriously wounded. The remainder turned as one and ran along the path. The first man was almost at the midway point when a second explosion erupted at his feet. He was blown to pieces, as was the man close behind. The third man was shielded and stayed on his feet but a rock the size of a football landed on his head and crushed it like a ripe tomato. Other rocks rained down maiming and injuring others.

Before the dust had settled hand grenades were lobbed down. Any screams and yells ended abruptly. The team stayed where they were, listening intently. So far it had not been necessary to show themselves and risk getting shot. A wounded man could easily be waiting below, determined to get revenge before he died.

After a few minutes Hunter cautiously looked over the edge. He saw nothing except fallen rocks and body parts. He scanned the area closely. Nothing moved. Over his radio he said, 'Take a careful look.'

Along the edge of the defile the team moved slowly, inching forward, taking a snap look. The gunshot was loud in the aftermath of the battle. A bullet struck a rock next to Napier's head and a chip of stone cut deeply across his cheek. In order to fire at his target, the man had stood up suddenly. Before he could drop back down out of sight Doug Tanner put a bullet in his brain.

Hughes and Hales arrived at the beginning of the defile and were working their way along, looking for live bodies. They reached the spot where the second explosion had occurred and gave the all clear.

'Prepare for the helicopters arriving,' Hunter ordered. He called TIFAT HQ and gave a sitrep.

'Excellent, Nick,' said the General. 'But you're not out of trouble yet. Their helicopters are five minutes out. Our Harriers are fully ten minutes behind them.'

'Roger that, sir. We'd better get ready.' At the bottom of the defile the team were checking the bodies of the dead men, searching for papers.

Claude Masson joined him. 'Boss, I recognise one of these scumbags.'

'Who is he?'

'Used to be a paratrooper with the Legion. Tough son of a bitch. One thing I remember about him, he was ultra right-wing.'

'How do you mean?'

'You know, the usual crap. France for the French, provided they're white. I'm sure he was thrown out for killing an Algerian in a brawl in a bar in Toulon.'

'Did he go to prison?'

Masson shrugged. 'Sorry, I can't remember.'

On impulse Hunter thrust a handful of passports at him. 'Take a look at these and see if you recognise anyone else.'

The sergeant quickly looked through them and looked at Hunter in puzzlement. 'I'm positive about one other and I'm almost sure I recognise a third.'

'Who are they?'

'Special forces. Or ex, anyway. You know what a small world we inhabit.'

Hunter nodded. He knew people all over the globe who were in special forces. Theirs was a close-knit world.

He'd just buttoned the passports into his top pocket when the first helicopter screamed into sight.

They were AS565s, known as Panthers. Built in France by Aérospatiale the Panther carried various externally mounted weapons, including air to ground missiles. The lead helo pilot made a grave error almost immediately. He flew in close to determine the identity of the men on the ground. Unfortunately for him, the TIFAT operatives he targeted were Badonovitch and Weir, the latter an Olympics standard rifleman. They already had their sniper rifles out and loaded with a specially constructed explosive bullet. They fired simultaneously and both men hit the helicopter. The bullets exploded on impact, killing the pilot outright. Out of control, the helo began to spin before crashing and erupting into flame less than a hundred metres from where the team stood. The other two 'copters swung down and away before the riflemen could take aim.

'Incoming!' Badonovitch yelled, seconds before a missile slammed into the side of the gorge. The explosion was huge. Tons of rocks were blown into the air, landing amongst the team, causing some minor injuries.

The helicopters hovered out of range and a second missile was launched at the team. It landed between Ruth and Frank Hales who were lying on the ground behind large boulders. The explosion sent a rock flying through the air striking Hales on the temple, killing him instantly. A second rock flew high and landed with a sickening crunch on Ruth's leg. She screamed in agony as her knee was crushed.

2

Men began to rappel out of the helicopters. Before the first touched the ground a Sidewinder missile flew into the side of the helicopter and blew it to smithereens. Debris and burning fuel tumbled out of the sky, killing the soldiers who were deploying underneath, preparing to attack. The cavalry, in the form of the two Harriers, had arrived just in time.

The other helicopter met the same end. When the second missile hit it, two of the soldiers had already reached the ground and were running in the direction of the defile. They had been expecting the helicopters to supply massive covering fire in the form of missiles and cannons. When the helicopters blew apart the two men stopped in shock. The first was killed by Badonovitch and the second wounded by Tanner.

The two Harriers flew over, waggled their wings and streaked north again, out of the country. They would be back on board the *Ark Royal* in time for tea.

Hunter had not waited to watch the action. Within seconds of hearing Ruth scream he was beside her, tearing open a first aid kit, frantically searching for an injection of morphine to give her. Don Masters was with him, rapidly undoing a bandage to wrap around the badly bleeding wound. Ruth was moaning, only semi-conscious, from the pain and shock of her injury.

Hunter injected a powerful pain-killer into her left thigh and calf. Within a few moments Ruth stopped moaning and passed out completely.

Apart from bruises and cuts none of the remainder were hurt.

A bodybag was opened and Frank Hales placed inside. Special Services never left the bodies of their own behind. Folding stretchers were quickly assembled. Hunter meanwhile was reporting to TIFAT.

Macnair acknowledged the report. 'The extraction helo won't get to you before tomorrow and then it'll take you to Brazil.'

'I know, sir. We're going to run for the river. We'll take the inflatables and head downstream as fast as we can. Please ask *Ark* for a helo to casevac Ruth. The doctors on board may be able to help.'

'How bad is she?'

Already the team were preparing to move out. Unable to trust his voice for a second, Hunter looked around him. It would be fast and furious to the river and all unwanted equipment was being abandoned. Guns and water were about all they would be carrying. Along with the two stretchers.

'Bad, sir. The knee is completely crushed. Bones right through the flesh.' He didn't say it but he didn't think Ruth would ever walk on that leg again. She would be lucky not to lose it from above the knee.

'Roger that. Get moving. We'll be tracking you. I'll let you know when the helo is on its way.' The General didn't bother telling Hunter that he was already embroiled in a diplomatic row for sending in the jets. To Macnair his people came first and diplomacy a very poor second. The helo would be sent in ASAP.

The team moved out while Hunter joined David Hughes next to the wounded mercenary. The bullet had hit him in the right shoulder and passed through, smashing the collar bone and leaving a gaping exit wound.

'Leave him,' said Hunter callously, 'and let's go.'

'I know him, boss,' was Hughes' startling reply.

At that moment the wounded man opened his eyes and said, 'Hullo, Taff. Fancy seeing your ugly mug here.'

'Save it, Fletcher! What outfit are you working for?'

The man looked at Hughes through narrowed eyes before replying. 'Fix my shoulder first and I'll tell you.'

Hunter placed his gun to the man's temple and said harshly, 'Answer the question or, by God, you'll regret it.'

'You wouldn't dare,' Fletcher gasped, the barrel digging into his skin.

Hunter could feel the adrenaline pumping around his body, making him giddy. 'Thanks to your mob one of my men has been killed and a woman seriously injured, you little piece of excrement. Personally, I'm more than willing to end your pathetic life. So I suggest you start naming names.'

The man could see that he meant it. Hunter's face was set as if it was carved from stone, his dark blue eyes almost black in their anger and hatred.

'I left Hereford last year and joined a mob who wanted heavy muscle. That's all there is to it.'

'Wait up,' said Hughes. 'I've been trying to remember. You were thrown out for attacking a black soldier. Another SAS man. A few of you were named as members of some sort of right-wing organisation connected to Le Pen in France.'

Hunter took the man's passport and checked it. It was genuine. 'So what were you doing in Suriname?'

'We were sent in to kill you after you stopped the drug shipment.'

'Who sent you?'

'No way – I've said enough. I know my rights. I'm a soldier and under the Geneva Convention . . .'

He got no further as Hunter hit him across the mouth with the barrel of his gun, breaking three of the man's teeth. Fletcher screamed loudly.

'Who sent you?'

'I swear I don't know.' The mercenary spat out blood and jagged pieces of tooth. 'We were hired by an outfit in Britain and sent here to cover the shipment of coke. I swear, that's all I know.'

Hunter could see he wouldn't learn anymore and he had neither the time nor the inclination to make him talk. He stood up. 'Let's go, Dave.'

Hughes nodded and the two men turned to leave.

'What about me?' Fletcher said.

'You can live or die for all I care,' Hunter said calmly, picking up the man's machine-gun.

'You can't leave me.'

'Your gun will be by the path,' replied Hunter. He and Hughes broke into a jog. As they ran, Hunter checked the weapon. When he dropped it near the jungle path there was only one bullet left. Hunter threw the rest away. He doubted Fletcher would live long as the wound was a nasty one and still bleeding. If a big cat or other predator chanced upon him he had a choice. Kill the cat or kill himself.

The team were well ahead and Hunter and Hughes opened up their pace. Hunter ran on automatic, his fear for Ruth all-pervading. He knew that the two team members at the river would be getting ready to move out, having been briefed by Macnair. One of the two, Matt Dunston, was a trained medic. More than that, he was a friend. He would have a drip ready and anything else he could think of. Thinking of Ruth made Hunter speed up again. Hughes didn't complain but kept along-side. The pace was crippling.

They caught up with the remainder of the team near the drop zone. Hunter ran alongside the stretcher bearing Ruth, who was still unconscious. The team changed carriers every fifteen minutes without breaking stride, eating up the kilometres to the river. They knew that once they got there they could rest.

Hunter checked their position. 'Two klicks, keep it up,' he called.

The knowledge put new heart into them and they picked up their flagging speed. Each man was drenched in sweat. Luckily they would be at their destination before dehydration became a problem.

Ahead of them they suddenly heard the deep-throated roar of an outboard motor bursting into life. Rounding a bend they found themselves at the edge of the jungle, the brown, sluggish water of the river in front of them. Tethered to the bank were two large inflatables, each powered by an Evinrude 120hp engine.

They quickly climbed on board. Ruth was handed over to Matt

Dunston's care. Hunter sat at the boat's console while Dunston was already feeling for a vein in Ruth's arm to feed a drip into her.

Hunter engaged the gears in reverse and backed away from the bank. The other inflatable followed, driven by Weir. They turned in unison and headed downstream. The river was a hundred metres wide and over three metres deep in the middle. On either side, the jungle formed a wall of green hiding the eyes of predators as they streaked past.

Dunston worked silently on Ruth's leg, muttering a prayer as he tried to reset pieces of the bone. But he knew it was hopeless. Eye contact and a grimace to Hunter spoke volumes.

Whenever the boat passed a low bank or shallows, alligators could be seen. They watched in total disinterest as the two boats flashed past, pushing 25 to 30 knots. Hunter's boat led. In the bows lay two lookouts watching for hidden obstacles in the water. Utmost vigilance was called for. The river had many branches and logs floating on or just under the surface. The remainder of the team were eating and drinking, each man with his weapon close at hand. The second boat followed in the wake, ten metres behind.

The deep-veed hull of the inflatables ate up the distance. On land they dealt in kilometres, now they were on the water, as at sea, they dealt in miles. A hundred and twenty remained until they reached the coast.

Occasionally they passed an isolated building, sitting forlornly at the water's edge. There was other river traffic, going both ways. Mostly slow and cumbersome shallow draft boats carrying people and livestock. The people on the boats saw the armed soldiers and watched stony-faced.

Hunter passed a sitrep to Macnair using his sat-nav.

'We're following your beacons on the screen,' said the General. 'The *Ark* is heading towards the coast at flank speed. As soon as a helo is en-route I'll give you an ETA. How's Ruth?'

'Not good,' replied Hunter, his tone flat.

'I'm arranging to have a surgeon flown down to *Ark Royal*. He works at San Diego hospital but has a reserve job with the SEALs at Coronado. Specialises is bones.'

'Thanks, sir.' Hope flared in Hunter. He should have known that Macnair would do all in his power to help. 'Any unusual activity around the river?'

'Not that we can see. It appears clear all the way to the coast but of course that can change at any time. I'm playing Suriname off against French Guiana and hoping they'll let you fall between the cracks.' He didn't tell Hunter he had already been on the phone to the Foreign Office to get the Foreign Secretary to threaten both governments if they tried to interfere. The FS was tough and enjoyed throwing his weight around when he could. He had let both governments know in no uncertain terms that any attempt to stop the team would have the direst consequences. He hadn't specified what, but had invoked the anti-terrorism mantra that had arisen since 9/11. *The enemy of terrorism is our friend; a supporter is our enemy; there are no bystanders.*

Of course that did not cover rogue elements in the armed forces of either country. Or even a general with too much pride who took it as a personal affront that the TIFAT team was in his country without permission.

Hunter began weaving the boat around a ferry that was crossing left to right, its decks packed with people looking and pointing. The diverse cultural mix of the Suriname population was evident – the people on board were of Asian and African extraction, as well as South American.

On each side of the river stood a motley group of houses, wooden and ramshackle. Flags hung in the still air announcing a customs post, although there were no signs of any officials.

Hunter checked their position. Eighty miles to go to the coast. Glancing back he saw that Weir had been relieved at the wheel of the second boat and Josh Clements was now driving. He indicated to Napier to take his place. Kneeling by Ruth, he took her hand. She was in a deep sleep and looked peaceful enough.

'How is she?' he shouted to Dunston above the noise of the engine.

His friend shrugged and pulled a face. 'It's not looking good, Nick.'

Hunter nodded. He was totally helpless and that was a feeling he hated. To occupy himself he collected the passports they had lifted from the dead men and went through them. They had eleven in total. Two British, two Dutch, one Austrian, two German, three French and an Italian. The names and faces meant nothing to Hunter. But they all had one thing in common. They all looked like tough sons of bitches.

Taking out the sat-phone stowed in the boat he put on earphones and face mask. Without them, struggling against the noise of the engine, it was impossible to have a conversation without yelling and asking for repeats.

'Isobel? Hunter. Can I speak to the General?'

'He's right here.'

'Nick? You seem to be making good progress. The helo is launching in five. It'll be with you in an hour.'

'Just the one?'

'Yes. For Ruth only. A paramedic is on board. He'll take care of her. As soon as you're in the open sea we'll lift the rest of you. There isn't time to take anybody else. We're beginning to get signal noise around your area. Nothing specific yet but something is stirring.'

'Understood. The reason I called is that the dead men are all Europeans. Matt is scanning in the passport details now and will transmit them as soon as he's finished. Get Isobel to do a trace. As far as we can gather, they're all ex-special forces. I suggest Isobel checks their reasons for leaving the services and more especially their political leanings.'

'Specifically?'

'Right wing, fascist, the usual garbage.'

'Will do. I'll also get Isobel tracking the money, their bank accounts, see what they throw up. Who their paymaster is.'

'Good idea, sir.'

'Good luck and be careful.'

'I will.' But Hunter was talking to a disconnected phone.

The closer to the coast they got the more traffic there was on the river. They were eventually forced to slow down to about half speed. According to the readout on the console they were still thirty-three miles from the coast when they head the clatter of a helicopter. A second later they saw a Sea King Mk 6, the roundels of the Royal Air Force painted on its side.

Napier throttled back to 10 knots and the helo hovered over them. Radio contact was kept to a minimum. With a maximum speed of 150 knots and a range of 450 nautical miles, the helo was being flown to its maximum parameters.

A hook reeled down and was touched by an earthing pole to remove the static electricity that had built up during flight. Matt grabbed the hook and snatched it on to a harness. The stretcher was whisked away in seconds. Ruth vanished in board and the hook reappeared. This time the bag containing Frank Hales' body was lifted away. With a lump in his throat Hunter watched the helicopter increase speed and head north, weaving around the bends, following the border between the two countries. Ruth would soon be in good hands.

Napier was already increasing speed back up to 15 and then 20 knots. Checking their position Hunter saw that they were only minutes away from the towns of St Laurent on the right bank and Albina on the left. He signalled to the boats to slow down as now the river was seriously crowded with everything from bum-boats to large ferries crossing in both directions.

The river was widening to the estuary and the raucous call of sea birds could be heard as they scavenged for food. The inflatables were down to 5 or 6 knots, weaving amongst the other traffic. The team was wary, keeping a sharp lookout for trouble. Their weapons were held close at hand but out of sight. They had stripped off their camouflaged jackets and trousers and now wore T-shirts and jeans, courtesy of the escape party. Every scenario had been addressed – the plan refined endlessly until finally Macnair announced it was time to go with it. Heads of departments had agreed. But they also knew that for all the planning, double-guessing and forethought there was no way they could foresee the unexpected. All plans were set clay, not stone, to be recast at any moment.

The houses on each side of the river were drab and in need of repair. The atmosphere of the villages was strangely Asian, the women wearing sarongs, their cooking smells wafting down to the riverside. Men thronged the waterfront on both sides and the noise of street vendors mingled with the sound of vehicles belching smoke through cracked silencers. The water was filthy and stank of open sewage. Dead animals floated on the surface, the ebbing tide taking them slowly to the sea. They were about half-a-mile from the river entrance and the open sea when a black and white customs boat pulled out from the left bank and headed directly towards them. On board were a dozen armed soldiers. They appeared to be natives.

An official waving a bullhorn ordered them to stop in the water.

Napier looked at Hunter who nodded. The boat slowed but was kept in gear.

'Put up your hands so I can see them.' The accent was heavy but the English was intelligible.

None of the team moved a muscle but sat looking at the approaching boat. The second inflatable had drifted to one side – far enough away to cause the soldiers to have to split their attention. From their scruffy uniforms it was immediately obvious to the team that they were dealing with poorly trained troops. The advantage could however also create a huge problem. Bad training resulted in poor discipline.

The boat was old, about forty feet long with a machine gun mounted on the bows. One man stood swinging the gun between the inflatables while a second nervously fingered its bandoleer of bullets.

Hunter assumed that the man standing on the open bridge with the bullhorn was an officer although it was difficult to tell from that range.

'What's the problem?' Hunter yelled up.

'You are in Suriname territory. I demand you come ashore for questioning.'

'We're in Guiana waters,' Hunter replied, 'and demand safe passage.'

'No demands *Inglês*!' Feedback on the horn caused a high-pitched squeal that would have been comical under other circumstances.

By now Hunter's inflatable was within fifty yards of the Suriname boat. All eyes were on him, just as he wanted. Bad discipline was working in the team's favour.

Hunter gave a hand signal and the team in the other inflatable grabbed their weapons. A single silenced shot hit the bullhorn and sent it flying into the water. The officer screamed loudly, cursing in the local lingua franca. Before the troops realised what had happened five guns were pointed at them from the other inflatable.

'Look behind you,' Hunter called. 'I think we have what the Americans call a Mexican stand-off. We'll cut you to pieces although you may get one or two of us.' He made another hand signal. A second silenced shot hit the windscreen of the boat and shattered it.

The distraction was enough. The troops turned to look at the other inflatable, allowing Hunter's men time to grab their guns. The sound of bolts being worked was ominous, making the Suriname troops more nervous than ever.

Hunter knew that he had to diffuse the situation quickly. One nervous finger on a trigger and all hell would break loose. Some of the team could be injured or even killed.

'Captain, I beg you, let us pass. Pride is not worth dying for and you would be the first. Tell your men to slowly put down their weapons. We don't want any trouble. We just want to get out of here.'

Hunter's inflatable had motored slowly towards the customs' boat. Now they were less than twenty yards apart. Hunter could see the nervous perspiration on the officer's face, his unshaved cheeks and thick moustache black against a deeply tanned face. His troops looked to be no more than teenagers.

Hunter used psychology, a face-saving gesture. 'Captain, I will happily pay a customs toll to let us pass. Five hundred dollars. Your choice. You can go into town to-night and have a good time or . . . you can die on this stinking water. What's it to be?'

The officer hesitated for only a second. The money would be most welcome. Theirs, after all, was a poorly paid and thankless profession.

'I take the money.'

'Good. Tell your men I'm coming closer. Tell them to put up their rifles.'

'No! I do not trust you. Advance *Inglês*.'

Hunter knew he had no choice. 'If they look like making a move, open fire,' he said softly.

Reaching into his pocket he removed five one hundred dollar bills and held them up for the soldiers to see. The troops, most of them unsure what was going on, relaxed when they saw what he was holding.

The officer was nervously licking his lips as he climbed down the ladder and onto the deck. His boat was three feet above the water line and he stood at the guard-rail as the inflatable nudged closer.

Hunter stood, feet astride for balance, his pistol in one hand, the money in the other. He took a gamble. Placing his weapon on the seat next to him, he used his free hand to hold the inflatable steady next to the boat. He held the money up to the man.

'No tricks, Captain. Or you will surely die.'

The man nodded. He'd had enough. This was meant to have been an easy task – arrest the men in the inflatables and hold them until further orders. These men looked like bandits – heavily armed, tough, unshaven, unwashed. He took the money, glanced at it and slipped it into his pocket.

'I suggest you reverse away while we move slowly towards the sea.' The nod Hunter received was sufficient. Like dogs bristling at each other they slowly disengaged, both sides ready for trouble. Napier turned the inflatable and moved slowly downstream, following the others who had drifted ahead. The customs' boat moved back towards the shore, the gap rapidly opening between them. The Suriname soldiers gave not so much as a backward glance. With the thinning of boat traffic and an opening of the estuary, the inflatables picked up speed. Within seconds they were flying along, pushing 40 knots.

They skirted around a couple of freighters that were coming into the river, passed two more that were also heading for sea and then they were out. The muddy, filthy water began to change colour and a mile from the entrance the blue of the sea greeted them.

The team exchanged rueful looks, thinking of Hales in his body bag. The operation was nearly over. The trouble was, there was always a price to pay.

Hunter reported to Macnair.

'Good work, Nick. That was money well spent. A Sea King will be taking off in ten. It'll be with you in an hour at the most. From the looks of things around you there don't appear to be any boats taking an interest.'

'What about aircraft?'

'Nothing on the usual radio channels. That doesn't mean you shouldn't be prepared, just in case. I've got two CAPS watching. They're at the twelve mile limit. Harriers.'

'Thanks, sir. That's a relief.'

'They're on the guard frequency. Anything comes near you and they'll be warned off. But only once. Ruth's ETA on *Ark* is six minutes.'

'Roger that. Any word on the names we passed you?'

'Yes. I'll have a full report forwarded to the *Ark* when you get there.'

'Roger that.'

The connection was broken and Hunter sat, deep in thought. Now they were away from the land the sky had cleared and a hot sun burned down. Canvas shelters had already been erected for shade and the breeze across the bows was pleasant on their faces. Most of the team had fallen asleep, the past few hours having caught up with them.

Hunter relieved Napier at the helm, pleased to have something to do. Dunston sat beside him, talking about Ruth's condition. Sipping from a bottle of water Hunter unburdened himself.

'I think she's crippled, Matt.'

Dunston looked hard at his friend. 'How do you feel about that?'

'We haven't tied the knot yet but my feelings and commitment are still the same. For better or worse, Matt . . .'

Matt smiled although he wasn't surprised by the answer. 'She'll need help and support, love and understanding. But no pity. Ruth couldn't stand that.'

Hunter nodded. 'You're right. What's the worst case scenario? She loses her leg. Hell, that's nothing compared to what a lot of people have to put up with.' He sighed. 'It helps, talking.'

Dunston tapped his shoulder. 'It always does, my friend. It always does. Prayer helps as well.'

Hunter smiled. 'I'll leave that to you.'

Dunston took no offence but smiled back. 'God listens, you know.'

Hunter said nothing. Their friendship went deep and wide with neither man trying to cram his beliefs, or lack of them, down the other's throat.

'Incoming helos,' said Hunter. 'Ten minutes out.' He raised his voice, 'Stand to, lads.'

They came alert and prepared to be lifted. They struck down the awning, and secured all loose gear. Lastly, they put on their security harnesses and waited patiently.

Two Sea Kings came into sight. Way was taken off the inflatables and the helos hovered above each of them. The winch was lowered, the hook earthed and then fixed to the eight-strand lifting strop. The inflatables lifted cleanly out of the water and even as they were being winched up the helicopters were turning and picking up speed. The inflatables went straight up to their locking positions on the starboard side of the 'copter. Each member of the team undid his safety harness and climbed inside the fuselage. When the last man was in and the doors shut the helos accelerated. Most of the team settled down to sleep. For Hunter it was a time for introspection. As the adrenaline subsided his thoughts turned to his past and his future.

He had wanted to be a naval officer ever since he could remember. Much to the amusement of the family he had spurned a business degree at an Oxbridge university and gone to Dartmouth instead. There he had elected to specialise in what was considered one of the toughest courses in the military – underwater bomb and mine disposal. He'd gone on to command minehunters before volunteering to join TIFAT. There had been no regrets. But now? With Ruth in her present condition, wasn't it time to re-consider his options? A top job in the family business almost anywhere in the world was his for the asking. He sighed. Somehow, it wasn't him. The truth was, he enjoyed what he did. With that thought he fell asleep, exhaustion finally taking its toll.

3

Intelsat and Inmarsat satellites which moved in geo-stationary orbit around the earth accounted for the vast majority of phone and fax communications traffic between countries and continents. Within countries, old-fashioned land lines, fibre optic lines and mobile communications systems carried billions of messages each and every day. ECHELON, the huge network of land-based intercept stations, intelligence ships and top-secret military satellites whirling twenty thousand miles overhead, hoovered up everything that was transmitted. It fed the information to the massive computer banks of the National Security Agency. There the advanced voice recognition and optical character recognition programs did their work. Using the Echelon 'Dictionary', key words and phrases were identified. The message was flagged and recorded and then transcribed for future analysis by highly-trained operators. Messages intercepted were automatically forwarded to the agency most likely to be interested in their contents. This process continued twenty-four-seven, all year round. Amongst the billions of words analysed, some phrase or sentence could help the world's security agencies prevent a terrorist outrage.

Following the horrendous events of 9/11 this type of surveillance had been stepped up as high as possible. Nothing was too trivial to be ignored.

The most important complex in Europe was at Menwith Hill near Harrogate in North Yorkshire. There were eight satellite dishes with names such as STEEPLECHASE, MOONPENNY and SILKWORTH. No transmission however small was missed or ignored no matter how it was sent. This collection of data would have been useless due to the overwhelming amount flooding in every minute if it was not for the highly advanced and incredibly sophisticated computer software that worked the recognition programs. Voice recognition software converted conversations into text messages for further analysis whenever a key word or phrase was identified. One system, code named VOICECAST, could identify an individual's voice pattern and automatically flag, transcribe and forward the conversation. When the relevant agency dealing with the subject was identified, the information was automatically disseminated by use of a prefix. If the information was for GCHQ, the UK Government Communications Headquarters at Cheltenham, it was given the prefix ALPHA – ALPHA. If the information was top secret the word UMBRA was added.

'Eyes-only' information for TIFAT, the relatively new International Force Against Terrorism, based at Rosyth in Scotland, was given the prefix YANKEE – YANKEE. During the last three months a vast amount of information had been passed to Isobel Sweeney, the information technology boss at the special services complex. Her task was to filter the information and pass it to her commanding officer, Lieutenant General Malcolm Macnair.

They called it morning prayers. Promptly each morning at 08.05 Isobel began an intelligence briefing in the auditorium, attended by heads of departments, deputies and all team leaders. The room had the latest and most sophisticated anti-listening devices in existence. Any agency or person attempting to eavesdrop would only hear loud white noise. Equipment used to try and listen in would be detected and tracked. The outcome was guaranteed to be very unpleasant for the eavesdroppers.

This Monday morning the auditorium was less busy than usual. Isobel's normally calm demeanour was absent. She had a great deal of bad news to impart. 'Gentlemen,' she waited for her audience to settle down and pay attention. 'It appears that the disturbing racist attacks experienced in recent weeks have been a mere prelude to something far worse. There have been literally dozens of race-based incidents in the past forty-eight hours. Seemingly random events – street fighting, clashes with the police, demonstrations with no apparent pattern and several very serious acts of terrorism with no prior warning to the authorities. The Intel we've downloaded is truly frightening.' Her plain face was now looking positively glum. 'We've never seen anything like it, ever.' She pressed a button on her remote control and a map of Europe appeared, filling the wall. 'Each star represents a recent terrorist act of one sort or another. I tried colour coding them but it was too complex. Leo is handing out detailed notes of each incident.' Leo was Isobel's right-hand man in the department and one of the first people to join when TIFAT was originally set-up. His expertise was primarily in hacking but he had also proved to be very adept at covering his tracks once he had broken into a computer system. Isobel often joked that if he had not been working for the organisation Leo would be in jail. Leo's riposte was always the same – they'd never catch him.

'I believe these attacks now represent a wave of terrorism – part of a pre-planned movement, rather than activity by individual terrorist cells. There have been over two hundred attacks in three months. Every single one has been carried out by known or recently identified Islamic terrorists. They are, beyond doubt, a part of the Al-Qaeda network but . . .' Isobel paused, unsure whether to voice what she really thought.

'Please go on, Isobel,' Macnair prompted.

Isobel shook her head. 'These incidents are definitely being carried out by Islamic fundamentalists and Muslims. There is no question about that. The proof is overwhelming.'

'So what's the problem? We're certain Al-Qaeda is involved, so presumably the dead hand of Osama bin Laden is still on the tiller?'

'I'm not so sure. You know my rule. If in doubt, follow the money.'

'And?'

Isobel shrugged. 'The trail isn't leading where it should.'

'Where should it lead?'

'To Saudi, sir. It usually does. But not in this case.'

Sensing Isobel's reluctance to commit herself further, Macnair moved on. 'All right. We'll follow up on that later. What about the latest incidents?'

'Thirty-three over the weekend. Leo will give you the details.'

She handed over the remote control and Leo began a run-through of shootings, bombings, stabbings, riots, robberies, car-jackings and muggings.

Macnair asked the important question. 'How many incidents did we have prior knowledge of?'

'Thanks to the new software,' Isobel replied, 'we knew probabilities but we had no details. Because we hadn't cracked the codes we were unable to act. But now, by marrying incidents to recorded messages, we're better able to identify what's going to happen.'

'I take it the software used was POLITICIAN?' the General asked.

'Yes, sir. As you know, we helped to develop it. It's now incorporated in the ECHELON system.' Registering the confused expressions on junior officers' faces, she explained. 'It identifies nonsensical chat. For example, one person says something like – *It's nice weather* and gets the reply – *Especially since it rains in Spain*. That was actually one conversation we identified and tied in to the recent riot in Barcelona. We have managed to identify code words and statements that fit every incident. This means we can be ready for the next event that occurs and possibly pre-empt it. Provided we get co-operation.'

'I don't doubt we'll get plenty from all the agencies,' Macnair said heavily. It had been a long time coming but, finally, territorial wars between the different security agencies world-wide were becoming a thing of the past. At the military level co-operation had, for a long time, been excellent. But between Britain's MI5 and MI6, America's CIA and FBI, France's DGSE and SGDN, Israel's Mossad and Shin Bet, and amongst the hundreds of other organisations, co-operation had been non-existent. Vital information that could have often saved countless lives and hundreds of millions of pounds in damage had been withheld. Thanks to the influence of TIFAT and the example set by Macnair, co-operation was much improved and, more importantly, more effective. The American President was also prepared to knock heads together to achieve co-operation, which helped greatly.

'Where does this new found knowledge leave us?' Macnair asked.

Isobel frowned, pursed her lips and decided to go for it. 'The scale of the attacks has climbed dramatically. We believe further attacks will take place in these areas over the coming week. They are graded one to five in order of likelihood. Five being the most certain.' Isobel proceeded to show a series of slides with probable places and dates.

'Good grief,' said Macnair. 'That many?'

'I'm afraid so, sir. They stretch from Ireland in the west to Greece in the east. And from Spain as far north as Norway and Sweden. Not a single EU country will be unaffected.' Isobel's careful preparation allowed a terrifying insight into the sheer range and scope of recent European terrorist activity and its numbingly fast momentum.

'Our political masters aren't going to like this one little bit,' said Major Jim Carter, TIFAT's Quartermaster and Macnair's right-hand man for logistics.

Several pairs of eyes honed in on a particular listing. 'What's that item in the Gulf of Mexico?' Colonel Hiram B. Walsh asked in a deceptive drawl. Late of the American Delta Force, he was TIFAT's second-in-command. In his late thirties, Walsh stood six-five in his bare feet and was as tough as he looked. With thinning fair hair swept back from a high forehead, he had a hooked nose that had been broken at least twice. His brown eyes had a perpetual laugh in them. Unless he was riled. Then they turned as hard as agates.

'We're working on it right now. All we know is that something big is being planned but we have no idea what. As soon as we get anything, I'll let you know.'

The briefing finished shortly after. The men filed out leaving Macnair, Walsh, Carter and Isobel alone.

'Why the hesitation over the money trail, Isobel?' Carter asked.

'Nothing matches with previous al-Qaeda patterns, Jim. We've been tracking currencies moving across the world for weeks now. The information sent in by Nick from Suriname appears to be a breakthrough.'

Macnair frowned. 'How can that be? What's the connection? We've established that the Suriname smugglers were all ex-special forces. All of them had been involved with extreme right-wing groups. Many had been dismissed from the services due to their white supremacy politics.'

'But here's the strange thing, sir,' said Isobel. 'The money leads in the same direction for both the Islamic fundamentalists and the white extremists. They're both being funded from the same source.'

'Are you sure?' Macnair saw the look on Isobel's face and held up his hand. 'Sorry. Any ideas?'

'None that make sense,' she said slowly.

'But?' Macnair prompted her.

'We need to find the ultimate source of the funds but I do have a theory based on what we've learnt so far.' To give herself time to think, Isobel stood up and poured coffees for all four of them. The others didn't rush her, knowing she would tell them in her own time. Sitting back down, she sipped her coffee and asked, 'What's the biggest problem facing Europe now?'

'In what way? Old nuclear weapons from the former Soviet Union?' Carter suggested. 'Iraq? The Middle East? India and Pakistan? Hell, the list is endless. Drugs, immigrants, Northern Ireland blowing up again? Need I go on?'

There were cynical smiles around the table.

'I meant *within* Europe,' said Isobel. The men nodded and she continued. 'We all know and understand the issues but the right-wing is really playing on the phobias of the electorate. The problem of immigrants is becoming serious. Elections are coming up in Denmark, Germany and France. In a year's time it will be Italy and Spain. What are the polls showing?'

There were sighs from the three men. There was no doubt

that the terrorist attacks taking place all across Europe were feeding the existing natural xenophobia of its people. A backlash was already taking place. Mosques had been attacked and fireballed, Muslims were routinely beaten up and women wearing the veil were being spat on and harassed. Muslim women no longer went out of doors unless protected by their menfolk. Gangs of youths armed with sticks and metal bars attacked immigrants en masse. Appeals to the police resulted in shrugs and token enquiries. Few, if any, arrests were being made.

'Clashes with immigrants are the ugly face of a broader dissatisfaction amongst Europeans. Ideological differences and terrorist threats are opening up a huge divide – people want to safeguard their way of life. The extreme right are either going to get into power or at least attain positions of significant influence across the continent. Here in Britain we're seeing serious trouble too. There were riots last night in Leeds, Bradford and Oldham.'

'And a mosque was destroyed in south London,' said Walsh, leaning back in his chair, his coffee forgotten on the table in front of him.

'If things continue as they are we will be forced into creating a fortress Europe,' said Macnair. 'We know what that will mean. The entire world will polarise. The rich West will pull up its collective drawbridges and the rest of the planet can go hang. Poverty and ignorance will inflame the masses who already live on next to nothing. Without Western aid they'll have even less to lose. War will be inevitable. The have-nots against the haves. Us against the Muslims. Countries such as India will side with the Muslim states as they will have nothing to lose. It's a nightmare scenario which some of our politicians understand only too well.'

'But the more clear-sighted politicos are fast becoming a minority,' said Carter. 'If things continue as they are for another year then fortress Europe could become a reality. The British government will be forced to go along, because if they don't they will definitely lose the next election. But people aren't fools. Europe's governments have been lying to us for years. We know that Al-Qaeda operatives have been coming into Europe along with the other illegal immigrants and the genuine asylum seekers. It is they who are now causing all the trouble.'

Isobel nodded. 'I agree al-Qaeda are responsible.' Isobel paused before she dropped her bombshell, 'But what if the terrorism was being *financed and orchestrated by Europe's right-wing?*'

The three officers looked at her in shock.

'Now there's a thought,' said Macnair slowly. 'Expand.'

'White extremists as the puppet masters? That would create exactly the atmosphere, the panic, we are witnessing now. Look at the lessons of history. Hitler's rise to power was achieved with a few well-placed bombs, lots of political posturing that placed the blame for Germany's woes firmly on the Jews and other minorities. A classic strategy that I know you've studied at staff college.'

Isobel knew the military was adept at learning from history in an attempt to prevent mistakes from being repeated. It was a shame, it was often said, that politicians didn't learn the same valuable lessons.

Isobel tapped into her computer and projected a new image onto the wall. 'You can see the way money has moved from banks in the Cayman Islands, British Honduras and Gibraltar to accounts in the cities on the left of the screen.' The list held almost every major city in western Europe. 'There are thirty cities each with several major banks holding accounts that we now *know* belong to the terrorists who committed the outrages of the past few months. By following the paper trail we've come back to the three banks you see here.' She flashed to the next screen. 'It comes as no surprise to find the Caymans and Honduras involved but Gib is too close to home for comfort.'

'Where does the trail lead from there?' Macnair asked.

'We're working on that now, sir. If I was to guess I would think a mainland, mainstream bank, probably more than one. The work we did that sent Nick and his team to South America also led us to the same banks. The DEA in the States helped us out there. It's thanks mainly to them that we found out about the Suriname operation. And that's only because the American Aluminium

Company have such a big stake in the country. As always,' she gave a little shrug, 'luck played a big part in identifying the banks involved. The men killed in Suriname all had bank accounts in those banks. *The same banks financing terrorism in Europe.*'

'Coincidence?' Walsh suggested.

'Perhaps, but I doubt it. There are tens of thousands of banks all over the world who would and do handle secret transactions. They know the money is dirty but couldn't care less. Whether it's stolen aid or drug money, the world's awash with dirty cash.

'You think it's too much of a coincidence?'

'I do, General,' said Isobel, with a firm nod.

'So do I. We must learn where the trail leads. Put everything you've got onto it.'

There was a knock on the door and a rating appeared. 'Sir, call for you. I told them you were in a meeting but they said it was urgent.'

'Who is it?'

'The Pentagon.'

Chantelle Suchard removed a red, peaked cap to reveal long blond hair tied in a pony tail. She smiled at the immigration officer who quickly stamped her passport and wished her a pleasant stay in the United States. She thanked him and walked out to the taxi rank. She was twenty-nine years old, an engineering graduate from the University of Rheims and held a private pilot's licence with over five hundred hours on twin-engined aircraft. However, her passion was the sea. She had been involved in diving and exploration since she was a teenager. It was while diving off Greece that she had been introduced to her current employer. One night, over dinner, she had shown her true political colours and they had become friends but not lovers. Since then she had done many and varied jobs for her boss, travelling the world, seeking excitement but always with an end goal in sight. She shivered with anticipation and pleasure. Soon, she thought, soon it will all have been worth it. The tantalising question was what she would do with all that lovely money. She salivated in anticipation.

* * *

'Malcolm, it's Colin Stafford.'

'Colin, I take it this isn't a social call.' A four-star general at the Pentagon did not make contact without good reason. Especially when Macnair realised it was the middle of the night in Washington.

'I wanted to bring you up to speed on an incident in the Gulf of Mexico.'

Macnair's grip tightened on the receiver and he pressed the loudspeaker button. 'You're on loudspeaker, Colin, with my heads of departments listening. We anticipated activity in the Gulf but have no specifics.'

'A liner has been hijacked. One of the Silver Star line.'

Macnair nodded to Isobel who was heading out the door. There was a lot of information she needed to pull.

'We'll get to work on it right away,' said Macnair. 'What can you tell us?'

'We received a radio message from the company's head office in Oslo. About four hours ago an automatic alarm was sent from the ship, the *SS Silver Beech*. Although it's rare for one to go off by mistake they didn't panic and began a series of checks. Each one panned out. There's no doubt that the ship's been taken over. Approximately ninety minutes ago they had the first direct contact with the hijackers. Somebody claiming to be a part of the al-Qaeda network radioed and told the owners to stand by for a list of demands to be forwarded to, listen to this baloney, the "decadent governments of a corrupt West".'

'That was all?'

'That's the lot. Oslo tried calling back but there was no reply on any channel. We've tried to contact the ship but every frequency is being jammed, including satellite connections and radio frequencies. It's a blanket blackout.'

'What are your plans?'

'We're sending a task force from Pensacola to investigate. Hell, it's hardly that. Two Coastguard cutters are getting up steam as we speak.'

'What role do you see for TIFAT?'

'You know there can be no negotiation with terrorists. If they give us the slightest cause I want to send in a team to take out the perps. You're the only outfit suited to this sort of thing.'

America could not go it alone. TIFAT had an international base and a mandate to operate without political interference. True, Macnair was accountable, but usually after the event, not before or during.

Macnair sucked his teeth. 'We've no assets available but I'll see what I can do.'

'None?'

'Sorry, Colin. Every team we have is out. You know what we're up against here in Europe. We're helping the internal security forces of practically every EU nation counteract terrorist attacks.'

There was a heavy pause. 'Okay. Get back to me as soon as possible, will you? If I have to, I'll send in a SEAL team from Coronado but the President isn't going to like it one little bit.'

'When will the Coastguard reach the liner?'

'In about ten hours.'

'Their orders?'

'Tell the ship to heave to and prepare for boarding. They'll send across a boarding party and find out what's what.'

'I shouldn't,' said Macnair.

'It's SOPs.'

'Colin, it may be standing operational procedure but it's highly dangerous. We've been monitoring signal traffic in the area because we knew something was being planned. Let us try and find out more before you go in at full charge.'

'I hear you, but as of now we've no choice.'

'How many terrorists are there on board?'

'We don't know. Apart from the one radio message we've heard nothing. We're re-routing all possible satellite assets to take a look. You can log in to everything we find.'

'PACER SKY?'

'It's being reprogrammed even as we speak. The whole kit and caboodle is over Afghanistan and monitoring the India Pakistan stand-off. It'll be in place in about thirty minutes.'

PACER SKY provided real time reconnaissance information

using radar, visual and infra-red detection equipment. The system's accuracy was phenomenal and still classified under the heading of top-secret.

'Is there anything else at the moment?'

'Nope, I don't think so. I heard about our man in Suriname.'

'Yes, we're really sorry. Hales' body is on board the *Ark Royal*. The Captain's making the necessary arrangements to ship him home. Who'll tell his next of kin?'

'We're doing that. He has parents living in New York.'

'All right. I'll speak to you later.' The two Generals broke their connection. 'Hiram, have Isobel make the necessary arrangements, will you? If his people don't need the money tell them to give it to a charity of their choice.'

Since its conception TIFAT had waged war against terrorists, drug dealers and criminal gangs. A war with rich pickings. Thanks to the skills of Isobel's department, hundreds of millions of pounds, dollars, yen and euros had been taken from the criminals' bank accounts and channelled into TIFAT's coffers. The funds had been used to good effect, buying state-of-the-art equipment from around the world to be used in the war against terrorism. If anyone was killed while on active service with TIFAT their next-of-kin received one million pounds. They were told it was the proceeds of a life insurance policy.

The meeting broke up and they each went about their duties. As in any modern organisation, paperwork was the bane of the General's existence and he was wading through his correspondence and action files when Isobel cornered him in his office.

'We've tried everything to contact the *Silver Beech* but it's no use. Whoever is on board has a very sophisticated and powerful jamming device. We've received information from the owners, including details of the ship and the crew. We're looking through it now.'

'Good. Anything else?'

'PACER SKY is on station and tracking. The liner is moving at a sedate four or five knots and will reach the USA in six days at their current speed.'

'Why so slow?'

Isobel shrugged. 'I've no idea.'

There was a knock on the door and Leo entered. 'Oslo has faxed through the *Silver Beech*'s passenger list.'

'Anyone of interest?' Macnair asked.

'Not yet, General. There are two hundred and forty-seven passengers and two hundred and twelve crew. We're cross-referencing every name right now. It shouldn't take too long.'

'All right, please let us know what you find. Have the lists been forwarded to other agencies?'

Leo smiled. 'Just about everyone I could think of. Would you like to see?'

Macnair waved him away with a 'No thanks'. He had complete faith in his men and women to do their jobs properly. If he didn't, they would no longer be working at TIFAT.

The General's direct line rang and he lifted the receiver. 'Macnair.'

'General, I have the PM for you. He's on loudspeaker in the COBRA office.' The Cabinet Office Briefing Room was where the most sensitive of political subjects were discussed. Briefings were usually attended by the majority, if not all, of the Cabinet, as well as their political advisers.

'Good morning, General.'

'Good morning, Prime Minister.'

The PM cut straight to the chase. 'What's your take on the situation in the Gulf of Mexico?'

'All we know is that a liner has been hijacked.'

'Are there any British subjects on board?'

Typical, thought Macnair. 'We don't know yet. We've received the lists of passengers and crew. Odds are they'll be mostly Americans and Europeans and so I expect some British are bound to be amongst them.'

'What do you intend doing?'

'I'm still assessing the situation. The Americans are sending in two Coastguard cutters to stop and board. Personally, I consider it foolhardy. The men who have taken the liner are not going to give up just because the USA Coastguard arrive on the scene. They may use it as an excuse to start trouble.'

'What exactly?'

Instead of saying how the hell do I know, Macnair kept his tone reasonable. 'I've no idea, Prime Minister, but somebody will be killed.'

'Are TIFAT getting involved?'

The mandate that Macnair held was, in effect, open warfare on terrorism. TIFAT's mantle often sat uneasily on the shoulders of the democratic governments of the West.

'Not directly, PM. We are currently co-ordinating the intelligence gathering and disseminating information to all interested parties. I have no operatives available at this juncture as they are all out on operations.'

'Right. Good. Thank you for that. Please keep me posted.'

The connection was broken.

'There is one team available,' said Isobel softly.

Macnair nodded. 'I know. Hunter's lot.'

4

The *Ark Royal*, 206m long, displacing 20,600 tonnes and capable of a speed in excess of 30 knots was the biggest ship in the Royal Navy. With the air squadrons embarked there were over a thousand men and women on board. As a consequence, the galleys ran night and day, cafeteria style.

Hunter had showered and dressed in clean shorts and T-shirt. The team had been kitted out in the NAAFI once Hunter had established a line of credit with the manager. Cabins had been allocated and the men were now taking well-earned rests. He sat picking at a meal of steak and baked potato but hardly noticed what he was eating, his thoughts on Ruth.

A surgeon had arrived from San Diego shortly after Ruth had landed and had gone straight to work.

The ship carried a fully-equipped operating theatre, manned by highly competent doctors used to dealing with serious wounds. Some of the best people in the world were working on Ruth's knee.

Waiting was so frustrating – the outcome so far beyond his control. He was worried and he didn't care who knew it. Hunter pushed his plate away and went and prowled the corridors outside the sick-bay.

After a while a junior doctor came out of a door and approached him. 'You're with the troops who flew in today, aren't you?'

'Yes. I'm the boss of the team. Hunter. Nick Hunter. Lieutenant Commander.'

'Ah! Right, sir. I didn't know.'

'That's all right. I work with an informal lot. What's happening to Ruth?'

'She's being well taken care of. Look, I've come out to get a cup of coffee. Come with me. There's nothing you can do here. They'll be hours yet.'

Hunter nodded, grateful for the distraction and the chance to learn more about Ruth's condition. The *Ark* was large enough to get lost in and strategically placed maps showing 'You are here' directed them. Enroute, the doctor introduced herself as Margaret Murray. She was in her mid-twenties and not long qualified. After a year at a shore establishment she was on her first sea assignment. She had removed her operating greens and was dressed immaculately in uniform. The gold braid on her shoulder boards with the red stripe in between gleamed, not yet tarnished by the salty air of sea time.

They went into the aircrews' mess. There were men and woman seated at tables, eating, drinking and smoking, going about their duties and their lives as usual. Hunter found the air of normality surreal, when Ruth was lying on the surgeon's table, in danger of losing her leg. 'Any idea when I'll be able to see her?'

'No. They've been working on her for three hours and I expect they'll be another ten or twelve . . .'

Hunter nodded gloomily. 'So long?'

'I'm afraid so. Look, the rock smashed not only her patella, her kneecap, but the surrounding bones and joints. They are taking out tiny slithers of bone and cartilage, cleaning the wound, fixing arteries and veins, and then rebuilding her bones. I've never seen anything like it. Believe me, if she was in a civilian hospital right now they would have amputated above the knee and had done with it.'

Hunter somehow managed not to blanch. 'I see.'

'This operation is pioneering stuff.' Margaret gulped her coffee. 'I need to get back. Will you be all right?'

He nodded, watching her go, sipping his coffee for a few minutes longer, thinking of the future. Ruth was such a strong, independent woman, how would the injury affect her? There was no way of telling. Finally, he stood up. He had work to do and brooding wasn't helping Ruth one iota.

He found Clements and Napier in a corner of the lower hangar, checking the gear they had brought back with them. Their weapons had been stowed in the ship's armoury and the inflatables collapsed and stowed.

Clements asked, 'How's Ruth?'

Hunter shrugged. 'They're working on her. We won't know anything for hours.'

'What's the score, Nick?' Napier was fixing one of the outboards to a tank of fresh water to flush out the seawater. 'Are we along for the cruise or are we being shipped home?'

'I've no idea, Doug. I'll go and see the Captain. He may know something. Have you seen Matt?'

'He's in the operating theatre, I think,' replied Napier.

Somehow Hunter wasn't surprised. Matt's paramedic experience would give him access. Knowing he was watching over Ruth made Hunter feel slightly better. 'Once the lads have had a decent sleep and something to eat tell them to take it easy.' Hunter stood in the hangar for a few seconds, looking around him. The ship was moving more slowly than he would normally expect and no fixed-wing operations were taking place, which was unusual. A moment later he arrived on the flight deck where a soccer game was being played. He saw that both Masters and Hughes were taking part. He grinned in spite of his worry.

Hunter ran up the stairs to the bridge. He attracted the attention of the Officer of the Watch. 'Permission to come on the bridge.'

'Granted.' The OOW held out his hand. 'Nick! Good to see you.'

'Hello, Jeremy. I hadn't realised you were on board.'

'Yep. I'm second ops. Let me introduce you to the Captain. Sir,' he turned to the grey haired man sitting in the captain's chair on the starboard side of the bridge, 'may I introduce Lt Cdr Hunter? Nick, this is Captain O'Neill.'

The Captain slid to the deck and offered his hand. 'Welcome aboard, Commander.'

'Thank you, sir. And thank you very much for your help. We wouldn't have made it otherwise.'

50

'All part of the service.' Holding up a signal clipboard O'Neill motioned for Hunter to follow him. 'I need to talk to you. You'd better come below.'

Stepping across the bridge he opened the door to the lift and gestured for Hunter to enter. Only the Captain used the lift and it was always on the floor where he was. It took him from his cabin up to the bridge or down to the operations room.

Once in his day cabin O'Neill said, 'Please, take a seat.' He sat at his desk. 'Do you know anything about the liner hijacked in the Gulf of Mexico?'

'No, sir. When did this happen?'

'A few hours ago. We're steaming towards the area, albeit rather slowly.'

'I noticed the ship wasn't moving at your usual speed. What are we doing? Eight knots?'

'Seven. At the surgeons' request, to give them the most stable platform while they operate on the woman.'

'Ah! Right. I see. Thanks, sir.'

The Captain shrugged. In his mid-fifties this was to be his last job in the Royal Navy. He was retiring in six months and looking forward to it. His craggy, narrow features and beetling eyebrows hid a keen sense of humour which, as a younger officer, had often got him into trouble. 'I received a signal a short while ago. Eyes-only-Captain. You're on notice to prepare to board the ship and take out the terrorists. That's all.' Shrewd eyes looked at Hunter. 'What do you need?'

If he was surprised by the announcement Hunter didn't show it. 'Secure communications to TIFAT, sir. My operators only.'

'Not a problem. I'll send for the Communications Officer. He can arrange it. What else?'

'I'll have my men check all the stores you have, sir, to see if there's anything we can use. I'll need permission to help ourselves.'

'No problem. The Supply Officer will sort it out. He'll give you anything you want.' The Captain smiled before adding the caveat, 'Provided you sign for it.'

O'Neill snatched a phone from a wall bracket behind him and

issued instructions. 'At this speed we won't be in the Gulf for days. Even if we increase to launch speed it would take too long to get you near enough to be of any assistance.'

Hunter nodded. 'I'm aware of that, sir. Is there a room I can use to brief my team?'

'Certainly. The aircrew briefing room is ideal. There's no flying for three days so you won't be disturbed. If there's anybody in there send them packing.'

'Thank you, sir.' Hunter stood up to leave.

'Good luck. Anything else, just ask.'

Hunter found Clements and Napier where he had left them. The soccer match was still in full swing. Hunter signalled Masters and Hughes that they were needed. They apologised to their team mates and joined the three officers.

'What's up, boss?'

'I'll tell you later. Round up the team and meet me in the aircrew briefing room in thirty minutes. Josh, Douglas, we need to find the communications centre.'

The *Ark's* Comms Centre was state-of-the-art, enabling communication with anyone in the world, anywhere and at anytime. Messages were automatically encrypted and, depending on how highly classified the message, were designed to withstand cracking by a sophisticated eavesdropper from eight hours to eight days. After that there were no guarantees. The power of computers was simply too great.

The *Ark Royal* was part of a task force and never travelled alone. Around her was a screen of three anti-submarine frigates and two anti-air destroyers. There had been so much interchanging of equipment in recent years that both classes of ship were now highly effective in either role. Hunter wondered if one could be detached.

The Communications Officer gave them a private cubicle and ran through the equipment with them. Hunter nodded his thanks and was soon talking to Isobel. She patched him through to the General. Ideas and information were exchanged and the contact broken. The TIFAT operatives sat in silent contemplation of their instructions for a few seconds.

'He's not asking much, is he?' Napier ventured finally.

'You could say that. I'd better go and talk to the Captain. You start briefing the lads. If we're to go, it'll be tomorrow night. And you'd better get a weather forecast.'

Hunter's meeting with the Captain was brief and to the point. Signals were already flying through the ether, giving orders, re-tasking the naval force. At the same time the President of the United States had issued his instructions and the logistical might of the biggest and best-equipped armed forces in the world was swinging into action.

Hunter went down to the briefing room. Detailed drawings of the liner had been sent, loaded into a computer and were already being projected onto a screen. The hijacked *SS Silver Beech* was nineteen thousand tonnes. It had five decks in total, four for the passengers' use. There were casinos, restaurants, a ballroom, cinemas, a range of shops, a theatre and on the top-most deck, two swimming pools. A golf range allowed fanatics the opportunity to hit golf balls made from a substance that dissolved harmlessly in seawater. Now the passengers' pleasure palace had become their prison.

'Since the hijacking nobody has been seen on the upper decks. There are no reports of casualties and to the best of our knowledge the ship is undamaged. We don't know how the terrorists got on board, whether they're fare paying passengers or were picked up at sea. The *Silver Beech* may have responded to a fake distress call. Isobel's lot are analysing the passenger and crew lists as we speak. Make lists of the gear we need. Brainstorm in pairs.'

At that moment the door opened and Captain O'Neill appeared. 'I've had a signal from TIFAT. I've brought it down to see if there's anything more you need.'

'We ought to get a move on, sir. I think we need to disembark to one of the escort vessels and head north as fast as possible.'

The Captain nodded. 'I came to the same conclusion after speaking to General Macnair. The *York* is the fastest ship in the task force. I've already detached her. She's steaming full ahead now. You'll transfer by helo.'

'Thank you, sir.'

'I gather a Lockheed C130 is being sent from San Diego.'

'Correct. There's specialist equipment which only Coronado or ourselves have.' Coronado was the base of SEAL Team 6, a source of highly-trained men to TIFAT.

'Well, rather you than me.' He looked at the tough individuals standing or sitting before him and nodded. 'Good luck to you.'

A chorus of thanks followed him from the room.

Throwing himself into the job of planning the operation enabled Hunter to put thoughts of Ruth to the back of his mind for much of the time. He was continually checking equipment, revising lists, talking to Macnair, or discussing the operation with the team. The job they were contemplating was highly dangerous. To drop from 25,000ft, at night, attempting to land on a moving target in the middle of the sea against unknown and armed terrorists was verging on the suicidal. The team had stealth, modern equipment and superb training in their favour. Hunter hoped it was enough to give them the edge they needed.

'Sir, the Pentagon's on the line.'

Macnair picked up the receiver. 'What's the news, Colin?'

'Bad. The cutters caught up with the liner and told them to heave to.' The American General paused, hating what he had to say next.

'How did the hijackers react?'

'The *Silver Beech* ignored the Coastguard until one of them put a shot across the liner's bows. At that moment passengers and masked gunmen appeared on the promenade deck. They opened communications on channel sixteen.' General Stafford paused again. This time Macnair did not prompt him. He had a sick feeling in the pit of his stomach.

'The bastards lined up men, women and children and shot them. Thirty innocent lives. Just like that. Then the bastards called on channel sixteen and told the cutters that if they were still within sight in fifteen minutes another thirty people would be shot.'

'What have the Coastguard done?'

'High-tailed it out of there.'

Macnair nodded. There had been no other option open to them. 'Any demands yet?'

'No, but the hijackers claim to have set a ring of explosives around the hull of the ship. Any trouble and they'll send the ship to the bottom with all lives.'

'Including their own.'

'Since when has that mattered to people like these?'

Macnair sighed heavily. 'You know this leaves us no option?'

'I know. We won't negotiate with terrorists under any circumstances. With the death of those passengers we have no choice. How are your team's preparations coming along?'

'It's all in hand. Their biggest problem is fatigue. They've been in the field for nearly a week and you know what happened in Suriname.'

'Tired or not, they're still the best we've got for this sort of operation. Are you in touch with Coronado?'

'Yes. All the special gear is being loaded. The C130 should be airborne soon. Hunter's team are transferring to *HMS York*. The ship will detach and make best speed for Trinidad. They'll helo ashore and be picked up by the Hercules.'

'Do you think this has anything to do with nine-eleven?'

'It would account for the slow passage of the liner. They would arrive in the US of A in time for some sort of commemorative attack. If that's their intention then I expect they'll be planning something pretty spectacular.'

The privately owned submarine had a crew of eight and could stay submerged for only ten hours. Designed and built by an Italian company, it was originally intended to take sightseers in comfort and safety down to depths of one hundred metres. It had a top speed of 8 knots submerged and each of the fifty seats, twenty five down either side, had a large port hole, for passengers to admire the wonders of the deep. For only two million dollars it had been a bargain.

Most of the seats had been removed and storage space created.

The original colour, a bright yellow, had been changed to a drab green. It was being transferred on the back of a pipe-laying ship, the *SS Goliath*, that was normally on charter to *Elf Nationale*, the French oil company.

The *Goliath* had departed Galveston in Texas twenty-four hours previously and was steaming at full speed towards the hijacked vessel. Already an exclusion zone had been set up around the liner and other Coastguard and United States Naval units had joined in the screen to keep away intruders. Nothing was being allowed within twenty miles of the *Silver Beech*.

Because of the electronic blackout created around the hijacked ship, the sub's rendezvous position had been established in advance. The crew was now working to a strict timetable.

Charles Gustav sat in the captain's quarters of the *Goliath* and looked at his assistant with narrowed eyes.

'You remain certain that all TIFAT teams are fully occupied?'

'We have accounted for all operatives. They are deployed in practically every country in Europe in one counter-terrorism operation or another. The exception,' he hesitated momentarily, 'is the team which wiped out our people in Suriname.'

'And cost me half a billion dollars.' Suppressed fury was betrayed only by the tell-tale white spots on Gustav's cheeks. He controlled his anger. Revenge would be all the more gratifying for the waiting.

Although Swedish by birth, Gustav was French by adoption, having moved to France in the late seventies. There he had begun to build his business empire. Now it spread around the globe like the tentacles of an octopus, encompassing everything from off-shore construction for the oil industry to huge media and publishing concerns. Known to be a billionaire many times over, Gustav was careful to hide his true worth from prying eyes, be they tax officials, governments or nosy reporters. He now used his wealth to finance his obsession – Europe inhabited only by white Christians and forced repatriation of all minorities. Second, third or fourth generation immigrants would be returned to the land of their ancestors. Whether it was Africa, India or any Muslim state, Gustav wanted them out of Europe.

The restoration of a white's only Europe would be a fitting tribute to the memory of his sister.

For ten years he had been working towards his goal and now it was within sight. Whilst Europe's politicians wrestled with strategic myopia, moral hypocrisy and futile wrangling for power, he, Gustav, was fuelling the tension between white and black. The anarchy building in the streets needed strong leadership to counteract it. Both political and military strength were called for and he, Charles Gustav, was the man to supply both. Over the years he had carefully nurtured politicians and military officers who had shown any sign of sharing his ideology. There had been mistakes over the decade but the challenges had served only to affirm his vision. The end of the Cold War meant that America's commitment to Europe was waning – she had her own battles to wage. Once American bases were shut down and all USA military personnel had returned to the States he would have greater freedom to act. Europe stood at a new dawn. There was wide disenchantment with conventional politics across the continent. Using his vast media empire, Gustav had continuously highlighted rising crime, threats to national security, rising unemployment, feeding on the electorate's paranoid fear of outsiders. He prided himself on the xenophobic reactions his red-top newspapers generated, increasing the sense of insecurity on both sides of the divide. Carefully plotting the rise in tension, his beautifully orchestrated flashpoints of conflict had led to a reawakening of extreme nationalism on a scale unprecedented since the Second World War.

Enlisting groups of skinheads and other fascist groups, and establishing networks of 'white-power' enthusiasts had given him particular pleasure. A complicated web of willing activists organised overt and covert attacks. Gustav had become adept at using his television and radio stations and newspapers to spread the message. And it was working. The disenchanted left were now voting for the right wing parties he surreptitiously helped to fund and establish.

His secretary, Duval, ever the observer, watched as Gustav stood up and paced the wood-panelled room, ten paces one way, ten the other. Lean and fit, an avid tennis player, Gustav had taken good care of himself. Now in his late fifties, he was a non-smoker and non-drinker. In all the time Duval had known him the Swede had never shown any interest in sex. His focus in life had been to make money, money to fund his dream of a whites-only Europe. At six feet three, he stooped slightly as though to listen more closely to what was being said to him. Those big, strong hands Duval knew had been used more than once to kill. Despite his shock of white hair Gustav's features were only saved from mediocrity by his eyes – a curious light grey which had a tendency to darken when angry. His tan was deep and even and owed nothing to the sunlamp. Gustav spent his time outdoors. He was a keen big game hunter, loved skiing and spent August on his yacht in the Mediterranean. There he dived for treasures from lost civilisations which he ceremoniously handed over to the Department of Antiquities in France. Let the French government argue ownership, particularly of those artefacts found in Egyptian or other African waters.

Ronald Duval had been his secretary for over twenty years. American by birth, Duval was of medium height and average weight. Behind immobile features was a first class mathematical brain which oversaw all of Gustav's business interests, allowing Gustav the time, energy and most importantly, the money, to pursue his objective.

Unknown to the Western authorities, one of the satellites which formed part of Gustav's media business also contained highly sophisticated eavesdropping equipment targeted at the security forces. He lacked the computer systems to break the codes as quickly or as accurately as Western governments but he enjoyed a great deal of success in interpreting them. It was imperative he knew TIFAT's movements.

The whereabouts of Hunter and his team was still a mystery, as all signals had been sent encrypted at the highest classification.

'Is everything ready?'

Duval nodded. 'We launch in two hours.'

'What's the shipping situation?'

'Nothing too close at the moment. We'll be well outside the exclusion zone when we put the submarine into the water.'

'And our Arab friends?'

'Have stayed in their cabins as ordered. They won't be any trouble.'

Gustav grimaced. 'They're Arabs. Excitable morons who through a quirk of nature own so much of the world's oil. If it wasn't for the West . . .'

Duval had heard the arguments before, many times. Over the years he had become inured to Gustav's rants. Twenty years ago Duval had been enthralled by the fierce intellectual arguments on race brought to bear by Gustav. But it was becoming increasingly clear that the man's senses were now totally warped, his former genius misdirected to the point that he was incapable of living in reality. Psychologists understood that such an obsession usually had its roots in childhood. In Gustav's case the root cause was found in the childhood of another – his sister. Duval thought about the file he had recently found. It's contents shocking and explicit, it explained Gustav's obsession.

Gustav's mother had died when he was young. A few years later his father had remarried. Unusually, Gustav and his stepmother had got on well together. She'd given birth to a daughter, named Katrina. A blonde, blue-eyed bundle of mischief. Charles had doted on her in spite of being seventeen years older. When Katrina was thirteen she had gone on a school holiday with her classroom friends to France. At the time, Charles had still been living and working in Sweden, attempting to buy his first local newspaper.

Negotiations had been at a crucial stage when he received the phone call from his distressed father. His beloved sister had been gang-raped and murdered.

It had taken nearly a week for the full story to be put together. The girls had been staying in a hostel near Royan in Western France. During visits to town they had been harassed by a group of youths. A gang of immigrants with little money and too much time on their hands. One evening the girls had become frightened and run away. Katrina had somehow become isolated from the rest. Her naked body had been found in a local park.

At first the pathologist refused to give Charles the details of the traumatic end of Katrina's short life. Finally he had relented when Gustav pointed out that the details would become known in court. Katrina had been raped by an estimated ten men. No orifice had been spared. She had bled to death. The information sent Charles Gustav over the edge of sanity for a short while.

No trial took place. DNA testing was still unavailable. Witnesses were too frightened to come forward even though the police were convinced of the identities of the ten youths responsible. A wall of silence protected them and the asylum seeking community closed ranks. The rapists varied in age from eleven to nineteen. Six were Algerian, two were Iraqis and two were Albanians. All were Muslim.

Charles' step-mother committed suicide exactly a year after Katrina's death. His father never recovered and spent the next three years vilifying all things Islamic, speaking out against immigrants at every opportunity. Most significantly, he gave Charles the money to buy his first newspaper on condition it reflected his xenophobic views. It did.

Charles bought another small paper and a commercial radio station. Just over three years after Katrina's death, his father was killed in a road accident. He had become a heavy drinker, looking for escape and solace in a bottle of schnapps. One winter's night he had been drinking. Driving too fast he had hit a tree. He had died on reaching hospital. Charles blamed the loss of his father on the immigrants who had killed his sister.

The money he inherited allowed him to expand more quickly. That was about the time he, Duval, had come on the scene. Duval had been auditing one of Charles' companies. Charles had made him an offer and he had accepted. They shared an intense dislike of non-white races although his own feelings were not as passionate as Charles'.

Since the death of Katrina, Charles had used his growing wealth to keep track of the youths who had abused and killed his sister. Much to Charles' chagrin one of the Iraqis died from a heroin overdose three years after Katrina's death. This prompted him to make his move.

In the course of the next three years, starting with the eldest, Charles had each man abducted. They died horrible deaths at the hands of a group of men who shared Charles' views. The men were paid handsomely for the work. There was only one condition attached. Before each man died he had to know *why*.

The last to die had been eleven at the time Katrina had been killed. He was seventeen when he bled to death from internal injuries inflicted by a pick-axe handle inserted into his rectum. It had taken him nearly twenty agonising hours to die. Charles had been there to watch, indeed to participate. Of the nine murdered, he had personally killed two of them.

Still Charles wasn't satisfied. He started a campaign against the families of the dead men, who had kept silent at the time of Katrina's murder. Houses were burnt down and people continually harassed. Two families, having received warnings that their children's lives were at stake, left France and returned to Algeria. It had been the beginning. From there it had been only a few steps to where they were today.

But a recent development had Duval truly worried. Using Arab fundamentalists to perpetrate these crimes in Europe – financing Islamic terrorism in order to turn the people of Europe against Islam itself – beggared belief.

Duval had made up his mind. After this, he was retiring. He had amassed a personal fortune of over fifty million dollars in various bank accounts around the world and he wanted to enjoy his wealth. Still the right side of fifty, he had so many things he wanted to see and do. And with that much money he could indulge his fantasies with the world's most beautiful women. This latest and most terrible act of terrorism was one step too far. America would never rest until they caught those responsible. And for the kind of reward that would be on offer, someone would betray him.

Duval's antennae picked up the question and he tuned back in.

'Are copies of the newspapers in yet?'

'No, sir. As soon as they are we'll get them. As requested, I spoke with the anchorman for 24 Hours.' The current affairs magazine was one of Gustav's flagship programmes and had been Duval's idea. Broadcast from 7pm to 8pm every day in every major European country, it was anti-immigrant, highly racist and right-wing. Frequently '24 Hours' was in trouble with the broadcasting standards authorities. Whenever there was a problem or complaint Gustav's print empire of newspapers swung into action, screaming that the minority interests of the immigrants were undermining the rights of the majority. The drip-feed of bigotry had led the people of Europe almost to the point of no return. Job losses were blamed on immigration. Poor housing? Blame the immigrants. No social security payments? Spent on the immigrants. Bad schooling? Overcrowded hospitals? Too much crime? Too many drugs on our streets? Judicial system too slow? Police stretched to breaking point? Everyone knew who was to blame. The immigrants.

The counter arguments, diversity of culture, much needed skills, highly intelligent, hard-working people prepared to do low paid, menial tasks, the backbone of health services across Europe, and so on, were lost in the clamour of perceived woes. Immigrants of all generations were finding it increasingly difficult to defend themselves. And now, with atrocities being committed across Europe by Islamic fundamentalists, the ideals of the right were being justified.

The cost of supporting the terrorists was huge though Gustav considered it money well spent. Funding Muslims to create their own ultimate destruction was a master stroke of genius. But even he could not afford the outlay for much longer. The loss of the Suriname shipment had been a terrible blow. Although his every instinct screamed for revenge against TIFAT, he knew it must be used as a major prop for the new regime he envisaged, its officers replaced by his own people. The possibilities were endless.

Gustav stopped pacing and looked at Duval for a moment before nodding. 'Check everything is as it should be and please let me know when the submarine is to be launched.'

Duval, dismissed, left the room and went up to the bridge. The Captain was sitting in his chair monitoring the dials arrayed in front of him. He looked up as Duval entered but said nothing. There was no love lost between the two men although they had only met the day before.

'How long to go?'

'Four and a half hours. I'll let you know when the sub's going in.'

'Good. Are the crew all right?'

'Why shouldn't they be? We may be short-handed but for a ten thousand dollar bonus they can manage.' His cut was twenty thousand and he was enjoying thinking about what he would spend it on while he sat on his bridge.

'Let's keep it that way.'

The ship had sailed with only a skeleton crew of six men. It was far too few for safety, in fact downright illegal, but the money on offer for a few days work was too great to resist. Apart from the captain and engineer there were four deckhands whose main task was to launch the submarine.

The *Goliath* was pitching into a long, low swell. Above, the sky was clear, the stars shining and a new moon was creeping over the horizon. The bridge-wing doors were open and Duval stood in the warm breeze for a few seconds, savouring the night. Thankfully the weather was in their favour. If there had been a high wind or a storm then the launch would have been next to impossible. As it was, everything was running to schedule.

A teleprinter clattered and the Captain heaved his bulk out of his chair and stepped across the bridge to take a look. It was the weather forecast. He scanned the map, read the information and grunted in satisfaction. A weak front was gathering in the north and would be sweeping across the Gulf in about twenty-four hours. Taking a file from the shelf above his head he put the report away. Perfect.

Duval was looking at him enquiringly.

'Weather forecast. Nothing to concern us.'

'Good. I'm going to check the sub,' replied Duval.

Aft of the bridge and accommodation, the deck was a large

flat area about a quarter of the size of a football field. Normally it was packed with pipes being transported to the oilfields but now lay empty, except for the submarine looking small and insignificant by comparison.

A tarpaulin covered the area and two people in overalls were walking around the outside of the sub, making last minute checks.

'Everything okay?'

'Yes, Mr Duval.'

Duval nodded. A pity, he thought. She was such a beautiful woman. It was a waste but unavoidable.

'All systems are go. The batteries are fully charged and the air scrubber has been tested.' Chantelle Suchard smiled, hiding her nervousness at what lay ahead.

'Excellent. We'll load in another two hours.' Duval left her to her preparations and returned to the bridge. It was his job, amongst many, to check and double check all arrangements. Nothing was left to chance.

The radar showed a few contacts and he questioned the Captain about them. They would pass well clear. So far everything was looking good.

Returning below decks he found Gustav reading copies of newspaper articles in English, French and Swedish, transmitted via satellite from his media empire. Gustav smiled with satisfaction. Governments were beginning to panic as Europe's citizens demanded action. In the previous twenty-four hours there had been nine incidents involving the deaths of white Europeans. The articles pointed the finger of blame squarely at Islamic fundamentalists. If it was untrue, who cared? A retraction of a story meant a small paragraph buried on page nine. The story itself made front page headlines.

'Excellent. By next week, the clamour will be overwhelming. With America under siege the President will have no choice but to withdraw his troops. That will leave the road clear for us.'

Duval nodded. It was impossible to have a whites-only Europe if American troops were stationed there. Too many of them were black. With the event Gustav planned for the anniversary of 9/11, the Americans wouldn't hesitate to fall back and protect their borders.

The phone rang and Duval answered it. 'We're at the drop-off point.'

'Good. Time to open the safe.' From inside the safe Gustav gingerly removed a round object about the size of a football. Hard, dark-brown and seamless, the sphere appeared to be made of plastic. In fact its whole surface was an aerial. Inside was a small detonating device that could be set off by a signal from a satellite or a transmitter. With one explosion, two litres of nerve agent would be released into the atmosphere. Contact meant death within three to four minutes – a horrible and painful death, with no available antidote. The toxic gas had a life of eight hours after which it was rendered harmless by oxygen in the atmosphere. From computer analysis Gustav estimated between 100,000 and 250,000 people would die in the targeted area – Houston, Texas.

Handing the sphere to his secretary he said, 'No mistakes, Duval.'

Back on the pipe deck Duval watched eight al-Qaeda operatives climb into the sub. The last man, a machine gun slung over his shoulder, waited for him. In his early thirties, Abu Al-Adil had a pathological hatred for all non-Muslims. He was a Saudi by birth and a fanatical follower of bin Laden by choice. Alive or dead, bin Laden continued to exert a huge influence across the Islamic world.

'Here is the toxin.'

Abu Al-Adil took the proffered sphere with breathtaking nonchalance and dropped it into a string-bag.

'You know what you must do?'

'Of course. We attack those whom Allah the All-knowing has cursed. Judgement is his alone but this deed will be a glorious tribute to his name.'

Duval kept a straight face. Their fanaticism appalled him. Once again he marvelled at Gustav's manipulation of their commitment to God. It was a master stroke.

Waving casually to Chantelle sitting in the pilot's position in the front of the sub, he stood and watched as the ladder up to the conning tower was removed. The hatch was closed and Duval ducked under the hull and paused for a second. Placing a high explosive onto the hull he pressed the micro-electric switch. The magnetic bond would be impossible to break without first removing the battery. He signalled the crane driver, the strops were raised until they took the weight and then the sub was raised into the air and swung gently outboard.

As the submarine dropped below deck level, Duval waved one last time to Chantelle. Reaching the water, the engine was started and, as the weight came off the lifting strops, the gears were engaged. The sub inched slowly backwards clear of the strop and away from the ship's side. There were no lights showing and almost immediately the sub sank from view.

Duval returned to Gustav who was nervously pacing the cabin. 'All done?'

'They are on their way to the *Silver Beech*.'

Something in Duval's inflection caused Gustav to step directly in front of his assistant. As always, he knew what was bothering him. 'Chantelle has been a very useful ally. She is also greedy and unscrupulous. The temptation to tell the Americans of my involvement would have proven too great.'

Duval nodded. But that also applied to himself. Did Gustav have similar plans for him?

5

The operation on Ruth's knee was still in progress. Hunter was shocked to realise that the surgeons had been working on her for nearly fourteen hours. Finally, Matt Dunston appeared, looking exhausted.

'All I did was stand and watch and occasionally fetch cold water for the doctors. What they're doing is amazing, pioneering stuff. They've rebuilt all the shattered bits of bone and literally glued them back together.'

'How much longer will they be?'

'Not long. They've almost finished.'

'What's the prognosis?' The briefest eye-contact betrayed the anxiety behind Hunter's question.

'No idea. She won't be running the marathon for a long time, if ever, but it looks as though she'll keep her leg.'

'Thank God,' said Hunter, feeling a terrible weight leave him.

Dunston nodded. 'Amen to that. Praying was all I was good for.'

'Well, it looks as if your prayers are needed again. I've a lot to tell you. Come on.'

In the briefing room Hunter went over the operation in detail. As soon as he heard the plan, Dunston said, 'I'm coming.'

Hunter nodded. He wasn't surprised. 'I figured you'd want to.'

Just then, Masters appeared with a wide smile, waving something in his hand. 'Look what I've found, boss. An ex-torch.'

Hunter grinned back. 'Excellent. That'll make searching for any explosives far easier.'

The ex-torch was an explosives detector, the size of a torch-light and powered by four ordinary batteries. Instead of a beam of light, it emitted an x-ray that also carried an explosive sensor beam. The unique, unstable atoms of an explosive could be detected by the ex-torch through walls and even steel up to an inch thick. If any explosives were found the green light on the base of the torch would change to amber or red depending on the power of the signal. The ex-torch was new on the market and although TIFAT had tested them, Hunter was surprised Masters' had found one on board.

'The Petty Officer Jack Dusty ordered it by mistake. It was slotted for return as soon as they got back to Pompey.'

'His mistake is our good fortune. Have you tried it out?'

'Yes, boss. Works like a charm. You'd better take it.'

'Thanks.' The torch was a godsend in the circumstances. Placing it on the desk, Hunter then thought better of it. In any sea it could roll off and be damaged. He packed it with his other kit, ready to go.

The phone rang and Hunter answered. The Officer of the Watch on the bridge informed him that the helicopter was ready to move the team to the destroyer, *HMS York*.

Hunter had one call to make before he left. He found Ruth in the sickbay, her face pale and wan, the pain she had suffered etched deeply into her face. A sickbay attendant sat next to her, thumbing through the day's newspaper produced by the ship.

'How is she?' Hunter asked him. 'Do you know how successful the operation was?'

'I can't say, sir, but here's someone who can.'

A tall, distinguished-looking man entered.

'Are you the surgeon who operated on Ruth?'

'Yes. How do you do?' He extended a long, slim hand that had a surprisingly strong grip. 'Surgeon Commander Fred Stewart.'

'My name's Hunter, Lieutenant Commander Hunter. Pleased to meet you, sir. Ruth's a member of my team.' He did not elaborate on his personal relationship with her. 'How is she?'

The surgeon shrugged and pulled an expressive face. He ran a tired hand through his greying hair. 'It's too soon to tell.'

'She will be able to walk again?'

'Oh, I should think so. Impossible to say yet how mobile the joint will be. It will, however, never be as good as it was. I fear her days in the front line are over. I understand from Matt Dunston that she's at TIFAT.'

'Yes.' If Hunter was dismayed by the news he didn't show it.

'Sorry I can't be more specific, but the reconstruction still comes very much under the heading of pioneering medicine. I've only performed it twice with our own people at Coronado.'

'Were those operations successful?'

'It depends on how you define success. One of the men had his foot shattered when a terrorist bomb went off in Bosnia. I put it back together again and he has maybe fifty, sixty percent articulation of the ankle. He's teaching with the SEALs and has just been promoted to Chief Petty Officer.' The surgeon paused, glancing at his sleeping patient.

'And the second one?' Hunter prompted him.

'Ah. Not so good, I'm afraid. A young man who had his heart set on becoming a SEAL. He was flying through the course. He even enjoyed Hell Week!'

Hunter nodded. He knew how tough the course was. Even after very careful selection, fewer than half the men passed. 'What happened?'

'A stupid accident. He was abseiling when his rope snagged and he took a bad fall. His left leg was shattered. I worked hard on that young man and he got about seventy percent use of his leg back.' Pausing again, he shook his head in sorrow. 'It meant he was out of the SEALs of course.'

'What happened to him?'

'He committed suicide. Decided there was nothing to live for. None of us had an inkling until we found his note. One of my failures.'

'And you can't be more accurate about Ruth's prognosis?'

The surgeon rubbed his bristled chin, fatigue evident in his kindly, brown eyes. 'If you mean, what's the worse case scenario,

I think she could have only partial movement of the knee. Even so, it should be enough so that she can walk without a limp. Sitting will be awkward, though not impossible. She'll have discomfort, twinges of pain, for a very long time, even after the bones have knit. In later life she will probably suffer from rheumatism in her knee but anti-inflammatory drugs will help. She'll be able to dance but probably not run. If I said any more, I'd be guessing.'

'Thanks for your honesty. I appreciate it.'

The surgeon looked at him shrewdly. 'Something tells me there's more to your relationship than just her being a member of your team.'

Hunter grinned wryly. 'We're planning to get married.'

'Well, congratulations. With the right support she'll come through her ordeal. Now, if you'll excuse me. I'd like to examine my patient and then get some sleep.'

Hunter nodded and the two men shook hands again. 'Thanks, Doc. Thanks very much.' With a final glance, Hunter left. Things were not as they were, but they could have been much worse.

Minutes later he was on board the helicopter and he and the team were being whisked across to *HMS York*. Now that Ruth's operation was over the task force was running at its more usual 15 knots with the *York* already twenty miles ahead with full speed rung-on. The destroyer turned to put the wind across her deck at green four-five, forty-five degrees over her starboard bow, and prepared to receive the Lynx Mk 8 she had despatched to pick up the TIFAT team. Hunter could clearly see her pennant number, D98, on the ship's port side and stern.

The helicopter made three trips back and forth to the aircraft carrier, ferrying the team and their equipment. Hunter was on the first flight and as soon as it landed he quickly made his way to the bridge.

Hunter asked permission to enter and stepped forward with a smile. Captain Brian Matthews returned the smile and the two men shook hands. 'Nick, what a pleasant surprise! I had no idea it was you who was coming. We'll go below and you can brief me. Officer of the Watch, I'll be in my day cabin. Let me know when the Lynx is returning.'

'Aye, aye, sir,' the Officer of the Watch acknowledged.

The last time Hunter and Matthews had served together had been on board *HMS Antrim*. Hunter had been a sub-lieutenant trying to earn his watch-keeping certificate, while Matthews had just been promoted to lieutenant commander and was the ship's navigating officer. Hunter had been his assistant for nearly two years.

With a welcome cup of coffee at his elbow, Hunter brought Matthews up to speed on what was happening.

'My orders were simply to detach and head at full speed towards Trinidad and that the team leader would brief me. You'll be sent ashore by helo the minute we're within range. As soon as you're disembarked we're to join the exclusion zone around the liner.'

'I would have thought the Yanks had sufficient ships for the job.'

'We make it an international affair, politically preferable, don't you know?'

Hunter nodded. 'Makes sense. As soon as the remainder of my men arrive we'll bunk down and get some sleep.'

'I'm afraid all we can offer are camp beds. Three of you can sleep in the sick-bay.'

'We'll manage. Thanks, sir. After nearly a week in the jungle this will be luxury. First though, I need to contact TIFAT and find out if they've any Intel for me.'

'I'll take you to the Comms Centre and then I had better get to the Ops Room. I'll also brief the crew. How much can I tell them?'

Hunter shrugged. 'The minimum.'

Matthews nodded. 'Pretty much what I expected.'

The submarine settled on its course at a depth of fifty metres. Usually, when taking passengers for a night trip, her powerful searchlights shone in all directions. Now she sailed in darkness, using sonar and cameras only. The monitor in front of Chantelle

Suchard showed a sea alive with all kinds of fish. Many of them were unknown to her but she had no difficulty recognising a tiger shark and a shoal of barracuda.

Chantelle piloted the boat in silence. She had nothing in common with the man in the co-pilot's seat. From the moment they had met she had loathed him almost as much as he disliked her. Arabs, their habits and rituals repulsed her.

Her eyes checked the instruments and she made a minute alteration of the dial for the automatic pilot. The electric motors ran silently, with only the faintest of vibrations indicating that they were operating. Outside, the sea was black, apart from the flashes of phosphorescent plankton which swept past the window. Three TV screens gave her a view ahead of 180 degrees. The small amount of light that did exist, even when the world seemed dark, was enhanced by computers which also added colour. The resulting pictures were almost as clear as daylight out as far as three or four cables.

Taking a sip of water from the bottle in the holder in front of her, she allowed herself to day-dream. The two million euros promised by Gustav would be very useful. She could pay off the mortgage on her apartment in the South of France and possibly buy a ski chalet. Or maybe a yacht? Something sleek. She could keep it in the marina at Golfe Juan near Cannes. Automatically, she registered the battery dials, the oil pressure, the atmospheric sensors analysing the air. Everything was working correctly. This had to be the easiest money she had ever earned. Meeting Charles had turned her life around. He had been generous in the extreme. Initially she had expected him to make a pass, but it never happened. Part of her was disappointed, but on the whole she was relieved. She liked keeping her business and private life separate.

She shared his dream, his goal. A whites-only Europe was something her parents had often talked about. Thinking of them, Chantelle's fists clenched involuntarily on the arms of her chair. Their car had been involved in a head-on collision on a mountain road in Bavaria. They had been killed outright. The occupants of the other car, two Kurds seeking political asylum from

Saddam Hussein's regime, had been driving a beaten up wreck, uninsured and without valid driving licences. One of the men had died and the other had walked away. He had not even been prosecuted. Bile erupted in her stomach. Six months later she had met Gustav. His rhetoric had been balm to her grieving soul. Chantelle forced herself to relax and checked the navigation data. They would be with the liner in three hours and ten minutes. She informed her co-pilot, Al-Adil, who merely grunted in acknowledgement. *Loathsome swine.*

Abu Al-Adil was busy with his own thoughts. He was looking forward to seeing his younger brother again, although their meeting would be brief. But they would have all of eternity together in paradise, God willing. His heart pounded in excitement. The name of Abu Al-Adil would go down in Arab history. He would become as famous as their exalted leader, Osama bin Laden, whose name was spoken with such reverence across the Islamic world. He had only one task, to get the *Silver Beech* to Texas. In order to do so every man, woman and child on the liner were to be used. If the Americans tried to stop them, he would kill the passengers and crew indiscriminately. It would keep the Americans away until it was too late. His eyes glinted with anticipation as he looked out of the darkened window, oblivious to the beauty of the sea around him.

As the submarine approached the rendezvous position, Chantelle took them up to five metres and raised a thin periscope above the surface of the sea. She had no need to look through old fashioned eyepieces. Instead an all-round picture appeared on screens in front of her. It was still dark, although dawn was not far away. She adjusted the magnification and there she was, gleaming white, at a distance of four miles. Chantelle plotted a course to intercept the *Silver Beech.*

The liner was travelling due north at a speed of 4 knots and Chantelle brought the submarine expertly to the ship's port side, paralleling the course and speed of the large vessel, before surfacing.

Al-Adil had gone back to join his men, and when she gave the signal, he opened the hatch. The sea was calm and the sub moved sedately alongside. Chantelle switched the power to diesel and began to recharge the batteries while the men passed up their equipment to others on board the liner.

Al-Adil did not even say goodbye. After a few minutes Chantelle realised there was no sound behind her and when she looked, she saw the lounge was empty. Angrily she climbed from her seat, closed the outer and inner hatches and sat back at her control console. Without a glance at the liner she turned the sub away and began to submerge. Once she was clear she sent a signal to Gustav. *Mission accomplished.*

Duval heard the insistent beeping and snapped awake. He checked the signal from Chantelle and went to find Gustav.

'Good. You know what's required now. Send for the helicopter. I want to get back to Europe as quickly as possible.'

Minutes later Duval appeared on the bridge with a mug of coffee and a sandwich. 'I brought you these, Captain. We should call the crew – the sub will be back soon.' After the submarine had been despatched the men had hit their bunks in anticipation of an early start.

In order to facilitate such a small crew, the only cooked food aboard the *Goliath* was a large pot of stew kept warm on the range in the galley. It was topped up from time to time by a tin of soup or casserole. Otherwise the crew ate bread, biscuits and fresh fruit. An urn of boiling water for hot drinks was also provided and it was into this that Duval had placed a powerful sleeping draught. As an afterthought he had added it to the stew and a flask of orange juice.

If he was surprised by the offer of the food and drink the Captain did not show it. Nodding his thanks, he wolfed down the sandwich and washed it down with the coffee. It wasn't as hot as he liked and he drained the mug in three swift gulps.

'Thanks.' He seated himself back in his chair and reached for the microphone to the tannoy system. He announced it was time to 'rise and shine', and to be ready to receive the submarine alongside in half an hour.

The crew arrived in the galley one after the other, tired,

yawning, keen to get the recovery over with. They helped themselves to juice, tea or coffee and a sandwich. None of them bothered with the stew. They were sick of the sight of it.

Satisfied that the men had drunk enough of the drug to put a horse to sleep, Duval went back to the bridge. He found the Captain fast asleep in his chair. Lifting the microphone he broadcast, 'Do you hear there? There's been a change of plan. The sub will not be returning for another three hours. I suggest you all return to your cabins and get some more sleep.'

The men, already feeling the affects of the drug, returned to their bunks. Gustav appeared on the bridge.

'I see the drug worked as expected. Have you contacted the helicopter yet?'

'Yes, sir. It'll be here in one hour.'

'Sufficient time for you to set the charges.' An accomplished sailor, Gustav ensured there was no shipping in the vicinity and altered course to the east. Increasing speed, he watched with satisfaction as the bow wave grew. He set the cruise control to 18 knots. Glancing at the bridge clock, he saw the time had come. The radio at the back of the bridge had been modified and carried a very-ultra high frequency signal on the back of a high frequency pulse. Its signal was picked up by a thin wire trailing from the submarine.

Chantelle, in accordance with her instructions, was at a depth of ten meters and had released the antennae buoy which now trailed behind the sub. In one minute Gustav would call her to confirm everything was in order and that the rendezvous point remained as originally planned. She checked the battery power. All systems were working correctly and in less than three hours she would be able to have a hot shower and a few hours sleep. She yawned happily at the prospect.

The submarine shuddered and suddenly she was wide awake, thoughts of a shower and sleep wiped from her mind. Coolly she ran her eyes over the gauges in front of her. What the hell had happened?

The engines were running smoothly, the life support system

was functioning, the sub was moving at 4 knots through the water and . . . and the depth was fifteen metres and increasing. She checked the gauge again, aghast. It was impossible. She checked the trim and the levels of water ballast and knew that she should have been on a level keel. Her hands flew across the console as she opened valves to dump water. The depth gauge was now showing nineteen, twenty, twenty-one metres and still going down. Finally it stabilised. The needle trembled at twenty metres and began to unwind back up. Nineteen, eighteen . . . *Come on, you bitch. Come on*, Chantelle prayed. Fifteen, fourteen . . . Yes! It looked like she was going to make it!

The needle stopped moving. For a heart-wrenching moment it was static, then it began to wind down once more. Chantelle sat frozen for a second and then checked the echo sounder. The sea floor was over two hundred metres away. If she hit there she would never escape alive. The submarine lurched, now at fifteen degrees to the horizontal and sinking faster all the time. She could hear cracking noises all around; the outer hull was breached and the inner one was feeling the strain. Grabbing the release valves she began to pressurise the submarine with air.

In the event of an emergency there were numerous means of escape. The sub was intended to carry fare-paying passengers and as such had fail-safe systems incorporated into the design. The rupturing of the outer hull was unheard of. Only an explosion could do that. An explosion! Cold certainty swept through her with the thought. Gustav was trying to kill her!

Her brain still struggling to grasp this betrayal, Chantelle moved quickly. If she were to escape the vessel whilst under the surface she needed to equalise the pressure inside and out. Then the escape hatches could be opened and she could swim to the surface using the emergency breathing masks. She cracked open the bottle valves as far as they would go, feeling the pressure increasing rapidly. Thank God she dived regularly, as otherwise she doubted her eardrums would have been able to take the pressure change.

In the passengers' lounge she whipped open the wheel above her head and let the hatch drop inwards. Frantically she pulled

down the emergency ladder and climbed the few rungs she needed
to reach the outer hatch. She turned the wheel and pushed with
all her strength. It wouldn't move. The sea pressure outside was
too great.

Glancing at the repeat depth gauge on the bulkhead panic
flared in her. The sub was at forty-eight metres and still dropping. She pulled open a tool box and grabbed the heaviest wrench.
Grunting with effort she attacked the air bottle bank. Her hands
and arms jarred as she smashed at the connecting pipes and
valves. Leaks appeared and the air escaped into the submarine
faster than ever. The pain in her ears was excruciating. She swallowed and tried holding her nose, blowing hard, trying to clear
them. Suddenly the pain vanished and she knew her eardrums
had burst. The gauge was at sixty metres when she dropped the
wrench and climbed back up to the hatch. Escape hood and air
bottle slung over her shoulder, she put her back to the hatch and
pushed until her eyeballs popped and her muscles ached with
the strain. Finally the seal cracked and water poured in but she
couldn't sustain the pressure and the hatch closed again. Taking
a deep breath she readied herself mentally and pushed again.
With a gut-wrenching, back-breaking effort she raised the hatch
an inch. Water poured in and the pressure in the submarine
suddenly equalised. The hatch opened and Chantelle, trembling,
climbed out.

Slipping the mouthpiece between her teeth and the hood over
her head, she began to swim to the surface. She knew that she
was 70 maybe 80 metres beneath the surface. She needed decompression stops but she had no idea how many, at what depth or
for how long. Briefly she contemplated what faced her when she
reached the surface, rising from that depth. For a second she
almost spat out the mouthpiece, but something forced her on.
The deepest she had ever been was 40 metres and that for less
than ten minutes.

Even as Chantelle had been desperately trying to escape,
hatches on the side of the sub had blown open and self-inflating
life-rafts had popped to the surface. As soon as they hit, automatic beacons started broadcasting and could be heard by ships

and aircraft many miles away. The United States Coastguard, on station around the liner, fixed the location of the beacons within seconds. Five minutes later a helicopter was airborne and heading towards her.

Swimming upwards through twenty, fifteen, ten metres, Chantelle watched the sharks begin to gather. She was trailing blood from a cut in her hand. The prehistoric predators were already circling. She had intended to hang in the water at ten metres until her air ran out, to help with her decompression. That was no longer an option. Fear clawed at her. Should she survive Charles Gustav would regret his treachery.

As she watched, one of the sharks, from the mottled appearance of its skin a tiger, came closer and almost touched her. Chantelle knew there was no escape. The sharks would be on her within seconds of reaching the surface. Again she considered spitting out the tit and breathing in water but she had a perverse, overwhelming desire to feel the sun on her face once more. Looking up she saw the yellow bottom of a life-raft, then a second and a third. Suddenly hoped flared within her.

Hitting the surface she swam frantically for the nearest inflatable. A black fin appeared, bearing down on her even as she grabbed the side of the raft. Kicking frantically she pulled herself inside the canopy and lay there gasping, tears in her eyes. After a few moments rest she gathered her wits and sat up to take stock. She found glucose sweets, water and a Very pistol. She drank a pint of water. As she lay quietly, gathering her strength, the pain struck. Her body convulsed as though an electric shock had coursed through her nervous system and she knew she had the bends. It passed but she knew another spasm would occur any second, then another, each worse than the last, until the pain was continuous and agonising. The solution was to grab the escape bottle and dive down until the pain ceased. But below the surface, the sharks were waiting. Gathering her wits, she ripped open the first aid kit and frantically searched through it. The hypodermic carried a warning. Use only in extreme emergency. Moaning, she broke the seal and rammed the needle into her biceps. She pushed the plunger steadily, emptying the narcotic into her system. Taking a second hypodermic she injected her thigh. Another spasm hit, worse than the first and she screamed in agony. When the third spasm came she was unconscious.

Chantelle didn't hear the helicopter, nor did she see the crewman being lowered and checking each raft. Hers was the third and final raft. As she was lifted into the helicopter and flown back to the ship, her condition worsened, the bubbles boiling in her blood causing irreparable damage to her nerve ends. She remained unconscious, unable to tell her rescuers the harm they were doing.

With 32 knots rung on, *HMS York* heeled sharply whenever the ship altered course. A warning pipe was made over the tannoy system to give the ship's company time to brace but even so a few bruises were inevitable. Hunter had spent most of his time on board talking with TIFAT HQ, planning, refining the operation, discussing options. As always, they were looking for a backdoor.

Reaching the liner safely was the most dangerous part of the mission. Once on board the team had at least some control over their destinies. Every precaution would be taken but the initial stage of the operation was risky in the extreme.

Macnair finally had a back-up solution. 'I've learnt that the nuclear submarine *USS Swordfish* is steaming at full speed for the area. It will arrive around midnight and take up station about half a mile astern of the liner. Its task is to watch and follow. The SEALs have emergency transponders which they're supplying with the other kit. If you fail to land on the liner, set off the alarm and the *Swordfish* will pick you up. Apparently they're accurate to within a few feet so there shouldn't be any difficulties. What's the weather forecast, Nick?'

'There's a weak front coming down from the north. Gusts are fifteen, twenty knots. It shouldn't be a problem, unless they hit at the wrong time.'

'Have you received a full list of the equipment Coronado are sending?'

'Yes, thanks, sir. It's as comprehensive as you'd expect. They're pulling out all the stops to help.'

'When the chips are down we know who our friends are. When are you leaving the *York*?'

'In approximately two hours. The C130 will be waiting at Trinidad when we arrive. Has Isobel learnt any more?'

'Some. The money trail definitely links Al-Qaeda terrorist acts in Europe and the smugglers in Suriname. Leo has managed to trace the cash to an account in a Jamaican bank which is actually fed from Paris. The sums involved are staggering.'

'Isobel's instincts were spot on as usual. I saw on the news bulletin that Seville's cathedral has been damaged.'

'The attacks are unrelenting now. Al-Qaeda have admitted responsibility for the bomb. The cathedral was built in the fifteen century on the site of a mosque, apparently. It's full of priceless art treasures. Now the Muslims are claiming the site for themselves; they're demanding a mosque be rebuilt there.'

'That's ludicrous, sir.'

'Of course it is. Islamic leaders all over the world reject the demands of these fundamentalist madmen. They've even said that Israel must cease to exist and all Jews must return to their countries of origin. They know none of it is possible. It's getting totally out of hand, Nick. We now have armed men guarding cathedrals and churches all over Europe. As many as a dozen people have been accidentally killed by armed police. The right-wing are in a feeding frenzy. There's a police presence at all major tourist sites, department stores, subways, airports, railway stations. It's even been suggested we deploy the military. Over two dozen mosques have been torched. In Germany a mosque was shown being set on fire on TV and the police stood and watched it happen. The situation's even worse in France. The gutter press are stirring it for all they're worth. The EU is talking about implementing legislation which will play into the hands of the bigots. Enough politics, Nick. You concentrate on the operation in hand and leave the big picture to me.'

'Roger that. Can you confirm that the hijackers have planted explosives on the ship?'

'That was the information given to the US Coastguard and I've no reason to doubt it. PACER SKY has been tracking and watching the liner for hours now. The only people we have seen on the upperdeck have been carrying weapons. Isobel is forwarding some of the images we've received. See what you make of them. They should be with you by now. There's also an interesting clip that Isobel cut out and sent. See what you make of it.'

'I'll go and have a look now, sir. Thanks.' Breaking the connection, Hunter walked thoughtfully up to the Operations Room. The *York* was in defence watches and half the ship was closed up and on duty. The helicopter was returning from its final trip from the aircraft carrier and would be arriving in ten minutes. The ship had been called to flying stations to receive it. Hunter stopped by the surface plot to see how busy the sea was around them. The marked contacts exceeded forty and he decided to stay away from the bridge which had been his next port of call. They would be busy dodging shipping and recovering the helo. He felt the ship slow down for the landing and made his way aft to greet the rest of the team.

They sat in an annexe of the Operations Room and looked at the pictures of the *Silver Beech* beamed in from PACER SKY. As always, the clarity was startling. Four terrorists could be clearly seen patrolling the upper deck with guns slung over their shoulders. Two were on the topmost deck while another two were on the main promenade deck, three decks down.

'Why are the men outside?' Hunter asked the group. 'Are they guarding against somebody trying to make a bolt for it, or an attack by us?'

Clements voiced his thoughts. 'Travelling at such a slow speed the ship's crew must know that they can launch lifeboats and life-rafts. I think it's to stop people escaping.'

Jan Badonovitch clicked his fingers and pointed at the screen. 'That's true boss, but I think they're looking out for submarines. See how they're leaning on the rail and looking at the sea. They fear a sub sending in special forces.'

'You could be right,' said Hunter. 'It's encouraging that nobody appears to be looking at the sky.' Hunter pressed a button on the console in front of him. 'The General suggested we look at the next bit of film and see what we make of it.'

They watched as the port lifeboats were slung out and lowered halfway to the sea. White awnings were thrown over the boats and fitted from one to the other, creating a canopy running a third of the length of the ship and projecting about twenty feet out. The screen split, the left half showing video, the right showing infra-red images.

A hot-spot appeared under the canopy. It was large and tracked alongside the ship. Smaller hot-spots appeared, evidently people. Probably passing items inboard. They quickly finished and the bigger hot-spot vanished.

'They've just been reinforced,' said Don Masters. 'I counted seven extra.'

'I counted eight,' frowned David Hughes. 'Though it was difficult to tell.'

'Makes no difference,' said Hunter. 'We've no idea how many were there in the first place.'

'That was definitely a submarine alongside,' said Claude Masson. 'But whose?'

'Good question, Claude,' said Hunter. 'We need to find out in a hurry. A submarine suggests an enemy government. And it also begs the question, what gear was taken on board? What nasty surprises do they have in store for us?' He let the thought hang in the air.

A rating knocked on the door and put his head round. 'Sir, the Captain wants you on the bridge.'

'Thanks. I'll be right there.'

Matthews, seated in his chair, was leafing through his signal pad when Hunter arrived. 'You sent for me, sir?'

'Yes, Nick. Two things. One, we'll be within range in an hour for the first sortie and two, take a look at this.'

Hunter took the proffered signal pad. It was a general message from the Coastguard to all ships relating the rescue of a survivor from a sunken vessel. They had located three large life-rafts in the area but nobody else was found. 'Where exactly is this, sir?'

'I need to plot the position but I think it's relatively near the liner. At least within fifty miles of it.' Sliding off his seat, Matthews added, 'Let's take a look.'

In the chart room the captain identified the correct folio and slid it from its drawer. Consulting the list on the front, he took out the appropriate chart, spreading it on the table. Using a parallel ruler and pencil he established the position of the liner and the life-raft.

'It's too close to be a coincidence as far as I'm concerned,' said Hunter.

'Me too. The signal says the survivor was a young woman. But where did she come from?'

'No idea. Have we pictures of the area prior to her being found?'

'Not yet. I've asked for them.' The phone went and Matthews lifted the receiver. 'Captain.' He listened for a moment and said, 'I'll be right there.' Replacing the phone he smiled at Hunter. 'The satellite pictures have just arrived. Let's go to the ops room and take a look.'

By superimposing a latitude and longitude lattice over the screen they were able to watch the movement of ships and small craft in the area for an hour prior to the appearance of the rafts. The film, in fast frame, took only seven minutes to view.

'There they are,' said Hunter. 'They appear literally out of the blue.'

'Obviously a submarine,' said the Captain.

'And I think I know which one.' Briefly Hunter described the film footage of the sub going alongside the *Silver Beech*.

'It makes sense but why and how?'

'I'd better radio the General. If I'm right then the sooner the woman talks the better.'

6

Chantelle groaned in her sleep. The bubbles of nitrogen in her bloodstream had grown to a devastating size and were trapped in her joints and spine. Nerve ends were being irreparably damaged. The effects of the powerful narcotic she had taken were wearing off and the pain was beginning to penetrate. Suddenly she snapped awake and screamed.

A medical orderly ran to her side. Chantelle writhed and groaned, tears streaming down her face. In a panic, he took another ampoule of a powerful painkiller and injected her with it. In a few seconds she lay quiet again, her screams reduced to a whimper. Immediately the medic telephoned the captain.

'What the hell is causing it?'

'I've no idea, sir. There's no obvious cause of pain – no broken bones, nothing. She could have ingested something, but . . .' he paused.

'What?' his captain prompted him.

'There's only one thing that fits, sir,' the medic said dubiously. 'But it don't make no sense. I think she's got decompression sickness. The bends.'

After a few seconds of thought the Captain said, 'It could be. But how did she come by the bends in the middle of the Gulf?'

'I've no idea, but it's the only thing that fits.'

'We've no chamber. She needs to be sent ashore. Good work, Hudson. I'll send the helo.'

Chantelle was airlifted to Galveston where a special unit dealt with diving accidents. She was pressurised in a diving chamber by a doctor who saw her pain easing almost immediately. However, he knew that it was too late. The damage would be permanent. Such a beautiful girl too.

Gustav checked the ropes securing the ship's master to his seat before he poured himself a cup of fresh coffee. Checking the radar, there were no other vessels inside fifteen miles. The radio burst into life and he heard the ship's call sign. Answering it, he established that the helicopter would be with them in fifteen minutes. He nodded with satisfaction. Everything was going according to plan. With the submersible and Chantelle gone and the ship and its crew following soon after, his tracks were being well covered. The helicopter crew would have no idea what was happening and would never make the connection between the events on the liner and him. After all, the world press knew the hijackers were Arabs.

'Duval appeared on the bridge. 'I've taken our bags down to the deck.'

'Good. Here's the helicopter.' Stepping outside he waved to the pilot who waved back as he lined up to land on the huge open deck. 'Let's go.'

The two men hurried aft in time to see the helo hover over the deck prior to touchdown. Gustav took a transmitter from his pocket, flicked a switch to arm it and pressed a button. Under their feet the two men felt a series of small explosions. They crossed to the helicopter and climbed on board, closing the door behind them.

'Let's go,' yelled Gustav at the pilot.

'Yes, sir.' The helicopter lifted off the deck and swung clear, the pilot heading east.

Gustav sat with Duval in the passengers' section and looked back. Already the ship was settling by the bow, the engines still working, the propellers driving the ship forward and down. Gustav quickly scanned the sea. There were no ships in sight, no witnesses.

*　　*　　*

'Sir,' Hunter advised Macnair, 'we're leaving in ten minutes. Somebody needs to question the girl urgently.'

'I've spoken to the Pentagon and they're informing the FBI. We need to leave it to them. Back to the job in hand. Once you're on board the liner, it's imperative you find the device that's jamming communications.'

'Will do. Anything from the passenger and crew lists?'

'The passengers appear clean. Nothing obvious. But the crew are a different kettle of fish. So far we've identified twelve members who are non-Christian, using false papers and references. Isobel received photographs from the shipping company a few minutes ago and is forwarding them now. You had better take a look, although I doubt they'll be much use.'

Matt Dunston entered the room and handed a sheaf of papers to Hunter. The photographs were passport size, obviously from job applications. Macnair was right. 'It's hard to tell one from the other, the photos are so bad, sir.'

'That's what we thought. Still, they may help. There's also an anomaly with one of the entertainers. A woman singer whose father was a Palestinian. She's never been in trouble but you never know. Trust nobody, Nick, apart from the master and his immediate officers.'

'Right, sir. And definitely nothing on the passengers' side?'

'No. If there is we won't be able to tell you unless you stop the jamming.'

'I appreciate that, sir, over.'

'Good luck to all of you. Out.'

Hunter said his farewells to Captain Matthews and soon afterwards was airborne and heading for Trinidad with half the team. The Lynx Mk 8 helicopter had a cruise speed of 125 knots and a range of 330 miles. Everything that could be stripped from the helo had been taken out or off. It carried no missiles, no torpedoes and no guns. Neither did it carry any seats. The five members of the team sat on the floor, along with some of their equipment. With all flying profiles laid down by the manufacturers, there was margin for error. On this flight most of that margin had been used up.

The flight took 2hrs 30mins and their air speed was a record breaking 139 knots. By the time they landed the engines were practically sucking air. It was still a couple of hours short of midnight and the main airport had closed for the night. A Hercules C130 had arrived earlier and the equipment that it had brought had been laid out in a hangar. Armed marines protected the area. Diplomatic egos had been stroked and promises of favours made and accepted. The US had *carte blanche* for the operation. Although Trinidad had the kind of aviation fuel used by heli-copters, for speed of turn-round the Americans had brought their gas with them. The Lynx was quickly refuelled and sent back to the *York*, which was already eighty miles closer.

Hunter was introduced to a Lt Cdr O'Connell, the boss of Seal Team 6, based at Coronado, San Diego. At 6ft 6ins he was taller than Hunter, with shoulders to match. His cauliflower ear and broken nose suggested an interest in boxing. The American greeted CPO Doug Tanner like a long-lost friend.

'So, how's it going with the limeys?'

'Not bad, sir. I just wish they spoke English.'

The two men laughed at the shared joke before O'Connell turned to Hunter. 'I've brought everything you asked for and some. I had my guys brainstorm the operation as well to see what we could come up with. There are one or two items we thought of that might come in useful, like flash-bangs. Also we brought two ex-torches.'

'Thanks. We've actually got one.'

O'Connell nodded. 'But they break easily. Have you used one of these before?'

'What is it?' Hunter looked curiously at the oddly-shaped weapon.

'Let me show you.' It was a peculiar looking gun, about the size of a .45 pistol, with an iron rod sticking out of the barrel. 'It attaches to your body using this harness. The bolt is fired via a powerful compressed air cartridge, attached to a thin line with a breaking strain of over eight hundred pounds. The line is contained inside the hollow butt. It will travel one hundred feet. When it reaches the end, the line pulls the bottom of the bolt, releasing a three pronged hook. If you pull the trigger a second time the line reels in and takes you with it. We developed it for exactly the kind of job you're going on now. I've got one for each of the team if you'd like to try them. We call them a hook-gun.'

'I appreciate it. They could come in useful. Anything we need to know about the wings?'

'Pretty much as standard. You've used the mark five?'

'Yeah. Okay, let's start working our way through this lot.' Hunter turned to his team.

But O'Connell wasn't finished. 'I also brought a consignment of Calico M-960As. Ever use one?'

Hunter shook his head as he hefted the machine gun in his hand. 'Nice. Light and well balanced.'

'It's the best the US of A has to offer. I brought fifty-round and one hundred-round mags. This is the concealable model where the barrel doesn't go past the fore-end. The helical feed mags are guaranteed not to jam. They're incredibly accurate and with this babe fitted,' O'Connell picked up a silencer, 'it's like a sheep farting in a high wind.'

'Okay. I'll try one, 'said Hunter. 'We'll let the rest of the lads decide for themselves.' As in Special Forces units the world over, the men had, and often stuck with, a favourite gun.

Although they had brought their weapons from the operation in Suriname, most of the team took the opportunity to try the American gun. Each man also carried a silenced handgun strapped to his side, either a Swiss SIG or a German Heckler & Koch.

The team began to sort out the remainder of the equipment. O'Connell had two of his men with him and they helped. Beacon frequencies were set and locators married up to orbiting satellites.

'Can you send Morse?' O'Connell asked.

'I'm a bit rusty but I reckon I can manage seven or eight words per minute,' Hunter replied.

'Good. I've got this as well.' The American handed over a small torch with a signalling trigger. 'The SSN following you are keeping a lookout from the time you jump. You can signal them with this. They can reply using the periscope. If you send, the most they'll do is a single flash in acknowledgement.'

'Okay. Though I doubt we'll need it.'

'You never know. Take it just in case.'

The remainder of the team had now arrived. Hunter asked the pilot of the Herky Bird for a weather update. The printout showed the weak front was deepening and that the wind for the area of the drop was now gusting 18–28 knots.

'Not exactly ideal jumping conditions,' said Dunston.

Hunter shrugged at his friend. 'No use worrying. Into the valley of death and all that.'

Dunston nodded.

Every precaution possible had been taken.

At midnight there was nothing left to do but depart. Once they were in the air Hunter established communications with TIFAT HQ and spoke to the General.

'Any information about the woman they rescued from the life-raft?'

'She appears to have the bends. She's being treated right now but it looks pretty bad. She needed help a lot sooner but they had no way of telling it was decompression sickness. She's still unconscious but we had a stroke of luck. The Coastguard sent a vessel to recover the life-rafts. We're trying to trace them now and it looks promising. We ought to be able to tell from the inflatables where they came from.'

'Good. Is *Swordfish* on station?'

'Affirmative. The ship has not changed her pattern of zig-zagging or altered her speed. There's no doubt that at this rate the *Silver Beech* will be arriving in Houston on the eleventh – the anniversary.'

'Precisely. If they're aiming to top nine eleven by an even greater atrocity then they must have something spectacular planned. Maybe a nuclear device.'

'Possibly, but we've put pressure on practically everybody in the world who could know anything about such a weapon and we've drawn a blank.'

'That doesn't mean to say they don't have one.'

'True. But you've no idea how hard we're shaking the trees and nothing's fallen out yet. No, I think it's something else.'

Hunter cleared his throat. 'Any news about Ruth, sir?'

'She woke up briefly and asked for you. But I gather she's sleeping off the anaesthetic still.'

'Thanks for what you did. Flying in the surgeon for her.'

'Forget it, Nick. We look after our own. You know the objectives.'

'Roger. Thanks.' Hunter broke the connection. How could he forget? Save the passengers and crew, take out the hijackers and last but not least, save the ship. A piece of cake.

Leaving the flight deck he joined the team as they were putting on their dark grey combat suits. Having slung their folded aerofoils over their shoulders they secured the straps. Each man checked a buddy, carefully. Their night-vision goggles were computer-chip controlled. They reacted fast enough in the event of a sudden bright light that the wearer wasn't blinded, unlike with previous models. Weapons were checked and secured. Flashbang grenades were distributed. The three ex-torches were tested by aiming them at a piece of plastic explosive. All three worked.

The team split into five pairs. Hunter would be jumping with Matt Dunston. They would leave the aircraft at one minute intervals, each pair jumping together. Beacons were checked once more, frequencies locked on again and personal communications tested. Then came the hardest part – waiting.

Gustav and Duval were ensconced in the first class lounge at Kingston airport, Jamaica. Their Air France flight had been called and they made their way to the plane. They had left the room before CNN reported the rescue of a woman from a liferaft in the Gulf of Mexico. The report was merely a foot note of local news and would not be broadcast again. Events in Europe and on board the liner were gripping the world to the exclusion of all other news coverage.

Gustav refused a glass of champagne, sipping a mango juice instead. He avidly scanned the newspapers for the latest information on Europe. He needed to read the response of the liberal masses. The reports were gratifying. Support for the right was growing while the threat to security was escalating daily. Extremist terror was no longer a brief intrusion into the life of the average European.

'Most satisfying.' Draining his mango juice he pressed the call button for the stewardess. She arrived with alacrity and he ordered a coffee. The plane began to taxi for take-off just as she arrived with the hot drink. In her haste to serve Gustav and return to her seat she spilt it over his left knee, staining his trousers. She was immediately very apologetic.

'Accidents happen,' said Gustav containing his anger with difficulty. White spots of fury lightened his cheeks and Duval placed a hand on his arm to calm him.

'Leave it,' said Duval to the stewardess, 'and go and sit down.' The young woman fled to the front of the cabin. 'Don't get upset, Charles. Everything is working perfectly. Focus on what's happening in Europe right now. Savour the taste of victory – your goal is only weeks away.'

'The stupid black bitch. She and her kind won't be working for our national airlines in the future. She'll be lucky to get a job cleaning toilets.' Unclenching his fists the anger drained from him as quickly as it had risen.

Duval pointed to the two items in the German paper, *Die Welt*.

'Let me see.' Gustav snatched the paper and read the articles quickly. 'Excellent. The Austrian police shot dead a dozen rioters, all foreigners. Ah, look at this. The Germans are pointing the blame for the riot in Paris on the Algerians. Five were killed, including a gendarme. Kill five, terrify fifty thousand. Excellent.'

'Not so loud, Gustav, we don't want to be overheard.'

Gustav looked around him, his mouth twisted in disdain. Five seats had black occupants and he dropped his eyelids to conceal his hatred. Settling back he closed his eyes. 'I shall doze for a while. Wake me when dinner is served.'

Macnair had briefed General Stafford at the Pentagon on the planned operation to retake the liner. As soon as the team was on board they were to go below to find the explosives. Once they had been made safe the team would clear the upper decks of the guards, take out those who were watching the passengers and get the hostages to the lifeboats. While the passengers and crew abandoned ship the team would track down the remaining hijackers and deal with them. Macnair acknowledged the high risk nature of the plan, but nobody knew what the consequences of the liner reaching America would be. This way at least there was a chance that many of the passengers and crew would live to tell the tale.

Macnair voiced his fears to Stafford. 'What if the team fails?'

'The President has given *Swordfish* orders. In the event of failure the submarine is to sink the liner. It must not reach America. We believe the hijackers have some sort of weapon of mass destruction on board. All the *Swordfish* needs is the hit signal.'

'What did the Captain of the sub say to that?'

'Nothing. He verified the order, but he'll carry it out.'

'The loss of life could be appalling.'

'But imagine the consequences should the ship dock. We know that Islamic fundamentalist groups have been working for years to get their hands on some sort of nuclear or biological weapon. Maybe this is it. Right now the National Security Adviser is recommending we bring our troops back to protect America. She's saying it's time Europe looked after itself.'

'And what do you say, Colin?'

There was a pause. 'I guess she's not far wrong. It's certainly a sentiment that most Americans share. Hell, we've pulled Europe's chestnuts out of the fire twice last century and a third time in Yugoslavia. It's time you stood on your own two feet.'

'You'd better have your President tell my Prime Minister.'

'He has, in no uncertain terms, about an hour ago.'

On that note the connection was broken. Macnair knew that the day was coming when the Americans would say enough is enough. While Europe supported welfare programs America was prepared to back its military. The States spent twice as much of their gross national product as Europe on defence. It was time European governments woke up to their responsibilities and shouldered their fair share of the burden.

Macnair picked up the telephone to Downing Street. He needed to brief the Prime Minister.

The C130 was at 25,000ft and circling. The waiting was almost over. Hunter stood in the cockpit behind the pilot's seat and looked at the picture on the screen. A down-link with PACER SKY showed the liner clearly. Cloud was beginning to build up and the picture fluctuated between video and infra-red. Four guards were still clearly discernible on the upper deck, one either side on the bridge wing, and one either side on the lower promenade deck about half way between the bow and the stern. They appeared to be lounging on the rails, looking out to sea, their guns slung over their shoulders.

'They look relaxed enough,' said the pilot.

'Let's hope they stay that way,' replied Hunter. 'What's the weather doing?'

'There are gusts pushing thirty to thirty-five knots. Cloud base is ten thousand feet, thin and scattered but building.'

'Time to go?'

'Whenever you're ready.'

'Okay. Let's do it. The longer we wait the worse the weather may get. I'd prefer to go in about two hours when their alert threshold is even lower but now is good enough.'

'A green in ten?'

'Fine. And thanks.'

'Good luck, buddy. We're rooting for you.'

Hunter nodded and went back into the cavernous hold. The team were at the farthest end and already getting into line. The jump lights changed from red to amber. With a last word to each of the men Hunter went all the way aft and stood next to Matt Dunston. A quick last check and they were ready. The rear doors stood open and the wind whistled around the cabin, making Hunter shiver. He adjusted his night-vision goggles, pulled on thin cotton gloves, ran a hand over the equipment he was carrying and waited. His mouth was dry in anticipation, more from excitement than fear. His tiredness sloughed off him like a shed skin as his adrenaline began to pump. He thought fleetingly of Ruth, saw the amber glow in the corner of his eye turn to green, felt the thump on his shoulder and he was walking off the ramp, throwing himself to his right, to port, while Dunston went left. Accelerating at 32ft/sec/sec he settled at a fall rate of 110mph, passing through 1,000ft every six seconds.

The wind whistled past his head and as he fell he looked at the readout on the electronic gauge he carried. The feet were unwinding fast and he looked up and back to see Dunston about a second behind him. They were both in the classic stabilised position for free fall – bellies down, arms and legs outstretched, legs slightly bent at the knees. From the height they had launched at they could see the dots of lights belonging to ships outside the exclusion zone around the *Silver Beech* but these were quickly vanishing under the horizon as their view of the world shrank rapidly.

The liner was steaming without lights but could be seen easily. The night-vision goggles gave a faint bluish tinge that was no more distracting than wearing sun glasses at noon. Down they arrowed towards the target which grew larger by the second. The faint buzz on his wrist told him he was at the correct height and the wing on his back deployed automatically. It opened with a snap, bit into the air and Hunter's feet dropped below him as he suddenly stood upright. He was at eight thousand feet and coasting gently downwards. Now he could feel the wind buffeting his body, causing the wing to rise and fall while he manoeuvred around the liner still over six thousand feet below.

Looking up he saw the black wings of the team, like huge bats, scattered across the sky. The wing they were using could be inflated using helium. The gas was contained in small high pressure bottles sewn into the lining, and controlled by two buttons on the small panel in front of each man, one to inflate, the other to dump as required. As the liner moved through the water a satellite picture of the ship was changed into latitude and longitude and relayed to each jumper. The wing automatically corrected its heading, taking into account wind speed and direction. It was only when they were within a hundred yards or so of the target that each man would take responsibility for his height, speed and the distance to travel.

Hunter eased the Calico gun on his chest and touched the safety. He would be landing any minute and he needed to be ready. Each member of the team knew where they were to land. The objective was to avoid the lookouts at all costs or, if that became impossible, to kill them before they gave the alarm. It was a tall order.

The wind suddenly gusted from the west, veered about thirty degrees and swung back again. Hunter swerved off course, corrected his bearing and added height by increasing the helium in the wing. He repositioned himself to land on the aft top deck of the liner, astern of the swimming pool. The ship was a hundred feet below him and about the same ahead. He gained a bit more height, corrected his course and aimed straight at the deck. At about fifteen feet he saw it was clear and turned to land. A gust of wind came along the bows, lifted him and sent him over the stern rail. He had missed the ship altogether and would land in the sea any moment. Frantically he pumped in helium and felt the wing lift. The air around him, deflected by the ship's superstructure, had no pattern to it. It was coming from all directions and he couldn't control the wing. One second the lowest deck was under him and then it was past. The ship was sailing on without him and the helium lift was not enough to give him another opportunity.

The hijacker, urinating over the side, froze in mid-arc as Hunter passed him under the stern.

7

Hunter fired the hook-gun straight at the hijacker. It missed, blossomed open and snagged on the middle of the guard-rails. Hunter threw the quick release switch on the wing's harness and the wing sailed away, vanishing into the night. The hijacker was reaching to unsling his gun from his shoulder when Hunter hit the water. He was pressing the trigger on the hook-gun even as he did so. Holding his feet in front of him, he swung in towards the stern of the ship. The line tightened and the harness around his upper torso pulled him in, like a fish being landed. His head broke the surface and he came out of the sea, his feet slamming into the hull. Shaking his head, he looked up in time to see the hijacker point his gun at him.

Matt Dunston had watched the drama unfolding and had changed direction. He was still about twenty feet above the deck when he released his wing. Plummeting down he landed with a sickening crunch on the terrorist's back, breaking the hijacker's neck on the safety rail. Crouching over the stern he saw Hunter walking up the side of the ship as the hook-gun reeled him in.

'Are you all right?' Dunston called in a loud whisper.

Hunter raised his hand, his thumb and forefinger forming in a circle. Okay. He climbed, dripping wet, onto the deck and stood there for a few seconds getting his breath back.

He tested his communications system with Dunston who answered immediately. 'Now we're inside the jamming device comms appear to be working.'

Bending down, Hunter turned over the body of the hijacker

and had a look at the face. He could not be sure but he thought he recognised one of the men in the photographs Macnair had sent. Checking the corpse's pockets, he searched for ID but found none. Heaving the body over the stern he stood up.

'Let's get the team together.'

Dunston grabbed his arm and pointed. Hunter stood in horror as two wings hit the water astern of the ship. Then a third. It looked as if the whole team was coming down into the sea. He counted them. There was one missing. He tried the radio but got no reply. He tried again.

'Boss,' a voice whispered in his ear, 'I'm on the top deck. One of the guards is pretty close.' Hunter recognised the voice of Jan Badonovitch, the Russian Spetsnaz.

Looking out to sea, Hunter saw the dark heads of his team bobbing on the surface. It looked like Macnair's backdoor was going to be needed after all. Ripping off his NVGs, he removed the signal torch from his pocket, pointed it aft and began flashing. Dash, dot, dot dash, dash . . . Laboriously he continued sending – Team missed. In water. Please rescue – he sent a single letter, kilo – dash dot dash – over. He was rewarded with a single, faint spark of light. He hoped the *USS Swordfish* picked them up all right. What in hell was he going to achieve with just three of them on board?

'Jan, don't speak. Click if you get my message.'

Click.

'The team missed the ship.'

Click.

'Can you come aft without being spotted? Two clicks for yes.'

Click, click.

'We're on the lowest deck at the taffrail. We'll wait here.'

Click.

Hunter and Dunston had pulled off their hoods and ditched the wings' harnesses. The night was warm and Hunter's clothes were already beginning to dry as the two men took stock of their equipment.

Badonovitch appeared a few minutes later.

'What happened?'

'The wind came out of nowhere, boss. I was lucky. When I realised I was missing the side I released my harness. I only just made it. Josh was right behind me one second and gone the next. He was about twenty, maybe thirty feet higher and that made all the difference.'

'Only one ex-torch, then,' said Hunter, testing it on a piece of plastic explosive. 'It works, thank goodness. 'Two flash-bangs and our personal weapons.'

'Plus PE and dets,' Dunston whispered.

'Damnation,' Hunter spoke with feeling. 'Well, the operation continues. We need to get between decks and down to the engine room.'

The team had memorised maps of the liner. The door behind them marked 'Crew Only' led to a flight of stairs.

Hunter cracked open the door and carefully looked inside. It was empty. A short corridor had two doors leading off either side and ahead lay the stairwell. Stepping inside, Hunter used the butt of his gun to smash the nearest light bulb and fitting. He destroyed the other two he passed, plunging the area into darkness.

The second door on the right was locked and bore a warning sign, declaring 'Danger – Electricity' printed in bold with a red forked lightning motif.

'The secondary electric switchboard for this part of the ship,' said Hunter. 'If we take it out, a third of the ship will be darkened.'

'Dawn is still four hours away. The darkness would help us,' said Dunston.

'I agree but I don't want to waste any plastic on it.'

'Not necessary, boss,' said Badonovitch, walking back from the stairwell, hefting a fire-axe in his hands. He took aim and smashed the curved point into the door before heaving on the handle. The door flew open and would have crashed into the bulkhead if Dunston hadn't caught it.

'Good work,' said Hunter. 'Keep a lookout, both of you, while I take care of this.'

Inside was an electrical switchboard with a master handle on the right-hand side. Along the board were rows of fuses, each one representing a compartment or other part of the ship. The schematic on the wall showed clearly that the board controlled all five decks and a third of the ship. Hunter pulled every fuse as quickly as he could and passed each handful out to Dunston who threw them overboard.

Having gained the advantage of darkness, they went down the stairs, Hunter leading, Badonovitch covering their rear. As they passed the emergency lamps fitted in the corridor they smashed each one.

Two decks down they came to a passageway that ran the length of the ship and was broken up by doors every ten paces or so. They knew that the cabins on either side were crew's quarters. In sharp contrast to the passengers' parts of the ship, the corridor was bare and lined with tiles. They checked a couple of the cabins and found them empty. As expected, the crew was probably held with the remainder of the passengers in one of the large lounges or dining rooms.

A third of the way along, they found the door marked 'Engine Room'. There were bound to be watchkeepers on duty and they would be guarded by hijackers. The engine room was the logical place to put explosives, so they had no choice but to go inside. They knew from the plans that the area stretched about a third of the ship. There were two huge diesel engines. In the event of a breakdown, they could be mechanically crossed over, enabling one to drive both shafts. Four generators created sufficient electricity to power a small town, but only two were ever in use at any one time. The watchkeepers occupied a sound-proofed office on the starboard side, near the middle. From there they monitored the myriad dials which ensured the ship's safety and the passengers' comfort.

Hunter cracked open the door and was immediately hit by a wall of noise. He took out a small mirror on the end of a telescopic handle and pushed it through, meticulously searching the space. There was nobody in sight and he eased the door open wide enough to slip through. The others followed. They found themselves on a platform, high above the space.

From their vantage point they could see inside the control room where two armed men were sitting. Three other men in overalls were evidently engineers. One of the crew spoke and pointed through the window. A gunman nodded, and the engineer, adjusting ear-protectors, entered the engine room. Hunter, looking down from three decks above, watched the engineer making his rounds. Even if the man happened to look up, it was doubtful the team would be seen. They were standing on a metal grill, in shadow. As the engineer finished and re-entered the control room, they descended the stairs. In seconds they were hidden from sight by the bulk of one of the main engines.

While Dunston kept guard, Badonovitch and Hunter walked slowly along the deck, Hunter aiming the ex-torch. Its green light turned amber and then red. Simultaneously, Badonovitch pointed out the missing deck-plate screws. With his knife, the Spetsnaz prised the plate up an inch while Hunter dropped to his stomach to took a closer look. It looked clear of booby-traps and Badonovitch lifted the plate.

The explosive was sitting against the hull. No effort had been made to hide it. Hunter lay for a few moments examining it and decided it was a bog-standard set-up. The plastic had one detonator which was sticking out about an inch. He recognised the type. American made, it could be set off either by a radio signal or by pulling out a percussion pin. Depending on the delay on the fuse, the detonator would explode anything from ten seconds to ten minutes later. Removing the detonator, he handed it to Badonovitch before lifting the plastic explosive clear. As they moved further along the deck, the torch changed again to amber and then red. Again, the screws were missing. It took only a few seconds to see that the set-up was identical to the first and to remove the detonator and explosives. They had removed a fourth lot when Dunston signalled. They just managed to duck down behind a generator before one of the ship's engineers appeared.

He walked straight up to where Badonovitch was hiding then stepped back in shock when he saw the Russian crouching there. Before the man could react, Hunter clamped a hand over his mouth and Badonovitch rose, putting a finger to his lips. The engineer nodded and pointed at a door. The four men hustled through it and found themselves in a sound-proofed secondary control room. For the team, the relief on entering the comparative silence was considerable.

'Who are you?' The engineer asked, excitedly, with a strong Dublin accent.

Hunter replied, 'Special forces. We need you to answer some questions. What's your name?'

'Mick O'Flynn. Second engineer.'

'How many hijackers are there?'

The Irishman was in his late forties, small, balding, with the sallow complexion of people who don't see too much sun. He screwed up his face and considered the question. 'I'm not sure, but there must be fifteen or so.'

If the team were dismayed at the number they didn't show it.

'Where are they positioned?'

'Here, the bridge and in the main dining room. Oh, and the galley,' he added as an afterthought.

'Are the passengers and the crew being held in the dining room?'

'Except for us three in the engine room. Do you know they put bombs under the deck plates?'

Hunter nodded. 'We found them. Are they only in the engine room? Or did they put them anywhere else?'

'I think only in here. Though I can't be sure.'

'Fair enough. We'll double check.' Hunter looked at his watch. 'How much longer have you got before the guards come looking for you?'

O'Flynn shrugged. 'I dunno. I've been out before and nobody's come after me. I don't think they like the noise.'

'I don't blame them,' said Dunston with feeling.

'Are the lights on or off in the dining room?'

'All on. It lets the hijackers keep a closer eye on them.'

'That figures,' said Hunter. 'All right, here's what I want you to do.'

*   *   *

The SSN picked up the remainder of Hunter's team about fifteen minutes after they hit the water. The men had collected together and waited patiently, treading water, shucking their gear, lightening their load. The submarine surfaced only yards away and they had swum across to it, quickly climbing on board. They had all been in and out of submarines so often it took only seconds to embark. The sub sunk quickly beneath the water again.

Clements reported to the Captain in the conning tower. 'Permission to come aboard, sir?' He saluted, dripping water onto the deck.

'Permission granted. What happened?'

'A hell of a wind came out of nowhere, sir, and we missed the target. I think my boss and two of the others made it okay. At least, there was no sign of them in the sea.'

'What do you want to do?'

'I'd like to contact my CO, sir, and tell him what's happened.'

'I see no problem with that. I'll get CPO Jones to show you the way to the radio shack.' The Captain, Henry Cabot, newly promoted and tipped for the top, was on his first patrol. His thin face was pensive. Shrewd brown eyes stared at Clements. 'How many of you are there?'

'Seven, sir.'

'We'll get you kitted out in dry clothes. What rank are you?'

'A Captain with Delta, sir, now seconded to TIFAT.'

'Any other officers?'

'One, sir. The rest are NCOs.'

'Okay. I don't suppose this'll be for long. The Exec can sort out bunks.'

'Thanks, sir.' Clements was shown the radio room and was soon patched through to Macnair.

'There's nothing to be done about it,' said the General. 'Knowing Lt Cdr Hunter he'll carry on with the operation.'

'I concur, sir. Is there any way we can get back there? We could take an inflatable from the sub.'

'Too noisy. They'll hear the engine. You'll either be shot to pieces or run down by the ship. Either way, the hijackers will shoot more innocent people. Our only hope is they get the passengers off before the shooting starts.'

Chantelle Suchard finally woke up. The pain had gone away although she felt discomfort through her whole body. She tried to move but couldn't. Immediately a hand touched her shoulder.

'Take it easy. You need to rest.'

'Where am I?'

'In a hospital in Galveston. In a decompression chamber.'

Tears welled up. 'I'm crippled, aren't I?'

The doctor was young. He still had to learn the art of speaking to a badly injured or sick patient. He hesitated.

'Please tell me the truth. I've been diving for long enough to know what a bad case of the bends will do to you.'

'Then in that case, yes, I think you will be crippled. We can't be one hundred percent certain. The bends affect people in different ways. It's a question of time. Your nerve ends have been harmed by the pressure of the nitrogen bubbles on them. Damaged nerves cannot be repaired. But the amount of damage depends on how long the bubbles were trapped in your joints. They will dissolve slowly out of your blood now, as we decompress you. We'll have to wait and see.'

Thoughts were hurtling around her head. Gustav, Duval, Al-Adil, the submarine. The outcome of the mission, justifying the target in her mind. Blaming herself for her stupidity. The terrible realisation of Gustav's betrayal. Above all was the knowledge that her life had changed irrevocably, forever. And Gustav was to blame . . .

Chantelle nodded. 'I must speak to someone. I have important information.'

'Calm yourself. You must rest.'

'Please. You must send for the police or the FBI or somebody.'

'I can't just send for the Feds,' the doctor almost smiled. 'I need a reason.'

'Is the death of a quarter of a million Americans good enough reason?'

'What?' His jaw dropped and he stared at her for a second before he realised his mouth was open and he shut it. 'What on earth are you talking about?'

'You know about the ship in the Gulf? The one that's been hijacked?'

'Sure. It's on all the news.'

'I know who did it and what they plan to do. You must get me somebody to talk to.'

'How do I know you're telling the truth?'

Chantelle thought for a few moments before answering. 'What do you know about me? I mean, how did you come to have me here?'

'A naval helicopter brought you in. They'd picked you up in the Gulf.'

'Precisely. And there was no ship I could have come from because I escaped from a sinking submarine. A privately owned one. The hijacked liner is carrying a nerve gas that the terrorists plan to let loose in Houston. It's lethal. The lives of hundreds of thousands of people are at stake.'

'How do you know?'

'I . . .' she was about to admit her part in the scheme when she had second thoughts about what she should say. She needed to think of a story that at least gave her a chance of going free. If the Americans knew of her involvement she could end up in the gas chamber. 'I can't say. Please, try and get the FBI to come and speak to me.'

'I'll see what I can do. First I need to take some blood and then I need to get out of here. I've been in the chamber long enough and I don't want to have to go into stop time. How's your hearing?'

'I've a buzzing in my head.'

'That's because you've burst your ear-drums.'

The doctor drew a syringe of blood, went through to the exit chamber and was decompressed back to the surface. The blood was taken for analysis while he went to find a telephone. He asked directory enquiries for the number of the nearest FBI office. He was surprised to learn that there was one in Galveston.

It was the middle of the night and all he got was an answering machine. Non-plussed he replaced the receiver without leaving a message. He hesitated for a moment and decided he could not leave the matter there even for a few hours until the local office opened. The girl might be lying, but the risk was too great to take. This time when he called directory enquiries he asked for the FBI in Washington DC.

Dialling the number the phone was answered immediately. 'FBI.'

'I . . . I'd like to speak to somebody, please. I have some information I need to pass on.'

The FBI took thousands of calls a day, many from hoax or crank callers. The female operator kept her voice steady. 'What is your name please, sir.'

'Sydney Carmichael.'

'Occupation?'

'Doctor.'

'Where are you calling from?'

'A hospital in Galveston. A patient has given me information which I think is important.'

The telephonist had already been tracing the call and the screen in front of her confirmed that the caller was telephoning from Galveston. 'Wait one second, sir. I am transferring you to an agent.'

'Smith.'

The doctor wondered for a brief second if that was really the man's name.

'Mr Smith, my name is Sydney Carmichael. I am a doctor at a hospital in Galveston.'

'How can I help you, Dr Carmichael?'

'I am treating a patient, a woman, who was picked up out of the sea with decompression sickness. She says she has information concerning the hijacked ship in the Gulf. She says it's very important that it's passed on to the appropriate authorities.'

'What information?'

'She wouldn't tell me the details. But I think she's genuine. She says that hundreds of thousands of lives are at risk.'

'Where is the woman?'

'In a decompression chamber. She has a bad case of the bends. She says she got them coming up from a submarine.'

'Right, sir. You can leave it with us, now. Just one thing. I'd appreciate it if you told no one about this. I'll have two agents with you ASAP. On behalf of the Bureau, sir, I thank you for calling.'

Replacing the receiver the doctor wondered if the man had been serious or whether he had been humouring him. What the hell! It was no longer his problem. He had patients to look after.

Fifty minutes later Dr Carmichael was visited by two agents who flashed their badges at him, identified themselves and immediately asked to speak to the woman.

Outside the decompression chamber he explained, 'You can talk to her via a speaker or you can go inside.'

'Inside?' Gail Gabonne looked askance at the idea. A striking woman in her late thirties, she looked as though she had been awoken early from a deep sleep.

'Yes. I'll show you.' Carmichael led the way into the room that contained the huge chamber, capable of holding half a dozen patients in comfort, as well as staff to treat them. 'You go through this door. We pressurise you, the inside door's opened and through you go.'

'No thanks,' said Gabonne. 'What about you, Barney? You going?'

Barney Sullivan shook his head. 'We'll speak to her from here.' He was older than his companion, grey haired and turning to fat.

The doctor demonstrated the microphone and loudspeaker. 'Press this switch and you can talk to her. Let it go and you can hear her. She only needs to speak and a microphone in the chamber picks up her words. If you listen carefully you can hear her breathing.' On the monitor they could see Chantelle lying on a mattress, covered by a thin sheet.

'Let me just check the time and pressure.' The doctor looked at the gauges and nodded. 'In fifteen minutes I bring her up another ten feet.'

106

'How long will she be in there?' the woman asked.

'Thirteen more hours. It's a slow process bringing somebody up from a bad bend. But she'll have to get used to waiting. She'll probably be in a wheelchair for the rest of her life.'

'Okay. Thanks.'

The two agents waited until the doctor had left the room. The woman pressed the switch to the microphone. 'Miss, can you hear me?'

Chantelle nodded and said, 'Yes. Who are you?'

'FBI.'

'I need to see some ID.'

'You can see my badge if you come to the little window.' The woman held her badge to the small, round port-hole.

'I can't. I can't move,' said Chantelle. 'I'm . . . I'm probably crippled.' The statement, expressed for the first time, was made less harrowing by the hope that it would gain her some sympathy. She had spent the last hour going over the possibilities in her mind. How to save herself from prosecution and yet nail Gustav? How to wreak her revenge and yet protect herself? She needed guarantees.

'We're sorry to hear that, miss. Please believe me when I tell you that we're FBI.'

Chantelle sighed. 'I believe you. Look,' there was urgency in her voice, 'that liner, *Silver Beech*, the one that's been hijacked, I know who's behind it. But I want a guarantee. If I give you the information, I walk free . . .' Chantelle seemed oblivious to the irony of her request.

'Why should we want to prosecute you?' Gabonne was genuinely puzzled.

'Because I know what they're planning to do.'

'And what might that be?'

'You must give me your guarantee first.'

'I'm sorry, miss. I'm not authorised to make deals.'

'Then get me somebody who is.'

'Why don't you tell me what it's all about first and let us decide.'

'No guarantees, no information.'

Gabonne turned to Sullivan. 'What do you think?'

'She's not the normal nutcase. I'd better call Jerry. He can call the shots from here on.'

Jerry Stapizki was the Senior Agent at their office. He was not at his own apartment but, unknown to the two agents, staying with a new girlfriend. The battery in his mobile phone had discharged and he was uncontactable. Sullivan gave up trying to get hold of him.

'What now?' he asked his partner.

Mick O'Flynn refused the offer of a gun. Instead he hefted a large wrench in his hand and said, 'They're sloppy bastards. They think because they've got the guns they've nothing to be afraid of. We'll take care of them.' He slipped the wrench into the long pocket in the side of his trouser leg.

'Okay, remember, lights out at precisely three-forty.' Hunter double checked with the engineer.

'Don't worry. You can count on Mick O'Flynn.'

'You'd better go back to the control room. And listen, Mick, don't look too happy. Remember there's a lot can go wrong.'

O'Flynn wiped the smile off his face but said, 'Aye, but not with you guys here. If there's three of you I figure there's thirty. But you ain't saying. It's okay.' He held up his hand, 'I understand – need to know. I've read enough books in me time.' Slipping out the door he left the TIFAT operatives to exchange wry glances.

They continued searching and found four more explosive devices each side of the hull. The amount of PE the hijackers had used would have taken the bottom of the hull clean away. The ship would have sunk in minutes. Hunter figured there were at least five maybe six kilograms of plastic, which made for one hell of an explosion. They left the engine room as unobtrusively as they had arrived. In one of the crew's cabins, Hunter opened a porthole and threw the detonators and PE into the sea.

For the next half an hour they searched the ship, looking for more explosives. Without the ex-torch it would have been a fruitless task. By the time they had finished, they were as sure as they could be that all the explosives had been removed.

The crew's quarters were empty. Not a soul to be found anywhere. At least not alive. They discovered six bodies, two of which were young women.

In the main galley, just as Mick O'Flynn had told them, they saw two armed guards overseeing the chefs. Keeping hostages fed and watered was easier than having to control hostages who were hungry, thirsty and ready to rebel.

The main dining room was full. People sat in chairs, at tables or on the floor with their backs to the bulkheads. They looked exhausted, woebegone. Many of them were trying to sleep as the long night dragged on. Standing at the round observation window in the door at the back of the room Hunter counted the terrorists, relaying to Dunston and Badonovitch in a whisper where each one was situated.

'Head count?' Hunter asked.

'Nine,' replied Dunston.

'I agree, boss,' said the Spetsnaz.

'Okay. Let's go and take a look on the bridge.'

Climbing the outside ladders used by the crew, on the upperdeck they paused. There was nobody there. The bridge was perched right forward with windows all round, giving the officers on watch a three hundred and sixty degree panoramic view.

Keeping low, Hunter darted up to the port, aft window and used his mirror to check the inside. He was slow and methodical, changing places five times before he rejoined the other two. 'I counted six hijackers and only two crew. One looks like he could be the Captain.'

'Why so many gunmen?' Dunston asked.

'They appear to be having a discussion.'

'What do we do, boss?' Badonovitch asked. 'Take them out?'

Hunter nodded. 'Jan, you and Matt take the port door. I'll take the starboard. Hold it! Someone's coming!'

The team crept like ghosts further along the deck and hid behind a lifejacket container. A further three gunmen appeared and joined the others on the bridge. The odds were now distinctly against the team and Hunter indicated they should go below. They descended two decks before they spoke again.

'There are too many on the bridge,' said Hunter. 'We couldn't kill them all before they started shooting the ship's officers.' He looked at his watch. 'Damn! The lights go out in five minutes if Mick is on the ball. We'd better be ready. You know which doors to go to?'

The two TIFAT operatives nodded.

'We'll have to clear the upper decks of guards later. Okay, let's go.'

8

Mick O'Flynn looked at the clock on the wall above the console. The other two engineers, with no knowledge of the TIFAT presence, were checking dials and making notes in their log books. The two gunmen sat nonchalantly, their machine guns across their knees, barely taking any notice. There were three chairs in the room, two facing the main console and one opposite the switchboard. From the switchboard the engineers controlled power throughout the ship.

O'Flynn turned to one of the gunmen. 'I need to check the ancillary pump.'

The Arab was about twenty, perhaps younger. He nodded his head and played with the butt of his gun, his hand never still as he nervously caressed the metal stock. Translating quickly for his fellow guard, an older, squatter man with a squint, he gestured towards the exit.

'All right. Go!'

O'Flynn nodded and opened the sound-proof door. Immediately, the noise in the control room was ear damaging. Leaving the door ajar, he stepped over to a tool box and lifted out the first and second layer of tools. The guards were now less than six feet away. He rummaged in the bottom. The two guards watched him for a second and then turned away.

Suddenly O'Flynn was very nervous. In the next minute he could be dead. Mustering his courage he slipped the heavy wrench from his pocket and took the two paces needed to reach the English-speaking hijacker. He raised the wrench and slammed it down on the gunman's head with brutal force. The Arab's skull caved in and he died instantly. The noise from the engine room had muffled the sound. The second hijacker wouldn't have known what had happened if he hadn't happened to look across at his friend now sliding to the deck, blood soaking his kaffiyeh and white shirt. The gunman sat in shock for a full second, not believing what he was seeing. Before O'Flynn could attack he sprang to his feet and started to bring his gun round on the engineer.

The other two engineers reacted quickly. The chief engineer, a bear of a man, threw himself on the other gunman, wrapping his arms around him. He didn't know or care what O'Flynn was up to but this was better than waiting for some stinking Arab to shoot him.

O'Flynn's first swipe with the wrench missed the second gunman's head but hit his shoulder, breaking it. The hijacker screamed in pain. O'Flynn changed his grip and his aim and this time hit the man on the temple. He went out like a light.

The third engineer closed the door. He was ashen-faced, shaking. 'What have you done? You fool, O'Flynn, they'll kill us for this.'

O'Flynn smiled. 'Special Forces are on board and are about to retake the ship.'

'What? What yer on about?' asked the chief engineer, his Glaswegian accent thickened by the rush of action.

'I'm telling you. I met them on me last lot of rounds. They want us to cut all power to the ship in,' he glanced at the clock, 'four minutes. That's when they're going to attack. There's a whole regiment of them. It'll all be over soon.'

The other two men smiled.

'Well done, Mick, you Irish git,' said the chief, clapping the smaller man on the back. 'I'll buy you as much whisky as you can drink when this is all over.'

'As long as it's Irish then I'll take you up on that kind offer. After we've switched off the lights we wait ten minutes and then put the engines out of action. They're going to launch the lifeboats and get the passengers and crew off.'

'Why would they need to do that if there's a bleeding regiment of them? They'll retake the ship and kill the swine.'

O'Flynn shrugged. 'I dunno. The man also said that we should be ready in case there's any trouble.'

'What sort of trouble?' the third engineer asked.

'How the hell should I know? He said trust nothing and nobody until we hear from him.'

The chief engineer picked up one of the machine guns from the deck. The gun was ready to fire with the safety off. He flicked it back on. Having been a marine during the Falklands war he knew, as he put it, one end of a frigging gun from the other. 'Okay. Cover the door. If anybody puts so much as his head through it we shoot it off.

The Senior Agent in Charge of the Galveston office was driving home a happy man and looking forward to a hearty breakfast of waffles, bacon and eggs, over-easy. He was salivating at the prospect. Jerry Stapizki, now in his mid-thirties, had trained as a lawyer before joining the FBI. Behind the wise-cracking and flippant manner was a clever and ambitious brain. He somehow managed to be popular with both his subordinates and his bosses, a feat almost unique in the history of the FBI. He was a serial womaniser, never staying long enough to have a meaningful or deep relationship. It suited his temperament and his ambitions. He was ready to move to any FBI office in the country if it furthered his career. Six feet tall, darkly handsome, he worked out regularly, drank only moderately, and had never smoked. If the FBI were to print a thumb-nail sketch of the ideal agent then Jerry Stapizki would be the role-model.

The first thing he saw when he entered his apartment was the flashing message light on his answering machine. He listened and phoned the hospital. Barney Sullivan brought him up to date with events.

All thoughts of breakfast were gone. 'I'll be there in thirty.' Replacing the receiver he hurried into his bedroom, shedding yesterday's clothes. Showered, shaved and dressed in a dark suit he was on his way in fifteen minutes, heading downtown. At that time in the morning traffic was light and he had no need to use his siren or lights. He stopped in the emergency parking bay, put the FBI Agent on-call sign in the window and hurried from his car.

Marching into the room containing the decompression chamber he introduced himself to the doctor. 'How long before she gets to the surface?'

'Seven hours and some minutes.'

'That's too long. I need to go in and talk to her.'

'You been in one before?'

'Sure. My hobby is scuba. I've never had an accident but we use a small chamber for training.'

'Good. If you take off your shoes and jacket, make sure you don't have any pens or anything with you. Oh, and I'd leave the gun if I were you.'

Stapizki nodded. 'You think she's on the level?' he asked his agents while he removed his shoulder holster and handed it to Barney Sullivan.

The agent shrugged. 'It's hard to be sure but if she isn't I don't see what she's got to gain from all this. I think,' he said slowly, 'she is. But how can you give her a guarantee that she won't be arrested? If she's mixed up in something serious?'

Stapizki shrugged. 'I can't. But like everyone else she's entitled to a fair trial.' He climbed into the outer chamber, the door was closed and the pressure began to increase. He took hold of his nose from time to time and blew down his nostrils, clearing the slight pressure in his ear drums and the twinge in his sinuses caused by lack of practice. The pressure equalised and he entered the main chamber. His first thought was that Chantelle Suchard was one of the most beautiful women he had ever seen.

She was watching him warily.

'My name is Special Agent Jerry Stapizki. FBI. Here's my ID.' He showed his badge and she looked at it carefully.

Handing it back to him she said, 'Thank you.'

'I gather you have some information to tell us.'

She looked at the agent for a few moments. 'I will tell you only if I am given immunity against prosecution.'

114

'That will be very hard to do.'

'Then it's no deal.'

Stapizki nodded as though that was perfectly reasonable. Then he said, 'I understand that whatever you know has something to do with the hijacked liner.'

'That's true.'

'Why don't you tell me what you know and let me judge the value of what you say. I'll then do my best for you in court. If it ever comes to that. It may not, of course.'

'Who makes that decision?'

'That's above my pay-grade. I just file the report.'

'But your recommendations will count for something?'

'I guess. Look, if you're in some sort of trouble then I may be able to help. I promise I will, if I can.' Stapizki had known many attractive women in his time and he could see past Chantelle's beauty to the manipulative creature behind.

She bit her lower lip. This was harder than she'd thought. Her confidence in Gustav had been so great, she had given no thought to the consequences should she be called to account for her actions. She had simply expected to get away with it. Her thoughts on how to handle her situation since regaining consciousness had been confused, vague. She was also doped to the eyeballs with painkillers which didn't help her to think clearly. How much did the authorities already know? Had they made the connection between the submarine and the liner? She would have to downplay her roll, but Gustav . . . She wanted him caught and tried. Vilified by the world. Crucified for what he'd done to her!

Her thoughts contorted her face. Stapizki thought the grimaces were caused by pain. 'Are you all right, miss?'

Chantelle took a grip on her emotions and gave a brief nod, her face a hard mask. She made herself relax. Now as never before she needed a cool head if she was to get out of this. The thought of prison caused fear to shudder through her. How much should she tell him? If she admitted knowing about the nerve gas she would go to prison for the rest of her life.

Slowly she shook her head. 'I must have the guarantee.'

'Look, miss, let me explain something to you. If the liner is going to be used in some way to cause the deaths of more innocent people then you're what is known as an accessory before the fact. You'll be charged as if you were responsible and believe me, if the crime is big enough you'll either go to prison for a very long time or you'll get the death penalty. We still have it in this state and we use it with monotonous regularity.'

Chantelle closed her eyes to hide the horror there. Dr Carmichael's voice came over the loudspeaker, informing them that he was reducing the pressure. For a few seconds the chamber was silent, apart from the hiss of escaping air. It gave Chantelle time to think.

'The men who took over the liner initially were joined by eight others. I was forced to take them out to the liner in a small submarine.'

'Forced? By whom?'

She shrugged. 'I didn't ask their names.'

'What nationality were they?'

'The men I took out to the liner were all Arabs.'

'How do you know?'

'They prayed on their knees four or five times a day.'

'Fair enough. And the men who you say forced you to take the sub?'

'I'm not sure.' Wanting to divert Stapizki away from that line of questioning, Chantelle added, 'I overheard them talking. They plan to hit Houston on September the eleventh – with an anniversary present.'

Stapizki looked at her steadily. 'What sort of present?'

Chantelle bit her lower lip, her mask slipping. 'I'm . . . I'm not sure.'

'What do you mean you aren't sure?' Exasperation made his voice hard.

'Look, I think they have some sort of nerve agent or gas. They have a ball which they treated very carefully. And,' she paused wondering what to say to convey the importance of her information while at the same time not letting them know *how* she really knew the facts. 'It was something the men said and the way they handled the ball. They talked of it killing hundreds of thousands of people.'

Shocked to the core, Stapizki kept his voice level. 'What nationality were these men?'

'I told you, they were Arabs.'

'That covers a lot of people. Were they Palestinians? Or Iraqis? Or Jordanians? What?'

'How the hell should I know? All Arabs are the same to me.'

'Ain't that the truth. Do you speak Arabic?'

Startled, Chantelle replied, 'No. Of course not.'

'Then how do you know what they said?'

Without thinking she replied, 'They spoke English.'

'I see.' Which made no sense to Stapizki. Whoever these men were they'd use their own language. So she was hiding something, only what was it? Whatever it was, he'd find out soon enough. Now he had to deal with the threat to Houston.

'Are you sure about the nerve gas?'

Now she had to be careful. 'As sure as I can be.'

Damn! 'Barney, you copy?'

'Yes, Jerry. I'll phone it in now.'

'Let's get back to the men who forced you to take the sub. Who were they?'

She shook her head.

'Does that mean you don't know or aren't willing to tell me?'

Chantelle licked her suddenly dry lips. She realised the more she said the bigger the hole she was digging for herself. 'I need to think.'

'Why don't you just tell me the facts? Everything?'

'I can't. I told you. I need to think.'

'About what?'

Again she shook her head, but then made a serious mistake. 'Not now. I want to use something to bargain with.'

'Why would you need to bargain if you were *coerced* into taking them to the ship?'

Realising her error, Chantelle replied, 'I don't trust you, that's all.'

'Miss, need I remind you that it was you who sent for us? As far as we know this could all be some elaborate hoax.'

'Why on earth would I do that?'

Stapizki shrugged. 'We don't know. But people do crazy things for crazy reasons.'

'I'm telling the truth.'

'Maybe. How did you come to be driving the sub?'

'I've said enough for now.'

'Where were you when you were apparently abducted?'

Chantelle said nothing. Normally intelligent and quick-witted, she knew she was getting into deep water. One lie would lead to another. *Was* leading to another. She shook her head.

'Does that mean you won't say or you can't?'

'It means I'm . . . I'm having difficulty keeping the facts straight in my head. I was unconscious for hours. I'm trying to help. You're wasting time. Please, I need rest. I'm exhausted.'

'This will do for now. I strongly recommend that you get a lawyer. If necessary we can appoint one.' Stapizki hadn't bothered taking notes. He knew the conversation was being recorded. Entering the outer chamber, he closed the door and waited for the pressure to return to atmospheric. Climbing out he took his shoulder holster offered to him by Barney and as he strapped it on he asked, 'Well?'

'She's lying through her teeth.'

He looked at the woman agent. 'Gail?'

'I agree. A great deal of what she said doesn't add up.'

'That's what I thought. But I do think she was telling the truth about the nerve gas.'

Gail nodded. 'So do I. I think the lack of co-operation is all about saving her skin.'

It was breakfast time at the White House, and the President was enjoying his grapefruit and black coffee. He treasured these few quiet moments, and was irritated when his phone rang. He grabbed the offending article, placed it to his ear and said, 'This had better be important.'

'It is, sir,' said his Chief of Staff. 'I have information on the hijacked liner. From the FBI in Galveston.' He quickly briefed the President, the only man who could make the necessary decisions.

'Jesus Christ! Then they have to be stopped now.'

'I agree, sir. We are in the situation room waiting for you. We have a specialist on nerve gas coming in who'll be here any minute.'

The President sighed. More often than not nowadays he wondered what lunatic urge had made him run for the job. It was bigger than any one man. The decisions he was called on to make every day were enough to last any normal person a lifetime. And it never stopped. Slipping on his jacket, he went down from his private quarters.

In the situation room everybody stood up as he entered. He indicated for them to sit and said, 'Let's get started.'

It took twenty minutes for the President to realise that he had no choice. The liner had to be stopped. He didn't dare wait for the TIFAT team to do its job. And anyway, what could three men accomplish? The ship could not be allowed to get any closer to the continent of the United States of America.

'Send the signal to the *Swordfish*. And tell the Captain he is not to surface under any circumstances in case the nerve gas is released. If people make it to the lifeboats and get away all well and good. If not . . .' he shrugged sadly. 'All right, people, let's get to it.'

The three of them were in position. Dunston said a short prayer for the men who were about to die and adjusted his night-vision goggles. On cue the lights throughout the ship went out. Automatically the emergency lamps fixed to the bulkheads came on. They cast a faint glow around the edge of the room but left most of it in darkness.

Consternation swept through the prisoners but the majority of them had the sense to stay where they were. Hunter stepped through the door, right behind one of the hijackers. The man must have felt a draught or perhaps sensed Hunter's presence because he began to turn. Hunter shot him with his silenced

119

Calico, twice. Once in the chest and the second time in the head. For no reason, consternation was turning to panic and one or two passengers suddenly stood up. Hunter shot another hijacker who was standing about thirty feet away. Another double tap ensured the gunman would never get up again.

Somebody screamed from further inside the room and now people began to move.

'Stay still,' Hunter yelled. 'Don't move or you could get hurt.'

Someone began to yell and curse. Hunter's third target had been cradling a machine gun across his chest and now he raised it as if to open fire. The man was backing towards the door behind him when Hunter took a snap shot. The bullet hit him in the shoulder and he fell backwards, his gun flying from his hand. He screamed something in a language that Hunter could not understand. A machine gun started firing, the noise devastating in the confined space. There were more screams as panic gripped the passengers and crew and they started getting to their feet. The gun suddenly stopped firing.

'Stay where you are!' Hunter yelled again. 'We've come to rescue you!'

Those people who were on their feet threw themselves back onto the deck, while some were pulled down by those who hadn't moved. Hunter dodged around inert bodies as he tried to reach the terrorist he had just shot. The man was frantically feeling around for his gun.

Hunter heard Dunston say through his earpiece, 'He's out, Jan, through the door behind you.'

'I'm after him,' replied the Spetsnaz.

Hunter saw the downed gunman touch the barrel of his machine-gun but was too far away for a clear shot at him. Innocent lives were in danger. He had wanted to keep things quiet for a lot longer but that was now impossible. He grabbed a grenade, pulled the pin and threw it at the terrorist.

'Flash-bang coming now,' he announced over his radio, warning the other two.

The grenade had a two-second fuse and blew up in the gunman's face. The noise and light were horrendous and people began to scream again. Hunter had closed his eyes tightly and put his hands over his ears. He opened them to see the hijacker, who had scrambled to his knees, falling back, his hands to his face. At ten paces Hunter put another two bullets into the man. This time he would not be getting up.

'Matt, you okay?'

'Affirmative. My three are down. Jan got two but the third went through the furthest door. Jan's gone after him.'

'Jan? Do you copy?'

'Yes, boss. He got away. He'll warn the others.'

'If they haven't heard already. Come back here and cover the door. Matt, you cover the entrance behind you.' He stopped transmitting and raised his voice. 'Listen up, everybody. Quiet, I said!'

Gradually silence descended over the room.

'Now listen to me. We're special forces . . .' he got no further as a ragged but heartfelt cheer went up. 'Please listen. The effects of the grenade will wear off soon. So sit quietly. We have to get out of here. There are still twelve or more hijackers to deal with.'

'Surely you can take care of them?' A man's voice queried.

'There are only three of us. Open the curtains. Dawn isn't far away. The lights will stay off but you should be able to see enough. Is there anybody here who's used a gun before?'

A dozen hands went up. Most of the male passengers were well into their sixties or seventies, although one or two appeared younger.

Kneeling next to one man he asked, 'Where did you lean to shoot, sir?'

'Vietnam. Colonel in a light infantry regiment. Kenyon's the name.' He held out his hand and Hunter shook it.

'Hunter. You out rank me, sir, but I'd appreciate it if you did what I told you.'

The old man smiled. 'Heck, son, that was a long time ago. You just tell me what you want me to do.'

Hunter had picked up the hijacker's machine gun and handed it to the ex-Colonel. Placing it into Kenyon's hands he said, 'This is the safety. Push it forward to off, back and it's safe. Take that door over there and keep a sharp lookout. Anybody comes, shoot first and ask questions afterwards. Okay?'

'No problem.' The Colonel turned to the woman on the floor beside him. 'Mary-Beth, you stay here.'

Matt Dunston and Jan Badonovitch were busy doing the same, distributing the terrorists' weapons. Three crew members had fought in the Gulf War and they quickly took up positions around the room. When they had the entrances covered Hunter identified the ship's officers.

'I'm the First Officer,' said a tall, blonde woman. She was strikingly good-looking with an air of authority about her.

'The ship will be slowing down in a few minutes and I want you to start getting the passengers off the ship. I've no idea how much fire power the hijackers have but it could easily be enough to turn the tables on us.'

'They have guards on the upper deck.'

'We know. We're going to take care of them right now. Jan, let's go. Matt, you stay here.' Hunter could see that the dawn was a sliver in the sky and the darkness of the room was already fading. Shadows were becoming more substantial. 'As soon as we send for you, come up in the order your lifeboat is called.' He looked at the First Officer. 'I take it they all know where to go?'

'Of course.'

'Good. I'll leave it to you to organise them. In the meantime, please wait for Matt over there to give you the nod. I'll radio him when it's time to move.'

'What happens when we're in the boats?' The First Officer demanded. 'We'll be very vulnerable. The ship could plough over us or they could use us for target practice.'

Hunter nodded. 'Don't worry. The engines will be stopped permanently. Let's go, Jan.'

The two men hurried across the room to the door leading aft and carefully opened it. The hail of bullets which smashed around the door sent them both diving for cover.

Moments earlier, Abu Al-Adil had been standing on the bridge and looking out at the faint hint of dawn with a great deal of satisfaction. So far everything had gone according to plan. In a few days the world would see that the Great Satan was as vulnerable as any other country. The infidels would pay for their crimes against Islam and for defiling the Holy Land. The events of 9/11 would fade by comparison. If the Americans tried to prevent the liner from entering port he would shoot the women and children. They didn't have the stomach to watch their people dying. Not, he thought, as we have had to do.

Unexpectedly all power to the equipment on the bridge went out. The radar stopped, the background hiss of the radio faded away, and the automatic pilot ceased functioning. The master of the ship instinctively grabbed the telephone and rang the engine room. There was no answer. He tried again. Still nothing, though he could hear it ringing.

'What is it? What's happened?' Al-Adil's voice was shrill. He fingered the machine gun slung across his chest, flicking the safety on and off.

'There's no answer from the engine room.' The ship's master, Johann Ericksen, looked at the terrorist with loathing. 'If my crew have been harmed . . .' He got no further. Al-Adil struck him across the mouth with the barrel of his gun, breaking his two front teeth.

'Shut up, you fool, or I'll kill you.' He turned to his men and said in Arabic, 'Saif, go to the engine room and see what has happened. Sulaiman, you go with him.'

The two men nodded and rushed away.

The ship's master lay on the deck, spitting blood from his injured mouth. Right then he would have given his soul to get his hands on a gun.

The ship began to yaw to port as the automatic steering gear disengaged. Without it the liner would continue in circles until her fuel was expended. Because of its battery back-up, the compass in the binnacle still pointed to true north. In the quiet of the bridge only the master heard it ticking as the ship's heading changed, each tick representing one degree. Honed by years of experience at sea he also felt the slight change as the ship slowed down even further. Whatever was going on, he hoped it was good news.

Al-Adil gestured with his gun. 'You! Get up!'

Laboriously, Ericksen climbed to his feet. He was a big man of fifty-eight and overweight from too much time on luxury liners where he was expected to mingle with and entertain the passengers.

Abu Al-Adil's skin was crawling. Something was happening and he had no control over it. The drugs he and his men had taken to keep themselves awake were making him edgy. As he prepared to deal Ericksen another blow, there was the faint sound of an explosion. Al-Adil rushed out onto the bridge wing to see what was happening. He heard the unmistakable sound of gunfire.

Who was attacking? None of the passengers or crew had guns. How had they risen up against his men? 'Mohammed, Ayman, go and see what is going on. If there is any trouble shoot some of the hostages. Go. Go!' He screamed the word a second time. 'Akmir,' he turned to his brother, 'stay here and guard these two.'

Al-Adil's younger brother nodded with relief. He was ready to die for the cause but not yet. Akmir envied his brother's courage, his willingness to sacrifice his life for Allah. Akmir hoped he would be able to equal him when the time came.

He looked nervously at the round plastic sphere sitting at the back of the bridge. He knew it contained the deadly nerve agent and it terrified him. Death from a bullet was one thing, death from the contents of the sphere was another.

By now Al-Adil noticed the ship's swinging compass. 'Captain! Get this ship back on course, immediately!'

Ericksen disengaged the autopilot and moved the joystick. The liner slowly turned back to starboard.

One of the hijackers burst onto the bridge, calling Al-Adil's name. There was a furious exchange of words. Al-Adil shrieked an order and the man scurried out again.

Composing himself with difficulty, he said, 'It appears that armed attackers have shot my men and are hiding in the dining-room with the passengers. No matter. We will kill them and then kill more passengers as a warning to any others.'

'You filthy swine,' began the master but stopped when Al-Adil pushed the barrel of his gun into the side of his face.

'Silence! Or I will kill you.'

'You need me to take the ship into harbour, you fool.'

'Your First Officer will do just as well.'

It was true but Ericksen wasn't going to let Al-Adil know that. Instead he played on his prejudices. 'You have met her. A woman! What does a woman know? We give them the positions and the titles to keep them quiet. She would make a mess of it.'

Al-Adil saw the sense in what Ericksen said and nodded. Flicking the safety switch on his gun he nonchalantly pointed the weapon at the back of the junior officer who had been keeping the watch and pulled the trigger. Bullets stitched up the young man's back and his white shirt was instantly saturated with blood. 'A warning, Captain, keep this ship on course. I will return directly. Watch him carefully, Akmir.' Al-Adil disappeared through the bridge doors.

Sickened to his stomach, Ericksen bent down, lifted the body by the shoulders and dragged it behind a curtain, into the chart room. He lay the dead man on the deck and went back to the bridge. The ship was again paying off to port and he corrected the movement. Anger and hatred seethed through him. There would be a moment, he promised himself, when he'd get his hands on the bastard.

Hiding on top of the control room, only a metre or so lower than the platform by the door, O'Flynn nudged the Chief Engineer who nodded. He had seen it too. The lights in the engine room, like the rest of the ship, were reduced to the emergency lamps. The one by the door cast a sufficient glow to show the movement of a silver handle and the door opening.

After a few seconds an armed hijacker appeared at the door. The wall of sound that hit him was mind-numbing, distracting to those who weren't used to it. The engineers waited nervously. The terrorist looked over his shoulder and appeared to be talking to somebody behind him. Then he came inside, stepping onto

125

the grill. He looked down at the control room but could see no-one in the darkness.

The man came on alone, his gun held out in front of him, his eyes darting back and forth. The two engineers waited no longer. Both started firing with their machine guns on fully automatic. The man died in a hail of bullets. Even over the racket of the engines the sound of the shooting could be heard. The second hijacker peered through the door. O'Flynn caught a glimpse of movement and altered his aim. His bullets ricocheted around the door, flattening on the steel, flying through the entrance. One bullet, bent out of shape, hit the terrorist in the arm and he flew backwards, his gun dropping from his nerveless grasp. The bullet had severed the muscle and smashed the bones, leaving the arm hanging by shreds of flesh and skin. The hijacker lurched away, blood pumping from the stump, his right hand gripping the wound. He was halfway along the passageway when he collapsed and died from loss of blood.

9

Macnair looked at the message from the Pentagon, originated by the FBI, and the blood drained from his face. Questions seethed through his mind. 'A nerve agent, Isobel! From where? How?'

Isobel shook her head. She had been sitting but now, in her agitation, she got to her feet and paced the office. 'How on earth did they get hold of a nerve agent?'

'Saddam?' The General ventured. 'Before the war?'

'I'm not so sure. We looked at the region very, very carefully. There's been not so much as a hint. Remember when we thought he was up to something?'

Macnair nodded. The West had been sure that Saddam Hussein was close to perfecting a nerve agent of a particularly virulent type. Although there was no proof, their suspicion was a near certainty. The King of Jordan had received a phone call from the President of the United States. As a result, a very nervous King had telephoned the Iraqi President. He made it absolutely clear that unless all production stopped within twenty-four hours and the Americans saw proof that it had stopped then Saddam's palaces were going to be wiped off the face of the earth. Saddam had tried bluster but without any success. He had received further calls from Iran, Saudi Arabia, Syria and even the Lebanon. Each leader made it clear that this was no bluff. Saddam had backed down gradually. He had been a past master at tweaking the tail of the American tiger but finally he had gone too far. Now he was history.

'If not Saddam, then who?'

Isobel shook her head despondently. 'We need to look elsewhere. But I've no clue where to even start. What about Europe?'

Macnair shrugged. 'Possibly. Do what you can. Have you seen the latest PACER SKY pictures?'

'No. They'll be in shortly.'

'Let me know when they arrive. I want to see what Hunter's up to if we can.'

Aboard the *Swordfish*, the SSN Captain, Henry Cabot, looked at the signal in resigned horror. He had been dreading receiving it and here it was. He sent an authentication signal which was immediately answered. He knew that the paper in his hands spelt the end of his career, whatever decision he took. He was damned if he acted on it and damned if he didn't. The fact was, the signal was a direct order from his Commander-in-Chief, and one he couldn't ignore.

'Exec, come round to a heading of zero four five. Increase speed to ten knots.' He lifted the receiver off the bulkhead next to the plot table. 'Forward torpedoes? Load numbers one and two with forty-eights. Yes, dammit! Live!'

'What's happening, sir?' his Executive Officer asked.

'We've been ordered to sink the liner.'

'What! We can't do that, sir! What about the passengers?'

'I know, Exec. I don't need reminding.'

'Why two torpedoes, sir? Why not one? One would give them more time to get off. We could save a lot of lives if we surface and help. Hell, we should send for the Coastguard to be ready to give assistance.'

'Nope. We stay submerged. If the ship sinks fast, so be it. If it stays afloat we are to stay away until a special team arrives by helicopter. Survivors in the lifeboats are to be left alone. The Coastguard are to stay clear.'

'In God's name, why?'

Cabot looked at the younger man for a few moments and considered telling him to obey orders. Instead he said, 'My best guess, Number One, is that the ship has some sort of weapon of mass destruction on board. There can be no other reason for such an order. The signal emphasises that the ship must *not* reach America. It's something we've feared for a long time and it looks as though it's finally come. So we stop it. And we stop it here. Understood?'

'Aye, aye, sir. I'll have a resolution for firing whenever you need it.'

'Let's get to work. Up scope.'

Hunter and Badonovitch were outside. There was no more gunfire. Slowly they climbed a set of stairs, the Russian guarding their backs. Hunter cast a wary eye over the edge of the deck and paused. It all looked quiet. Taking another step took his head above the protection of the top stair and all hell broke loose. A machine gun opened fire and a swarm of bullets splattered into the metal stairwell, bouncing into the night, winging past Hunter's head as he dropped below the skyline. A nano-second glance had located two gunmen. One to the left behind a ventilation shaft, a second behind a life-jacket stowage container.

'You okay, boss?' Badonovitch whispered.

'Yes. There are two of them.' Hunter slipped a grenade from a pouch, pulled the pin, counted three and lobbed it into the air between the two gunmen. It erupted at knee height. Hunter dived over the edge of the deck and rolled behind the container. He could hear nothing. Cautiously he inched forward. Both men had disappeared. He signalled the Spetsnaz who quickly joined him.

They continued to make their way along the deck towards the stern. In order for the passengers to escape safely they needed the lifeboat decks cleared of terrorists. Halfway along Hunter heard a noise, a faint scuffle, more imagined than real. He signalled and both men froze, listening. They heard it again. Cloth on cloth. Somebody easing cramped muscles. There was a faint clunk, metal hitting a solid object, from the other side of the lifeboat davit nearest to them.

Hunter slithered slowly on his belly across the deck. Stopping, he listened and sniffed. Now he could smell the man's scent, a mixture of tobacco smoke and sweat. Another couple of feet and he glimpsed a red and white checked kaffiyeh. Hunter slid out the knife he carried in his right legging and moved cautiously forward. The terrorist had his back to him, leaning on the railing, looking back and forth at the deck below. Some instinct must have warned him. As Hunter rose to his feet a pace behind, the Arab turned his head. Instead of clamping his hand over the man's mouth and shoving the knife under his ribs and up into the heart, Hunter found himself looking into the gunman's eyes. Swinging the knife from knee height, Hunter rammed the blade into the man's throat and up into his brain. The gunman collapsed onto the knife, the razor-sharp, serrated edge sawing into the jaw bone. Quickly he lowered the body to the deck. The snicker of a safety catch had Hunter throwing himself flat onto the deck with a bone jarring, breath taking thud.

Hunter turned onto his back in time to see Badonovitch shoot the second Arab through the head with two silenced shots.

'Thanks, Jan.'

'Anytime, boss. Always a pleasure,' the Russian grinned.

Quickly now, as time was running out, they scoured the remainder of the decks. They found nobody else. Hunter looked at his watch. It was time to abandon ship.

It had been O'Flynn's idea. He had wracked his brain trying to think of an easy way to put the engines beyond use. Their instinct was to fix machinery, not wreck it. It went against the grain but it had to be done. The Chief Engineer had reluctantly nodded. At the agreed time they stopped the water cooling pumps. Quickly the engines began to overheat and the room filled with the cloying stench of burning oil. In minutes the engines began to growl and grate as metal rubbed on metal. The temperature gauges shot up and warning bells began to clamour. O'Flynn grinned humourlessly; the noise would be repeated on the bridge. He hoped it was sowing panic amongst the Arabs.

After a few minutes O'Flynn hit the emergency stop buttons and the noise ceased. Blessed silence descended and the men removed their ear protectors. The ship began to lose speed and steerageway. Without forward movement, the stabilisers became useless and the liner settled beam onto the swell, rocking gently.

'They won't be started again in a hurry,' O'Flynn said sadly. 'Time to go, so it is.'

The three engineers made their way up the steps and into the corridor. They hurried aft and stopped at the door to the outside deck. Cautiously they opened the door. The dawn was as silent as a crypt. Stepping onto the upper deck O'Flynn went to the taffrail and looked down. The ship was dead in the water.

With the lightening of the day came rain squalls and an increase in the wind. The *Silver Beech* was now rocking a few degrees either way, with a steady list to port as she drifted broadside on to the wind.

The engineers stood quietly in the dark, terrified of a confrontation with the hijackers, while at the same time relishing the opportunity to shoot the bastards. A door opened slowly. They couldn't see who it was and so they waited. A figure appeared and took a hesitant step over the combing. In the strengthening light they saw it was the First Officer.

'Ma'am,' whispered O'Flynn, 'over here.'

The passengers were leaving the dining room, one behind the other in order of their lifeboat numbers, to avoid confusion once they reached the upperdecks and began to launch the boats. Doorways along the route were covered by armed passengers, with Dunston and Kenyon bringing up the rear. It was the ex-colonel who noticed the nervous young woman passenger reach into her handbag and take out what looked like a revolver. In the half-light he wasn't sure at first, but as she began to raise and point it at Matt Dunston he knew. Kenyon threw himself into Dunston and knocked him to the deck as the woman opened fire. The bullet sailed harmlessly between them, missing the TIFAT man by a hair's breadth. Before she could shoot again Kenyon fired a short burst of his machine-gun. The last round hit her in the middle of the forehead, creating a third eye.

People began to yell and scream. More shots were fired. Passengers and crew dropped in terror, some dead, others injured. Dunston scrambled to his feet and lurched along the corridor, stepping over and around the casualties. Although it was growing light the corridor was still gloomy. Dunston, wearing his goggles, could see as clearly as if it were broad daylight. Two men who had been amongst the passengers were firing revolvers indiscriminately at the cowering crowd. One of the armed crew shot the furthest gunman, killing him. The second man turned his gun on the crew member. Dunston yelled loudly and the man looked over his shoulder at him. Dunston shot him in the back, between the shoulder blades. The bullet severed the man's spinal cord and smashed him to the floor. An elderly male passenger leapt on top of him and ripped the gun from his hand.

The hijacker turned his head and said in English, 'God is great.'

'Mine is, not yours,' said the man. He put the end of the barrel to the hijacker's forehead and pulled the trigger. There was an empty click, the hijacker smiled at him and died. 'Rot in hell,' said the silver-haired grandfather with feeling.

The liner's medical staff administered first aid to the wounded and shook their heads over the bodies of three of the passengers. Distraught relatives were crying while others were cursing.

'We need to keep going,' said Dunston. 'The sooner you're all off the ship the better.'

The words were hardly out of his mouth when a machine gun started firing and bullets flew along the corridor, thudding into the bulkheads on both sides. Running back, he yelled, 'Close the door!'

The order was superfluous as Kenyon and another man were already doing just that. The bullets suddenly ceased but could be heard hitting the metal watertight door like angry bees. Miraculously no one had been hit. They hammered the door clips home as tight as they could.

'That should hold them for a few seconds,' said Dunston. 'Follow the others and get off the ship.'

'What'll you be doing?' asked Kenyon.

'Helping the other two. We'll keep the hijackers away while you escape.'

'No, son, I don't think so. William Kenyon never ran from a fight in his life and he isn't about to this time.'

'Sir, we don't have time to argue,' Dunston began . . .

'Then don't, you're just wasting your breath. Come on, we'll close each door as we move back.'

By now the passengers were milling around the stern of the liner, fearful of other terrorists appearing. A figure suddenly popped up on the higher deck and gestured. 'Time to go! Man the lifeboats!' Hunter gave an encouraging wave and then was lost to sight as he darted back towards the bow where the sound of gunfire suddenly rent the morning air.

'Sir, firing solution. Locked on.'

'Thank you, Ben,' Cabot said to his executive officer. 'Fire one.'

'Fire one, aye, aye, sir.'

The submarine gave the slightest of shudders as a mark forty-eight torpedo left the tube.

'Fire two.'

The second torpedo started on its way.

'Time to impact?' Cabot asked, checking the stop-watch hanging around his neck.

'Twenty-six seconds, sir,' his XO answered immediately.

'Agreed.'

'Something strange is going on, sir,' a sonar operator reported. 'The ship is slowing down. And I'm no longer hearing any engine noises.'

'Up scope.' Cabot twisted his gold-leafed, baseball cap backwards and bent to meet the periscope. He adroitly adjusted the lens and lined up on the *Silver Beech.* 'What the hell . . .'

'What is it, sir?' The Executive Officer asked, praying for a miracle, a reason to halt the firing.

'They're abandoning ship. The lifeboats are being lowered to the water.'

'Sir, we must abort! If a torpedo hits while they're alongside we'll blow up the lifeboats and kill hundreds.'

Cabot, white-faced, had already reached the same conclusion. Turning to the Fire Control Officer he ordered, 'Stop both weapons!'

'Stop both weapons, aye, aye, sir.'

The order was passed along the wire to the torpedoes and both engines ceased. The torpedoes slowly sank to the seabed, automatic switches cutting out the firing sequence, isolating the explosives and the firing mechanism. Cabot looked at his stopwatch. There had been less than two seconds to impact. He took another look through the scope.

'The boats are at sea level. Some are disengaging and moving away. They're staying close to the side and heading towards the ship's stern.' Adjusting the magnification he took a closer look, focusing on the figures he could see on the deck. 'There's a fire-fight going on. One of the men on the bridge wing is leaning out. He's shooting at the people in the boats.'

Cabot paused, considering his orders, before muttering, 'What the hell. Take her up XO, man the forward gun. It's time we lent a hand.'

Al-Adil stood in shock as the lifeboats began to be lowered down the side of the liner. He hesitated for a few seconds only. With a snarl of rage he reached into his pocket. Withdrawing a small electronic device, he extended its aerial and pressed the button at its centre. Nothing. He pressed again. Still nothing. No explosion ripping out the hull and sending the ship to a watery grave, along with its passengers and crew. If the transmitter wouldn't work then they must set off the charges individually. He screamed instructions at his brother, Akmir, who nodded nervously. With a second hijacker, he rushed down the stairs, heading for the engine room.

Akmir was terrified out of his wits. Whatever he had expected it hadn't been this. Glorious martyrdom was one thing, ignominious death was another. He was a coward, he realised, something he had not been prepared to admit even to himself, never mind his heroic brother, Abu.

On the pretext of tying his shoelace he paused and gestured the other man ahead. He rushed around the corner straight into the arms of Matt Dunston. As the two men collided, Dunston recovered quickest. He rammed the palm of his left hand into the Arab's nose. The upward blow broke the cartilage at the base of the nose and sent it with devastating effect into the man's brain. The hijacker's scream was cut off abruptly as he staggered backwards, almost knocking into Akmir. The youngster didn't wait to see what was wrong. He turned on his heels and fled as fast as he could, back the way he had come.

Pausing at the stairs to the bridge he was suddenly terrified of facing his brother. What could he say? They had been heavily outnumbered? He shook his head in despair. Abu could always tell when he was lying. He didn't know how long he stood there, in an agony of indecision. Another noise startled him and he fled once more. Amidst the mannequins of a luxury boutique he found a small cupboard. He crawled inside, closing the door behind him. He sat in the darkness, ashamed yet so thankful to be alive.

Hunter was hard pressed. Heavily outnumbered, he and Badonovitch were trying to hold back heavily armed fanatics who didn't care if they lived or died. The hijackers' objective now thwarted, all that was left to them was to kill as many of the passengers and crew as possible before they escaped. Already two of the passengers who had stayed to help had died.

Al-Adil was cowering by the bridge wing screaming orders to his men, directing their efforts.

Matt Dunston radioed Hunter and Badonovitch. 'I'm working my way along the main corridor, back towards the dining room. I've got the engineers with me. We've taken out one hijacker but a second escaped. We'll attack from below. Try and distract them.'

'Roger that. But hurry, Matt, things are getting hot up here.' That was an understatement. The hijackers were becoming desperate as the lifeboats began to appear at the stern of the ship and move slowly away to safety.

Hunter, Badonovitch and four of the passengers were concealed behind protective barriers, waiting for an opportunity to return fire. The hijackers were moving slowly but steadily towards them. Soon there would be no hiding place.

'We need to move, boss,' said Badonovitch, crouching behind one of the lifeboats' davits.

'I know. Count of three. I'll use the last flash-bang and then we attack.' Hunter paused, 'One, two . . .'

'Boss! To starboard . . . Do you see what I see?'

Hunter glanced quickly over his right shoulder and a broad grin broke out. 'The US Navy to the rescue. Flash-bang now. Keep them distracted.' He snatched the pin from the grenade and lobbed it along the deck. It erupted with a loud bang and a blinding magnesium light that gave Hunter and the others the opportunity to return fire. Out of the corner of his eye Hunter saw men appear in the submarine's conning tower. A heavy machine gun was placed in its bracket before firing commenced.

Al-Adil continued to rant, screaming at his men to press the attack, his attention focused on the stern of the ship. He was watching the lifeboats slipping away. The sun was now just below the horizon and the sea was an early morning, undulating grey. The wind was gusting 15 to 20 knots and intermittent rain squalls were passing over every few minutes. He was on the port side of the bridge wing and couldn't see the submarine to star-board. When the sub's machine gun began shooting his men were caught in a cross-fire and they were forced to retreat towards the bridge. Al-Adil saw three of his men virtually cut in half. Another two were badly wounded as they broke cover and ran for the relative safety of the bridge.

The terrorist leader screamed at them to attack but it was to no avail. They were brave men but not totally foolhardy. They reached the bridge and Al-Adil rallied them with a mixture of haranguing and threats. There were still eight of them unscathed while two were wounded. Their average age was twenty-two.

'Remember the words of the prophet. Peace be to you who persevered. Worship the Lord until the certain end comes to you. Which is better – this Hell or the Garden of Immortality?' After a few seconds he stopped and said softly, 'Let us die doing God's work.'

He looked at their unshaven, bleary-eyed faces. 'We have

nowhere left to go, my brothers. We charge down the port side, hidden from the submarine. Achmed, you and Abdullah lead. I will see you and your descendants in Al-Janna!'

The two men nodded, knowing that they would be the first to die.

The submarine, left without targets, had stopped firing. Unknown to the hijackers, Hunter and his men had closed to within a dozen metres of the bridge while Matt Dunston and the engineers were walking quietly up the stairs behind them.

Forgotten in the mêlée was the master of the *Silver Beech*. He was hidden in the chartroom, holding a heavy, metal roller-ruler in his right hand. Old-fashioned and little used, it helped to train officers in the basics of navigation. It weighed around half a kilo and felt good in his hand.

Al-Adil yelled and his men leapt to their feet. Achmed and Abdullah reached the deck outside the port bridge door before being shot to pieces by Hunter's party. Urged on by Al-Adil the rest began to advance. One of the passengers was hit, giving heart to the Arab gunmen. The terrorists knew they had to end it soon and so began to close on their enemy.

Matt Dunston and the engineers, reaching the bridge, opened fire into the backs of the hijackers. Al-Adil, having dived for cover, worked his way around the front of the bridge and came in behind Dunston. He shot dead the third engineer before Ericksen rose and smashed the ruler across Al-Adil's arm, breaking the ulna and radius with a loud snap. Al-Adil's scream could be clearly heard above the noise of the guns. Even so, he flung his gun at the master's head, catching it a glancing blow. Grabbing the container of nerve gas, he knelt on the deck with it between his legs, snatched a knife from a sheath at his side and plunged it into the plastic.

Outside the firing ceased, as the last of the hijackers was killed. The door was slammed in Dunston's face by Ericksen. His words left them numb.

'He's let the nerve gas loose. Don't come in.' The master darted across the bridge to the other door and slammed it shut. They were watertight doors and the seal was complete. The gas would slowly permeate the ship. But before it escaped to the outside he hoped the authorities would have time to deal with it.

He looked at Al-Adil with contempt. 'You lose.'

Even over the sound of the rising wind outside, both men could hear the faint hiss of the escaping gas. Ericksen was consumed by fear but he was damned if he was going to show it to Al-Adil. This had been his last cruise. With no family, and after a lifetime at sea, he had been dreading old age.

Al-Adil had been chanting prayers, holding his injured arm and rocking rhythmically back and forth. His eyes locked on Ericksen's, projecting all the hatred and intolerance of his warped beliefs. Suddenly he arched his back and let out a piercing scream of pain. His eyes watered and mucous erupted from his nose. The tears turned red as small blood vessels around his eyes began to burst.

Ericksen, a few metres away, looked on in horror. Al-Adil's death throes continued, the Arab thrashing around in unspeakable agony. Unable to watch his suffering any longer, Ericksen moved towards the terrorist. Grabbing the hijacker's gun he checked the safety, saw it was off and blew Al-Adil's head apart. He looked out the window as the sun burst over the horizon, showing a cloudy sky and a rainbow stretching across the heavens. Feeling nauseous and disorientated, he placed the barrel in his mouth and pressed the trigger.

Hunter had immediately understood the implications of the master's warning and had despatched the surviving men to close all outside, watertight doors. They ran around the ship, in a hurry to complete the job and get off, but aware of their duty. If the gas could be contained, even for a few hours, they would do it.

Once they were finished they took to a lifeboat, moving away from the ship's side, heading up wind, towards the submarine.

They were helped on board by the crew. Within minutes Hunter was reporting to Cabot.

'So the nerve gas has escaped?'

'Yes, sir. We watched it killing one of the hijackers. The ship's master shot himself, knowing he too was contaminated. He was a brave man. He saved our lives by closing the bridge doors.'

'Indeed. All right, Lt Cdr Hunter, I'll signal Washington for instructions.'

'May I suggest a flash message, sir? We also need coastguard help around here to keep other boats and ships away.'

'Thank you, mister, I do know my job. For your information the US Coastguard is on its way to pick up the survivors in the lifeboats.'

Chastened, Hunter merely nodded.

'Your men are up forward if you'd like to be reunited with them.'

Recognising a dismissal when he heard it, Hunter nodded and went forward to find the remainder of the team. He would signal Macnair later.

Less than ten minutes went by before the Captain made his announcement. 'Do you hear there, all hands. We have been ordered to sink the liner as quickly as possible. We will fire four mark forty-eights in two minutes.'

This time there was no stopping the torpedoes. The warheads slammed into the liner's hull at one and a half second intervals. The bottom blew out of the luxury ship and it sank within three minutes in water only eighty metres deep.

Akmir Al-Adil felt the huge explosions and wept. For long seconds fear held him in its grip and he was unable to move. He prayed fervently to Allah. Water seeping into his hiding place broke the paralysing grip of his cowardice and he pushed open the door. Crawling out, he ran for the stairs to the bridge. He stumbled as he reached the top and fell to the deck. His eyes took in the sight of his dead brother and the ship's Captain. Suddenly he arched his back with a gasp and collapsed in agony. For Akmir, there was no considerate non-believer to put him out of his agony.

Hunter and his team made their farewells and were flown by helicopter to Houston in Texas before flying back to the UK.

Thirty-six hours after the *Silver Beech* sank they found themselves back in Scotland at TIFAT Headquarters, Rosyth.

Expecting to see Ruth, Hunter asked where she was.

'She's being flown to Tel-Aviv,' said General Macnair.

Whatever he had been expecting it wasn't that and the surprise showed in his voice. 'Why there, sir?'

'It was at her own request, apparently. The Israelis do have about the finest trauma surgeons in the world. Her father arranged it.'

Hunter nodded gloomily. Ruth's father, David Golightly, was now opposition spokesman for defence. He was a critic of the current right wing in power and unpopular, particularly with orthodox Jews. But he still had a great deal of influence and would use every ounce of his power to get the best help for Ruth, his only daughter.

'I'll try and phone her later.'

'It's the middle of the night,' said Macnair kindly. 'Leave it until the morning, afternoon her time. It'll be the best time to speak to her.'

Hunter nodded agreement, though some instinct was setting off warning bells.

Macnair interrupted his thoughts. 'We saw some of what went on from the PACER SKY pictures. I've also read your report. I think congratulations are in order.'

Hunter shrugged. 'It was a pity those passengers had to die.'

'It couldn't have been helped, Nick,' said the General. 'As it was, deaths were at a minimum.'

'Have the hijackers been identified yet, sir?'

'We're still working on that. The boffins have declared the area safe and salvage will begin soon so we might learn more, but I doubt it, somehow. If we can't ID them from photographs we may have luck with the pathologist reports.'

'How can a pathologist help to identify the men?'

Macnair lifted his hands in a show of uncertainty. 'I asked the same question. I was quoted the maxim, we are what we eat. They'll be able to tell which part of the world they're from and even their countries of birth from things like the fillings in their teeth and the constitution of their innards.'

'Who do you think we're dealing with, sir? The Iraqis? Saudi fundamentalists? The Palestinians?'

'None of the above. Isobel is working on something right now and we've information from the FBI which may or may not be useful. Only time will tell. In the meantime I suggest you go home and get some sleep.'

Hunter nodded, weary to the bone. The emotional roller-coaster of the last few days, followed by twenty-four hours of travelling had taken their toll. His inclination was to bunk down in the cabin he had at the complex, but he also wanted to see his father and talk with him over a stiff drink.

It was a fine September evening, an unusually wet few months having given way to a warm and pleasant Indian summer. Collecting his grip, he slung it into the boot of his old MGB, then spent a few minutes folding down the roof and stowing it away before climbing in. The deep, throaty growl of the engine failed, on this occasion, to give him any pleasure.

At the main gate he returned the salute of the sentry and pulled away, driving up past *HMS Caledonia* and through the narrow winding lanes. Fiddling with his radio, he found BBC Radio 4. A heavyweight interviewer was giving a British politician, whose name he didn't catch, the third degree. It was the usual waffle. Bombs were exploding across Europe, people were being killed and injured and hundreds of millions of euros of damage were being sustained. Yet all the politicians could manage was a plea for calm.

The wind ruffled his dark hair as he arrived at the main road and headed for Kincardine Bridge. Once over the River Forth he hit the motorway and put his foot down. Knowing Ruth was so far away in Israel left him feeling unsettled. He hadn't had the opportunity to talk to her since her injury. What was she thinking? Feeling?

In spite of his gloomy thoughts and overriding concern for Ruth, he couldn't help but enjoy the feel of the sun on his face as he turned off the motorway and headed towards Loch Lomond. He adjusted the sun shade and ambled along behind a string of vehicles, slowed down by a heavily laden tractor and trailer carrying round bales of hay.

It was nearly 18.30 when he arrived at Balfron. The pretty village nestled amongst farmland near the Campsie Hills, which formed a rugged backdrop to the surrounding area. Near the bottom of the hill he turned into the drive of the white house belonging to his parents. The rear garden stretched back an acre and was well tended. His parents were sitting outside enjoying the evening sun, glasses of wine on the table in front of them. Seeing him pull in they both smiled and rose, hiding their worry behind their effusive greetings.

Being home was somehow enough to reassure him that the forced separation from Ruth was no insurmountable obstacle. Hunter, seeing his parents, was struck not for the first time by how contented they seemed together. Sian and Tim Hunter had met when Tim was writing the story of the Griffiths family at the end of the sixties. He had been a reporter with *Time* magazine and commissioned to write a book about Sian's dynastic family who had influenced European politics for so long. The book, *A Million Tears*, had been short listed for the Pulitzer, missing it by a very narrow margin. Now retired, Tim was still passionately interested in world politics and liked nothing more than a healthy debate with his son over a dram or two.

While his mother fussed over him, getting him a glass of wine, Hunter sat at the table, smiling wanly at his father.

'You look all in, son. It must have been a tough trip. How's Ruth?'

'I don't know. She's been taken to a hospital in Tel Aviv. I'll phone David in the morning and get the number to call her.'

'Be sure to give her our love,' said his mother. Sian Hunter was still an attractive woman, despite the grey streaks in her black curly hair.

Tim Hunter nodded, his blue eyes sombre in his lean face.

'So what have you been up to?' his mother asked.

Hunter hesitated for a second. He had known he would be asked and had been thinking about his reply. He kept few secrets from his parents, but he didn't want to worry his mother too much. His father was different. Over a late whisky he often filled in the bits he had omitted earlier.

He began his tale. It continued while they barbecued marinated pieces of chicken which they ate with baked potatoes and salad.

His story finished with the meal. His parents sat in shocked silence, absorbing what they had just learnt.

Typically, Tim Hunter's grasp of the situation was immediate and incisive. 'If they are using weapons of mass destruction,' began his father, 'you need to find out who's behind it and fast. The world-wide ramifications are enormous. Where did the gas come from? North Korea? China? The Middle East? Each one means a possible scenario with horrific consequences. America is not going to stand idly by and let a rogue state threaten them with WMDs.'

Hunter took a gulp of wine and refilled his glass. 'We know. But so far we haven't identified a target to go after.'

10

-

They were walking alongside the River Endrick. Hunter's dog, a golden Labrador named Winston, was eagerly rushing back and forth, torn between tantalising smells and his desire to spend time with his master. Hunter whistled and the dog stopped by his side to have his ears stroked.

'Something tells me,' said his father, 'that you're putting on a brave face about Ruth's injury. How bad is it really?'

'I didn't want to worry Mum too much, but it's pretty serious. Ruth's crippled but we don't know to what extent. Certainly she won't he able to operate at TIFAT any longer, unless it was in some sort of admin job and I can't see her settling for that.'

'Nor me. There is a bright side.'

'Tell me, please. I've been looking for one since it happened.'

'If you still love her . . .'

'Of course I do,' Hunter interrupted. 'The accident hasn't changed my feelings for her.'

'I'm glad to hear it as she's a wonderful girl. There's absolutely nothing stopping you marrying her. She can live here, while you continue working for Macnair. You could even go back to general service.'

'After TIFAT I doubt I could settle for general service. I think fighting terrorism is a worthwhile job while being another seaman officer in the Royal Navy won't amount to much.'

'You could leave.'

'And do what?'

'Whatever you put your mind to.'

'Nice try, Dad, but I think I'll stay with Macnair for a while longer.'

They walked a short distance in companionable silence, before Hunter senior continued. 'You know I've stayed friends with my old cronies at *Time* magazine? Apparently they've had a tip-off. They're working on a story that suggests the trouble erupting all over Europe like a plague of boils is being orchestrated by a group of right-wingers.'

Hunter nodded non-committally.

'You knew?'

'General Macnair is working on the same theory. How did *Time* find out?'

'You know journalists. Nothing's safe from their prying eyes and inquisitive tongues. Hell, nearly all intelligence gathering these days amounts to nothing more than a bunch of analysts reading foreign newspapers from across the world. By piercing together snippets of information our security services can usually discover what's going on. Good news magazines work in the same way.'

'I'll pass it on to the general.'

The two men began to retrace their steps, slowly, enjoying their time together. Back at the house they had a final night-cap before Hunter retired. He had a restless night, in spite of his tiredness. When he left the following morning he felt jaded and out of sorts.

There was no sign announcing TIFAT's Rosyth base as The International Force Against Terrorism. Instead, it was still known as *HMS Cochrane*, anonymity being the order of the day. Hunter, dressed in the naval uniform of a lieutenant commander, a rank he'd held for two years, was thinking about his conversation with his father. If he hoped to be promoted to commander, he would need to return to the navy proper, a prospect he didn't relish. He knew he had several options – some very tempting ones. His mother's family were rich beyond avarice, owning and operating many businesses world-wide. They would find him a senior manager's job, somewhere, one that suited his organising talents. After all, his training as an officer in the RN would stand him in good stead, regardless. But would it be enough? Only, he realised, if he had Ruth by his side.

In his office, he spent the first hour going through paperwork. File after file he annotated with his initials and dropped into an out-tray. He was bored with it long before he was finished but he persevered. Nowadays, a modern fighting force lived by its paperwork.

He made four attempts to phone David Golightly in Israel but without luck. Each time he left a message and his number. At 10.00 he went to the wardroom for stand-easy. Being a weekend there were few officers around. He was helping himself to coffee when Isobel and General Macnair arrived.

'Any news on Ruth?' Isobel immediately asked.

Hunter shook his head. 'But I've had an interesting conversation with my father.' He related the theory of the *Time* journalists. 'He gave me copies of e-mails he's received. It's all circumstantial so far.'

'We've acquired information in a myriad ways. By combining data drawn from bank accounts, credit cards and other sources, we've pinpointed certain individuals who fit the profile. Now the FBI report on the submarine survivor confirms it. We think a man by the name of Charles Gustav is behind it,' said Macnair. 'Did you catch the news this morning? About the rallies in America protesting about their troops being in Europe.'

Hunter nodded.

The general went on, 'I can't say I blame the Americans. Stopping the liner was a close call. We might not be so lucky next time. Now the Cold War is well and truly a thing of the past there is no reason why Europe shouldn't police its own borders.'

'We've relied on the USA for too long, sir,' said Hunter.

Macnair sipped his coffee before replying. 'I think those times are passing fast. The storm being whipped up in the States right now could turn ugly and the Americans could pull out before we're ready.'

'But that'll make them more isolationist than ever,' Hunter argued. 'They already have enough trouble taking the international community along with them as it is.'

'Be that as it may, the majority of Americans believe we aren't pulling our weight in Europe and the rest of the world – and they're right. If Europe needs to take military action on a big scale, can it?'

'No. Not without the States.'

'Precisely. And if they left us to our own devices can we expect them to come to our aid?'

'It would be highly embarrassing even to ask.'

'Right again. So we have to keep them with us. The West must have a united front at all costs. Never mind the reality. The *perception* is all-important.' Macnair paused and then added, 'We need to confirm who's responsible for the attacks in Europe and the attempted attack on America and deal with him. In accordance with our mandate.'

'I thought the finger of blame was pointing squarely at Charles Gustav.'

'Unfortunately we've no definite proof. Isobel is working on the problem right now. The woman they pulled out of the sea, Chantelle Suchard, has given us some information to work with. But she's holding back.'

'Why would she be doing that?' Hunter asked.

'There's no doubt she's lying about her involvement. If she's to escape a long jail sentence she needs to cut a deal. I believe that's what they're discussing right now. In the meantime we carry on as usual.'

By lunchtime Hunter had caught up with his paperwork and had still failed to contact Israel. He was beginning to wonder if Ruth was deliberately trying to avoid speaking to him. *But why?* He decided to work out his frustration in hard physical exercise. In his cabin he changed into running gear and set off at a steady, mile-eating pace around the perimeter fence of the base. His speed would have placed him as a contender in the London marathon. He was about ten minutes into his run when a figure fell in alongside him, matching him stride for stride.

'Hullo, Matt,' Hunter grunted.

'Save your breath, Nick, you'll need it.'

147

Hunter grinned in spite of himself and imperceptibly increased his speed. Dunston matched him easily. They kept going, working up a sweat, stretching themselves. Hunter marvelled at the older man – at his stamina and toughness. Matt's friendship was a constant in his otherwise turbulent life. Not only was he one of the fittest men that Hunter knew, he was also one of the toughest. Although he was an ordained minister, and the base's Chaplain, Matt had started life as an officer with an infantry unit and then transferred to the Special Air Service. He had seen action all over the world – and had medals to show for it. He had taken Holy Orders in his thirties and rejoined the military after completing his studies. Evil, Dunston argued, could not be battled by turning the other cheek. Anyone who argued that Jesus was gentle, meek and mild had mis-read their bible.

After approximately twenty miles they came to a panting halt. They limbered up some more and then began a series of fighting katas, mixing different styles from different disciplines, looking for the advantage. Their movements were fast, each strike deadly, pulled at the last nano-second, avoiding damage. One or two blows were mis-timed and reached their targets, bruising flesh. After fifteen minutes they called a halt, exhausted.

'I needed that,' gasped Hunter, bent over, his hands on his knees, sucking in air.

Dunston, in a similar pose, looked up, smiled and said, 'Me too. There's nothing like it for clearing the cobwebs.'

The two men made their way back to the wardroom and their cabins to shower and change. What little activity there had been around the base had died away to nothing now the afternoon was so advanced. Those who were duty watch would be glued to a football game on TV or in their cabins with their heads down, catching up on their sleep.

Hunter chose to doze for a while and as dusk was falling snapped awake, thinking immediately of Ruth. He showered and dressed before going to his office and phoning David Golightly. This time there was an answer. 'David? It's Nick. How's Ruth?'

Was it his imagination or had there been a moment's hesitation?

'What can I tell you, Nick? They've got her resting. The knee appears to be knitting together but she's in a good deal of discomfort. She's on heavy sedation and has been ordered to remain still. Our doctors are amazed by what the surgical team who operated on her have managed. And as you know, we have some of the best surgeons in the world.'

'When can I speak to her?'

Again a pause. 'I don't know, Nick. It'll be at least a few days. Perhaps longer. The knee has to be kept absolutely still to give it time to heal sufficiently so that small movements won't matter. She is literally tied down and heavily sedated. Look, as soon as she is able, I'll get her to call you. Deal?'

'Thanks, David, I appreciate it.'

They exchanged a few more platitudes and hung up. Hunter had planned to return to his parent's home that evening but was tempted to make his excuses and stay in the mess. He was in no mood for small talk. The thought made him feel guilty as he had seen very little of them over the last few months. Reluctantly he decided to make the journey back to Balfron.

The following morning he returned to TIFAT and, for the first time in a long time, he went to Sunday Service.

It was conducted by Matt Dunston, and, as usual, was well attended. After the service, which included a prayer for Ruth's full and speedy recovery, the officers adjourned to the wardroom and the other ranks to the bar in their mess.

Hunter stood with a dry sherry in his hand making small talk with some of the others when General Macnair joined them. With him was a Member of the European Parliament, Christine Woolford, the General's 'other half', as she was delicately referred to by the members of the wardroom. An attractive woman of medium height, Christine's best features were shrewd eyes and a wide smile.

On this occasion however she wasn't smiling. 'Nick, I'm so sorry about Ruth. I hope she recovers fully.'

'Thanks, Christine.' Hunter quickly changed the subject, feeling strangely ill-at-ease. 'How long are you staying with us?'

'A few days. Malcolm and I intend getting in a round or two

of golf before I have to return to the bear pit of Strasbourg. Do you play?'

Hunter shook his head. 'Afraid not. I've tried but somehow the game does nothing for me. I'd rather be on the rugby field.'

Christine chuckled. 'Dear Nick, you can't do that all your life. Golf you can play to a ripe old age.'

Hunter smiled back. 'In that case I'll take it up when I'm a ripe old age. You know the General is supposed to be a good player?'

Christine cast a quick glance at Macnair's back and made sure he couldn't overhear. 'I know,' she said in a quiet voice. 'He told me. Warned me, more like. What he doesn't know is that I'm off scratch. I played professionally when I was in my twenties. Before politics enticed me into its embrace. I think Malcolm is in for a wee surprise.'

Hunter chuckled. 'I love it. Where are you playing?'

'Banchory. A course called Inchmarlo. One of the directors used to be in the RAF. He's sent a standing invitation to all members of TIFAT to play there.'

The General joined them and asked if either wanted a refill. They both declined.

'I gather you're away for a few days, sir,' said Hunter.

'Until Wednesday.'

'Playing golf, I understand.'

'Yes, I'm looking forward to it. It's been a while. I used to have a single figure handicap but I expect it's more like fifteen or sixteen nowadays.' He frowned. 'I did ask, but you never told me. What's your handicap?' He was looking speculatively at Christine but Hunter answered for her.

'Christine was just telling me, sir, that's she's very rusty. It's been an age since she played. She was hoping you'd go easy with her.'

Macnair chuckled. 'Of course I will. Ah, Hiram, a word.' Macnair moved away to talk to his second-in-command.

Christine winked at Hunter.

The Sunday took its usual quiet course. This time Hunter did decide to stay at the base. In the bar before dinner he met a glum faced Lieutenant Napier, wearing his mess undress.

'You on duty?' Hunter asked him.

The Special Boats Service officer nodded. 'Worse luck. I had a hot date in Dunfermline, as well.'

'I wouldn't have thought it possible. Not in Dunfermline.'

'You'd be surprised,' said Napier, darkly.

'I'll take the weight, if you like,' Hunter offered.

'Are you sure?'

Hunter nodded. 'I'm staying on board anyway, so I may as well. You go while I get changed.'

Napier turned to the barman, 'Put Mr Hunter's bar bill on my tab, please, and I'll sign for it in the morning.'

'You'd better go before I change my mind.'

'Thanks, Nick. I owe you one.'

Hunter went back to his cabin and changed into his mess undress. He phoned the duty senior rating and the guardroom at the gate to let them know he was now the duty officer, then wandered back to the wardroom bar.

There were only half a dozen officers present. After dinner Hunter and Dunston whiled away the evening playing snooker. Dunston thrashed him soundly. The ten o'clock news bulletin depressed both men. It seemed unending. Atrocity after atrocity was being committed Europe-wide and each time the finger of blame was being pointed firmly at Muslim fundamentalists. Analysis by the TV pundits blamed immigrants and Islam. Inflammatory rhetoric was being used which only a short while earlier would have been considered racist and quickly stamped upon. Matters were becoming uglier by the hour.

Over a nightcap in the bar, Dunston said, 'The sad fact is, even moderate people who recognise the benefits of a multi-cultural society are becoming Islamaphobic. The growth of fascism in Europe is terrifying.'

Hunter nodded gloomily. 'It's so well orchestrated. We *have* to find out who's behind it. According to the latest intelligence signal there have been another fifty-eight incidents resulting in eighteen deaths, dozens injured and millions of euros of damage and all this weekend. There are marches planned next week in every European capital.'

'Pro or anti-Muslim?'

'Both,' was the chilling reply.

'They can't be allowed to go ahead,' said the Chaplain.

'They can't be stopped,' said Hunter. 'It's their right. And any government trying to stop one or the other would be in political trouble. If they ban *both* it could be the fuse to a powder keg.'

'With what result?'

'Virtually all-out war, I should think. Whites against blacks and coloureds.

'Is it al-Qaeda?' Dunston asked.

'They're certainly doing the damage. But are they behind it? Not according to Isobel and the General.'

'So you go with the Gustav theory?'

'I think I do. But how on earth did he get the Muslims to do his bidding?'

'Maybe they don't realise exactly what his agenda is. Al-Qaeda and the other fanatics don't see beyond being anti-West and pro-Islam. They don't discuss the implications of their actions. They're destroyers, not builders. Look at the ravages people such as the Taliban inflicted on Afghanistan. And Gustav, if he's the man we're after, will ensure he's kept himself at arms length from the atrocities.'

Gustav closed the folder of newspaper articles with satisfaction. Everything was working as planned. His country of birth, Sweden, was at last talking about stopping immigration. Repatriation was high on the agenda of all the mainstream political parties in Europe. Furthermore, a change in European law was at last being contemplated. Controversial in the extreme, but for Gustav long overdue – collective responsibility for a criminal act by a non-European. On the release of a convicted felon, the whole family was to be deported back to their country of ethnic origin. Algerian-Dutch? Back to North Africa. Pakistani-British? Back to Pakistan. Draconian in the extreme, there was furore in the European Parliament about the measure. He still had some persuading to do with a few of the MEPs but he was sanguine the law would pass. The dossiers he had been compiling for years were now proving invaluable. Blackmail, bribery and coercion were wonderful tools. Once the law reached the statute books the bloodshed in the streets would be as great as anything he could hope for. He would have a whites-only continent if it was the last thing he achieved. Enlargement of the European Union might have been on the agenda but the idea was fading fast. Story after story about the West being swamped with immigrants, particularly Muslims, was being spread. They were hitting the newspaper headlines and the television news broadcasts practically all day and every day. Public opinion was now firmly on Gustav's side as to where the ills of Europe lay – at the doors of illegal immigrants, asylum seekers and economic migrants. His hands clenched tightly, crumpling the papers he was holding. Unwashed, uneducated, *filth*!

There was a discreet knock on the door. 'Come in! Ah, Duval, any news?'

'Not yet, sir,' replied his secretary. 'The assassination,' he glanced at his watch, 'is scheduled for just over an hour's time.'

The raised eyebrow spoke volumes and Duval nodded. 'Relevant details have been taken care of, sir. Evidence of his affiliation will be found in his hotel room.'

'Excellent. It's a pity such a popular politician with strong right-wing views has to be sacrificed. But he will benefit the cause so much more by his martyrdom.'

Duval placed sheets of A4 paper on the desk by his employer's elbow. 'These reports relate to incidents that have taken place in the last hour. You may like the third item in particular.'

Gustav glanced down the paper and then read with evident enjoyment. A mosque on the south side of Glasgow had been torched. Burnt to the ground. Neither the fire brigade nor the police had arrived in time to be of any assistance. Initial reports suggested five, perhaps six, people killed. All Muslim. All elderly. All with children and grandchildren born in Scotland. Excellent.

General Macnair and Christine Woolford had arrived in Banchory the previous evening, too late even for a quick round of the nine hole course. Instead, after a leisurely breakfast, mid-morning found them in the clubhouse discussing the championship course with the club's professional. Local rules about out of bounds, water hazards and obstructions were discussed. Some of the idiosyncrasies of a few of the holes were mentioned and then it was time to start. The course wasn't busy and Macnair and Christine wandered out to the first hole.

Macnair breathed in deeply. 'Perfect. This has to be one of the most picturesque views in the country. An ideal spot for a golf club.'

'I couldn't agree with you more. Is that the first green?' Christine pointed into the distance.

The first hole was known as Queens Drive and was a par four. The distance for the men was 284 yards, for the women 251 yards.

They had tossed a coin to see who played first and Christine had won. Much to Macnair's surprise she placed her tee in the man's position.

'My dear,' he said, 'you tee off from down there.' He pointed.

Christine nodded and smiled. 'Indulge me. I just thought it would be better fun to play together.'

Macnair looked at her appraisingly and suddenly laughed. 'You never did tell me your handicap.'

Christine took her stance and addressed the ball. Her club swung in a perfect arc. The ball sailed straight down the fairway. She turned to him and smiled sweetly. 'It's scratch.'

'Somehow,' Macnair said, bending to place a wooden tee in the ground, 'I thought you were going to say that.'

Macnair's superior strength was, in the long run, no substitute for Christine's greater skill. By the time they had played the fourth hole, known as Loch Hope, Macnair was two down. They had halved the first and second. He had lost the third to a birdie and Christine took the fourth, sinking a thirty-foot putt. She had smiled beatifically when she'd done so. With two such committed and driven people the game had become one of no-holds-barred, each playing to the utmost of their ability. Macnair's rustiness was fading fast, and he was regaining some of the ruthless skill he'd honed years earlier. Christine played

154

with the concentrated passion which in the past had taken her so close to the highest echelons of the game. While they were starting at the ninth hole, known as Glencommon, Macnair's telephone rang.

'Blast!' The warbling note distracted him and he hooked the ball to the left, into the rough, close to the trees. He answered in a bad humour, eager to be rid of the intrusion. 'Macnair.'

'Sorry to disturb you, sir' said Hunter, 'but we have a situation developing and I needed to talk to you.'

'What is it?' he asked testily.

'A group of Muslims have taken Glasgow Cathedral and are threatening to blow it up.'

'That's a police affair. Nothing to do with us.'

'Normally, sir, I agree. But in view of recent events on the continent I thought you might want us involved.'

Macnair was deep in thought. There had been over two dozen similar situations and the outcome had been the same every time. Historic buildings had been destroyed and many of the police involved had been killed. Even negotiators who had approached to talk to the terrorists had been shot. Hostages had been used to prolong the incidents – in order, it seemed, to ensure maximum publicity. All the hostages had been killed. He remembered the incident in Rheims. A group of children sent out of a church were gunned down as they approached the police barrier. All the children and several bystanders had died. They had never been negotiable situations.

Christine caught his attention and pointed. Others were waiting to tee-off, their impatience becoming evident. Macnair grimaced and waved them through.

'Have we been asked for?'

'Not as such, sir.'

'Meaning?'

'We've been told by the Chief Constable of Strathclyde to keep away. Quote, "he doesn't need gung-ho types like us queering his pitch and causing needless death and destruction".'

'What's your analysis?'

'We've discussed this situation in detail. There's no doubt in

155

our minds what the outcome will be. If we don't go in those hostages are as good as dead already.'

Macnair sighed. The devil of it was, Hunter was right. 'How soon can you move?'

'In ten, sir. We've been getting prepped. I have a team of six ready to go. The helo is cranked up and ready for take-off. But the CC was adamant when I spoke to him. He was in no mood to listen to me.'

'Have you a number for him?'

'Yes, sir. His mobile.' Hunter relayed the information which Macnair jotted down on the back of his score card.

'Get going. Leave this to me. You know what you have to do.'

'Yes, sir.'

Christine was looking at him quizzically and Macnair explained the situation as he dialled the Chief Constable's number.

'Blackwater.'

'Ah, Chief Constable, this is General Malcolm Macnair. I'm . . .'

'I know who you are.' The tone was abrupt and angry. 'I already told your people that this is a police matter and we don't want your help.'

'Be that as it may, you're getting it.' Macnair kept his own temper in check. 'I am giving you the courtesy of this phone call to allow you to change your mind.'

'Listen to me, General. This is a police action. We don't need your cowboys charging in and causing the deaths of innocent people. This takes time. We negotiate and do our damnedest to protect lives and property. In that order. And these people, whoever they are, deserve a fair trial. We don't need your lot judging and passing sentence with a bullet.'

'Now listen, Mr Blackwater, under normal circumstances I'd agree with you. But you know that there have been similar incidents all over Europe resulting in innocent deaths and destroyed buildings . . .'

Interrupting again, the Chief Constable said, 'I'm aware of that. We had a similar situation last year and negotiated a peaceful outcome. And I can do it again.'

'I remember the incident, Blackwater, and it was expertly handled. But this is entirely different. Then you were dealing criminals. These are fanatics who *are ready to die*.'

'What utter nonsense. Not on my patch, Macnair. I can end this peacefully or by sending in my own ARU.'

Macnair knew that the Armed Response Unit was highly trained and effective in normal policing incidents. But he also knew that this wasn't one of those times. The man was a fool.

'Now I'm saying this only once, Macnair. Stay away and don't bother me. I have work to do.' *Click.*

Christine had heard Macnair's side of the conversation. 'I take it he doesn't want to play ball? What are you going to do?'

'Fire my big guns, call up a helicopter and finish the round while we wait to be picked up. Would you mind packing our cases and driving back to Rosyth? I'm going to Glasgow. Sorry our break is cut short.'

Christine smiled wryly. 'Duty is a concept I understand.'

11

Hunter, Dunston and four others were airborne. There were no other operatives to spare. Burg Schwarzkopf was flying a modified Lynx helicopter. As soon as they were in the air he called Air Traffic Control at Glasgow.

'Glasgow this is Tango India Foxtrot Alpha Two, over.'

'This is Glasgow, authenticate, over.' Authentication codes changed according to the date and time of day.

'I authenticate Charlie Mike Bravo Sierra.' Schwarzkopf folded away the secret tables and slipped them into a side-pocket.

'This is Glasgow, what are your requirements, over?'

'Priority to land near the Royal Infirmary, over.'

'Approved. All aircraft are being routed clear of the area. Good luck. Out.'

'We'll be there in twenty minutes,' Schwarzkopf announced over his communications system.

Hunter radioed Isobel at headquarters. 'Has the General taken off yet?'

'Two minutes ago. Not best pleased. He lost the game. Am patching you through now.'

'Sir? Hunter.'

'Nick, the Assistant Chief Constable is now in charge. I've briefed him precisely on what's required. He appeared relieved that we're taking over responsibility.'

Though he was itching to know how Macnair had side-stepped Blackwater, Hunter knew it was wisest not to ask. 'Any special instructions, sir?'

'None at present. Don't go in until we get a clear picture of what's going on. Did you get a plan of the building?'

'Affirmative. Isobel got it for us. Even as cathedrals go, it's a very large and beautiful building.'

'Which is why it must be saved.'

'What's the priority, sir?'

'Your ears only, Nick. My instructions are the building. There are twelve hostages and an unknown number of terrorists. More people are killed on our roads every two days than are at risk in the cathedral. The building has been there for over nine hundred years. It is irreplaceable. The site itself has been held sacred for over fifteen hundred years. It's no contest I'm afraid.'

'Roger that, sir. Have there been any messages from the terrorists yet?'

'Not so far. We're still waiting to hear their demands. Waste of time, of course. We won't negotiate with them under any circumstances, as they well know. This is revenge for the mosque which was torched in Glasgow yesterday. Wait, Nick. I'll be right back.'

Hunter's earphones went dead and he sat pensively. Who, he wondered, had given the order to save the building at the possible cost of innocent lives? Well, he was the man on the ground. As far as he was concerned he'd save lives and damn the consequences.

'Nick? Macnair. Where are you?'

Hunter looked down. 'Coatbridge is on our right, sir. Ten minutes out at the most.'

'Don't go in. Go high and stay high while I try and sort out a few problems. The terrorists have made contact. They've said that if they see the slightest sign of military personnel they will kill three of the hostages.'

'They won't know we've arrived, sir.'

'Unless they have somebody on the outside watching events. Which is most likely.'

'Roger that, sir. How is the evacuation progressing?'

'It's going on apace. But there are thousands of people to move out, a whole hospital to empty. That takes time. Seriously ill patients need a great deal of surgical support and nursing.'

159

'If this incident follows the pattern of the others, the terrorists must intend to demolish the cathedral. I've studied the plans. It will take a lot of plastic to destroy it completely.'

'We have to assume they can do just that.'

'I agree, sir. But the amount of explosives needed means that the peripheral damage could also be huge.'

'I'm aware of that. So?'

'If the terrorists are aiming for maximum publicity then the sooner they detonate their explosives the more people will die. Particularly if evacuations are still going on.'

'Then why haven't they done so already?'

'Maybe they intend to milk more publicity out of it first. The more television and radio reports the better, as far as they are concerned.'

There was a few seconds silence. 'I agree. That makes sense. The journalists will howl like stuffed pigs but I'm pulling the plug on them right now. I'll talk to the Assistant Chief Constable.'

'What about freedom of the press, sir?'

Macnair's reply made Hunter grin. He tapped Schwarzkopf on the shoulder. 'Burg, go high, stay high. We need to get a better picture of what's going on.' He changed frequency. 'Isobel? How are the satellite pictures coming?'

'Not good, Nick. I don't understand it. There's a definite huddle of people in the Chapter House – the hostages I suspect, but I can't trace anybody else.'

'What? That's not possible!'

'I've checked the equipment and it's working perfectly.'

'Could the terrorists be hiding amongst the hostages?'

'Not according to my count.'

The solution hit them both simultaneously. Hunter voiced the thought. 'Aluminium.'

Terrorists world-wide were becoming wise to the ways of governments and the bag of tricks they had developed in counter-terrorism. Heat-seeking satellites read the ambient temperature and that of any object or living body in the locale. It was so effective that the shape and size of the body, and any movements, could be measured and followed. One way to counteract the system was to wear clothes impregnated with aluminium. Older style prototypes were uncomfortable and rustled but the new outfits coming into use had overcome these drawbacks. So far, to the best of the West's intelligence services' knowledge, no one outside government organisations had the new design.

Macnair called back. 'The police have been warned. If anyone looks or smells like special forces or army they'll detonate the bomb and kill the hostages. They must have someone on the *outside* who would tip them off. I've got the ACC working on that right now.'

'What should we do, sir?'

'Do you have the portable heat-detector with you?'

'Yes, sir.'

'We can't risk you being recognised for who or what you are. And we don't know yet who the mole is on the outside. I have an idea.' The General gave his instructions. All operations of this sort were developed in three separate stages. The decision to go was made at the highest level and ordered by the senior officer. Then planners debated, argued, plotted and finally issued the outlines and guidelines for the operation. The third stage was okayed by the man in command on the ground. He had the right to veto a plan or an operation at anytime if he thought it was unworkable or too dangerous. Such a veto was a decision he would make perhaps once, at the most twice, in his career. After that he could look for a new occupation. Hunter's acquiescence to the General's idea was paramount.

The Assistant Chief Constable was named Graham Baldock. Unlike Blackwater his high-flying and younger superior – who had just been called to the Home Office at a moment's notice – he was an old fashioned cop. He had come up the hard way, through the ranks, serving his time. He was due to retire shortly from what was, by any yardstick, a highly successful career. Shrewd, hard-working, in his middle fifties, Baldock's neatly cut grey hair was hidden beneath an old-fashioned fedora hat. Despite a bulbous, drinker's nose, Baldock was teetotal and had been all his life. Drink had killed his father at an early age and the son had sworn an oath to his mother that he would never imbibe. He still kept his word even after she, too, had died. As far as he was concerned Blackwater's removal was a godsend. The pompous ass saw this as an opportunity to further his career, disregarding the safety of his men, the prisoners and the possible destruction of the cathedral. With great difficulty he had somehow managed to keep a straight face when his superior was called to London.

The possibility of an outsider watching what they were doing had occurred to him and he was already combing the area for possible suspects when Macnair had called. The ACC liked what he was told.

A control vehicle had been placed next to the statue of the missionary David Livingstone. Baldock knew he and his officers were too close to the cathedral. If it blew up the falling masonry would probably kill everybody in a wide radius. The M8 motorway was closed in both directions, and barriers had been set up as far as a thousand yards from the area.

Looking moodily at the large scale map pinned to one wall Baldock pondered the problems they were facing. The biggest was the Royal Infirmary Hospital, right next door. There were operations taking place which could not be interrupted, as well as critically ill patients who needed to be moved to other hospitals. Those who could be discharged were being sent home, while alternative beds were being arranged all across Scotland. Anger erupted in the ACC's stomach like acid. Nothing on earth justified this sort of atrocity.

Around him, senior officers were busy giving orders and relaying information. As each building was cleared it was marked with a yellow highlighter. Baldock sighed. There were too few coloured yellow.

Turning to Chief Superintendent Douglas Matthews he said, 'Doug, I want the press moved right back. They have to go behind the barriers as well. The concession to film is now withdrawn.'

He and Matthews had joined the force together and had been friends all their adult life. 'Is that wise, Graham? They're going to howl like . . .'

It was an indication of the pressure the ACC was under that Baldock snapped, 'Just do it, all right?' He was immediately contrite. 'Sorry. This is the biggest incident we've ever faced. Tell the press it's for safety reasons.'

'But it isn't?'

'No. It makes good sense operationally. I'll fill you in later.' He was about to say something else when he thought better of it. Instead he took his assistant to one side, out of hearing of the busy control van, 'We've a helo coming in. TIFAT. I want them taken into the hospital nice and quiet. They'll be in civvies, not combat gear. They're setting up an observation point on the top floor of the Royal, overlooking St Mungo's. There's going to be a news blackout imposed ASAP. We must isolate this incident as far as possible. It may buy us time.'

Matthews nodded. To him it made little sense but he would follow out his instructions to the letter. 'Where do we want the helo to land, sir?'

'As far away as possible and still get the passengers here double quick. What the . . .' Both men heard the unmistakable thwacking noise made by a helicopter in flight and dashed outside. Baldock felt a surge of anger as the helo came in to land close by. The bloody fools! Perhaps Blackwater had been right. Maybe they were just a bunch of cowboys. Then the helo turned and the unmistakable sign of the red cross was displayed. The Lynx continued turning as it came into land, ensuring, with a three hundred and sixty degree sweep, that its insignia was unmissed.

Schwarzkopf had landed in a field to the east of the city where the TIFAT team had quickly decorated the sides of the helicopter with a white banner and red cross. They had changed out of combat gear and into jeans and tee-shirts, before pulling on white medical coats and hanging stethoscopes around their necks. The disguise was Isobel's idea. The hospital was the logical place to set up an observation post. The equipment the team would be using was contained in white boxes marked with a red cross, the paint still drying. If there was somebody on the outside watching, an open approach was better than a clandestine one.

To add to the subterfuge, the helicopter was to be used to ferry the seriously ill to other hospitals, a refinement Hunter had dreamt up only minutes earlier. Isobel was already informing the hospital authorities that the helo was available and patients were ready to move. Six stretcher cases plus six staff could fly out. The same information was being relayed to the police control caravan, as well as to the radio and television stations. It was the last piece of news that was to be broadcast on the siege. After that the news blackout would be enforced.

With satisfaction Hunter saw the police moving away the hordes of press, live TV cameras and still photographers. After a good deal of angry argument from the brave but bloody-minded reporters, they gave ground. The policemen and women had been given their instructions. They were not to take no for an answer. If anyone refused to go they were to be arrested. Just for a few hours, freedom of the press and civil liberties were to be suspended. Anyone refusing to move out of their homes was also to be removed, for their own safety. They could kick up a fuss afterwards. Those fitting a certain profile were to be arrested and their property searched. The criteria? Muslim or foreign nationals in properties over-looking the area. As for search warrants, a state of emergency had been declared and different laws were in force.

So far nobody had been arrested.

Hunter ignored the uniformed ACC beyond a brief nod. Already stretchers bearing seriously ill patients were being wheeled out. Hunter and the rest of the team helped them into the helicopter. At the same time they moved their equipment onto empty stretchers and began walking towards the hospital's main entrance. The team quickly disappeared into the throng of evac-uees now milling around Castle Street.

The team were met at the entrance by a worried-looking man who introduced himself as the Director Of Administration.

'You understand our requirements?' Hunter asked.

'Yes, yes, certainly. Please, follow me.'

A lift took them up three floors. They soon found themselves in a small ward with six empty beds. The ward's windows overlooked the Cathedral of St Mungo's, a glorious sight in the sunlight.

They began to assemble their equipment. Priority was given to a high-powered heat-seeker that resembled a TV camera. While it was being fixed to a tripod and aimed at the cathedral a second device was placed on a table and switched on. It looked like a normal radio but was in fact an eavesdropping device of amazing complexity. Every frequency within five miles was being sucked up and transmitted back to Isobel at Rosyth. There, computers were listening to every conversation currently taking place on a telephone, mobile phone or radio within that radius. Leo had programmed the software to identify certain words, certain languages and foreign accents. The system was hampered by the fact that foreign correspondents were reporting on events even though they couldn't see what was going on. It was hoped that the news blackout would quickly change all that.

Hunter stood at the window, powerful binoculars to his eyes, scanning the ancient cathedral. It was, he realised, quite stunning in its majesty.

'Claude, you got anything on that monitor yet?'

'Yes, boss. I think the hostages are in the furthest corner. I'm just comparing it to the map.' He pointed. 'Here. They're in the Chapter House.'

'Just as Isobel said. Found the perps yet?'

'I've focused the sight all along the building at maximum power. Faint heat spots are showing up and we're comparing them to other possible sources.'

Frowning, Hunter stared at the monitor and then pointed. 'That looks like a head.'

'I agree,' said Lt Napier.

Matt Dunston looked intently at the tiny points. 'I think you're right. So they're definitely wearing aluminium suits.'

'Seems like it,' said Hunter. 'Jan, how are you getting on with the ex-torch?'

'The light is flickering green to amber. That's because we're so far away. We need to get a lot closer,' the Spetsnaz replied.

'It can wait,' said Hunter. 'At least we know there are explosives, we just don't know where or how much.'

Hunter's phone rang.

'Nick? Isobel. We've got a possible contact. A conversation has just been intercepted in the five mile radius – in Arabic. From the readouts I would say that one of the people speaking was in the cathedral and the other very close by.'

'How close?'

'I can't tell exactly. It's a little bit odd, to tell the truth. This isn't an exact science for locating message transmissions but I'd expect the target to be within, say ten yards.'

'And?'

'The signal appears to have been sent from the clear ground to the east of St Mungo's. But that's been evacuated.'

'Could it be somebody in one of the flats behind, watching?'

'It's possible,' Isobel sounded doubtful.

'But you don't think so?'

'No, to be honest, I don't. Could someone be hiding in the cathedral grounds?'

'Possibly. But it's not a location I'd choose. Is it a radio or phone signal?'

'Mobile telephone. We've tried tracing it but no luck. It was reported stolen a week ago.'

'Stolen? Where from?'

'Somewhere in Glasgow.'

'Which police station was the report made to?'

'Let me see.' There was a pause while Isobel checked her computer. 'Maryhill.'

'Okay, thanks.' He broke the connection and relayed the information to the others.

'Matt, can you nip down and have a quiet word with the ACC? Ask him to come and talk to me. Make sure he knows it's a request.'

Dunston, dressed in a grey suit and dog-collar, nodded. 'Leave it to me.'

While he was away the others continued examining the faint thermal images on the monitor. Each one was marked on the large scale map they had of the cathedral. They double checked.

None of the images appeared to have moved very far. That was the good news. The bad news was there appeared to be eleven terrorists in all.

Hunter reported to Macnair.

'Okay, Nick. I'll be with you in fifteen minutes. We're landing at Port Dundas. I'll walk from there. Tell ACC Baldock to expect me. I don't want to be held up by some over-zealous P.C. Plod.'

'Will do, sir. In fact, he's just walked in.' Hunter broke the connection and smiled to the ACC, his hand outstretched. Both men shook hands, each assessing the other.

The ACC, apparently satisfied, smiled. 'This gentleman in the vicar's costume politely asked me to come and speak to you.'

'Thank you, sir,' said Hunter. 'The dog-collar is real, though. He knows the cathedral pretty well but he's also one of us.'

The ACC looked as surprised as he felt and re-appraised his initial opinion of Dunston who had seemed to be such a tough son-of-a-bitch when they'd met.

Hunter explained about the intercepted phone signal and Baldock looked suitably shocked.

'You realise what this probably means?' The ACC asked.

Hunter shrugged. 'It could be a bent policeman.'

Baldock nodded. 'Leave him to us. If it is, whoever he is, I'll have his balls.'

Hunter shook his head. 'I've a better idea. We need to buy time. It's now eighteen hundred and darkness is still three hours away. If these terrorists follow the usual pattern they'll balance killing hostages against the maximum publicity achievable. Which means that sometime in the next hour or so they'll set off the explosives. Loads of media coverage and lots of bodies. How long will the evacuation take to finish?'

'Hours yet. We have to search every building. The hospital is a nightmare. You just can't rush so many people, especially if they're bed-bound. The staff are doing their damnedest but there are only so many lifts and so few volunteers to push the beds, trolleys and wheelchairs.'

'I suggest we find this bent copper and feed him some mis-information,' said Hunter.

'What do you propose?'

'Tell him the evacuation is taking a great deal longer than expected. That there are still many hundreds of people in the surrounding buildings. Tell him it will take until well after midnight to make a dent in the numbers.'

'That won't stop them detonating the explosives,' said Baldock. 'Hell, it may even encourage them to set them off now for maximum effect.'

'Here's the clincher,' said Hunter. 'You also say that the news blackout imposed under section eleven of the Official Secrets Act is already being questioned by the newspapers. A special court is sitting in Edinburgh right now to discuss the pros and cons. Say you think we're going to lose. That the press will be swarming around the cathedral before the night is out. Emphasise it will be world-wide coverage and that you're bloody angry about it. That may hold the terrorists for a few hours.'

'I need to find the traitor first,' said the ACC.

'Broadcast it to all your force as a sitrep. He's bound to transmit the info to those in the cathedral. Now we know which frequency he's on and where to look we can listen in.'

'He may not tell the terrorists what's going on,' said Baldock.

'True,' said Hunter. 'But the mis-information is too important not to pass on as it means the perps are guaranteed world-wide coverage. If he doesn't, contact Maryhill and find out if they have any Muslim or Islamic personnel. Match them with whoever is in the grounds. Oh, and see if there are any Arabic speakers.'

'He or she will probably have moved by now. The sweep of the open spaces is complete and everybody is now working at emptying the buildings.'

'It's definitely a man. That was confirmed.'

'Nick,' said Dunston. 'I've just thought of something. As far as the terrorists are concerned, what would be the worst case scenario?'

'They get taken out before they can set off the explosives,' said Hunter.

'And how do you guard against that? You have a man on the outside with a transmitter as well, just in case. If it all goes pear-shaped he presses the button and up it all goes. That's what I would do. Either way the cathedral is destroyed.'

Hunter nodded gloomily. 'Is it likely to be the same man?'

'I should think so. They can't have that many assets on the ground in Glasgow.'

'Don't you believe it,' said the ACC. 'We've had a huge influx of immigrants from all over the Middle East in the last two years. Any number of them could be al-Qaeda supporters. And probably are.'

'In that case search anybody who looks of Arab extraction,' said Hunter. 'If he has anything on him that could possibly send a signal arrest him and hold him incommunicado until this is over. But my bet is, it'll be the man who telephoned.'

'How do you intend to infiltrate the cathedral?' asked the ACC.

'We've found a way in. One thing, sir,' said Hunter, 'we may not be taking prisoners. Does that present you with a problem?'

'No. I hate paperwork,' came the response. 'Now, if you gentlemen will excuse me, I have a lot to do. I'll speak to you later.'

'One more thing,' said Hunter. 'My boss, General Macnair, is arriving soon.'

'I'll see he gets straight through.' On that note the ACC departed.

'Think it'll work?' asked Doug Tanner, a frown on his normally cheerful face.

'We can only pray,' said Dunston.

The American SEAL grinned, his white teeth shining in his black face. 'That's your part-of-ship, Matt. We leave all the hallelujah stuff to you.'

'With you lot that's a full time job.'

The ACC went downstairs, sucking an antacid drop. Yet again his anger had erupted in bile. That one of his men could be helping these scum was beyond his comprehension. Well, he knew just the man to finger the likely culprit. But first of all he would up-date his men.

Back in the control van he said to Superintendent Douglas

Matthews, 'The media barons are up in arms. A special court is sitting right now in Edinburgh challenging our exclusion of the press. We'll try and keep them at bay for a few hours but I've been told we're going to lose.'

'Damn,' Matthews said with feeling. 'The last thing we want are reporters and cameras all over the place.'

The ACC sighed theatrically, 'That's the price of freedom and democracy.'

The Superintendent looked at his boss is surprise. He knew Baldock's position on civil liberties – the rights of the guilty at the expense of the innocent he called it.

'I want to tell everyone what's happening. Put me through on the universal channel, will you?'

A few moments later the ACC was speaking to hundreds of officers who were busy in the area. 'The evacuation is taking a lot longer than expected. I've been speaking to the hospital authorities. We don't expect the building to be emptied before tomorrow morning. The evacuation of patients cannot be rushed. So just keep things moving along at the present pace. Secondly, I have news regarding the press blackout. I'm not happy about this but we can expect the cameras back here around twenty-three hundred or shortly afterwards. Unfortunately, this will play into the terrorists hands, giving them global media coverage. Be that as it may, I want a peaceful resolution to this affair. We will co-operate with the media and at the same time try and establish contact with the men in St Mungo's. I want no precipitate action unless they start killing hostages. If they kill even one person we go in and we go in hard. As long as the prisoners live we'll try and talk to the terrorists and establish their demands. Oh, one more thing. Well done, all of you. I'm proud of what you've achieved to date. That is all.'

Baldock broke the connection and looked into the frowning face of his friend and colleague. The ACC placed a finger to his lips and gestured to the door. Outside he casually looked around to make sure nobody could overhear him. 'There's a mole and we think it's a copper.'

'What!' Matthews was scandalised. 'Are you sure?'

'As sure as we can be. Find Ali for me. He knows all the Muslim coppers – maybe he can suggest which scumbag is to blame.'

Ali al-Faruq was Glasgow born and bred. His father had immigrated to the West from Saudi Arabia in the nineteen sixties. With a medical degree from Oxford al-Faruq senior had gone on to become one of Glasgow's most respected and eminent plastic surgeons. Ali had shown no desire to follow in his father's footsteps and instead had taken a law degree. Being a lawyer hadn't suited his temperament and eight years earlier he had joined the police force. Fast-tracked because of his education and special skills – he spoke four languages including Arabic – he had quickly made Inspector. He was tipped for the top and was widely expected to be the UK's first ethnic minority Chief Constable. He was the type of man that an old-fashioned copper like Baldock would normally heartily dislike. But in this case Baldock had the highest regard for the man, respected his beliefs and thought him a good policeman. He was a devout Muslim, although he never paraded his beliefs in the other coppers' faces. There had been a lot of comment about his rise through the ranks but it had been richly deserved. Lesser men had talked about quotas and ethnic minorities getting the best jobs and political correctness leading the way. Only Baldock had known better. Al-Faruq had proven to be a superior police officer in every way.

'Ali is over by the barriers in Duke Street,' said Matthews.

'I'll find him myself.'

The ACC walked out of Cathedral Square and along John Knox Street, deep in thought. If the cathedral was destroyed it could never be replaced. The expense alone was one thing, but there were no longer artisans capable of re-building such a magnificent edifice.

He spotted al-Faruq on his mobile telephone a short distance from the barriers, one hand against his ear, talking softly. The Inspector was in uniform and looked up when the ACC approached. He said something in what the ACC assumed was Arabic and broke the connection.

'Important call?'

Al-Faruq was a good-looking man in his early thirties. Tall, slim, black-haired, brown-eyed and still a bachelor, the ACC knew that many of the policewomen in the force would have gone to bed with the man if he had given the slightest hint. But he had played it straight. He never mixed pleasure with business. His girlfriends had all been from outside the force.

'My mother. I was explaining I would be home late.'

Years of training told Baldock that al-Faruq was lying. The ACC's nose was twitching and he had learnt to trust his nose in cases like this. Realisation hit him like a thunderbolt but he knew instinctively. Al-Faruq was based at Maryhill.

Was the man a traitor? Baldock thrust his hands into his jacket pockets, his fists clenched tightly as he fought down an almost overwhelming desire to smash the answers out of the handsome face before him.

'Everything all right?' Baldock managed to ask without betraying the emotions coursing through him. He checked his watch, to give his expression a chance to settle.

'Ah, yes, sir. Everything is fine. I em . . . heard your broadcast.'

The ACC pulled a face. 'Can't be helped I'm afraid. It's going to take even longer than I said but I didn't want to dishearten the troops too much. But I meant it when I said if they kill one hostage then we go in hard. Immediately. There'll be no waiting for the cameras to arrive. In many ways I'm hoping they'll give me the excuse. I would have liked this over before the media got back, one way or another.'

'Do you know when the press will get back here, sir?'

Baldock nodded. 'I've been speaking to our people at the court in Edinburgh. They think they'll manage to delay matters until around midnight, but definitely no longer. So anytime after that.'

'I see, thank you, sir.'

'I'll speak to you later. I'm just going to have a word with the armed response unit.'

Armed policemen surrounded the cathedral. It would be their task to storm the building if they were ordered in. Or so they thought. Baldock had no intention of enlightening them. He spoke

172

briefly to the Chief Inspector in charge and returned towards the control van. Once he was out of sight he hurried instead to the hospital entrance. Within minutes he was with Hunter and his men.

He was introduced to General Macnair who had just arrived and was being brought up to speed with events.

Baldock asked, 'Have there been any more phone calls?'

'Yes,' replied Hunter. 'One.'

'At what time?' The time given confirmed his suspicions. Although his gut instinct was proven correct, Baldock was devastated – who *could* be trusted? 'The man we want is Inspector Ali al-Faruq. He was using his phone then and I didn't believe his story. Damnation! His involvement makes matters even worse.'

'Why?' Hunter frowned. 'The strategy appears to have worked. We've bought time and . . .' He held up his hand. A phone was ringing and, glancing at the display, he said, 'That's Isobel at HQ.'

'He's used the phone again,' prophesied Baldock.

Hunter listened to Isobel and hung up. 'You're right.'

'He told the perps that the press are away until midnight?' Baldock hazarded.

Nodding, Hunter asked, 'How did you know?'

The ACC repeated his conversation with al-Faruq.

'Good,' said Macnair. 'In that case it's time to go over the battle plan.'

12

It was dark at last. Or as dark as any city becomes once the sun has set. At 22.30 the city was plunged into total darkness as an electricity blackout hit the whole conurbation of Glasgow.

Hunter and the team had changed into grey attack gear. They moved like ghosts out of a rear entrance of the Royal Infirmary and into the grounds of the cathedral. Each member was in contact by personal radio, both with Macnair and back to Isobel at H.Q. Satellites were passing overhead, focusing on the cathedral, recording silently. The heat-seeking camera installed by the team displayed an almost static image. Eleven faint shapes scattered around St Mungo's Cathedral.

Each team member carried an ex-torch and was working his way around the building, holding the torch close to the walls, looking for the slightest indication of plastic explosives. Here, even through the great walls of the cathedral, the torches worked effectively. The indicator lights were firmly on amber and flickering to red. By cross-referencing the angles of the beams they identified eight locations. The information was relayed back to H.Q. A few minutes later Isobel called back.

'There are explosives in the eastern arm, in the Presbytery and Feretory.' The former, Hunter knew, had been the ecclesiastical and spiritual court, while the latter housed the portable shrine for relics of saints.

'Roger that,' acknowledged Hunter.

'A second lot is in the Chapter House, in the north-east corner. The remainder are fixed to the four main pillars opposite the

174

Blackadder Aisle and to two of the lesser pillars in the centre. We've tried to estimate how much explosives there are and it must be hundreds of pounds.'

'Easily enough to raze the cathedral to the ground.'

'The cathedral, the hospital and every building in about a half mile radius I should think,' said Isobel.

'Agreed. Thanks.'

On the north side of the building, protruding like a small arm, lay the Sacristy and Treasury. Near its ancient wall was a metal plate, a metre square, leading down to the main drains. With oxygen masks and night-vision goggles in place, the team quickly prised up the plate and vanished, one by one.

Their ingress was watched by a dark-haired man standing on the far side of the grounds. He reached for his mobile. *They had been lied to! Special Forces were going in.*

Assistant Chief Constable Baldock stood in the shadows with Superintendent Matthews. They too had watched the team vanish into the ground. Normally they would have seemed like dark ghosts against the grey stone cathedral walls but the two senior officers were wearing NVGs borrowed from their own force. Inspector Ali al-Faruq was equally plain to see. He had just removed the phone from his pocket when Baldock approached him.

'Ah, Ali, there you are,' said the ACC. 'We need you back at the control van straightaway. Something has come up.'

'Yes, sir. I'll be right with you. I just have this call to make.' Al-Faruq knew he could make the call in front of his superiors as he would be speaking Arabic. He almost laughed out loud at the irony of it. His anger though, was making him tremble. If his companions didn't stop them and delay matters until the press arrived he would set off the explosives himself, as soon as he was at a safe distance.

Baldock was standing near the Inspector. For a big man he could move extremely quickly when he needed to. Even as al-Faruq began pressing buttons on the phone the ACC sprang forward. The small cosh he held in his hands was illegal but it had saved him on a number of occasions when facing down some of Glasgow's hard men. The blow to the upper forearm was hard and numbing. His hand paralysed, al-Faruq yelped in shocked outrage and dropped the mobile.

Chief Superintendent Douglas Matthews wrestled al-Faruq to the ground, twisted his arms behind his back and quickly fitted handcuffs. He ensured they were just tight enough to cut off his prisoner's circulation. 'Not bad for a couple of old men,' he said to the ACC.

Baldock chuckled. 'You're right there, Doug. Read the bastard his rights and take him away. Get him out of my sight before I do him some real damage.'

'This is an outrage . . .' al-Faruq began but got no further.

The ACC kicked him in his ribs. 'Shut up, you traitor. You're a disgrace to your uniform and your family. You've betrayed your people to the scum in there,' he gestured to the cathedral.

Making no attempt to deny it, al-Faruq said, 'And what of the greater betrayal to Allah and Islam? The obscenity of policemen standing by and watching my mosque being burnt to the ground by ignorant savages who are not fit to clean the shoes of Muslims. That is a far greater betrayal. There is only one true faith. And it will prevail over all the earth . . .'

'Search him,' said Baldock.

In al-Faruq's pocket they found a small radio transmitter with a switch and a button.

'It looks like that chap from TIFAT was right. He does have the transmitter.' Baldock bent down and grabbed the supine Inspector by the scruff of his collar. Rage gave him strength and he jerked the man to his feet. 'You're going down for the rest of your life, al-Faruq, you bastard!'

His prisoner laughed. 'You've nothing on me, Baldock. Nothing that will convict in a court of law. If you do get to court it'll be circumstantial. I found that transmitter lying in the grass and was about to bring it to you when you attacked me without provocation. You two are the ones going to jail.'

'Shall I tell him or you?' Baldock asked his friend.

'Let me, please, Graham. But not until I can see his face.'

Matthews was looking forward to watching al-Faruq listen to his own voice on tape. The case they had was watertight and al-Faruq would be lucky to ever leave prison alive. His fellow prisoners would see to that.

Gustav had been watching his own channels on TV – nine screens in a phalanx filling an entire wall. Every channel shared footage of the cathedral in Glasgow. His TV companies across Europe and beyond were 'on message', communicating live, describing events of the latest outrage in Norwegian, French, German, Swedish, English, Walloon . . . the polyglot babble filled Gustav with deep satisfaction. Immigrants were blatantly destroying European culture as evidenced by the atrocities already committed and epitomised by the outrage in Glasgow. Once the cathedral was destroyed there would be no turning back. The acts of terrorism would continue until the right-wing were in power across Europe. Then they would pounce. Draft legislation, conceived by him over the decades, honed and polished, the finest details thoroughly researched, would come into force. Islam would be outlawed. All mosques would be shut down forthwith. Muslims would be forced to leave Europe and return to the land they claimed as their country of origin. If a third generation German could describe him or herself as Algerian-German then so be it. They could return to Algeria. Let them, he thought, eat sand.

There was a knock on the door and Duval entered.

'Anything new on the Glasgow affair?' Gustav asked.

'No, sir. We can expect something to happen at any time.' He looked at his watch. 'It is half past eleven now, so it is half past ten their time. It can't be much longer.'

'Are the press releases ready?'

'Yes, sir.'

'The politicians and commentators comments?'

'Of course. This will be the most savage attack to date. We've doubled and in some cases trebled the tallies of dead and injured and highly exaggerated the cost of the damage. The vitriol against the Muslims will be so great that no politician in his right mind will speak up on their behalf. The news from America is also good. The populace is baying for the repatriation of its troops from Europe. They are demanding that their own shores be protected, saying its time we Europeans stood up for ourselves. Our press release will be saying the same thing. With a concerted orchestration of public opinion on both sides of the Atlantic the present administration will have little choice.'

'Is everything in place to disengage our connections with the followers of Islam?'

'Yes, sir. I have only to send the orders down the computers. The electronic walls and cut-offs we designed will slot into place. No one will be able to trace anything back to us.'

'In that case we will send the instructions after the destruction of the cathedral.' Gustav chuckled. As political structures disintegrated and alliances shifted, now was the time to make the break, before the pressures of secrecy multiplied out of control. With current technology it was almost impossible to work out who the real enemy was. How easy to cast suspicion elsewhere. Black holes, viruses, trap doors . . . child's play. 'This is indeed excellent news. I think a little celebration is called for.'

'Herbal tea, sir?'

'No. Open that bottle of one-hundred-year-old brandy.'

If he was surprised, the ever faithful secretary didn't show it.

The team had walked, bent double, underneath the cathedral all the way to the Blackadder Aisle. The drain cover inside yielded to a slim jemmy forced in from one side and slowly pulled down. According to the infra-red information supplied by the general there was nobody in the area. But they moved silently and cautiously nevertheless. A fibre optic camera lens was slipped through the minute crack. The picture and sensors confirmed the room was empty.

Badonovitch lifted the cover clear and Tanner hoisted himself into the cathedral. He took the cover out of the Russian's hands and held it while the rest of the team quickly followed. Replacing the cover he followed the others to the stairs that led to the half landing and the crypt. The cathedral was in pitch blackness. Without their NVGs they would have been working blind. At the back of their minds the question was, did the terrorists have the benefit of goggles too? A clock chimed a soft ding-dong twice. Hunter checked his watch. 23.30 precisely.

The team were awed by the cathedral's interior. It was worse than sacrilege to think that its immense beauty, its serenity, could be destroyed at any moment. It was so silent that nobody dared to use their personal radios. All they could do was listen for Macnair who was watching the infra-red, heat seeking monitor.

Hunter pressed the send button twice. Macnair immediately responded. 'They haven't moved. From their positions they would be able to smash a window and shoot at anybody approaching the cathedral. They're relying on being warned from the outside. It's still as we thought. If we attack the whole building goes up.'

Hunter clicked twice again. From supposition and information from previous attacks, they knew the terrorists would leave no one alive. Prior to detonation, the prisoners would be shot. Probably just as they were exiting the main door. That would bring the police down on them like a ton of bricks and the resulting explosion would kill as many of the force as possible. It was a clever plan, if you didn't intend living.

The indicator light on the ex-torches glowed red when briefly flashed on in the stygian darkness. Dunston slid across the floor to the Crypt. From there he could see along the Nave and back to the Choir, Presbytery and Feretory.

The least damaging explosives were those in the Chapter House. If they went off they would kill the hostages but probably not destroy the cathedral. The four pillars underpinning the crypt were the priority. If they were destroyed the damage would be total and irreparable. Masson, Napier, Badonovitch and Tanner followed Dunston while Hunter went into the Nave. Four catchments of explosives, two either side of the Nave, were Hunter's responsibility. His dilemma was that the explosives

179

were out in the open – and there was a terrorist between him and the target.

The outer door was solid oak but was approached through a vestibule with a glass door either side. Hunter stood at the side entrance normally used by visitors. A terrorist was kneeling on a prayer mat, facing east, preparing himself spiritually for the conflict ahead.

Hunter moved very slowly and very carefully. He knew the location of the other terrorists. In theory only one other man was in a position to see him. He eased behind a pillar, out of sight of the kneeling man and looked to his right. There he was! At the north wall, also on his knees – praying! He was wearing old-fashioned NVGs, which temporarily blinded you if a bright light were shone upon them. Nonetheless effective under normal conditions. Hunter watched the terrorists preparing their souls for departing this world, ready to greet the majesty of the Prophet. This was the edge they could only have dreamed of. Hunter grinned mirthlessly. Prayed for.

Suddenly he was aware of a presence alongside him and found Dunston by his side. Hunter pointed to the two kneeling men. The chaplain pointed at himself, then at the man on the north side. Hunter nodded and moved further along the Nave, intending to come around behind his target. Using the pillars as cover, he flitted across the stone floor. At the main entrance he stopped. There were two terrorists on the floor above the door, one on either side, but he was in their blind spot.

He approached his target. The aluminium in the man's clothing rustled loudly as he lifted his body and prostrated himself once more. Hunter inched closer and was only feet away when the man began to arch back up. At the top of his movement, Hunter stepped forward, clamped a gloved hand over the terrorist's mouth and slid a blackened blade under the man's ribs and into his heart. He died without a sound. Hunter eased the body back to the supplicant's position. He sent three clicks down his transmitter.

Macnair immediately responded. 'Nick, one dead terrorist?'
Click.

'Good. The explosives in the Crypt have been dealt with. Jan went back into the aisle to speak to me. It's semtex. Three detonators, each wired to a receiver. No booby traps. They're going after the others on the upper floors. Matt has just called in. He's dealt with his target. You're clear to go after the other explosives in the Nave.'

One click. Hunter moved silently to the nearest pillar fitted with plastic explosive. A brief glance told him all he needed to know. He even recognised the detonators. New Mark 10s, supplied courtesy of the Ministry of Defence to anybody willing to pay the price. Short lengths of electrical wire connected the dets to a receiver. He cut the wires and pushed the ends into the PE. To a casual glance, the explosives still appeared ready to go. Looking across at Dunston he received the OK sign and nodded. He made four clicks to Macnair.

'You and Matt have dealt with your explosives?'

One click.

'Excellent. The two terrorists on the floor over the main door are down. I'm watching the screen now. Two of our men are approaching their targets. The one in the upper part of the Sacristy and the other in the Central Tower.' There was a few seconds delay. 'Both men have been shot.'

Neither Hunter nor Dunston had heard anything. Hunter acknowledged the information.

Macnair continued. 'That leaves the five we have on screen. Two are still either side of the stairs leading to the Chapter House and two are behind the main pillars either side of the Presbytery. The fifth man is moving. He's now approaching the Crypt. I think he's going to check on the others.'

Hunter sent a click. The man was walking towards him. He would pass within feet of the pillar Hunter was hiding behind. The distinctive rustling of the aluminium clothing came to Hunter's ears, virtually drowning out any other sound.

Maybe it was instinct. Something warned the man and as Hunter stepped forward the terrorist turned to look straight at him. He was opening his mouth to yell a warning when Hunter dived forward and slammed a shoulder into his midriff. Hunter had been expecting a vicious fight. Instead the terrorist collapsed

181

under him. Hunter had no difficulty slamming the haft of the knife into his temple, knocking him out. He reversed his action and was about to ram the knife into the man's throat when he realised how slight the body was. Pulling off the unconscious terrorist's goggles he saw it was a young girl. Hesitating, he knew he couldn't do it. He pressed a finger to her carotid artery for a few seconds and induced a deeper unconsciousness. She should still be there when he came back for her.

The noise had caused consternation in the Presbytery. A voice called out. 'Fatima, are you all right?' No reply. 'Fatima, answer me.'

'Flash-bangs,' ordered Hunter softly into his throat microphone. 'On two. One . . . two.'

The silence of the cathedral was abruptly shattered as the heavy grenades clattered amongst the pillars surrounding the Presbytery and Feretory. The team cowered down and closed their eyes as wild shooting began. As the grenades exploded, the bangs and bright lights were overpowering in the quiet darkness of St Mungo's.

The team moved fast, Hunter and Dunston along the southern wall, Masson and Napier along the north. Badonovitch and Tanner went straight through the Choir. The two terrorists were firing blindly, screaming at the tops of their voices. The bullets from their machine guns splattered against stone and ricocheted around the walls. The team took aim and fired silenced shots. Two taps each. Six bullets into each terrorist, any one a killing shot. The firing ceased abruptly.

Screams were heard from the Chapter House and already Hunter was diving over the floor, bullets flying above his head. Just as suddenly they stopped. Now the screams were mixed with voices begging for their lives. The terrorists were turning the guns onto the prisoners.

A harsh voice called in Arabic. A second replied. Hunter reached the steps, saw two terrorists on his right, behind a supporting pillar. Both carried transmitters.

'God is great!' One of them screamed as Hunter shot him twice in the head.

The other man dropped to his knees and looked up at Hunter. 'Too late.'

Hunter felt a presence at his shoulder and dropped to one knee, thinking one of the team was with him. He saw the terrorist press the button on the transmitter. Nothing happened. The man pressed again. And again. He looked up at Hunter, snarling his hatred. Hunter was inwardly calm, a feeling unlike anything he had ever had before. He shot the man in the neck. The terrorist flew backwards, blood pumping from his wound, the transmitter dropping from his hand.

Hunter leapt into the room and picked up the transmitter, placing it in his pocket for safe keeping. As the prisoners realised they were unharmed, one by one, they stopped screaming. Many had been temporarily blinded and deafened by the flashbangs.

'You're safe,' said Hunter. 'Just rest for a while. Your sight will return to normal – along with your hearing. Stay where you are and we'll try and get you out of here as soon as possible.'

He looked up as Dunston appeared in the doorway. There was nobody else there. Hunter shrugged. He could have sworn somebody had been right behind him.

Hunter radioed Macnair with a sitrep.

'Excellent. Are all the terrorists accounted for?'

'Yes, sir. One is still alive. A young girl. Sorry, I couldn't bring myself to kill her.'

Macnair was silent for a few seconds. 'That's all right, Nick, I understand.'

'I'll apologise to the ACC.'

'What for?'

'Leaving him with paperwork to do. It's pitch dark in here, so we'll lead out the people we've rescued. I think it will be best if we remove the PE and the other gear.'

'Is there much?'

'I'd say ten or twelve kilos in each pile, tamped down like a collar around the base of the pillars. Luckily we had a mis-fire. The devastation would have been beyond belief.'

'What happened?'

'We didn't make it to the Chapter House in time. Somehow it didn't go off. None of the detonators worked, otherwise we'd have a different tale to tell. Certainly all hostages would have been killed or seriously injured.'

'It was a high-risk strategy Nick, but one we had to take.'

'I know that, sir. We were lucky, that's all I'm saying.'

'Well, we need and deserve luck sometimes. Leave the girl to the local police.'

'Will do, sir.'

Dunston was already organising the evacuation of the cathedral. When the door opened the ACC was waiting to greet them. Hunter showed him around St Mungo's.

'We'll take the explosives,' said Hunter, 'and let you have a report. I'll estimate the amount of devastation I think would have occurred had the terrorists been successful. The evidence will be presented in written format with no court appearance. You know that, sir, don't you?'

'Yes, I do,' said Baldock. 'And thanks. The City of Glasgow owes a debt it cannot repay.'

Hunter nodded and smiled. 'The girl is over here.' Leading the way to the south wall he showed him the unconscious figure.

'She's only a wee chit of a thing.'

'That may be, but she can pull the trigger of a machine gun with the best of them.'

'Any ID?'

'No idea. We haven't looked. They're all yours now. Sorry about the paperwork.'

Baldock's Glaswegian roots showed when he was either under stress or happy with his lot. 'Laddie, think nothing of it. It's been a pleasure to know you.'

At that moment General Macnair joined them. 'We'll bag up and get out of here. Burg is on his way back from Ninewells Hospital in Dundee and will be here soon.'

The clock over the main door chimed ding-dong three times. Exactly fifteen minutes had elapsed since they had entered the building.

The semtex was placed in separate bin bags, the receivers were tagged to each detonator and placed separately. All other equipment was collected. As they stood in the Cathedral Square waiting for the helicopter, the lights came on all over Glasgow, revealing a lot of grinning faces.

From his plinth, David Livingstone looked down as serenely as ever.

When they arrived back at TIFAT HQ they found the ward-room bar open, food ready and bottles of whisky and beer laid out. They needed to unwind, to let the adrenaline work its way out of their systems. The debrief would come in the morning.

Dunston found Hunter nursing a large whisky and in philo-sophical mood. A couple of whiskies later, the reason for his ruminations emerged.

'You know, Matt, I envy you.'

'You surprise me. You have more than most men, Nick – surely you're the one to be envied?'

'Material things, the career, yes. But you have an inner peace, a contentment that comes directly from your belief. Everything is so clear to you. Sorry if I'm not making much sense but I've had three, or is it four, of these?' Hunter waved his glass.

'As with anything else, Nick, faith is something you have to work for.' Dunston sat opposite his friend, a low table between them, and leaned forward. 'I think hard and I pray even harder. Others will tell you about Jesus extolling us to turn the other cheek, to forgive our enemies. But the bible also tells us of a vengeful God who makes demands on us and expects us to obey. Otherwise we can expect retribution. If not in this world, then certainly the next.' Dunston took a gulp of his own single malt and continued. 'I have as many doubts as the next man but I work at it. I want to believe and so I do. I have a deep convic-tion that I have an important role to fulfil here are TIFAT. I don't hate or even dislike Moslems. But I do hate the corruption of a great religion for earthly ends. Hell, enough moralising. It shows I've had too much to drink. Time, old boy, to hit the sack.'

The following morning the whole team were at their desks at the usual time, following morning prayers. If anybody was suffering a hangover nobody was admitting to it. Hangovers were for wimps.

'Nick,' Napier put his head around Hunter's door, 'we're off to Barry Buddon. Coming?'

Hunter looked at his in-tray of paperwork. 'Getting rid of last night's PE haul?'

'Yes – we've taken the serial numbers and Isobel is trying to trace where the dets, receivers and transmitters came from. Burg's taking us.'

'Okay. The fresh air will do me good. Give me ten minutes.'

Barry Buddon was a point of land between Carnoustie and Monifieth that defined the north east of the Firth of Tay. It was a firing and explosives range consisting of sandy hillocks and salt-laden earth. The helicopter landed mid-morning and the team were soon engaged in setting off the semtex and the detonators. The PE in each firing ring had been weighed and indeed found to be 12 kilos. They used a small amount to light a fire and boil water for coffee while the PE was split into 4 kilo piles and exploded by a single detonator.

It was time consuming work. Four kilograms still made for a loud bang and they didn't want to disturb too many of the locals. By the time coffee was ready they had set off seven explosions. By lunch time only the PE from the Chapter House was left.

'I've brought extra dets and a firing circuit,' said Hunter, 'since this lot didn't go off in the cathedral.'

'I'll try it first, boss,' said Badonovitch, 'otherwise we'll have to blow the dets as well.'

Hunter nodded.

The first four kilos went off as normal. As did the second and the third. As each explosion erupted Hunter found his mouth becoming drier. He remembered the presence he had felt at his shoulder – but there had been nobody there. He

186

remembered the terrorist pushing repeatedly at his transmitter button, calling out to Allah. He also remembered the overwhelming feeling of calm and peace that had descended on him and he wondered.

13

Jerry Stapizki straightened his tie, ran his fingers through his hair and entered the room in the hospital. Chantelle Suchard was sitting in a wheel chair, a book unheeded on her lap. Her hair was lank and she had lost a good deal of weight.

'How are you feeling?'

In a bitter voice she asked, 'How do you think I feel? I'll be stuck in this wheelchair for the rest of my life. I hope,' she added, 'your jails are cripple friendly.'

Stapizki shook his head. 'Nope. I'm afraid not. But we've no shortage of murderesses to help you up and down the iron stairs. I can just see them, carefully tucking a blanket around your legs, putting you on the toilet, helping you into bed . . .'

'Bastard!' Tears sprung to Chantelle's eyes.

'What do you expect?' The FBI agent leant against the wall and crossed his arms.

'I've co-operated fully. Told you everything I know. Charles Gustav is the brains behind the unrest in Europe. He planned the attack so that American hysteria would force your troops to be withdrawn and brought back here. And it's happening! He was right!'

Stapizki nodded. 'I fear my fellow countrymen are nothing but predictable. Which is why we have to move fast with the information you've given us. Here, you'd better read this.'

Taking an envelope from his pocket he thrust it into Chantelle's hands and stepped back Tentatively she opened the legal sized envelope and withdrew a single sheet of paper. Unfolding it, she read slowly, with obvious trepidation. Finally she looked up at him with confusion in her eyes.

'What does it mean?'

'It's pretty clear. There's to be no trial because of your co-operation. Cognisance has been taken of the fact that you're crippled from the waist down, but the return of feeling in your upper body was entirely down to the treatment you received here at the hospital. You should consider yourself lucky under the circumstances. Many felt you hadn't deserved the help you received in view of your role in Gustav's plans. However, you are to be kept in a safe place while we continue to debrief you.'

'How long?'

Stapizki shrugged. 'Until we're satisfied you've nothing left to tell us. It won't be pleasant, I assure you.'

'And after that?'

'You'll be deported. You'll never be allowed back into the United States again.'

Tears trailed down her cheeks and she awkwardly wiped them away with the back of her hands.'

Stapizki reached for a box of tissues and placed them in her lap. 'It's out of my hands now. You'll be moved in a few hours. Don't worry, there'll be medical assistance available if it's needed.'

She nodded. 'I've been racking my brains for anything else I can tell you about Gustav but he operates strictly on a need-to-know basis. His homes, the ones I've mentioned already, are all I know about.'

'What the hell does a man want with seven houses?'

Chantelle shrugged. 'He needs a base in the countries he visits most regularly. The house in Palermo is new.'

'Why Sicily? I'd have thought he'd get too much attention from the Mafia.'

Chantelle smiled. 'There's sense in Charles' madness. Think about it, the Mafia want a whites-only Europe more than anybody. All black and Asian criminal gangs taken out at one stroke? Europe for Europeans affects more than just legitimate businesses. The white crime cartels will clean up, big time. He's there to get that message across to them. After all, the Italian government are in the pockets of organised crime.'

The FBI agent nodded. She wasn't telling him anything new on that score. But the Gustav slant was interesting. It made sense. The crime cartels wielded a great deal of power in many parts of the world, including the good old US of A.

Chantelle had obviously been using his silence to think too. She had one trump card to play and as a gesture of good will she decided to deal it. 'He's got a boat. A small ship really. Called the *Stockholm*.'

'Where does he keep it?'

Chantelle shrugged. 'All over. It cruises between Scandinavia and the Med with a professional crew. It's big enough for a helicopter pad.'

'What does he do for fun? To enjoy himself?'

Chantelle looked startled. 'I . . . I hadn't thought of that. I've never seen Gustav enjoying himself. Never relaxing with anybody. And I have never seen him drink alcohol. He's . . . obsessed.' She halted then began again. 'He's totally driven by his ideology, fanatical about a whites-only Europe. He'll stop at nothing.' She frowned and then added, 'It's almost as if for Gustav the world ceases beyond Europe. He sucks in assets, money, raw materials and gives back as little as he can. He was . . .' again she paused, searching for the right words, 'uncomfortable when he was in America. He couldn't wait to get back to Europe. It was most peculiar to see such a sophisticated man so ill at ease outside what he considers his environment. I've never known anyone else like him.'

'Any women in his life?'

'No, I don't think so.'

'Any sexual liaisons of any kind?'

'He's not homosexual. And if you mean boys and girls, the answer is no. Charles thinks paedophiles should be hung or castrated.'

'Finally, one redeeming characteristic. Okay, you rest now. You're looking tired. I'll be back later.'

She nodded, too dispirited to care.

*   *   *

Macnair read the FBI report with interest. Chantelle Suchard's information confirmed all the research Isobel had done on Gustav. The tip-off about the ship was new though. It was probably owned by a series of companies, all offshore and virtually untraceable. He would need to find the *Stockholm*.

The list of houses tallied with what they already knew. But currently Gustav wasn't located at any of them. Macnair allowed himself to play Devil's Advocate for a moment. Even if Gustav was killed, would it be too late to stop the backlash against non-white Europeans and immigrants? Macnair knew there was a critical mass element. At some point it would become unstoppable, no matter what they did. Gustav and his news media had to be destroyed. To do so he needed overwhelming evidence that the atrocities being committed throughout Europe were actually being perpetrated by the very people who were denouncing Islam and the immigrants. Evidence that stood up in court. It had to be in-your-face, irrefutable, shocking, strong enough to force right-wing newspapers, television and radio stations to come down firmly on the side of the non-white Europeans. To admit that they were an asset to whichever country they were settled in.

Of course he had an ally in the European Parliament. The only trouble was, if Christine stood up and made any accusations, no matter how well founded, her life wouldn't be worth a wooden euro. He balked at the idea of using her. Yet time was of the essence.

Elections were due in Germany, and soon in France. A shift to the right in either country would prompt the same in other democracies. And although Italy and Spain weren't due to vote until next year, anything could happen to force an election. Italy was on a knife edge as it was. If her government lost any more parliamentary motions they would *have* to have a General Election.

Was there time to get a man on the inside of Gustav's organisation? To steal as much information about Gustav's main supporters as possible? With that knowledge Macnair could decapitate the right-wing hydra. Knowledge at that level could divert an international tragedy. Shaking his head, Macnair lifted the red phone on his desk which connected him directly to the Prime Minister. He was aware of the limit of his mandate.

The Prime Minister knew immediately that the call would be the harbinger of bad news. Malcolm Macnair only rang when it was serious.

'Prime Minister, sorry to trouble you.'

'I've just been reading your report on the operation at St Mungo's. Good work.'

'Luck played a significant role, PM.'

'I didn't like to say so, but you're right. What's particularly gratifying is that TIFAT has been kept out of it. The ACC is claiming that his police team did the work.'

'Yes. It's better that way. Thanks for getting the Chief Constable off our backs.'

The PM chuckled. 'Think nothing of it. We called him to a COBRA meeting as a matter of great urgency. The pompous ass was full of it. He was extremely upset at the success of your operation. It was almost as if he had wished you'd failed and St Mungo's *had* been destroyed.'

'It would have been if we hadn't made our move.'

'Agreed.' The Prime Minister sighed. 'The galling fact is, we appointed Blackwater. So I can't even blame the Tories.'

Macnair chuckled. 'That's what comes of being in office for so long. Eventually the buck does stop with you.'

'On that note, why have you called?'

Macnair brought the Prime Minister fully up to date. He listened attentively. His lawyer's training stood him in good stead at times like this. When Macnair had finished he was silent for a few moments.

'I don't know if I can sanction that. I'd never get it past the Cabinet. My own party is already leaping up and down in agitation as it is. They still haven't learnt the lessons of the past. Immigration, crime and perceived inequalities are making the working class rebel. That's why the Home Sec must get tough on bogus asylum seekers. And we must stop the atrocities being committed. Even if they are being orchestrated by Gustav and his men, the Muslims are being seen to carry out the acts. And in politics it's people's perceptions that count.'

'I'll leave the politics to you, sir. I can't think of a better idea than the one I've put to you.'

'Oh, the idea is first class – but I won't be able to sanction it.' The PM's words were clear.

'What about your blessing?'

'That you have – unofficially.'

'It's probably for the best. This way we can keep a lid on matters for as long as possible. The fewer people who know the better.'

'Why, General, you aren't suggesting my Cabinet leaks are you?' There was humour in the question.

'No more than a colander, sir. Even if we don't have your sanction, you can help ease matters considerably. There is one important factor. At the right time you will need to make a great deal of political noise across the world. We need to muster every pundit who will come down on our side. Have every talk show in Europe decrying the fascists, while supporting Europe's non-whites. I can't stress how important public opinion will be. Already I think it's too close for comfort. Gustav is winning hands down unless we do something drastic – and quickly.'

'Leave that to me. When you're ready, I'll get Alastair to push all the right buttons, he's good at that.'

Macnair chuckled. The Prime Minister's Press Secretary was *very* good at pressing buttons.

Hunter was sitting in the church in Balfron, his home village. He slouched down in the front pew, his feet outstretched. He was alone and deep in thought. His experience in the cathedral had shaken him. Not the action and the violence. He was used to that. But that feeling he'd had. And the fact that the transmitter hadn't worked. The experience had caused him to seriously question his faith, or lack of it. He knew he was trying to find a rational explanation where none existed. Intellect alone couldn't unravel mysteries pondered for centuries by greater men than he.

He didn't expect an answer to his musings and he wasn't surprised when he didn't get one, though he felt the benefit of time spent in contemplation. He stood up and walked out the front door, taking a little of the peace and solitude he had found with him. Maybe, he thought cynically, I'd better start behaving as if there really *is* a God.

Walking down the hill he enjoyed his stroll back to the house. His parents were out at some dinner party or other. He'd been invited but had cried off. He badly needed some time to think. And plan. Macnair's latest idea was so crazy it might just work. But the ruse was exceedingly dangerous, before, during and after. Who would be the best people to trust for this one? The decision was quickly made. Matt, Jan, Doug Tanner and Douglas Napier. Tanner would be perfect, being black.

His parents house had been extended out from the kitchen and Hunter effectively had his own quarters. He sat at a desk, a whisky near at hand, a synopsis of the operation on his lap. He considered the different options available to them. Three of Gustav's houses were no use. They were too isolated. After the operation there had to be a way of removing the bodies. So that left four other possibilities. Another factor was actually locating Gustav. Well, that wasn't his problem, it was Isobel's, and he had the utmost faith in her.

The four houses which seemed best suited to their purpose were Munich, Oslo, Fontainebleu and Spiez. Isobel had found architects drawings and had satellite photos of all the properties. The operation in each case would be almost identical, differing only in the detail.

His glass of whisky was sitting untouched by his elbow and he raised it to his lips to take a sip. At that moment his sat-nav phone rang. With a curse he placed it to his ear. 'Hunter.'

'Nick, Isobel. Gustav will be spending the next two days at Spiez.'

'When does he arrive?'

'As near as I can tell, about midnight tonight their time. One hour ahead of us.'

'I'll be back in an hour. Do we have any contacts in Switzerland?'

'A bit of luck, really. We have someone MI6 used twice a few years ago. His father was a Royal Naval officer, his mother Swiss. He lives in a small suburb of Thun known as Uetendorf. In Altelsweg Strasse.'

'How reliable is he?'

'For what we want, we think he'll do. He's a bit of a playboy but the sort you can rely on in a difficult situation. He's proven that on more than one occasion. He took a bottle in the eye a few years ago in a fight involving one of Six's men. He was trying to calm the situation. I'd say, reading his record, tough enough when required.'

Hunter wasn't convinced. 'And do we definitely need him?'

'He's on the spot. He's also got a speed boat licensed for the Thunersee. More importantly he's got a house you can hole up in. Saves using hotels. Nick, think it through. It's your op. Over to you.'

'Thanks, Isobel. I'll see you soon. What's his name?'

'Oliver Michael. There's a note here in his record. Known as Olikins.'

Hunter replaced the receiver in disgust. *Olikins! What sort of a stupid name was that?*

He poured the whisky down the sink, wrote a brief note to his parents and climbed into his MGB. He broke the speed limit all the way back to Rosyth.

In the briefing room he found the General, Isobel and his team. Macnair stood in front of his hand-picked audience and said, 'This is probably the most difficult and ultimately dangerous job you can possibly undertake. Lieutenant Commander Hunter will have briefed you on the outline. No doubt he can now fill in the detail. Nick?'

'Thank you, sir.' Hunter got to his feet and stood with his hands behind his back. 'We've got all the props we need. It will come down to your acting ability. You've all seen enough people killed in your time, so you know how to react. Just go with it. You know the difference with the mags. Don't mix them up.'

That earned him a chuckle, though they were all aware of the deadly earnest behind Hunter's words.

'Where are we kipping when we get there?' Doug Tanner asked.

Isobel looked at Hunter who shrugged. 'With some toss-pot called Olikins.' His expression earned some real laughter.

They continued discussing their options until there was no more to say.

The briefing over, the men left. Hunter was already at the door when Macnair called to him. 'Nick.'

'Sir?' Hunter paused in the doorway and looked back.

'You know the priority. It is absolutely vital we get the information. No matter what the cost.'

'Yes, sir.'

'Be careful. Other agencies will be after the same thing. We've a big enough problem as it is, with inter-agency fighting still going on, in spite of the fine rhetorical speeches following nine-eleven. There's a lot of resentment from our American cousins, especially the CIA, because of the funding that's being re-directed to us. Five and Six are watching us like hawks. You can't rely on them. Not for this one.'

Hunter nodded and left. He was only too well aware of what was at stake.

The next flight out of Scotland to Zurich the following morning was British Airways. In the hold was a diplomatic bag, though to call it a bag was a serious misnomer as it was in reality a large, well-packed trunk. Its contents had little to do with the world of diplomacy either. The team drank the coffee offered by the stewardess but ignored the disgusting excuse for breakfast. They dozed most of the way. Like all soldiers they had learned to sleep whenever the opportunity presented itself. You never knew when you would next get the chance.

Their journey through Zurich customs was quick and effort-less. They were met by a lackey from the British Embassy who took charge of their gear and transport. Soon after arrival they were in a Mercedes People Carrier on the autobahn, heading for Bern and then Thun. There was little talk. Their driver wasn't cleared to hear anything they had to say.

Two hours later they pulled off the autobahn and found themselves in a small mixed industrial and residential area. They stopped alongside an Audi S6.

Their driver pointed at the house door, handed over the car keys and walked away. He was, they decided, a man of few words. Another diplomatic car had followed them to pick him up.

There was no need to ring a bell as the door opened within seconds of their arrival.

Oliver Michael was late twenties or early thirties, blond-haired, clean shaven, about six feet two. His appearance certainly wouldn't hurt his playboy reputation any, Hunter conceded. He had broad shoulders, narrow hips, a square jaw and brown eyes. His handshake was firm.

They went up two flights of stairs and into a spacious living room. 'I've two bedrooms upstairs, a room next to this and the space here. I hope that's okay?' Michael smiled. 'And the coffee maker is over there.'

'Thanks,' said Hunter. 'Can I ask what you've been told so far?'

'Enough, I think. I have been out on the lake this morning looking at the target.' Seeing the team's concerned glances he hastened to reassure them. 'I had a skier behind me and a camera locked onto the house. Will that suit you?'

'Thanks,' said Hunter. 'We aren't used to working with non-combatants. Sorry.'

'That's okay. I learnt a great deal from my father.'

'He was Special Forces?' Dunston asked.

'No. Merely paranoid.' The quip earned Michael a few smiles. 'I think we should take a recce this afternoon. In the meantime I've got my people asking questions in Spiez.'

'Is that wise?' Napier queried.

Oliver Michael grinned. 'Is any of this wise?'

Nobody answered.

'Why are you called Olikins?' Tanner asked.

The grin on Michael's face was quickly replaced by a scowl. 'Let's get this straight. That's a pet name, used only by my mother. The guy from MI6 overheard her and started calling me that to rile me.'

There was more to the story and Napier asked. 'What happened?'

'He returned to England with a few loose teeth. Call me Oliver or Oli.'

'Oli,' said Hunter, 'I have to ask. What's the smell?'

Tanner laughed and answered for their host. 'That, boss, is the all-pervading smell of cannabis. Lot's of it, if I'm any judge.'

'I have an industrial-sized growing room under here. All perfectly legal, so don't look so worried.'

Charles Gustav had landed by sea-plane on the Thunersee. He was in a foul mood. He hadn't been fooled by the police reports. The whole affair at the cathedral had TIFAT written all over it. Well, they'd interfered once too often. He would up the stakes, bring forward every operation he had in the pipeline by at least two weeks. His original idea to control the organisation had evaporated. TIFAT would be history as soon as political power was where it belonged.

In the meantime, en route to his yacht in the Mediterranean, he was forced to spend a couple of days at Spiez. He hated the place. He had bought it only because he needed a legitimate address in Switzerland The house was built on stilts, between the shore and the lake. Underneath was a boat pen, holding two speedboats, each capable of speeds up to 100kph. Not so fast when you considered there was no speed limit on the lake and that the police patrol could reach over 130kph.

He was there to transfer money into dozens of different bank accounts all over the world. Funding terrorism was an expensive business. Normally the transactions were done via computer and passwords, but he was becoming more concerned daily about his personal safety and the security of his operations.

Rumours were beginning to circulate. Soon he would have to instigate a full-scale propaganda offensive of misinformation and denial. Not a problem to a man in his position. He was still vulnerable if the wrong people snooped too closely, in spite of the safeguards he had in place. Because of the debacle in Glasgow his intention to break all ties with the Muslim terrorists he was using had been put on hold.

It was lunchtime, the day was warm and sunny. The view was breathtaking but Gustav was oblivious to the natural beauty around him. He was sitting on the balcony, a cup of coffee cooling at his elbow, carefully studying a flip-pad on his lap. Each page contained meticulous details of a new operation. As he worked through them he marked the corner of the page with a tick or a cross. A tick indicated that the attack could be brought forward. So far he had made almost two dozen ticks although he was less than a third of the way through.

The sound of a speed boat caught his attention. He scowled across the water at the source of the intrusion. Less than a hundred metres away he saw a boat with three men and one skier. They were all laughing, joking and yelling in German. They appeared the worse for drink but it could just as easily have been mere high spirits. It was too early in the day even for a German to get drunk.

Turning his head he addressed the man in dark glasses standing behind him. 'If they get any closer go and warn them off. Explain that the first hundred metres of water is private.'

'Yes, sir.' There was no inflection, and almost no discernible accent. René Faubert was six feet six inches tall, blond haired, broad shouldered and without a trace of fat on him. He spoke seven languages fluently and until recently had been a Captain in the fabled Vatican Guard. More money and limitless travel had persuaded him to join Gustav. That and his deep hatred of foreigners, Muslims in particular. His guard detail consisted of himself plus five others. All tough, utterly ruthless and completely committed to Gustav and his cause. When Gustav was in Europe he always travelled with them, their task was to protect him. In the words of the American Secret Service, to take the bullet if necessary. It was what they were paid to do.

Faubert spoke into his lapel microphone. A few seconds later the deep throated roar of a powerful engine could be heard under their feet and one of the speed boats nosed into the open.

The boat with the skier was now less than fifty metres away, paralleling the shore and taking no notice of either the house or the boat approaching rapidly from the shore.

'*Sie da! Hier ist Privateigentum – scheren Sie sich weg!*' On board the speedboat the man next to the driver stood up and waved at Hunter and the others.

'*Ich verstehe Sie nicht!*'

The pantomime of not hearing or not understanding lasted a few more exchanges, by which time the boats had drifted to within thirty metres of the house. Gustav was now standing by the rail watching, bristling with anger. He turned to Faubert and said angrily, 'Get rid of those clowns.'

The message was relayed and this time things changed out on the water. The man had stopped yelling and drawn a gun. He ostentatiously drew back the bolt. The gesture was enough to cause the other boat to speed away, Hunter and Napier making rude gestures at Gustav's men, playing their role of obnoxious tourists to the full.

'Did you see Gustav?' Hunter asked.

'Yes,' said Napier. 'And I've got some excellent pictures of the layout. As well as close ups of his men. I'll get them off to Isobel and see if we can match their identities.'

'Thanks, Oli,' Hunter said to the boat's driver.

He was rewarded with a grin and then a sober observation. 'If I had known guns were going to be involved I'd have doubled my fee.' He was silent for a few seconds, 'But then twice nothing is still nothing. Ah, well.'

'You aren't getting paid?' Hunter asked in surprise.

The Swiss shook his head. 'The General asked for a favour and I was happy to oblige, this time.'

'You know Macnair?'

'Sure. Have done for a few years. I've helped him out once or twice before as well as your lot at MI6.'

'Still – no fee . . . Isn't that taking altruism too far?'

'I don't believe in what Gustav is up to. Where does it end? You can't chuck people out of their homes and countries because you don't like the colour of their skin.' Shaking his head he looked keenly at Hunter. 'Are you going to tell me what's really going on or do I just tag along for the ride and hope for the best?'

Hunter pursed his lips, thought for a few seconds and then said, 'We're going to need you tonight so it's only fair you know what's going down.'

Above the roar of the engine he briefed Michael. If he was surprised he didn't show it.

Tanner skied all the way back to the small marina where the boat was kept. They tied up, piled into Michael's black Audi, and drove back to Uetendorf.

That afternoon snippets of information came through from Michael's informants around the picturesque village of Spiez. As far as they could tell, the household consisted of a married local couple, a cook and factotum, plus eight male visitors – Gustav, a secretary and six tall, apparently armed bodyguards. This was only the third time the house had been used in two years.

'Okay, that'll do us,' said Hunter. 'Call off your people, Oli. We don't want to warn Gustav.'

Michael nodded and made a call, speaking heavily accented *Schwiezerdeutsch*, practically unintelligible, even to fluent German speakers like Hunter and Dunston. They went over their plans once more and carefully selected the equipment they would require. All that was left was to wait until the early hours of the morning. Hunter tried telephoning Ruth but had no joy in getting through to Israel. He gave up after his fifth attempt and like the rest of the team settled down to sleep. For once sleep evaded him for some time.

It was 01.00 when they quit the apartment. They were dressed in dark civilian clothing, their combat jackets stowed in the trunk of Michael's Audi. Hunter, Dunston and Michael went to the marina to take the boat while the rest travelled in the Mercedes to Spiez. It would be a two-pronged attack.

14

Hunter sat next to Michael as he eased the boat along the shore. He was in direct contact with the team and Isobel back in Rosyth. Satellite infra-red pictures were being relayed to a small monitor on board. The whereabouts of the house's occupants were clear. One couple asleep in a small annex to the main house were, they guessed, the cook and handyman.

Identification had been received on three of the images sent to Isobel – Gustav, Duval and the ex-Vatican Swiss Guard, Faubert. Two of the others could be ex-SF, one a French Legionnaire, the other from the Royal Marines Special Boats Service. Of the others there was no inkling.

Three of the guards were patrolling the area, two indoors and one on the balcony. The remainder were asleep in different bedrooms. The lake house was as silent as the grave.

Michael's boat puttered to a stop before the noise of the engine reached the shore. Hunter and Dunston sat with their oxygen rebreathers on, purging their bodies of carbon dioxide. After two minutes they cleared the black bag that sat across their chests and slipped into the water. They quickly left the surface and swam around the shore, only a few metres under the water. The depth was sufficient to ensure that any cameras, infra-red and light-enhancing equipment didn't see or sense them.

The two men surfaced under the boat shed. Silently they clambered onto the nearest speedboat and stripped off their diving gear and dry suits. They checked the silencers on their weapons and went up the solid concrete steps to the balcony above. Hunter led the way. A guard was standing with his back to the house, looking out across the lake, diligently using binoculars, sweeping the area and then glancing at the TV size monitor on a table next to him. The combined light-enhancing and infra-red camera showed nothing moving on the water.

The distance to the guard was too great. The monitoring equipment was state-of-the-art, so it was safe to assume that the man carried a quick-response alarm on him that he could reach instantly. The night was so still that the man's movements, cloth on cloth, could be heard faintly. To cross the open space undetected was nigh on impossible. Hunter decided to try it. Stepping onto the wooden balcony from the shadows of the stairwell, Hunter was ready to shoot if necessary. The single pace he took was enough. The guard was already turning to see what had caused the intrusion when Hunter shot him. Two rounds, one into the heart, the other into the head. The gun made a sound like a sheep coughing on a faraway hillside but the guard's body fell with a clatter that was heart-thumpingly loud in the night.

Hunter contacted Napier. 'Are you ready?'

'Negative, boss. We're still checking the alarm system. We've placed the plastic. And we've glued the door and windows of the annex shut.'

'Roger that.' Hunter didn't waste his breath telling Napier to hurry. They each knew their job and what was expected.

Ten minutes elapsed before Napier confirmed, 'Ready.'

'Okay. Hit it and drive them this way.'

Gustav had paid a handsome price for his privacy. The house stood in splendid isolation far from other houses in the area. The shaped charge that blew open the front door and took out a downstairs side window was barely heard a hundred metres away.

Hunter and Dunston entered the house by the simple expedient of opening the balcony door and stepping inside. Over their radios Isobel's voice came clearly to all the team. 'Everybody's awake and moving. The two guards are hurrying towards the break-ins. One will pass the main stairway any second now.'

Hunter stood on the third stair and waited. The guard appeared and Hunter shot him twice, both head taps. He fell dead, his blood a black pool reflecting in the moonlight streaming through the window.

The second guard, the only other person sufficiently awake to react fast enough, was approaching the blown door cautiously, his gun held straight out in a two-handed grip. Napier was in the doorway, crouching, his NVGs showing the man as clearly as daylight. Two shots dealt with him. Europe was heading towards the most appalling bloodshed and violence and it had to be stopped. The men guarding Gustav were well-trained professionals. They were the sort you didn't give a second chance to.

By now the remaining three guards would be wide awake, fully alert, armed and dangerous. Isobel was able to tell them the location of each individual. Two of the images were static, the other three were on the move. It was safe to assume they were the remaining guards.

Badonovitch and Tanner appeared in the door and followed Napier into the house. The corridor was long, with rooms opening off on both sides. The house layout was, in effect, upside down, with the living quarters built on the upper floor to take advantage of the views. The bedrooms were downstairs. A door was opening cautiously on the left.

Napier let loose a hail of gunfire from his silenced BXP South African sub-machine gun. The bullets thudded into the door and wall and hit the guard along the arm and in the side of the head. He flew backwards across the room.

One down. Two to go. It was vital to leave Gustav and Duval without protection.

Isobel's voice was heard once more. 'Two of them are at the end of the corridor, by the door leading to the basement. They've split up. One is going up the back stairs while the other is crouching in the doorway to what I'm fairly certain is the basement.'

The time for finesse was past. Napier hurled a flash-bang along the corridor and as it exploded he pulled the trigger on his gun back two stops to fully automatic. Twenty rounds of 9mm Parabellum bullets followed the searing white light and loud bang. The guard was hit in the arm and leg, blinded by the while light and deafened. But like the professional he was, he attacked back. Tanner killed Faubert, shooting another hail of bullets across the prone figure of Napier, who had thrown himself to the floor.

Badonovitch took off up the back stairs. Dunston had already turned around and rushed back to meet the last remaining guard. He was caught in a trap between the two TIFAT men and died quickly.

Reports were made on their personal radios. The way was clear to Gustav and Duval.

Hunter stood to one side and tapped on the door of one of the bedrooms. 'Come out with your hands up or we shoot,' he said loudly in German.

The door was practically blown apart as a machine-gun, unsilenced, opened fire. Taking a grenade from a pouch, Hunter threw it through the shattered wood. It was still in the air when it exploded. There was a loud scream and Hunter followed the flash-bang into the room. Gustav was on the floor, his eyes screwed tightly shut, in obvious distress.

Hunter hauled him to his feet and sat him on the bed. The two men were alone for a few moments.

'Who are you?' Gustav demanded. The white spots in front of his eyes were fading and the ringing in his ears was easing. If he was afraid he wasn't showing it. Over the decades he had been in many tight spots – a man of his convictions attracted enemies. But this time he realised he would need more than luck to emerge with his skin in tact. 'More to the point, what are you? Special Services?'

'*Das ist unwichtig,*' said Hunter.

'Speak English. I can hear the faint accent. But of course, you people are all multi-lingual now, aren't you? Who do you work for? TIFAT? Are you Macnair's bunch?'

'Very good, Mr Gustav.'

Gustav squinted up at the soldier standing in front of him. His vision was clearing and he could make Hunter out. Just as he thought, all brawn and no brains. What would it take to get him out of the situation he was in? Time was running out! 'What do they pay you, eh? What's it worth to risk life and limb for an ungrateful government?' There was no response so he decided to try the Islamic card. 'Lost any comrades in the war against the Muslims?' Still no reaction. 'I will pay you ten million pounds sterling to let us go.' Now he got a reaction.

'That's a great deal of money, Mr Gustav. Two million for each of us.'

'Enough so that you can vanish and live a very happy life.'

'It does sound like it. And it's very tempting.' There was doubt in Hunter's voice and Gustav allowed himself a small smile. It never failed. Greed was a very powerful motivating factor.

'The problem is,' said Hunter in a heavy voice, 'that my men have principles.'

'Every man has his price.'

'Some men cannot be bought, Mr Gustav, no matter how much you offer.'

'Perhaps,' said Gustav, hearing the hesitation in Hunter's voice.

'Let's go, Mr Gustav,' said Hunter, keeping his voice deadpan.

The rest of the team were inside the house, ostensibly searching it. The couple who looked after the house were safely glued up in the annex.

Hunter used his radio to call the team back to the balcony. When they trooped up they stood with their backs to the low balcony railing.

Hunter untwisted the silencer off his machine gun and changed the magazine. He said in a loud and harsh voice, 'Drop your weapons. All of you.'

'Nick! You can't be serious,' said Dunston. 'What on earth are you up to?'

'I've just been given ten million reasons to let Mr Gustav go.'

'If you do this we'll hunt you down wherever you go. You'll never enjoy the money,' said Napier.

'Nick,' there was pleading in Dunston's voice, 'I know you've had your last warning from Macnair. But you can go back to general service.'

'And you know if I do,' Hunter replied brusquely, 'that my career is over. There's nothing left. A few years at sea and then early retirement. I'll be washed up with nowhere to go.'

Gustav and Duval were following the exchange in some confusion, hope coursing through their veins.

'But this isn't the way,' said Dunston.

'I'll take my chances,' said Hunter in a calm voice. He knew that Duval's and Gustav's eyesight would be fully clear so this was the moment. Hunter opened fire. The stream of bullets hit his comrades across the chest. Blood flew everywhere. All four flew backwards over the railing and into the water beneath. The chatter of the gun had been loud in the night.

'My God!' Duval spoke in awe.

'Ten million, I think you said, Mr Gustav?' Hunter casually walked to the railing and looked down, as did Gustav. They were in time to see the bodies sink beneath the water, the weight of their clothes taking them down.

Below the surface each member of the team slipped a hand to the cord they wore around their necks. From the cord hung a steel device shaped like a pen. It incorporated a small mouthpiece that they could grip between their teeth and seal with their lips. Twisting one end opened the oxygen flow and in the warm, dark water of the lake they swam silently away, hugging the bottom, leaving no tell-tale signs.

Gustav, suspicious as ever, stood and watched the water for some minutes. By now, in the moonlight, he could see the lake's surface. Instinctive caution and years of watching his back made him wary. He suspected that all was not as it seemed. Minutes later, however, none of the bodies had resurfaced and his doubts began to dissipate.

Hunter stood dispassionately by his side. 'Their clothes and equipment will have dragged them down. It'll be days until they come back up, depending on how bloated their bodies become.'

'What was that about your career?' Duval asked.

'You heard the man. I'm washed up as far as the navy and

TIFAT are concerned.' Hunter paused for a few seconds before adding, 'I may as well tell you. I was overheard saying that I believed Europe should be for white people. That all immigrants should be deported and all blacks sent back to their country of origin. If their great grandparents came from Nigeria that's where they should go. I said it to the wrong person. I was reprimanded for my views. Since then Macnair has been picking on me all the time. So I knew I had to find a way to get out. As soon as we knew you were behind the unrest in Europe I knew I had my solution. Those men I just killed were, shall we say, the more liberal minded amongst us? Hell, you saw for yourself, one of them was black. But you should know, Mr Gustav, that many of my colleagues think like I do. Or, I should say former colleagues.'

'How do I know you're telling the truth?'

'How do you know?' Hunter allowed incredulity to sound in his voice. 'I just killed four men, for God's sake. How much more proof do you need?'

Gustav nodded thoughtfully. 'So it would seem.'

Hunter thought for a second and said, 'Get one of your men to hack into the Ministry of Defence computer and look me up. It'll all be there.'

'I may do that.'

'We need to get away before the police get here,' Hunter said.

'We? Where do you fit into all this, Mr Hunter?'

'You've no bodyguards and nobody to help you until you get away from here. You arrived by sea-plane didn't you?'

'You're particularly well informed.'

'That's our job. We plan every operation carefully and to the nth degree. We always know what's happening.'

'And what about your HQ?'

'They'll think I'm dead along with the others. And as long as they think so, at least until we have the right governments in power, I'm safe. Do you want my help or not? I'm happy to just wait until morning, collect my money, preferably in a banker's draft, and get the hell out of here. Or we leave together.'

Gustav hesitated. He could certainly use somebody as ruthless and with as much apparent ability as Hunter, but on the other hand, could he really trust him? Time was wasting as Gustav pondered the question. Either he was as he seemed and therefore an ally or he could help them escape and Gustav could deal with him later. A dead Hunter would have no use for ten million pounds. The faint sound of sirens coming along the lakeside road from the direction of Interlaken stopped him in his tracks. They could see the flashing lights of a string of police cars.

'With what's happened here the police will hold you long enough for TIFAT to find you. Then it'll be too late.'

Gustav nodded. 'All right. It's time to go. What do you suggest?'

'We take one of the boats into Thun. I have a car parked in a marina near there.' Hunter could see him hesitate.

'That's very fortuitous,' said Gustav.

'No, it's not,' Hunter replied. 'It's simply a well-conceived plan. I'll get the boat flashed up while you and Mr Duval get your clothes and any bags you need.' He looked at the fast-approaching cars. 'And I suggest you hurry.'

With the three of them in the speedboat they took off straight across the lake, leaving a wide wake behind them. Neither Gustav nor Duval noticed the TIFAT team sitting quietly in their boat, watching. Gustav had apparently swallowed the bait.

Dunston reported back to Rosyth. There was no need to give chase as they knew exactly where Nick was going. What was more, the car had a tracking device fitted in the trunk which was easily read by satellite. Hunter also had a similar but smaller device fitted in each of his shoes. Unfortunately, the car was Michael's Audi, and his pride and joy. However, he had been promised a replacement – with all the gadgets he seemed to like so much – if the car wasn't recovered.

They were soon at the marina and Hunter put the boat in Michael's empty berth. At the car, Hunter stripped off his combat gear and put on a white shirt and charcoal grey suit. The tie he took from his pocket was dark red with a faint stripe. He took his time tying it. Gustav became impatient.

210

'Please hurry, Mr Hunter.'

'We can't fight our way out of Switzerland, Mr Gustav, but we *can* bluff it if we're stopped. We'll dump all the military gear here and drive away normally. You've got your passports? Good, then let's go.'

Hunter opened the driver's door and settled behind the wheel. To his surprise Duval sat next to him, with Gustav in the back. Considering what the two men had been through, Hunter was further surprised by how relaxed they seemed. If their *sang froid* was a sham, they were extremely good actors.

'Which way do you propose we go?' Gustav asked.

'Bern, Neuchâtel, Pontarlier. That's where we cross the border into France. The border's manned but cars are very rarely stopped. If an alert goes out, I think we can expect things to be different. The customs are good, well trained and armed. Will the police be able to connect you to the house on the lake?'

Gustav's reply was short and to the point. 'No.'

'What about the staff?'

'They know me only as Mr Steinway. They *believe* that's my name. The house cannot be traced back to me, Mr Hunter.'

The car moved onto the autobahn and accelerated towards Bern about twenty minutes away. The first roadblock they hit was on the outskirts of the capital. There were two cars ahead of them and they pulled up behind. The cars were quickly allowed through and the Audi drew up beside an unthreatening and unarmed policeman. Hunter wasn't fooled. The armed police were there, watching, careful, unobtrusive.

'*Guten Tag.*' The policeman touched the peak of his hat.

'*Grüss Gott,*' replied Hunter, not to be outdone with the courtesies.

Their conversation was in German. Papers and passports were presented, due respect was shown to Charles Gustav, his secretary and their chauffeur and they were waved through.

Hunter pulled sedately away, staying within the speed limit, bearing right onto the E25 minutes later. To reach Neuchâtel they pulled off the autobahn and onto a two-lane highway. In the early morning the roads were deserted and they continued to make good time. Dawn was breaking when they arrived at the customs post five kilometres before Pontarlier.

Already a long line of lorries had built up. Trade between Switzerland and France was prolific. Many trucks from Italy and Austria used Swiss roads to avoid the high tariffs on French motorways. Extra hours of driving were often considered well worth the price. Normally the lorries went through without any delay. Customs were cursory unless they were looking for something specific and acting on a tip-off. What they *did* check was that the vehicle was displaying this year's badge showing the driver had paid the one-off fee for the licence to drive on Swiss motorways.

Hunter patiently switched off the engine and settled down to wait. Looking over his shoulder he said, 'You can go back to the restaurant if you wish and eat breakfast. This is going to take a long time.'

Gustav looked at Hunter and said, 'I am not a man used to being kept waiting. Duval.' He nodded to his secretary who immediately climbed out of the car and walked the hundred metres or so to the customs post. He was back within minutes.

'Pull out and go ahead.'

In truth, Hunter had expected little else, but he managed to plaster an impressed look on his face. Gustav merely stared back at him.

The car was waved straight through.

'We'll stop at Pontarlier for breakfast,' Hunter announced.

'We keep going,' said Gustav.

Hunter looked at his new employer in the rear-view mirror and said, 'I've been going all night. I need sustenance. I need carbohydrates, protein and caffeine. And not necessarily in that order. You need me fit and alert. You've got TIFAT after you, Mr Gustav, and they won't give up until they get you. It may take them a while to learn that you've survived the attack. But when they do and when they find the team they sent after you is missing, presumed dead, then there isn't a rock you can hide under where they won't find you.'

Gustav blanched. Fear was a wonderful motivator and an even

212

better clouder of judgement. It would help to keep the initiative with Hunter, at least until Gustav felt safe again. The Swede nodded as the car pulled up outside a large alpine hotel and restaurant. Although it was early there were already several cars and lorries parked outside.

Locking the car and pocketing the key, Hunter led the way inside. The layout was typical of the region. Heavy tables and high-backed bench seats were in serried rows. The air was thick with smoke and the aroma of freshly cooked food. There was nothing as politically correct as a 'No Smoking' area in this French stop-over. The middle-aged, and somewhat frumpish waitress quickly took their order. The coffee was served in moments.

'Where are we heading?' Hunter asked, after an appreciative sip of his drink.

Gustav sat pondering the question for some moments before replying. 'I'm still not entirely sure I trust you Mr Hunter.'

Hunter broke a bread roll, added butter and took a mouthful with relish. 'That's up to you. We'll wait here. The banks open around nine. I want you to arrange a banker's draft for the ten mill. I know you can do it. After all, a deal is a deal. Then I'm out of here. You make your own arrangements. A taxi will take you to Besançon. You can get a train from there to anywhere you wish.'

'That's a great deal of money, Mr Hunter.'

'I'll need every penny of it, if I'm to hide from TIFAT. They take a dim view of betrayal, Mr Gustav. And particularly the murder of their own people. You, on the other hand, can never hide. Your only hope is to get your people to power. To break TIFAT before they come after you. But you'll have to move fast. Their mandate is world-wide. And they are the best force ever conceived. They have enormous resources and backing from governments all over the world. General Macnair has access to Presidents and Prime Ministers, although to the best of my knowledge he has never abused the privilege. They know they can trust him and rely on him. His men will follow him to the ends of the earth. He has a natural gift for leadership.'

'Except with you.'

Hunter pulled a sardonic face and shrugged. 'The exception that proves the rule. You don't have to believe me. Quite frankly, I don't care. I did what I did because I believe in your cause. I'll happily take the money, then let you battle it out and decide what I do depending on the outcome. You win and I settle back in Europe. You lose, I sail the high seas and settle in a land far enough away that TIFAT won't know where I am.'

'Is there such a place?' It was Duval who asked the question and for a second it took Hunter by surprise. Then he realised the significance of the question. Duval wanted to know if there was a bolt hole he, too, could use.

'New Zealand would be a safe bet. Japan, if you've got enough money. Although it would have to be Tokyo. You'd easily get lost in the crowds. A small town in the mid-west of America is an equally good bet, especially if you've got the right passport and a green card. I have both.'

'You seem to have planned your options very well, Mr Hunter,' said Gustav thoughtfully.

'I'm a careful man. It's why I've lived so long in a very dangerous job.' He allowed some bitterness to creep into his voice. 'I've risked my life dozens of times for my country and for what? Forty thousand a year and a silver gong they pin on me every now and then! There's a good lad, go and save us yet again. And if you live we'll give you a crappy pension. But if you die! Great news! We'll give you a wonderful funeral with all your friends and colleagues there to say goodbye. If you're unmarried your pension dies with you. A wife? That's different. We'll give her half.' In his anger Hunter crushed a bread roll to pieces, scattering crumbs across the white tablecloth. *A nice touch*, he thought.

The waitress returned with their meals and Duval, without prompting, instructed her to clean up the bread crumbs. Hunter's apparent anger faded as quickly as it had materialised and he settled to eating the scrambled eggs and bacon while it was still hot.

214

Gustav watched Hunter closely for a few seconds then made up his mind. 'Which would you prefer? To be on my payroll or to accept the ten million?'

'How big is the payroll?'

'Half a million euros a year.'

Hunter stopped chewing, took a sip of coffee and said, 'I'll take the ten million. If it's all the same to you.'

Gustav threw back his head and laughed. 'Excellent. The right response. I would never trust a man who gave up the chance of so much money for a cause. Duval, arrange for a banker's draft in Mr Hunter's name – to be ready when we arrive in Palermo. The job is still yours if you want it.'

'What job, exactly?'

'Head of my personal security.' Gustav smiled. 'You were responsible for permanently retiring the last man who held the post.'

'You mean René Faubert?'

'You knew his name?' Gustav's surprise was evident.

'TIFAT found out within seconds of us transmitting his photograph to HQ.'

Gustav nodded. 'Of course, the boat, yesterday. Your idea?'

Hunter tried to look modest but failed, miserably. After a few seconds of apparent thought he nodded. 'You've got yourself a deal, Mr Gustav. This way,' he allowed himself a tight smile, 'I get the best of both worlds.'

At Gustav's shark-like smile Hunter felt a shiver go along his spine. He knew he couldn't trust the man an inch. Reaching into his pocket, Hunter took out a small-scale map of Europe. He pointed at the map.

'We're here. Palermo is all the way down there. It's a long drive.'

'And one I don't intend taking,' said Gustav. 'The sea-plane was a charter. It was due to pick us up tomorrow. We can easily arrange for it to meet us somewhere else.'

Hunter nodded. 'I presume you were in Switzerland for a purpose. What business do you still have here?'

Gustav stared at him. 'That's a very astute question, Mr Hunter.

All I need is a major bank in a city or large town. Switzerland was merely convenient. I like their banking laws.'

'Lyon is two hours away. It's still early so the traffic won't be too bad. Even rush hour in this part of France is hardly more than a tractor and an over-laden lorry or two. Will that do?'

'It will be perfect.'

'How long will you need in Lyon?'

'Duval?'

'I'll have everything encrypted and ready to go. I can use the bank's computer, so not more than ten minutes. I'll have it all on a disk.'

This time Hunter really was impressed. 'You can get a bank to let you do that? To download information into their system without first checking what's in it?'

Duval frowned as though the question was beneath his understanding. 'Of course. We have established routes through the banking system which we use regularly. We pay a hefty premium for it but it is invaluable. Especially when you consider the sums of money involved. All major banks have the same facilities for large customers. It's like . . . like tentacles that weave across the world, one leading to another, smaller tentacle that eventually gets to the end user. Highly sophisticated and highly effective.'

'That will do,' Gustav snapped. Duval had the good grace to blush.

'If I'm to look after your personal safety then I need to know what's going on. I can be of more use to you then.'

'In theory, you are correct, Mr Hunter. But we will proceed slowly. One task at a time. Your first task is to get me to my destination safely.'

Hunter nodded. 'Fair enough. In that case we had better go. We'll fill up with petrol and while I drive I'll think about getting you safely to Sicily.'

Duval dropped a hundred euro note on the table and the three men departed. This time Gustav sat in the front while Duval occupied the back seat. He was soon busy using his lap-top computer, filling the quiet, high-powered car with an irritating, irregular tapping. By the time Hunter had filled up with petrol,

Gustav had found a radio station playing light classical music which helped to drown out the sounds from the back.

Hunter settled down to enjoy the drive. *So far, so good.*

15

At Lyon Hunter drove around until he found what he was looking for. Less than a block from an international bank he pulled into a multi-storey car park.

When they got out of the car, Hunter said, 'I'll be a few paces behind. When we get to the bank I'll see you inside. From there on you're on your own. I'll be sitting opposite the bank at the café I pointed out. I'll have a newspaper. If it's open in front of me then it's safe to come out. If you can't see the paper then stay in the bank until I'm quite certain there are no problems.'

'What sort of problems are you expecting?' Gustav asked, frowning.

Hunter shrugged. 'I'm just being careful. We have no idea what TIFAT knows right now. It may be everything or nothing. By assuming it's everything we'll live a lot longer. Trust me, I know what I'm talking about.'

Gustav nodded. This time there was a hint less arrogance about the man. Hunter's continual drip-feed of TIFAT's omnipotence was beginning to wear him down.

'And if there are any problems?' Duval asked, licking his lips. The thought of TIFAT close at hand was also beginning to get on his nerves.

'We'll have to cross that bridge when we get to it. I've no weapon and, quite frankly, don't relish the idea of a gun battle in the middle of Lyon. We wouldn't get very far. One of the reasons I picked this bank is the car-park. More importantly, the back entrance leads directly onto a side-street. If I'm not here then go out the back door and wait for me. I'll get to you as soon as I can with the car. When you go through the rear entrance, directly opposite you'll see a bar with a plate glass window. Stand in the window and watch for me. I'll only be gone if I'm seriously unhappy about what I see. And one more thing . . .' He paused and looked at each man in turn. 'I'm alive today because I take precautions. Extra precautions. I will always err on the side of caution. Faubert didn't, which is why he's dead. Better to *look* stupid than to *be* dead. I hope you both understand that.'

Reassured, they both nodded. It made good sense to them.

'While you're in the bank please inform the aircraft hire company that we will require the plane in southern France somewhere. You'll pass to them exactly where no later than close of business today. In the meantime, you wish the plane to be pre-located at Port-de-Bouc on the south coast.'

'Why there?' Gustav asked.

'It's a safe place to land and in easy reach of Montpellier to Monaco. That's where we'll spend the night. Somewhere on the south coast.'

'That's a long way to travel,' Gustav protested, though only half-heartedly. Hunter's thinking intrigued him.

'First of all we'll be on the move, therefore a more difficult target. Secondly, we need to stop for the night and there are so many large and anonymous hotels right along the coast we'll be virtually invisible. Thirdly we can go in-land by car or steal a boat and head out to sea. Which means the plane can come for us and land without any restrictions.'

Gustav nodded, further reassured. He liked what he was hearing.

They walked purposefully along the pavement towards the bank. The streets of Lyon were packed with people going to their work. Early shoppers filled the wide pavements. At the bank, Hunter watched as Gustav and Duval were immediately greeted by what looked like a senior member of staff. So, thought Hunter, Duval's computer also incorporated a mobile phone system. He grinned. Why wasn't he surprised?

219

He picked up a *Figaro* from a street kiosk and went across the road to the café. The outside tables were only half full and he selected one next to the pavement, with a clear view of the bank. Across the street Duval put his head outside the door and looked over to him. Hunter ignored him. He ordered a large *café au lait* and a croissant and settled down to enjoy both with his paper. Ten minutes later he had finished eating and drinking. He had already paid his bill and so he stood up and walked away. Gustav seemed relaxed now, happy to go along with Hunter's plan. Now it was time to apply pressure. Emotional roller-coasters were ideal for keeping a man off balance. They helped to prevent clear thought.

Back at the car park he paid for the exit ticket at an automatic dispenser. Next to it was a telephone. He was through to Scotland within seconds and reporting events to date, along with his plans. There were no specific instructions for him. The tracking devices in both the car and his shoes were working correctly.

He drove out of the multi-storey and around the city. Lyon had a complicated one-way system and it took him several minutes to get to the street he wanted. Gustav should have finished the transactions by now, and have realised he wasn't at his position in the café. Hunter was in no hurry – let them stew for a while. Cars were parked on both sides of the road, half on the pavement. Driving slowly, he approached the bar behind the bank. He braked and the door flew open. Gustav and Duval hurried out. They piled in and Hunter drove away, tensed over the wheel, his eyes flicking everywhere.

'What happened? Where were you?' Gustav asked.

'I suggest you get down. I had to leave fast. I saw two men I recognised along the street from the bank.'

'Who were they?' Duval asked as both men slid down in their seats.

Hunter suppressed a grin. 'They were both from TIFAT. A Captain Clements and a Sergeant Masters.'

'I'll check the names on the Ministry of Defence computer later,' said Duval.

'Did you look me up?'

'Yes. It made interesting reading. There was a recommendation you be given SNLR, whatever that means.'

Hunter laughed. 'Services no longer required. It looks like I jumped before I was pushed.'

'You didn't tell us you'd hit a senior officer.'

'Nothing to tell. The man was getting on my nerves. Let's leave it at that.'

'How did TIFAT get on to us so quickly?' Gustav asked.

'As I've told you, their resources are incredible. I can guess, though.'

'Then guess,' the Swede ordered.

'They will have blanketed Switzerland with satellite coverage. Every phone call and radio transmission will have been listened to. Certain words will have triggered an automatic response. If the police or customs had reported that you had passed through, which is highly likely, then they'd know about it immediately.'

'But how did they get those men here so quickly?'

'Easily. We have a number of operations going down in this part of the world, mainly to do with anti-Muslim unrest. It would be a piece of cake for Macnair to move operatives into the major cities. After all, where else would we be? He'll also have the local gendarmerie looking for us. We have to be more careful. I think we had better get rid of this car. It's too conspicuous.' Hunter was on thin ice and he measured his words carefully. 'They were doing exactly what I'd expect them to do. Searching for somebody, without firm knowledge of where they are, is a hit or miss affair. Usually the latter. But you'd be surprised how often a chance sighting happens. And I for one won't take a risk. Ever. Please remember that, Mr Gustav and you'll live to a ripe old age. I think you can get up now, gentlemen. We're clear of the city.'

'What now?' Duval asked.

'We stay off the motorways. The pay booths can be alerted and we could easily get caught. We'll stop at Vienne thirty kilometres away. There I suggest you use cash and buy new clothes and toilet gear. It'll be safer if we split up. It will look peculiar, three men together shopping. I'll dump the car and buy us train tickets for Marseilles.'

221

Gustav was quiet for a few minutes and then he said, 'I'd like you to stay with me, Mr Hunter. Duval can shop alone.'

'Fair enough.' Hunter settled behind the wheel a little more comfortably, satisfied with his progress to date.

Vienne was relatively quiet after the bustle of Lyon. Hunter parked the car in a side-street and the three men walked away from it without a backward glance. Hunter and Gustav went to find a men's clothing shop while Duval located the railway station.

Shopping didn't take long. Much to his chagrin, the small town didn't boast the *haute couture* garments Gustav preferred. He finally settled on a sports jacket and trousers. He also bought two sets of shirts, underclothes and socks. His hand rasping on his chin convinced him of the need for a razor and shaving cream.

Hunter bought shaving gear, boxer shorts and a couple of white shirts. He also found himself a blue tie with a tasteful motif. The suit he was wearing was new and still looked immaculate. Gustav bought a small suitcase, Hunter a leather holdall. Outside the shop they were joined by Duval. He told them that the express south was due in forty minutes. They arranged to meet at the station buffet inside the terminal and Duval went inside the shop.

As they walked along the street Hunter dropped the red tie into a waste bin. Gustav looked at him with a raised eyebrow.

'Ties are a give away for a description.' Hunter didn't elaborate and Gustav didn't ask.

The train departed on time. They sat in a first class compartment, Duval and Gustav side by side, Hunter opposite. They were in the end carriage, next to the engine. Hunter sat facing the length of the train, so no one could approach without being seen. To his travelling companions, Hunter's vigilance was entirely convincing.

'Why don't we take it in turns to wash and brush up?' Hunter suggested. 'There are facilities directly behind us.'

Gustav heaved himself to his feet and Duval moved to let him out.

Once he was away Hunter said, 'Would you like a coffee or something stronger?'

'What did you have in mind?'

'A couple of aperitifs from the restaurant car. What does Mr Gustav drink?'

Duval shook his head. 'Nothing. He's teetotal. Usually. Occasionally, a very special brandy, but I have only ever seen him drink it twice in ten years.'

Hunter nodded. 'In that case I'll forego any alcohol. I don't want to upset the boss. I'm going to walk the train. Take a look at the other passengers. Now we're moving we should be safe enough but as I keep saying, you can't be too careful. I'll be back in ten minutes. All right?'

Duval was tired and merely nodded. 'You know your job,' he said, accepting that Hunter was now part of the team.

Moving effortlessly along the speeding train Hunter arrived at the restaurant car. Using a credit card he telephoned Scotland and reported where he had left Michael's Audi.

'We've got it located. I take it you're on the train?' Isobel said.

'That's right. Did you track the transactions at the bank?'

'Doing so now. Take care, Nick.'

Hunter broke the connection and continued his meandering along the swaying carriages. Turning round he picked up three coffees at the restaurant car and returned to find Gustav back in his seat and Duval away.

'Everything all right?'

Hunter nodded. 'If there's anybody on board, I didn't recognise them. More importantly, no one appeared to take the slightest notice of me. I think we can relax until Marseilles. If you can, I suggest you get some sleep.'

Gustav nodded. 'Not a bad idea. I won't bother with the coffee.' He reclined his seat and closed his eyes. Fairly soon a gentle snore suggested he was in a comfortable doze.

Duval returned. Seeing his boss asleep he downed his coffee and settled back to do the same.

Hunter sat quietly for a few moments thinking about Ruth. Then he stood up and went for a shave and wash. Back in his seat he closed his eyes. He was beginning to feel bone weary. But the closer he got to Gustav's lair the more alert he needed to be. Then sleep would become more problematical – and possibly more dangerous.

The call for the first sitting at lunch woke all three of them.

Back in Scotland, Leo and Gareth, Isobel's 'right and left hands', were doing a superb job. The instructions given to the computer at the bank in Lyon were easily identified by means of a time selection program. Breaking the code was child's play – it only took twenty minutes. Following the paths the money and orders took was relatively simple. Doors in the paths were either circumvented or opened – and always closed behind them.

Isobel updated Macnair continuously. Knocking on his door she handed him another report. 'Thank God Nick made contact – the bank transfer in Lyon has highlighted several new tricks Gustav has up his sleeve. Although everywhere's operating on a state of heightened alert, the intelligence agencies would never have learned of these attacks until it was too late. Another two identified. That makes thirty-three in all.'

'Is the time-scale still the same?'

'Yes, General. The attacks are scheduled to take place within the next five days. And all across Europe. The usual targets – churches, three banks, a cathedral in Spain, four aircraft bombings and seven hijackings.' Isobel shrugged. 'You've got the list. One thing I find very significant; the money to fund the violence is all passing through Saudi banks. The program is closing down right behind the transactions once they arrive in Saudi. If we weren't so close we'd lose them. But then the track becomes very interesting indeed.'

Macnair sat back in his chair and waited patiently.

'The paths become so obvious it's child's play to follow them.'

'Hardly that,' argued Macnair, 'but I take your point.'

'It's like the computer equivalent of a three lane motorway straight back to the Arabs.'

'Neat,' said Macnair. 'Presumably providing enough proof that Arab fundamentalists are behind everything.'

'You've got it, sir. The evidence would convince anybody. Gustav has covered his tracks extremely well. There's a good deal of nascent anger mixed with ancient hatreds out there right now and it'll get a lot worse. The havoc these fresh attacks will cause beggars belief. A lot of innocent people are going to die unless we do something.'

Macnair placed his hands behind his head and said. 'It's our job to stop the attacks. But we'll need a lot of help.'

'Who?'

'Nato. I'll contact Brussels and speak to George.'

'You've always maintained that Nato isn't equipped for work like this. The requirements are too specialised.'

'I know. We'll put some of our men with each Nato detachment.'

'Sir, *nobody* is going to like that. Not Nato and certainly not our people.'

'I don't have any choice, do I? We're stretched about as thin as possible if we're still to function. We're down to a skeleton staff here and right now I'm having to recall troops who are long overdue for leave. Every Nato country from Belgium to Turkey is involved with the exception of Canada. There are three operations alone in the United States.'

'America can look after itself.' Isobel sounded callous but both of them knew what she meant. It was the one Western country that took its security seriously. 'They have the resources and the manpower to do it.'

'Where are our weakest links?'

'I'd have to say Belgium, Greece and Portugal. And not necessarily in that order. Of the rest, I don't see the Icelanders or the police in Luxembourg being much use. Apart from that, we ought to be able to contain what happens because of the detailed information we have. We know where, what, who and when. It can't get much better in intelligence terms.'

'That's what I thought. What's the latest on Hunter?'

'He's on a train heading for Marseilles. Gustav and Duval are with him. He's now Gustav's new head of security.'

Macnair summoned up a grin. 'Good for Nick. Let's hope he

225

gets us what we want. Okay. Leave this with me. I've got calls to make.'

Lunch was superb, considering they were on a fast moving train. Nobody drank anything other than water followed by coffee. Hunter's steak was the best Aberdeen Angus, once more available now that France had lifted it's illegal embargo on UK beef imports into the country.

'When we get to the next stop,' Gustav instructed Duval, 'buy as many newspapers as you can find.'

'I can download from the internet,' he offered. 'The world's an electronic village square.'

Gustav waved his hand. 'You know I don't like reading off the screen. Get me the hard copy. Which town is next?'

'Valence,' Hunter replied. 'And this looks like it.'

Duval hurried to the door and was waiting for the train to stop. He alighted quickly and rushed to the kiosk selling newspapers. He grabbed one of each, threw a fifty euros note to the man behind the counter and hurried away.

The Algerian nodded his thanks and pocketed the money. He would say a special thank you to Allah at evening prayers.

The doors were already closing when Duval climbed back onto the train.

Hunter was speaking to Gustav. 'The plane can wait for us at Port-de-Bouc. We'll spend the night in Marseilles – it's big and anonymous. I want to hire a car. Something powerful, just in case.'

'Then do so,' Gustav frowned. He hated being bombarded with petty detail.

'They will want credit card and passport details. The passport is no problem. I have a false one. The credit card, unfortunately, is in my real name. The instant I use it TIFAT will find out.'

Gustav looked up from yesterday's Washington Post in some surprise. 'I thought you had all this planned?'

Hunter scowled. 'To have a false credit card you need money, big money. When I get my ten million, I'll have sufficient credit cards to satisfy me. More importantly, ones that will match my new passport.'

'What do you suggest?'

'Duval can hire the car. A big Citröen or Peugeot. We also find a hotel. Not too big and not a flea-pit either. Near the harbour where the pleasure craft are berthed. We'll also take a twenty-four hour hire on a fast speed boat.'

'Why?'

'To give us options. A car along the coast or a boat if we need it. A car can be followed, a boat less so, especially if they aren't ready for it.'

'You sound as though you expect somebody to be waiting for us,' said Gustav. The feeling of safety he had been enjoying after the good lunch was fading fast.

'I don't expect anything,' Hunter corrected him. 'But I plan for all eventualities. It's the only way. Believe me.'

'Oh, I believe you, Mr Hunter. And I like your thoroughness. Now if you will excuse me, I would like to get back to my newspapers.'

Hunter nodded and sat back in his seat. Gustav and Duval read the news. Both men appeared satisfied by the stories they were reading. Hunter read the English and German papers.

One item came as a shock and was in all the newspapers. In France a new draconian law had just been passed. In order to claim citizenship you had to prove that at least one great-grandparent was French born. Without it you were no longer considered *vraiment Francais*. And your passport was to be amended accordingly. Many immigrants, first, second and even third generation, were beginning to panic. If they didn't leave now would they be able to get away later with their money and possessions? Political unrest was mounting. Acts of violence against innocent people were becoming commonplace. More and more often, if the victims involved were non-white or non-European, the police stood by and watched. Europe was fast becoming a powderkeg.

Tapping the paper in front of him, Hunter asked, 'Did you know about these new French citizenship laws?'

Gustav looked at him in some surprise. 'Yes. I helped draft them. They are merely the start. We will tighten the screws at every opportunity until all non-white foreigners leave. Do you have a problem with that?'

Hunter forced a smile. 'Not at all. I hope to see the rest of Europe following France's lead soon.'

'You will, Mr Hunter. Believe me, you will.'

Hunter nodded his satisfaction and continued reading, seething with anger. He decided to interrupt their evident enjoyment. 'I need some cash for expenses,' Hunter said to Gustav, who nodded to Duval. The latter reached into his briefcase and extracted a wad of notes, counting out five thousand euros in mixed bills. Hunter pocketed the money.

The train pulled under the huge canopy of Marseilles railway station and glided to a smooth and silent halt. The three men stood, stretched cramped limbs and prepared to disembark. Hunter went first, paused in the doorway and glanced along the platform. The main concourse was only a few metres away and was teeming with people of various shapes, colours and dress. Marseilles was one of the most cosmopolitan cities in Europe and had, by far, one of the most diverse populations. Many of her inhabitants were from North Africa, stretching from Morocco to Egypt. But vast numbers came from former French colonies south of the Sahara.

Hunter cast a glance at Gustav as they forced their way through the throng. The Swede was having to work hard to keep the distaste off his face. When a black woman, in native dress, bumped into him and turned to apologise, his look of venom caused her to back away with fright. Gustav actually shuddered at the contact.

Hunter walked around the suitcases and boxes of goods piled up at the travellers' feet, deliberately weaving a complex path to the main entrance.

Half way Gustav caught him by the arm. 'Can't we go straight outside? The smell of these . . . these cattle disgusts me.'

Much to Hunter's amusement Gustav was looking ill. He was pasty white and sweating. Hunter wondered what had caused such a deep-rooted xenophobia. 'It makes it more difficult for a man with a rifle to predict our path and shoot you.'

'I'll risk it. Just get me out of here.'

Next to the huge entrance Hunter paused at a kiosk and bought a guide book, this being his first visit to Marseilles.

Within moments they were in the warm, humid air of the bustling city. Even here there was little respite. Beggars approached with hands held out, others offered trinkets for cash, still more had oranges and slices of melon for sale. The one thing they all had in common was their dark complexion. Gustav looked like he wanted to be sick.

Deciding it was time he earned his money, Hunter went to the front of the taxi queue and pushed aside the man about to climb in. As the man turned to protest Hunter thrust a hundred euros note into his hand. He looked at it in astonishment before nodding his thanks. By this time Gustav and Duval were in the car and Hunter climbed into the front passenger seat.

The driver turned to protest at the rough treatment of his potential fare but thought better of it. Hunter didn't look like a man to argue with. Besides, he had also seen the money exchanging hands.

'*Ou partir, messieurs?*'

'Drive,' Hunter said in English. He looked back over his shoulder as the car pulled away, his eyes scanning the train station.

The driver was a scrawny African, with grey curly hair. He had his window open and was smoking. A torrid mouthful of French from Gustav caused the man to go rigid with tension before contemptuously flicking the cigarette away. '*Comme vous voulez, monsieur.*'

The Gare St Charles gave way to the Place Victor Hugo. It was packed with cars apparently heading aimlessly in different directions. The driver got them through by the judicious use of his horn and middle finger. He paused on the Boulevard Charles Nédelec and looked over his shoulder.

Duval waved a hand indicating straight on. Gustav looked fixedly out of the window. Hunter suppressed a smile. He was flicking through the pages of the guide book and said, 'Quai Des Belges.'

The journey continued in silence. It was only a few kilometres to the Vieux Port. They could probably have walked it as quickly. The streets were packed with people, all carrying suitcases and boxes, all going towards the port. It reminded Hunter of the stories he had read about the Jews leaving Germany in the late thirties. Some had had the sense to get out before it was too late. Most hadn't and had perished.

The taxi deposited the three men at the edge of the old basin. The previously run-down dock area in the decaying city had been transformed during the past decade with European aid. Now fashionable bars and restaurants stood side-by-side with *avant-garde* theatres, small clothing boutiques and ship's chandlers. Looking along the basin from where they stood, they could see the picturesque forts guarding the entrance to the port, Fort St-Jean on the north bank and Fort St-Nicholas opposite.

By now it was early evening and the sun was setting on a warm and humid day. Down both sides of the Vieux Port many tramp steamers were berthed. Filing up the gangways were families – men, women and children, people of all ages – none were white. The bright colours of the Africans contrasted sharply with the white robes and black chadors of Arab men and women.

'Good riddance,' said Gustav with satisfaction. 'Like animals into the ark.' He looked at his secretary, 'We will need to find a way to speed up the process.'

Hunter found the thought chilling.

'Where now, Mr Hunter?'

'The Hotel de Ville. Three star, central, anonymous. Around the corner on the Quai de la Tourette are a number of boat-hire places and over there,' he pointed to the other side of the road, 'is a car-hire.'

The hotel was only a few hundred metres away on the Quai du Port but the pavements and streets were completely packed with people. Climbing out of the taxi, they left it stranded in a sea of humanity. They had to fight their way through the throngs, piles of baggage in their paths. Children were crying, their parents subdued in the oppressive atmosphere. *They're scared*, thought Hunter. *Terrified*. For the first time Hunter felt the fear at grass roots level. After the deaths and destruction of recent weeks, terrorism was no longer a vague concept. It had forced its way into people's lives. He listened to them. They were nearly all speaking French. Idiomatic French. Hunter felt rage surging through him at the injustice of it. If he needed more proof that Gustav had to be stopped, then this was it. These people were abandoning their homes, their livelihoods, their friends, even, for many, their culture. Their French culture. Many talented people were leaving. Doctors and teachers, writers and singers. And many were hard workers prepared to do menial tasks for a pittance, tasks many whites refused to soil their hands with. It was a long-term disaster in the making.

They finally reached the hotel. The foyer was packed and Hunter had to shoulder his way to the desk. The harassed staff ignored him until he took a fifty euro note from his pocket and held it flat with his forefinger. Within seconds a man appeared in front of him.

'*Monsieur*? *Vous désirez*?'

'Three rooms for one night,' Hunter said.

The man switched smoothly to English. 'I am sorry, sir, there are no vacancies. You can see. Many people are waiting to take ships away from France. The city is virtually full.'

'How much for your best rooms?'

'*Desolé*, monsieur, sir, I must repeat. They are taken.'

'I will pay ten times the normal rate for one night.' Hunter pushed the note across the desk where it was expertly palmed.

'Excuse me for one moment, sir.' He turned away and hurried into a back office. A few seconds later another, older man came out and crossed the reception area to Hunter.

'You said ten times?'

'Cash.'

'Alphonse.' He spoke in a loud voice, 'You have made a mistake. Get the rooms ready immediately. *Voilà, enfin*! Sir, I am very sorry. If you and your companions would take a seat in the bar I shall arrange to have the three best suites made ready immediately.'

'Thank you.' This time Hunter slid a thousand euro note over and it too vanished as though in the hands of a magician. Cynically he wondered if palming money was one of the skills you learned when working in a hotel. 'This is a token of my thanks. The bill will be paid separately.'

The man beamed his appreciation.

The bar was also crowded and they stood in a huddle just inside the door. Hunter heard a phone ring and looked up in time to see the barman answer it and glance in their direction. He hung up the receiver and waved to them and pointed.

A small corner table with a reserved sign suddenly had three chairs placed around it. A dish of olives and an ashtray magically appeared. Hunter led the way, shouldering his way past protesting men who took one look at him and decided not to protest too much.

A ten euro note took care of the waiter. Drinks were ordered. A pastis for Duval, coffee for Gustav and sparkling water for Hunter. He sat with his back to the wall, playing at being a bodyguard.

'Once we have our rooms, we pay the bill and you, Duval, go and see about a car. I'll see about a boat. Incidentally, the room is ten times its normal price.'

'What!' Gustav was infuriated. 'You should have cleared . . .'

'Mr Gustav, take a look around you. These people, or some of them at least, have money. They will already have tried bribing their way to a room. I'm told the city hotels are full with so many people leaving France. I don't fancy a park bench because I suspect they'll all be full too. What's it to be? Pay or go?'

Gustav scowled and then nodded. 'You did the right thing. I must learn to trust your judgement more.'

Hunter nodded in satisfaction. 'One more thing. The banks are open late. I would like my ten mill before close of play today.'

Gustav emphatically shook his head. 'That is not possible. Truly. It will be arranged in Palermo.'

'Not good enough. Fix it for first thing in the morning. Okay?' He directed the question at Duval who looked at Gustav. Gustav nodded imperceptibly.

'Yes. It will be done,' said Duval.

Hunter found it interesting that Gustav was prepared to part with ten million pounds yet protested about the cost of a hotel room. Perhaps he didn't believe Hunter would have the chance to cash the cheque.

16

Walking towards the Quai de la Tourette was a nightmare. The streets and pavements were jammed solid with people and cars. The air was filled with noise and above the strangely dehumanised mass, there came the occasional loud shriek of a ship's whistle as yet another over-laden vessel left the quayside. As soon as the space was empty another came in. Many of the luxury yachts and boats that were normally berthed there had left for safer harbours. Too many had already been stolen.

In a small boutique Hunter bought a pair of shoes. He ditched his old pair in a rubbish bin after removing the location transmitters from the heels. The shoes were clearly visible for some lucky tramp to find. The transmitters he crushed beneath his heel. Walking along the road he carefully scuffed the soles and uppers of his new shoes.

Hunter had to walk a good kilometre until he found what he was looking for. The small office had a plate-glass window festooned with pictures of boats for hire and sale. The shop was due to close shortly but Hunter took no notice of the scowl that greeted him from its only occupant.

In passable French he said, 'I see you have boats for hire?'

The man's English was home-grown. 'Yeah, mate. What're you looking for?'

'Scouse?'

'Near enough. What can I do for you?'

'I'd like to hire a speedboat.'

'We're closing. Come back tomorrow.'

Hunter settled himself more comfortably into the chair he wasn't offered and said, 'I need it for tonight. I'm planning a moonlight ride with a very attractive woman, and I want something fast and smooth.'

The man was in his early twenties, casually dressed, with long fair hair and a deep tan. He spread his hands in an apology and lifted his shoulders. 'I'm sorry, mate, I can't help you.'

He sounded genuine enough but Hunter persisted. 'Money's no object. Name your price. How about five times the normal fee?'

The man blew out his cheeks and shook his head. 'She must be a hot date but it ain't the money. We don't have anything for hire.'

'But the signs in the window . . .'

'Just for show. Don't mean nothing. They pull the punters in and we persuade them to take something they may not really want. You know how it is.'

Hunter nodded. He knew. 'What would you normally charge for a good speedboat with a small cabin?'

'It depends. Top-of-the-range, about twenty euros an hour. Plus petrol and a deposit.'

Hunter guessed that was well at the top end but said, 'I'll pay fifty euros an hour and pay for a full twelve hours. Cash.' He enjoyed spending Gustav's money.

That made the young man sit up and take notice. 'How long do you want the boat?'

'Not that long.' Hunter managed a smirk.

'Okay, leave it with me. I'll make some calls. You'll have to leave a deposit. Same again. Non-refundable.'

'Nice one, sonny, but no. I'm giving you a good deal as it is.'

His reply was greeted with a grin. 'You can't blame a man for trying. Two doors along is a bar. I'll join you there as soon as I can. Name's Steve.'

'Nick.'

Hunter nodded and left. The bar was packed and Hunter had to elbow his way to the counter. He was in need of a drink but he settled for a small beer. He went to the window and looked out. The streets were still thronged with people, the ships filling up and leaving. The air of desperation sickened him. Hunter's fist clenched tighter around the glass handle as he took another sip of beer. He'd just drained the glass when Steve entered.

'Got one!' he grinned. 'Want to see?'

Hunter nodded and placed his empty glass on a nearby table. Outside they made their way along the street and past the huge cathedral that dominated the skyline.

'Down here.'

Hunter was led into a side street and down some steps. A solid looking metal gate blocked their path. Steve took out a bundle of keys and selected a heavy brass one. He pushed open the gate and said, theatrically, '*Voila!*' The path led down to a small stone lined inlet, about three metres wide and six long, in which sat two boats.

Steve pointed to the nearest boat, low and sleek, painted a glistening maroon with white go-faster stripes down the sides. There was no cabin, but Steve said, 'The seats fold down and the mattresses fit for a perfect union. If you get my meaning. Want me to show you the controls?'

'Please.'

It only took a few minutes. With another key Steve unlocked a special clamp on the fuel leads and used a third key to start the engine. It burst into life with a deep-seated roar.

'She'll do a hundred and forty kilometres an hour. But I'd go a lot slower than that. In any sort of weather she's an unstable bitch. But there's a cove about ten minutes down the coast, full of buoys. You can tie up to one of them. It's usually deserted at night. Most of the boats go back to their marinas after dark. You unlock that grill when you want to leave. Close it behind you afterwards, will you? They're a light-fingered, thieving lot around here.'

'Of course. This is fine. We'll leave the boat here. On the way back to my hotel, I'll drop the keys through your letterbox. Fair enough?'

'Sure.' Steve unthreaded the keys and held them in his hand. 'Mullah?'

236

Hunter reached into his pocket and extracted the notes. He counted them into Steve's hand and added another hundred euros. 'For your trouble.'

'Hey, thanks, man. You're all right.'

Hunter doubted he would feel the same when neither the boat nor the keys were returned in the morning.

They switched off the engine and returned to the street above. 'I go this way,' said Steve and set off with a jaunty swagger, waving goodbye as he did so.

Once Steve was out of sight Hunter returned to the boat. There were too many locks hindering the boat's passage for his liking.

All Hunter had to do now was to panic Gustav and Duval into taking the boat. It all, he thought, added to the melodrama. But first things first. He found a telephone and rang Scotland. He was soon explaining the situation to Isobel.

Returning to the hotel he found both Gustav and Duval in Gustav's suite. It was pleasant enough, a large en-suite bedroom with a comfortable sitting area.

Hunter sat on a hardback chair. 'Did you get a car?'

Duval nodded. 'A Ford Taunus.'

'I'd have preferred a French model. Can I have the keys? I'll check it out and park it properly.'

'Properly?' Duval frowned at him.

Hunter asked, 'How easy is the car to get away? Is there room to manoeuvre? Or is it hemmed in, like practically every other car on the street?'

Duval tossed the keys to Hunter with bad grace. Gustav nodded his approval.

'I've got us a boat.' Hunter explained exactly where it was. 'If anything happens and we split up make for it. I'll meet you there.' He stood up. 'I'll be back soon. Where's the car parked?'

Hunter found the Taunus near the Avis car park. As he'd suspected, there was a vehicle parked hard against the rear bumper and a second too close to the front. If he had to drive away in a hurry he wouldn't get very far. Unbeknown to Gustav the need would become a certainty in the next twelve hours. Unlocking the door, he climbed in and started moving the car back and forth, opening the gap front and back, inch by inch. He was careful not to set off the alarm in either of the other vehicles. Eventually he managed to pull away and drove around until he found what he was looking for. An empty space on the corner of a one-way street. Nothing could park behind him. He noted the street name and wandered back to the hotel. On the way he stopped for another watery beer, one of the few alcoholic drinks the French made badly.

In the hotel he explained where the car was parked and the quickest way to it.

'I'm going to get some sleep,' he announced. 'If you need me, you know which room I'm in. However, I'll be out some of the time.'

'Doing what exactly?' Duval asked.

'Checking. Walking the hotel and the streets. I've left enough money at the desk to buy their loyalty in case someone comes in asking for us. But you never know. TIFAT may come and offer them something more.'

'More money, you mean?'

'No. Their lives. Breakfast at eight, I think.' Hunter bade the men goodnight and left, enjoying the melodrama.

'He's very efficient,' said Gustav to his secretary.

Duval nodded. 'Then why don't I trust him?'

Gustav smiled. 'For the same reason I don't. I can't quite put my finger on it, but he doesn't ring true.'

'You saw his record.'

'Even so, it's all too smooth. Once we get to Sicily we'll have to take another look at our friend Hunter. Have you made the arrangements with the bank?'

'Yes. He can have his cheque.'

'Let's ensure he doesn't get the chance to spend it. The message is sent?'

'Yes. The fun will start later tonight.'

Hunter lay with his hands behind his head for a few seconds. Everything he could do had been done. Now he needed to panic

Gustav some more. Keep him off balance. Stop him thinking. Use fear.

He was soon asleep but came wide awake just after midnight. Sliding out from his bed he made his way to the balcony that overlooked the Old Port. Opening the doors he stepped outside. The screams and yells he had heard, muffled by the glass, now came clearly to his ears. People were running along the street in panic. The slowest were being trampled by those behind. The bravest were jumping into the water to avoid being hurt, while others tried to take refuge behind cars and in doorways.

Looking up the street Hunter saw a gang of men, waving what looked like baseball bats, coming in line abreast, two deep. Hunter almost expected skin-heads sporting nazi insignia and steel-capped boots. But from the street lights he could see that they were dressed in civilian clothes, jeans and tee-shirts for the most part, but there was no doubt that these were trained men. Either soldiers or riot police. Hunter suspected the latter from the way they were using their bats. Heads and bodies were being broken before his eyes and there was nothing Hunter could do but stand and watch.

He was aware of a presence on the balcony next door and he turned to see Gustav and Duval step out. Both men had wide smiles on their faces. Gustav noticed Hunter and said, 'An inspiring sight, don't you think, Mr Hunter? Soon, French soil – no, European soil, will be free of these parasites.'

Hunter managed to sound normal when he said, cheerfully, 'It does my soul good to see it. Well, goodnight again.' Going indoors Hunter sat on his bed, his head in his hands. *Bastards*! He knew, somehow, that Gustav was behind the riot. How had he organised it right under his very nose? He shouldn't underestimate Gustav's power – it could prove fatal. Climbing back into bed he lay for a while listening to the fading sounds of the attack. Finally he drifted into an uneasy sleep. At 04.00 he snapped awake.

Shaving and showering took only minutes. He put on a clean white shirt, the blue tie and the charcoal grey suit. Cautiously he opened the door and peered out. The corridor was as quiet as a crypt.

He went down the back stairs to the basement and out the tradesman's entrance. The streets appeared deserted but in almost every doorway he passed he heard muffled sobbing, the groans of children and adults in pain. He was glad he didn't have far to go. The Opéra was less than a kilometre away.

He went the long way around. After a while he knew he was being followed. He took different turnings but there was always somebody there. Just hidden, a ghost almost. He grinned and ducked into an alleyway. He didn't have long to wait.

'Nice one, Jan.'

'Hullo, boss. We thought we'd try and surprise you.'

'You almost did. Good try though. Where are the rest?'

'Nearby. Follow us.' Badonovitch and Doug Tanner led the way.

In a back street they found the rest of the team from Switzerland. They had been joined by Claude Masson and Peter Weir.

Dunston shook Hunter's hand.

Hunter gave them the information they needed, including the numbers of the rooms in the hotel.

'What time do you want us?' Napier asked.

'Come into the hotel at eight o'clock. We'll be in the restaurant having breakfast. I'll see you. Let us escape out the back entrance. We'll go through the kitchen. The car is parked here.' He pointed to his street map of Marseilles. 'And the boat is here.' He continued the briefing. 'You all got that?'

'Sure, boss,' said Badonovitch, 'only I can't remember which magazine to use.'

There were a few chuckles and Hunter said, 'In that case, Jan, aim high.'

Hunter telephoned Gustav's hotel room at 07.00. 'I suggest we go down for breakfast in forty-five minutes. We're due at the bank at nine o'clock. Bring your briefcases in case we have to move fast.'

'You fuss too much, Mr Hunter. It is beginning to annoy me.'

'Suit yourself. But I learned I live longer that way.' He hung up with a wide grin on his face.

They sat at a table in the far corner of the dining-room. Neither man had brought his briefcase. They were already becoming blasé – which suited him. He sat facing the door that led to the foyer. He ordered a cooked breakfast, wondering if he would have time to eat it. The orange juice was freshly squeezed and the coffee freshly filtered. He enjoyed both.

Duval and Gustav sat with their backs to the room and the foyer. Gustav leant forward and said, 'Mr Hunter, why are we sitting at this disgusting table? Everytime the door swings we hear the noises from the kitchen. The waiters push through and cause a draught. It is most unpleasant.'

'Look, Mr Gustav, if you want to sit somewhere else then please do so. Only this is the safest table in the room. I can sit with my back to the wall, the door to the foyer is across what will shortly be a crowded room and we have an escape route. I would rather suffer a little discomfort than a bullet.'

'You talk such arrant nonsense. If they were going to find us, they would have done so by now. Nobody is going . . .'

'You're wrong.' Hunter ducked his head. 'The men at the window are from TIFAT.'

The only members of the team that Gustav and Duval hadn't come face to face with were Masson and Weir. They were now looking through the door and straight at the three men.

'Rubbish!' Gustav said with anger, looking over his shoulder. 'They are just two ordinary . . .'

He got no further. A bullet hit the wall above his head, fired by Olympic Gold medallist, Peter Weir. Other bullets were fired but none came near them, a fact altogether missed by Gustav and Duval in their panic to follow Hunter into the kitchen. Shoving staff out of the way, knocking over pots and pans, Hunter caused as much confusion as possible in his attempts to delay their pursuers. The yells and screams merely added to the chaos, although nobody tried to hinder their passage.

'Out! Out! Out!' Hunter yelled at the two men, hustling them through the back door. As he followed, a gun fired and he ducked, the bullet clipping the wood next to his ear.

Gustav and Duval were now in a funk. With no weapons, all they could do was flee.

'Come on, this way.' Hunter led and they followed on his heels. He took them straight towards the car, a five minutes mad dash along the side of the road, missing the pedestrians, avoiding the traffic. Angry motorists beeped their horns and used the entire panoply of Gallic gestures which the fleeing men ignored. Approaching their car, Hunter was aiming the electronic key when another bullet hit empty ground just in front of them. Diving into the driver's seat, he had the engine started and in reverse before the other two had closed their doors. Another bullet hit the bonnet and ploughed a furrow along the gleaming paintwork. To the uninformed the impact seemed highly dangerous. Hunter knew the bullets had only fifteen percent of explosives in them. They lost their power as soon as they hit the slightest of objects. Nobody wanted innocent people killed.

The car turned onto the main road, backing into another vehicle, smashing its grill and bonnet, stopping it in its tracks. More bullets flew. Hunter swerved across the road and drove up it the wrong way. He flashed the lights, the hazard indicators were working and he kept his hand pressed firmly on the horn. Swerving around car after car they ran out of luck about halfway along. An overloaded lorry careered across their path and smashed into them, bringing them to a halt.

Hunter threw open his door. 'Move it!' he said loudly over his shoulder.

The two men needed no urging. They fell out of the car and lurched after him. Although not young Duval and Gustav were reasonably fit but in no way trained and so they shambled along behind Hunter as he lengthened his stride. People were standing and staring as they ran down the middle of the street, in between the traffic which had come to a halt following the accident. It had taken skilful driving to hit the lorry as Hunter had, making it appear that the other driver was to blame.

'Not far now,' he encouraged them.

Both of them were gasping, sweating, Duval most of all,

although he was a good ten years younger than Gustav. A bullet
hit the tarmac and both of them began to run faster.

Hunter had the keys to the metal gate in his hands by the time
they arrived at the small boat pen. He fumbled with the lock as
a bullet hit above his head. He managed to get it open and tore
down the steps.

Inserting a key into the ignition the engine burst into life as
the other two fell into the boat. Hunter slipped the berthing ropes
and pushed the lever into forward. The boat surged ahead, hit
the grill, unlocked by Hunter the previous night, and smashed
it open. The grill bounced back and scraped a deep gash along
the port side, right down to the white fibre-glass hull.

The powerful engine was already picking up speed and the
boat was beginning to lift onto the plane. Hunter ignored the
10kph speed limit.

Where the narrow, stone-lined inlet turned north to the open
sea, men wearing balaclavas appeared behind them and opened
fire with automatic weapons. Bullets hit the side and stern of
the boat but did no real damage other than to the paint work.
Already the boat was moving out of range. It shot into the main
channel under the bows of a departing coastal vessel and Hunter
threw the wheel hard to starboard, just missing the over-laden
ship. In impotent anger the ship's master sounded a series of
short blasts on its horn.

They flew past the old forts as the boat edged its way up to
100kph. Although the water was flat there were small ripples
across the surface and the boat skimmed over them, a faint judder
passing through the hull. As in all ports, departing ships had the
right of way and just outside the entrance there was a long line
of old and not-so-old coastal vessels waiting to enter. These ships
were there to take the dispossessed away from Europe. Even in
times of misery and hardship there were those who would make
money. In this case, a fortune.

Gustav and Duval lay in the stern, on the deck, leaning against
the rear seat, their legs outstretched. Slowly they were beginning to recover their breath and their strength, the sweat drying
on their faces.

Hunter was concentrating on driving the boat. At such a fast speed it was easy to turn too hard and overturn, a problem less experienced helmsmen had encountered many times – often with fatal results. He throttled back to a more sedate 50kph. After a few minutes Gustav struggled to his feet and clambered into the seat alongside Hunter.

'How did they find us?' he called loudly.

Hunter shook his head. 'TIFAT operates on a need-to-know basis, Mr Gustav. Some things are way beyond my pay-scale.'

'We got away.'

Hunter turned his head and gave Gustav a penetrating look. 'We were lucky. I wouldn't have placed odds on us escaping. Would you?'

Gustav returned the gaze for a few seconds and then shook his head. 'No. You were right. We have to be very, very careful.' He didn't elaborate.

'Mr Gustav, humour me. You are so close to achieving your objectives for the good of all white Europeans,' the words stuck in his throat but he persevered, 'just go along with what I tell you. Your ideas will soon shape the reality of a new Europe. I'm determined to make sure your interests are looked after and to ensure your safety.'

Gustav looked ahead at the unfolding scene of a pleasant Mediterranean morning and licked dry lips. If it hadn't been for Hunter, he and Duval would be dead by now.

The team vanished into the backstreets of Marseilles. They removed balaclavas and placed their weapons into the trunks of their cars which were parked on the top floor of a multi-story car park and still empty at that time in the morning. Like all good commuters, the French filled up from the bottom first.

They were in high spirits when they drove away. Dunston and Napier got out at the Hotel de Ville and went inside. Dressed in smart business suits they looked as though they belonged.

They didn't bother with Hunter's room. The corridor was empty and neither man bothered with finesse. A heavy shoulder to each door of Gustav's and Duval's rooms and they were in. They quickly collected together the men's few belongings, including Duval's laptop, and met in the corridor once again. Unhurriedly they walked down the stairs and out of the front entrance. As before, the quayside was packed with people and they had to elbow their way to where the cars were waiting.

Roads all across the city were closed. Police cars were speeding in all directions with their lights flashing and sirens blaring. The team were stopped at one roadblock but their diplomatic passports saw them waved through. Soon after they were at the British Consulate, 24 Avenue de Prado.

A Queen's Messenger took charge of the bags they had lifted from the hotel. Within minutes, the same official was taken in a consulate car to the airport. He was booked on an Air France flight to Paris and on to Edinburgh, where he would be met by a member of TIFAT. Isobel and her team were waiting ready to unravel the secrets held in Duval's computer.

In the meantime, the team left the city for a small private airfield about twenty kilometres inland. Schwarzkopf was waiting for them with the helicopter. They were due in Réggio Di Calabria at the toe of Italy later that day.

The Port-de-Bouc was a natural harbour adjacent to the Regional National Park of the Camargue. Gustav's hired sea-plane, a twin-engined Griffin Land-Water II, was the only one there, tied to a buoy about fifty metres from the shore. They approached the plane but it was empty. They had not been due to leave until 10am.

'What now?' Gustav asked.

Hunter felt a good deal of satisfaction that the question was directed at him. He raised an eyebrow. 'Now we finish our interrupted breakfast. We can't do anything else.' Easing forward on the throttle he took them in towards the sandy, gently sloping beach.

The bow of the boat grated onto the sand, still a few metres from the water's edge. Hunter took off his shoes and socks and threw them onto the beach. Duval and Gustav followed his lead and removed theirs as well. While they did so, Hunter climbed into the warm water and took hold of the small anchor and chain kept in the bow. The others joined him and they dragged the boat well up the beach. He left the keys hidden in a small compartment under the driver's seat just in case the boat was returned to Steve. Somehow, Hunter doubted it.

Picking up their shoes and socks they trundled through the sand and onto the pavement. Sitting on a nearby bench they dried their feet and replaced their footwear. There were quite a few pedestrians walking along the promenade, many with small dogs on leashes, out for their morning constitutional. The dogs fouled the pavements and gutters, the mess ignored by their owners. It was all so normal.

'We'll head over there,' said Hunter, indicating a restaurant with tables and chairs outside, where a small clientele was already beginning to gather.

Hunter ordered breakfast and ate with gusto. The other two picked at their freshly baked croissants, but drank copious amounts of orange juice and coffee.

When they had finished, Hunter said, 'Let's take a stroll. We'll wander the town. You two go together while I follow. We'll be less conspicuous than three men walking together. I'll be right behind but you may not see me. Before we leave, I should ask. What about your briefcases? If they're handed in, is there anything incriminating in the contents?'

Duval managed a grin. 'If anyone tampers with the laptops, a program cleans the soft and hard drives completely and utterly. Unlike most systems mine really works.'

'Excellent! TIFAT know too much as it is.' Standing up Hunter indicated for the men to go ahead. He followed, keeping them in sight for the most part, allowing them out of his sight from time to time. The ruse permitted him to access a payphone in a *Tabac*. He was quickly through to Scotland. Having warned Isobel about the computer system, he was back on the street within two minutes.

Gustav and Duval were clearly unhappy and nervous. Hunter on the other hand enjoyed his stroll. At ten minutes to the hour he indicated that they should head back to the beach. There a small, yellow inflatable dinghy was now tied to a strut on the aircraft.

Duval waved to the plane and was instantly rewarded by an arm appearing through the cockpit window and waving back. A few seconds later the inflatable was heading for shore.

The co-pilot made two trips, first with Gustav and Hunter and then with Duval. Hunter insisted on the arrangement. He had no intention of being left behind. By the time Duval reached the plane the engines had been started and pre-flight checks finished. The co-pilot let go the buoy and puttered around to the door. With a practised movement he climbed aboard and pulled open a dump valve in the side of the boat. The boat collapsed and he dragged it inside where it was neatly stowed.

The Griffin was luxuriously fitted. With only eight seats it was possible to recline them fully and sleep almost as comfortably as in a bed. An attentive blonde stewardess offered them light refreshments, which they declined. Having ascertained that the distance to fly was 350miles and would take approximately one hour and forty minutes, Hunter wondered briefly what lay ahead before falling asleep.

17

The sea-plane landed to the north-west of Palermo. It taxied across the calm water to within a few metres of the hull of a luxury ship. It was, Hunter realised, the *Stockholm*. She was about 200ft long. Details flashed through his mind from the information garnered by Isobel. Dead weight 2,000 tonnes. Widest beam 65ft. Cruising speed 25 knots and a possible top speed in excess of 36 knots. Helicopter deck. Twenty state rooms. Crew of thirty. Beautiful and very expensive.

The hull was a deep blue with a white stripe along the plim-soll line matched by a second line just under the lower deck-edge. This deck held the helicopter pad and hangar. A further two decks tiered upwards, the top one starting from halfway along from the stern. All three decks ended in a sheer wall, topped by the bridge, thirty feet from the bow.

There was no need for the inflatable. They were met by a sleek launch manned by two sailors wearing pristine white tee-shirts and trousers.

A short while later Hunter found himself in a starboard state-room. Its opulence was awesome. A four-poster bed dominated the room, set against the aft bulkhead. The room was en-suite and boasted a balcony big enough to take a table and four chairs. A teak cabinet held a well-stocked bar, which would do a world cruise-liner justice. As he stood there contemplating his surroundings there came a knock on the door. A steward appeared. He carried a complete set of fresh clothing over his arm.

'Mr Gustav's compliments, sir, but I've come for your clothes.'

'May I ask why?' If he was surprised, he didn't show it.

'Orders, sir,' was the enigmatic reply.

Hunter nodded and stripped to his underpants. He threw his clothes onto the bed and slipped his shoes back on while he reached for a bathrobe.

'Your shoes and pants, too, sir.'

Hunter decided it was time to get angry. 'What the hell for?'

'I don't know, sir. I was told to get your clothing as soon as you came on board.'

Hunter fully understood the reasoning behind the request but he intended to play the injured party for a bit longer. 'Tell Mr Gustav I want to see him right away.'

'Oh, I can't do that, sir.' The steward reached behind his back and brought out a gun which he now pointed at Hunter's midriff. 'Please be sensible, sir.'

Shrugging, Hunter tied the belt of the robe tighter, slipped off his boxer shorts, shoes and socks and held out the shoes to the man. When the steward reached for the shoes, Hunter hit the gun arm aside and quickly disarmed him. 'Pick up that lot and get out. And don't wave a gun in my face again.'

Sheepishly the steward did as he was told. When he got to the door Hunter called to him, 'Here.' He lobbed the gun, causing the man to fumble with the clothes and drop a shoe. Hunter watched him leave before going for a shower. They'd find nothing.

Wearing white trousers, a white open-necked shirt and loafers on his bare feet, Hunter left the cabin. The corridor ran fore and aft and was heavily carpeted. His was the end cabin and to his left he could see a gleaming open deck with a swimming pool and separate jacuzzi. He went right, towards the bows. Hanging between each door was a painting, modern art of the kind which Hunter disliked but knew to be expensive. He assumed correctly that they were originals. At the end of the corridor he stepped out onto a large balcony that overlooked the bow where passengers could stand and watch as they entered harbour or ploughed their way through the seas. A circular set of stairs led to the lower deck. A notice on the gate said it was for the use of the crew only. Looking behind him, Hunter saw separate stairs which led to a balcony above. He knew the owner's suite was to be found there. Looking up further and leaning out, he could make out the bridge windows and bridge wings. An officer was standing on the port wing looking down at him. He didn't respond to Hunter's cheery wave.

He went down the stairs to the bow and looked into the clear blue water. The white anchor chain led into the depths and vanished in a shimmering haze. A few dark shadows darted around the chain and further down he could make out rocks on the bottom, stark against the barren sand. He had an over-whelming desire to put on a diving set and plunge into the crystal clear waters. To forget the danger he was in if only for a little while.

He continued around the deck, along the port side and as far as the helicopter pad, where he loitered at the stern and looked towards Sicily. The sea was fairly dotted with boats, sailing vessels and powered craft of different shapes and sizes.

Apart from two sailors who watched him as he went past, ignoring his friendly nod, he saw nobody. Halfway along the starboard side he found a doorway that again said 'Crew Only'. He went in. Although not nearly as opulently decorated as the guests' quarters it still looked well appointed.

Moving along the corridor he came to a door marked 'Crews Mess' and entered. Half a dozen men sat at a table littered with Styrofoam cups, smoking, drinking and talking. Along one wall stood a cafeteria-style, stainless steel counter with clear plastic shelves, holding plated food. Aware of the men watching him, Hunter walked over to take a look. He helped himself to lobster salad and cold water from a cooler. Nodding to the men he took a seat at another table.

One of the crew stood up and approached him. 'What are you doing here?' The question was asked truculently. About Hunter's height, blonde and muscled, his accent suggested he was Swedish or possibly German. Hunter decided it was the former.

'What's it to you?'

'I ask the questions. I'll ask you again . . .'

He didn't get any further. It was time, Hunter decided, to

stamp some authority on the crew. The man was standing next to Hunter's chair. Hunter drove his fist hard between the man's legs, practically lifting him off his feet. He gurgled, clasped his hands in front of him and sank to the floor with a loud gasp. His face had turned a mottled green and yellow.

Hunter pointed at the two nearest men. 'You and you, carry him to his cabin.' When nobody moved, Hunter hit the table with the flat of his hand and yelled, 'Now! And listen up! I'm in charge of Mr Gustav's personal security. From now on what I say goes around here. I go where I like, when I like. Do I make myself clear?'

One or two nodded nervously. The two men he had pointed to stood up and went to help their moaning companion. They too were blonde and muscled. From the few words Hunter heard them exchange it was clear that they were Swedish.

'You,' he pointed at another man, 'where will I find the Captain?'

'On the bridge.' The words were uttered between clenched teeth.

'You have a problem?' Hunter stood up nonchalantly and stepped to one side of the table.

The other man did likewise. 'Yes. That was a cowardly attack. You gave Kurt no chance.'

'I'm giving you one.'

The man was in his middle twenties, an inch or two shorter than Hunter but broader in the shoulders. From his toned muscles he obviously pumped a lot of iron. He glanced at the men still at the table before launching his attack. It was no contest. Hunter moved as hard and as fast as he had ever done in his life. The man stood stock still for a second or two and then keeled over with a loud crash, smashing his head on the deck. Hunter wasn't even breathing hard.

'I repeat, I'm in charge of Mr Gustav's personal security. When I say jump you ask how high. Got it?' This time he didn't raise his voice and had the satisfaction of seeing them nod nervously. 'When I ask a question or want information it will be for a good reason. My only concern is our leader's well-being.'

He left, perfectly satisfied with the little encounter he had just engineered. They would not be so quick to question him from now on. All he had to do now was deal with the ship's Captain. He would have to be tackled in an entirely different way.

Along the corridor near the bow he found a set of stairs. He ran up them and found himself on the bridge. A man in white uniform with gold stripes on his shoulders looked up when he walked in.

'Captain?'

The man was leaning over a desk, a pencil in his hand, a ship's log book lying open.

'*Ja*. I am the Captain.'

Hunter stepped forward with his hand outstretched. 'My name is Hunter, Nick Hunter. I am in charge of Mr Gustav's personal security.'

The Captain ignored the hand and turned back to what he was doing. 'I know who you are.'

'Captain, I don't care if we get on or not. I have only one concern and that is the safety of Mr Gustav. Your concern is the safety of the ship. Mine takes priority. I hope you clearly understand that.'

'I take my orders from Mr Gustav only. No one else.'

'Captain, I had hoped we could resolve any differences or difficulties amicably. If need be I can speak to Mr Gustav.'

The man tensed and then straightened up slowly. He looked at Hunter. He was about forty-five, tanned, fit looking with brown hair and grey sideburns reaching to his lobes. His was the fitness of the tennis courts and the ski resorts, though a small belly was beginning to fight against his muscle-tone.

He seemed to be thinking over Hunter's words. After a few seconds he nodded. 'That won't be necessary. Mr Gustav's safety is also my main concern. Followed by the ship and her passengers.' He held out his hand. '*Kapitän zur See* Jürgen Novak.'

'Good,' Hunter smiled. 'Then we'll get on famously together.' Hunter shook the captain's hand. There was no answering smile.

General Macnair replaced the receiver on his desk and sat looking at it for a few moments, as though there was something more to learn from staring at it. Leaning forward he pressed a button on his internal intercom. 'Jim, can you spare a minute?' The request was the equivalent of a senior officer's command. Carter would give Macnair as long as the General wished.

'Take a seat. I've spoken to Nato. They've been co-operating fully, or at least, as fully as we can expect. Until now.'

'What do you mean, sir?'

'I just had Hiram on the phone. He's in the Netherlands. In Rotterdam.'

'Yes, sir. Staking out a police station.'

Macnair had no need to tell Carter why the police station was a target. A week earlier there had been an attack on a super-market in the Dutch city. It was in the centre of the Muslim enclave and catered primarily for local people who worshipped Islam. It sold mainly foods which were specially prepared or imported from Muslim countries. Such strict adherence to Islam had led to trouble in the past, and the supermarket had become the focus for hatred by gangs of the city's skinheads and neo-nazis. Now the shop had been attacked and torched to the ground. Three Muslims had lost their lives and many more had been hurt. The Dutch police had been late in responding. When they had arrived at the scene they had done little apart from make a half-hearted attempt to stop the violence. There had been no arrests.

Since that night there had been sporadic unrest in the city and more people had been killed, mainly Muslims, but also a white Dutch couple and their baby. The blame had been laid at the door of Islamic extremists. According to the information Isobel had collected, the police station was now a target and due to be attacked that night.

'Hiram met with a Nato major, a Dutchman, which is appropriate under the circumstances. He promised a contingent of troops to help contain the problem and back up the men in the police station.'

'Sounds reasonable.'

'Except none of the troops have appeared. The attack is in three hours and Hiram can't find the officer.'

Carter allowed the surprise to show on his face. 'What gives?'

'We know Gustav *needs* Muslim success. He needs white people killed and injured to prove that everything he's saying is true. He needs death and destruction in Europe on a scale great enough to convince Europeans of his goal. I hadn't realised how far Gustav's influence had already extended. If he can pull Nato troops out of action what else can he do?'

'What are you proposing to do about it, sir?'

'Our best bet of holding the lid down – until we get the information we need from Hunter – is to stop any Muslim success. Once we can show that the real mastermind behind the attacks is Gustav and his right-wing cohorts we can swing back public opinion. But if we lose the battle in the next few days then it could be too late. No matter what we say and do the hatred will be too deep and too raw.'

'Not to mention the hatred the Muslims will have for us, sir.'

Macnair spoke fervently. 'The hatred has been there for centuries, Jim. I'm only interested in today. We keep the peace, or what passes for peace, across Europe. Whilst we do, our politicians will have to work harder at appeasing the fears of the majority. Whether they like it or not. Re-deploy Dunston and his team.'

'But, sir, that'll leave Nick without any back-up!'

Macnair nodded. 'I'm aware of that. But they are wanted elsewhere. I need every man I can trust. Hunter will be on his own for a short while. Hopefully, it won't be long enough for him to get into any serious trouble.'

Dunston and his men flew to Rome airport, 300 miles away. From there they were dispersed, to assist at forthcoming attacks. Isobel was downloading information even as they were in the air. Dunston was lucky. His destination was Fiumicino, Rome's international airport. There he met David Hughes in deep discussion with the airport's chief of security.

'Matt, meet Sylvestre diSilvio.'

The two men shook hands. DiSilvio was short and fat and smelt strongly of expensive aftershave.

'I am very please to have you here,' were diSilvio's opening words. 'I have been given much details and I am very worried. What should we do? The General Manager wants to close the airport.'

'I don't see how that will help,' Dunston frowned.

'He say that if the airport closure is on the radio and television then the attackers won't come.'

'That's wishful thinking,' said Hughes, 'and highly unlikely. Mr diSilvio, it doesn't work like that. These men are coming here to attack the airport. We know that their primary target is the American Delta flight due in at nine o'clock. They want to kill Americans but they will also kill anybody else who gets in their way. This is a suicide attack intended to cause maximum death and destruction. Closing the airport is not an option.'

Nodding his round head, diSilvio said, '*Si, si*. But my manager . . .'

'I'll talk to him,' said Dunston, soothingly.

The door opposite burst open and the General Manager bustled in followed by a retinue of staff. There followed a heated argument between him and diSilvio. The Chief of Security appeared to be getting the worst of it. While this was going on, completely ignored, the two men from TIFAT stood to one side. After a short while Dunston telephoned Macnair and explained the situation. He replaced the receiver. The phone rang a few minutes later while the two Italians were still arguing.

Dunston answered and then held the receiver towards the General Manager. It took three attempts to attract his attention.

'I am too busy now,' he said angrily.

'Prime Minister? He says that he is too busy to talk to . . .' He got no further.

The GM tore the phone from his grasp. There were a series of *Si's*, a lot of gulping and no further arguments. The General Manager replaced the receiver, looking older than his sixty-three years by about a decade. 'What do we do?'

'Ask your staff to leave while I brief you. Just you and Mr diSilvio, please.' The GM's entourage left the room. 'This is an operation of containment,' said Dunston. 'The biggest risk is to innocent bystanders, either other travellers or their family and friends. So we have to isolate the terrorists.'

'How?' asked diSilvio.

'That's what we're here to work out. We know the attackers are coming in on a train from Rome . . .'

'How do you know this thing?' diSilvio interrupted.

'From our intelligence sources. We even know which train the terrorists will be on. If we wait until they arrive at the terminal then they will be able to disperse across the railway station, into the adjacent multi-story car parks and even get into any of the three terminal buildings. A lot of people could be killed and a vast amount of damage done. How many planes are usually at the terminals?'

'Eighteen, possibly twenty,' diSilvio answered.

'Some will be embarking passengers, others disembarking. Some planes will be ready to leave and others arriving on the hard-standing. A concerted attack by the terrorists could be enough for one of them to get to a window overlooking the area. One man with a grenade launcher is all it takes to create a vast amount of damage and loss of life.'

'You are painting a bleak picture,' said the General Manager.

Dunston raised his hand. 'The only place that we can contain them is on the train.'

The relief on the General Manager's face would have been comic if the discussion hadn't been so deadly.

DiSilvio said, 'It is an express, direct from Roma. It will not stop until it reaches here.'

'Then we stop it . . . where?' Dunston asked.

'Acilia,' diSilvio replied. 'What do we do then?'

'These people have to be stopped permanently,' said Hughes. 'Otherwise they'll regroup and come again. And next time we may not have the advance intelligence to stop them. We know that they are members of al-Qaeda, and are fanatics. So we have no choice.'

Dunston nodded. 'My colleague's right. We also need to enter the train with overwhelming force. It's the only way. These people will be travelling alone or in pairs. We know that they will *look*

Middle Eastern. They will have bags nearby, either above their heads or on their laps, or next to them. We go in with a lot of noise and we contain each carriage. What's the situation with manpower?'

DiSilvio looked sheepish and shrugged.

'What about police or army help?' Hughes asked.

'I swear I had it arranged but they have been called off,' said diSilvio. 'An hour ago.'

'There's nothing we can do about that now.' If he was dismayed, Dunston didn't show it. 'How many men do you have here?'

'We need them to protect the airport,' protested the General Manager.

'Why?' Hughes asked in his quiet Welsh voice.

The ludicrousness of his statement was apparent even to the GM and he lapsed into silence.

'Luckily we have a shift change coming up,' said diSilvio. 'I can gather thirty, perhaps thirty-two armed men and a few women.'

'How many carriages will there be?' Dunston asked.

'Usually fifteen,' answered diSilvio.

'How busy will they be at this time of the evening?' Dunston asked.

'Half full, I should say.'

Dunston looked at his watch. 'The train departs in just over an hour.' He looked at the General Manager, 'Sir, can you get the railway authority to cut the train in half?'

'I don't know. Why?'

'These are modern open carriages, yes?'

'Of course. The best in Europe,' the Italian boasted.

'With only two people for each carriage anybody in the middle would be able to draw a weapon before we get to them. I want to avoid a bloodbath if I can help it. We need at least four men to rush in and to quarter each carriage. If we can manage even more then all the better. Any questions?'

There were none.

'One more thing. We do *not* tell anyone else what the operation is about,' said Dunston.

'I not understand,' said diSilvio.

'Get your men in position but don't tell them why we're there until it's time to go. We can't afford any word of the operation being leaked to the terrorists.'

The General Manager stood straighter and was about to remonstrate with Dunston at the idea that there could be a traitor in their midst when he thought better of it.

Colonel Hiram B. Walsh, late of Delta Force and now second-in-command at TIFAT was not a happy man. He was in a meeting with a senior police officer in Rotterdam's main police station. The officer was not happy either. The antipathy between the American and the Dutchman was almost palpable. They came from diametrically opposite viewpoints to the same conclusion – the other man was a fool.

Inspector Paul Schroder was Dutch, tall and thickset with a spreading waistline held in by a residual fitness from when he played professional football. He had learnt only an hour earlier that his station was to be attacked by Muslims. He knew and understood the reason for it and had expected back-up from either the army or other police units. None was forthcoming. Indeed, Schroder had been looking forward to catching the Islamic scum, as he put it, in a trap. Now there wasn't going to be one. The building they were in was practically Gothic. It would be a nightmare to defend against armed men, particularly if the reports on their opposition proved true.

'We need to evacuate,' said Schroder. 'Let them come and destroy the building. At least my men will be alive.'

Walsh couldn't argue with that. It was precisely what he would do and so he nodded. However, 'There's one problem with that.'

Schroder raised an inquisitive eyebrow.

'They won't stop with torching this place. We know that twenty plus, fully armed men, are going to hit this building. They have automatic guns, grenades and probably a missile or two. If they meet no resistance what will happen? They'll go on the rampage. This area is predominantly white and middle class. It would trigger a killing orgy and it's your task to stop it.'

'But why have I no support?'

Walsh was aware that Schroder was not the brightest policeman he had ever met but such stupidity was breathtaking. 'Normally, you would have had no prior knowledge of the attack, would you?'

'True. The only intelligence we have been given is from TIFAT.'

'Would you have been ready for an attack?'

The man looked uncomfortable for a second before having the grace to admit, 'No. But we would have responded very quickly. With the tension around nowadays we are better prepared than ever.'

'You'd have been too late,' Walsh said quietly. 'The likelihood is you'd have been wiped out. You still could be. How would you describe this station? Pro-fascist? Anti-immigrant?'

'You can call us what you like. The men I've got here are all true Europeans. We believe this is a white continent for Christians. Muslims should go back to where they come from.'

Walsh didn't bother replying. 'You've been set up, my friend. Your men stood by and watched the supermarket being burnt to the ground while Muslims and non-whites were killed. Well, the situation is about to be reversed. The deaths of white policemen will ensure a frenzy of anti-Islamic, racist feelings.' Walsh stood up and stretched cramped muscles. 'The trouble is, you don't realise who you're dealing with.'

Schroder was about to protest but thought better of it. He needed Walsh right then.

'Believe me, Schroder, the men who are responsible want the deliberately engineered deaths of Dutch citizens. Particularly the deaths of white, Christian folk. Right now there are millions of Europeans who think like you do. When your deaths and those of others like you hit the TV screens, people will flock to the cause. Europe could easily become a whites-only continent. Except *you* won't be alive to see it. Do you live locally, Schroder?'

'What?' The policeman was looking dazed but he replied. 'About two streets from here.'

'If this station is attacked and destroyed, do you think it'll stop there? With your police officers dead who's to stop them rioting? Killing more innocent white people?'

Schroder's bleak gaze was answer enough.

'We need to be ready for them. How many men do you have on duty?'

'Eight, at this time of the night. I only came in because of you.'

'Weapons?'

'Sticks, CS gas and side-arms.'

'Not much against a heavily-armed and fanatical terrorist group three times stronger. That map,' he pointed at the wall, 'is your jurisdiction, I take it?'

'Yes. We are in the corner, here.' Schroder pointed with a stubby forefinger at the map behind his head. 'This is our normal patrol area, except when we are in hot pursuit. But any robberies or murders that take place within the red lines are dealt with from here.'

'How do you get on with the other stations? The other senior officers?'

Schroder shrugged. 'All right, I guess. We have different opinions, we sometimes argue when we meet. On the whole we agree that our problems are caused in great part by the immigrants. Some want a radical change, others think . . . differently.' There was no need to ask Schroder which option he preferred.

'Could they help you? Send men?'

Schroder thought about it for a few seconds before he reluctantly shook his head. 'They are already stretched too thinly. Crime has gone up in the last few years to such an extent that there are never enough officers available.'

'What about off-duty officers?'

'Yes. That is a good idea.'

'It's just after nine now. According to our information we can expect an attack any time after one o'clock. Get me somebody I can trust to come outside with me. I want to take a look around. In the meantime, round up as many of your officers as you can. And don't let any go off on some crime bust. Tonight, the criminals can have it their own way around here.'

*   *   *

The plan they settled on was not ideal but it was the best that Dunston and Hughes could come up with under the circumstances.

The train, half its normal length, left Rome station ten minutes late. The carriages, seven of them, were between half and three-quarters full. Profuse apologies were broadcast to the passengers about the delay and the cramped conditions. Trouble on the line ahead was blamed. The train travelled more slowly than usual. After a few minutes another broadcast informed those on board that there would be a delay at Acilia because of a power failure. But the delay would not be too great. Many, many apologies.

There was indeed a power failure at the station. All the lights had been extinguished. The train stopped and the doors hissed open. There was a silence as nobody got on and nobody got off. After all, this was not a scheduled stop.

Then it erupted.

Clad in full riot gear, two airport security guards, wearing flack-jackets and carrying Beretta Model 12S Italian sub-machine guns, issued after 9/11, stepped quickly through the doors.

Some of the men yelled in English, 'Don't move! Police! Don't move!' Other officers screamed the same in Italian. They rushed along the carriages, pointing their guns and yelling.

There were no obvious targets. The people sitting in their seats looked suitably shocked and frightened. A quick search showed nobody carried weapons. The few people with Middle Eastern or North African passports were few. They were searched and questioned closely but to no avail.

Hughes took Dunston to one side. 'Matt, something's wrong. Our intelligence is too good. You know that.'

Dunston nodded, frowning. He caught a look. A smirk. Whose was it? He looked around but saw nobody acting oddly. But there *had* been something.

'The airport! Let's go! I hope we're not too late. Mr diSilvio, warn the airport. They can expect an attack at any time.'

The men ran from the station and bundled into cars. With screaming tyres and over-revving engines the cars sped towards the airport only a few kilometres away.

The vehicles screeched to a halt outside the main terminal and the men ran into the concourse. Armed and dressed as they were, they made a frightening sight, sending the passengers screaming and panic stricken towards the exits. As Dunston stopped indecisively, near the moving stairway, shots were heard coming from the upper level. He and Hughes bounded up the steps as more panicked people streamed down. Hughes was at Dunston's left shoulder, each man covering the other. A grenade went off and the screams turned into the high-pitched sound of the injured.

They were on the viewing floor. On the other side of the room a plate glass window blew out as an automatic weapon opened fire. Around a pillar, the TIFAT operatives saw a masked man shooting out the glass of a window while next to him a second man was raising a rifle to his shoulder. On the end of the barrel was the unmistakable lump of a grenade.

Dunston and Hughes opened fire simultaneously. They cut the terrorists down before the grenade was fired. More shots came from their left and they ran towards the noise. By now the area was clear of innocent bystanders but the floor was littered with the bodies of the dead and wounded. Blood was everywhere.

More firing and glass smashing came from around the next corner. The two men slowed down and approached carefully. It was a repeat of the scene they had just witnessed. They fired their guns. Dunston's shot hit the man with the grenade launcher in the shoulder, deflecting his aim just as the terrorist pulled the trigger. The grenade missed the wing of the Airbus it was aimed at and hit the tail. As it went off, pieces of shrapnel smashed into the plane's tail. If it had hit the wing, the aviation gas-filled conflagration could have resulted in many deaths.

Dunston fired again, killing the man. Hughes' first shot had been lethal. More firing was heard in the distance. It tailed off to sporadic shots and then silence.

Dunston turned to Hughes and said, 'We failed, Dave.'

An hour later Dunston contacted TIFAT HQ and reported to Macnair. It was a sorry tale. Thirty-three innocent people killed, a further forty-two injured. Six terrorists had died and two were wounded. The wounded men were in custody.

'What went wrong?' Macnair asked.

'They were warned, sir. I don't know who and how but I'm sure of it.

Hiram Walsh had fifteen Dutch officers. Two others had turned up, but were either drunk or on drugs and had been sent away again. The officers bore only side-arms, Belgian Browning BDA 380s specially manufactured for the police forces of Western Europe. The magazine held thirteen, 9mm Shorts, and was useful at close quarters. Walsh knew they were completely inadequate for what he envisaged was ahead that night.

'You know the situation,' he addressed the police officers. 'They will be coming and they'll be coming in hard. This is a suicide mission as far as these men are concerned. They are here to cause maximum damage and the maximum number of deaths. Once the station is taken care of they'll attack the civilians in the area. You'll see grenades, automatic weapons and petrol bombs. They must be stopped at all costs.'

The officers sitting in front of him nodded with varying degrees of enthusiasm. This was *not* what they had signed up for.

'Sergeant Baedecker and I have scouted the area.' Baedecker was an ex-military policeman, who had proven to be a useful man to have around. 'And we have a strategy of sorts. It's vital we capture some of their weapons. It's possible they have Stingers, but they will have grenades and at least one, maybe two, launchers. The men with those weapons are our priority. The area will be lit-up as much as possible. They may have Night Vision Goggles; we certainly don't. All the lights will be on in the station but nobody will be inside. We'll be hiding in the streets. Sergeant?'

Walsh handed over to the burly Dutchman. Baedecker had spent fifteen years with Nato and knew his stuff. Of all the men in the room, he was the one Walsh could rely on.

Midnight found the officers deployed around the area. The police station sat in a square, surrounded by shops with residential apartments above. The streets were one-way and ran north to south, east to west, cutting off the station like an island. Cars were parked alongside the pavements and would remain there until the morning when a no-parking ban came into force. Around the station cars could park only if they were there on police business. Currently there were two in front of the building and two behind. The station could be approached from any direction, by anyone. This was, after all, one of the freest societies in the world. It also had one of the biggest proportion of immigrants in the Western hemisphere.

The police sat in nondescript vans or crouched hidden in doorways. They had the four streets leading to the square under surveillance and were in constant touch by personal radios. And they were very, very nervous. Walsh noted again the difference between TIFAT operatives and even well trained men.

The attack began around 02.00.

18

Aboard the *Stockholm* Hunter had feasted with Gustav and Duval in a splendid dining-room off the main salon and bar. Bisque was followed by fresh skate, vegetables and three different potato dishes. Cheese and fruit followed. A superb white wine had been offered. Hunter and Gustav drank water.

'I am so sorry about your clothes,' said Gustav over coffee. 'An accident with the drier, I believe. We've had to destroy them.'

Hunter waved a nonchalant hand and said, 'It doesn't matter. Somehow I never expected to see them again.'

'Good. Then we understand each other perfectly.'

'I think we do, Mr Gustav. However, I am still waiting for my cheque.'

'Ah, yes, the ten million. Duval?'

The secretary reached inside his shirt pocket and withdrew a folded piece of paper. He handed it across to Hunter.

Opening it, Hunter saw that it was made out in euros and was near enough to ten million Sterling as to make no difference. 'Thank you.'

'My pleasure,' said Gustav. 'After all you did save my life. Twice.'

'The second time was on the house. I was looking after, shall we say, my investment?'

Gustav chuckled. 'Very good, Mr Hunter. I gather you've been introducing yourself to the crew?'

'I take your safety very seriously, Mr Gustav. When I give an order I expect it to be obeyed. That way you'll have a better chance of survival. Trust me, I know what I'm doing.'

Gustav smiled. 'Of that I have no doubt.'

'Sir, I need to know your movements. I have arrangements to make for each destination. I also need to see about recruiting more help.'

'All in good time, Mr Hunter. All in good time. For now, be assured that I am staying here. I have everything I need. World-wide communications, every comfort conceivable and perfect safety. Come, let us go and see the good news.'

The room on the other side of the bar was a fully-fitted cinema. The ship could receive every television station in the world that broadcast via satellite and Gustav was soon flicking through the channels. Whatever he was looking for he didn't appear to find. 'Duval, try the BBC and Reuters.'

'Yes, sir.' Duval left the room.

Hunter walked over to one wall which was lined with the very latest DVDs of films only just out on general release. 'You have an eclectic selection.'

'My guests have very different tastes.'

Gustav went back to flicking through the channels while Hunter sat down again and watched. Duval returned ten minutes later.

'There have been a dozen episodes so far. Mainly in the east. Greece. An Orthodox Church and a museum destroyed. A number of other killings and attacks. Nothing of major importance.'

'Anything on Rome or Rotterdam?'

'No, sir.'

'Paris? Stockholm? Madrid?'

'No, sir. It's still too early.'

'All right. As soon as you get something, let me know.' Gustav went back to channel hopping, ignoring the other two men.

Hunter stood up. 'I'm going to take a look outside. I want to get a better feel for your security. Mr Duval, may I have a word?'

Duval followed him outside, closing the door. Hunter asked, 'Where's the armoury?'

'What?'

'The armoury. You must have one. Right now if we came

under attack I can improvise one or two weapons but they'll be about as much use as a chocolate teapot. You must have some real armaments stowed away somewhere. Somewhere a cursory customs examination won't turn up.'

Duval hesitated for a second before nodding. 'We do. But I need Mr Gustav's permission to show you.'

'Then get it. I can't emphasise enough how much danger he and by extension you and I are in. If TIFAT come after us we're in deep trouble. Believe me. I'll be on the upper deck. I want to recce the ship and anchorage and work out a plan of action. Meet me on the bridge in ten minutes.'

Before Duval could argue Hunter walked away. It was a small, almost imperceptible victory, but he had established that he took orders only from Gustav, not from his lackey.

Walking around the deck it was obvious that nothing could save Gustav in the event of an attack even by the most amateurish troops. Hunter bounded up the outside ladder to the bridge wing and stood admiring the view of the island, now directly ahead of the ship. Duval found him there a few seconds later.

'I'm to show you the armoury,' he said without preamble.

'Good. In the meantime we should flash up and get out of here. I cannot protect Mr Gustav if we are at anchor. If special forces came in now there would be nothing I could do to stop them, Duval. Nothing.'

'But they have no idea where we are.'

'Do you want to bet your *life* on it? We need to keep moving. I can talk to the Captain and work out a racetrack.'

'A racetrack?' Duval shook his head, confused.

'A course we can follow all night. Keep moving. Stay safe. I need to know how much fuel we have and what speed we can maintain and for how long. The higher the speed the better.'

Duval nodded. 'I'll speak to Mr Gustav.'

'You also need to talk to the Captain. He won't listen to me.'

Duval led the way onto the bridge where Novak sat in his captain's chair. 'I would like you to give Mr Hunter all the information he requires. Then prepare to get under way. Mr Hunter will tell you where we are going.'

267

'Yes, sir.' If Novak resented his orders he gave no indication.

Duval left the two men. Hunter bent over the chart table and studied the local Admiralty chart for a few seconds. 'We want to be away from these shipping lanes. Out of sight of land and moving at a reasonable speed. How much fuel do we carry?'

'We're pretty much topped off. I filled the tanks in Palermo before coming to anchor.'

'What range does that give us?'

'Three thousand miles at fifteen knots. Less at higher speeds. Fifteen is our optimum cruising speed.'

Taking a pair of dividers Hunter measured off distances. 'If we establish a racetrack twenty miles south of Sicily we'll be out of sight of almost all the shipping lanes. Say fifty miles in each direction. Better yet, three hours in each direction.'

'Why? We're only wasting fuel.'

Hunter was about to explain as he would have done normally but decided it was time to exert a little authority. 'Does that present a problem? Endanger the ship in any way?'

'No. Of course not, but . . .'

'No buts, Captain. If I give another order, I don't expect you to ask questions. You're responsibility is clear, as is mine. So you do as I tell you provided it doesn't hazard the ship.'

The Captain had been bending over the chart but now he straightened up, bristling with anger. 'I do not care for your tone, Herr Hunter. As the Captain, if I ask a question, then I expect an answer.'

Hunter too straightened up and looked at the Captain squarely. 'You'll get one if I think you merit it. This once I will tell you. But only this once. A moving target is much harder to hit. Right now special services divers could be arriving under our keel and we'd know nothing about it. Or they could be parachuting in for all we know and the first indication we'd get is when they start shooting. At least if we are under sail they'll find it a damn sight more difficult. Is that understood?'

'*Ja. Ich verstehe.*' The Captain had lapsed into German.

Hunter was about to reply in the same language then thought better of it. 'Speak English, man.'

Struggling to hide his contempt, Novak said, 'I understand.' Quickly he added, 'I also agree. I can get us underway in thirty minutes.'

'Make it fifteen and we'll get on a lot better. I need to see the armoury. Get somebody to take me there.'

'We have a lookout on the upper bridge. He can show you.'

Hunter shook his head. 'I'll go and speak to him. Get two more men as sentries. They can accompany me to the armoury. It's time we sharpened the crew up around here.'

The armoury was deep in the ship, on the starboard side. Hunter entered through a door in the engine room. It was long and narrow, with room to walk past cage after cage of weapons. It was almost as well stocked as TIFAT's.

Hunter carried a bunch of keys in one hand, each one colour-coded to match a locked cage. One of the crewmen pointed ahead. 'Behind that door is where we keep the plastic.'

'Let's take a look.' Hunter unlocked the door and went inside a storage locker big enough to stand upright in. On the starboard side were racks of slabs of plastic explosive, while on the port side were different types of boxed detonators. Each was individually held in a round, padded slot, ten dets to each box. 'I've seen enough. Let's get topside.'

They had arrived at the engine room and Hunter was locking the door when the four big diesels began to burst into life. The men hurried. The noise level was nerve shredding. By the time they closed the engine room door behind them all four diesels were operating. Through the soles of their feet they could feel the chain rattling as it was shortened, prior to being raised.

Back on the bridge, Hunter found Duval as well as the Captain. 'Is Mr Gustav still in the cinema?'

'Yes. He's watching the news. He agrees with your strategy.'

'One more thing. We need to have the men fully armed at all times. The guns, if they remain locked in the armoury, give us about as much chance as a snowball in hell.'

'The sentry we have on watch is carrying a sidearm,' Duval argued.

Hunter snorted in derision. 'Useless. They need to have something with real stopping power. And they need to be ready at all times. From now on the men sleep with their guns. Leave it to me. I'll make all the arrangements, but first answer me this. How often has Mr Gustav been on board?'

'This is the first time in nearly a year.'

Hunter nodded. That explained a lot. The Swede obviously felt safe on the ship and his security man, Faubert, hadn't had an opportunity to implement the most commonsense of precautions. Hunter knew that what he was suggesting would have occurred to either Duval or Gustav at some point. Better to come from him as he continued to establish his *bona fides*.

The anchor was raised and the ship got underway. It was past 02.00 when they reached the area Hunter had suggested they patrol. On the way, he had taken members of the crew down to the armoury to find suitable guns. The choice was staggering. Hunter decided to issue Austrian Steyr TMPs. It was a close-quarter gun and had been in production for less than ten years. For himself, Hunter chose a Steyr AUG Para, an assault rifle. Three times heavier than the TMP, it held a magazine of 32 rounds and was far more accurate with a much longer range. He slung the gun over his shoulder, barrel pointing down, cocked and primed. He only needed to flick the safety to be able to fire the weapon.

He had all the men, except the crew on watch, assembled in the crew's dining room. 'From now on you keep your guns with you at all times. Raise your hands if you've used this type of gun before.' He wasn't surprised to see every man raise a hand. 'Have you all served in the armed forces?' They all nodded. A few smirks were exchanged.

Hunter nodded and smiled. 'Good. That makes my life a lot easier. From now on the ship will operate in two watches. You'll either be on watch and alert or eating or sleeping. As far as we know nobody knows where Mr Gustav is and hopefully we'll keep it that way. But just in case . . .' Hunter continued his briefing. 'One last thing. Keep your guns safe. Don't have one up the spout and make sure the safety is on at all times.' It would give Hunter a half-second advantage. He hoped it would be enough.

Down in the cinema, Hunter found Gustav watching CNN, glued to what was happening on the screen. It looked like the aftermath of a street battle.

Gustav glanced over at Hunter and said, 'A police station in Rotterdam. Terrorists attacked it twenty minutes ago. Eight policemen have been killed.'

'And the terrorists?'

'Wiped out.' Gustav spoke with a degree of bitterness in his voice. 'I had hoped for a great deal more damage by the Arabs. And a lot more Dutch fatalities. But they were stopped at the police station.'

Hunter kept the anger out of his voice. 'Are there any details?'

'Rotterdam's Chief of Police has been speaking. The fool! All he had to do was follow orders. I wanted the station isolated and wiped out. Our Muslim puppets would have then gone on a killing spree in the area before being taken out by other police units. But they were stopped too soon. It is unbelievable.'

'Who stopped them?' Hunter asked.

'I don't know. But I will learn the answer soon.' The phone interrupted him. 'This is probably my source now.'

Gustav answered and held a short conversation in Dutch. The language was close enough to German for Hunter to be able to follow it. Gustav made it clear that he was angry with the low death rate among the police. He hung up, scowling at Hunter. 'It seems your former colleagues have interfered once more. A man named Walsh. Do you know him?'

'Of course. Colonel from the American Delta force. Second in command. Tough as hell.'

'He won't be bothering us again.'

'What do you mean?' Hunter asked. 'He's dead?' Somehow he managed to keep his voice steady.

'No. Merely wounded. A bullet in the leg and arm. He organised the policemen outside the station. When the Muslims attacked they were surprised from the rear and sides. The Chief of Police has had no option but to praise the action. A classic way of defending against greater odds, so I understand.'

Hunter nodded. 'Makes sense. That's what I would have done.

271

Take out the terrorists and then take their guns. No police force in the world is equipped to deal with heavily armed terrorists. I take it the Arabs were heavily armed?'

Gustav grunted. 'The best money can buy. It should have been a walk over. The stupid swine cannot be trusted to do the simplest of tasks.'

Hunter refrained from answering. It was a ludicrous and unjustified comment born of ignorance of urban guerrilla warfare. Knowing Col Hyram B. Walsh as he did, Hunter suspected it had been one hell of a fight. He only hoped Walsh would survive. Leaving Gustav to his browsing of TV channels, Hunter decided it was time to properly explore the ship. He had hopefully proven beyond a shadow of doubt that he only had Gustav's safety at heart. The arming of the crew, the movement of the ship, all pointed clearly where his loyalties lay – the well-being of their leader.

He found what he was searching for on the top deck, directly below the bridge; the communications room. He tried the door. It opened at his touch and he went in. There were two men sitting there. One had on earphones, the other sat at a desk. A heavy calibre Colt Anaconda revolver lay on its wooden surface. A second after he had entered, the gun was pointing in the region of Hunter's belly button. The hand holding the gun was as steady as a rock.

'What's the latest?' Macnair asked as Isobel entered his office, obviously exhausted.

Isobel poured herself a cup of coffee and took a mouthful. 'Ugh! It's like tar.'

'I'll make some fresh,' Macnair spoke impatiently, 'but tell me the news first.'

'It looks like Gustav has only been playing with us up till now. He has really upped the ante in recent days. There have been twenty-eight incidents. In all of them we managed to take out the terrorists but we've suffered a lot of casualties. So far the totals are one hundred and ninety-eight terrorists dead, eighteen wounded and seven captured. On our side we've had thirty-eight civilians killed, nineteen policemen, seven soldiers and four – as you know – of our men.'

Macnair nodded. Four good men, each killed in separate incidents. Sergeants Maguire and Estephan, Corporals Hanson and Jarvis – Irish, Portuguese, Canadian and American. Good men. Hard to replace. They would be sorely missed.

'What about the nerve gas aboard the *Silver Beech*? If there are Weapons of Mass Destruction out there we need to know who's producing them and where they're coming from.'

Isobel shook her head. 'General, we've been everywhere. About the only place left is North Korea and I don't see it somehow. The Americans have been leaning very hard on anybody and everybody who could even remotely have supplied Gustav with the biotoxin. Nothing.'

'Do we yet know what the gas is?

Isobel shook her head. 'From the description of the deaths of Al-Adil and the liner's master we surmise that sarin is one constituent. But there is something else which we are unable to identify.'

'Okay. Back to the big question. Who? North Korea?'

'It doesn't make any sense. They want back into the international fold. And they have no love of Islam. No money in the world would be sufficient compensation if the Americans find out they were involved.'

Macnair sat back and put his hands behind his head. He was groggy from lack of sleep. He rested his eyes for a second and then snapped wide awake, sitting bolt upright. 'What if he manufactured the stuff *himself*? Start re-examining all Gustav's companies. Holdings within holdings. Doesn't he own a chemical manufacturer or something?'

Reaching for the file on his desk he flicked it open, running his finger down a list of names. 'Here. A chemical company. And here. An ecological company. What the hell does an ecological company do?'

Isobel shrugged. 'God knows. May I?' She took the file and checked what was written against the names. 'He sold them . . . oh, a year ago.'

'Did he indeed? Or did he just go underground with them? Check it out as soon as you can, please. And try and find out what it was the companies produced.'

'Yes, sir.' Isobel stood up, the coffee forgotten. 'Any news on Hiram?'

'He's going to be okay. One bullet went through his thigh and a second caused a flesh wound in the upper arm. Lost a lot of blood. Looked worse than it was. The hospital said, and I quote, "We'll discharge him in a few hours to protect our nurses".'

Isobel smiled. 'That sounds like Hiram.'

'What about the ship?'

'It's ploughing a furrow in a piece of the Med about twenty miles south of Sicily.'

'At speed?'

'Fifteen knots or so.'

'Figures. Hunter protecting Gustav. I just hope it's enough to keep him safe as well, till we get him some back-up. Check out those companies.' Where on earth could Gustav have got that gas from? And which was worse? A rogue state selling the stuff to him or Gustav making it? It was really no contest. If Gustav had control over its manufacture and hence had unlimited access, then the threat he posed was mind-numbing.

19

'Point that gun the other way or I'll ram it up your . . .' Hunter didn't get any further as the hammer of the gun was cocked back with a loud click.

'You were saying?' The man was mid-thirties, blonde, muscle-bound and by his standards, tough. His hooked nose had obviously been broken at least once. He spoke English with an accent that sounded vaguely Scandinavian.

Hunter did the unexpected. He raised his arms, put his hands behind his head and said, 'You've got me.'

The man obviously felt in control. He stood up from behind his desk and walked around, a grin on his face. He knew who Hunter was and what Hunter had done but liked the feeling of control he was experiencing with a gun in his fist. He wondered how Hunter would react to a hard poke in the belly with the barrel. His curiosity made him step too close.

Hunter brought his hand down hard, jamming his thumb between the gun's hammer and the breech. Clasping his hand around the man's fist, Hunter twisted the gun through 180 degrees so that it was pointing at the man's stomach. The trigger guard had torn the skin off the man's finger and blood dripped steadily onto the deck.

Hunter smiled. 'If I take my hand away the hammer will strike the cartridge. It may or may not be sufficient to set it off. What do you think?'

The man stood stock still, sweat appearing on his brow while Hunter continued to smile at him.

'What I suggest,' Hunter spoke conversationally, 'is that you gently let go the gun and give it to me. This takes a Magnum point four-four cartridge and is one of the most formidable close-quarter guns in the world.'

The man let go. Without breaking eye contact, Hunter felt the cylinder latch on the left side of the frame and pulled it to the rear. Swinging out the cylinder he pushed the ejector rod and dropped the bullets into the palm of his hand. He swung the cylinder shut and dropped the weapon onto the desk. As it was a trigger retracted hammer block, there was no safety catch.

'You're bleeding all over the deck.' Hunter's voice was still as measured. 'I suggest you clean it up.'

The man nodded nervously. He still didn't know how it had happened. One second he had the English bastard at the end of his gun and the next he was looking down its barrel. Putting his skinned finger into his mouth he took out a spotlessly clean handkerchief and knelt to wipe up the few drops of blood. He looked up nervously at Hunter, expecting a kick in the teeth at any time. Instead all he got was a smile.

'Good,' said Hunter. 'We're on the same side. Please don't point any more guns at me, the next time I may not be so under-standing.'

'Nobody is allowed in here without Mr Gustav's express permission,' the man with the headphones said. He licked his dry lips. He had witnessed the move but couldn't believe it either.

'I suggest,' said Hunter, 'you add my name to the list. Please make sure your reliefs know it. Otherwise I won't be so gentle. You're the operator and you, I take it, are the guard.'

By now the guard had regained his seat behind his desk, feeling safer with a barrier between him and Hunter. He looked longingly at the stainless steel revolver and wished he could start again. Only this time he'd shoot the swine and ask questions after.

'The Colt is a good choice,' said Hunter. 'It's ideal for close work. Real stopping power. But if you are going to point it at somebody make damn sure you are able and willing to use it.'

The guard nodded. Hunter handed him back the bullets. 'Load

it. It's useless without them.' Turning to the operator, Hunter said, 'I want to know about our communications set-up. I assume they're world-wide and can be encrypted?'

Hunter spent the next ten minutes with the operator, making it clear that he knew what he was talking about, building up a rapport with the man. Once the operator's nerves had eased, they joked about being able to send Morse even in this day and age. Now almost anybody who understood computers could use the equipment in the room. It required only a bit of time with the instruction manual to learn what to do.

Even so, Hunter ensured he received a quick lesson on one or two pieces of gear.

'Do you carry an emergency transponder?' Hunter asked.

'Sure. It's operated by this button, and fires out the side of the hull. If we're sinking it'll stay attached down to a few thousand metres. The emergency signal covers all the usual frequencies from UHF to VLF so it reaches near and far.'

'Good. Let's hope we never need to use it.'

'Amen to that, sir.'

Good, thought Hunter. He had the man's respect; the 'sir' proved it. So he would have his obedience. Hopefully.

He had done what he had come to do, established a right to be in the comms centre. Now it was time to leave before any awkward questions were asked. Or he was found there by Gustav or Duval and had his right of entry immediately rescinded.

'Good night to you both.'

Both men returned the salutation as Hunter went back into the corridor. He spent the next twenty minutes roaming the vessel, ostensibly checking the disposition of guards around the ship and who was on watch. He quickly sized up the operation. There was no engineer. The officer of the watch monitored the engines from the bridge. Any problems and alarms rang on the bridge, in the engineer's cabin and in the main mess. Engines could be shut down using controls on the starboard side of the bridge. Fire sprinklers worked automatically, water or inert gas, depending on the location of the conflagration. The *Stockholm* was fully automated and needed only a very small crew to run effectively. In two watches, the ship had many spare hands to act as guards. In fact there were ten of them, scattered throughout the top decks.

Hunter had a word with each man. His message was always the same. 'They'll come from the sea. Fast inflatables. Very vulnerable. They won't have a chance. Trust me.'

By the time he had finished his pep talks the guards were jumpy, just as he had intended. Peering at the sea, imagining what wasn't there, they were tense and on edge. TIFAT wouldn't come from the sea, when they *did* come. Or so Hunter hoped.

There was nothing more he could do for an hour or two. It was time to get his head down.

At 04.30 he was up again and prowling the ship. All was quiet and nobody saw him passing. The cinema was empty so he supposed Gustav had gone to bed. A quick search convinced him that the information he was looking for was not to be found. There was only one thing for it – a detour to the engine room.

The corridor outside Gustav's quarters was brightly lit. Hunter used a screwdriver to unscrew the light fixing and gingerly took out the bulb. It was hot. A quick shake and he heard the filament break. He replaced the bulb and the fixing, leaving that part of the corridor in shadow. Gently he tried the door handle. He moved it so slowly it took a full minute to twist all the way back. Using his other hand he eased the door open, millimetre by millimetre. The room was dark but he still took his time. It was minutes before the door was wide enough for him to slip through. Equally gently he closed it behind him. Standing for a few moments to let his eyes become accustomed to the deeper gloom, he gradually began to make out the hard edges of the furniture.

The opposite side of the cabin had a door to Gustav's sleeping quarters. The room Hunter was in was luxuriously furnished with a huge desk in one corner. Using a masked torch, lifted from the engine room, Hunter rapidly went through the drawers but found nothing of use. He found a lap-top computer and was about to switch it on when he had second thoughts. If it was properly secure then as soon as Gustav switched it on himself he would know somebody had tried to get into the machine. And it wouldn't take a genius to guess who that somebody was.

Behind a painting he found a locked safe. It had a combination lock and key. He had no skills to open it so he left it alone. Twenty minutes later he was back in his room, lying on his bed, hands behind his head, deep in thought. There had to be another way.

He slept until 05.50. After a shower and shave he dressed, armed himself with a cup of coffee and went up to the bridge. There were three seamen officers who were qualified to keep watch, including the Captain. As he knew, the First Officer was on watch.

'My name is Hunter,' he introduced himself.

The man nodded warily. He wore two gold stripes on his shoulders. Hunter guessed he was mid-twenties, European but not British. He was stocky, black haired, fit looking. Sitting in the captain's chair, he watched Hunter with a mixture of trepidation and interest. 'My name is Jacob Hernstein.'

'Jacob, I'm a qualified watchkeeper. If you'd like to take a break I'll relieve you for an hour. The cook's up and making breakfast.'

Shaking his head, the officer said, 'I think not. The *Kapitän* would have me hanged.'

Hunter wasn't surprised but he'd thought he'd try. 'Okay. I'll be in the chartroom. I need to work out where we're going and discuss our options with Mr Gustav.' The words were meaningless but the officer, used to obeying, merely accepted them at face value.

The chartroom was accessed via a door at the back of the bridge. It contained a full portfolio of charts covering the world, a rack of used ship's logs and a bookcase of maritime publications. It also had a navigation computer that Hunter was very familiar with. It only took seconds to instruct the machine to print out every port of call the ship had made during the previous two years and to give the date and duration of each stay. The laser printer spewed out the information and Hunter quickly pocketed the A4 sheets. Lifting an atlas from the rack he tucked it under his arm before returning to the bridge.

A magnificent dawn was breaking and he stood for a few seconds next to Hernstein, awed by the sight. He could see from the other man's face that he too was enthralled.

'There's nothing like it, is there?' said Hunter.

'Mmm?' Hernstein glanced at Hunter before returning his attention to the sunrise.

'This time of morning, at sea, watching another day breaking. People who have never been to sea have no idea how truly beautiful it is.'

The officer nodded his head. 'I agree, it is magnificent.'

'I'm going below to get another coffee and look through this atlas before speaking to Mr Gustav.' Hunter left with a smile. It wasn't much but he had connected with Hernstein. Begun to build a little rapport based on a mutual passion for the sea. It could make the man hesitate at the wrong moment. *Would it be enough?*

Back in his cabin, Hunter quickly scanned the printed lists. Most of the names were of major ports around Europe. There was one he didn't recognise. Pozzallo. It took only seconds to find in the atlas. The southern end of Sicily. One visit. Three weeks before the attack on the liner. Interesting, thought Hunter, but was it the answer he was looking for?

Isobel found Macnair in the briefing room with many of the teams just back from their operations across Europe. They were all agreed on what had gone right and, more importantly, what had gone wrong. Across the continent TIFAT operatives had been fighting desperately to contain the damage Gustav's attacks could have wrought. The deaths of four of their number cast a pall but they had been lucky. Many more could so easily have died.

Seeing Isobel enter the room and gesturing, Macnair excused himself and left the debriefing to Jim Carter.

'Fresh coffee, this time,' the General greeted her.

In his office he put on the coffee maker. 'Hiram will be back in a few hours. Burg is picking him up at Edinburgh airport.'

'Good. Thanks.' She took the proffered mug. It was black,

strong and sugarless, just as she liked it. 'We tracked down those companies you were interested in. They were both closed down about a year ago after Gustav ostensibly sold them. One was definitely involved in some sort of genetic engineering but exactly what we don't know.'

'What about previous employees?'

'Ah!' Isobel smiled. 'We thought of that. So we looked up the tax records of the companies. They were both UK based which made it marginally easier. We identified twenty-five former employees from the more likely of the two companies – Genotech Laboratories.'

Macnair, his own coffee in hand, sat behind his desk and waited patiently for Isobel to continue.

'What we found is very interesting. And statistically impossible on two accounts. After the company closed, seventeen employees left the UK. But,' Isobel paused significantly, 'the remaining eight employees, within a period of less than six weeks, were all dead.'

'What!' Macnair jerked upright, spilling coffee onto the floor. He ignored the rapidly expanding stain and asked, 'Are you sure?'

'Positive. One died in a house fire, four perished in separate car crashes where no other vehicle was involved, two were mugged and one was shot. The muggings and shooting are still open files with the police forces involved. It can't be a coincidence. Somebody had those people killed.'

'Gustav.' The general screwed up his face, concentrating hard. 'What jobs did they do?'

'Drivers, lab-technicians, a secretary . . . No major players. They ranged in ages from late twenties to early fifties. There's nothing connecting them apart from their work with Genotech. The other peculiar fact which cannot be coincidence is that none of the men were married. They don't appear to have any families or close relatives.'

'Any idea where they went?'

Isobel smiled. 'An inspired piece of work by Leo. He compiled a list of those who had emigrated and went into every social-security computer in Europe to see if they were to be found.'

'And?'

'They work for a new company in Italy. Sicily, to be precise. We are trying to trace ownership right now but I'll bet a pound to a penny it'll be Gustav's. He has a house there on the north side of the island.'

'I won't take your bet. Do we know where in Sicily?'

'A little place called Íspica. It's seven or eight kilometres from the southern most tip of the island.'

Macnair was busy with his computer, calling up Sicily, typing in the name of the place. He pointed at the screen. 'There it is. Just to the north of a small port called Pozzallo. Get the satellites on it, will you?'

'I've issued instructions already.'

Hunter needed to get the information on Pozzallo to TIFAT HQ. The bridge's state-of-the-art radio system would suffice. But how to gain access without alerting the officer of the watch? The goons in the communications centre meant it was a no-go. But this was absolutely vital information. He wasn't one hundred percent certain, but it might let Isobel look in the right direction. Was it worth the risk of exposure to tell her? Possibly. The trouble was, looking at Sicily on the chart, Gustav could have chosen any of a hundred places to manufacture the deadly nerve gas. Anywhere from Catánia in the east to Caltanissetta in the west. But that made no sense. The ship could have gone into a closer port. He stared down at the chart. No, it would be somewhere local. Ragusta, Módica, Íspica, Rosolini . . . But which one? There was only one thing for it. He would have to find an excuse to get ashore and take a look.

Isobel walked into Macnair's office pushing a wheelchair. 'General, look who I've found.'

Macnair bounded to his feet. 'Hiram, my dear fellow, but it's good to have you back.' The two men shook hands. 'Can I get you anything?'

'No, sir. I'm fine. The wound in my arm is nothing and the bullet went straight through the top of my thigh. It missed the bone, thankfully. And it was a steel tipped bullet so the entry wound and exit wound are the same size. About as big as a dime.'

'You were lucky,' said Macnair. 'By the way, I've spoken to Bragg.'

Walsh's detachment of Delta Force was headquartered at Fort Bragg. 'Thanks, sir.'

'It seems they're going to put you up for a Purple Heart.'

Walsh groaned. 'God, how embarrassing.'

Macnair grinned. 'That's what I told them you'd say. Can't be helped though. Wounded in action and all that. Now,' Macnair became serious, 'are you ready to get back to work?'

'Sir!' Isobel began to protest, 'Hiram needs proper rest. I only brought him in to say hullo.'

'Thanks, Isobel, but I'm okay. I'm ready, sir. I learnt a lot in Rotterdam. The rot in the police force is widespread. They talked only because Gustav hung them out to dry. They lost half their men in the fight and won't support him any longer. Quite the reverse. We ought to be able to take advantage of the fact.'

Macnair nodded. 'Will they testify?'

Walsh grinned. 'You bet your life they will. In exchange for immunity.'

'From prosecution?' Isobel asked, puzzled. 'But they haven't done anything wrong. Not in the legal sense.'

'Isobel's right,' said Macnair. 'The only criminals are the Islamic terrorists. And Gustav for financing them. But techni-cally the police forces and armed services who agree with Gustav are not guilty of any crime.'

Walsh nodded. 'All along they've been counting on the right-wing coming to power in Europe. If that happens then they would definitely be safe. But if we stop Gustav then who's to say laws won't be changed to punish those same men for supporting the idea of a whites-only Europe? They don't trust the politicians. And who can blame them? It's because of Europe's politicians you're in this mess.'

Macnair nodded gloomily. What the Delta Colonel was saying not only made sense but was, without doubt, the case. Damn all politicians! Europe was a complete quagmire with its immigration policy. No wonder there was a backlash.

'We've contained Gustav for now,' said Macnair. 'The blood-bath he'd envisaged hasn't happened. I don't know how many more fundamentalists he has on his pay-roll but he must be hurting by now. Especially in light of the number that have been killed or arrested.'

'Which means he might try to do something desperate,' said Isobel.

'Precisely,' agreed Macnair. 'Like let loose with more WMDs. Any news about the factory on Sicily?'

Isobel shook her head. 'Nothing. I've learnt that they closed down the original business because of the level of animal rights protesters the company was attracting. Italy doesn't have the same problem. Besides which, it seems the local Mafia has given the place its blessing and support. A lot of money has gone into the area, thanks to the company. We don't know who the ultimate owner is but my money is still on Gustav. We've no proof of the WMD manufacture. As far as the public is concerned they do genetic experiments, looking for cures to certain ailments. Stem cell work and all that. It's highly controversial but with huge potential.'

'Is it possible that's what the place is really being used for and we're making complete asses of ourselves?' Walsh asked the question the other two had also been considering.

'Anything's possible,' replied Macnair. Glancing at his watch he added, 'Tea is being served in the wardroom. Let's go across and I'll bring you up to date on a few facts. The bottom line is, we can't be certain. And we can't go ahead without proof.'

Finally, Hunter had an ideal excuse to go ashore in Sicily and he wasted no time in speaking to Duval about it. If he could convince the secretary then Gustav would be all the easier to persuade. He found the man in the upper salon, standing at a window, staring out to sea.

'I've been giving more thought to a possible attack while we're at sea,' said Hunter without preamble.

Duval appeared to snap out of a trance. 'What did you say?' he frowned.

'I think it is all too possible for special forces to attack the ship using fast raiders. Now, we'd give a good account of ourselves but it would be a good idea to get some real fire-power. Heat seeking missiles and heavy machine-guns would be useful.'

'And what do you suggest?' There was no hiding the sarcasm in Duval's voice, 'That we call in at our local supermarket and buy some?'

'No. I suggest we go ashore in Sicily and ask your friends in the Mafia. They can get us what we need.'

Duval looked dubiously at Hunter for a few seconds, then said, 'We're already headed for Sicily. I'll see what I can do. Though I doubt we'll have the time to meet them.'

Hunter frowned. 'When was it decided that we were going to Sicily and why wasn't I informed?'

'Mr Gustav doesn't consult his bodyguard about his movements. He issues instructions. We carry them out. He only made the decision a few minutes ago. I'd stay out of his way for now, if I were you. He's absolutely furious about the reports we've received from Europe. The attacks we orchestrated have, to a large degree, been foiled by your ex-colleagues. Mr Hunter, we have lost many of our,' here Duval managed to crack a smile, 'shall we say, friends? The useless swine. Many of them have been killed and others arrested. Thanks to Mr Gustav's foresight, the cells operate in isolation; none of the attacks can be traced back to us. However, insufficient damage has been done to sway public opinion to the extent we hoped. So we have to go to Sicily.'

'What's on Sicily?'

'That, Mr Hunter, is not for you to know. Meet me on the bridge in half an hour. I need to speak to Mr Gustav.'

Recognising a dismissal when he heard one, and not prepared to make an issue of it just then, Hunter left the room. He went quickly along to the bridge where he found the Captain sitting in his chair. A glance at the chart told him all he wanted to know. The pencilled course headed straight to Pozzallo.

'Can we get alongside?'

Novak looked at Hunter with irritation. 'Yes.'

'It would be safer if we stayed offshore, steaming.'

Novak looked at Hunter for a second or two before replying. 'Believe me, Mr Hunter, we will be perfectly safe alongside. If anyone came within a hundred metres of the ship they wouldn't live longer than a minute or two.'

'How can you be so certain?'

'Trust me, I know.' The Captain turned his head to look back out to sea, binoculars in hand, scanning ahead of the ship.

Another glance at the chart showed that they would be near Pozzallo in about ninety minutes, alongside shortly after that. If he was right, then Hunter guessed that they were going to pick up more nerve gas. Gustav had to be stopped, no matter what.

Hunter offered to take the watch, but was curtly refused. Nevertheless, he stayed on the bridge until Duval arrived.

'Care to tell me what's going on?'

'We are going into Pozzallo. There we will be met by some friends, who will escort us to our destination. We will be away from the ship for less than an hour. When we return we will put to sea immediately. Captain, please arrange to take on fresh provisions. Mr Hunter, you will escort us. Please select three other men to accompany us.'

'And my recommendation that we need heavier weapons? Missiles?'

'Mr Gustav feels it won't be necessary. That we have all we need.'

Hunter was about to argue then thought better of it. What the hell. He'd only suggested it as an excuse to get ashore on Sicily. And here he was, being handed the perfect opportunity.

'I'd say,' said Leo, looking at the picture, 'that the ship is heading for Sicily. More accurately, Pozzallo.'

Isobel stood at her assistant's shoulder and watched the screen. 'It looks like it. And that's right next to Íspica where we think Gustav's factory is located. Of course, he could just as easily be going to any one of a dozen or more ports once the ship has neared land.'

'It's not likely,' replied Leo. 'Otherwise they'd go straight there. What's that?' He pointed at the screen. 'There's another and another.'

'Looks like small craft to me,' said Isobel. 'And they're heading fast towards the ship. See if you can get better pictures.'

Leo's fingers flew across the keyboard, hammering it, issuing instructions to the satellite orbiting hundreds of miles above the Mediterranean Sea. Slowly the picture zoomed in on the smaller targets about ten miles ahead of the ship. The small boats were closing fast.

'They're carrying armed men. Looks like soldiers. They're either reinforcements for Gustav or they intend to attack him.'

'There's nothing we can do about the former,' Isobel said. 'But if they are on the attack, where did they come from?'

Leo plotted a hypothetical course backwards. All three tracks converged on a civilian ship steaming south and currently just off the south-eastern corner of Sicily.

'Doesn't tell us anything. They could be anybody.' Isobel frowned at the screen.

Hunter spotted them on the radar first. Grabbing binoculars he scanned the sea. Rigid raiders and coming in fast. Where the hell had they come from? And who were they? One thing was certain. They weren't TIFAT. The primary objective had not yet been achieved. It was vital they learn where the WMDs were sourced. Killing Gustav might not be enough to stop his organisation; not if they retained access to Weapons of Mass Destruction.

Nobody else had noticed what was happening until Hunter grabbed the microphone to the ship's tannoy system. 'Do you hear there? Stand-by to repel boarders. We are under attack by three fast boats coming in from ahead. All off-watch men muster on the upperdeck. Do not, I repeat, do not show yourselves until the boats are close in.'

'What the hell!' *Kapitän zur See* Novak looked at Hunter in shock.

Duval, too, stood frozen to the spot, unable to move.

'Take a look,' said Hunter. 'You can see them without glasses now.'

Three black spots were approaching on the horizon, taking shape, hardening in the late afternoon sun. Each boat held half a dozen men. They were well armed and opening out in a pincer movement.

'Are they guests of yours?' Hunter asked Duval.

'No, of course not.'

'I don't care who they are. They have to be stopped,' said Gustav appearing on the bridge. 'Mr Hunter, annihilate them!'

20

'Hold your fire until I tell you,' Hunter shouted. 'Stay down and out of sight. When I give the word open up with everything you've got. Remember your weapons are short range and don't waste any rounds. Shoot at the engines. Try not to kill anybody.' Now, he thought, I'd better try and save a few lives.

His Steyr AUG Para was three times as long as the weapons carried by the crew and far more accurate. He slung the gun across his front and went out onto the starboard bridge wing. One boat was at about green four-five, one right on the bows and a third at red four-five. The shot he was attempting was extraordinary difficult because of the rate of change of the target's relative position. A glance through his binoculars confirmed one motor. A big one.

Settling his elbows on the top of the safety rail he squinted along the barrel. He had set the sight for 200 metres. A second later the bow of the boat came into his sight, then the engine, and he fired. The gun was on single shot. He missed. He readjusted his aim and waited for the boat to appear in his sight again. It was now at 150 metres. Bow – motor – fire. The bullet smashed into the engine and it stopped almost instantly. The men in the boat opened fire with a withering blast. Bullets struck against the sides of the ship and shattered glass on the bridge.

'Hard aport and increase to full ahead,' Hunter yelled.

The Captain did as ordered and the ship began to pick up speed. By now one of the boats was within 100 metres and thirty degrees on the starboard bow, turning to keep track. Because of its speed and the way it was bouncing across the water, its occupants couldn't open fire. The men in the inflatable Hunter had stopped were still shooting but now they were being hampered by the second rigid raider edging into their sights. Their fire was tailing off.

Hunter fired three times in succession and saw the top of the second boat's engine blown away. The boat surged to a halt, giving its occupants a more stable platform and they opened fire. The *Stockholm* was still turning, its speed increasing, and she was now stern on so that the bullets struck harmlessly at the hull.

Looking at the wake, Hunter guessed they were approaching 25 knots or more. The third boat was almost alongside, its occupants throwing grappling hooks upwards at the starboard rails. The ship's crew didn't wait for orders. They leant out and opened fire from close range. It was a turkey shoot. The men in the boat didn't stand a chance. Hunter shot out the third engine and the boat floundered but not before many of the eight men on board were wounded or killed.

'Stop firing! Stop firing!' Hunter yelled. Though some of the crew did as ordered others continued shooting until the boat was out of range.

One man was still taking pot shots when Hunter stalked up to him. He grabbed the gun, tore it from his hands and swiped him across the side of the head with it. 'When I say stop, I mean stop,' he snarled. 'You bloody fool! We don't want to make enemies of special forces or whoever the hell they are. They have long memories and a longer reach. They'll hunt us down one by one to get revenge for what you stupid swine just did. This is a short term situation. Once Mr Gustav's people come to power we will have to work with these men. We don't want them to resist us any more than necessary.' He gave up. He could see from the man's obdurate look that his message wasn't getting home. Instead he stalked back to the bridge to have it out with Gustav.

By now the ship had turned again, giving the stopped raiders a wide berth, before continuing its journey towards Sicily. On the bridge he found Gustav, looking deadly serious. Novak was trying hard not to smile.

'Of all the stupid . . .' Hunter began but Gustav raised a hand to stop him.

'I wish an explanation, Mr Hunter. Why did you not just kill those men?'

Hunter understood the Captain's smirk and had difficulty controlling his temper. 'You really are the biggest bunch of moronic thugs and dickheads that walk,' Hunter began.

'How dare you speak to me like that,' Gustav began but Hunter interrupted him by prodding his finger into the other man's chest.

'I dare, *Mr* Gustav, because your thugs have just endangered all our lives. I couldn't care less about their lives. *Your* life I'm paid to care about and *my* life I care about very much. We don't know who those men are. Suppose they are CIA or MI6? Or Special Forces from one of a dozen countries? They harbour grudges. They'll come after you no matter what. And it won't be a big splashy death. It'll be quiet and subtle and the head-lines in your own papers will be that you died of a heart attack or an accident. And why? Because you killed their mates. Inter-service rivalry is one thing, support for your oppo is another. Word has got out that you're behind the troubles and they know where you are.'

Gustav stared at Hunter, weighing his words. 'You may be right, Mr Hunter. I appear to have underestimated you again.'

'Well make it the last time! Now, tell your crew and this idiot of a Captain that from now on they do what I tell them. That way you may just live long enough to enjoy the fruits of your labours.'

Gustav nodded. 'Duval. Issue the orders.'

From the expression on Duval's face, Hunter didn't think he'd have any more trouble with the American.

'Now, will you kindly tell me what's going on?' Hunter spoke in a reasonable voice. 'So that I can plan what we do?'

'I have to visit one of my companies on Sicily. It is near to where we are berthing.'

'Where?'

'That doesn't matter,' Gustav shot back with a flash of his former haughtiness. 'Suffice to say that I will not be there for long.'

'Total time?'

'No more than an hour.'

'Make it less. Captain, I want to see a chart of the harbour. You go alongside and drop us off but be ready to leave fast. Those troops came from somewhere and that could be anything from a tramp steamer to a nuclear submarine. Or even an aircraft carrier.'

'An aircraft carrier?' Gustav queried.

'Yes. Part of the American Sixth Fleet, which operates almost continuously in this area, keeping an eye on the Middle East. Those men we just stopped could even now be whistling up rein-forcements. And I don't mean another raiding party but aircraft that'll blow us to kingdom come.'

The other three men looked nervously out of the window as if expecting an attack at any second.

'You won't see them,' said Hunter, 'until the rockets start landing. Captain, our only chance is full speed for Sicily. Even the Americans won't open fire on an unarmed ship in a port belonging to one of its allies.'

Kapitän zur See Novak pushed open the throttles of all four diesels as far as he could, trying for every fraction of a knot of speed. What Hunter had just said made eminent sense.

Macnair, alerted by Isobel to the attack, was already on the tele-phone demanding explanations. He was getting nowhere. The Secretary-General was apologetic but he had no more intelli-gence than TIFAT. Of course, he agreed with Macnair, until the source of the nerve gas was found Gustav had to remain unharmed. He also agreed to try and find out what had happened.

Isobel rushed back into his office, uncharacteristically without knocking. Macnair had just replaced the receiver and greeted her with a raised eyebrow.

'It was a combined Op, General, CIA and the French.'

'How do you know?'

'We intercepted some signal traffic. They're spitting blood.

292

Five of their men have been killed and two seriously wounded. They want Gustav dead.'

'The fools! Okay, Isobel, leave it to me. I've more calls to make.'

The CIA at Langley wouldn't or couldn't put him through to the Director and so he had to go via the Pentagon. He finally managed to track down General Colin Stafford.

'Macnair? What can I do for you?'

Hearing the formal tone in the senior officer's voice Macnair modified what he had wished to say. 'Sir, you heard about the attack on Gustav's ship?'

'Yes. I have just received a request to blow the bastard out of the water. We're considering sending in a couple of F14s.'

Macnair tightened his grip on the receiver as though he was trying to crush it. 'Sir, you can't do that.'

'Don't tell me what I can and cannot do, General.'

'Listen to me, Colin,' Macnair changed tack. 'We have to find out from where Gustav got the nerve gas and to destroy the source at all costs.'

'I hear you, Malcolm,' Stafford said more reasonably, 'but the CIA and the French are screaming blue murder.'

'They shouldn't have gone in. This is our job. TIFAT's. Not theirs.'

'Well, as they see it you aren't doing very much. And they saw an opportunity to stop Gustav.'

'What will that achieve?' Macnair's tone was icy. 'This isn't about one man any longer. He may have funded the Islamic fundamentalists initially but now half of Europe is backing him. Tens, maybe hundreds of millions of ordinary people think he's right. Many are political leaders. The bandwagon is rolling so hard and fast it's almost unstoppable. If Gustav dies now what will we say? That the French and Americans killed him? That'll go down well with his supporters. Or how about more disinformation and we blame the Muslims? Or Europe's right wing? Whichever way you play it we'll lose and the tidal wave of change that Gustav has created will be unstoppable. What's more the WMDs would still be in their hands.'

293

'So what is it you're suggesting?'

'His control of the print and TV media has been almost total. In effect, we're fighting a propaganda war. We need absolute proof that Gustav has created WMDs for use in Europe. We have to discredit him and his followers with an overwhelming blitz in newspapers, on radio and television. When the silent majority learn how they've been duped and to what length Gustav and his cohorts were prepared to go, they'll turn away in revulsion. But we need time to prepare. And we need Gustav alive for a while longer yet.'

Stafford was silent for a few seconds, pondering Macnair's words. 'I hope,' he said finally, 'you know what you're doing.'

'So do I, Colin. So do I. Now please, call off the dogs.'

The sun was setting as the *SS Stockholm* entered the small port. There was plenty of water under her keel and sufficient room for her to dock – just. Normally Pozzallo would have been full of fishing boats and a few private yachts but, unknown to Hunter, the local Mafia had arranged for the harbour to be emptied.

Standing on the port side, watching the land slip close by, Hunter could appreciate the Captain's delicate handling of the ship. When the first heaving line was thrown, the ship's bow and stern thrusters were already pushing the hull towards the wall. Men with guns helped to tie up the ship alongside.

Three large, black saloon cars with tinted windows waited on the quay. There were no sightseers, nobody out strolling or sitting in either of the two small cafés. He looked around the port. There was just enough room to turn the large vessel.

Entering the bridge, Hunter said, 'Captain, I take it that normally you'd make a sternboard and turn once you were in the open sea?'

'*Ja*. That is correct.'

'Can you turn here? That way we can save a few minutes.'

The Captain pondered the question before nodding. 'If we use ropes to warp the ship around. With the thrusters it should be possible.'

'Good. Then please do so while we are away.'

Minutes later Hunter, Gustav and Duval were in one of the cars, three of the crew followed behind. In the lead car four armed Mafiosi led the way. The driver of Hunter's car was an ill-smelling oaf who reeked of stale wine and cigarette smoke. His grin showed broken and discoloured teeth. Nothing was said as the cars accelerated away from the tiny village.

At the edge of the buildings the road branched right along the coast and left inland. They veered left towards the mountains. Ten minutes later they were approaching a main road that circumnavigated Sicily. On the other side of the road was the small town of Íspica. The cars swept right towards Rosolini and, a kilometre along the highway, turned off the road. They halted in front of a locked gate with a guardroom to one side. The driver in the first car spoke to the armed guard and the gate opened electronically. The perimeter fence was brightly lit with arc-lamps placed every fifty metres. Running along the top of the fence and leaning outwards were strands of wickedly sharp-looking barbed wire. A patrol of two armed guards with large, brutish dogs walked briskly along the fence. It was, Hunter concluded, well protected.

'What about staff security?' Hunter asked. 'How do they get in and out?'

If he noticed the exchange of glances between Gustav and Duval he showed no sign.

Gustav shrugged. 'There is no harm in you knowing. The staff live on the premises, in an underground complex. It is extremely well equipped.'

Hunter was surprised. 'And they put up with that? What about recreation?'

Gustav smiled with satisfaction. 'These people are extremely well paid. The job lasts a year. We bus in, what shall we call it, entertainment? Yes, just the word. Every Saturday.'

'What about the female staff?'

'They're all men,' came the blunt reply.

There had been no sign announcing the company and there was no name on the building's façade. When he alighted from the car Hunter could see that it was a brand new, single story edifice, about a hundred metres wide. What was most disconcerting from his point of view was that there were no windows. Even the door was solid.

'Mr Gustav and I will go in alone,' said Duval.

As Hunter made a move to follow them, Gustav put a hand on his arm. 'You will stay here too, Mr Hunter,'said Gustav. 'I will be perfectly safe inside. And we will be less than ten minutes.'

Knowing when not to argue, Hunter nodded. 'Spread out and keep your eyes open,' he told the other bodyguards. 'If the men who attacked us knew we were on the ship then they might be tracking us and know about this place.' He turned back to Gustav. 'Please hurry.'

His words galvanised Gustav and he hurried towards the door, casting nervous looks around him. Duval followed, equally perturbed. The fact was, Hunter *was* concerned. Whoever had attacked the ship could come after them again. If so, a firefight would be most unwelcome, he thought, with complete understatement.

Gustav and Duval were back within five minutes. Duval carried a holdall which appeared full though not heavy.

'Open the trunk,' Hunter ordered the driver and stood at the back of the car. He took the bag from Duval and placed it inside the car. Quickly running his hand over the simulated leather he felt three round shapes each about the size of a football. His blood ran cold. Any lingering doubts disappeared.

'Let's go, let's go,' Hunter chivvied them as they piled in and took off with a squeal of tyres.

The return journey to the ship was uneventful and less than thirty minutes after leaving Pozzallo they were back in the port. The ship had been turned and was pointing towards the open sea. Only a bow line and stern line held her alongside.

Hunter had taken a step towards the gangway when a gun was shoved into his side. He stopped in bewilderment. 'What the hell . . . ?'

Gustav turned to him with a smile. 'I am sorry, Mr Hunter, but I'm forced to terminate your employment. Forthwith and with immediate effect. You won't be coming with us.'

'But . . .'

The blow was hard and he didn't see it coming. As he sank to his knees he was engulfed by blackness.

'Take him away,' said Gustav. 'I want to learn everything he knows. About me, our organisation and about TIFAT.'

Hunter came to slowly. His head hurt like hell and when he tried to move shooting pains flashed from his skull down his shoulders and arms. Nausea washed over him and he fought hard to keep it down. He lay still, collecting his thoughts and his strength. What was niggling at him? That was it . . . why was he still alive? Information! Gustav needed to know what he carried in his head.

Gustav must have planned it all along. The nerve gas! Christ, the man was a maniac.

Slowly Hunter became aware of his surroundings. He knew that a blow to the head was a lot more dangerous than shown in film stunts. You didn't just get up and walk away, fully functional. Permanent brain damage could be sustained which could result in epilepsy, tunnel vision or a host of other problems. Even paralysis. He realised that he was lying on his back, on something soft. There was a smell of earth and fish. An odd combination. Perhaps the blow had affected his olfactory nerves? He was on some sort of rough cloth. His fingers moved, gripping the fabric. His brain suggested he was on a pile of sacks and he didn't question it.

Tentatively he moved his legs and his arms. He touched the side of his head. It felt sticky. With a great effort and a stifled moan he sat up. He placed his head between his hands and threw up all over his feet. They appeared to have taken his shoes. He sat still and tried to open his eyes. He couldn't and panic welled up in him, threatening to engulf him, but he fought it down. Blood, he thought. Slowly he collected saliva in his mouth and spat into his hand. He wiped his right eye and the lid flickered open. He pulled the left lids apart and blinked owlishly around him.

It was dark. Not pitch black but it was obviously night time.

He was in a shed of some description. Images and thoughts tumbled through his mind. Yes, he was on a pile of sacks. Over in a corner there appeared to be a pile of lobster pots. One window cast pale, white light from a full moon. There was utter silence and then a cat meowed faintly.

Standing up with difficulty, Hunter felt the room spin and collapsed back onto the sacks. He felt sick again but controlled the urge to vomit. His mouth tasted like the bottom of a bird cage. This time when he stood he stayed on his feet. He shuffled across the packed earth floor.

The outline of a door was clearly discernible. He heard running water and followed the sound. The hut was large, maybe ten metres by seven or eight. About three metres high. The roof was pitched and what looked like tanks lined one wall. The sound of water was coming from one end of the tanks. When he got to them, his eyes now accustomed to the gloom, Hunter saw they were open topped and full of water. He reached in and wet his hand. It was cool. He tasted it. Salty! Gingerly he leaned forward and washed his face and then his head. The side of his head stung like hell. Taking a deep breath he ducked his face into the water. The cold reduced the pain and cleared his mind. He saw something moving in the tank and in alarm lifted his face. Tentatively he reached in and, with his sleeve rolled back and the water up to his elbow, felt the hard body of a lobster. He lifted it out and saw that its claws were tied shut. Dropping it back into the water he continued searching.

By the door he found a tap and turned it on, slowly, careful not to make too much noise. He washed out his mouth and drank copious amounts of fresh water. He was beginning to feel like the living again. The side of his head had a bump the size of a small egg. When he touched around it, it felt painful but hard. Thank God. If it had been even the slightest bit soft he knew he would have been in serious trouble. Though he was in agony, he didn't think his skull was cracked.

His next priority was to get out of there. He went to the window and stared out but could see nothing. Realising the panes of glass were grimy with dust, he rubbed a spot clean. He had assumed he was near the coast and sure enough, in the distance, he could see the sea, shifting restlessly in the moonlight. It was maybe a kilometre away. Perhaps two.

There didn't appear to be any guards outside. The building was in a clearing, surrounded by trees. Not high but widespread, bushy. Olive trees, he guessed. He tried the door, opening it very, very slowly. It took an age but eventually the gap was wide enough to put his head through. Cautiously he looked out. Nothing stirred. Nobody yelled and no one shot at him. He stepped outside, straining his ears, listening to the sound of the night, trying to distinguish between the breeze in the leaves and any alien sounds. He heard nothing untoward.

He was surprised there was no guard. Maybe, he thought, they believed they'd hit him so hard he'd stay unconscious.

The ground outside the hut was scrub – stony but predominantly sand. Packed earth showed where vehicles regularly came and went. He walked around the hut. The olive trees were set about fifty metres away. They surrounded the area, except where a track led towards the sea. He went down the track, picking his way carefully, the ground uncomfortable on his shoeless feet. About two hundred metres from the hut he saw a gate, three or four metres high. Then he saw the glinting of moonlight on a high, wire-linked fence. When he got closer he saw it was topped with barbed wire, similar to the wire he had seen around Gustav's factory. *Curiouser and curiouser.*

A clink followed by what could have been a footfall sounded close by. Hunter ducked down behind a small bush. He could smell tobacco smoke. He heard someone walking slowly with a measured step, only a few metres away. Was this the guard?

A man appeared, on the other side of the fence, a rifle slung over his shoulder, a cigarette cupped in his hand. Pausing beside the gate he looked along the track, towards the hut and away from the sea. Then he continued walking. After a few seconds, Hunter heard a second guard. This time he had stopped and the unmistakable sound of a man urinating came to Hunter's ears. Every thirty seconds or so an armed man walked past where he hid. He was sure the sixth man was the same person he had seen the first time. He watched them go round again. There was no doubt. Five guards! But that made no sense! No sense at all!

Why have five men guarding him when two would have been more than enough? Then it hit him. They weren't guarding him. They were guarding the premises. But that was equally nonsensical. Whoever heard of guards on a lobster farm? And armed guards at that.

When the coast was clear for a few seconds he retreated the way he had come. He needed to think. Nobody guarded lobsters. Not on Sicily. Not with guns. But they did guard drugs. He was suddenly alert. That was it! Drugs! What better method of distribution? The heroin could be smuggled across Europe in tanks containing lobsters stuffed with packets of heroin. It was callous and cruel but highly effective.

Back in the hut, he ripped strips off the sacks and wrapped them around his feet like bandages. Tying them around his ankles, he tried walking. They were uncomfortable but adequate.

Hunter searched the place. He needed a diversion. There must have been room for hundreds of lobsters and he quickly ascertained that the tanks were full. What was the situation? Were the lobsters full of heroin and ready to go? Or had the heroin still to arrive? Or was the heroin in-situ and yet to be put into the lobsters?

It had to be the first or third. Otherwise why have such a heavily armed guard? Apart from the tanks and the sacks there was nothing else in the hut. Except the lobster pots! They were piled high in the furthest corner. He went across to examine them. There were dozens. He pulled them away from the wall. At the back he found a packing case with hasp and lock. It was a flimsy looking affair. Even so, as he tore at the lid, Hunter felt shooting pains stabbing through his skull. Reaching in, he dragged out a handful of small, clear plastic bags. He took them across to the window and examined them. They were filled with a white, crystalline powder. It didn't take a genius to work out it was heroin.

Feeling in his pockets he looked for something to use. They had been emptied of everything, including his passport. In the lining of his jacket he felt the crinkling of the paper he had hidden there but it was no use to him in this situation. He searched the hut more thoroughly. What he needed was a fire. In a corner he found a broken blade from what he guessed was a scythe. It was about half a metre long, rusty, blunt.

Taking the steel blade he went outside into the moonlight. He found a flat stone and dragged it along the blade, clearing away the rust. He rubbed hard and soon saw clean metal shine through. Hitting the steel, a small spark flared briefly.

Hunter returned to the hut and made his way to the container of heroin. He dragged it across to the pile of sacks. Tearing off a piece of the cloth, he shredded it finely. He placed the rusty blade amongst the threads and struck it with the rock, using a sweeping motion, down the blade, rapid but not too hard. The sparks flew and fell amongst the hessian threads. He could smell smoke, faint but there. Bending down he blew gently on the sack while still striking the blade. The threads burst into flame and he fed more pieces onto the fire. The sacking smouldered, billowing thick smoke into the air before bursting into flame.

He lifted the heroin and placed it in the middle of the sacks. The wood of the container began to catch fire and he left the hut, satisfied he had done all he could. Taking two of the empty hessian sacks, he hurried along the track towards the gate until he came to the only bend. There he found a thick bush, behind which he scraped a shallow hollow using the broken blade. He worked frantically, expecting a yell from one of the guards at any moment.

He lay down with the hessian sacks covering him and waited. The yell wasn't long in coming. He heard a chain rattling and the gate being thrown open. Running footsteps thundered past him and he looked at the retreating backs, silhouetted against the flames that had spread to the wooden walls. He counted five of them.

Hunter rose to his feet, the sudden movement causing him to stagger, pain shooting across his head. He tried running towards the gate but each step caused a thudding in his temple and he was forced to walk quickly instead. He lengthened his stride, reached the gate and was about to hurry away when he paused. The padlock and key were still hanging from the chain, forgotten in the guards' haste to save the heroin. Pulling the gate to, Hunter locked the padlock through the chain and threw the key into the bushes. It wouldn't stop them but it might slow them down for a few minutes.

There were no houses to be seen and the track meandered down a steep hill towards the coast. He looked around for a few seconds but couldn't see a vehicle. He decided to cut straight down the slope instead of following the track. In the moonlight it was easy to see where he was treading.

The ground was reasonably smooth going, stony and scrubby with small bushes and an occasional olive tree. The sacking around his right foot came loose and he stopped to retie it. While he did so, he looked back. Flames and sparks were shooting into the sky as the roof collapsed. He would have grinned if he didn't hurt so badly.

He was halfway down the hill when he tripped and fell headlong. He lay there for a few seconds, too dazed to get up. The world was spinning, his head throbbing and he just wanted to shut his eyes and go to sleep.

Get a grip, damn you, he told himself. *Get up! Now!* Groaning he pushed himself to his knees and then staggered to his feet. His vision was blurred and he waited until he could see again to walk straight. The dizzy spell passed and his vision cleared. He carried on downhill, crossing the track from time to time, getting nearer to the sea. Suddenly the land flattened just as he walked out from behind some low bushes. To the right lay a two-lane highway. He stopped to take stock. The road was at a cliff edge and he looked down at the endlessly undulating water of the Mediterranean. To the left was darkness while to the right he could see the glow of street lights. They looked to be a long way away but he knew he had no choice. He started in their direction.

After staggering along for a few minutes he became aware of the sound of an engine over-revving. Looking ahead and behind, he couldn't see any sign of a car or other vehicle. Then he looked up the hill. Headlights were cutting a swathe of white along the hill, following the track. The guards were on the move. Hesitating for only a second he made up his mind. He wanted the car.

Hunter hurried back to the track. On either side of the road there was a ditch, to drain away surface water during thunderstorms and flash floods. He found two rocks, both fist sized and scrambled down into the dry ditch. He was only just in time as the car's lights suddenly lit up the scene.

In his haste, the driver was driving erratically. Even so, he had the presence of mind to stop at the road. He was close enough for Hunter to see that he was alone. The guards must have split up to search for him. He looked right, away from Hunter, the car moving slowly. Hunter lobbed the rock in his left hand onto the bonnet of the car. It struck with a loud clang. The driver instinctively hit the brakes hard. The engine stalled, Hunter grabbed the door handle, ripped the door open and smashed the other rock into the side of the man's head. It was hard and effective. The sickening crunch of the blow was loud in the still night.

Hunter dragged the guard out and laid him on the ground. Quickly he rifled his pockets. He found a fistful of euros and a credit card. Pocketing both, he was about to roll the body into the ditch when he caught sight of the watch on the man's wrist. With delight he realised it was his old Rolex and he unclasped the metal hinge, sliding it off. Putting it on his own wrist he glanced at the time – 03.38.

The man was still breathing and Hunter decided to leave him where he was. If he was found he may yet live. If he hid him in the ditch it was less likely. I must, he thought, be getting soft in my old age.

Straightening up, a wave of dizziness and nausea washed over him and he held onto the roof of the car for a few seconds until it had passed. With a huge feeling of relief he climbed into the car and sank onto the seat, fumbling for the keys. The car was an old Fiat that had seen better days but it was a godsend. Turning the key, the starter motor whirred and then jammed. He tried again. This time the engine started.

He was putting the car into gear when he saw the barrel of a rifle resting on the floor, against the passenger's seat. Picking it up he quickly checked it over. It was the ubiquitous Russian AK47, easily recognisable by its banana-shaped magazine. He checked the safety, found it was on and slid it two positions to single shot. Pulling back the cocking handle he ensured a round was in the chamber before placing the rifle on the seat, the butt facing him.

Engaging first gear with a loud grating noise he set out along the highway towards the loom of lights in the distance. He was feeling light-headed but at least the throbbing pain had subsided to a dull ache. With his foot on the floor, the car increased speed, the needle flickering between 50 and 90kph. The oil pressure gauge was equally as erratic but at least the engine temperature needle was steady. Regrettably it was in the red.

21

The signpost said *Agrigento 8kms*. The name meant nothing to him. The only thing he was sure of was that he was on the south side of Sicily, but where exactly? A few minutes later he came to another signpost pointing inland to Agrigento, now only 4kms away. He ignored it and stayed on the main highway. The more distance he put between himself and the guards the better. He checked the fuel gauge and frowned. It was showing full. That wasn't possible and so he surmised it, too, was broken.

The next big town was Sciacca, 80kms away. He'd hole up there and contact Scotland.

He had travelled halfway when wisps of steam began to emanate from under the bonnet. With a curse he pulled over. By a process of elimination he found the bonnet release under the passenger's side of the car. Once he had the bonnet open he took a look. By now the moon had set. The sky was brightening as another day dawned and Hunter could just see the cap on the radiator. Tentatively he touched it. It was red hot. Opening the boot, he searched for a water bottle but found only the jack and a worn-looking spare wheel.

The car was a rust bucket, held together by its paint. Hunter found a rock and used it to smash apart the hinges holding the bonnet in place. He dumped the bonnet over the cliff. The road was on a slight decline and he released the handbrake, gave the car a shove and jumped behind the wheel. The car moved slowly, picking up speed as the decline increased. The cold air sweeping over the open engine helped to cool it more quickly as the car free-wheeled slowly downhill. The momentum lasted for ten minutes before the road levelled and then began to rise again.

Hunter stopped and got out. The radiator cap was much cooler and Hunter unscrewed it. There was no eruption of water and no steam. Stretching on his toes, Hunter urinated into the radiator, grateful he had drunk so much water while in the shed. He replaced the cap, climbed into the car, started the engine and drove away. Without a bonnet, the noise of the engine was about twice as loud as it had been.

Each time he crested a hill he switched off the engine and coasted. The sign *Rio Plátani* warned him that a river crossing lay ahead. He slowed down and pulled over to the side. The fast moving river was only a few metres away down a gentle incline. Driving to the water's edge, he stopped, letting the engine cool for a few minutes. Leaning his head back against the seat he shut his eyes and promptly fell asleep.

It was a combination of a heavy truck roaring past and the rising sun that finally brought him around. With a jerk he was wide awake, groaning at the uncontrolled movement of his injured head. Climbing out of the car he went down to the river. The water looked clean enough but he didn't dare drink it. Instead he washed out his mouth, ducked his head into the freezing water and held it there for a few seconds. When he looked up, dripping water, he felt better.

He had made two journeys with water cupped in his hands to put into the radiator before he saw a rusty tin. The cola can speeded up the process. Climbing into the car he started the engine, drove up onto the road and continued his journey in the strengthening daylight. Although he felt better for his short nap he was angry with himself. He didn't have time to sleep.

The town of Sciacca was off to the left and less than a kilometre away when the radiator erupted. Hunter kept going. Steam hissed out for a minute or two before it evaporated completely. The car began to jerk as bearings over-heated. *Just a few seconds, that's all I ask*, he prayed. Ahead he could see a large hoarding advertising a new time-share complex being built on the site.

By now the car had developed a serious case of the judders

and he put the gear lever into neutral and let it coast. It stopped
a few metres short of the sign and he clambered out. He pushed
the car behind the hoarding and out of sight. Briefly, he thought
about taking the AK47 with him but realised it was impractical.
There was no way he could carry it without it being seen.
Reluctantly he stripped it and walked away from the car, distributing pieces of the gun as he went. The last thing he wanted
was for some Sicilian child to find the weapon.

Macnair was in the operations room. 'Where's the ship?' he
barked at Isobel, his weariness evident in the abruptness of his
manner.

'Continuing towards the western end of the island.'

'Are we sure it docked in Pozzallo?'

'Yes, General, according to the satellite pictures.'

'So Íspica looks a good bet?'

'It does but we still can't be absolutely certain.'

Macnair sighed. 'I know. But do we have any choice?'

It was a rhetorical question. The buck stopped with Macnair
and it was his decision alone to make. He had compromised. A
TIFAT team was in the air in a Hercules C130 and heading for
Italy. It was fully equipped and ready to go as soon as the
General could confirm the target. The team was led by Matt
Dunston who had only arrived back a few hours earlier. All the
men had barely been debriefed before they were on their way
again. They could, Macnair had told them, sleep on the plane.

It had sounded callous but in fact campbeds had been taken
on board and the team were soon fast asleep.

Macnair's mobile rang and he answered. 'Nick! Where are
you?' The General listened to what Hunter had to say. 'Excellent.
Good work. Stay where you are. I'll have Matt with you ASAP.
I have to go. I've work to do.'

Breaking the connection he looked into Isobel's enquiring eyes.
'Hunter confirms the factory is in Íspica. He also witnessed
Gustav leave with three spheres of the biotoxin.'

'Where is Nick?'

'Hiding in a hotel in a resort known as Sciacca.' As he spoke,

Macnair was busy with his computer. A map of Sicily appeared on the wall screen in front of them. 'There it is. On the south coast. Nearest airport is on the west coast near Paceco. We'll divert the Hercules there. I need to speak to Nato and see if we have any liaison officers with the Italian army on the island.'

'Why, General?' Isobel asked.

'The Mafia are probably after Hunter from what he told me. We can't trust the police and even some elements of the Italian armed forces are suspect. But if we can get a Nato officer to baby-sit him, he should be all right.'

'Nick needing a baby sitter?' Isobel couldn't keep the surprise out of her voice.

'He's hurt, Isobel. He's fallen unconscious twice in the past hour.'

Hunter had telephoned from the railway station. His original idea had been to find a small hotel but he realised that the Mafia, if they were looking for him, would easily track him down. Instead he had gone down to the still deserted beach. He had sat in the shade, on a sun-lounger, for a few minutes, to regain his strength and promptly passed out. Whether it had been the effect of his head wound or sheer exhaustion, he had slept for an hour. When he had awoken the sun was well above the horizon and people were about. At a nearby stand-pipe he had washed his head and drunk some water before going back into town. He had bought shoes and some fresh clothes in a shop on the sea-front before returning to the beach. In a Gents toilet he had changed, and had dumped his old clothes in a waste bin. He had remembered to remove the piece of paper from his jacket lining. Gustav's cheque – well, he was certainly earning his money now.

In a chemist's he had bought toiletries and Aspirin – downing four. After he had freshened up he felt almost human again. He had returned to the nearby sun-lounger for a few minutes rest. He had lain back, telling himself it would only be for a few seconds and had promptly fallen fast asleep. This time he had been woken by somebody shaking his shoulder.

With a start he had looked into the swarthy face bending over

308

him. Before he knew it, he had the man on his back, in the sand. He was leaning over him with his arm drawn back, before he realised the man was gibbering with terror. He had merely wanted to collect the rent for the bed.

Hunter had apologised profusely, paid him, added a tip and left the beach. He went shopping again. This time he bought stationary, drafted a quick note and posted the ten million pounds cheque to his off-shore bank account in Jersey. It was a subsidiary of the family's bank, Griffiths Buchanan Plc. He wondered idly if the cheque would clear. He walked to a different part of the beach, where sun-worshippers were already gathering, and paid for a day's hire of a lounger. In the shade of an umbrella he settled down and slept again, this time until half the morning had wasted.

A beach-side café provided excellent coffee and pizza. The coffee helped to wash down another two Aspirin. Back on his lounger he slept until the middle of the afternoon. When he awoke his head was no longer throbbing. The pain had faded to a dull ache. That disappeared within a few minutes of swallowing more pills. The bump was definitely going down and was less painful to touch. A scab had formed over the cut.

More coffee and food left him feeling more alert than he'd been all day. He was sitting at a table outside the café. Two similar establishments were to his left. To his right was the entrance to a small port and marina. Masts swayed in the swell and rigging and bunting flapped in the breeze. People were scattered across the sandy beach, some in the sun, others under the shade. Hunter noticed two men walking up and down the beach, looking at the sun-worshippers. These were no holiday-makers. For a start they wore suits. But they were also interested only in the men rather than the topless women and they were moving quickly.

Hunter nonchalantly walked back to his lounger, the men were still around fifty metres away. Discretion being the better part of valour he headed for the beach toilets. Opening a cubicle, he locked the door behind him. He had just sat down when he heard somebody slam open the first cubicle door. Then the second. His

309

door was hit hard. A voice called something in Italian. He didn't reply. Instead he straddled the toilet and stood back from the door. There was an almighty crash and the door flew open. If he had been sitting down it would have smashed into his right knee.

They weren't really expecting any trouble. They were after a man who was badly hurt or so they had been told. He was unarmed while they carried guns. They were Mafiosi while he was a stranger. And this was *their* island, *their* town. Nobody dared stop them. Or even try.

Hunter kicked hard. Not between the man's legs but all the way up to his chin. A bone shattered and the man collapsed with a scream, his hands to his face. The second man had already moved past Hunter's cubicle and was pushing open the end door. As his friend hit the wall he turned with his jaw open, his hands by his side.

Hunter was already out of the cubicle and stepping towards him. The man stood still in utter astonishment, unable to believe what he was seeing. Too late he reached for his gun. Hunter's palm swept upwards and took the man in the nose, breaking the cartilage, thrusting it into the front lobes of the brain. The man collapsed, his arms and legs moving like jitterbugs. They stopped when he drew his last breath.

Reaching under the man's jacket, Hunter removed a revolver and slipped it into his belt, pulling out his tee-shirt to cover the gun. He removed the Sicilian's wallet and dumped it in the holdall. Grabbing the man by his belt and jacket lapel, he put him into the nearest cubicle. The door didn't go all the way to the floor and he reached under, grabbed the man's leg and pulled it against the door, jamming it closed.

The first man had drowned in his own blood. Hunter took the Sicilian's gun and dumped it in the holdall before disposing of the second body in the same way. A wave of dizziness washed over him and he rested for a few moments before he went back out into the sunshine. The irony of sudden death and a beautiful day wasn't lost on him.

There was a small veranda and wooden platform outside the

door and he paused in the shade to look around the beach. No one else appeared to be other than they seemed – holidaymakers enjoying themselves.

Macnair had told him to stay where he was. That the team would come for him. But it was too dangerous. It would only be a matter of time before the bodies were found. But where could he go? The Mafia were obviously looking for him and next time he might not be so lucky. It was only the incongruity of men in suits walking up and down the beach in the heat of the day that had alerted him so quickly. Another dizzy spell came on and he put a hand out to support himself. When it had passed he was aware that his head was hurting again and he took more Aspirin, swallowing them dry. He wandered slowly back to the café for a drink for all the world like a tourist without a care. Ice-cold fresh orange never tasted so good.

Gustav and Duval were the sole passengers on the craft speeding away from the side of the *Stockholm*. Marsala on the western tip of Sicily was less than one nautical mile away. The ship had slowed but not stopped for the launch. It continued on its way as soon as the boat left the side, quickly returning to its cruising speed of 15 knots.

Only one man accompanied them. He steered the boat expertly into the port and alongside the wall. A large limousine was waiting and the three of them disappeared into it, hidden behind its tinted windows. They carried no luggage, except for the holdall containing the three plastic spheres filled with the nerve gas.

Macnair wished Hunter would phone again so that he could bring him up to date on events. He was unable to find a Nato officer and had decided not to trust anybody in authority on Sicily. So the operation would be hard and fast. The one piece of useful information he'd received was that Nato was staging an exercise in the Mediterranean. Under the control of the American Sixth Fleet, units from seven Nato countries were taking part. They would be invading a deserted piece of Greece, using amphibious forces and landing craft. Thousands of personnel were involved in a simulated invasion of another country. There were two reasons for the exercise. The first was self-evident – to train the armed forces of the world's democracies. The second was a not-so-subtle reminder to the rest of the world that the West still had the power to project its will should it be necessary.

On Macnair's wall map, now focused on Sicily, the Hercules was shown lining up to land. The *SS Stockholm* was shown but here was a slight anomaly. She was a few miles short of where he expected her to be.

Time was of the essence. At present it didn't look as though she was heading for any particular port, unless it was out of the Med. That was always a possibility. On no account could the spheres with their deadly contents be taken ashore. God alone knew where they could end up.

Isobel phoned his office. 'I've had Porton Down on the line.' Macnair recognised the significance of the location – it was the home of Britain's Defence Science and Technology Laboratory. 'They are suggesting the gas used on the liner is a mixture of sarin and ricin. If it is, there is no known antidote.'

Macnair sighed, thanked her and hung up. He telephoned the PM and they agreed. They would meet in the Cabinet Office Briefing Room in four hours. He next phoned the Director at Porton Down.

Was there anything else he could do at this stage? Under the guise of taking part in the Nato exercise, the team was being picked up at the airport by a Sea King helicopter from the task force. It was waiting for them and would be in the air only minutes after the Hercules landed. Customs had already been alerted to ignore the plane. Immigration didn't warrant an alert. Travel across the borders of Europe was virtually unrestricted, even for the military. Or perhaps, especially for the military.

Macnair stood lost in thought, staring at the projected wall map. He'd dealt with everything. Had he missed anything? It was an uncomfortable thought with so much at stake. Not just the lives of thousands if Gustav used the gas, but the future of

Europe as a multi-cultural, multi-ethnic mix of people. Indeed the very future of democracy hung in the balance.

Hunter sat in the café and kept a close eye on the beach. He saw no other suspicious characters. So far three people had gone in to use the toilets but none had re-emerged, panic-stricken and hysterical. There was a public phone in the café but it had an out of order notice on it and Hunter didn't want to draw attention to himself by asking to use the café's phone. But time was passing and he needed to talk to Macnair. He had already checked the other two bars for a public phone but without success. He could, he supposed, walk towards the town and find the nearest phone booth. The sudden appearance of two black sedans, driving fast, racing down towards the beach made his mind up for him.

Hunter stepped into a doorway. As the cars passed him, he saw the ominous black rods of gun barrels appearing in the windows. Each car held four men. The cars screeched to a halt and the men emerged, fanning out over the beach. Within seconds a gunman entered the Gents toilets. He rushed out excitedly, yelling. It seemed to galvanise the others and they moved quickly, one man to each of the cafés, the others along the beach.

Unnoticed, in the distance, a small dot appeared on the horizon, rapidly growing larger. It stopped, out of noise range and hovered low down, the roundels of the Royal Air Force indiscernible from the beach. None of the gunmen even looked in its direction.

Hunter, looking towards the sea, had seen the helo and had known instantly who it was. His problem was that between it and him were the Mafia. Already the shops' shutters were coming down and doors were being locked. He saw the waiter who had served him earlier come out and point along the road in the direction he had taken, speaking and gesticulating excitedly.

The man he was speaking to said something in a loud voice and the other gunmen converged on the road, guns at the ready.

Hunter was about sixty metres away and had his back to a glass door. As he tried the handle a woman's face appeared and she locked it. He gestured at the door to let him in but she shook her head and angrily indicated that he leave.

313

Looking cautiously out he saw it was too late to make a run for it. The men were strung out across the road and advancing steadily towards him. Hunter knelt down and opened his holdall. For the first time he took a closer look at the guns. One was a Spanish Llama Comanche, not very old, holding six rounds of .357 Magnum bullets. The other was a battered and worn looking French Manurhin MR73, also holding six rounds of the same ammunition. The longer barrel of the Spanish gun convinced him it was the one to use first. It was probably more accurate at the longer range while the French gun's unique roller-bearing trigger system made for a smoother and faster action.

Gunfight, he thought, *at the OK Corral*. They still had no idea where he was, which was evident from the way they were looking into the doorways. What surprised him was the total arrogance they displayed walking down the street. But then, he figured, the police had probably been told to stay away from that part of town. And one man alone wasn't going to frighten them. Especially if he was unarmed or armed only with a couple of revolvers. They had automatic weapons.

A man appeared on the other side of the road, to Hunter's left, and started pulling down the metal shutter to his shop. One of the gunmen yelled something. The shopkeeper turned with a startled look on his face and scuttled inside. *More like High Noon*, thought Hunter.

He lay on the ground in the doorway. Luckily the glass windows of the shop front sat on solid stone about half a metre high. Out at the edge of the pavement a metal lamp post stood tall, shielding him slightly from the gunmen across the street. Cars were parked on the other side but on Hunter's side there were no vehicles. By now the pavements and street were completely deserted.

With his eye at ground level Hunter took a quick look. Forty metres. Close enough. It was time to discourage them. To buy some time until reinforcements arrived. A glance at the sky wasn't encouraging. The helicopter had vanished.

One gunman was walking the pavement directly towards

314

Hunter and another was a few metres to his right. The remainder were strung across the street. He knew that left-handed his chances of hitting either target was a lot less than if he used his right. To use his right hand he had to show more of himself than he liked. So be it. Two double taps and back in. Resist the temptation to continue firing. Two seconds maximum. By which time the remaining men would have collected their wits and opened fire with automatic weapons. Then he'd retreat through the glass door which, he was sure, would be smashed to pieces in the hailstorm of bullets. One bullet was all it would take to finish him. It was now or never.

He rolled out, the gun in his right hand, cocked and ready to fire. His left hand immediately cupping his right fist, he came up on his elbows and aimed. His sudden appearance shocked the man he was aiming at into immobility. Hunter was pulling the trigger when the man threw his hands in the air with an anguished cry and fell forwards. Hunter hadn't heard the shot being fired. His own gun stayed silent as he watched the eight Mafiosi fall. Hunter's shock turned to pleased surprise when he saw a man appear along the road. The unmistakable figure of Dunston strolled towards him.

Lowering his hands he dropped his head onto his arms with relief. A feeling of dizziness swept over him and he had difficulty getting to his feet.

As though from a distance he heard Matt Dunston ask, 'Are you all right, Nick?'

Hunter nodded. 'Thanks, Matt, you arrived just in time.'

'We were waiting for you to make your move. We saw the play going down from the chopper so figured what you'd do. We rappelled down and took up position. It was, as the Yanks say, a turkey shoot. Let's get you out of here. We've a lot to do.'

The helicopter landed on the still-deserted street and Hunter climbed aboard, followed by the team. He was not surprised to find that the original RAF pilot had been replaced by Burg Schwarzkopf. For such a covert operation TIFAT used its own men.

Schwarzkopf was gently raising the collective as the last man climbed through the door. He pushed forward the cyclic and the helicopter took its characteristic nose-down aspect and surged out to sea. The remainder of the team were pulling off their ski-masks, grins on their faces.

'Good job you've got a hard head, boss,' shouted Lt Napier.

Dunston was already checking Hunter over, feeling for the tell-tale sign of a slightly soft feel to the bone around the skull. If he was hurting, Hunter didn't show it.

'It should have had stitches but it's healed over,' announced Dunston. 'Does it hurt?'

'A bit,' Hunter admitted. 'I've taken a few Aspirin.'

'I'll give you a local anaesthetic. That'll hold it for a few hours. You up to coming on this jaunt?'

'Sure. Have you got kit for me?'

'In the corner.'

In the team were Claude Masson, Doug Tanner, Don Masters, Jan Badonovitch and Josh Clements. The Delta captain handed a holdall to Hunter.

Over the internal headphones they heard Schwarzkopf say, 'The General's on line one, Nick.'

Hunter flicked his communications switch to one. 'Sir? It's Hunter.'

'Nick, glad you're in one piece. Matt will brief you. We're shadowing the *Stockholm* and won't go in until you've taken out the factory. It must be razed to the ground.'

'Yes, sir. What about the personnel?'

'Hold them until the Americans get there. They're spiriting them away. It'll be up to them whether the scientists stand trial for crimes against humanity.'

'Roger that, sir. I'll let you know how we get on. Out.'

Macnair was flying into Heathrow when he spoke to Hunter. Landing, he was met by the police. A car, alarms and lights flashing, whisked him into London and deposited him at No 10 Downing Street. There he was introduced to Dr John Williams, a scientist from Porton Down, a tall, distinguished looking man of about fifty. Along with the Prime Minister were the Defence

316

Secretary, Home Secretary, Deputy PM and Chancellor of the Exchequer. All had sombre looks on their faces.

Williams sat at the end of the table. He had no props, no papers. 'Shall I begin?'

The PM nodded.

'It's important to understand that this is all guess work. Do you know anything about ricin?'

The men shook their heads. The Home Secretary stroked his beard and said, 'Only that we've found traces of it recently in London and that we think there is a quantity out there somewhere.'

Williams nodded. 'Ricin is a natural toxin found in castor bean husks. A million tons of the beans are processed every year for oil used as an industrial lubricant. About seven percent of the residue is ricin. So it's easily obtainable. The husks need only be ground into powder, dissolved and then dried into crystalline form to be deadly. Death from pure ricin takes thirty-six to forty-eight hours and is caused by circulatory and respiratory failure. It's not contagious and by itself makes a lousy WMD. However,' the doctor paused, 'mixed with a nerve agent such as sarin and with whatever else is in the gas then it becomes far more deadly. What we suspect,' again he paused and added, 'and this is *pure* speculation, is that the third gas is relatively heavy. So when released the mixture will stay at ground level.'

'Why is that?' asked the DPM.

'Maximum fatalities,' was the stark reply.

'What sort of numbers are we talking about?' Macnair asked.

The scientist shrugged. 'Impossible to tell. We've programmed various scenarios into our computers,' he paused again, licking dry lips.

'Well, man,' the DPM asked impatiently, his strong Yorkshire accent grating in the quiet room.

'If released in an underground station it would kill everyone there and then infect other places as it drifts with the draughts through the network, ultimately causing thousands of deaths. If released in the open the breeze could disperse it over a wide region. We've done some "what ifs" on the computer.' He looked down at the sheet in front of him and paused. 'With average weather and winds for this time of year a city the size of Manchester would experience ninety-five percent fatalities within twenty-four hours.'

The helicopter landed on a deserted spot, away from prying eyes. It was too early to attack. A guard was posted and the remaining team sat over hot drinks, exchanging stories of the last couple of days. When it was time to go, they dressed in their Nuclear, Bacteriological and Chemical Warfare Suits. Fully enclosed from head to foot, refined gas masks hung from their necks. The masks could be used in the conventional way, filtering the outside air, or by turning a handle, they could be used in a closed-circuit mode. Then the wearer would breathe pure oxygen carried in a small cylinder strapped on the back. Thanks to a unique scrubbing system, the oxygen was reused until it was fully depleted. This meant that the bottles had an endurance of about twenty minutes for an ordinary person. For the physically fit that time span was extended to around thirty minutes. The team could squeeze out at least forty minutes thanks to the controlled breathing techniques they had learned as divers.

With the helicopter four thousand feet up and two miles out they bailed out. Their wings deployed and they swooped down like huge bats, hardly noticeable against the moonless sky. It was barely 21.00 and moonrise was at least three hours away.

Their NVGs showed them the way and they deployed in accordance with the plan of attack. Dunston landed behind the guardhouse. The man inside was looking out, down the road. Unaware. Dunston wrapped up his wing and approached the glass door in the back wall. Gently he tried the handle. The door opened and was only slightly ajar when the guard looked over his shoulder. His jaw dropped in shock as Dunston threw caution to the wind and smashed the door wide. He gestured with a Glock 19 in his hand for the man to raise his hands. The guard did as he was told. Dunston didn't see him lean against a red button protruding from the side of a table. A low but intense two-tone hooter sounded. The guard grinned.

Dunston wiped the smile off the man's face with an open-edged stroke of his hand into the guard's neck. He collapsed, unconscious.

'Sorry, lads. I didn't see that one.'

'Never mind. Hit it!' Hunter ordered.

Explosives kneaded along the sides of the front doors blew the hinges. Badonovitch pushed the middle of the doors with his shoulder and they smashed to the ground with a loud bang. They stormed in. A short corridor faced them. At the far end glass doors were already more than half covered by a metal shutter, rolling down.

The plans Isobel had lifted from central records in Rome had been pored over by Dunston and the team prior to departure. The building above ground was less than twenty percent of the total and consisted of the foyer and storage rooms. The remaining structure was underground. The first subterranean floor was made up of public rooms, the second of combined bedrooms and sitting rooms and the third held the laboratories. Eighteen servants worked at the establishment, one per scientist. How many of them were armed guards?

They knew that every door and internal window had steel shutters which closed at the press of a button. They also knew that the steel shutters were much tougher than the walls. The team had brought with them round, metal mines, packed with explosives, eight inches in diameter and two inches thick. The flat base of the charge was surrounded with thick soft rubber, one inch wide. When pressed against a reasonably smooth surface, like a wall or a door, a small thumb-operated pump quickly sucked the air out and made a seal. The mine stuck to the surface like a limpet. It could be exploded by timer or remote detonator, the preferred method for this operation. The explosive was shaped to go into the surface, creating a jagged, circular hole, about three feet in diameter. Two were used, either side of the door, to devastating effect, the explosive power smashing into the wall.

A flash-bang grenade was thrown through each of the holes. Hunter dived through the one to the right, Napier dived left. Both men had guns ready, on full automatic.

In their NBC suits and respirators they looked like beings from outer-space. Aliens invading an antiseptic and tranquil haven of peace. Two men stood in shock, disorientated by the grenades. Both were fit looking and armed. Two taps each took them out.

They had entered a large foyer, carpeted and plush enough to be found in a five star hotel. To the left of the reception desk was a corridor. Again a shutter was rolling down, rapidly sealing off the door. It was like being encased in a tomb.

There were doors around the foyer leading into toilets and storerooms that were quickly checked. Nobody and nothing of interest was found. A lift was situated in one corner, the indicator showing it was on the lowest floor. They called it up, ready for any nasty surprises. When it arrived they found a man huddled in the corner, away from the door. He was about fifty, scholarly looking. He wore black-framed glasses, his grey, receding hair swept back. He was shaking with fear.

'Don't shoot! Don't shoot!' He held up his hands. The fear wasn't an act.

'On your feet and move outside,' ordered Clements.

'American? You're an American?' The relief was clear in the man's voice. 'Oh, thank God.'

'Shift it.' Clements prodded the man outside and into the waiting arms of Dunston. There the chaplain handcuffed the man with plasti-cuffs and made him sit on the ground. Two minutes of conversation had Dunston on the radio to the others.

'Listen up. According to the man I've got here, the scientists are being held under coercion. Promises made by Gustav haven't been kept. The guards are there to keep them in line. The laboratories are numbered one to four and are confirmed as being on the lowest floor. Number three contains the gas. Number two is where the antidote is being created. From what this guy is telling me, I think it would pay to get as many of the scientists out alive as possible.'

'Why?' Hunter asked.

'Because the antidote hasn't been perfected yet. And Gustav has definitely left with three containers of the virus.'

'Do we know what's in it?' Hunter asked.

'A mixture of sarin and ricin plus a new super toxin. They call the mixture SRX. I'll let the General know.'

'How many guards and how many servants are there?'

There was a pause before Dunston came back on. 'Bad news, I'm afraid. Even the servants are armed. There are eighteen of them in total and eleven scientists.'

'Does he know where they all are?'

'Negative. Although some of the scientists will be in the labs.'

'Roger that,' Hunter acknowledged.

'There are fewer scientists than we expected, boss,' said Masters.

'Yeah. I was thinking that. Matt? Ask your guy where the other scientists are.'

'I can answer that, Nick,' said Dunston heavily. 'Six of them have been killed. By the guards. As an incentive to the others to give Gustav what he wanted.'

'Whatever happened to old fashioned bonuses?' Napier asked.

The door past the desk was the main entrance to the complex and mines were placed either side, blowing holes in the wall. In the confined space they paused to let the dust settle. The portable thermal imager showed that the corridor beyond was empty. They climbed through the holes to find themselves in a short corridor with a stairwell leading down.

22

'*SS Stockholm, SS Stockholm*, this is warship. Heave to immediately and prepare for a boarding party.'

'Warship, this is the *Stockholm*. I protest. I am lawfully going about my business in international waters. You have no right to stop me.'

'This is warship. I say again. Stop your engines immediately or be prepared to be fired on. You have two minutes.'

'Warship, this is the *Stockholm*. If you do I will have you arrested and in court. The world's media will take a dim view of your actions. Are you American or English?'

'Look behind you, *Kapitän zur See* Novak.' The words were spoken with contempt. 'Perhaps you recognise the flag of the country where you are registered.'

During the exchange the Stockholm's engines had been put to full ahead and the ship was gathering speed. Through his binoculars Novak focused on the stem of the frigate that was a mile astern and coming up on his quarter. He knew that in a straight race, the *Stockholm* could outrun the naval vessel. The blue and yellow cross of the Swedish flag came into sight.

Even as his brain registered the colours, the captain experienced palpitations of shock. Screaming blue murder at the Americans or the British for human-rights violations was one thing. Sweden, famous for its neutrality, was another. It had been pure inspiration by Macnair to suggest using the Swedish frigate to the Secretary-General of Nato. The Swedes, for the first time in history, had been exercising with the fleet. It was part of a political softening up process to persuade the Swedish people to come into the fold at long last. Their neutrality meant that for too long Sweden hadn't been pulling its weight in the world. Especially now with the all-too present dangers faced by Western democracies.

Novak had his orders. Keeping to international waters, the *Stockholm* turned away from the frigate. Gustav had said that the likelihood of even the Americans firing on them were slim. The Swedes? Forget it. There was not a dog's chance in hell. It was therefore all the more shocking when a solid shot, 4.5 inch round, slammed into the midships section of the ship. If it had been a high-explosive shell or a missile the devastation would have been horrendous. As it was, the shot went through the port side of the ship, hit number two diesel and smashed it to pulp.

The Captain's shock and torment were so great that he stood still for a second, unable to take it in. He launched himself at the radio and began sending a Mayday signal saying the ship was under attack. Unknown to Novak, a blanket jamming was in force from an American stealth bomber, ten miles above the ship.

The next two shells hit the bows. Both at the waterline. The sea began to flood in and the ship slowed down. However, the *Stockholm* didn't slow fast enough. She drove the water into her hull and began flooding, settling with a forward momentum that would take her a full nautical mile before reaching the seabed. Before giving the order to abandon ship the last thing Novak did was to let loose the emergency beacon.

When the ship finally settled, on her side, in a rocky region of the Mediterranean, the beacon was floating on the surface, forty metres above the seabed.

Dunston came back on the radio. 'Listen up. More bad news. I've just been told that an alarm connects to somewhere else on the island. It will bring the Mafiosi in hordes, according to my friend here.'

'Can you whistle up reinforcements?' Hunter asked.

'I've already done so. Two stealth fighters are inbound to ride shotgun plus a contingent of marines will be arriving by helo. The fighters will be here shortly. The ETA for the marines is one hour at best.'

'Okay folks,' Hunter said, 'let's shift it. I don't want another firefight with the Mafia if we can help it.'

At the bottom of the stairwell they found another shutter, fitted across the whole width of the corridor. Close examination showed that the shutter was embedded into the wall either side. They would have to go through the metal. They moulded plastic explosives into a Toblerone shape and tamped it down around the steel shutter. The explosion was not clean and the circle of metal was still held in place by tiny bridges of steel. A hefty kick pushed it clear.

The thermal imager showed two men were somewhere on the other side. Hiding behind the shutter, Hunter fed in an optic fibre camera and checked the area. He was looking at a short corridor leading to a T-junction. A shadow moved on the floor.

'Come out and you won't get hurt,' Hunter called. 'This is a Nato contingent of special services. Come out with your hands in the air.' Nothing happened.

If the people inside expected a flash-bang then they would know what to do. By sitting in a foetal position with heads bowed, eyes shut and hands over the ears it was possible to avoid most of the damage inflicted by the grenade. Hunter had no intention of risking any of the lives of his team if he could help it. He threw in a high-explosive grenade that detonated as it passed the junction. Badonovitch and Weir went through the hole like rats up a drain-pipe. They reported two armed guards, both dead.

Quickly they checked the corridor was clear while the rest of the team followed them through. There were five doors either side of the corridor, each signed clearly, indicating the room's function. The thermal imager found four people in the room marked cinema. According to the sensor, two were in the furthest left hand corner, lying on the floor. A third was cowering in the near left hand corner and a fourth was kneeling opposite the door, partially protected by something. The team placed a mine either side of the shuttered door and blew two holes. Gunfire erupted from inside the room and sprayed the first hole with bullets. Through the second, Tanner saw the gunman kneeling behind a stuffed armchair. With his Glock 19 on automatic he fired six shots, killing the man.

'Come out with your hands up,' said Hunter in a loud voice.

Three men appeared. They varied in age and physique but one thing was sure, they weren't guards. They clambered through the holes.

One of the men stood erect and with a certain dignity asked, 'Who's in charge here?'

'I am.' Hunter replied.

'You can take your ridiculous gas masks off, there is no danger.'

With relief the team took off their masks. Sweat covered their faces and streaked down their cheeks. The masks were uncomfortable at the best of times and in action they were a downright nuisance. In the right circumstances however, they could save your life.

'Who are you?' Hunter asked.

'My name is Joachim Dietrich. I am in charge of the research scientists. We have been held prisoner by Charles Gustav for nearly a year.'

'Save it,' said Hunter. 'We need to get out of here. The Mafia could be arriving any time. But first we need to find the remaining scientists, so tell us where they are and quickly.'

'I refuse to be spoken to like that.'

The team looked at the little scientist in utter astonishment. He was barely five feet, rotund almost, with a smooth, hairless face and a bald head. His innocent appearance belied such unbelievable gall. 'I insist you take us out of here now. Our rescue is of the utmost importance. Otherwise your superiors will hear about this and I warn you . . .'

He got no further. Josh Clements had the man by the throat and lifted him up on his toes. 'Listen you little slime ball, we know you've created germ warfare here intended for use in Europe. If any innocent people die you'll be tried as an accessory to mass murder. You got that? And if you don't end up in court I'll put a bullet in you myself. Understood?'

The little man, his eyes bulging with fear, nodded vigorously.

'Now answer our questions and then you can go outside.'

More nods. Their questions were answered promptly. They learned that the doors could be opened individually from inside or from a master switch in the foyer.

'Matt? Three scientists on their way. There's a master switch for the shutters. Find out where it is and I'll let you know whether we want to use it. At present, with the men locked inside, we have better control. Oh, and cuff them,' said Hunter over the radio.

'Roger that.'

'All quiet?'

'So far. If things change I'll let you know.'

'We're left with seven scientists and fifteen uglies all on the two floors below,' said Hunter. 'Let's go.'

The next shutter yielded to the same treatment. The corridor was empty.

'Boss,' said Badonovitch, 'I think these shutters are delaying tactics while the guards pray for the cavalry in the shape of the Mafia to arrive.'

'That's what I think too, Jan. What's your point?'

'Maybe we should just seal the whole lot and get the hell topside.'

'That's occurred to me as well. Ten minutes max before we leg it. Okay? Josh, Claude and Don go straight for the next stair-well while we clear the bedrooms and sitting rooms.'

Hunter used the thermal imager to check each of the rooms. In one room they found one person and in another they found three. The rest of the rooms were empty. In both cases the images suggested the men were cowering away from the doors. Hunter used one mine on either side of the doors and blew them simultaneously. At the end of the corridor the other team's explosion was heard.

'Come out with your hands where we can see them,' he yelled.

'Don't shoot! I'm coming out.' A bespectacled man came out of the first room with his hands up. He had scientist written all over him.

'Jan, cover him while we see who's in the other room.' Raising his voice, Hunter called, 'Are you coming out or not?'

'Yes! Yes! We're coming. Only don't kill us.'

The three men crawled through the hole. They all had a number of things in common. A pallor that indicated a lack of sunshine, a soft outline that spoke of too much good food and not enough exercise and they all wore glasses.

'Get them out of here, Jan,' said Hunter.

'You're British!' one man exclaimed.

'Save it for later. Now go!'

Hurrying along the corridor they were at the stairwell when they heard firing. Cautiously they went down in time to see Clements throw a grenade through the hole they had blown in the shutter. The fragmentation grenade erupted and the firing ceased. Using the optical camera they checked to see one body lying in the corridor, the walls covered in blood.

Unlike the other rooms, the four labs had windows into the corridor which were shuttered. They also had entry-phones either side of the doors. According to the heat sensor Lab 1 held one person.

Hunter pressed the button on the entry phone. 'You in there. Open the shutter and come out with your hands up. If you don't open the shutter in ten seconds we'll come in.'

The heat-sensor showed the person inside change from a round blob in the far corner of the room to an erect figure. It came slowly towards the door and paused.

Hunter decided to give the figure a prod. 'Our sensors show you to be at the door. Open it and come out.'

There was a second's delay and then the shutter rolled slowly upwards. The man on the other side was in his thirties, wearing a white coat and spectacles. He was raising and lowering his hands in some sort of supplication when he reached under his coat for a gun. Masson had been ready and shot him between the eyes.

'He had too much tan,' the Frenchman said.

The sensors showed two occupants of Lab 2. Using the entry-phone Hunter repeated his request that they come out. The two figures remained where they were, apparently crouched behind something, on the other side of the room.

Explosives were attached to the wall either side of the door and blown. Automatic guns opened up from inside and bullets poured through both holes. Ricocheting off the wall opposite, they were a deadly danger. Two fragmentation grenades were thrown in and the shooting stopped as soon as they exploded.

That left Lab 3 where the deadly gas was concocted. Hunter used the entry-phone. There were six men inside as far from the door as possible. One of them came forward but suddenly collapsed in a heap. Tiny flecks of red light on the sensor's screen left the team in no doubt that he had been shot.

'Gas masks on,' said Hunter. 'I don't like this.'

Uncomfortable in their masks once more, Tanner said, 'Boss, I propose we go to oxygen.'

'Agreed.' The team turned on the valves isolating them from the air around them.

Explosives blew two holes through the wall. As before, gunfire erupted from inside the lab and peppered the wall behind the team with bullets. There was no time for finesse. A couple of grenades were thrown in. As they exploded, a huge scream rent the air. The firing stopped and Hunter pushed a fibre optic camera into the furthest hole. Looking at the monitor, he was trying to understand the picture he was seeing.

Two men in white coats were climbing dazedly to their feet. The younger of the two called out. 'Don't come in. The germs have been released. For the love of God get away before you're exposed.'

He suddenly arched his back and collapsed with a scream.

The men of TIFAT were amongst the bravest in the world. They had put their lives on the line often enough and proven themselves in tight spots again and again. But this was different, hideous, insidious. The gas killed in a terrible way, leaving you to die in fear and agony. And although they were suited up, wearing respirators and using their own oxygen supply, they didn't wait. Hunter paused to commit one last act of kindness, lobbing in two grenades to where the men were lying, screaming in agony. At the stairwell they each threw incendiary devices into the corridor. One floor up, Napier was already setting explosives with a two-minute delay while on the next floor Clements was doing the same.

On the ground floor they placed a third pile of PE before escaping the building. The incendiary devices went off causing a huge fireball that engulfed the laboratories, incinerating the gas and setting fire to the building, killing those left alive. The explosives sealed the stairwells.

The team herded the scientists away. They walked awkwardly because their arms were pinioned behind their backs. Dietrich protested continually while the others had the good sense to keep quiet.

'Look!' Masson pointed ahead of them.

Coming along the road were headlights. Four, maybe five sets.

'What do you think, boss?' asked Badonovitch.

'I think we've got company. Nighthawk this is Team One, over.'

'One, Nighthawk, over,' Schwarzkopf replied immediately.

'We've got company.'

'I see them. The F-117s are thirty seconds away. I'm vectoring them in now. Duck real low. Out.'

'You heard the man,' said Hunter. 'Into the ditches either side of the track.'

While the scientists cowered in trepidation the team readied for a firefight. As was the case with American stealth fighters, nobody saw or heard anything. The strike aircraft carried laser-guided bombs which could be dropped with great precision. Five car loads of Mafiosi were blown to Kingdom Come without the occupants knowing what was happening.

The F-117s circled upwards, barely noticeable except for the flickering stars in the sky.

'All quiet again,' said Hunter to Burg.

'Roger that. What now?'

'Come and get us. We need to get out of here.'

The team rested up on an American aircraft carrier, the *USS Ronald Reagan*. The ship, pennant number CVN 76, was a colossus of the sea. Its firepower was awesome, its protective screen of warships greater than the navies of most sovereign countries.

When the team landed, they were assigned beds and promptly forgotten about. The scientists were taken to the Admiral's quarters where they were treated like dignitaries. Except that their complaints about how they had been abused by their rescuers fell on deaf ears. Finally even Dietrich stopped harping on the subject. Already arrangements had been made to fly the scientists to America to continue their research. A red carpet was quietly being rolled out for them.

Macnair was awoken from a deep sleep by the ringing of his phone. Groggily he answered it. Within nano-seconds he had snapped wide awake. 'Are you sure?'

Carter broke the bad news to his boss. 'As sure as we can be, sir. The Swedes have just signalled us. Gustav left the ship with Duval hours ago. He's on Sicily somewhere.'

'And the spheres of SRX?'

'The Captain doesn't know. Claims he's just a simple mariner going about his duties.'

'I bet. And what do the Swedes say?'

'They're back-peddling like fury, sir. You know what they're like. Big on human rights.'

Macnair grunted. 'Human rights of the criminal, not the ordinary citizens.'

'You've got it, sir. They're crapping themselves about the whole affair. Think they've gone too far. Shouldn't have done it, and so on. The usual drivel.'

'They'll hang their angst out and make themselves a laughing stock. Hunter still on the aircraft carrier?'

'Affirmative, sir. Probably having breakfast about now.'

'Okay. We need to check it out. Any chance we can get our hands on the Captain of the *Stockholm*?'

'I doubt it, sir.'

'Where is he?'

'On the frigate. The Swedes are already flying lawyers out to him.'

'What! Jesus wept! Don't they know the stakes we're playing for?'

'They do, sir. But it's no use.'

'What about holding him under some terrorism law until we can lift him?'

'I've suggested that to Downing Street. But they say if the Swedes won't play ball there's nothing we or anybody else can do about it.'

'Okay. We need to check out the ship. Do we know where it is exactly?'

'Yes, sir. An emergency transponder was sent out from the side of the hull and is floating on the surface. We have its signal loud and clear.'

'Okay. I'll get on to the Pentagon.'

Hunter didn't hear his name being announced over the tannoy system. He and Dunston were having breakfast in the wardroom. A meal only the Americans could manage – waffles, eggs, bacon, washed down with mugs of excellent coffee.

'You're up, Nick. You're wanted on the bridge,' said Schwarzkopf, walking up to the two men.

'Me?' Hunter frowned. 'Must be another man of the same name.'

'Nope, I don't think so,' said Schwarzkopf.

With a sigh Hunter arose from the table and went over to the nearest bulkhead. An internal phone was fixed to it with a list of extensions pinned alongside. He dialled the bridge.

'Second Officer of the watch.'

'My name is Lieutenant Commander Hunter. I came on board last night. Am I wanted on the bridge?'

'Just a second, sir. Let me ask.'

Another voice came down the phone. 'That you, Lieutenant Commander?'

'If you mean Hunter and am I from TIFAT, yes it is.'

'Good. This is the Captain.'

'Sorry, sir. I had no idea.'

There was a chuckle. 'That's all right. You're flying off in half an hour.'

'Yes, sir. Am I allowed to ask where I'm going?'

'Yep. You and your team are diving on that ship the Swedes sunk yesterday. I've been ordered to give you all the help and equipment you need. We carry a contingent of SEALs on board as well as ordinary divers. So we've got a wide range of gear. Stay where you are and I'll send someone to find you. In the meantime, I'll get your men together.'

'Yes, sir. Sir, I recognise the hand of General Macnair behind this. Can I go to the Comms Centre and contact him?'

'Sure. Tell one of the mids to take you.'

Hunter hung up and returned to his table. 'Eat up. We're wanted.'

'What's up?' Napier asked, sitting down at the table, a tray of food in front of him.

'We're going diving on the *SS Stockholm*.'

'What for?' Clements asked.

'I don't know yet. I need to talk to the General. I'm off to the Comms Centre.' He stood up as a midshipman came through the door and approached him.

The mid saluted nervously.

Hunter glanced at the junior officer's name tag and said, 'Midshipman Hibetson, you here to show me the way to the Comms Centre?'

'Yes, sir. Captain's orders, sir. Follow me please, sir.'

They got lost twice, which was quite normal on a ship of that size. But they eventually found the right place, in the midsection and close to the bowels of the ship.

It took a call to the bridge before Hunter got the authorisation he needed to enter and use the equipment.

Macnair briefed him quickly.

'But sir, five minutes with Novak would tell us all we need to know.'

'I am aware of that, Nick, but no-can-do. The Swedes are digging their heels in. And the more we push the more obdurate they're becoming.'

'What a waste of time. Has anybody asked them what they intend to do should Gustav release one of the containers of SRX? Or, heaven forbid, all three?'

'No response other than banging on about the human rights of the individual no matter what crime they've committed.' There was no mistaking the anger in Macnair's voice.

'Where's Gustav now?'

'Gone to ground. We're pulling out every stop to find him. Our best guess is he went ashore on Sicily.'

'How can you be sure, sir?'

'That's it – we can't. We were tracking the ship off Sicily when it appeared to have lost ground at one stage. With hindsight, it's likely Gustav went off by boat, and the *Stockholm* picked up speed again.'

'Good enough. Could he have already left the area?'

'With his resources? Easily. Private plane. Private ship. Nick, we're assuming he's on the loose with the SRX. But we have to make sure. Get to the *Stockholm* and check all the likely places those containers could be hidden. You're the only one who's been on board and knows where to look.'

'Okay, sir. I can check out his stateroom and the safe. After that the task is too big.'

'I agree. If the SRX isn't there and you don't see any sign of Gustav's body then we can assume he's out there somewhere with the stuff.'

'He's out there. Believe me.'

'I know, Nick. But let's make sure.' Uncharacteristically Macnair added, 'I've been ordered to make the search. Our politicians are clutching at straws. They live in hope. So just do it.'

A strange calm had descended over Gustav, a clarity of thought focused entirely on his ultimate commitment. The Swede was sitting in his house outside Bagheria, to the east of Palermo. He felt relatively safe, believing the obfuscation he had created covering its purchase to be impenetrable. Despite everything, he prided himself on his discipline and self-control. Outwardly nothing had changed. Inwardly his anger erupted like acid in his stomach. Ranting and raving would help no one. Rational consideration was required. Never in his life had he experienced so many set backs.

His contacts in the Swedish government were keeping *Kapitän zur See* Novak out of his enemy's hands but that might not last. He had to move fast. His frustration was mounting. Messages and phone calls he had been making all afternoon were going unanswered or ignored. He was almost sure that on two occasions the bastards on the other end had hung up on him. His grip on the glass of Evian water tightened imperceptibly. He'd pay them back. Once his people were in power he'd teach them the meaning of loyalty.

He could feel a momentum of resistance growing against him – TIFAT had discovered too much and time was running out. He had no idea how Macnair and his organisation had done it but he'd find out. It was now imperative that he strike the death blow. The Arabs would take delivery of the SRX shortly. The havoc its release would cause would be enough to make the white Christians of Europe rise up as one and sweep the Muslim filth into the sea.

Gustav sat back in his chair and took slow breaths to calm himself. He did so by going over the intended targets in his mind. One container was to be detonated at an American base in Germany, near a town called Paderborn. A second was to go off in the Paris Metro and a third . . . He stroked his eyebrow. The third was the one that gave him the most pleasure. It was to be detonated near the British Houses of Parliament. After all, it was from Britain that most of the opposition had come.

Duval came into the room. 'All done, Mr Gustav. The spheres are on their way.'

'The couriers?'

'As agreed. They don't know what they're carrying. They'll make the deliveries and leave immediately.'

'Excellent.'

Flying the SRX to their destinations was no longer an option. With the heightened tension of recent events and the possibility that customs were looking for them, it was too great a risk. The open borders of Europe were the perfect solution. It would take longer but was far safer.

*   *   *

Ursula Fritberg was an eye-catching blonde, nearly six feet tall, her features dominated by attractive blue eyes. She was a lesbian and ultra-right wing. The latter was well known in the proper circles. The former she kept a secret. She was looking forward to the train journey from the toe of Italy up to Germany. Thirty lovely hours cocooned in First Class, watching the scenery unfold. The idea was balm to her restless nature. And one never knew. There was always the possibility of a little sexual adventure.

Olaf Gustav was Charles' brother. Always in the background, content to live in the shadow of his older sibling, he was totally different in appearance. Olaf was average in every way. From his regular features, to his average height and weight. It was said of him that he would be lost in a crowd of two. Over the years this had stood him in good stead. He was a tabloid journalist of the lowest denominator. He had often been in company that literally forgot he was there. Many indiscretions therefore came to his ears. Reporting tittle-tattle, unconfirmed rumours, putting two and two together and coming up with five was his speciality. The high and not so mighty were his targets. His column was syndicated across Europe, mainly in his brother's newspapers, and often made fillers on TV and radio broadcasts. Information for potential blackmail he passed directly to Charles. Like his brother, he was a rabid right-winger. He believed fervently in a whites-only Europe and was prepared to do anything in his power to help his brother meet that goal.

He would travel by private boat to Marseilles, then by TGV to Paris. At 300kph he would be in France's capital in three hours. Time enough to enjoy a long and leisurely lunch. It was perfect. He would deliver Charles' package to the restaurant in Malmaison and then hit the hot-spots. He was looking forward to it. Damn Charles' instructions to leave immediately. Paris was just the place for his type of fun.

Clive Holmes was a disgraced civil-servant. Discovered sending British National Party propaganda over the internet from his office, he had been summarily dismissed. His guts knotted up at the memory of it. The black bitch had enjoyed telling him to clear his desk. He had appealed of course but it was no use. The government had closed ranks and he was out after fifteen years. No job. No future. No pension. Always on *their* side. The black swine. The sooner Britain returned to its Anglo-Saxon roots the better. Conveniently, he had forgotten that he had been in the civil service at the lowest grade with no hope of advancement. Holmes would tell anybody who cared to listen that the blacks, browns and Chinkies had been promoted over him because of so-called affirmative action. Well, he'd show them!

Tall, brown haired and brown eyed, he was good looking, with a dimpled chin. He kept fit by working out in the gym whenever he could. He had a boyish charm and an inane grin that women found alluring. It wasn't until they got to know him better that they realised he really was as stupid as his grin suggested. He spoke in slogans, passionate about race issues but with no substance to back his arguments.

He too was travelling by boat, but to Nice. He'd take the TGV to Paris and then change to Eurostar. He would arrive in London in the evening and make his way to Shepherd's Bush. To a particular restaurant where he would hand over the parcel. His instructions were to leave the country immediately. He always obeyed orders. It was easier than having to think for himself.

23

Two large inflatables were lowered onto the gently undulating sea. The team members were winched down. They were already kitted out in wet-suits and had only to finish pre-dive checks of their bottles to enter the water.

Badonovitch in one boat, Masters in the other, put the 120hp outboards into position on the transom and started each one. They burst into life with a deep-throated roar. In seconds they had the *Stockholm's* transponder in one craft and had lashed the inflatables together. There was a party atmosphere about the team. This was something they loved doing. Diving in clear water, from a stable platform, under a warm sun, with a job to be done. Perfect.

Dunston and Masson would stay in the boats. The others would dive in pairs, secured to each other by a two-metre long rope attached to their left upper arms. Communications would be by voice from throat mikes. Hunter was buddied with Badonovitch, Masters with Tanner and Napier with Clements. They had different tasks to perform. Hunter was to look for the spheres of SRX, while the other two pairs were to set charges inside the ship's armoury and blow it to smithereens. It was too tempting a target for terrorist groups should they ever find out where the ship was and what it was carrying.

The sets they were using were state-of-the-art. The gas, heliox, was computer controlled to ensure the right mix of oxygen and helium for the appropriate depth. They had three hours, near enough, at fifty metres before they had to worry about decompression stops.

'Are you sure you're up to this?' Dunston asked Hunter, as Badonovitch helped him on with his set.

'Sure. I can't wait.'

'What about your head?'

'It's okay. Ready, Jan?'

'Yes, boss. Waiting on you.'

The two men slid over the side of the inflatable and into the warm water. Not for them the flashy back-flip with lots of show, splash and disorientation once you hit the water. They checked each other for leaks in their sets, gave the OK sign to Dunston and left surface. Once under the water they checked communications with Masson and followed the line down to the ship. Within seconds they could see its ghostly outline. Around them swam fish of all shapes and sizes which ignored them as easily as they ignored the fish. A small amount of oil or diesel was leaking from the ship. It wasn't enough to develop into a slick, and dissipated as it rose to the surface.

The *Stockholm* was at a list of about 45 degrees to starboard. Around her, curious denizens frequenting that part of the Mediterranean were congregating. Some had already found nooks and crannies to move into, intending to live there until they were either driven away or their prey no longer came near. Unerringly, Hunter led the way into the ship. It was eerie swimming in through the port side, the door latched open, fish swimming in and around the high-tech bridge. Already a thin layer of silt was beginning to form on the surfaces.

The lamps on their heads illuminated their way down to the next deck. There they were surprised to discover that the battery operated emergency lights fixed along the walls of the corridors were still operating. Water tight and with their own power supply, they were good for up to 96 hours.

In Gustav's stateroom, Hunter and Badonovitch unclipped their buddy-line and while the Spetsnaz searched the cabin Hunter set PE around the safe.

The explosion took off the hinges and Hunter was able to pull the door open. It was empty. Totally empty. He felt around, disappointed but not surprised. His fingers touched an imbedded lifting ring. Curling his finger around it he lifted a lid and inside found a locked box. He put it in the string bag he had dangling from his dive-belt.

He and Badonovitch continued searching but found nothing. Duval's room was also empty. The other staterooms were bare of everything except furniture. Not a single personal item was found.

The bridge yielded very little. Hunter took the latest log and the disc from the satellite navigation system. A safe on the bridge was opened simply by using a key hanging on a nearby shelf. Inside they found the Captain's passport and some money. Both were taken.

Throughout the search they had been reporting to the surface. They knew that the other two teams had finished and were on their way back up. Hunter acknowledged the information and told Dunston that he and Badonovitch were doing the same.

It was glorious to swim upwards, heading for the sun dappling the surface. Diving gave Hunter a sense of freedom, of entering another world. Hitting the surface the two men made the OK sign, slipped off their sets and handed them into the boat. A kick of their fins and a heave and they flopped into the bottom of the boat.

'How'd it go?' Hunter asked Clements.

'No problems. We ran the whole lot to one detonator with a back-up. It's a thirty hour delay. That'll give the clean-up vessel plenty of time to get here.'

'Good. We don't want any more pollution than is absolutely necessary.'

The clean-up vessel would literally suck up the surface of the water, filter out any oil or diesel and spit the seawater back out. It was highly effective, provided it was in the locale when the spillage was in the early stages.

'We'd better let the General know what we've learned,' said Hunter. 'Which is precisely the square-root of nothing.'

They were mid-way between Sardinia and Tunisia. While the divers had been down, Dunston and Masson had erected shades over the boats. Now the men settled down to a cold buffet, iced drinks and a short wait. Burg, who had been piloting the helicopter, after dropping them in-situ, had flown on to Cagliari to refuel, the carrier having continued on its planned route. He was due back shortly. In fact, they heard his approach as new instructions reached them from TIFAT HQ.

Macnair had spoken to the Prime Minister in the morning. They agreed it was time to go on the offensive. The PR offensive. Press releases already agreed, written and refined to the nth degree, were to be distributed that afternoon, in time for the evening news across the whole of Europe. A 4pm conference was called by No10. That was unusual in itself. TV, radio and the printed press all agreed to send their top people. In journalistic code if an announcement was a Jimmy Young it was interesting but not bad. A Jeremy Paxman was bad but not earth-shattering. A Kate Adie or a John Simpson meant very bad, head for the bunkers. The word went out this was a Kate Adie and John Simpson combined.

Other European leaders were to make the same announcements. Certain facts were now clear and TIFAT's role was crucial. This was to be an orchestrated attempt to accuse the ultra-right-wing of terrorist attacks across Europe. Evidence was produced, mostly thanks to Isobel, that the attacks were paid for and planned by Charles Gustav and his associates. And the Prime Minister was as good as his word. He had given Macnair every possible support. The news release was hard-hitting, factual and shocking in the extreme. A huge propaganda machine moved into operation, led by the British and strongly supported by the European Parliament, spearheaded by Christine Woolford. She was well briefed by Macnair and in turn she had given the facts to other MEPs who now supported her. From left-wing Social Democrats to right-wing Conservatives, an awareness that they were fighting for the very existence of democracy and tolerance in Europe made them ready, willing and able to battle their corner. They were united against the ultra-right-wing and the xenophobes of every European state.

Macnair clenched his fists in anger. He had to stop Gustav. *But where the hell was he?*

As if in answer to a prayer Isobel rushed in. 'General, GCHQ just traced a call from Gustav to somebody with a mobile in London.'

'Are you sure it was Gustav?'

'Positive. They did a voice match.'

'Where is he?'

'Somewhere in Bagheria in Northern Sicily. We are getting all the details now. Leo is pulling detailed maps of the place and we've re-programmed the satellites to take a look.'

'Are you absolutely sure he's there?'

'As sure as we can be. Unless he's used a land-line from some-where else, phoned to the house and routed the call via there. But I don't see it somehow.'

'What was the gist of the call?'

'In a nutshell, to hurry up an operation. He didn't say what it was. He sounded rattled but,' she shrugged, 'still over-confident. We also received a floppy disc of information from Nick. We're working on it right now.'

In fact Gareth was working on it. He had been told to be careful, in case there was any self destruct mechanism in the program should anybody try and access the information without the right passwords. It was just as well he was prepared. As soon as the program was opened it threatened to wipe itself clean. Gareth set about constructing a mole that would break through and spit the information out of a window he would construct. He was, put simply, a genius.

The house sat in the folds of two hills, about three kilometres from the north coast of Sicily, south of Bagheria, and inland of the A20 motorway. The helicopter flew high, waiting and watching. The next part of the operation called for careful timing. A combination of satellite and infra-red pictures showed there were a number of people in a guardhouse at the main gate. Gustav's property was surrounded by a high fence and, from the information gleaned by TIFAT, it was probably electrified.

At the house, a huge sprawling hacienda, there were at least a dozen people. Some would be guards, others merely local help.

Unfortunately there was too much at stake to worry about the lives of a few who may or may not be innocent. The team was going in hard and fast. But first they had to wait for the Americans.

'Two minutes,' Burg told the others. 'One minute. Tally ho.'

The helicopter swooped down out of the sky just as a stealth fighter dropped a series of smart bombs along the southern wall of the house. A second F-117A took out the guardhouse with one hit.

The dust was still mushrooming when the helicopter landed a few metres from the house. The team poured out, weapons ready, moving fast but carefully towards the smashed walls.

One, two and then a third figure staggered out, coughing, choking on the dust. Masters and Clements ran around the front of the house. Badonovitch and Napier went to the western side, Masson and Tanner went east. Hunter and Dunston approached the shattered walls. Schwarzkopf took charge of the two men and one woman who had appeared. Making them lie down, he handcuffed their hands behind their backs.

An automatic gun opened up and the team threw themselves to the ground. It had been fired from a window in the east side of the house. Masson was killed outright, while Tanner was hit in the side. He returned fire, setting down a barrage that allowed Clements to come around from the front and lob a grenade through the window. The firing was abruptly cut off.

Dunston kept low and dashed across the open ground to see what he could do for the injured men. It took only a second to confirm Masson's death. Ripping open a triangular bandage, Dunston strapped it around the entry and exit wounds in the left side of Tanner's abdomen. The blood looked healthy enough and Dunston hoped no vital organs had been hit.

'Stay put,' he ordered Tanner, who merely nodded.

Hunter was picking his way into the house. From the infra-red sensors it appeared that there were people upstairs, moving around. There were others in a room in the front of the house. Schwarzkopf was at his shoulder, covering him.

In spite of the bombs the house remained standing. Practically all of the southern wall was blown away and they could see bits of bodies lying in the debris. Where were Gustav and Duval?

More shooting started from the front and Hunter and Schwarzkopf followed the sound. A door took them into a large open space from which other rooms led off. In the middle was a staircase. The infra-red sensors confirmed three people in the room ahead. Nobody was showing up in their immediate area. They darted across to the door. Hunter cracked it open and the pilot threw in two grenades in quick succession. The resulting explosions stopped the firing.

Hunter used his personal radio to check the situation with the rest of the team. They all agreed. There appeared to be only two people left alive in the house, in an upstairs room. Hunter and Schwarzkopf made for the stairs. The sensors confirmed survivors were at the end of the house, on the western side. A short corridor was faced by a solid door. Two people were hiding behind it.

Hunter tried the door handle. The door opened on silent hinges. A cautious look made him step into the room, his Glock 19 pointed at Gustav. The Swede was seated behind a desk in the corner of the room. To one side sat Duval. The secretary was nervous. Gustav, as always, was ice cold.

'Ah, Mr Hunter, I might have guessed it would be you. You keep turning up at the most inopportune moments.'

'On your feet, Gustav. You're coming with us.'

'I don't think so, somehow. I have already contacted my friend, the Chief of Police at Palermo and asked for assistance. No doubt help is on its way even as we speak. You can argue it out with him and his men.'

Hunter shook his head. 'You couldn't be more wrong, Gustav. The Italian government has warned both the Mafia and the local law enforcement agencies to stay out of this fight. Unless they want a clampdown the likes of which they have never seen before. Believe me, no one is coming to your aid.'

Gustav licked his lips. The utter confidence with which Hunter spoke rattled him. Duval looked positively sick.

'I need some information and I need it fast,' said Hunter. 'Where are the spheres of SRX?'

'I don't know what you're talking about.'

'Don't play games with me, Gustav, I haven't time.' Hunter had crossed the room and was standing in front of the desk. 'Where are they?'

'I don't . . .'

The Glock was on single shot. Gustav sat with his hands splayed on the desk in front of him. Hunter pressed the barrel of his gun onto the little finger of Gustav's left hand and fired.

Gustav screamed in pain and shock. Blood spurted across the leather desk top, leaving a red stain. 'You'll pay for that,' Gustav snarled, reaching into a pocket for a handkerchief. The white linen, wrapped around the stump of his finger was turning bloody.

'I will shoot off each of your fingers and then start on your feet,' said Hunter.

'Fool,' said Gustav with a sneer. 'Have you any idea how powerful I am? Who I control? As soon as we've taken power I'll have you, Hunter. You'll live to regret ever crossing swords with me.'

Hunter shrugged indifferently. 'It's over, Gustav. Within,' Hunter glanced at his watch, 'half an hour, a media blitz will start. Names will be spelled out. Your involvement will be clear for all the world to see.'

Gustav snorted in derision. 'Do you not realise that I would foresee such an eventuality? Anything that's said against me personally or my movement will be denied. Many men and women in high places will come out on my side, whether they wish to or not. I've ensured that. And once the Muslims have let loose the nerve gas, who will have the upper hand? Europe will panic. The people will believe what I tell them because they *want* to believe. That's the beauty of propaganda.'

'The people of Europe will believe the truth. The evidence is conclusive. After all, you are the one who hired the scientists to make the filthy stuff. Or do you deny it?'

'Of course I don't deny it,' Gustav said with scorn. 'It was the only way to ensure white Europeans will rise up and throw the coloureds and the non-Christians out.'

'Did you get all that?' Hunter asked into his throat mike.

'Yes,' said Macnair. 'Loud and clear. The picture is a little fuzzy but it will do. Isobel says she can clean it up digitally.'

'What's going on?' Duval asked, fear making him speak out.

Hunter pointed to his shoulder. 'This is a camera lens and this is a microphone. Gustav's confession has just been sent via satellite to TIFAT HQ. It will be broadcast later today.'

Gustav was shaking with hatred. 'I'll claim you made it up. Used actors to dub my voice. Synthesised my face using computers.'

'Gustav, Gustav, Gustav,' Hunter spoke in mock sorrow, shaking his head, 'you still don't get it. If you don't tell me where to find the spheres of gas I'll kill you. You won't live to see a glorious new dawn breaking over Europe. And neither will you,' he added, looking at Duval. Hunter blinked hard. A wave of dizziness was sweeping over him again. Damnation! He had thought the after-effects of the head wound had passed.

'I'll tell you all I know,' said Duval, 'in exchange for immunity.'

'Shut up, you weakling,' hissed Gustav. 'Remember which race you belong to – if you're going to die, at least die with some dignity. Tell them nothing.'

'Charles, your mind is diseased. Your obsession has become a mania. Your idea of a whites-only Europe is . . . ludicrous. Anyone with half a brain can see that. And setting off weapons as heinous as the SRX gas proves you're mad.'

'You will not speak to me like that,' Gustav hissed, standing up and leaning his weight on the desk. His eyes were bulging.

Hunter couldn't see properly but he'd heard the exchange. His eyesight was clearing when he saw the small calibre gun appear in Gustav's hand. Hunter shot him in the elbow, shattering the joint. The gun flew from Gustav's hand and he screamed in pain once more.

An image of Ruth and her damaged leg sprang to Hunter's mind. In a cold rage he fired twice more in rapid succession. He blew apart Gustav's knees. The Swede collapsed unconscious.

Duval was watching in horror. Hunter now aimed his gun at

the American's left knee. 'All right, Duval, talk. Where are the containers being taken?'

'I don't know.' He saw Hunter's finger tighten on the trigger and he yelled, 'Wait! It's true! I tell you I don't know. Gustav made all the arrangements. But I do have extremely valuable information about his organisation. About the people in power who are in his pay. Hunter, for God's sake, I'm a walking data bank.'

'We'll come to that later. Right now we need to find that SRX before a humanitarian disaster happens.'

'I know who has them. I can give you their names, their descriptions.'

'But you don't know where they are going?'

'No! Gustav kept that secret. He was becoming paranoid. He was keeping more and more things to himself.'

'Or maybe he was beginning not to trust you,' said Hunter. 'Burg, check on Gustav.'

The pilot moved around the desk and knelt by the body. 'He's still alive, just.'

Gustav opened his eyes and said in a rasping whisper. 'It will be too late. *You* are too late. The uprising will start. My death will change nothing.' Blood was pooling across the floor, the metallic smell all pervading. Gustav struggled, trying to lift his head but collapsed again. Schwarzkopf checked his pulse, looked at Hunter and shook his head.

'That just leaves you, Duval,' said Hunter.

'I'll do all I can to help. But I want immunity.' Duval looked at the body and shuddered.

'What about a bullet in the brain?' Hunter aimed at the secretary.

Duval flinched but said, 'Then you'll never find the SRX.'

Hunter lowered his gun. The bloody man was right. 'I'll see what I can do.'

'Not good enough. Speak to Macnair. Tell him I can be of great help in the present situation but I want a guarantee that I won't be prosecuted.'

Hunter knew Duval's unique knowledge of Gustav's movement

would be invaluable. His co-operation might well save thousands of lives. 'Show me some sign of good faith. Let me give the General something.'

'Like what?'

'Like the names and descriptions of the people carrying the SRX.'

Duval's forehead furrowed in worried indecision but then he made his mind up. 'All right. Their names are Ursula Fritberg, Olaf Gustav and Clive Holmes. I know the targets too. Ursula Fritberg's is the US army base near Paderborn. Olaf's is the Métro in Paris and Holmes' is to be set off somewhere in London.'

'Olaf Gustav? Any relation?' Hunter nodded at the body.

'His brother.'

'Did you see the three of them?'

'Yes. I handed them their instructions in an envelope. Along with some money for expenses.'

'And you don't know what those instructions were?'

'No, I told you. Charles was becoming extremely secretive with his plans. It was beginning to lead to disagreements between us.'

'Disagreements?'

Duval shrugged. 'Listen, Hunter, I've been looking for a way out for months. This makes it easier.' He cast a glance at Gustav and shuddered. Standing up, he went into a bathroom and returned with a towel. He threw it over Gustav's body. Blood began to soak into the cloth.

Hunter used his sat-phone to call Macnair. He briefly reported what had happened and what Duval had said.

'Actually, Nick, we've had some luck,' said Macnair. 'That disc you sent us has a raft of information which we can use. However, one small file contained three itineraries. Until now they made no sense. I'll phone you back in a few minutes.' The connection was broken.

The team were deployed around the house, creating a defensive perimeter. There was no telling whether the Mafia *would* stay away.

While Hunter waited for the General to phone, Schwarzkopf

went downstairs to help put Masson into a body bag and stow his body in the helicopter.

Macnair phoned within five minutes. 'This all checks. The itineraries are headed with the initials of each person. Ursula Fritberg is on the train for Paderborn and is just now crossing the German border. I've arranged for her to be picked up while the train is moving. That way she cannot escape. Unfortunately, the other two are a different problem. Olaf Gustav has already arrived in Paris. We know where he's going so we'll have him met at the restaurant. Clive Holmes is already in London. Likewise we'll pick him up at the drop.'

The arguments raged wide and deep on some TV shows. Bitter rhetoric turned into fisticuffs. It was good for ratings but dreadful for democracy.

The existence of the SRX filled containers was not disclosed. The rioting taking place was bad enough. If the populace became really terrified it would escalate out of control. Minorities in inner-cities were building barricades to protect themselves and their communities. Skinheads and other fascist groups were on the rampage, throwing petrol bombs and firing illegal guns. The police in some areas tried to control the problem. In others they stood back and watched.

There was no doubt in Macnair's mind that everything hinged on stopping the release of the nerve gas. If the spheres were found and the attacks stopped then it was possible democracy could win. If they were let loose by Islamic fundamentalists then it wouldn't matter what proof or information was shown to the public. It would be too late. Muslims would pay the price. There would be no stopping the anger flooding into the streets. The current exodus of non-whites leaving Europe, bad though it was, would become a flood. Gustav would have won.

Ursula Fritberg was feeling pleased with herself. She would be changing trains at Frankfurt in fifteen minutes. She had enjoyed her journey. The food had been very good, the wine palatable and the large brandies the night before had helped her sleep soundly. There had been a slight delay at the border but it hadn't amounted to much. A cursory look had been given to her passport but it was more for form than anything. The train had made an unscheduled stop at Darmstadt but it had only been for a few seconds. She wondered idly why they had stopped.

There were two men walking along the carriage, though not looking in her direction. Alarm bells rang in her head. Something was wrong. *What? That was it*! They *weren't* looking. Men always looked at her. She stood up with a feeling of alarm and turned away. She found herself staring into the eyes of a stranger.

He greeted her with the words, 'You are under arrest.'

She heard them as if from the end of a long tunnel as her world shattered. The SRX was found in seconds.

Olaf found the drop-point, an Algerian restaurant in a run-down part of Malmaison. The clientele were mostly non-whites and Muslim. Two tables were particularly boisterous. One white man was celebrating his divorce with three other white friends, while a black man, with three mixed-race friends, were celebrating his stag night. Both parties had obviously drunk too much before arriving at the restaurant, although the men had barely touched the wine that had been placed on their tables. They had eaten though, picking at their food, laughing too loudly, being a nuisance. The sooner they left, thought the owner, the better.

Olaf Gustav entered carrying a bag. He looked around nervously. In a corner of the restaurant sat two men. Swarthy-complexioned, Arab looking. Silent men who kept glancing towards the door.

Gustav's brother walked towards them. He was halfway across the crowded restaurant when the eight raucous customers suddenly stood up and drew guns.

'Police! Police! Stay where you are! Do not move!'

Olaf Gustav stopped in horror and looked over his shoulder. The guns were levelled at him. He couldn't help himself. Urine ran down his leg and puddled at his feet.

The two Arabs sitting in the corner had leapt to their feet and were reaching for guns they carried in holsters under their armpits.

The French police didn't hesitate. The two men were gunned down even as Olaf Gustav was being thrown to the floor and handcuffed. A senior policemen grabbed the bag. Relief flooded through him when he saw the container of SRX gas.

From Sicily the team flew by helicopter to Naples. They took Duval, a laptop computer and a handful of floppy discs. Macnair had assured the American that he would do everything in his power to keep him from prison. Provided he co-operated fully. When they arrived in Naples, a Hercules aircraft met them and they changed from one plane to another in record time.

Once the team was in the air they did what they always did in these circumstances. They slept. They had been expecting to fly straight to Scotland and so it came as a complete surprise when they were diverted to Heathrow.

Hunter was informed by the pilot of the change of destination and he radioed Macnair.

'Bad news, Nick. We got two lots of the SRX but the third has gone missing. In London.'

24

Ex-civil servant Clive Holmes made a simple error. He failed to take account of the hour difference between the Continent and the UK. He arrived an hour early at the restaurant in Shepherd's Bush. Situated in a side street off Charecroft Way, its owners boasted that the food was suitable for the most observant of the Muslim faith. The two Arabs he was to meet were not yet there. In fact, the restaurant was empty. It was only just 6pm and the evening rush was yet to start.

Nervously Holmes sat down to wait at a corner table. He wasn't there for long before a kitchen door opened and two men approached his table.

'You have it?' The younger of the two asked.

'Who are you?' Holmes replied. If he was nervous he didn't show it. A total lack of imagination helped a great deal in circumstances like these.

'We know you have something for us. Hand it over.'

'How do I know . . .'

'Do not play games with us. Give me the bag.'

Holmes shrugged. He'd done what he was supposed to do. He handed the bag over.

The two men walked away, through the kitchen door. Holmes sat there for a few seconds and then got to his feet. Time to leave. He walked out the front door, bumping into a large burly man. Holmes apologised, as did the man who stepped around him. He had taken two or three paces when he heard a voice.

'Excuse me.'

Holmes looked over his shoulder.

'Aren't you Clive Homes?'

'Yes. Do I know you?'

The words were hardly out of his mouth when he was looking down the barrels of two revolvers. Armed police came pouring out of a plain white van parked next to the kerb. He was hand-cuffed and in the back of the van before he knew what was going on.

It only took a matter of minutes to get him talking. He'd had no idea what he was bringing into the country. No, he didn't know the two men he had given the bag to. He assumed they had left through the back entrance.

The police raided the restaurant but there was no sign of the SRX or the two men. Three illegal immigrants were taken into custody. At Bow Street Police Station their photographs were scanned into a computer. Two proved to have links with al-Qaeda. Their self-appointed leader, Hamad bin Thani, made clear their position. He demanded to see their lawyers and refused to talk until one was present. The offer of the duty solicitor was turned down. The Arabs had names and phone numbers of specific lawyers they wanted to represent them. The police recognised the names immediately. Apologists for terrorists under the guise of human rights, these particular solicitors would be a thorn in the sides of the police when they tried to extract information from the men arrested. The Superintendent in charge had a flash of inspiration. He telephoned Macnair.

Hunter met the police at Heathrow. The three men were handed over to the team who were kitted out in full battle dress, including black ski-masks. They looked terrifying – as indeed they were meant to. Macnair had been explicit with his instructions. A WMD was out in the streets of London somewhere and these three men had knowledge of its whereabouts. No matter what it took, they *had* to get the information.

The prisoners had been arrogant, offensive. Their attitude suddenly changed.

'What are you doing? You cannot hand us over to these men,'

screamed Hamad bin Thani. 'I demand to see my lawyer.'

Clements took hold of bin Thani by the throat and snarled into his face. 'You don't exist, scum. You're ours.' He shoved him towards the back of the Hercules which was sitting with its tail-gate open.

The other two men were herded after him.

'Superintendent,' said Hunter, 'please forget you ever saw them. And look after Mr Duval for us.'

'Saw who?' the Superintendent quipped, turned away and then suddenly walked back. 'Do whatever it takes. My family live in London. And don't worry about Duval.'

On board the plane the men were secured to their seats. Bags were placed over their heads, the feeling of claustrophobia adding to their fear.

'Where's Jan?' Hunter asked.

'On his way, boss. He'll be about five minutes. The police had a little difficulty finding what we wanted,' answered Napier.

'But he got them?'

'He did.'

A police car drew up and Badonovitch leapt out. From the trunk he took three bags, slung them over his shoulder and ran up the ramp. As soon as he was on board the door was closed and the pilot asked for permission to take-off. The Hercules was given priority but even so there was a delay of three minutes while the runway was cleared. As soon as enough height was gained the Hercules headed for the Channel before turning west.

Hunter went through the brief files the police had handed him. Two al-Qaeda men and a third unknown but definitely an illegal and probably Saudi. Did he have anything to do with the WMD? Perhaps. Certainly the al-Qaeda men would know something.

The Geneva Convention was clear on the treatment of both prisoners of war and civilians. The trouble was the enemy they were up against didn't fit into any of the categories as laid down by international law. With the images of the American treatment of Iraqi POWs fresh in his mind, Hunter hated what they were about to do. He knew the rest of the team thought likewise. But with so much at stake there was no choice. He hoped the threat of eternal damnation would make the men talk.

Pulling the bags off their heads he watched as the men sucked in air, half-suffocated by the restricting bags. Hate and fear mixed in their faces. They were released from their seats and pulled upright. Their hands were tied to the parachute rail above them.

'Who has the nerve gas?' Hunter asked bin Thani.

'I do not know what you're talking about. You cannot do this. I demand you take us back to Heathrow and allow me to call my lawyer.'

'Let me explain something to you,' said Hunter. 'And please listen very carefully.' He hated what he was doing but knew that he had no choice. Time was of the essence. Tens even hundreds of thousands of lives were at stake. Grimly, he hit the man as hard as he could in the solar plexus. The man screamed in agony as the air erupted from his lungs. He was gasping, unable to suck air in, unable to curl over to relieve the pain.

Hunter turned to the second man. 'Your name is Omar al-Faud. Correct?'

'I tell you nothing. We demand . . .' He screamed as Hunter repeated the blow.

'Mr Ayman Zubaydah,' Hunter spoke almost conversationally, 'I hope you will be more reasonable?'

Zubaydah responded with a torrent of Arabic.

'Don't you speak English?'

The al-Qaeda man answered. 'No! I no speak English.'

'In that case we have no further use of you. No more questions to ask. Understand?'

The man nodded vigorously.

'That surprises me as you claim not to speak English. Jan!'

Badonovitch approached carrying one of the bags. He opened it and took out a dead piglet. The three Muslims looked at the pig in utter horror. Badonovitch took the suckling and hung it around the neck of Zubaydah, who was now gibbering.

'I speak. I speak English good.'

'Sorry,' said Hunter, 'you're too late.'

Badonovitch wrapped canvas around the pig and the man's

body. The other two looked on in complete shock. Chains were wrapped around Zubaydah's legs, all the way up to his chest.

'Do you see that indicator?' Hunter pointed to an altimeter over the port side door.

None of the Arabs responded. Hunter grabbed bin Thani by the hair, lifted his head and pointed. 'Do you see it?'

'Yes,' he croaked. 'I see it.'

'Do you know what it means?'

'No.'

'It means we are twenty-five thousand feet high. I can tell you we are in the middle of the English Channel, heading west-south-west.' He used his internal comms set to speak to the pilot who confirmed there was no shipping in the vicinity. Gesturing to Masters and Clements, Zubaydah was freed from the parachute rail. He was picked up and carried to the port side of the aircraft. A door was opened and he was thrown out unceremoniously and still alive.

Hunter managed to hide his emotions. He loathed what he was doing so much that he felt sick. But they had to find the SRX and there was no time. 'I don't know how long he lived,' he smiled through his mask at the other two, who were staring at him like rabbits trapped by a snake. 'But he probably didn't die until he hit the water.' He paused and then added as though it was an afterthought, 'Of course he'll never go to heaven. Never mind, he's got a pig for company for eternity.'

The faces of the two men reflected their complete devastation. Hunter stood and watched them for a few seconds, saying nothing.

Looking bin Thani straight in the eye, Hunter said, 'I want to know where the SRX is. It's a virulent form of biotoxin that will kill many, many thousands of people, indiscriminately. Christians, Hindus and Muslims alike.'

'I . . . I don't know.' The al-Qaeda terrorist was staring at the door through which Zubaydah had vanished, as though expecting him to reappear at any moment.

'If you have nothing to tell us, then you're of no use to us. You'll go the same way as your friend. Then al-Faud can answer my questions. I can promise you two things. You will scream all the way to the sea and you will have company. Jan.'

The Spetsnaz brought forward another bag and tipped the carcass of another piglet onto the deck. Both Muslims stared at it in horror.

'You won't be going to Paradise, that's for sure,' said Hunter. 'So your friends and family won't be there to greet you. Or to see you when it's their turn to die. Who will protect you then from the torments of hell-fire?'

Bin Thani dragged his eyes from the pig and looked at Hunter with hate. 'What kind of man are you,' he asked hoarsely, 'who can condemn a man's soul to eternal damnation?'

'One who finds a loathsome swine like you even breathing the same air as ordinary people an abomination. I'll do whatever it takes to save the innocent lives you are condemning to so horrific a death. I've seen the gas in action and it's a terrible way to die. In fact, your death will be pleasant by comparison. Jan,' Hunter tilted his head towards bin Thani.

The Arab screamed loudly and fainted. A mug of cold water thrown in his face revived him.

'I am running out of time and patience. Now, where is the SRX?'

'I swear I don't know,' bin Thani screamed at him.

'Jan.'

The Spetsnaz tied the hindquarters of the pig around bin Thani's neck. Screaming hysterically the Arab finally managed to say, 'He knows, not me.' He moaned and added, 'For the love of Allah, take it away.'

While Badonovitch removed the pig Hunter turned his attention to Omar al-Faud. 'You know? Is that right?'

'I know nothing! Nothing!'

Hunter appeared to be considering the man's statement and after a few seconds he sighed. 'In that case, we have no use for you. Jan . . .'

'Allah is merciful. Judgement is his alone!'

Hunter grabbed the Arab by the throat and rammed his head against the side of the plane. 'You bastard. Don't talk to us about

God's judgement. You intend to murder innocent men, women and children and for what? You perverted piece of filth. I told you I've seen the gas kill. I *know* what a horrible death it is. Now tell me where to find the SRX.'

The Arab stayed silent. Hunter nodded to Jan who picked up the pig's carcass and walked toward al-Faud.

'All right! All right, may Allah curse you. It is in a mosque in Lambeth.'

'What's the address?'

Al-Faud mustered his courage for a few more seconds but as Badonovitch placed the pig's snout against his cheek he yelled out the location.

'When is the attack going to take place?'

'Tomorrow! Tomorrow, I swear!'

'Where?'

'At the Houses of Parliament.'

Now that he had started to talk, al-Faud found it easy to continue. He gave the names of the two men who were to carry out the attack but all he knew about the timing was that it was planned for the afternoon.

Hunter radioed Macnair and told him what they had learnt.

Macnair acknowledged the information and said, 'You know what to do.'

'Yes, sir.'

Turning to the two men, he said, 'We wait and see what happens.'

The plane droned westwards, past the tip of Cornwall. An hour later, Macnair called back. 'He was telling the truth. Unfortunately, one of the men escaped with the SRX. He went through an underground passage to a house five doors along and got away. The police have picked up about twenty people who are refusing to talk. And there's no way we can get them to tell us what we need to know as their solicitors are already on the scene.'

'What now, sir?'

'Try and get more details. The Houses of Parliament cover a large area. The gas could be released anywhere at anytime. See if they know any more.'

'Roger that, sir.'

In spite of more threats they got nothing further from either man. Hunter came to the conclusion that they knew nothing more. Which made sense. Information cut-outs were the corner-stone to any terrorist act.

'You may get to heaven after all. But I doubt it.'

At Hunter's nod the two men were released from their cuffs and allowed to sit. He offered them each a drink of water which they gulped down thirstily. The poison, a derivative of curare, was fast acting and both men died within seconds.

The team wrapped chains around the bodies and threw them out of the plane. The carcasses of the pigs followed separately. Had the two men been allowed to live the uproar about their human rights would possibly have drowned out the screams of terror of the innocents killed.

Already the Hercules had banked around and was heading north, for Edinburgh. There was nothing more they could do. However, their plans were changed by a call from Macnair. The plane was being sent back to Heathrow.

When it landed they were met by the same Superintendent who had seen them off. He had already been briefed on what the team had learnt.

'So why are we needed?' Hunter asked, puzzled.

'We need sharpshooters. We've identified vantage points over-looking the square. Peter Weir and David Hughes are on their way here with four rifles. Some sort of specialist sniper guns?'

Hunter nodded. 'Probably. Weir's a superb shot and Dave Hughes is no slouch, either. The other men I can offer are Don Masters and Josh Clements.'

'Can the rest of you be in the Square?'

'No problem. What about undercover police?'

'It'll be crawling with them. Men and women. Undercover operatives are one thing. Special services quite another. And God alone knows what we'll be up against.'

The day's beauty mocked the possible horror ahead. It was warm, the sun was shining, clouds scudded across a blue sky.

Parliament Square was busy with Londoners going about their business, as well as tourists coming to wonder at and photograph one of the most famous buildings in the world. Visitors faced one disappointment. Big Ben would not be striking that day. The clock and the bells were stopped, so the press announcement said, for necessary maintenance. At that time of the day, many politicians, mostly unknown, were heading to one of the heavily subsidised restaurants or bars for lunch or a drink. It was business as usual for the vast majority of people.

It was precisely noon.

Matt Dunston and Hunter strolled around the square, to all intents and purposes in a deep discussion, enjoying the weather. Dressed in light grey, pin-stripe city suits, and wearing ties, they appeared the epitome of successful businessmen or middle-ranking civil servants.

About half the men and women walking in and out of the square were plain clothes police. Some, members of the armed response unit, carried concealed weapons. Others were there to look and report. They walked down the streets that led into the square and out again desperate to identify the possible terrorists before it was too late. Loiterers on Westminster Bridge stood and gossiped, watching the people walking across. One thing they knew was helpful in their search. The man or woman they were looking for would be carrying a bag big enough to hold the deadly SRX sphere.

The road had been closed to all traffic. It was causing chaos in the area but it removed one of their biggest headaches – a vehicle with the nerve gas hidden inside. The terrorists would *have* to approach on foot. But they were also gambling the attack was still taking place around Westminster.

Dunston and Hunter were leaning on the parapet of the bridge, watching, searching, aware that time was passing. With a life-time interest and love of all things nautical, Hunter's eyes were drawn to a boat coming downstream. It was sleek and fast looking. A mean machine, he thought, capable of a hell of a turn of speed.

He turned around, his back to the river. So far five men and three women had been unceremoniously lifted, hustled into an unmarked police van and had their belongings searched. Each time the search was done quietly and efficiently. Nothing and it was fast approaching 13.00. The attack could come at any time and the afternoon was stretching far ahead of them.

There was no other way into Parliament Square apart from along the streets and over the bridge. Unless it was by boat. The thought had hardly taken hold when he looked over his left shoulder, his heart hammering. The boat was tied up next to the clock tower. Looking closely he could see the faint shimmer of the engine still running, the sunlight catching the faint stream of cooling water over the starboard quarter. The two men, non-white, Arab-looking, had just stepped ashore. One was carrying a small holdall!

They were perhaps thirty metres away, out of sight of the Square and the police.

'Matt, I've got them.'

The words were hardly out of Hunter's mouth before one of the men looked up, straight at Hunter. It was an instinctive recognition.

Hunter was reaching under his coat for his Glock while the man was reaching for his own gun. Hunter beat him to it. He drew his gun and fired twice, both shots into the man's body. Dunston had reported the sighting and police were converging on the area. The surviving terrorist threw the holdall back into the boat and jumped in after it. He let go the single rope holding the boat alongside and rammed the throttle forward. The boat took off like a Formula One racing car.

Hunter cupped the gun in his left hand and took aim. As he pulled the trigger the boat jinked to starboard and back to port. Hunter missed. He pulled the trigger again and kept firing. The boat was now passing under the bridge and in desperation Hunter leaned over and fired his last shot. The bullet missed the man but hit the steering cable just as the driver swung the wheel to port to avoid a slow moving barge. The strain snapped the wire and the boat careered out the other side heading obliquely for the left bank. Hunter took off, sprinting as fast as he could though he knew he had no hope of catching up with it. Through his earphone, he was aware of Dunston briefing Peter Weir.

The Olympic marksman was in the tower housing the bell known as Big Ben. At this point the Thames was flowing south to north. From his vantage point, Weir could see east over Westminster Bridge and north along Victoria Embankment. David Hughes was in the other quadrant of the tower and covered Parliament Square and south along Millbank.

Weir held an Accuracy International AW-AS-98, 7.62mm calibre rifle in his hands. The Arctic Warfare-Australian Special Forces model was called the most boring rifle in the world due to its accuracy. The glass he was using was a Schmitt and Bender sniper scope.

The boat flashed into sight. Weir took aim and fired at the fast moving target. The shot hit the terrorist in the left shoulder and threw him against the windscreen. He fell back and hit the throttle into reverse. The sudden change cut the engine and the boat turned a few more degrees towards the bank, out of sight of Weir. Seeing the boat slowing down gave Hunter hope.

He was running on the path alongside the river, towards the moored ship, *Tattershall Castle*. His feet pounded the concrete, resonating in a harsh throb in his skull. Pedestrians screamed as he passed. The police ran after him, though the nearest back-up was Dunston, a hundred metres behind. Hunter had changed the magazine in his Glock and fired two snap shots at the boat which was now gently bouncing against the side of the bank, still moving. They missed the driver who was frantically trying to restart the engine. Hunter's breath was coming in ragged gasps and his vision was blurring. *Damnation*! *Not now*!

The boat's momentum was taking it past the bow of the *Tattershall Castle* as Hunter caught up with it. Hunter didn't stop to think. He had no time. He vaulted the railings and prayed for the best just as the engine coughed and caught.

Hunter's feet hit the smooth stern and he tottered on the edge, in danger of falling into the water. With a superhuman effort he flung himself forward onto his knees and then tumbled head-long onto the backseat.

The boat was increasing speed, bouncing from the river bank to the hull of the *Tattershall Castle* when it shot past the stern of the moored ship. The driver wrenched the wheel to starboard before realising it had no effect. He let go and made a grab for the bag. It was closed and he fumbled with the zip.

The boat began to turn to starboard, following the bend in the river and headed straight for *HMS President.* The SRX container fell out of the bag and landed next to Hunter. With a snarl of triumph, the terrorist reached inside and brought out a radio transmitter.

Hunter's arm snaked out and an iron grip crushed the Arab's hand around the hard plastic box, preventing him pushing the send button. Squeezing with every ounce of strength he possessed, Hunter heard the man's fingers cracking. The terrorist screamed and reached with his other hand for the transmitter. Through a haze Hunter saw the movement and desperately hit the man in his wounded shoulder, using a clenched fist like a hammer. The Arab screamed again but his fanaticism gave him the strength to continue reaching for the box. This time Hunter aimed more carefully and brought his fist down in a smashing blow across the terrorist's shoulder, into the bullet damaged bones. There was a crunching sound as the bones parted and the Arab screamed in utter agony. The Arab's strength was fading fast as Hunter pulled the man to him, half turned and used his elbow to devastating effect, hitting him in the nose, breaking it, driving the cartilage flat across his face. The man collapsed, unconscious.

The boat, up on the plane, was now only yards away from the grey side of *President.* Hunter was on his knees in the stern and the sphere was rolling along the backseat. If the boat hit the steel hull and exploded it was possible the SRX would be released. Not that he would know anything about it, as he'd be dead from the impact.

He grabbed the sphere, curled himself around it and fell over the side, holding it tightly to his chest. He hit the water and swam down into the filthy Thames. The boat hit the side of *President* with a tremendous collision, breaking the fuel linkage at the engine, spraying petrol over the hot casing and causing an enormous fire ball. The terrorist's body was burnt to a crisp.

Hunter hit the soft mud at the bottom, the container of SRX burying up to his elbows. The current pulled him away and the smooth sphere slipped from his grasp. Swimming upwards, Hunter reached the surface, looked up at the sky and passed out.

He didn't feel a boat-hook snag his collar and pull him to the side of a police launch. Nor was he aware of the hefty police constable hauling him on board. His pulse was checked along with his breathing. Mouth-to-mouth was deemed unnecessary. After a few moments he came to with a groan. Trying to sit up, he felt the world spin, gagged and brown bile vomited from his stomach.

'Are you okay?'

'Yes. At least, I think so. Christ, I hurt like hell.'

'Take it easy.'

'The SRX! I hit the river bottom with it. It's buried in the silt.'

'Don't worry. Our police divers will find it.'

Hunter nodded and passed out.

Epilogue

Duval's testimony was crucial. Details of Gustav's involvement in fomenting the right-wing backlash against Muslims convinced the majority. However, among a small percentage of the population there was still a deep simmering hatred of the minorities who had come to the West. Politicians were forced to confront the issues and tackle them properly for the first time – to be honest about the problems Europe faced. Race relations had been set back a generation and work was now needed to foster the understanding and tolerance required to live in harmony and peace. At the same time, Muslims in particular and other minorities in general, were being made to confront their own attitudes to religious tolerance and integration.

All races and creeds knew how close they had come to an utter catastrophe which would have resulted in complete polarisation. And it wouldn't have stopped in Europe. It would have spread across the world, whites forced out of Muslim countries, Christians evicted, Hindus ostracised. Where would it have ended? Thinking about it gave Macnair nightmares.

Duval escaped prosecution. He moved to the Seychelles and lived quietly in complete luxury. His book about the rise and fall of Charles Gustav bombed. He made no attempt to write anything else.

Sylvestre diSilvio took early retirement from his position as Head of Security at Rome Airport. He divorced his wife and moved into a luxury villa with his mistress with whom he'd been

364

having an affair for nearly three years. Isobel tracked down his bank accounts and found in excess of three million euros which she quietly purloined. DiSilvio's mistress left him when she discovered he no longer had any money. Acting on a tip-off, the police raided his villa to find him dead, hanging from a rope tied to the balcony surrounding the inner courtyard. Foul play was suspected but never proven.

The cheque for ten million pounds cleared through Hunter's offshore account. The money had been paid to him by Gustav and was legally his to do with as he wished. He used it to pay the members of TIFAT a bonus. It meant that nobody had to worry about their credit cards and overdrafts, at least for a while. Only Macnair, Carter and Dunston knew where the money came from. Carter told the men it was payment from a grateful government for what they had done. They didn't really believe it, but what the hell.

Isobel, as she had done so often in the past, raided Gustav's bank accounts searching for hidden assets. There was very little there. Much of it had already been raided. Isobel guessed Duval had beaten her to it. Worse, she couldn't track where the money had gone. Some of Gustav's companies collapsed. Others survived because their infrastructure kept them going. The more unsavoury and right-wing of his publications prospered, although the readership was down.

The scientists settled in Los Alamos. There, at a top secret military establishment they continued with their work. Weapons of Mass Destruction were developed along with supposed antidotes. The antidotes provided the excuse for the research. As so often was the case, the hypocrisy of the West knew no bounds.

The crew of the *SS Stockholm* were freed. No case to answer. Damages were awarded by the Swedish government to each of the men. They could live on the proceeds without ever having to work again. It took the French Secret Service, working with the CIA, a year to kill every one of them. Each man knew, before he died, why it was happening. The lesson, like all lessons, was only meaningful if others learned from it. The message was quietly disseminated to all those who needed to know. Sweden was invited to take part in future Nato exercises but declined.

The letter waiting for Hunter from Ruth gutted him. In naval parlance it was known as a 'Dear John'. In it she explained that it would be a long time before she could walk again, that probably she never would without aid. She didn't want to be a burden. She would always love him but it was for the best. She didn't want him to try and contact her. She was truly, very sorry.

He wasn't prepared to let it go at that. He knew she was hurting, emotionally as well as physically. Ruth valued achievement and independence over everything. Hunter had thought their love counted more and he made several attempts to contact her but she refused to accept his calls.

When he finally gave up he got exceedingly drunk. The powerful painkillers he was taking contributed a good deal to his condition. A tongue-lashing from his father left him in no doubt about what he needed to do. Macnair granted him a month's leave and Hunter left for Israel as soon as he could.

The End

A Million Tears

by Paul Henke

1890. Murder and intrigue have forced the Griffiths family to flee their native Wales. They leave behind a village devastated by a mine disaster and the oppression of the Victorian ruling classes.

Their subsequent adventures represent the American Dream. With bravado born of necessity, Evan Griffiths builds a business empire – retail, transport, banking, real estate – in the frontier town of St. Louis. With an inherent sense of justice, and the support of his beloved Meg, he forges a political career. But on his right hip, Evan carries a gun. No one will ever hurt his family again.

In Wales, David yearned to travel, dreamed of discoveries. Shipwrecked on a coral island in the South Seas, he discovers himself.

His brother, Sion, dreams of flying, craves freedom and adventure. But will his dream – and Sion himself – die in the lawless hinterlands of the Wild West?

Through meticulous research, author Paul Henke expertly braids together fact and fiction, recreating the Frontier of America. With consummate ease, he conveys a vivid sense of life at the turn of the century, weaving the thread of history – and the lessons it can teach us – through his narrative.

The vitality of Henke's fiction is mirrored in the energy of his vibrant characters. On his vast canvas he captures their triumphs and their tragedies. In 'A Million Tears' he unveils the portrait of the remarkable Griffiths Family. A gem to be treasured.

ISBN 1-902483-00-6

The Tears of War and Peace

by Paul Henke

It is 1911 and David Griffiths is in Wales, bored and lonely. He travels to London at the behest of their family friend, John Buchanan, to start a new business in banking. There he gets caught up in the suffragette movement and falls in love with Emily. Against the backdrop of women's fight for votes and the looming First World War, the Griffiths build a vast, sprawling company encompassing banking, aircraft manufacturing, farming and whisky distilling.

The enmity of a German family follows them tragically throughout this period, leading to murder and revenge. At the end of the war, thanks to a change in the Constitution, Evan is invited to run for President of the United States. The family rally round for the most important battle of Evan's life.

With the Brown-shirts running rampage across Germany, David and Sion are soon involved in a battle for survival.

Sir David Griffiths is a colossus of a figure, striding across the world and through the century, a man of integrity and bravery, passion and dedication. Determined to win, nothing comes before the family.

The story is as compelling as ever. Historical fact woven into the fictional characters makes a breathtaking tale of adventure you will not want to put down.

ISBN 1-902483-03-0

Silent Tears

by Paul Henke

Silent Tears is full of passion and adventure. You will be captivated as three generations of the Griffiths family struggle to meet the challenges of their time.

From the depths of the depression and the rise of fascism to the abdication of Edward VIII and the Spanish Civil War, Henke's meticulous research brings the period and vibrant characters to life.

David, powerful and dynamic, at the centre of political intrigue, his love for the family is put to the ultimate test . . . Meg, his mother, stalwart and determined, guides the family with humour and devotion . . . and Susan, beautiful and tempestuous, fighting for justice. No sacrifice is too great for those she loves.

Packed with excitement, Silent Tears is a masterpiece. A novel that vibrates with sheer narrative power and relentlessly builds the emotional pressure until it explodes in a firestorm of passion and high-octane adventure. A spellbinding epic.

ISBN 1-902483-05-7

Débâcle

TIFAT File I

A Nick Hunter Adventure

Following a summit meeting in Paris an alliance of interested countries form an elite fighting force to combat terrorism throughout the world. Based in Britain and under the command of a British General, the team is made up of Western, Russian and other non-aligned countries' special forces.

Without warning the terrorists strike. A group of bankers, politicians and industrialists are taken prisoner off the coast of Scotland and the new, untried force is sent to search for them.

The Scene of Action Commander is Nick Hunter, Lieutenant Commander, Royal Navy, an underwater mine and bomb clearance expert with experience in clandestine operations.

The enemy is one of the world's most ruthless and wanted terrorists – Aziz Habib! Hunter leads the team against Habib, backed up by two computer experts: Sarah from GCHQ and Isobel, hired by the General to run the IT for the new force.

While stock markets take a pounding and exchange rates go mad, the state sponsoring the terrorism is making a fortune. It has to stop. At all costs.

This is non-stop adventure from beginning to end. A riveting story told by a master story teller. You are guaranteed not to want to put it down!

Débâcle mixes fact with fiction which will cause you to wonder, how true is this story? Did it really happen?

ISBN 1-902483-01-4

Mayhem

TIFAT File II

A Nick Hunter Adventure

Israel faces imminent destruction, nuclear Armageddon. A series of kidnaps, bombings and senseless murders have left her isolated from her allies and threatened by enemies of old. Unknown to all but a few, the situation has been orchestrated by multi-millionaire Zionist, Samuel Dayan. His vision of a Greater Israel will be carved from the charred ruins of the Middle East.

But Dayan is up against the international anti-terrorist organisation, TIFAT, and our hero Nick Hunter. To the age-old struggle of Good against Evil, author Paul Henke adds state-of-the-art communications technology and computerised warfare. In a desperate race against time, Hunter and his team of hand-picked specialists deploy satellite intelligence and high-tech weaponry to track Dayan to his lair.

The plot twists and turns in a series of setbacks, betrayals and mind-blowing developments. Myriad minor characters deserve story-lines of their own.

Relentlessly building the tension, Henke strips his hero Hunter of all resources but those within himself – knowledge born of experience and the inability to give up. Hunter simply must not fail.

ISBN 1-902483-02-2

Chaos

TIFAT File III

A Nick Hunter Adventure

Ambitious Alleysia Raduyev has inherited the family business – the largest crime cartel in Georgia. Operating on the classic theory of supply and demand, she caters for her customers every desire – narcotics, arms, prostitution, forced labour. Her payroll has extended to include lawmakers and law enforcers. No one is safe from her tyranny and oppression.

Power base secured, Alleysia moves on to her next objective – the formation of a super crime cartel, whose actions will result in global chaos. As a deterrent to those who would oppose her, she chooses the ultimate weapon – three nuclear warheads.

Desperate to prevent a new, anarchic world order, the West declares World war III against the cartels and their terror organisations. As violence escalates, the now battle-hardened troops of TIFAT are pitched against their toughest adversary yet.

Spearheading the battle is Lt. Cdr. Nick Hunter, the fearless explosives and diving specialist seconded to The International Force Against Terrorism.

The latest TIFAT novel is a clarion call to the Western world as it comes to grips with the realities of modern terrorism.

ISBN 1-902483-04-9

A Million Tears

The Tears of War and Peace

'Henke isn't just talented, but versatile too. His books are very convincing. As good as Stephen King, Wilbur Smith, Tom Clancy and Bernard Cornwell.'

Burton Mail

'Read them and weep.'

The Stirling Observer

'He's one of the best new writers we've had in ten years.'
The Burton Trader

'A family saga with non-stop adventure from beginning to end.'
Tony Cowell, *PressGroup UK*

Débâcle

'A gritty political thriller . . .'

The Times

'A rip-roaring thriller from the world of terrorism and espi-
onage.'

The Wee County News

'The readers will be hard-pressed to distinguish fact from fiction
in Paul Henke's latest blockbuster.'

The Press and Journal

'A political thriller that combines international terrorism, the
military and high finance. A roller-coaster of a thrilling ride.'

The Sunday Post

'Has that absolute tang of authenticity – a rattling good yarn.'

Chris Serle, *BBC Radio*

'Non-stop action from beginning to end.'

BBC Radio Manchester

'A political thriller that rivals Tom Clancy.'

The Stirling Observer

'Move over Tom Clancy. Henke has turned his own amazing
real-life experiences into blockbuster novels.'

The Sun

Mayhem

'A non-stop action adventure set in Scotland and the Middle East.'

The Edinburgh Evening News

'A fast moving tale of terror and destruction set amidst the charred ruins of the Middle East. An international force exists to fight terrorism. Terrific realism.'

The Stirling Observer

'The hero, Nick Hunter, embarks on a non-stop roller-coaster adventure from the Scottish Highlands to the Middle East. Henke is being hailed as the next Wilbur Smith.'

The Aberdeen Press and Journal

'Mayhem is a classic airport thriller. It's a veritable page turner and a cracking read.'

The Milngavie & Bearsden Herald

'A cracking good yarn. Non-stop action from beginning to end.'
Central FM radio

'Fiction becomes fact in Paul Henke's action thrillers. A superb read.'

The Northern Echo

TIM FITZHIGHAM is an unassuming sort of bloke. He likes a beer, gets rather flustered around pretty girls and finds it impossible to hold down a proper job. He had an interesting childhood: a house in Norfolk that sank into the fens, a cottage in Derbyshire with a leaky roof and a worrying ancestry going back to the Doomsday Book. In later life he hindered farming in both Hertfordshire and the West Indies. Now, he's the Commodore of Sudbury Town Quay in the County of Suffolk – the only landlocked port in the country. He has the ancient title of Pittancer of Selby Town in the Ridings (the only person other than the Queen to distribute money on Maundy Thursday), and is a Freeman of the City of London and the Company of Watermen and Lightermen of the River Thames. He's set precedents in paper boats, suits of armour and running up volcanoes; although to look at, he's more like an escaped cast member from the Muppets. Tim is also a Fellow of the Royal Geographical Society and a multi-award-winning Perrier-nominated comedian. His shows sell out wherever they appear and have kindly been made 'critics' choice' in various newspapers.

OH, AND DID I MENTION THE SMALL MATTER OF ROWING ACROSS THE ENGLISH CHANNEL IN AN ANTIQUE THOMAS CRAPPER BATH?

OTHER BOOKS BY THE SAME AUTHOR

FICTION

BIOGRAPHY

VOLUME III: Pig Keeping in the West Indies
VOLUME IV: Paper Boat
VOLUME VII: The Man Who Discovered the Kama Sutra
VOLUME VIII: My Cufflinks Box: Its Vital Importance

GENERAL
A Splendid Haul
Willets and the Dark Tunnel
Poetry: A Word of Guidance
Keeping Pig Keepers
Pennyquick and the Fallen Men
Black Death in The Family
The Correct Uses of Gin
Moses Chamawam and the Great Ice Robbery
Lepers' Squints: A Monograph
Mistakes in Medieval Wool Gathering
The Conker: A Failed Experiment in Diet
My Top One Hundred Conker Recipes
The Decline in Domestic Manners Since 1270

OTHER PUBLISHED BOOKS BY THE SAME AUTHOR

· · ·

ALL AT SEA

ONE MAN. ONE BATHTUB.
ONE VERY BAD IDEA.

BY

TIM
FITZHIGHAM

preface
publishing

The FitzHigham Papers: Volume V

This paperback edition published by Preface 2009

11

Copyright © Tim FitzHigham, 2008, 2009

Tim FitzHigham has asserted his right to be identified as the author of this work
under the Copyright, Designs and Patents Act 1988

First published in Great Britain in 2008 as *In the Bath* by
Preface Publishing
1 Queen Anne's Gate
London SW1H 9BT

An imprint of the Random House Group Limited

www.randomhouse.co.uk
www.prefacepublishing.co.uk

Addresses for companies within The Random House Group Limited
can be found at www.randomhouse.co.uk/offices.htm

The Random House Group Limited Reg. No. 954009

A CIP catalogue record for this book is available from the British Library

ISBN 978 1 84809 026 2

Penguin Random House is committed to a sustainable future for
our business, our readers and our planet. This book is made from
Forest Stewardship Council® certified paper.

Printed and bound in Great Britain by Clays Ltd, Elcograf S.p.A.

Typeset in Great Britain by Palimpsest Book Production Limited,
Grangemouth, Stirlingshire

For my family,
here and gone.

A blank page.

Every manual should have one.

CONTENTS

FOREWORD

This is the true story of how out of hand things can become from a very simple starting point. It covers the two summers when I tried to become the first person in history to successfully row the English Channel in a bath. I pursued this aim with the innocence and drive of a five-year-old and the mess this created is contained in the following volume.

I've tried to remember the events of those two summers and the intervening winter as well as I can. I may have mixed up a sandbank here or a tide or date there but I've tried to decipher my notes of the time (written with very badly damaged hands) to the best of my abilities to capture the story as truthfully as possible. I apologise in advance for any mistakes I've made, but the truth of the bath remains, like the trip itself, eccentric. I do hope you enjoy reading it.

There are a few people to thank, in no order and leaving most of the more important ones out: my friends and other animals. PBJ, Janette, Mary and all at PBJ. Charlie Viney and all at Mulcahy & Viney. Patient Trevor and all at Preface. Jeremy, Karon and Joe.

The theatres, kind reviewers and audiences that have kept me out of gaol all these years. The clowns who make it such a joy to make people laugh and have guided me endlessly. The Clan. St Chad's College. LFH. The team of hardened drinkers who inspire me. The bar staff who inspire them. And, the bath team – this is our story.

Finally, I'd like to thank the skippers of all the massive tankers and container ships in the English Channel that narrowly missed me.

Signed under the moon with the ice rapidly melting in the glass.

Tim FitzHigham
Tangiers, 1843
(on 26 February 2008)

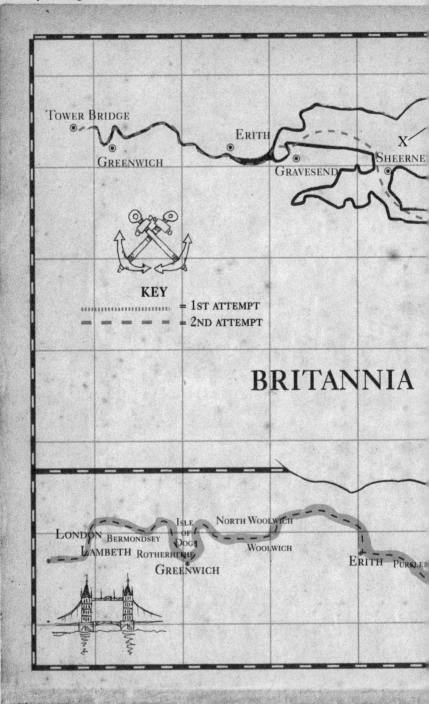

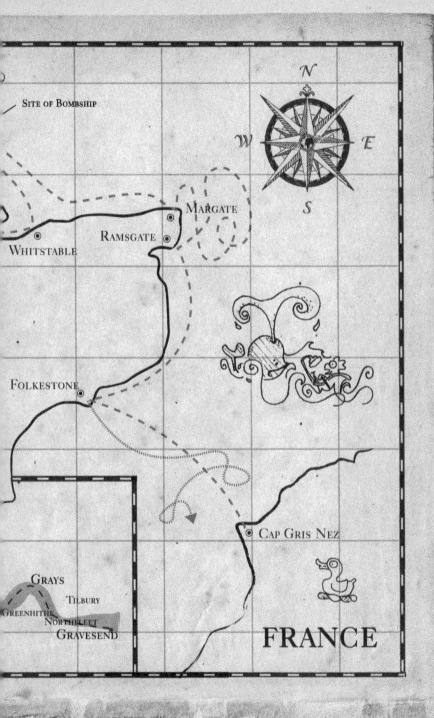

SITE OF BOMBSHIP

N

W E

S

MARGATE

WHITSTABLE RAMSGATE

FOLKESTONE

CAP GRIS NEZ

GRAYS
TILBURY
GREENHITHE
NORTHFLEET
GRAVESEND

FRANCE

INTRODUCTION

MUCH SIMPLE PLEASURE

There are few things in life as good as the warm embrace of a well-drawn bath. Steam swirled soporifically around my nostrils, rising up to form complex weather systems round the dead hanging plant above me.

I lay back, waves gently lapping the islands of my knees, thinking of the most luxurious bath time I'd been involved in. Easy: a huge bath I'd shared with three beautiful women, playing hunt the soap.

I was three and they were four, two and one respectively.

I'd been bathing for many years semi-professionally. It started in Norfolk. I was born in what is now the lunatic asylum in King's Lynn. There seems to be some confusion about the exact date it changed but at the time I arrived there, I'm told people are fairly sure it was the maternity unit. I was taken back to a large bath in the fen. The fens of Norfolk are a flat land with big sunsets. They were claimed out of the sea by Dutch engineers in the 1600s using clever dikes and are now a slightly tamed version of a swamp. In the 1970s, when I was born, not many people lived there and socially it was still run like medieval England. There was a Lord, who lived a long way away, a Sir, who might live closer or even run things locally and, failing both of these, there'd be a Squire who would run, and probably own, your village. Where we lived wasn't even a village, it was much smaller and more chaotic. Places too tiny and eccentric to be villages in Norfolk are called droves. Being a really little one of those, it didn't even have a squire. In the absence of sane alternatives, our happy drove made do with my dad.

I loved bath time in Norfolk. I was normally found in, what I remember as, a permanently sunlit orchard. I'd be playing, well, more sitting or bouncing, before being taken up for my bath. My mum and I had songs for everything and there was a bathing one, too.

The Norfolk house we were living in had been gradually slipping into the fen for years. Normally they build houses in the fens on large oak rafts but somehow someone had forgotten this. Many of the walls leaned quite badly and there were rooms that were shut off from us as they'd gone under. Our house was miles inland but sinking fast. When I was two, my sister arrived and joined me in bouncing and baths. I gave her my favourite bouncing chair and Dad converted an old wooden beer barrel into a castle for me. In line with my designs (I was three at the time so they may not have won an architectural award) he even cut gothic windows into it. I moved in with a large ginger stray – a cat I loved called Oscar.

By the time my barrel got gothic windows, the main house was faring less well. The wall near the main staircase was leaning nine feet to the perpendicular. Dad finally accepted this might be a bit unsafe. Accompanied by much booing and hissing from me we left the bath in Norfolk to sink gently into the fen, along with the house that surrounded it, and moved to Derbyshire. Dad took the large oak gateposts from Norfolk with us and made the dining-room table from them. The bath in Derbyshire was much smaller, more awkward and much, much colder. The countryside was also considerably higher with numerous humps and mountains. At first I didn't like it and registered my protest by painting violently on walls all over the house when no one was looking. I found hills very frightening as in Norfolk I'd never met them.

However, over many baths, snow-laden mornings in winter, gorgeous mists hanging over stone walls in spring, warm, sunny summers and golden-leafed autumns I came to love Derbyshire. It was a very happy place. My grandparents on my dad's side lived there and my granny was one of the funniest, most beautiful things in the world to me. She and her oldest friend Elsie had me in non-stop tears of laughter with stories, songs and jokes. One was all about how they'd been drilled in the war to defend Derbyshire with an antique Gatling gun, no instructions and some rather soggy ammunition. Somehow it went off and the ensuing chaos of the story made me laugh till I hurt. The memory of Granny telling how she and Elsie flailed around behind the butt of this mighty weapon trying to work out how to stop it as it spewed ammunition all over the Derbyshire countryside still makes me smile, even now.

Derbyshire became too much of a distraction from my baths, so we moved to Hertfordshire as Mum got a post there. She's a priest and her career has given my dad some great moments. Striding up to people at parties who didn't know what Mum did, he'd open with, 'as I said to the vicar in bed last night . . .' before looking on at the total bafflement that met him. Now she's been made a canon it's led him to a rich seam including anything ending with 'you're fired', many lines involving short or long fuses as required and several others which, if you ever meet him, will not be more than a few seconds away.

In the holidays I'd go on bathing tours, great plumbing progresses of the country, staying with eccentric relatives who only had outdoor wells, godparents who taught me to surf and debonair great-uncles and -aunts who would take me out for lunch and let me read books.

Hot steam wrapped about my ears.

Throughout all these holidays and various baths, I'd always come back to the one in Hertfordshire. My parents' Hertfordshire bath is the finest I've ever found. It's huge and wide and really comfy. Not so big that it's impossible to keep hot, but not so small that you need a degree in yoga to use it. It has no complicated or ostentatious plumbing; it's really just solid and decent – rather like my parents. This was the bath in which I now found myself.

Coming round from dozing lazily I attempted the most complicated of bath-based manoeuvres: letting some water out of the plug while simultaneously topping up the bath with new, hotter water. It didn't work very well. It never does for me. I lay back into the hot, watery arms and turned my mind to my current problem – a problem that was dogging me with cat-like stealth.

In 2003 I'd broken the world's oldest maritime record kayaking down the River Thames in a boat entirely made of paper. I'd discovered the original record in a footnote while reading a book on poets in the reign of James I (or VI, I'm not going to take sides on the issue here). The record had been set in 1619 when the Thames Water Poet, John Taylor, made it 40 miles down the river in a paper boat using two large dried fish for the oars. This record had slightly obsessed me for years. So, during a very wet March, in the worst weather seen on the Thames in 40 years, I'd set out to go 41 miles and raise £500 for a charity called Comic Relief. When I stepped off my 100% recycled paper boat, 384 years after John Taylor, I'd gone 160 miles in what was rapidly becoming a soggy mass of papier mâché held together with gaffer tape and luck. The paper boat finish was televised on four continents and raised in excess of £10,000 for the charity. This was way beyond anything I'd thought remotely possible and ignited in me a passion for boats, water and adventure that I didn't know I had. Admittedly, I'd always done things slightly differently from those around me, but a succession of teachers, friends and relations had tried to keep this tendency in check. I'd been more embarrassed that I seemed to see the world sideways than proud of it. The triumph of the paper boat was that I normally kept my imagination under wraps. This time I'd let it fly and the results were great.

Bath water nibbled seductively at my earlobes as the problem raged round my head. I was reflecting, with all the brilliance of a cracked mirror, on how to follow up the adventure in the paper boat. The problem was: what could I do next? Anything seemed possible but I just couldn't decide what. If the world was my oyster, I was having difficulty opening the shell.

The paper-boat adventure had been a hugely successful, joyous trip into the absurd. It had combined the three things I loved most: outdoor adventure, raising some cash for a cause and making people laugh. It had challenged me and taught me something new. Before the paper boat, I'd never been in a kayak and certainly never dreamt I'd get to take one the whole length of the mighty River Thames. However, when the journey finished, it had left a hole.

To that point, I'd spent my life wandering around bumping into experiences, feeling a bit lost and trying to find something useful to do. I'd made a career out of temporary jobs, while I tried to escape towards doing something in comedy or acting. I'd been lucky; I'd loved it all (with the possible exception of a very brief, dyspeptic spell cleaning drains with no proper equipment).

Trying to find something to do in life had in itself been a great life. However, in the wake of the paper-boat trip it now felt something was missing. Being out on the water in the middle of challenge had made me smile and, desperate as a frisky bullock demanding entry to a pasture of cows nine months before the calving season, I wanted more.

Legend records a graveyard where elderly elephants instinctively go to lie down and die. Similarly, whenever I need to think really hard, I always head to my parents' Hertfordshire bath, draw it and lie down. Many of my best and worst plans had come to me in the bath that now cosseted me. I looked up at the dead plant in the hanging basket for inspiration: none came. And the bath water had got cold again. With only mildly less success than before, I attempted to top up the bath again.

What could I do?

I took a sip from the now warm glass of gin left on the table next to me. As I reached over to put it back, it knocked against the bath. There was a muffled thud. It was as though the bath had spoken. I tapped it again. There was a cast-iron work of genius nestling beneath my buttocks. I'd do something with a bath. People always seem to be sitting in bathfuls of beans for charity: no challenge there.

Then in a flash it hit me. I could row it. A Noël Coward song about a man rowing an India Rubber bath across Lake Windermere ripped into my head.

Like Archimedes before me, in that instant, I discovered something that I wanted to do. I would take a bath, put oars on it and row it across the English Channel. I felt called, driven, motivated. I would become to sanitaryware what the Wright Brothers were to aviation. I would be the Captain Webb of baths. Synapses in my brain snapped and whirred into life. Fireworks of ideas shot out of the bath and bounced off the walls in the tiny bathroom. I was hooked.

I've become aware over many years and countless projects that I have the potential to become a little obsessive about things. It's something I've always tried hard to control, so now, when an idea comes to me I normally give it ten minutes' thought to try and talk myself out of it. Within ten short minutes, the bath plan had totally taken hold. This idea was not only a goer, it was a belter.

I burst into the drawing room to see my parents not even sketching; they looked up, shocked. I left the drawing room and returned to the bathroom. Putting on a dressing gown to cover my nudity I left the bathroom again and re-burst into the drawing room. 'I'm going to row the English Channel in a bath for Sport Relief.'

Mum sat looking a bit stunned. Dad responded first, 'Well, your great-grandmother was the first lady to swim from Folkestone to Dover, or was it Dover to Folkestone . . . or perhaps it was Ramsgate?'

'Really, Dad?'

'Yes she was called Lilius; although in the draconian times when she did it, swimming costumes were so big she probably floated most of the way on an enormous pair of bloomers. Still if you make it, it'll be another first for the family.'

Dad smiled, Mum still looked a bit shocked. I closed the door and triumphantly dripped back to the bathroom, leaving my parents feeling much, I suspected, like a less mathematical version of Mr and Mrs Archimedes.

A litter of questions popped up. I had no money to fund the project and above all, didn't have a spare bath. My first attempt to get one was not a resounding success.

'Dad, you know I need a bath to row the Channel . . .'

'Yes . . .'

'Can I borrow the one in the bathroom?'

'No.'

CHAPTER ONE

VIBRATING PIPES

'I climbed Mount Everest – from the inside.'

Spike Milligan

Back at my desk, problems and questions carpet-bombed me. I didn't know anything about the sea, would that be important? Would it be possible to make a bath really float? What was the procedure for rowing the Channel? Was there anything legal that had to be done? These and many more questions entered the fray until the dogfight of problems diving and weaving above me had developed into a real scrap.

At the time I was working off and on in a temp job for the civil service. After work one night, I met up with an old friend called Jack. I'd been trying to keep the bath idea a secret, as I didn't really have much of a clue how to proceed at that stage, but seeing Jack I suddenly blurted out, 'I'm going to row the English Channel in a bath for Sport Relief.'

Jack looked on wide-eyed, similar, I imagine, to a frog that's swallowed a wasp. He rallied and in a voice pitched much higher than his normal one responded, 'Off you go then . . .'

Sipping his beer, his eyes relaxed and the incisive brain I've always rated him for hummed and revved into a higher gear.

'How are you going to pay for it?'

'Erm . . . I hadn't really thought about that in huge detail.'

'I'll get you a list of bathroom companies. One of them might sponsor it.'

With Jack-like efficiency the list arrived the next day. I started at the top and began phoning bathroom companies. No one was interested. A third thought I was mad, another third that I wasn't serious and the third third thought both.

My phone rang, it was Jack: 'Have you got the list?'

'Yes. I've been phoning them all day. It's not going very well . . .'

'Have you got to the last page yet?'

'No, why?'

'Have a look at the "T" section.'

'Oh my . . . are they still in business?'

'It seems so – I think they might be the ones for you.'

'I'll give them a ring . . .'

I put down the phone and picked it up again immediately. The ring tone on the other end seemed to take longer than a BT engineer but finally a female voice answered, 'Good afternoon, Thomas Crapper and Company, how may I help you?'

Stifling a giggle, I put on the stentorian voice I'd been perfecting in tests for the civil service, 'I'd like to speak to someone in charge . . .'

'I'll put you through. May I ask what it's about?'

'I'd like a bath.'

After some holding music, rather pleasingly Flanders and Swann, a soft midland accent rolled into my ear, 'Good afternoon, Warwick Knott, General Manager, how can I help?'

'I'd like one of your baths please.'

'Certainly, what sort of bath would you like?'

'A strong one; I need it to withstand the English Channel.'

'What?'

'I'd like to row the Channel in it.'

'Oh good . . . I'll put you through to the Managing Director.'

After more Flanders and Swann, a clipped officer's voice arrived with martial precision at the end of the line, 'May I help you?'

'I'd like one of your baths please.'

'Certainly, what sort of bath would you like?'

'A strong one; I need it to withstand the English Channel.'

'What?'

'I'd like to row the Channel in it.'

'Very funny, Ronnie, I've really got to go, I've got quite a lot to get done this afternoon. Goodbye.'

The line went dead. I paused. Who was Ronnie? I picked up the phone and dialled again. The same female voice answered.

'Good afternoon, Thomas Crapper and Company, how may I help you?'

'It's me again, I seem to have got cut off, please can you put me through to the Managing Director again?'

'Certainly.'

'And tell him I don't know who Ronnie is . . .'

The officer's voice came back on the line.

'I'm sorry, I thought you were a friend of mine. Now what can I do for you?'

'I want one of your baths to row across the English Channel to raise money for a charity called Sport Relief.'

'That was what I thought you said the first time . . .'

I waited for another rebuttal.

'If you're really serious about this, I think you'd better come and see me.'

'Perfect. How about the day after tomorrow? Where are you?'

'Just outside Stratford upon Avon.'

Two days later I drove up to Stratford, looked at the instructions I'd been given, then left Stratford and headed south. Somewhere on the way I missed the turning. Somewhere on the way back I missed it again but on the third time found the understated gateway I was looking for. I drove up the track. On the left was a cricket pavilion and in front of that, following the original designs laid down by God, a pitch. To one side of it were cricketing nets and a tree: so far, so perfectly English. On the right of the track were fields with a stream running through them and various sheep masticating nonchalantly and discussing the effects of unexpected car arrivals on ovine digestion.

Pulling into the car park I was unable to park. Baths overran all the parking spaces. There must have been 200 parked there in all. I'd reached the bath version of the Promised Land. Over the other side of the baths, ahead of me and slightly to the left, was a double gate to some sort of stabling. To the right of the gate, another smaller drive and a large rhododendron bush, was another smaller building. A plum-coloured sign announced to the world that this was the head office of the world's greatest bathroom company: Thomas Crapper & Company. Crapper's Head Office was as eccentric and beautiful as you might expect. Beneath the sign was the main entrance. Either side of the door, where other lesser companies would have stone lions, bulls or other animals proudly standing rampant, stood two massive, stunning Victorian urinals. The overall effect was clear: you have found the HQ of an ablution legend.

I rang the bell. A Bond girl answered the door. I took a guess and assumed her to be the owner of the voice that had first picked up the phone.

'Good afternoon, Thomas Crapper and Company, how may I help you?' confirmed it.

'I'm here to see the Managing Director, it's about a bath.'

'Oh, sorry, he's out for lunch at the moment ... oh, no wait, here he is now ...'

I turned around and saw, coming down the drive towards me, a bearded man, in his mid to late thirties, riding a penny-farthing bicycle. One enormous, oversized wheel at the front, one tiny one at the back, seemingly added as an afterthought – they are lethal death contraptions, famously fiendishly difficult to ride. The bicycle we now know as normal, with two wheels of the same size, is actually called 'the safety bicycle' and was invented due to the huge numbers of penny-farthing-related deaths in the Victorian era. The most experienced person I'd ever seen on a penny-farthing was an old photographer in Derbyshire. He used to wobble round the village fêtes and garden parties of my youth in an entirely unconvincing manner. However, riding down the track towards me was the apotheosis of penny-farthing riding. This was a steady, commanding performance. The bearded man even took the speed bump at the end of the track without flinching. In that moment I knew we'd get on.

He slowed down and dismounted with episcopal serenity and, holding the penny-farthing in one hand, extended his other to me.

'You must be Tim. I'm Simon Kirby.'

We then entered the lavatorial equivalent of the old curiosity shop, and turned right up a staircase. At the top was a tiny office engulfed by an enormous desk. Simon sat on one side of it and I squeezed in behind the other.

'Now, what do you mean you want to row the Channel in a bath?'

'Just that. I want to try it to raise cash for a charity.'

'Seriously, are you serious?'

'Very.'

'Right! How can we help?'

I outlined what I wanted from Simon and he agreed with all of it.

'I'll do some maths and be in touch. I'm supposed to say, "I only wish I could come with you in the bath", but nothing would make me want to do that.'

With that he gave me a tour of the offices and various sheds of the Crapper empire before I left for the drive back to London.

Driving back, it dawned on me I needed to make a very important call. A significant problem had been growing steadily in my mind: I knew nothing about the sea or anything to do with maritime navigation. It was becoming obvious to even my very dim intellect that this would be something of a handicap so I'd need help.

I picked up the phone and dialled the Royal Navy and by mistake got put through to an Admiral, Rear or Vice – I'm not sure which. Several members of the family had been in the Navy and I'd always been taught that it was naval courtesy when talking to a sailor to start the conversation with the question: 'How are your futtocks old man?' I had no idea what a futtock was but did not wish to be discourteous so as the voice on the end of the telephone said 'Hello,' I launched in.

'How are your futtocks old man?'

There was a wheezing chuckle before the voice said, 'At their furthest reach dear boy, at their furthest reach.'

I paused. Now what? I was having a conversation that I didn't understand a word of. 'I need advice on rowing the English Channel.'

'Then I'd say you'd come to the right place.'

After this slightly odd beginning, our conversation went amazingly well. We really got on. I inferred that the man on the end of the phone had actually, or was soon to be, retired from the Navy but seemed very keen to help. Then came the awkward bit. We'd been talking for about half an hour about wind, sea and currents, none of which I'd really understood, and still I hadn't mentioned the bath. I really needed this man's help so didn't want to scare him off but I also had to tell the truth. Finally I took the bullet squarely by the horns.

'This boat that we're talking about trying to get across the English Channel . . . I should probably tell you, it's a bath.'

The line went dead. I'd really blown it. I'd lost him. I was just about to hang up when the line crackled into life.

'Well, same rules of navigation apply dear boy, I'm on board.'

I now had an Admiral (Rear or Vice) (probably ret.) to help. Later that week I was with another old sailor and told him I'd used the question, 'How are your futtocks old man?'

Instinctively he replied, 'At their furthest reach dear boy, at their furthest reach.'

I looked at him, with much the same ranid expression Jack had used in observing me earlier in the month. 'That's exactly what he said.'

'Well, it's a bit old-fashioned but he said it because it's the correct naval response to the question, "How are your futtocks old man?"'

'That's fantastic but what does it actually mean?'

'Well, that's the thing, Tim, nobody actually knows.'

There it was: an almost forgotten Britain in a nutshell. The Admiral and I had just begun a conversation with phrases that neither of us understood but that both of us were too polite and locked in etiquette to admit we didn't understand. The bath project was going to be great.

The Admiral (ret.) suggested I find someone else to advise me as well as him. He had to be away quite a bit over the next few months and would be uncontactable. During these times he wanted to be sure that someone would be there to help me. This was a great idea; the only question was who? Someone would have to take me from a total maritime novice to being capable of taking on the Channel. They would need top naval knowledge and the patience of a saint: two qualities very rarely compatible.

Thinking it through over the next couple of days, a single name bounded into my head. I'd known Dominic Hurndall for years. He had been in the Navy and risen to the rank of Lieutenant Commander before leaving to attend various top-level beer-based discussions with me at university. At college, Dom was something of an enigma. While I'd spend summer holidays playing around, losing temp jobs and teaching, Dom would go back into the Royal Navy and protect my freedom to do so. He made me laugh with tales of windsurfing gone wrong and his determined attempts to take up the trumpet. However, when it came to maritime stuff, Dom was the most knowledgeable person I knew.

In distinguished competitions he'd raced against my friends' older brothers. They all rated him as a truly great sailor. Once, he successfully skippered a boat to victory in the prestigious Fastnet Race.

The fact Dom had an ability, consistently proved at college, of being able to calmly explain stuff to me without wanting to throw me out of a window was also truly important. It was becoming very obvious that without Dom, I'd really struggle on the bath trip. I picked up my phone.

'Dom, are you about for a beer?'

Even though he's a very old and close friend, as I bumped into the table inside the door of the pub, I realised I was oddly nervous about seeing Dom. The more I'd thought about it the less possible the bath project seemed without him. This had to go well.

Returning to the table with beers, we began chatting about all sorts of stuff. In fact everything under the sun that didn't involve baths or Channels. Eventually, I thought I'd just have to bite the bull and said, 'I've got a plan ... sort of charity thing ... a bit like the paper boat ... but I'm going to need your help.'

'What is it?'

'Well ... I want to row the Channel and I know nothing about the sea.'

'Should be fairly straightforward. I could teach you what you'd need to know.'

'Hmmm ... I want to row the Channel in a bath.'

Dom looked as shocked as Jack. Then laughed out loud.

'That's a brilliant wheeze. It's going to be tough and I'm not sure you'll make it but I'd love to help.'

Dom had joined the team and I'd found an officer to run plumbing command.

'Have you checked with the French? They own half the Channel.'
'Good point. I'll get on to that . . .'
'Another beer?'

I'd invented a new maxim, 'hard drinking leads to success at sea', and attempting to prove it, the next night I met up with a man called Douglas. I didn't know Douglas well. He'd been to a talk I'd given about the paper-boat trip and after it, he gave me his card. He was some sort of boat designer and said that if ever I needed his help I only had to ask. Before going to the pub that evening I finally checked out the website address on his card with my coal-fired laptop. It turned out Douglas was not just some sort of boat designer but a multi-award-winning boat designer. Asking a reputable boat designer to put his reputation on the line for a floating Crapper bath was a big call. Asking a multi-award winner at the top of his profession to do it would be almost impossible.

We met in a pub just off Lots Road near the harbour in Chelsea. I bought beers and sat down opposite Douglas. In our short acquaintance I'd already become aware that he was one of life's most cheerful people. Every time I'd seen or spoken to him he'd had a huge smile on his face. He seemed a man consistently one beat away from a gut-wrenching peal of laughter.

We talked about all sorts of stuff, found common ground and drank lots of beer. Several beers in, I thought it might be time to chance my arm.

'You know how you said you'd be up for helping if I had another idea?'

'Absolutely.'

'Well . . . I've got one.'

'What is it now: a paper sail? A loo-roll Armada?'

'I want to row the Channel in a bath.'

There was a beat. Silence. Douglas burst into hysterics. He came up gasping for breath. 'Brilliant. I'm in. What do you need?'

'Well, do you think a bath can actually float and do this?'

'Erm . . . I don't know. Have you got a pen?'

Together we drew countless designs on beer mats for the rest of the night. The more beer we drank the sillier the designs became and the more we laughed. Design mark 2B made us laugh so much we hurt doing Hamlet impressions in the style of Sean Connery, Roger Moore and Mrs Thatcher. Via several versions of the mark 8, we finally finished the night on a totally implausible design: the mark 12E.

Two days later my phone rang. It was Douglas.

'Mate, I've really got it.'

'Still? Oh dear. My hangover's just clearing.'

'No, I've got the design. I've been working on design 12E.'

'Was that the good one?'

'Absolutely.'

'Perfect.'

'I'll pop it in the post.'

'Brilliant work, mate. Fancy a beer after work?'

'Great idea . . .'

Waking up somewhat later I remembered Dom's words about checking with the French. Now I had the designs of one of the country's leading boat designers, I was bound to be fine. I tried to look up the French Coastguard and was somewhat surprised that I couldn't find one. I phoned the French Embassy.

A slick diplomatic Gallic voice answered the phone, '*Bonjour*, the Embassy of France.'

'Ah, *bonjour*, excuse me for asking but where is the French Coastguard?'

'At the coast. Guarding.'

'Perfect. Of course. Do you have any contact details for them?'

'But of course.' He rattled off the contact details of the French Navy.

'Erm . . . I don't think I want the Navy, I rather need the civil Coastguard.'

'We have no civil Coastguard in France.'

'I don't mind if they're rude, I just need to . . .'

'What?'

'I just need to talk to whoever it is in France that is the equivalent of the British Coastguard.'

'This is the Navy in France.'

'Thank you so much for your time. Or, should I say, *merci beaucoup*.'

'Pardon?'

'*Merci beaucoup*. I think it's "thank you" in French.'

'Oh sorry, *bien*, *desolé*. I didn't understand you. *Au revoir*.'

I thought I'd better check my new information. Perhaps I'd not been clear with the man from the Embassy and he'd got confused. I dialled the Admiral.

'It seems it's the French Navy that I should be talking to about the Channel crossing not the Coastguard.'

'Right. There's no Coastguard in France. They let the French Navy do it. They have to give them something to do. It's not good for national pride to have to disband it so they turned it into a Coastguard. I think it does a few other bits and bobs too.'

'Right-ho, thanks . . . I'll phone them.'

It was 2004 – the 100th anniversary of the Entente Cordiale – or the centenary, in the pre-decimal system of measurement. Signed on 8 April 1904, the Entente Cordiale was a series of agreements between France and the UK attempting to put an end to the rivalry that had dogged the two nations up to that point and usher in a new era of peaceful co-operation[1].

I thought: what better way to celebrate 100 years of love between our two great nations than to row the waterway that separates us in a giant piece of sanitaryware? With the fervour of a terrorist, I wrote to the Prime Minister to tell him of my plan. I didn't hear back. Then I picked up the phone and dialled the French Navy.

'*Bonjour* . . .'

He went on in French. This was something I'd not bargained for. Fairly early in the conversation it became obvious even to me that the French Navy spoke nothing but French. I did GCSE French, or as it should be known 'French for the stupid', and being stupid, passed with flying colours. The course was themed around a series of books: the first one was called *Tricolore*, the second was called *Encore Tricolore*, then they ran out of words to rhyme with 'Tricolour' and for the third book settled on *Tricolore Trois*. As it was written on the book cover as *Tricolore 3* I always suspected it was probably pronounced '*Tricolore* Three' but arguing this with my French teacher would have been less pleasurable than my castration and probably lead to a similar result.

---

[1] Together with the other two of the Triple Ententes (Anglo-Russian and Franco-Russian) it paved the way for World War I but that's not important in the bath story and was certainly not the intention when it was signed.

The *Tricolore* series had irreparably drummed into me how to ask the way to the station: '*Où est la gare?*' I remember repeating the same phrase over and over again, yet at no point in the whole murderous series had I been taught the one phrase that would have been actually useful to me: 'Hello sir, I would like to row the English Channel in a bath, please.'

I tried hard to improvise. I knew the French for 'hello'. I knew the French for 'sir'. I even knew the French for 'I would like'. Surpassing myself linguistically, and in the spirit of the Entente Cordiale and basic politeness, I'd even looked up the French for 'the English Channel'.

The French, somewhat surprisingly, don't like calling it 'the English Channel' but don't seem to feel justifiably able to call it 'the French Channel' either. Mysteriously they call it 'la Manche' which translates as 'the Sleeve'. I discovered later that the same word – the Sleeve – with a slightly different accent shift or a *Carry On* style eyebrow wiggle is also a slang term in France for condoms. In England, slang for condoms is 'French letters'. Knowing this, everything became clear.

'Please' is easy in French and again had been drummed into me, coupled like the passenger carriage to '*Où est la gare?*' So the only hurdle I could see was the verb 'to row'. Cursing myself for not being better at French and desperately flipping through the dictionary I heard the naval man on the end of the phone repeat helplessly, '*Pardonez moi, monsieur, mais je ne comprends pas.*'

I found the 'R' section, ran my finger down the page and apprehensively shut the dictionary. A bead of sweat appeared on my forehead. I felt nervous, self-conscious, dishonest and cagey: the classic signs that a stout-hearted Briton is milliseconds away from attempting French.

In a French accent developed through a lifetime of using English I said, 'Hello sir, I would like to row the English Channel in a bath please.'

What actually arrived in the ear of the French Navy man was, 'Hello sir, I would like to fight a condom across a bath if you please.'

The naval man clung to his mantra like a monk in a whorehouse, '*Pardonez moi, monsieur, mais je ne comprends pas.*'

I had to think fast. The education system of Thatcherite Britain had failed me at the first hurdle. What option was left to me? Politely, I tried slowing down my questions, which did not help. I tried using monosyllabic words[2], which still did not help. Then I tried the age-old trick of the Briton abroad and raised my voice. This really did not help.

Finally, desperate to communicate, I attempted mime to try and get my point across. Innovative mime was my best shot and would have worked had we not been separated from each other by a phone line. I finished in my best French by thanking him for his time and asking if he knew the way to the station before putting the phone down.

I phoned the Admiral back.

'It's no use, Admiral, the French speak nothing but French.'

There was a short pause on the end of the line then his voice rattled into life like a sabre.

'They're lying, Tim!'

'What?'

'The French Navy must by law speak English, as English is the international maritime language of the sea.'

'Has anyone told the French that?'

The line went dead for a moment before he thundered, 'Yes: Nelson. At the battle of Trafalgar.'

I tried to stifle an irresistibly British giggle not knowing if the Admiral was making a joke or not. I got it right. He was serious.

The indignant thunder continued, 'This is rotten behaviour; he was playing a cruel trick on you. The animal is probably now laughing about it down the mess with his other officers. Your mistake was to try and speak French at him in the first place.'

I put down the phone to the Admiral irritated with the cunning officer of the French. However, I decided in the spirit of what I was trying to achieve that I'd play his game for as long as I could. I needed to find someone who spoke French like a native.

I was in London that weekend and left my flat to wander round the corner to grab some milk. On the way back a lady sashayed down the road towards me, looking not unlike Audrey Hepburn

---

[2] It is one of the greatest achievements of the English language that the word monosyllabic, used to describe words with a single syllable, does itself contain five syllables. I love footnotes.

in *Breakfast at Tiffany's*. She came closer and smiled. I smiled back.

'Liza!'

It was a staggering coincidence – in its defence, all I can say is that London is a very small place sometimes.

'Hello Tim, how are you? Do you fancy a cup of tea? I only live down the road.'

'Lovely idea, I've even got milk, if that helps . . .'

'I'm sure I've probably got some, too, but that's very sweet of you.'

It had been ages and ages since I'd seen Liza. In fact, the last time I'd seen her, she'd been one of history's most radiant and happy brides.

'How is Ed?' I asked of her implausibly tall, stunningly nice husband.

'He's great, although he's out today – he'll be so sad to miss you. Fun bumping into you, I've got loads of news. This way.'

The list of people who are genuinely sad to miss me can normally be limited to the parents of girls I've fallen foul of, staring down the barrels of shotguns and cursing their aim. However, Ed is one of the rare exceptions and I couldn't believe of all the days to bump into Liza I'd managed one when Ed was away. Nevertheless, it is always a blissful joy to see Liza and plus I have a golden rule in life: never turn down the offer of a cup of tea.

Inside, we drank tea, laughed and nattered. There really was loads to catch up on, especially the news that Liza was pregnant. I had missed so much by being away in paper boats. During our second cup, a dark force began to muster on the dull edges of my brain. This dark force grew, developing into an army of thought before bursting out of my mouth, 'Liza . . . you speak French don't you?'

'I should, I grew up there.'

That was what I'd been trying to tell myself to remember.

'I even went to school there and everything.'

My mind flashed to Liza's 21st birthday party years before. I knew it! It was in France.

'You couldn't do me a favour could you?'

She laughed. 'As long as it's not running the marathon as I'm not sure that's good for the baby.'

I explained my chronic lack of French and what I was trying to achieve.

'I mean I think it would be semi-OK. I probably could just about be understood if I practised really hard at it but I just want someone who can speak it like a native as we've got to be absolutely clear with them so they can make a judgement on it.'

'I'd love to give them a call.'

This had been a blinding flash of inspiration as although Liza can quite justifiably be compared to Audrey Hepburn in appearance, her voice is even prettier than that. She could put honey into early retirement. If there were a weapon that was guaranteed to charm the hearts of French Naval Command, I'd just found it. She did have a warning though.

'I think it might be tough as they're not really on the same wavelength as us on this sort of thing.'

A day later my phone rang. It was Liza. 'They're not convinced at all. He says he'd like to see some plans.'

Douglas might have been drinking with me the night it was conceived but, as it turned out when the plans arrived, he was justifiably a multi-award winner. The plans were brilliant: totally meticulous down to the last degree. As finely expressed as the sayings and equations of Wittgenstein. He had taken beer-mat design mark 12E, thought through the problems, solved them and made the craft that now appeared on the paper seem more indomitable and seaworthy than the *Ark Royal*.

Pleased at being able to sort this one fast I said, 'Sure, what's the fax number?'

The next day Liza called to tell me the news.

'Right. It's taken quite a bit of talking but he says his advice is clear and it's the advice of his government: they're not happy about you rowing the Channel but that goes for anyone. He said the French government don't like anyone swimming or rowing the Channel at all and their official position is that no one should do it. They can't understand the English fascination with it. However, people ignore that every time they swim or row the Channel. So he says, bearing that in mind, if you're willing to take the risk and promise to have a safety boat near you, there's nothing he will do to stop you.'

'Thank you Liza, that's really good of you. Can you phone him and say I'd like to call to thank him personally.'

'Sure.'

Fifteen minutes later I heard the now familiar foreign dialling tone, then a click.

'Hello. This is Tim FitzHigham just phoning to say thank you for your help.'

'No problem. Sorry I couldn't understand you before, I thought you were Dutch.'

What I wanted to say at that point was not what came out of my mouth: 'Thank you for being so understanding and I promise to undertake this safely.'

'It will be hard but we hope it goes well for you. I'll put some documents on the fax for you.'

'Thank you. I'm looking forward to it.'

His English was not great but at least he was now using it. This all seemed like a huge step in the right direction.

I put down the phone and called Liza back.

'Thank you so much. They even spoke English this time.'

'They like it when you make an effort.'

'They seem fine with everything.'

'I think he was impressed with the plans. That seemed to swing it. However, I feel it's only fair to warn you that although they are fine with it today, the French have been known to change their minds.'

The bath plan was coming together and the spirit of the Entente Cordiale was very much alive and kicking in the 21st century. Hurrah for the French.

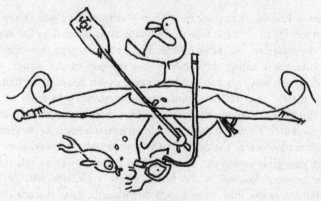

CHAPTER TWO

ROW, ROW, ROW YOUR BATH, GENTLY TO THE SEA . . .

'Give me a camel and I can get anywhere.'

Gordon of Khartoum

From an early age, I'd spent years trying to learn to row. I'm qualified to be a rower: I went to university. That should count. My college was famous for its rowers. While there, I spent weeks during both the Michaelmas and Epiphany terms under the river, obsessed with trying to master rowing. I remember my coach on the riverbank screaming encouragement, as only the truly deluded can, while I heroically turned the boat over and sank it in a variety of impressive ways. I transformed capsizing into an art form: the slow-motion capsize; the one where I'd fake that I was going to capsize on the *left* before righting myself just long enough to hear him shout enthusiastically 'well done', then flipping it over effortlessly on the *right*; and my favourite: capsizing while doing up my shoes. To be that bad takes talent.

Rowing should be a simple and beautiful thing. In an ideal world start with legs fully extended so your bottom is furthest from your feet, push your hands down to lift the blade from off the water (this is known as the release). Then you turn the blade (known as feathering) so that the face of the blade runs parallel to the surface of the water as you move up the stroke to the top of the slide. This is sometimes called the recovery. At the top of the stroke, your sliding seat can't go any further towards your heels. Your buttocks are nearest your feet and your arms outstretched in front of you. In this position square the blades so that they're now at right angles to the water. Then pop the blades down into the water in the glorious moment known as the catch. Pushing your bottom away from your feet you glide down the slide with as much power as possible to the moment known as the finish where your legs will be fully extended again. Push your hands downwards, raise the oar up out of the water and you're back at the release. Simply repeat the process until you've either won the race or crashed into the bank. It involves balance, speed, strength and mental toughness. Rowing is justifiably called the sport of kings.

It didn't seem to matter how many times the above details were explained to me, I could not get it right. Somehow the blades contrived to be feathering when I was trying to catch or I finished as they were at the recovery. Sometimes it was the boat that would make things difficult by demanding my attention at the top of the stroke when I was administering to the finish. Through all these problems I never once blamed my tools.

Once I went out rowing on the coldest day of the year. I kicked snow off the landing stage where they launched the boats. It went into the river in snowball-sized lumps and sank in snowball-sized lumps. Never before had I made it back to the bank without capsizing but my coach thought that this would be my great day. I had managed eight strokes without capsizing the week before (my personal best) and so everything seemed in my favour. It really was freezing cold and there wasn't another boat out that day. I could see my own breath as I pulled out into the centre of the river. I took a couple of strokes and didn't capsize. Just six more and I'd equalled my personal best. The river was racing, carrying me with it. I felt the boat run underneath me, this was how rowing was meant to be. The water made a pleasing sound as I successfully managed another one; in a flash I'd strung an extra three together before attempting the tricky seventh stroke.

With the poise of a prima ballerina I gently rotated the boat just less than 90 degrees right to hold it half above and half below the water's surface. I paused long enough to wave politely at the bank before serenely flipping it the remaining 90 degrees and slipping under the icy water. I gulped for air; only ice came. I was upside down, still attached to the boat, racing downstream in freezing cold water. Would I drown first or die of cold? I managed to get my head above water, gasped down air and swam desperately for the bank.

Clearly worried about me, my coach shouted from the bank, 'Go back for the boat! Don't come back in without it!'

I'd forced that normally mild-mannered man to hit the tone of a drill sergeant. I was too cold to argue so turned back to get frost-bite and fetch the boat.

'If you can find the blades too, that would be good, only with you learning to row we're getting short of them in the boat house!'

I got the boat and one oar back to the bank but was really cold. I knew it was serious when he looked and me and said, 'I think you'd better get back up to college and hope the hot water's on . . .'

I didn't hear the rest of what he said. I knew where I should be: safely in a hot shower, wrapped up in a bosom or buried beneath a mountain of towels. Mainly, safe on land.

That evening, as I went into the dining hall, the rest of college laughed. The clear imprints of my bare feet in the inches of snow formed a path running up from the riverbank to the college. They stood out like neon monuments to stupidity beside the many sensible shoe and welly prints coming home from lectures. It was now commonly known that if there were footprints in the snow, I'd been learning to row again.

When you win a regatta the boat club lets you keep your oars as a mark of respect. It's a big honour. At the end of that year as a mark of irony the Boat Club Captain presented me with a broken oar simply for having survived a capsize on the coldest day of the year. Embarrassingly, following that there was even a college four[3]

---

[3]For those people who don't row, me among them, a four is the most common unit of rowing crews. Single rowers are called scullers. They row in a racing boat made for one called a scull. Two rowers is a pair. Four is a four and eight rowers is an eight. Whoever patented this system was a man of staggering charm.

named after me. The 'Higham First Four'[4] was the slowest crew on the river and finished triumphantly last in every race. I hate irony but I was never even good enough to row for them.

That night I sat swathed in blankets, my still-numb feet in a bowl of hot water, as close as it was possible to be to my radiator. As I drank warm Coca-Cola that night (we were told this prevented the Weil's Disease, rife in the river[5]), I mused that it might have been better if I had died or drowned earlier than face the ignominy of my failure.

If my life had been a Hollywood movie I would have turned it round the next morning, learnt to row, trained to 'Eye of the Tiger', won the Henley regatta and married Jennifer Aniston with Adam Sandler gurning in the background. It wasn't Hollywood. I continued to capsize for three more weeks before I gave up rowing for ever, invented drinking croquet and discovered alcoholism.

Sitting at my desk, I snapped out of the reminiscences of a capsize ninja. The campaign of problem carpet-bombing stepped up another gear. The terrifying memories of my career as a serial sinker reminded me that there was a problem to climb bigger than the Matterhorn: I couldn't row.

I started a list, as there were now so many problems I began to run the risk of not even being able to remember them. Forgetting my problems would in itself be a problem. I put 'Having too many problems and forgetting one of them' at the top of my new list. Underneath this I wrote, 'No money to fund the project'. Beneath that I wrote, 'Not speaking French well enough'. Next on the list was, 'A total lack of even basic knowledge of the sea and maritime matters'. Finally, shuddering, I added, 'I can't row' before slumping back in the chair.

---

[4] The 'Higham First Four' colours were green and palatinate – a kind of pinkie purple – quartered. I was known as Tim Higham at college. FitzHigham simply means 'Son of Higham' and always seemed such a mouthful and so awkward to spell that I didn't use it back then.

[5] The Coca-Cola does not have to be drunk warm but I was cold – also I'm sure having thought about it that another brand of cola would be equally effective but at the time we all thought Coke had magical powers to ward off Weil's Disease. I've suggested this to the Coca-Cola empire as a marketing strategy but am yet to hear back from them: 'Beat Weil's Disease – drink Coke!' (cue jingle).

I've never liked thinking about problems. The main reason for this is that, like a mummy rabbit and a daddy rabbit who love each other very much, when you have two problems very often they suddenly become six. Sure enough just as I was thinking this, a sixth major setback popped out: I was chronically unfit.

I'd had a brief moment of sobriety and fitness during the paper-boat challenge. This was largely inflicted on me by my loving cousin and had been a short flash of sunshine in the violent storm of my utter unfitness. Also, if you've never rowed, you are unaware of the very high level of fitness it requires. Rowers are among the fittest athletes on the planet. This problem was serious, what was I supposed to do?

Jack had now left frog-like shock far behind him and swung into action.

'I've found you a rowing machine, you know one of those training Ergo things, at nearly no cost . . .'

It belonged to a girl we'd known from university who was going abroad and couldn't take it with her. She was a great rower at college and also very beautiful. I get terribly shy around beautiful women and had always found her impossible to talk to. Still, beauty is dulled by age, I thought as I rang the doorbell at her flat in Clapham. Besides, I'd grown up, so wouldn't be shy this time.

When the door opened the eyes that met mine beheld a stammering, nervous apparition that looked like the logical result of breeding a Fraggle with *What-A-Mess*. They blinked, opened again and managed to mix bemusement with a slight giggling twinkle. If anything she'd got more beautiful with time.

'Oh, hi Tim . . . it's upstairs.' She looked at me as I stood stammering on her doorstep. 'Come in.'

We dismantled the Ergo and I took the first bit down to the car. We agreed it would be called Betty. Arriving back at the top of the stairs to fetch the second bit she looked thoughtfully into the distance.

'So, Jack says you're going to row the Channel. That's a really tough challenge – personally, I don't know anyone who's managed that.'

'Erm . . . neither do I, really.'

'I don't remember you being much of a rower at college – in fact Tim, did you even row?'

'No,' I lied.

Thank goodness, she'd obviously left before I took up sinking. I hate lying but thought it was better to leave her with the impression that I was someone with great rowing potential, untapped at college, rather than embarrass myself further with the truth. The door closed on the stunning eyes and I tried to cram the second half of the Ergo into the back of my battered car. At least I now had something to train on. That had to be a step in the right direction.

Driving away, this one positive soon turned negative. I was the worst rower in the history of my college with the balance of a cowpat (in the words of my long-suffering coach). Yet insanely, now I thought I could take on the trickiest single-seat rowing challenge in the world.

The car turned into a rabbit warren as another problem surfaced. I needed to find someone to foot the bill for Jack's 'nearly no cost' and help pay for the Ergo. The Thomas Crapper money was specifically tied up in bathroom products and I'd budgeted nothing for training costs. Bother. Getting out of the car I pulled out my list and wrote 'Hopeless at budgeting' underneath 'Chronically unfit'. On the plus side, both of these qualities do qualify me for one thing: being Chancellor of the Exchequer.

After unpacking the Ergo, I arrived back at my desk and pulled out my phone.

'Hi, is Kenny there?'

Kenny was the kind newspaper editor who fought so hard to help me with the paper-boat project. The paper boat almost failed to happen several times and Kenny had been instrumental in making sure it came off. Through these trials, including my rotting skin and near death, we'd become great mates. He's got a brilliant sense of humour and is the only man I know who is merely four generations removed from a caveman (his ancestor was a nook-dwelling highland shepherd). I felt sure he'd help.

'You've got another plan? Oh good . . .'

He managed to say 'oh good' in a way that combined several emotions: the first, 'not another of your plans, Tim, the last one almost got me sacked'; secondly, 'it's bound to be a cracker – what's the plan this time? Paragliding strapped to a piece of toast?'; and thirdly, 'of course I'll be involved – what do you need?' That's the thing about truly great friends, you know what they mean and can always rely on their help.

'Fancy a beer after work?'

Over a few of London's finest we laughed about the paper boat. If he'd not decided to edit newspapers, he'd have been writing jokes. At one point only two people thought the paper-boat plan could work and both of them currently sat either side of the pub table.

'So what's the plan this time?'

'I want to row the English Channel in a bath.'

'Of course. What do you need?'

With a dry smile, little chuckle and sip of beer Kenny had joined the bath team. Over a couple more beers we discussed the various things I'd been putting in place so far before Kenny said, 'Why stop there, Tim? Why not row it all the way to Tower Bridge? In fact, I bet you one pint of beer you can't make it from France to Tower Bridge in that bath.'

His words were strangely reminiscent of the ones that had almost got me killed in the paper boat but, thinking only of beer, my brain knee-jerked into a response so quickly that it kicked logic in the crotch.

'You're on!'

In my head and not having checked the charts, Tower Bridge didn't seem that far away from Folkestone, Dover or wherever it was that you stopped when you'd rowed the Channel. I pulled out my list and wrote, 'Check where the Channel finishes'.

Later I would discover that in just two ill-chosen words, I'd lengthened the aim of my journey by 170 miles to win a single pint of beer.

Over the next few months I embarked on a gruelling drive to get fit. I looted bookshops and read tonnes of books on fitness. One advocated, 'Always run in trainers'; another, 'Find some comfy boots'; a third, 'Never run in boots'. Spurred on by this clarity I read a fourth, 'Cycling or swimming is good, running is not.'

In darkened corners of bookshops all over the place I found books on rowing technique, too. They seemed just as unified in their thought. One, 'Sliding seats are a must for long-distance rowing'; another, 'Never use a sliding seat for long-distance rowing.' A third, 'Meat cleaver blades are best for rowing at sea', and a fourth, 'Meat cleaver blades are very damaging to your back over long distances, this is especially true when rowing at sea.'

As well as being confused by general fitness and rowing books I also read books on diet. The first one said, 'Always start your day with a bowl of cereal'; another, 'Never eat anything but fruit before midday.' I decided these books were cunningly designed to make me stay in bed till after midday, on the phone to a broker buying shares in a cereal company. I was stumped. No two books had the same advice.

There's a senate of faceless and formless beings that always get quoted by others when the quotee needs validation. This senate is known simply as 'They'. They say 'a little knowledge is a dangerous thing' but the same also seemed to be true of too much opinion in a field that demands more clear research. I'd taken to eating both cereal and fruit before midday just to be on the safe side.

I sat in the old barn at my parents' house looking at the piles of totally confusing and expensive books (I hadn't budgeted for them either). If there's no clear lead on how to get fit, there's no wonder we have an obesity problem in this country.

I gazed over at where I'd proudly assembled Betty the Ergo. During all the months I'd been reading about getting fit, Betty had been sitting unused. I was becoming PhD-level educated on the confusing subject of getting fit but had absolutely no practical knowledge. To think this over further, I went to the pub.

That Thursday night I was going to stay with my friend James in Putney. Jimmie is a very safe bet to talk to about fitness as he regards any form of physical exercise at best as insulting and at worst permanently damaging. As often happens in families, his brother is a super-fit soldier. Jimmie had just got back from weeks away touring as an actor and as usual was full of great stories. After a good night drinking and nattering we went back to his flat. Following more laughter and a nightcap I dropped into bed. I was sleeping in the room his older brother had stayed in a few days before.

I woke up the next morning with a hangover they wrote about in the Bible and, through eyelids lined with sand, glanced over at the bedside table. On it was a book called *Fit for Life* by Sir Ranulph Fiennes. This was one fitness book I'd not read.

With my head beating like a marching band and Jimmie groaning in the room down the corridor, I slowly began to read the first chapter. Midway through, I suddenly got the urge to make a cup of hot tea with lashings of milk and sugar. Then following the advice in *Fit for Life* Chapter 3 about having as little milk as you can and no sugar in tea, I took the milky sugared tea back to the kitchen and made the first cup of black tea I can ever remember having.

I poured in the water. Steam rose off the nefarious dark brew below. Tentatively I lifted the cup to my lips. There are people who would rather lose a testicle than drink tea black and I was among them. I took a slurp. It wasn't too bad, but hard to tell with just a slurp. I blew over the surface of the tea then took a bigger slurp. Like a wine connoisseur I swilled it round my mouth to try and work it out. It was much more bitter than I'd expected. A third gulp passed my lips. My mind was made up. I liked it. It felt somehow pure. In just three sips of tea that book had struck more of a chord with me than all the others put together. Like St Paul on the road to Damascus, I'd been transformed, only in Putney with a huge hangover.

As I went back to bed with my gorgeous black tea and read the rest of the book, the single chord turned into a number-one hit. It's a regime suggested by a man I've always admired. This gave me inspiration through example. It's also a very practical set of guidelines and suggestions. It gives you advice to achieve whatever stage of fitness is appropriate to you. The main thing I liked about it was the suggestion that you should find what works for you and, most importantly, stick to it.

Finally, with *Fit for Life* manacled to my side, I started training in earnest. I only realised the terrifying level of my chronic unfitness when I started to train. Betty the Ergo was an incredibly cruel mistress. I started gently. I'd arrive in the old barn at my parents' and spend some time stretching. Then I'd spend time begging Betty not to hurt me too much, before mounting her and doing 3,000-metre distances. It may sound like a lot but 3,000 metres is a relatively short distance. It's the blink of an eye to someone seriously wanting to row the Channel but I wanted to build up my ability to do this and not pull any muscles, tendons etc before attempting longer distances.

I didn't have rower's shoulders, or, in fact, strong shoulders of any sort, and my lower back wasn't used to Ergos – this is traditionally the area that gets a lot of punishment in rowing. So many people I knew had started training on macho impenetrable distances, pulled something in the first week and had to give up rowing for ages. To keep any hope of rowing the Channel alive, this could not happen to me.

After a while I progressed to 6,000-metre distances. At this point I added weights, more stretching and running, to build all the various muscles and support the Ergo training. Betty was the most unflinchingly vindictive of women. I discovered quickly that one of the main challenges of an Ergo is mental.

Finally, I was up to pulling decent times at 10,000 metres with running, stretching and weights. This was the regime I kept up, pounding away as much as possible to try and maintain the level of fitness I'd achieved. At the time I was working in another temp job at the Foreign Office in London in an attempt to pay off various booksellers. I had to leave the house at 6.30 a.m. and arrived back in at 8 p.m. It was one of the more demoralising things to come in from a full day at work and realise I'd got 10,000 gruelling metres to pull on the Ergo.

There was another significant problem. As well as training and temping I had a very precious girlfriend.

It was a very hot day in late summer when I'd first seen her. I was staying with a cousin who was studying for a Masters. I'd gone to pick him up after college one evening. In a meadow behind one of the halls of residence some people he knew had organised a lazy game of rounders. I hadn't realised we'd be seeing anyone else so was still in a pair of eccentric bright orange tartan trousers. I was testing them to see if he and I could get away with them as the new family tartan. As we lived in the middle of nowhere (nowhere being deepest rural Wiltshire) I'd assumed I could test them in private.

I wasn't sure I could meet his friends wearing something quite so inexplicable but he insisted, supportively, 'What are you talking about? I've barely ever seen you wear something appropriate.'

We arrived at a barbeque; a friend of his was cooking. As the greatest smell on earth filled the air, my cousin introduced me to his friends and there she was. My cousin smiled ingeniously and left us. I followed my usual protocol on these occasions of stammering, trying to disguise it with a joke and looking at the floor. She laughed at the joke and at the same time unleashed a devastating smile. She was blonde, foreign and was studying at the college too.

We were called over to play lazy rounders. Oddly enough, lazy rounders is a game I'm normally quite good at. The main reason for this is that I'm left handed and very often there are fewer fielders in the place where I want to hit the ball and in lazy rounders no one can be bothered to move around so I normally manage to score fairly well. We were on the same team and she teased me and laughed throughout the game but, I noted with interest, smiled quietly when I scored.

After everyone got bored of rounders and dispersed to eat, chat and drink, the gentle haze of a hot English summer evening descended on the meadow. I threw her a rugby ball; she caught it and threw it back. Probably as a girl, it's not the most romantic thing to have a rugby ball thrown in your direction but such are the peculiar courtship rituals of the English gentleman.

Within weeks, something of a land-speed record for me, we'd got together. Scared by how effortlessly well it was going I conformed to a horrid, shameful stereotype and bolted.

Oddly, and in a series of genuine coincidences, similar to bumping into Liza that day with the milk, I'd kept bumping into her on Valentine's Day each year. In Battersea one Valentine's, I popped out to buy some bread and arriving at the baker's, the only other person in there was her. Other, greater thinkers would have seen this as an omen; I merely filed this under 'Odd' in my head and buttled on with life.

I always move fast in affairs of the heart and a mere two years after first bolting I finally asked her out for supper. Within a day we were totally happy and inseparably together. There hadn't been a single moment of unhappiness since then, just rather sickeningly joy, happiness and smiles.

She had been with me throughout the paper-boat adventure and was now preparing for the bath trip. I'm not sure either of us realised quite what an inconvenience to us spending time together it would be but throughout it all she had been brilliantly understanding and selflessly, guilt-inducingly supportive. In the foreign land that created her, they clearly made women well. What a girl.

Betty had finished giving me the pounding of my life for the evening. Later, as my muscles tingled, like fingers on a frosty morning, I lay back in bed. This was an arduous period of training. I listened to the birds. I was positive. Probably due to the previously unseen levels of exercise-induced happy hormones running round my brain, although it could have been because my punishing training regime was going really well. I was now getting very fit.

There was just one slight oversight in my indomitable training regime. I'd still not actually trained in a boat.

CHAPTER THREE

IN A BEAUTIFUL PEA GREEN BOAT

*'Rowing seems to me to be a monotonous pursuit, and somehow wasteful
to be making all that effort and be going in the wrong direction.'*

Peter Ustinov

With my training going so well, I turned my attention to other
matters. During lunch hours at the Foreign Office, I'd been hunting
for a boat maker to turn the plan Douglas and I had made into a
reality. Many boat makers had not believed it possible and most
had laughed me off the phone. Some had not even taken my calls.
Without a boat maker to help me adapt the bath I was stuck. I
didn't know a keel from a stern; I certainly couldn't adapt a bathtub
to withstand the high seas.

As a result of the paper-boat trip I'd been made an Honorary
Freeman of the ancient Company of Watermen and Lightermen of
the River Thames. This may not mean a lot to many people but on
the river it's important. The Watermen are respected. They have
trained for seven years to gain the right to captain freight and
passengers up and down the Thames.

I like being a Waterman as it's not some glorified old buffers' club
but a hard-working organisation. Currently, the European Union is

trying to strip them of their rights in order to make the Thames less safe. However, hopefully the common sense of hundreds of years will win out in the end. Watermen know everyone on the Thames.

I stood outside the Foreign Office in King Charles Street under the statue of Clive of India with my phone pressed to my ear and called Waterman's Hall.

After a brief chat and catch up with the assistant clerk, she put me through to the Clerk of the Watermen. He's the Company's chief administrator on a day-to-day basis and through the paper boat, I'd got to know him quite well.

'Hello, Colin? It's Tim – I need someone to help me adapt a bath to go across the Channel.'

'The bath's not made of paper is it?'

'Not this time.'

'Have you heard of Mark Edwards? He's your man – he once reconstructed a 17th-century Dutch submarine design using a couple of Thames skiffs and some wax.'

'So you think he might help?'

'I think he's the only one who might help. I'll find you the number . . .'

I made repeated attempts to phone Mark and finally, after leaving the phone to ring for what must have been close to a world record, a thick London accent answered.

'Hello?'

'Hi, I'd like to speak to Mark please.'

'Oh . . .'

The phone hit something and I heard the same voice disappear off into the distance shouting, 'Mark!' I held. Eventually a lighter voice with a slight West Country twang came on the line.

'Hello, this is Mark.'

'Hi, Colin at Waterman's Hall gave me your number and suggested I call, I need a bit of help . . .'

I arranged to see Mark for a beer one night after he'd finished work. I thought it might be best to explain the bath project to him face to face. As it happened Douglas was in town that night so said he'd come along too. I arrived in Richmond, got out of the car and was just about to pay the meter in the car park on Friars Lane. A voice behind me shouted, 'You don't have to pay that now, it's after time.' Douglas was early.

'Hi mate, thanks for coming.'

'Thought it might be useful if I was here. We can talk about it in boatie terms.'

We walked down Water Lane and passed the White Cross pub on our left. Ahead of us was the bridge and in front of it a floating restaurant.

'Stunning isn't it.'

My mind was fixed on how to get Mark to convert the bath for as little money as possible. It was only when Douglas mentioned it that I became aware of how beautiful Richmond looked in the warm evening light. We walked down the river's edge past a few slipways towards the floating restaurant. On the towpath, running parallel to the river, were a series of boathouses. Most of the doors were shut but out of the remaining open one came a man, about 5' 8", with shortish brown hair and a bounce in his step.

'So you're going to try and row the Channel then,' he smiled, wryly.

It was true; Watermen did know everything[6].

'How did you know?'

'I was speaking to Colin the other day. Fancy a beer or a glass of something?'

Douglas, Mark and I sat at a picnic table outside the boathouse in the setting sun and talked things through. Mark is the latest in a 300-year-old line of craftsmen operating in the original boat maker's workshop under Richmond Bridge. The workshop is partly under the arches and was built with the bridge.

Mark was in full flood. 'The story goes that to encourage business, the bridge company gave a free or low fixed rent concession to the original occupant of the boathouse. He was a Waterman, see, and they're always clever, so this first boat maker registered his rent-free concession in the name of his young grandson. So, to the great annoyance of the bridge-building company, the boat-making business thrived on the same low rent for the lifetime of three generations of the family until the original grandson died.'

---

[6] I discovered later that officially, Mark had not been sworn in as a Waterman for some reason or other, but in a day-to-day sense he's very much a waterman through and through.

'How old was he?'

'Oh, a ripe old age ... over 70. Then his son took it on.'

Mark chuckled. He was a Cornishman who came up to the Thames as an apprentice, fell in love with the river and had stayed there ever since. After a long evening together and many laughs, he agreed to help make the bath float.

Douglas and I left the boathouse and walked back along the towpath.

'I think he'll do a great job for you.'

I looked back to see Mark sitting under the arches outside his boathouse sewing something or possibly doing a bit of ropework and knew Douglas was right. Boat makers had sat doing rope work and sewing cushions there for over 300 years before going up the hill. Mark was as much a part of Richmond as the bridge he sat under. I felt comfortable with him. There was total serenity in the scene.

'Yes. I think he will.'

I'd been stretched for weeks. Tiredness at my brutal regime was beginning to affect both my training and job. Finding Mark was the camel that broke me. Mark was located in Richmond, I was training in Hertfordshire and my temp job was in Whitehall. I couldn't pin down my job, keep up 10,000-metre Ergos, weights, running, see Mark and undertake the huge organisational backlog that was building up all at once. I took out an overdraft, stopped the job and started spending time at the boatyard.

As arranged, within days of our first meeting I arrived back at the boathouse. Richmond by the river was just as serene and stunning as before. I walked along the towpath to the boathouses and was met by a paint-addled youth wiping his nose on his hand.

'Hi, is Mark about?'

What to the untrained ear would constitute a cockney accent, but perhaps not the same one that originally picked up the phone, emanated from somewhere beneath the paint, 'Think he's somewhere in there . . .'

He wafted a hand vaguely over his shoulder and wandered off in the direction of what had once been a boat. I walked over to one of the arches and entered. This time the boathouse was the antithesis of serenity. This was foreign, chaotic and confusing. In every nook and cranny, there were similar paint-, grease- and sawdust-ridden young lads pawing over bits of boat in various stages of repair. Not one of the boats in their capable hands looked like it would float.

I shouted above the din of various tools scraping and loud music blaring out of an old stereo, 'Has anyone seen Mark?'

The eyes of several youths darted up to view me suspiciously. One raised his head. 'Think he went out ...'

I nodded sagely. 'If he comes back, tell him I'm in the teashop.'

I left for the teashop under another of the arches and ordered a cup of tea.

'Milk and sugar?'

'No thanks, I'll have it black.'

'Are you sure?'

This had been happening a lot.

'Yes, thank you for asking.'

'Really?'

'Yes please.'

Time went by. I made a few calls and read a bit before going back to the boathouse. Again, there was a loud din of combined humming, scraping and discord as now there were two stereos tuned to competing radio stations.

'Has anyone seen Mark?'

The same youth raised his head.

'Think he's in his office.'

'Thank you ...'

I stood motionless.

'... Where's his office?'

One of the youths, who was covered in wood shavings, smiled and put down the scrapey thing he was using. 'I'll show you.'

We went further into the bowels of the boathouse arch and turned left through a door kept shut by a large fishing weight rigged up as a counter balance.

'Hi Mark, when did you get back?'

'I've been here all the time. You're late.'

The wood-shaving lad smiled. 'I think the lads have been playing tricks on him.'

He left the office and Mark laughed. Over the coming days I

tried to understand the boathouse. It seemed to comprise the master boat maker, a couple of carpenters (one of them a master carpenter) and myriad apprentices who may or may not turn up on any given day. It's not a company in the modern corporate sense of the word, more a loose collective of interwoven friendships and interest groups. To an outsider it was hard to believe that this still existed in modern London. This was an ancient world that had continued rampant and unchecked since at least the 1700s. Since then they've used the same tools, sat on the same seats and drunk the same tea. This gives the place a feeling of solid familiarity, confidence and over three centuries of washing up.

All the invoices were still written by Mark in beautiful copperplate handwriting. It was like walking into *Oliver Twist*. The apprentices always seemed to be borrowing from, and lending money to, each other and to their various girlfriends who hung around outside the boatyard. When they'd finished that game for the day, they'd borrow money from Mark against their wages. One had seemingly advanced his wages well into the next year. Yet Mark still lent him money if he asked. Tolerance like this doesn't exist anywhere else except in the most exclusive city banks. There was such a complex matrix of who owed money to whom that I became certain there was a fiver that had never actually left the boathouse but had simply been passed around between them to cancel out one debit or incur another.

It wasn't easy fitting into such a closely knit world. I floundered, attempting to fetch numerous glass hammers, left-handed spirit levels, and waited for the kettle to boil at plug sockets that had long been disconnected. Many of the apprentices thought the entire project of rowing the Channel in a bath was an enormous wind up. They seemed to think I was some sort of trickster who would eventually reveal that the entire thing was arranged just to make them look silly.

Things turned round in a single day. A very big man wandered up the riverbank towards where I was working with the apprentices. He'd either got back from a day's work on one of the freight ships downriver, or seven years in prison. From looking at him, it was hard to tell. I'd heard the apprentices talking about him earlier, they respected him – he was hard. I felt nervous as he heaved his way towards us. There was a noticeable awed hush in the workshop. My first thought was to look for the nearest exit. In any kind of confrontation, this man would win.

'So, are you Tim?' he said with a gruffness that suggested aggression.

'Yes,' I said, although finding the fine line between 'said' and 'whimpered'.

For a big man he moved fast. I saw a blur in the fading light of the workshop. The next thing I knew I'd been engulfed in a handshake that drew me into a mighty hug that even a bear might think twice about. I stood back shocked.

'I read all about the paper boat, I've even got the paper cuttings in my cab [the cabin of the freight boat]. As a Waterman apprentice, you've made us proud – well done.'

The apprentices were almost as shocked as me.

He turned to them. 'You know he's a Waterman?'

The apprentices were now *as* shocked as me. I hadn't mentioned my Freedom of the Company to them but it had obviously been in the paper. One of them wiped his hand across his face.

'Really?'

The big man replied, 'Yes. And it's rare that is . . . an honour . . .'

I knew it was fairly rare but it seemed it was rarer than that. With one handshake and a bear hug I never looked back in the boatyard. They seemed to have accepted me. Now I got to ask newer apprentices to fetch the glass hammer. They even let me in on the tricks they were planning for Mark. It was a great time. I got to see the medieval craft of the boat maker up close; an old world that just manages to co-exist with the new one. I think some of them still thought the entire bath plan was a ruse to make them look silly but now it seemed they felt they were in on the gag.

I was now commuting between my parents' house in Hertfordshire, where Betty the avenging angel was living, and the boatyard in Richmond. Less than ideal, as Richmond was on the other side of London. Short of moving to Richmond or finding somewhere else to be able to train for free I had no choice. Hertfordshire was shrouded in a quiet tension between my mother and me. Normally, Mum and I get on really well. She's wonderful in my eyes; I've loved her since I remember anything. When I was small, she used to take out a guitar and sing to me beneath the trees – I loved that, real Julie Andrews-style mothering. Just great. I have a very special mum but I'd noticed there was a tension in the air. I didn't understand it. What was causing it?

I'd come up with another plan to raise cash for a charity. She'd loved the last one and was pleased at the amount of money that had been raised. I'd discovered a new sport and was getting good at that. Mum was a great rower in her day so it couldn't be that which was causing the tension. I was on the Thames every day. Mum rowed on the Thames and loved the river, so it couldn't be that. The plans were moving ahead really fast, which had to be good. There were problems but they were all being sorted. The bath plan was irrevocably in motion and nothing, it seemed, could stop me from actually having a chance of completing it. With all these positives, she should be happy. I was really puzzled. Bearing in mind the open, brilliant relationship I have with my mum, I asked Dad.

'I think it's something to do with your Uncle Tony . . .'

Uh-oh. That was a big problem. How had I forgotten it? For someone who is normally quite thoughtful, this was a staggering lapse. It wasn't even that I'd forgotten him; I just hadn't thought through the impact on my family of my current decisions in relation to him.

Uncle Tony or Great-Uncle Anthony to give him his full name was my grandma's older brother. Handsome, strong, clever and a crack shot. Like many men of his generation, when World War II started he joined the Royal Air Force. His plane was shot down over occupied France but in a stroke of luck, uncharacteristic in the family, he was able to land it safely and get his crew out.

I am from the famously blond-haired looks-a-little-like-Gonzo-from-the-Muppets side of the family. Great-Uncle Tony was from the ravishingly good-looking, dark-haired, dark-eyed side of the family. Also unlike me, he spoke fluent French. Before the war he'd always had some gorgeous European lady to escort somewhere and this helped his skills as a linguist greatly. So finding himself trapped in occupied France he impersonated a Frenchman. Disguised by his dark hair, tanned skin, fluent French and with a twinkle in his eye, he managed, remarkably, to get his crew (none of whom spoke French) across occupied France with a mixture of cunning and charm. Arriving at the coast he put them in a boat and, being a schoolboy rowing champion, he decided to row back to England.

It's always made me feel very small when I hear stories like that: the incredible courage and bravery of very ordinary people. He rowed the Channel to escape from the Nazis. With exhausted relief, when he saw the white cliffs he shouted to his crew, 'I'll swim the rest of the way . . . race you . . .' Then he jumped overboard. This was typical of the man, a sense of fun even during danger. His crew made it back to the UK and all went on to become top-ranking officers in the RAF. They've all talked of his extraordinary bravery and courage in getting them out of the situation. Uncle Tony, having saved them, was never seen again.

A couple of months later there was a break-in at my grandma's family house and his things, including almost every photo of him, were stolen. It may have been a coincidence that his were the only things taken but if it was, it's always struck me as being a very incredible one.

It was particularly hard on my grandma who was then left to wonder if he was perhaps still alive. Many attempts were made to find him, involving everyone from Winston Churchill to the French Resistance. All had their twists and turns and all sadly ended fruitlessly. Mystery continued to shroud my heroic pilot great-uncle and he was finally added to the memorial at Runnymede as being still missing in action 65 years on. He would have liked Runnymede as it overlooks the Thames, a river on which he too rowed as a schoolboy with some success.

Realising I was now attempting to row the very stretch of water where Great-Uncle Tony was last sighted hit me hard. The family story of his disappearance, the one picture of him I'd seen when I was small, the expression on my grandma's face as she looked at the image of the brother she'd lost, all ran through my head.

My family had already lost someone they loved to the Channel. How had I been dimmer than a candle in a sock? I sat in Hertfordshire alone, with thoughts of cancelling the project. Running it through my mind, I realised I couldn't. Things had already gone too far.

I sat thinking of things I might be able to say to try to console Mum. None of them were any good and most of them didn't even make sense. 'Don't worry, Mum, I'm a better athlete than him . . .' That wouldn't work. 'Don't worry, Mum, I've got a better boat than him . . .' If the first one wouldn't work, this one was just pie in the sky.

It was no good. There was only one course of action left to me. I must get on with beating the Channel and make very sure I made it back. In the moment of my new resolve I felt oddly very close to a man I'd never known.

Arriving back at my desk I was again hit by the nagging feeling that there was someone important I'd forgotten to talk to about my plan. I phoned Dom.

'Is there anyone I should have spoken to that I've missed?'

'I don't think so, you've checked it with the French Navy and the English Coastguard . . .'

'Bother. I knew it.'

I picked up the phone and checked they were in before speeding off down to Dover. I'd forgotten to talk to the English Coastguard and it was vital to get their support. I was not sure of the legal position. Could they legally stop me from going? This meeting was going to be tense.

Before leaving I'd glanced furtively at their website. Their catch-phrase is 'Safer lives, safer ships, cleaner seas.' Nowhere on the website were baths mentioned. But what shipping could possibly be cleaner than a bath?

I waited in reception. Very promptly a man in a smart cap and epaulettes arrived. He spoke as punctually as he clearly kept time, 'Merryweather.'

'Is it?'

'Droll. I get that a lot being in this line of work. Now what is it you wanted?'

For a meeting that I knew would be tense I'd not started well. My opening gag had gone down like the LZ 129 Hindenburg. I followed him up a staircase into a room with a stunning view.

'Wow, you can see the whole Channel from up here.'

'You should see the view from the other side. Shall we sit down?'

The conversation continued going badly until suddenly, there was a single beam of light. He'd read about the paper-boat trip.

'If you can make it that far in a paper boat, you must be able to skipper almost anything.'

I had a chance.

'Funny you should say that Mr Merryweather . . . have a look at these plans.'

As he scrutinised the Douglas plan, he explained the situation in this country. It was somewhat different to the one in France. In the UK it turns out that legally the Coastguard (or the MCA, as they now like to be called) cannot actually forbid you from rowing the Channel. However, they can stop you if they find you're being a danger to other shipping, yourself or infringing maritime law. I really wanted the Coastguard to back the bath project. As I knew nothing about the sea, I felt it would be good to have them in my corner.

The meeting finished with the words, 'My official advice is that you do not row the Channel, but if you ignore that advice I suggest you get the help of the Channel Crossing Association.'

There was an association for crossing the Channel? Why had I not known about this before? This is the downside of embarking on totally tangential adventures with no experience. I could have got right to the water's edge, crossed the Channel and at no point even heard of the Channel Crossing Association. Wiser men, even other comics, would have put 'Channel crossing' into Internet search engines and come up trumps. Using complex prediction systems at my birth, both the Shaman and Sibyls were fairly unanimous that I was never destined to be defined as a 'wiser men'. I stared at him blankly.

'Channel Crossing Association?'

'Yes, they're the experts. Sure you've been speaking to them already but just thought I'd mention it. Do you fancy a tour of the station?'

Touring the MCA station at Dover, amid all the very high-tech radar systems and computer equipment that keeps that Channel safe, I realised that this would be a very difficult challenge indeed.

'The Channel is the busiest shipping lane in the world.'

'So I see . . .'

'Some of these tankers have a stopping distance of over 25 miles.'

'Imagine taking a driving test in that in Stevenage . . .'

Again I heard faint cries of 'Brace! Brace!' as the Hindenburg went to crash but this time Mr Merryweather cracked a smile. Further into our time together I felt able to tell him my full plan.

'Ideally, I'd like to make it round the coast and up to Tower Bridge.'

'That's a heck of a trip. I wouldn't make it but good luck to you.

I'll wave when you come past Dover. In fact if you make it to here, I'll even come down to the shore myself and shake you by the hand.'

I left the Coastguard in Dover and drove back up from Kent to Hertfordshire. As soon as I got through the door, pausing only to fire up my laptop, I typed 'Channel crossing' into Google. Sure enough, up popped the website for the Channel Crossing Association.

I picked up the phone and in a brief conversation established they were based in Kent, near Dover. I left the house, turned the car round and drove straight back to Kent. Driving back there, I made a note to move to Kent.

I drove through a wood, out the other side and down an implausibly small rack[7] (could have been a toad) with pasture on either side. 'This is a stunning part of Kent,' I thought as I missed the turning I wanted. After the world's first 57-point turn in the narrow rack I went back down to the turning I'd missed.

I went up the drive to find a house, built in the late 70s with a conservatory on one side, a garage and in the field next door, two llamas nonchalantly chewing in a barn. I knocked on the door and heard a muffled, 'Come in.' I found myself in a hallway. A stocky frame of between 5'8" and 5'10" (let's call it 5'9") with an off-white grey beard, hair and very wide shoulders approached. Duncan Taylor threw out a hand. My first impression of him was one of strength; he looked stoic and solid, but above all strong.

'You must be Tim, do come in. Tea?'

His words came in the lovely undulating, lyrical accent of that part of Kent. I nodded nervously and we went to the kitchen. I was nervous, because even a brief look at their website had convinced me that the chances of getting a serious organisation like the Channel Crossing Association to back the very silly plan of rowing their precious Channel in a piece of plumbing were slim. To me, Duncan had the aura of a man on the verge of using phrases involving the devil, intemperate weather and ice skates.

'Actually could I have mine black?'

'Are you sure?'

---

[7] A thing that's not quite big enough to be a road but just too sophisticated to be a track.

'Yes, thank you, it's quite nice when you get used to it . . .'

While the tea brewed, I filled him in on the paper-boat journey, stressing the safety aspects of it and leaving out the bits about getting trapped in locks, near-death experiences and almost drowning. He nodded, smiled and laughed but with the air of a man who thought that the most important thing in the story was the safety. I mentioned the llamas.

'Yes . . . I'm only head of the Channel Crossing Association some of the time. In winter I fish and for the rest of the time farm llamas. They're great, I'll take you out to meet them later.'

We took our cups and went into the next room.

'Now, how can I help?'

I pulled out all my bits of paper, including the Douglas plan, maps that I'd made out of photocopies of the road atlas and names of people I'd talked to.

'I really want to row the Channel for a charity called Sport Relief. Then I'd like to row round Kent and up to Tower Bridge. I think that by being on the water for longer I might make more money for them.'

I didn't mention the bet with Kenny to win a beer. I wasn't sure I knew Duncan well enough yet to let him into that part of the plan. He looked through all the pieces of paper and sat back in his chair.

'This seems like a great plan. I'd love to be involved. In fact I've never been that far up the Thames before so it'll be quite an adventure for me, too.'

He smiled and stood up.

'I'll go and find some proper charts.'

Then there was an awkward pause. Not just a pregnant one but the kind that takes days in labour to sire and leads the mother of this pause to curse the day her husband got her tipsy and suggested an early night.

'There's just one more thing . . . I'd like to try and row it in a bath.'

Even the midwife of the mother of the pause, paused. The entire room shifted. Duncan turned looking half puzzled, half cross. All the joy had vanished.

'What!?'

'I thought it might be a problem.'

Duncan sat straight back down.

'I think we'd better have a very full and frank discussion, Tim. Taking a bathtub across the busiest shipping lane in the world is a very reckless, stupid thing to do. With the way the current works you basically would be very hard-pressed to make it across anyway even if it wasn't such a bad plan. At the Channel Crossing Association we're primarily concerned with the safety of all, what we call, unorthodox crossings.'

'I can see the bath is pretty unorthodox.'

'By unorthodox I mean crossings of the Channel that have to be supported. It's a term we use for this type of crossing. What did the Coastguard say?'

'He said I should talk to you . . .'

'Well, I'm glad you did. This plan simply will not work. I can't see it happening. It's incredibly dangerous.'

Somewhere in hell, Satan reached for his ice skates.

The conversation continued for several very painful hours; me constantly looking on the bright side, thinking how much money we could raise for charity and how much fun the whole project would be. Duncan constantly looking on the practical side, thinking how much the court cases would cost and how much chaos the whole project would cause. The conversation was not going well and as the Coastguard had made very clear, I needed Duncan to be able to go ahead.

Eventually, he put down one of the various bits of paper or shipping guidelines he'd been reading and, looking at me oddly, said, 'You're really serious about this.'

'Yes.'

'It won't work.'

'I'm not saying it will. I'm just asking you to give me the best possible chance to try.'

He paused.

'Good. I just had to check. It's a terrible plan and you're bound to fail but I'd rather I was there to try to make sure you don't get killed. Let's go to the pub for a celebratory meal.'

'What?' My words came out feebly.

'I'm in! Let's go and celebrate.'

'What?'

'We're going to get you across that Channel in that bath and up to Tower Bridge – or at least be there when you fail. I'm in.'

With that, we left for the pub down the rack, pausing only to say hello to the llamas and tell them the good news.

I was in a state of shock and awe. Not even burning the top of my mouth on the pub's own brand 'mild' mustard or catching a glimpse of my own nostrils caused by a second helping of 'the mild' was able to shake me out of it. I had got the serious and efficient Channel Crossing Association to back me in an attempt to cross the Channel in plumbing. I was stunned.

We had a great lunch plotting all aspects of the bath plan and especially ways to try and make it as safe as possible. After coffee, we walked back up the toad to the car. Duncan hugged me goodbye.

'Great to meet you. I'm really looking forward to this. We'll speak soon.'

I drove off down the rack towards the wood. I felt so dazed I was a hazard to other road users. Pulling over, I parked the car, got out and slumped down on a nearby picnic table.

I'd done it. I thought getting Duncan on side would be simply impossible and now I'd not only got him to back the project but also found a kindred spirit.

Over the next few weeks Duncan and I set to work phoning the French, the Coastguard in Dover, rifling through paper work and discussing charts. Sometimes we'd work together as the sun poured into his study window in Kent. Other times we'd work apart. The project was now gloriously moving forward on every front: Duncan in Kent, Mark and the lads up in Richmond and me flitting between the two.

Duncan spoke fluent French, so I could leave the brilliant Liza to give birth, which was the main thing on her to-do list that month.

This was a golden time in the project. There were no obstacles; everything was running faster than a racehorse with ginger beneath its tail. The French Navy and her officers, far from being true to their petty, bureaucratic stereotype, were being as kind and helpful as it was possible to be. As Duncan was the first to point out it was difficult to tell if this tremendous bonhomie was due to an exhibition of Gallic *fraternité* rarely seen by English eyes, or the case of port we sent them as a present.

One morning I arrived to see Duncan for one of our plotting sessions; he looked drawn. 'We're in trouble, Tim.'

'What?'

'The French have changed their minds.'

'What?'

'They've updated the shipping guidelines.'

'What?'

'Have a look at this . . .'

There on the paper in front of me was devastating news. The representative of the French Navy had kindly sent us an update on the shipping laws and guidelines of France. In front of me in black and white, plain to even my limited understanding of French: no bathtub rowing in French waters more than a mile and a half off the French coast.

'In light of my plan, this is a bit of a blow.'

'It's more than that, Tim. It means it's over.'

'Can we phone them?'

'We can give it a go . . .'

Duncan sprang to the phone. His repeated negotiations were turned down flat. The French position was very clear. If I attempted to row a bath more than a mile and a half from the French coast-line, I would be arrested by the French Navy and tried under martial law. This could lead to a lengthy stay in a French naval prison without the slightest need to trouble civil lawyers or justice. It seemed a very harsh position to take. The French Navy had invoked emergency powers and gone from being totally supportive to totally obstructive.

Later that day, my phone flashed into life. It was Liza.

'How's it all going?'

'Not the best this end, how's being pregnant?'

'Still going. What's up?'

I explained the situation, the Navy, the total *volte-face* and big legal hurdle we now faced.

'Tell you what, I'll give them a buzz if you like, just to check it all.'

Brilliant. Perhaps it was all a mistake. Perhaps Duncan's French was not as good as Liza's. Perhaps the French Navy would respond better to the soothing purring of an expectant mother than the working French of a Kentish fisherman.

I spent an agonising half a day while Liza tried to get hold of the French Navy. I didn't know what to do. Should I stop the work on the bath in Richmond and accept defeat or assume that Liza would win through and carry on with planning my dream? It was an afternoon of total ambiguity and the thing about being totally ambiguous is, practically, you don't get a lot done.

Finally, Liza phoned back. 'They really have got a bee in their bonnets about this. They're just not going to budge. I really tried but they're sticking to it. I'm really so sorry.'

So there it was, even the glimmer of hope had been snuffed out by an industrial-sized wind fan. The law was in place. The French Navy planned to defend its shores to the silt. The bath project was over.

Some would say my celebration of the 100th anniversary of the Entente Cordiale was perfect. It had hit the wall: unable to continue due to two totally opposing national viewpoints on sanitaryware. It was finished.

Somewhere in a quiet moment in Hertfordshire, my mother breathed a big sigh of relief.

CHAPTER FOUR

RING A RING O' ROSES, A POCKET FULL OF RED TAPE

*'A common mistake people make, when trying to design
something completely foolproof, is to underestimate
the ingenuity of complete fools.'*

Douglas Adams

The challenge was off. I refused the main course of depression but nibbled gloomily at the starter of being less than buoyant with lashings of melancholy on the side. I sat at home in my village in Hertfordshire, deep in thought. I'd spent months of time, effort and money planning the trip with the total knowledge and support of the French Navy only to have them change their minds. The old enemy had reared its ugly two-faced head. Foolishly, I'd believed the original happy face before being confronted with the cold sneer of the real one. I felt like Henry V clutching at tennis balls. Game, set and match to the French. I was totally beaten. The bath project was over.

Like Henry, I raged in private and damned the French for their lack of truth and honesty. Like many Britons before me I'd expected too much of our Gallic brothers and found them lacking. It would

47

be too easy to fall in with the stereotype of the French as the nation of inconsistent, wine-swilling, cheese-eating surrender monkeys but when you're confronted with the side of their character that had been shown to me, it's hard to find fault with the analysis. I'd believed in the Entente Cordiale and the European ideal of a brotherhood bound by a common purpose. This had failed. My faith in Europe was smashed. The entire European Union seemed less a united team, more a warring extended family squashed together, shouting and screaming on a long car journey. The total *volte-face* made no sense. France had proved herself to me as a nation totally lacking logic.

After half an hour of seething about the French Navy's lack of logic, I smiled wryly. There's not a great deal of logic in attempting to row the world's busiest shipping lane in a bath. Still, I felt as I looked, like a black Labrador during the days immediately after being spayed. I'd not just wasted my own time but had drawn an entire team into this complete nonsense.

I sat motionless, devastated: another victim of the perfidious French. Planning and working to a ridiculous goal is the thing I love the most. Taking apart those plans is the thing I hate the most. With a hand made of lead, I telephoned Mark and asked him and the apprentices to stop work on the bath. The next phone call was to Kenny.

'You sound a bit down, what's up?'

'It's all off . . . the whole bath thing. The French have changed their minds and there's simply nothing I can do.'

'Damn! They've just changed their minds . . . just like that?'

'Yes – I can't take on a whole other national government and expect to win.'

'I'm sure you've tried everything.'

'Yes . . . Look, I know there are costs and stuff and I'll pay for as much of it as I can. It's not fair for you to have a bill for this complete nonsense, especially as it's not now going to go ahead.'

'Don't worry, we can sort all that out later. The main thing is, not to get too down. Why don't we go for a beer in a few days to celebrate the idea that got away . . .'

'Thanks, mate.'

A similar call to Simon; later I phoned Douglas and Dom, both of whom were as down as me about it. After a few more phone calls I'd totally dismantled the team and the project was finished.

Many of the people involved said the words 'British', 'Grit' and 'Spirit' and suggested doing it anyway. Many phrases starting with 'The French be damned . . .' or similar drifted into my increasingly downcast ear.

It is 26 August 1346. Somewhere on a hillock in France, people shout and scream, a chaotic melee scrambles around trying to make sense of what is around it. Following a bet with his brother to win a pint of beer, one man avoids the volleys of arrows, runs forward and throws down a glove. He shouts something medieval about crushing France before charging at them.

I'm descended from that man (pint bets obviously run in the family), he fought with the Earl of Northampton (who basically seemed to own him), survived the battle of Crecy and true to his word, the French were crushed that day. He was there on the day the then Prince of Wales won his feathers.

This was uppermost in my mind as I listened on the phone. There's obviously something deep within me that is designed to tease the French: a gene reaching back nearly 700 years.

The downcast team had tapped into some part of me designed to test French resolve. Yet, forcing the French hand would not just endanger me but other members of the team. I'd probably be arrested, but so too would the members of the support crew. If my stupid risk hurt others, it's not a risk that should be considered. At the bottom line, the bath was just a project to raise some cash for a charity; it was never meant to escalate to this level.

To a symphony of 700-year-old bones turning disapprovingly in their graves, I phoned Duncan to thank him for all his work.

Laughing, he said, 'Just a shame the bath isn't a registered British Shipping Vessel, then you could row it where you like.'

That was the only line of the conversation I remember, which shows how hard it hit me. I put down the phone to Duncan and my brain started whirring.

Ever since I first saw the piece of paper it seemed bizarre that an entire country would alter their law just to stop me trying to complete a charity project. I couldn't believe that a sovereign power would specifically victimise me in this way to try to stop me from raising money for a really good cause. As a nation, to deny the right of a citizen to attempt something to help others is as far from the ideals of Rousseau and Voltaire as it was possible to be. *Liberté*, *égalité* and *fraternité* it certainly was not. I resolved to take this up with the French President if I ever met him.

However, that one line from Duncan led me to think that perhaps I'd got it all wrong. Perhaps the French were testing my resolve. Maybe they were saying, 'Tim if you're really serious about this stupid bath plan – prove it!' except obviously they'd have said it in French. A strong possibility arose in my head that they were just playing the time-honoured Gallic game of 'Red Tape'.

Whenever I see red tape something makes me reach for the scissors.

To look at what Duncan had said another way, if I could get the UK Ministry of Transport to include the bath on the shipping register I could row the Channel and no one could stop me.

Somewhere in the civil service a telephone rang.

'Hello, sorry to disturb you, I'm sure you're very busy but I need to talk to someone about shipping licences . . .'

'I'll put you through.'

I waited. This could be crucial.

'Hello . . .'

'Hello, I need to try and register for a shipping licence.'

'Have you checked our website?'

'Yes, but this is something of a special case.'

She sighed, bored. Clearly legions of the self-important trying to get onto the small ships register had created scepticism.

She sighed again, in case I'd misinterpreted the first one. 'Why?'

'It's a bath.'

There was a pause.

'Go on . . .'

Very carefully I explained the situation with the bath and the French Navy. I also explained that it was a charity project and that the Channel Crossing Association and the Coastguard had been consulted and as far as anyone could see we were doing our best to ensure the safety of the whole scheme. There was another pause.

'Are you serious? Or is this one of those wind-up things?'

'No, I'm very serious.'

'Send me some pictures.'

She hung up without committing either way. As it was a choice between sitting at home feasting on a diet of self-doubt or going out and taking pictures I picked up my camera and headed off to the boatyard in Richmond. Mark came out.

'How do you want to take her?'

'I think the more nautical we can make her look the better. What about putting her in the water and taking the front end of the bath?'

'The one with the taps?'

'No, the other end. We'll take that and if we shoot from the ground up it'll look a bit like one of those early P&O posters.'

I sent off the pictures. The bath didn't quite look like the leading ship in the P&O fleet but as much like a realistic ocean-going vessel as we could make her appear. This was my only chance to get the bath project back on. Would they grant her a shipping licence? I spent two days thinking of nothing else. In an office somewhere in the civil service a phone rang again.

'Hello. We spoke a few days ago, it's about the bath and the Channel.'

'I've got your pictures. I've made some calls.'

Would she grant the licence? She still sounded bored. Perhaps that was just a character trait? But she hadn't put the phone down; it seemed a good sign.

'We'd need to insist on a few modifications to grant the shipping licence. It's just if anything went wrong, we'd look very stupid – we're prepared to look a little silly as it's in a good cause but we can't cut all the corners. Have you got a pen?'

Originally they asked for a total change of plan, effectively turning the bath into a boat. I objected and suggested another tack. They changed that and sent it back. This was classic old-school horse-trading. A Grand National of phone calls took place between us.

'We'd need to insist on some sort of buoyancy aids, like on a catamaran, in order to give it an outboard and more stability.'

'Great – I'll have a Victorian black-and-white tiled bathroom floor.'

'Erm . . . right . . .'

Or, 'We're going to have to insist on a masthead.'

'Right, I'll make it a showerhead and have it plumbed in, would that count?'

'Erm . . . yes, I suppose it would.'

And, 'You're going to have to have a waterproof enclosed area for the electrics for the lighting you must have.'

'Super, I'll have a washstand built. That'll store them and I could have taps plumbed in on top of it and a shelf for shampoo . . .'

More sighing. At every turn I'd think of a way of trying to stay true to the original bath plan whilst still acceding to their requests.

'You've got to fly the Red Ensign flag – don't tell me you'll make a bath towel out of it?'

'Absolutely not. Who'd make a bath towel out of a Red Ensign? Outrageous!'

'Oh and you're going to need an anchor.'

'Great.'

The anchor would add weight but it might come in useful. The compromise we agreed was the closest to my original intention they would allow. It would enrage bath purists in that it was more a bathroom than a bath but on the plus side it was a bathroom that was a registered British Shipping Vessel with an SSR Number.

I was in Kent with Duncan. With joy we telephoned the French to tell them I'd passed their red-tape initiative test, the bath was a ship and the challenge was back on. Somehow, they didn't seem as pleased as I thought they might, but accepted that legally I could now row it across the Channel.

The bath challenge had come back from the brink.

'Celebratory lunch at the pub? The bangers and mash is lovely, they make their own mustard you know.'

My eyes and nose watered at the mere mention of the famous locally made 'mild'.

'I should probably make some calls . . .'

I hit the phone again and Mark got to work on the raft of changes to the bath. Kenny and Simon smiled, Dom got out the charts for more planning and Douglas sank a beer in delight. The team were back together.

With all these changes to make, my place seemed firmly to be at the boatyard. It was hard work but a lot of good fun. Each day after working on the bath I'd get to take out a skiff and row as far as I could up river and back again. The boats were all moored on a pontoon next to the floating restaurant and were looked after by a swarthy, strong-looking apprentice called Luke. I've never been more impressed by anyone else on the water. Luke seemed semi-amphibious. He wandered along boat tenders, leaped between skiffs and punted and rowed as though he had been born in the water. Mark was an impressive oarsman but Luke had the magical poise and effortless balance of a swan. He seemed more at home on the riverbank than an otter – it might just have been me but he looked a bit like one too.

'Mark says you can take out that boat . . .' He pointed to an old Thames skiff.

Another paint-stained apprentice called down from the towpath, 'Nah, Luke, Mark said to send him out in that one . . .'

He pointed down at a thinner boat, shaped more like a racing scull.

Luke laughed and turned to me. 'You wouldn't make it back in that . . .'

I must have looked down as he quickly added, 'I mean, with this tide. Here, take this . . .'

The Thames skiff is a totally bombproof boat. Not that it could actually withstand a bomb but in that they're almost impossible to capsize. Whether they'd hold up in the hands of a professional rowing submariner like me was a different issue. I cast off from the pontoon and spent many happy hours rowing in circles near Richmond Bridge.

The incredible thing was that I didn't capsize once. I fell in lots, especially getting into and out of the boats. In fact there was a week where Luke made a few quid betting people that I'd fall every time. He won. Once I even managed to fall in simply by trying to stand on the pontoon.

I was thrilled, wet but thrilled; I'd improved from capsizing to falling in. It's a slim distinction but a promotion nevertheless. Up to this point, my training to row the Channel had been entirely land based. Now, finally, half a year in, I was training in boats. Over weeks, I graduated from circles to ovals, then to ellipses and finally to a wobbly line.

My first wobbly line was a huge success. I remember Luke standing on the pontoon looking shocked. I was so pleased that I carried on, pulling upriver of the bridge. This was uncharted territory for me. Hours later I returned to Luke at the pontoon.

'You must have been miles. How far up did you get? Teddington? Hampton?'

'Erm . . . actually, just around the bend up there, then I got a bit stuck. I freed myself then got caught in a fishing line from the bank and it took ages to get out of that . . . then I tried pulling against the tide but couldn't and it took me further away so I had to wait for it to turn before I could make it back.'

Luke and the other apprentices laughed and teased me affectionately before we tied up the boats and went home for the night.

My wobbly lines turned to straight ones and, eventually, I managed to make it up to Teddington and back. Finally, progress. Gin-soaked fast launches passed me on the way, their captains slurring hoards of abuse, less than clearly believing that anyone as inept as me must be drunker than them, or stupid. Someone should invent L-plates for the river.

Improvement came fast now and very soon I was rowing up to Teddington and back several times a day. I couldn't believe I'd ever found it hard. I even took Mark's racing skiff out a few times and even that didn't capsize me.

I began to see a pattern. With unerring planning and the enthusiasm of an extremist, every time I went out rowing, a blue-and-white speedboat would appear. Like Nelson and de Villeneuve we fought: him for maritime supremacy and me for the ability to stay upright. He laughed as I floundered in his wake and a couple of times turned impressively to pass again and finish me off. Each time I bobbed, wove, lost the oars, banged my knees and did everything I could to capsize but amazingly didn't go under. He smirked as he turned away from our daily skirmish, swilling lager from a can and leaving me to locate the kneecaps I'd lost. I wonder if de Villeneuve drank lager?

During one of these skirmishes my phone rang in the violently rocking skiff.

'Hi, Kenny.'

'How's the training going?'

'Erm . . . pretty well . . . well, sort of OK.'

'Someone in the office lives in Richmond you know.'

'OK, it's a disaster really but I'm getting a bit better.'

'Is the bath in any kind of shape yet?'

'It's coming together, just there were a lot of things to change but we're getting there. It's not done yet but I think it would float.'

'Can you get it to Berkshire tomorrow? Only I think I've found a couple of rowing coaches who might be able to help.'

'I'll sort it.'

I needed all the help I could get. I rowed back to the pontoon. Mark, the apprentices and I carefully modified one of the boat trailers using a sledgehammer. Following this precision engineering, we manhandled the unfinished bath off the trestles. Getting the bath onto the trailer, even on the towpath, took much longer than expected and an hour and a half more than planned. In darkness I left Richmond and set off back to Hertfordshire. I slept violently and the next morning woke early. Following instructions I set off towards Berkshire.

On the way I phoned Mark. 'Is it going to be all right putting her in the water?'

'She'll be fine. All the structural stuff is done so she's going to float. We've got a long way to go, see, but she's going to be great. I gave her a polish last night while you were out rowing.'

'Thanks. Speak later.'

The sun was shining, there was a wind in the air and white tops to the choppy peaks of water on the lake at Eton Dorney. Just two months after my first non-capsize rowing outing, I stood on the banks of the country's leading rowing facility. The massive project to create the Eton College rowing lake was finally finished. The College has created a top stretch of water for rowing.

The road leading up to the lake undulates gently. Either the man who designed this loved hillocks or even the road had been engineered specifically to reduce the bounce you get with a boat trailer. I pulled the car to a stop and surveyed the scene. It was like seeing the future and in the middle of it stood the massive frame of Sir Matthew Pinsent. Of course he was just Matthew Pinsent then but his frame was still massive. Standing beside him were the rest of the legendary Great Britain Men's Olympic First Four: James Cracknell, Steve Williams and Alex Partridge.

To a man who had only learnt to row two months before, this was an awesome sight. This was serious; Kenny had obviously got me some pretty amazing coaches if they were sharing a lake with the GB Squad.

A man walked over. 'You must be Tim – I can tell by the bath. I'm Shane.'

'Hi ... are you going to be coaching me?'

'Did Kenny not say?'

'No.'

'You'll be with the guys.'

'What?'

I stood stunned and realised my mouth was open. If there had been crops around me, they would all have been safe from crows.

'Come on over and meet them.'

I followed in silence to meet the Great Britain Men's Olympic First Four. We faced each other divided only by a vast chasm of experience. Matt was the first to shake me by the hand. I'd met both Matt and James before, in fact we almost collided with each other when I was coming down the Thames in the paper boat but I'm very forgettable and they've got a lot on their plates so they didn't remember it. When I reminded them, they immediately cracked a smile.

'So you're at it again,' said Matt.

'You nutter,' added James.

I nodded, smiled and met the others. If it's possible to be *very* speechless, I was. I'd only managed to keep a scull upright for the first time two months before and here I was with the greatest rowers in the world. It was a surreal situation. I'd just walked into a very tight unit. Matt seemed to be the most focused man in the world. His entire mind seemed already on the finish line at the Athens Olympic just two short months away.

James was enthusiastic about everything. He asked me lots of questions about how it all worked and before I fully figured out how to answer, he'd said, 'Want to go out on the lake?'

'Do you want to come too?'

'Absolutely.'

The bath needed special oars, as the original ones were now not long enough due to the new tiled floor adaptation. Mark and I had only just roughly made them the evening before.

I'd never rowed in the bath before. I was about to take my first strokes with an Olympic champion standing quietly on the bath-room floor, leaning on the roll top and quite genuinely looking over my shoulder.

I looked at James, he smiled. 'Let's see how she performs.'

I took a deep breath. After a lot of debate Mark had caved in and installed a sliding seat on the bath. I slid up to the top of the stroke, squared the blades, dipped the oars in and pulled back. I was so very nervous. Luckily, I didn't catch a crab[8]. With huge relief I took a couple more strokes. We were making headway up the lake.

Nervously, I turned to James, 'What do you think?'

'You've got a good action.'

Hooray: something for my gravestone.

'But the bath is such an awkward shape and it seems really heavy – is it heavy? It looks like it's making you finish quite high too.'

It had felt to me like I was finishing high compared to the skiffs and sculls, but I didn't know what I was talking about so it was great to hear it from him. Sharing a bath in the middle of the lake, James and I were getting on really well. He's such an approachable character. I felt very at ease in his company, as we joked, laughed and splashed about. It was as though he was the older brother of someone I'd known for ages. There was something that had been troubling me for a bit and I thought James was the man to trust with it so I asked him.

'It's a bit personal this, and erm . . . sorry, but I've got no one else to ask. But, um . . . how do you cope with the chaffing down below?'

'Well, what clothes are you wearing to row in, as it could be that?'

'Mostly, an old college rowing lycra and a jumper.' The lycra is like an all-in-one bathing costume that rowers and other sportsmen wear, made famous by starring in the 1988 Olympics with Linford Christie's lunchbox.

'Anything else?'

'Just my boxer shorts, shoes and socks.'

He smiled benevolently like an older brother, then paused. 'Maybe don't wear the boxer shorts.'

With what I know now about rowing I can only guess just how hard James very kindly suppressed his laughter. Boxer shorts are worse than useless for rowing. All they do is add an extra layer of fabric, get wet and rub against your skin. The best thing to wear for rowing is nothing at all. Wearing boxer shorts to row, all you get is increased chaffing, pain and a less-than-happy girlfriend.

---

[8]'Catching a crab' is what they call it when you miss a stroke. I was so confused the first time I heard someone say it to a bloke, I asked how his girlfriend was coping with the news.

A crowd had gathered on the landing stage. There was a television camera there and some people from the newspapers. I carried on rowing and asking James more questions. He was the most experienced rower I'd met and I wanted to get as much advice as possible from him. There was a whistle from the landing stage and a shout. We looked over. Matt was signalling for us to come over. I pulled on the oars and rowed us back in to where Matt, Steve and Alex were giving interviews to the newspaper people and television camera.

As we pulled into the landing stage, I heard Matt say, 'Let's put a stop to these ideas now, I will not do anything that mad for Sport Relief or any other charity.'

'What piece of equipment do you most recommend for Tim?'

'A straitjacket!' Matt never misses a beat.

Next, they spoke to James who replied, 'You wouldn't catch me doing anything like that.'

To underline this, six months later, James crossed the Channel on a surfboard before rowing the Atlantic.

Steve Williams was next up. 'We've just met him and he's clearly a little bit loopy . . . but good on him.'

Being rowers they were all aware of the challenge that lay ahead of me and gave me tips, advice, training ideas and a rubber duck.

Matt really hit home. 'What length Ergos are you doing?'

I puffed out my chest. '10,000 metres.'

'That's about six miles. If you're going to make it across, you want to look to up that to 25-mile ones. In fact you should really be looking to do 25 miles at least every other day.'

It may sound harsh but I could see he was right. He gestured to the lake, smiled and continued, 'Off you go then. Get a few miles in now.'

They all shook me by the hand. Matt was the last of them. 'Good luck, we'll be thinking of you . . . you loony.'

I wished him luck in the Olympics.

They wandered round to the sleek-hulled four that sat moored to the landing stage next to the one we'd been on with the bath. I sat on the other landing stage with the bath watching them. They got into the four and put their oars in the gates. With a snap I realised this could be the race of a lifetime and got into the bath.

They pulled off a little way from the landing stage, went up to the top of their slides, squaring the blades ready for the start. I pulled level with them and did the same. For once five minds, not four, imagined they were at the start line of the Athens Olympics; four in a racing boat and one in ablution equipment. There was silence on the bank but you could tell there was tension amongst the spectating grass. The turf held its breath, someone shouted and we were off. The GB First Four got off to quite a start but in the early stroke the bath held them. As we powered up the lake at Eton Dorney conditions were choppy – that had to favour the bath. The bath came back at the GB First Four but within ten metres of the start the First Four had pulled into a commanding lead. On the bank, turf accountants tore up betting slips.

I was still going up the lake as they passed me going back the other way. As I was still sweating on my second length, the GB First Four had already finished, got out, stored the boat, cracked open the golf clubs and were walking off to pitch and putt as a reward. It had been a tense race and at the start line was quite close, but by the way they were walking off to play golf I could tell the bath had lost.

I grimaced to myself, cursed the fact I'd not been rowing since I was an embryo and carried on sculling in the bath. Rowing the Channel was going to be tough. There'd be no pitch and putt for me till the Channel had been vanquished. This had been great training for the Olympics: if the Committee ever listened to my requests and took bathtub rowing into the Olympiad I'd be ready. If only the boys could leave the rest of the world as dead in the water as they'd left the bath.

Some days later, I was very sad to hear that Alex Partridge had punctured his lung and could no longer compete at the Olympics. Alex seemed a very good man to me. It's a proper measure of respect that the rest of the crew named the boat they raced in at Athens after him. Alex's injury was a very stark reminder of just how tough rowing is on your body.

I drove back from Berkshire with the sense that things were possible but harder than I thought they might be. People refer to sculling the Channel as 'the pinnacle of single-seat rowing'. Before meeting the GB Squad these words meant nothing real to me. Having seen people at the pinnacle of the sport I realised there was a mountain to climb.

The only problem, other than my fitness mountain, was the weather. The English summer is famous for its rain. Rain was fine for me to row in. Like a man who's just eaten locally sourced 'mild' mustard in a pub in Kent, wind was my main enemy.

June brought two possible 'weather windows'. These are days when the conditions are good enough to contemplate the trip. During those, the bath sat on trestles at the boatyard as Mark, his apprentices and I worked round the clock to try to get the changes completed. It was deeply frustrating to have great weather and spend it, dry in a bath on dry land. Now, all I wanted was to get out to sea and finally attack the Channel.

Leaving Mark to carry on, every other day I'd get out and complete 30 miles, either on the river or on the Ergo. These training sessions were as much about the mental challenge as the physical one.

On the plus side, while working on the bath and training hard, I did have time to deal with one vital question: what to call her? To get the final licence, the bath had to have a name. For the majority who don't know the ins and outs of the paper-boat trip I'll try and explain this bit quickly. Anyone who has read about the paper boat, flip a couple of paragraphs.

In 2003, I set off to break the world's oldest existing maritime record in a paper boat. The record was set in 1619 by a Royal Waterman so I decided to follow the 400-year-old etiquette of writing to Her Majesty the Queen to ask for Her permission to attempt to break the record.

To my total amazement Her Private Secretary wrote back. I think he was shocked that anyone could be bothered to follow pre-decimal etiquette. Also, it seemed the Palace were pleased that someone was trying to do something positive and raise a bit of money for a charity. King James the VI or I (still not taking sides on the issue) had chosen the name of the first paper boat. In my letter I'd rather cheekily asked if Her Majesty would like to choose the name for the new one. After various letters going back and forth and the Machiavellian antics of the then Lord Chancellor, too off track to go into here, the name 'Lilibet' was decided upon. This was the name given to the Queen by Her father when she was a child. It brilliantly summed up the whole childish nature of the paper-boat trip.

I now wrote to the Palace again and after various letters, the name 'Lilibet II' was approved for the bath. Again the name perfectly captured the childish nature of the quest. It summed up the total unawareness of failure you have when you're five years old and the indomitable belief in right and truth that comes from being able to spend time under a blanket with your favourite soft toy if things go wrong. It also made the bath feel like a sister to the paper boat, and having had such a good time in that boat, this was a good omen.

With the changes to the bath completed, my licence from the Ministry arrived just in time for the weather to turn really bad.

Like a small child or neurotic girlfriend at Christmas, I ripped the envelope apart. There it was, my entry into the world of the serious mariner. In black and white with a Royal Crest at the top: 'Certificate of British Registry', registered under the 'Merchant Shipping Act of 1995 and Merchant Shipping (Registration of Ships) Regulations of 1993, as amended'. Her small shipping registration number was SSR111694 and her Hull ID was ME034. But, more than all of this, *Lilibet II* was a bathtub.

What I liked most about the whole licence was that, although *Lilibet II* was a third-of-a-tonne Thomas Crapper bath, she had been put down in the paper work as, and forever in the eyes of Whitehall would remain, a 'sports boat'. Who says civil servants don't have a sense of humour? A member of the legendary Whitehall 'Joined Up Drinking' club had obviously filled in that part of the licence. There was a covering note. In it the thoughtful men and women at the Ministry wrote that they expected the French Navy might wish to see the licence so suggested I keep it with me at all times, even and especially, at sea. To help me, they'd made sure that my licence was waterproof. This genial five-carat gold, laminated civil service foresight is what made Britain great.

The bath was finally ready to hit the water. Mark and I decided that since she was now a ship, we should follow the launch procedures for pagan vessels. I emailed a deluge of druids to find out how pagans launched them. The druids mainly seemed to be in America and were all very accommodating on the email from their wooden laptops. However, the sounds of mahogany keys tapping away across the Atlantic failed to produce one conclusive ceremony but a host of ideas for them. To bring some order to the druidic chaos, I decided to combine their suggestions with the recognised procedures for launching large ocean-going vessels in the late 1800s, namely: put the vessel on the slipway, find someone religious to say prayers, get someone in a big hat, smash champagne over the hull and watch the ship gently glide into the sea.

I invited the druids to come and do the religious bit. They said they were very keen to come so we picked a date they could all make. Brilliant: the religious part was sorted.

As a boy growing up in Derbyshire I lived near the lovable, idiosyncratic small market town of Wirksworth. My mind flitted back to running around the hills outside the town with various other boys and girls, one of whom was called Thomas Crapper. He had a brother called Alan. I'd not seen Tom since we were very small but I was always struck with how calmly he bore the stigma of such a comedy name. He was a few years

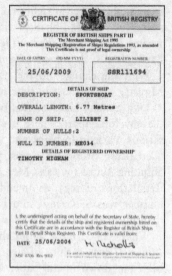

CERTIFICATE OF BRITISH REGISTRY

REGISTER OF BRITISH SHIPS PART III
The Merchant Shipping Act 1995
The Merchant Shipping (Registration of Ships) Regulations 1993, as amended
This Certificate is not proof of legal ownership

DATE OF EXPIRY (DD-MM-YYYY)   REGISTRATION NUMBER

25/06/2009   SSR111694

DETAILS OF SHIP
DESCRIPTION: SPORTSBOAT

OVERALL LENGTH: 6.77 Metres

NAME OF SHIP: LILIBET 2

NUMBER OF HULLS : 2

HULL ID NUMBER: ME034

DETAILS OF REGISTERED OWNERSHIP
TIMOTHY HIGHAM

I, the undersigned acting on behalf of the Secretary of State, hereby certify that the details of the ship and registered ownership listed on this Certificate are in accordance with the Register of British Ships Part III (Small Ships Register). This Certificate is valid from:

DATE 25/06/2004   M Nicholls

MSF 4706 Rev 9/02   For and on behalf of the Registrar General of Shipping & Seamen

older than me but had been one of my great friends when I was small. If I could find him now, perhaps he could launch the bath.

Unsurprisingly, Simon at Thomas Crapper & Co didn't have a number for him. Bother. I remembered he'd gone into the Army but I wasn't sure which regiment. Again, bother. I thought he was based somewhere near Bath (surely a sign) but couldn't remember the address. I phoned a few friends from that time whose numbers I still had but no one was in touch with him. My options for finding him were getting slim. After a few days of trying the Army, Bath and the 'old friends' route I was stumped.

Then my mother suggested, 'Why don't you just phone his mum?'

Why didn't I think of that? Another example of sack-smothered candle-like dimness. The mother grapevine never ceases to amaze me. Like mighty animals calling across the savannah, mothers never lose touch with each other.

'Hello, Mrs Crapper?'

Within minutes I was on the phone to Tom. He'd love to come and launch the bath. Could he bring his fiancée? Turns out I was right; Tom was in the Army and is now a Major.

After a few nights where, like a small child, I was too excited to sleep, the day of the great bath launch arrived. I jumped out of bed with the drive of a toddler. My beloved girlfriend opted to stay gently snoring in bed; there was no shifting her. At the time I thought it was because she was a heavy sleeper but on reflection it could be that for the previous few evenings she'd had to deal with something like a cross between Tigger and Zebedee and had wisely had a stiff whiskey or three before turning in. Alone, I raced to the river at Richmond. Mark was there, making sure everything was ready: the apprentices ran around seemingly as excited as me about getting *Lilibet II* to the slipway.

The first hitch of the day occurred when the druids phoned on their timber mobiles to say they would not be turning up. Some had woken up late, some had not realised you needed to turn up for flights and some seemed to still be out from the night before. This lack of druidical organisation and planning may explain why Christianity got the upper hand in the race of religions.

With sadness, I thought we might have to skip the religious part of the ceremony.

'Hey man, what happening?'

A lanky Rastafarian lumbered towards us, his dreadlocks shoved up into his multi-coloured knitted hat.

'We're launching a bath.'

'Cool man, cool, irie man, I stay. Irie.'

He lit a form of Rastafarian incense, took a long drag and stood swaying at the top of the slipway. He'd probably just left the group of druids still out from the night before. He leant on one of the guide ropes to steady himself in prayer, the bath juddered on the slipway and Mark trapped his hand under it. The Rastafarian prayed in the medium of gravity and fell over; Mark screamed in Anglo-Saxon and at that moment the unmistakable form of Major Crapper bounded out of the early morning mist.

'Hello Tim. Your plans seem to be going as well as ever.'

I don't remember ever being surrounded by excitable apprentices, upside-down Rastafarians or swearing Royal Bargemakers in any of my early vintage Derbyshire plans but Tom's memory of that time is probably better than mine.

'You haven't changed a bit.'

In fairness, neither had he. Wearing an eye patch, I could have picked him out of a line up at 500 yards. Together we extracted Mark from under the third-of-a-tonne bath and prevented him from evangelical behaviour towards the Rastafarian using the medium of his fist.

From beneath the dreadlocks, 'Peace man, irie . . .'

Mark reached for a boat hook; I got there first. I don't think Mark is cut out to be a Rastafarian. The Rasta, who as it turned out was called Kenroy, seemed placidly unaware of any problem. He got up and examined his incense stick. It had become bent into an L-shape in the fall. He quietly sucked on air to himself, re-lit it and continued to sway gently. The smell of his incense was soon joined by the smell of his steadily burning beard.

'What's the best thing about being in the Army, Tom?'

'Well there's lots but I suppose being able to pick up the phone and say, "Hello, Major Crapper" and no one can laugh . . .'

After a lifetime of people laughing at your name I could sense the triumph.

'. . . unless they're a General.'

I could sense that from triumph, occasionally, a merry General would command defeat. As we were talking I pulled out a bottle of champagne and gave it to Tom. Suddenly, Mark came to life. His years of launching boats on the river leapt forward unchecked.

'She can't be launched by a man, that's bad luck.'

Thank goodness Tom had the foresight to have a fiancée.

'Would you do me the honour?'

She sprayed champagne over the taps of the bath brilliantly. The bath started to roll down the slipway.

Extinguishing his beard, Kenroy began to sing: 'Iron, like a lion in Zion . . .'

He swayed, bobbed and moved to his own beat as the bath entered the water. We all shared the rest of the champagne in mugs before Mark suddenly and solemnly tossed one of the cups out into the river.

'It's for the gods of the river, to give you good luck when you get back up to the Thames. We always must feed the river god otherwise he gets angry.'

One apprentice turned to another. 'Ah, that's why we're always short of mugs . . .'

They'd obviously never searched for them in the Eiger of mugs in the sink. Major Tom and I spent the rest of the morning messing about in the bath. It was the biggest relief of the project to date. Despite all the problems, setbacks and near failures, the bath was finally having her morning in the sun.

Nothing could stop me now.

CHAPTER FIVE

HE MARCHED THEM DOWN AGAIN

'I like to give my inhibitions a bath now and then.'

Oliver Reed

The bath launch had left me feeling totally invigorated. I arrived home to find a roughly shaped package held together with lashings of parcel tape.

I was doing the bath thing to try to raise money for the charity Sport Relief[9]. The Sport Relief gimmick that year was to give each fundraiser one sock at the start of your event (with 'Doing it!' printed on it) and the second one (its pair) when you finished the event (which said 'Done it!'). Sir Ranulph Fiennes had suggested that a pair of good, thick socks was the key to most endurance challenges and this worried me. If I only wore the Sport Relief sock (given to me for starting) while doing my event, I'd have one bare foot and that surely couldn't be good. I'd written to Ranulph and asked him what he suggested.

---

[9]Sport Relief is Comic Relief's younger, fitter sister charity, they alternate years. I had completed the paper-boat challenge for Comic Relief the year before and the bath started as a Sport Relief project. This seemed appropriate as there was a serious sporting part to the rowing.

I slit open the parcel in front of me and a note fell out.

> Dear Tim,
> All the very best with your challenge. Wishing you success,
> good fundraising and not too many blisters!

It was signed simply 'Ran'. He'd added, with a modesty that made me smile, '(Fiennes)' – the brackets are his.

Enclosed with the note was a good, thick sock for my other foot: a typically brilliant, practical and thoughtful response. Other people found out about this and soon I had a small washing line of socks. Ran's good, thick sock nestled next to Dave Gorman's old football sock, a short sporty number from James Cracknell, a boxing sock from Ben Fogle, socks from Ingrid and Chris Tarrant, and flapping on the end, a shocking tie from Richard Whiteley.

Ingrid kindly also sent me a rubber duck, which I named Bernadette[10] and took with me on all my training exercises. I was shocked by how people had kindly thought of fun ways to show their support for what I was trying to achieve. I felt really encouraged before my big trip to the bathroom.

There were still some practical things to be sorted as well as getting the vital 'weather windows'. We still had to find a seaside base of operations. It was all well and good having the bath on the river at Richmond but if the weather improved we'd waste up to six hours, getting her out of the water, loading her on a trailer, driving to the sea and unloading. Duncan Taylor suggested using Folkestone; Dom wasn't sure as Dover seemed a better bet to him; I simply didn't have a clue. Duncan was our cross-Channel expert, so Dominic politely caved in and I agreed to use Folkestone.

Using Folkestone created one added complication. Unlike Dover, Folkestone's harbour is tidal, which means it only has water in it twice a day. The rest of the time it's not a harbour, more a malodorous mud flat with stranded ships balanced on it waiting for the water to come back and make them float again. With Folkestone, you could only get the bath and support boat out to sea in those two

---

[10]Bernard was the rubber duck I'd had since I was small and Ingrid and I thought it would be nice if he had a girlfriend.

daily windows of opportunity. With the way the tide works, one of those daily windows is normally at night. Dom realised this and had I known more about the sea, I'd have seen this could be potentially very important. However, I knew nothing about the sea, so was blissfully unaware. I'm not sure this was Duncan's best piece of advice. It was not the end of the world, but would make things difficult or impossible if we needed to get out to sea fast.

My staggering lack of knowledge and understanding of the sea had played its first crucial part. I knew about tides, I'd seen them on the river and understood how they worked in twice-daily cycles. I even knew about tides at sea. I'd lost my shoes to one once when I was six. But I didn't have the experience or knowledge to understand how the tides might impact on a boat, harbour or bathtub. I'd never seen or heard of the concept of a tidal harbour. For once I'm not going blame my dimness, just a total lack of experience. Many cross-Channel rowers start from Dover for precisely this reason.

The English Coastguard had suggested it and the Channel Crossing Association and French administration insisted on it: *Lilibet II* must undertake and pass a 10 km sea trial.

I'd been watching the weather. Trying to learn as much as possible from Dom about how it all worked. High-pressure ridges seemed to be important. I'm still not sure exactly how, but the normally sanguine Dom seemed to experience a lot of high-pressure ridges as he manfully tried to explain remedial weather to me. Weeks went by without any suitable weather windows. All this time I carried on training on the river at Richmond, getting more despondent as the days went by.

In my understanding of the weather, it seemed, if it was sunny in Richmond, it was bad on the coast. If it was raining in Richmond, it was bad on the coast. If it was windy in Richmond, it was bad on the coast and if it was bad weather in Richmond, it was bad on the coast . . . unless it was good weather at the coast. The main thing I learnt about weather was that to try to predict it is like trying to herd amoeba.

Finally mid-June arrived and with it a phone call from Duncan. 'I think we can give the sea trial a go tomorrow. Can you get the bath down here in time?'

That's the thing with weather. Like a master card player, it always seems to declare itself at the last minute.

I turned a romantic night in into a frowning feminine face and a peck on the cheek goodbye as I sped off to Richmond.

The scramble to load the bath was even more hectic and chaotic than it had been before the modifications. Trying to get a third-of-a-tonne piece of plumbing to behave long enough to trap her into coming onto the sledgehammer-modified boat trailer taught me how primary- and prep-school teachers must feel every day of their lives.

Just when I'd got one bit of the bath under control another bit tried to escape off downriver. As I dived to try and render that bit governable a third bit led the first bit off to another area of mischief. Thinking my best plan was to deal with the bit I'd got acquiescent first, then the two naughty bits later, I tried looping a foot round the fixed point of the trailer. This great plan led to a splosh and me, upside down, wearing the muddy riverbed as a hat. Finally, the apprentices and I tamed the unruly bath but it had taken the better part of an hour and a half. During this debacle, the tide had risen and the car, standing solid as a carthorse attached to the boat trailer, had water running in and out of her exhaust. The car didn't respond to the many polite requests I made to start her. So now we had the bath on the trailer, the trailer attached to the car and a car that wouldn't start due to water in her pipes.

Rallying a few people on the bank we tied a rope to the front of the car and the scratch tug-of-war team pulled the car, bath and trailer out of the river. Although time was short I thought it might be best to leave it for a moment to drain. I went back to checking ropes on the trailer and packing wadding round the bottom bits of the bath where it touched the ropes so it didn't crack. After a moment of deep prayer I turned the key in the ignition, the car started first time. Brilliant. Only an hour and a quarter later than the time I'd planned to leave.

Early the next morning I arrived on the outskirts of Folkestone. After a swearing bedecked tussle with a one-way system designed by Satan himself and several quizzical phone calls to Duncan, I missed the turning I should have taken for the fifth time. Finally I discovered the tiny arch through which I was meant to drive to find the slipway. Driving under this holy grail of traffic features I arrived at the harbour. I stepped out and felt the cool of the sea breeze on my face. In a Hollywood film this would be a romantic, inspiring scene, as they'd leave out the multitude of lost cars tooting in unredeemable damnation, stench of the harbour and swearing native pedestrians.

Before going to find Duncan I took a moment to look out at the sea. Finally, I could see it, the English Channel. Of course I'd seen it before, I'd even crossed it before, a couple of times by ferry, but this was my first sight from Folkestone of my nemesis.

'Something of a false alarm I'm afraid.'

'What?'

'I've just been talking to some mates out at sea and there's a howler coming in, we're not going to get the sea trial in before it hits.'

Brilliant: a totally wasted day. Trying to be buoyant and not take my unbelievable feelings of frustration out on him, I had a drink with Duncan. Predictably, we chatted about the unpredictability of the sea. Then I attempted to turn the car and boat trailer round and set out back to Richmond. I made such a mess of it that I managed to totally block up Folkestone Harbour. Luckily, Duncan hadn't left.

'Do you want me to have a go for you? It's a bit awkward.'

After un-sticking the trailer from the various shops and cars of Folkestone I set off for Richmond. Arriving late, Mark, the apprentices and I unloaded the trailer and floated the errant bath back on the river. As we were walking back to the boathouse my phone flashed.

'I think we can give the sea trial a go tomorrow. Can you get the bath down here in time?'

Mark growled. I sighed, 'Leave it to me . . .'

For the second time in 24 hours the car got flooded and, diving hopelessly at a line, I had another fitting with the muddy riverbed hatter. As dusk fell on Richmond, we left the bath half tied to the boat trailer and, wiping mud from my eyes, Mark and I went up the cobbled street for a pint in the Waterman's Arms.

'Same again tomorrow?'

'I hope not.'

Of course Mark was right. After manhandling the bath into place, speeding off down to Folkestone, feeling the sea breeze on my cheeks and hearing the melodic sounds of local swearing in my ears, a rather sheepish Duncan said, 'Nope, it's not going to happen again today, you see those little white peaks on top of the waves?'

'Yes.'

'We call those galloping white horses, it means there's a storm coming.'

Again I arrived back at Richmond totally exhausted. I knew I must look tired as Mark said, 'Don't worry about the bath, me and the lads'll stick her back in the water, you go off home to bed.'

Very sound advice.

I was woken early the next morning by my phone. 'Tim, it's Duncan, this time I really think we've got a chance. Can you get the bath down here in time?'

It's true; fishermen really do get up unbearably early in the morning. I dredged myself out of bed and reached for my trousers and rowing lycra. I wasn't even sure Mark would be at the boat-yard when I got there, that's how early it was, but I thought if I could just find a couple of early-morning fitness enthusiasts on the river I could load the bath and leave a note for Mark.

I arrived to find Mark opening up the doors of the boatyard under the arches. I'd never been there early enough to see this before.

'I've got a weather window for the trial today. I'm so sorry, can we get the bath out of the water . . . I know it's a pain but I've really got to get this done . . .' Not sure why I was breathless, but I was.

'That's lucky.'

'What?'

'I thought this might happen.' Mark flashed the cheery and slightly mischievous smile I'd come to enjoy from him. Behind him was the bath, still loaded on the trailer from the night before. I was exhausted already that day but so relieved to realise that I didn't have to go through the great irritant of having to load her again. I actually remember smiling, something I hadn't done for the last few days.

We hitched the trailer to the un-waterlogged car and I sped off to Folkestone. I'd like to write, 'It was a sunny day', but it wasn't, it was overcast, with not much wind in the air and the sea state I was told was two. I didn't know what this meant but guessed it meant two out of ten, ten being the worst possible sea state and one being the best.

I miraculously found the Elysian arch after only one miss but then failed to reverse the boat trailer down the slipway. I got out of the car and Duncan kindly had a go at it. The slipway at Folkestone is really tricky (that's a polite way of putting it). It's not designed for boat trailers. It's a makeshift slipway that probably had its roots in launching small craft that could be carried by hand.

There is a much better inner slipway but that doesn't get the water till very high tide and to reverse down that one you have to block the one-way system. Blocking the one-way system in Folkestone is not recommended unless you're a prizefighter or a lemming suffering from vertigo and needing an alternative to jumping.

My only choice was the narrow, outer slipway. Duncan had the knack. He politely asked the early-morning drinkers at the pub next door to the slipway to stand up from their tables. He then cleared their tables away, moving them a safe distance down the street. I would never have thought of asking them to move, and if I had thought of it, I would have got an insurance quote first. They seemed quite used to it, like it was the normal way of launching boats. They were so drunk at that time in the morning that even the bath seemed normal to their addled eyes. Duncan then talked to the fishermen at the café opposite before moving the piles of what looked like lobster pots that were stacked up on the slipway. He was good at this. He'd done it before. I looked on with the impressed awe that Luke Skywalker levelled at Obi Wan Kenobi.

Then he got back in the car, reversed the boat trailer down the slipway and into the carefully stacked pile of lobster pots, while hitting a befuddled pub patron gently with the front of the car. A ranting exchange later, he pulled the car back up to the top of the ramp, lined it up and reversed again. This time, he made it perfectly, conquering the world's most difficult boat trailer reverse.

We unloaded the bath onto the water and tied her off to the slipway. This was the first time the bath had sat in the sea. I drove the car and trailer back up the ramp, parked and paid the extortion money to the meter. We re-situated the tables and straightened out the lobster pots before I bought a drink for the couple of inconvenienced pub patrons. Using her slipway instantly explained why it's rare to meet a serious mariner who has ever set sail from Folkestone.

Duncan started up his boat. It was a very old-fashioned craft and has the only clinker-built hull still left in Folkestone Harbour. He was justifiably proud of this, and with the amount of money he spent keeping this treasure above the waterline, he had a right to be. I jumped down into the bath and got everything ready. I remembered I'd forgotten the oars. In all the excitement of putting the bath in the water, I'd forgotten the oars. This was a very significant oversight. True to my own form I'd have left them in Richmond;

today I'd only left them strapped to the car at the top of the ramp. This was a sign; today would go well. As Duncan brought his boat round I ran up the ramp, collected the oars, checked I'd paid the meter and ran back to the bath.

Duncan shouted over, 'Let's get this started!'

The sea trial was vital. The bath and I had to complete 10 km out at sea. This is just under 6.5 land miles or just over 8.5 sea miles. To satisfy the French Navy, I had to complete it in kilometres, miles would not count. Normally, they make cross-Channel rowers do this to check they are actually fit enough to row the distance. In my case it had been made very clear to me that it was not just to see if I could make the distance but to check how this most unorthodox of unorthodox crafts would cope at sea. If the bath failed, Duncan would not risk the Channel Crossing Association in a battle with the French and would withdraw his support boat. Even as a Registered British Shipping Vessel with no engine, legally, I needed a support boat to cross the Channel. Without it I was stuck. Also the English Coastguard had made it very clear that without the knowledge, experience and support of the Channel Crossing Association they too would take a very dim view of my crossing. Essentially, for the legal reasons I've paraphrased above, without passing this sea trial, the bath project was off. The stakes were high.

Duncan increased the throttle on his engine, I gripped hard on the oars and we were off.

My first time rowing out at sea was a totally pivotal moment in the plan. It was every bit as important as the first time I managed to row without capsizing – an epoch. And just like the first time I managed to row without capsizing – an epoch I'd left until very late in this plan. What if I couldn't do it?

As I struck off towards the harbour arm at Folkestone, my action was nervous, jerky and very inefficient. All my senses worked way too hard, I overreached at the catch, went up the slide too fast, or too slow, and all in all felt very self-conscious. The sea didn't help. It kept moving down when I wanted it to stay flat and up when I thought it would stay down.

I've only experienced the gut-wrenching awed and confused feelings I felt on my first day rowing at sea once before. That time, I was sitting on a bench under the clearest starlit sky. It was a cold night; snow shone on the ground and reflected off the frozen lake. The girl sitting next to me bathed me in her dark effervescent eyes and stuck her tongue into my mouth. The agonising first few seconds of that moment, as I tried to work out the rules of that new game and at the same time take in and deal with those startling, wonderful feelings were exactly the same as my emotions as I swerved hopelessly around the water at Folkestone and proficiently crashed into the harbour arm. Rowing now, as kissing then, I was engulfed with sentiments that normally only enter the mind of a man newly departed an aeroplane one parachute short of a successful landing.

You'd think that rowing at sea would be like rowing on a river, but it's not. The sea consistently moves in three dimensions. It's like chasing a frog around a waterbed. When you're rowing on the river or a lake, it's a relatively flat surface. There might be a bit of current on the river or some chop on the lake but basically it's flat. You come up and down the sliding seat, pop your oars in at the top of the stroke and pull back, rolling the seat backward, horizontally to power yourself forward. Rowing is the only high-speed sport where you strain every sinew to power forwards as fast as you can, not looking where you're going and facing backwards. The entire power movement in rowing is horizontal. At sea, there's no horizontal. It shifts constantly. This makes it impossible to get any kind of decent strokes together: the enforced rhythmlessness of a hippo playing maracas overtakes you.

The sea allowed me strokes when it wanted me to take strokes. It moved itself when it didn't want me to take strokes. It somehow contrived to put air where the water used to be midway through strokes and generally conspired to make me catch crabs with one or both oars almost every stroke. I saw Duncan's face. He looked on from the support boat, powerless to assist me, with deep concern etched into every furrow. He didn't say a word but it was obvious he was thinking: He's not going to make it across the harbour let alone the Channel.

With this added pressure and the sea playing with me, things were bad. I should have hated the sea with every stroke I took. Every bit of my being should have wanted to get off the water and away from this embarrassment. The thing was, I loved it. Like a battered spouse, the more the sea threw at me, the more I loved her for it. I wanted to learn. Every time the sea moved the water away from me I adjusted the oar to meet the challenge and very slowly began to feel like I was riding the sea. The sea was a particularly frisky horse with ginger up its nethers, but it was one that I was learning how to tame. By constant concentration and watching every second where the water was going on both sides and repeatedly altering my hand heights to match the sea's peaks and troughs I was getting control. Even when the water rose on one side and my hand lowered to counter that, I still had the upper hand. I even began to glimpse rhythms in the sea's contrariness. Somewhere in the Nile Delta a hippo led a conga line to the strains of 'La Cucaracha'.

Every moment I spent out at sea was a joy. I was there: a speck in an ocean, constantly battling to stay in control and every second I managed it was a triumph. It was wonderful out there surrounded by beauty. Somehow, now I'd got my bearings I felt part of it. Duncan looked relieved.

'You're getting the hang of it now,' he shouted through the wind.

Now I knew he thought I could do it. I had to row 5 km out and 5 km back to complete the ten. I was not very clear on what a kilometre was, but I knew it was less than a mile and thought we must be about 5 km out by now. We'd been out there for a while when the wind picked up.

'That's good. Let's turn her round and head back.'

Great. Going back never seems as far as going somewhere. I turned the bath round and made for Folkestone. This gave me a stunning view. Now there was no Folkestone to see. All I could see in front of me as I rowed to Folkestone, facing away from it, was the sea. It stretched out before me until it blurred with the mist and became the sky. All that faced me was cold blue of different shades with the odd plume of white: the beauty was breathtaking. There's no past or future at sea. That day, there was just me and the sea locked in the present with each other for company.

Concentrating hard, I made it back to Folkestone, tied off the bath, got the car and messed up reversing it down the ramp. Duncan tied off and arrived at my side. We moved the now-horizontal patrons of the bar and their tables, shifted the lobster pots again and Duncan reversed down the slipway. With obscene difficulty, the two of us managed to float the bath onto the trailer. The tide helped as little as possible, as she wanted to get out of Folkestone as much as I did. We managed it. I'd never manoeuvred the bath onto the trailer with only one other person before. This was quite an achievement. I made a mental note of what we'd done. Finally, we tied her down and I drove the car up the ramp.

At the top I parked the car near Holy Grail Arch and the loading the bath symphony for two men, a trailer, car and tub concluded to the slurred clapping of the patrons of the pub, one of whom even shouted, 'Encore.' Actually, on reflection, he might have shouted 'wanker': difficult to tell with the slurring. I broke into a jog back to Duncan as a bottle whistled past my ear.

'I thought we were going to have to call the whole thing off at the start but you really got the hang of it. Well done.'

'Thank you.'

My eyes shone with the awed enthusiasm of a child given its first helium-filled balloon. I rolled the words mellifluously round my mouth before I let them out.

'My first 10 km at sea . . .'

'We actually only managed 6 km.'

'What!'

Somewhere a helium-filled balloon burst.

'Now, there's a few things we need to say about the bath . . .'

This sounded less than ideal.

'. . . She can't turn well enough; if we get stuck in an emergency I can't tow her; the fastenings holding the ropes are fine on the river but . . .'

'Let me get a pen and paper.'

I was trying to give myself a chance to think, to find something positive.

'So there's the turning, towing and fastenings issues . . . anything else?'

'I'm not sure that the prow will stand up under duress at sea; she's not stable enough . . .'

The list went on and on to depressing infinity and beyond, finally finishing with, 'Look, Tim, why don't we just get you a normal boat, and you row the Channel in that? You've clearly got a good chance with the skill you showed today. But in that thing, you've not got a hope. Tim, this is a failed safety test, and even if you hadn't failed it – rowing the Channel in that is just not possible.'

Personally, I'd been passed as fit on the safety test but the bath had totally failed. I think Duncan wanted me to know just how hard it would be to row the thing out at sea, and it was, but now I'd had a taste of it, I wanted more. I met his eyes firmly with mine, they locked on to each other; there was a pause while I thought of what to say.

'It may not be possible to row it in the bath, but all the same, I'm going to try. Let me get a pen and we can write these safety failings down and sort them out.'

I got the bath back up to Richmond and Mark was woeful. He looked through my list, 'How can they fail her? Why do they want that? This seems like a really bad plan to me . . .'

Now we began even more tweaking to the bath to get it to stand a chance of passing the next safety test. Many of the things we'd been forced to change to get the shipping licence were the cause of the problems we now faced but we just had to adapt our plans to include them and yet still modify the bath for safety.

We added stronger fixings for the rope work. We strengthened the prow by adding more struts and braces to the inside of them. This made the whole thing even heavier but again it seemed I was being left with little choice. We made massive, strong lines to enable us to tow the bath better and created a rudder system to help with the steering.

Mark looked up, 'Monkey's fists.'

'What?'

'She needs monkey's fists.'

He left me bemused and headed into the boathouse. I watched with amazement as Mark proceeded to twist and turn the rope around the front of the prows. He created two massive intricate balls of rope.

'They look like the cufflinks you get in posh shirt shops.'

'Nope, those are Turk's Head knots, these are Monkey's Fists.'

It takes a black belt in knot tying to tell the difference but apparently it would make towing the bath behind another boat safer. We worked hard for days and days on the modifications. All this time the sun shone down and glorious weather reigned supreme as the bath sat in bits on the riverbank.

Late one night, following a golden Oriental sunset, Mark and I finished the bath. Finally the modifications were completed. With this amazing weather, getting a new date for the sea trial quickly was going to be easy.

We looked down in the increasing dark at the bath on the bank: the two buoyancy aids resting on the trestles; the black-and-white tiles above that with the various bits of rope work coiled neatly. Just below a Monkey's Fist on one of the buoyancy aids Mark had proudly painted *Lilibet II*. Sitting in the middle of the tiled floor, the copper of the Victorian slipper bath glimmered in the lingering light. Like the back of a racing leopard, the rim curved from the low end with the taps, up to a beautiful arch at the head end. Behind that in the slight breeze, the Red Ensign flag tried to puff itself away from the small mast. Rising up from all of this, and glinting in the light from the newly turned on street lamp, was the showerhead. Like two gleeful five year olds Mark and I looked at each other.

'Get a bucket of water and let's test the plumbing.'

We put a bucket beneath the floor where we had installed a small pump to suck water up from the river and into the showerhead plumbing system. We looked at each other and Mark flicked the switch to turn the pump on.

'It works!'

A few short showers and much laughter later, both wet, we went up the hill to the Waterman's Arms.

Dominic had always maintained the success of the whole plan hinged on good weather. The bath was completed just in time for the worst July weather on record since World War II. Storms lashed the South Coast and more than 13,000 homes lost electrical power. Churchill achieved his aim with weather like that from a bath, but his was fixed to the floor of Number Ten Downing Street. The storms continued. Lashing the country as a whole. Even homes as far away as Wales lost power. The gods conspired against me. Perhaps I shouldn't have had a Rastafarian at the launch but opted for the more traditional Church of England cleric.

After weeks of weather so bad I couldn't even train on the river, I got a phone call from Duncan Taylor.

'I think there's a real chance we can give the second sea trial a go tomorrow. Can you get the bath down here in time?'

I shuddered. I'd heard this before. Mark, his apprentices and I loaded the bath in the pouring rain onto the bath trailer. I sped down to Folkestone as rain bounced off the windscreen in drops the size and weight of hailstones.

I arrived in Folkestone and started with a chat from Duncan. 'I'm really sorry Tim, I know how you feel about this but if the bath doesn't pass this one, that's it. We have to look at you rowing in a normal boat or not at all.'

We began a movement of the unloading the bath symphony with an especially enlarged grunting, sweating and swearing section. The only person whose spirits were lower than mine was the pub patron whose drink I spilt. I re-parked the car, paid the hush money, ran back down the slipway and tripped over a lobster pot. I picked myself up long enough to jump on to the bath, slip and fall in the water. On the plus side, the sheet rain had stopped and just as Duncan predicted, the sun poked round the wisp of a dark cloud. The dark cloud and the sun had a momentary battle of wits before the cloud retreated and the rain was no more. I pulled myself out of the mephitic water, soaking wet. Although the rain had stopped, the net result was the same. I was wet.

'Stop messing about Tim, we're up against it, let's get out there.'

On the last sea trial I had triumphantly conquered the sea. Now I was a natural. It came as a bit of shock to find that I was still as awkward and terrible at rowing on the sea as I had been the last time. Sailors talk about 'getting their sea legs'. I'd never understood what it meant but I certainly didn't have mine. The bath and I did a brilliant impersonation of a rabid drunk trying to walk the line as we zigzagged out of Folkestone. Various fishermen looked on and laughed. I couldn't tell if they were laughing because I was rowing a bath or because I was terrible at rowing a bath. I consoled myself that this confusion was a similar problem to that which dogged Spike Milligan and swerved violently into the harbour arm. Looking to see if Duncan noticed, at least now I knew what they were laughing at.

The one positive thing I found was that it took me less time to get used to rowing at sea this time. Last time I only got it after about an hour or even an hour and a half. This time, after a devastating first half-hour, I'd got it under control.

After five nerve-racking kilometres Duncan shouted, 'Right, that's it, let's go in and have a chat!'

What did he mean? Had it passed or hadn't it? Could I finish this project or not? The words seemed to hang in the air. He gave them no qualifying statement.

I turned and made for the harbour arm. I tied up the bath, moved patrons, their tables, spilt more drinks, got the car, fought the tide to load the bath, nearly flooded the car (again), spilt lobster pots, reset tables, settled patrons and bought more replacement drinks with my heart tied in knots. Had the bath passed? Still no word from Duncan: he scribbled furiously on his sheet of paper and said nothing. I finished paying for the replacement spilt drinks at the pub. It was amazing how custom appeared to have picked up in that place. Whereas the first time I bought replacement drinks, there were only three drunks, now there were between 15 and 20. Somewhere in the dark recesses of my mind, a penny rolled a tiny bit closer to the cliff.

Duncan still said nothing.

'Well?' My nervousness was horrible.

'She's passed. Not with flying colours but she's passed. Well done. I feel I've got to say she's still not going to make it across the Channel and I think you're mad for trying but if you want to try – I'll back you.'

I could have hugged him. On reflection I wish I had. *Lilibet II* had passed her second sea trial. She's a third-of-a-tonne, un-aqua-dynamic piece of ablution equipment. She was never going to pass with flying colours but a pass was a pass and that was all I needed.

'Shall we check the weather forecasts for tomorrow?'

We got into the cabin of his boat and checked the weather. I so wanted it to be good. I finally had a bath that had passed, I was fit, I was even in Folkestone and ready to go; all I needed now was a weather window. Yes, it was British summer time and the weather had been stoically awful to celebrate but surely I was owed just one good day of weather. Just one chance to try to finish this and get across the Channel.

I didn't understand a word of the weather forecast. Dom had spent days trying to teach me whether a Dogger was worse than a German Bight or explain why a Viking never met FitzRoy at Trafalgar without the slightest success. Yet, thanks to Dom I could now make the right approving noises, I just thought of sampling jam and purred. Duncan looked up from writing things down in a book.

'We've got a weather window tomorrow. If you want to try it, let's go then. I'll complete the final checks on my boat.'

'I'll give you a hand if you like before I go and complete the final checks on my bath.'

'Polish the taps you mean?'

'Check the plug is in!'

There was a jovial sense in the air as we started the final checks on Duncan's boat. Finally, after months of planning, setbacks and disasters I was just one night-time away from attempting the plan I'd tried so hard to create.

I phoned Kenny, Simon, Comic Relief, Dom, Douglas, the Admiral, Mark, my girlfriend, family and the rest of the team to let them know we were on final standby to attempt to go with the weather window the next day. Everyone was as excited as me about it. Dom prepared to plot the course. Kenny prepared a journalist and photographer to come down. The others raised their glasses and sat back in their chairs. The bath Channel plan was on.

As I was doing this, Duncan made calls, too. He phoned the various people he knew he must: the Coastguard, Harbourmaster, French Navy and the others at the Channel Crossing Association to let them know about it. When we'd both hung up from our respective calls we popped the hatch and started work on the final checks to his boat's engine. There was a huge sense of excitement and the kind of childish enthusiasm that strangely makes you feel slightly nervous. I knew Duncan felt it too as he slipped and dropped his screwdriver into the running engine. It made a noise like a cow caught in a fence, shuddered and stopped.

'Is that bad?' I'm not an engineer.

'It's going to mean a complete new engine.'

'Before tomorrow?'

'No. Tomorrow is off.'

Finally the bath had passed her safety tests, I'd got a perfect and near-impossible-to-find weather window, I'd beaten every obstacle that had been thrown at me including circumnavigating the labyrinthine web of French bureaucracy: and one slip of the fingers had scuppered my support boat. I could not attempt the Channel without one.

The entire venture was up in the air again.

Chapter Six

GLOWERING LIKE THE MOON

*'The English Channel is a ditch and will be crossed
as soon as someone has the courage to attempt it.'*

Napoleon Bonaparte

What I know about engines wouldn't fill the back of a stamp, but even I knew this was disastrous. Duncan reached for his mobile.

'Hi. My engine won't start . . .' He wouldn't admit the mishap to his fisherman mates. 'Are you and your boat free tomorrow?'

There was an agonising pause. Without a support boat I couldn't take advantage of the good weather we'd got after two long months.

Duncan put his hand over the phone. 'He's just checking his diary, Tim . . .' The diary checking took a disturbingly long time. How many giddy social engagements could one fisherman have? Duncan broke into my thoughts. 'He says he's got a bunch of bankers to take fishing.'

'Shouldn't that be a wunch of . . . ?'

Duncan looked blank and returned to his phone. 'Can you get out of it?'

Another pause. Duncan turned to me. 'He says how much, Tim?'

I had my new support-boat skipper.

Duncan Taylor had seen me through my troubles with the French government, helped rejig the bath's design and been the one skipper I'd found who, although not believing the project entirely feasible, was willing to give it backing. He seemed genuinely sad about not coming with me.

The following morning I woke far too early. Obsessed with getting to the quayside in plenty of time I'd arrived with hours to spare. I paced up and down running through final checks. Bananas? Check. Toothbrush? Check. Why had I packed a toothbrush? I was interrupted by a shout and glanced up to see a burly stereotype of how a fisherman should look lumbering towards me.

'I'm Andy. It really is a bath!'

A plate-sized hand was thrown out. Andy's handshake felt like a bear hugging an ant. He retracted his paw. My new support-boat skipper was a man boasting language so rare and raw it would make the Chairman of the Selection Committee for Undiscovered Words at the Oxford English Dictionary dive for his notepad. I'd no idea about his seamanship but took confidence from his salty demeanour. Just from the grease on his overalls I was sure this man knew the Channel brilliantly and would help me get across.

'I'll fetch my boat.'

Andy crashed away and another new member of the team arrived. Gavin Trevan is a friend from home. He'd finished his exams and was in that one Elysian summer we get of having nothing to do. He'd decided he'd come along on the support boat. Kenny had sent a reporter and photographer who now fetched up as well. The reporter pulled out his pad and pen.

'Can I have a interview before you set off? This new record you're about to set. Has it ever been set before?'

I suppressed a smile, mumbled, 'Err . . . no,' and carried on mixing the vile energy drink I'd invented using cranberry juice, sugar, salt and various other bits and bobs.

The plan was that I'd be towed across to France from Folkestone as this was the harbour in which Duncan had suggested I base the bath. Arriving there, the bath would be detached from the support boat and I'd row it back to Dover as this was a fair few miles further north-east up the coast from Folkestone and would mean I was closer to London. This would help when setting off on the round Kent leg of the journey. It had been cleared with the French authorities, the English

Coastguard and Channel Crossing Association. Everyone was happy.

My phone rang. It was the French Navy, I assumed calling to wish me *bon chance*. The officer on the line informed me that, on that specific day, it was now totally illegal to row anything from the French coast to England. It sounds fantastic and implausible – I'm still questioning it – but it was exactly what happened. This is the crucial difference between having a Coastguard who act inside civil law (England) and having the Navy to look after the coast (France). Their Navy can immediately invoke emergency powers and they'd done just that. It didn't matter if *Lilibet II* was a bath or Registered British Shipping Vessel; the new powers counteracted both. I coolly observed it was a remarkable coincidence that these powers had come into play today. He made no reply. I tried to reason with him, making everything much worse. Due to an act of bureaucratic malice I couldn't understand, my entire plan appeared to be in ruins.

'But Monsieur, how can it be illegal to row from France to Dover when it is not illegal to row from Dover to France?'

'By saying "not illegal" do you mean legal?' This from a man who just six months before had professed not to speak or understand a word of English.

'Exactly, Monsieur . . .'

'*Alors*, Tim. It does not seem *logique*,' he confessed. 'I will call you back.'

We all waited for *logique* to triumph.

My phone rang again.

'You are right. It is *illogique* to say you can't row from France to Dover but you can row from Dover to France. So now it's illegal in France to attempt to row from Dover to France. *Je suis desolé*.'

A slim possibility flashed through my mind.

'So it's not illegal to row from *Folkestone* to France?'

'*Non*.'

'Then I'll do that.'

Hammered by black-belt extreme logic the French Navy caved in. Realising the position they'd taken was at best untenable, when I'd offered them Folkestone they'd taken it. This was the opposite way across the Channel to the one I'd planned but I'd still have rowed it. Due to protracted negotiations with the French I was now hours late starting out but if the weather held it wouldn't matter.

My brass Victorian showerhead gleamed as I rowed out from

Folkestone Harbour in the early morning light. Plumbed in, I could take showers on the briny. I looked up at it fondly only to see it snap off on the low swing bridge of the inner harbour. Damn. I dived into the water and passed it back to Andy for storage. I would have to do without the en suite.

Rowing hard, I inched my way beyond Folkestone's harbour wall. The buildings on the shore became smaller and less distinct. I was at sea, a lone engine of industry amid a mass of calm. It was a beautiful experience. As I looked round me that sunny morning I'd never felt happier. All the troubles and crises that had plagued me evaporated as I pulled towards my goal. Finally, I understood the call of the sea. I looked over at my support crew, a body of men handpicked for their intimate knowledge of the Channel and brilliance at sea. One of them leant over the side of the boat, waved cheerily and vomited violently into the calm blue. The reporter joined him. Andy waved sheepishly.

Two-fifths of my crack team were blowing chunks into the ocean. I tutted to Bernard my rubber duck. He gave me his usual glazed look back, but I thought I saw my disappointment with the support crew reflected in the shiny, enamelled paint finish of his googley eyes.

I checked my watch. After several hours of rowing it was still ten to seven in the morning. It had failed due to the salt water. Having a concept of time was vital to rowing the Channel. All the complex navigation theorems (including the key Speed versus Time equations that Dominic and I had slaved over) were now going to be impossible. But one of the support crew came to my rescue. I'd begun to notice that he was vomiting regularly and each time he threw up I shouted for the time. He was chundering roughly every half-hour. As a unit of measuring time at sea I'm not sure the Royal Navy would have been thrilled, but it was good enough for me.

The English Channel is the busiest shipping lane in the world. More ships and tankers plough their furrows up and down this stretch of water than anywhere else. To avoid crashes, and make life easier for the French and English authorities, it's divided into two lanes – a bit like a massive dual carriageway with a central reservation in the middle marked by large red and white buoys. I wished I'd known just how busy it was and cursed myself as I pulled into the first lane.

You can read statistics about the sheer enormity of tankers but it doesn't necessarily mean anything. Seeing these leviathans for the first time is something else. They are absolutely enormous – up to a mile long. Many have stopping distances of 20 miles, so on land if you put the brake on at Nelson's Column you'd come to rest in Hatfield. Practically speaking, it means that by the time they've got close enough to see you and applied the brakes, they have passed through where you were and someone from the shipping line is phoning the undertaker. Some tankers have turning circles of 25 miles, which means if they want to do a U-turn in the English Channel they can't. I was crossing the world's busiest shipping lanes at right angles to the traffic flow in a piece of copper plumbing. It was like playing 'chicken' on the M1 riding a snail.

I mention this because around midday my worst nightmare happened. A tiny blue dot on the horizon turned out to be a mile-long behemoth bearing down on me really fast. Would the tanker follow theoretical naval law and give me right of way? Or would it smash me to smithereens? Trapped in my comic conceit, was I about to die chasing a punchline? Maniacally I increased my stroke rate; effectively I was a slightly arthritic worm trying to outrun a cheetah.

My mind, however, raced much faster: where had I put it? My hands shook slightly with the adrenaline. I opened the washstand and rifled through it. Nestling in the bottom, next to the shampoo was my early warning device. All captains must have one. Mine was red and shaped like a large party hooter. This was bound to save me. Sucking in air, I paused before blowing it as hard as I could.

No effect at all. I blew it again: zero impression. There was nothing I could do to get out of the way. I prepared for death. All was lost.

With one last throw of the dice, the following frantic conversation took place over the radio: 'I'm in a *bath*! Back down! BACK DOWN!! Over?'

Total silence.

A throaty, Dutch-sounding voice eventually came back: 'Are you alone?'

What was he offering? To soap my back?

To my amazement, and for the first time in maritime history, a tanker backed down for a piece of plumbing on the high seas, creating the 'FitzHigham Precedent'.

With huge relief I noted the massive bow waves – previously equal on both sides – suddenly became unequal. That meant she was turning to avoid me. The tanker passed within half a nautical mile. When dealing with something that size at sea, this had been a very close shave. Baths are cunningly designed to keep water in and the wash from the hull engulfed me. Soaking wet and bailing like a dervish, I couldn't find it within me to complain. I'd narrowly avoided being killed and cursed myself again for not installing a toilet on the bath. Smell the fear? I was sitting in it.

The water was now less choppy and my strokes easier. Soon it was like rowing on a lake again. I'd made it to the 'central reservation' dividing the shipping lanes. The support crew threw up in celebration. I shouted across for the time, they called back between chunders. I'd made it halfway across the Channel in about the same time as it had taken the female record holder to complete the crossing. Her boat had weighed the equivalent of three bags of sugar, my bath weighed a third of a tonne. This was going well. I was ahead of the schedule Dom and I had worked out. As I punched the air in triumph, my watch flew off my wrist and sank. In the depths of the Channel there's a small area where it's always ten to seven.

I'd now lost even the semblance of time. I looked down at my state-of-the-art compass. The shop told me it had glow-in-the-dark directions and even worked upside down. I now discovered that the one thing this expensive piece could not do was find magnetic north. I gazed at the uselessly spinning needle. It could be that the copper was confusing it. Or simply that it was total rubbish. I grudgingly accepted that my compass had also failed. I now had no method of telling direction or time. I had a vomit-festooned support crew. I'd narrowly avoided being scuttled by a tanker. My rubber duck was nervous and my showerhead had snapped off. These things were less than ideal; but, very much on the plus side, I could now see France. I hadn't noticed her at first. She slowly rose up behind me with all the cunning subtlety of a Parisian whore. I looked over my shoulder. There it was: the clear, defiant, beautiful Gallic coastline was beckoning me in. Nothing could come between us now.

The storm started slowly at first. Spots of rain, turning to drizzle, the sun haring off behind clouds, wind getting worse. Bernard turned to me and said, 'I'm just going out and may be some time.'

I steadied him and carried on pulling through the increasingly deteriorating weather.

'Will you give up?' yelled the reporter through the spray.

'Giving in is not an option,' I yelled back.

He made to write it down, slipped and vomited.

Things were becoming quite tough. I'd now been rowing for over
six hours and my body was in crisis. My hands had lost a lot of
skin and my nethers were deplorable. The least said about my
buttocks the better. I was very tired. In good weather I was sure I
could have driven myself on, forcing my battered frame up and
down the sliding seat, but my physical problems got worse with
the storm and my spirits were getting low. Andy screamed over the
spume that he thought it was time to call off the attempt. I repeated
my mantra about never giving in, pulling through what had now
become a brisk Force 4 and would soon leap to a full-scale Force 6.

The indispensable *Reed's Nautical Almanac* describes the various
sea states. At the time, I had read no explanations of sea states
above a Force 3 or 4, as those were the very worst I'd been told
to expect. A Force 3 suggests winds of 7–10 knots (defined as a
'gentle breeze') with wave heights of 0.4 metres. Force 4 suggests
winds of 11–16 knots (defined as a 'moderate breeze') and wave
heights of one metre. Even a one-metre wave is challenging in an
ocean-going bath. What I now found myself in was a Force 6
described as winds of 22–27 knots with wave heights of up to three
metres. But definitions in a book are useless when confronting
nature face to face. The wind now pivoted to go not with the tide
but against it, driving the sea into an army of vicious white-topped
waves. In froth-tipped choppy short waves like that, getting any
kind of oar purchase is impossible. I was seeing Duncan's galloping
white horses up close. The storm was deploying all its troops and
had just unleashed the cavalry.

Mist surrounded the bath and now I lost sight of my support
crew. The waves responded by getting much bigger and crashing
down on the bath. I bailed frantically. In the now dense fog, my
perception sharpened. Things were not going according to plan.
One particular wave was so violent it ripped the copper off the roll
top exposing a nasty, serrated edge.

A massive wave threatened to tip me over. As the bath lurched
to my left, I dived to the right to keep it stable. The bath paused,

before slamming back down onto an even keel. My relief was short lived. The moisture on my shoulder was warmer than the water. I looked down. I'd cut my shoulder quite badly on the serrated edge. Blood seeped through the lycra sweater. When you're drenched with water blood doesn't stay long on your skin, but it was coming out thick and fast. The arm began not to respond properly. This could have been the shock or the cold chill of the wind but I began to suspect it was something to do with the cut. Obsessed, I carried on pulling with my remaining good arm towards where I had last seen the French coast.

There was a horrible clunk below, a sound like a muffled gunshot, and a rip. The bath juddered in the water. All I knew at the time was that it felt like we were getting lower on my left-hand side. Something – a log? – had hit the bottom and ripped a hole in one of the two pontoons designed to keep the bathroom floor afloat. This was serious. I'd seen Errol Flynn movies as a boy. What Flynn did in these situations was light a cigarette and toss things overboard. With my good arm I hurled the tool kit, First Aid box and the crappy tracking system overboard. The bath was now leaning well down to the left. I grabbed an oar with my right hand and continued rowing for France. I'll be fine, I thought. I can make this. I'm British. When I look back on this it was insane.

The rudder cables became useless and I lost my ability to steer. I was helpless amid the swirling maritime mass of industry. The sea had turned malevolently dark. What had once seemed friendly was now a violent monster trying to kill me. Three-metre-high waves crashed down on top of me.

I wasn't terrified or even scared. I didn't have the luxury of time. To be scared you have to realise that you're in danger and dwell on how things might end. That takes time. I spent every second I was out there making constant adjustments to my seating position. When not doing that, I'd be concentrating on how my hand would drive the oar through the water. Most of all I'd focus on what I could do to try and keep the bath up in the water.

Wave after wave rained down. I screamed at God. If he answered, I couldn't hear him over the ocean's noise. Facing the terrifying walls of water punching down on me, I realised that I'd soon be another member of my family lost in the Channel. More than anything else that realisation spurred me on. I found some last reserves and pulled to where I thought France must be. There was a gap in the fog and waves, and a moment of calm. I think, bizarrely, the sun even shone briefly. I heard voices: not the siren voices I'd been hearing in the spray, but very human, very alarmed, voices.

'Bloody hell! There he is! Bloody, bloody hell!'

The support boat had sighted me through the mist. Later Andy told me the reason he'd been able to find me at all was that with one arm and a sinking bath I'd been rowing in a giant circle.

Andy threw a line. I dived to get it and missed. Everything was now happening in three vivid dimensions. One moment Andy and the support boat were below me down a watery slope. The next they were way above, then hurtling down at me. Many times I watched them powerless in a trough or threatening to crash on top of me. Boat and bath were swilled round, forced above and below each other, battling the sea.

Trying to catch a line in this situation with one good arm is not easy. Eventually I got it. Straining hard they dragged me beside the support boat, mystified why I was so heavy. In my defence I'd lost a lot of blood and wasn't thinking clearly which might, in some way, explain what happened next. It turned out that the reason I seemed so heavy was that I had storm-lashed myself to the bath, dementedly prepared to go down with my vessel. They had pulled alongside the support boat not just me, but a third of a tonne of sinking sanitaryware.

Andy held my good arm, slashing through the cords which bound me to the bath. Both of us were totally focused on what needed to be done, rather than speculating on the mess we were in. He pulled me up and over the side rail of the support boat, landing me on the deck like a stunned mullet. Now the pain hit me like a fist, but I knew if we were not very careful we'd lose the bath altogether. Nursing my wounds was not an option.

I ran to the side and caught hold of one of lines attached to the bath and clung on to it. It was the only thing holding the bath to the support boat. Without my weight to keep it upright in the water, it had gently flipped over. Desperately, I looped the rope in my hand to the rail and Andy got hold of the other one. The bath's flag floated away from our grasp. A desperate lunge with the boat hook and I'd caught it. Losing the flag was unthinkable. The waves whipped up again, the spray cutting into my cheeks, and the bath finally rolled beneath the waves. Just one pontoon was now still visible, the rest lay below water. Through biting spray I saw Bernard sinking out of sight and leant out to where I'd last seen him, clawing the sea. Andy grabbed me as the boat lurched again, hurling me back on deck. Without him I'd have followed Bernard to a watery grave. With my one good arm Andy and I attached the bath to the side of the support boat as the wind, rain and waves lashed us from all sides. At this point both of us firmly believed that the sea would claim not only the bath but support boat as well.

It turned out we were in French waters, four tantalising miles from finishing the trip. Any decisions about what we should now do had to involve the French authorities. Reaching Calais wasn't an option. Due to the delay at the start caused by all the negotiating with the French on what was – and wasn't – legal on that day of the year, I'd missed the weather window. It is very fair to say that, being only four miles from completing the challenge, we probably would have finished before the storm hit. Without the negotiating, we'd now have all been tucked up, safe and warm, in a nice French port waiting out the storm with a Croque Monsieur, a bottle of red and the words 'good job we're not out in that' ringing comfortingly in our ears.

We made contact with the French. Their attitude was 'I told you so . . .' Ironically, it was the very time taken earlier that day, by the same French administrator, telling me that if it went wrong he would be saying 'I told you so . . .' that had led to the fact that it had gone wrong, and which now gave him the chance to say 'I told you so . . .' However cross I felt at his sneering delivery, I suppressed my anger and dealt with him with sunny courtesy. Even under immense strain, politeness is vital. In the true spirit of liberty and fraternity the French then refused us permission to land at Boulogne, before suggesting that their solution to this was to put explosive charges on the bath and blow it out of the water. They claimed the bath was a danger to all other shipping, a questionable assertion given we were now out of shipping lanes. When I pressed them they maintained blowing up the bath would deal finally with the bath question. They even offered to provide the detonative charges.

With a badly injured arm and the whole situation in chaos and confusion the storm lashed in again. Things were unclear and worrying. Phone calls and radio conversations went back and forth between us, the French and Duncan in Kent.

Andy had been mostly silent since I arrived on the support boat. He looked at me, 'I've not seen a rowing effort that bloody gutsy in the bloody Channel before. You sort this and I'll make sure that damned bath gets back to the UK.'

I wasn't thinking clearly, but went back on the radio[11] to the French Navy man, 'Just to remind you, Monsieur, that the sinking of a Registered British Shipping Vessel without the permission of the Captain will be taken as a bit of an act of war . . .'

Pin-drop silence on all frequencies in the English Channel followed. Back in Dover you could just hear the Coastguard saying, 'Could you come here a moment sir, there might be a problem.'

Supremely exhausted, blissfully unaware of the ramifications of what I'd just said I stood motionless in the cabin of Andy's boat.

I flicked the switch on the radio, '. . . Over?'

Silence reigned until the Frenchman finally came back on the radio. Under maritime law I was right. He gathered himself and said, 'You are the Captain, may we have your permission to sink her?'

'Absolutely not.'

We may have been stuck in the Channel in a hideous storm with a disabled bath hanging off the stern, but now we were having fun.

Andy broke into a grin. 'Right. Let's get this crapping Crapper back to Folkestone. Go and check that that bloody thing's still tied on. This is going to be *fucking* rough . . .'

The crew of the support boat were now in a terrible way and I felt for them. Were it not for me and my foolhardy plans they never would have been in this terrible situation. However the problems with the French authorities had turned any ill feeling within the boat towards those outside it. We worked hard in our common goal of getting the bath back to Blighty.

Ships then came from the other Channel nations to help us. It was very moving and proved that it's not just Britain but all the other nations along the Channel's shore that don't like the French.

---

[11]For clarity I've made this a single radio conversation as there were lots of simultaneous conversations flying back and forth on several mobiles and using various different radio frequencies making it very hard to be sure which part of which conversation occurred on what apparatus.

The sea continued to batter us. One moment the bath was tied up behind Andy's boat, the next it had slipped a line and was broadside across the bows, flying towards the cabin at warp speed. It was a horrid crossing back.

The storm was now Force 7 or 8. When you're in the middle of them it's difficult to measure these things accurately, but it seemed very bad to everyone on that boat. I don't get seasick, so Andy kept turning to me to do things. My competence at sea was being radicalised by this terrible punishment and a real rapport developed between us. Although we'd only known each other less than a day, Andy and I had bonded. He could see how difficult things were becoming for me and suggested that I went below and as the weather was now easing slightly, I agreed. I slumped onto the bed below deck and immediately jumped up again. There was no skin left on my buttocks. I lay on my front, nursing my shoulder as it hung over the edge of the hard, thin, foam mattress. It was a nasty throbbing mess. I passed out. Coming round, I found my scrotum bleeding, joining my shoulder and hands. This was the lowest point of my journey so far. Whichever way you looked at it, whatever gloss I put on it, at a very basic level I'd failed to do what I had set out to achieve. I sat below deck and tried to text the people I loved, but my swollen fingers weren't able to frame words on the tiny keypad. I finally managed to construct something approximating a message and clicked 'send'. There was no reception.

The support boat lurched down in the water; I hit my shoulder and passed out again. Coming round, I found myself in a strange world with no smiles. A world that didn't have the colour yellow. A world that never heard laughter. A world totally of my own making. As well as failing I'd almost lost the bath and narrowly avoided declaring war on France. I couldn't begin to think how I could come back from this. There was no money to stage a second attempt. My body was going to need some serious medical attention before I'd even be able to sit on a chair with ease let alone attempt the Channel again. The bath had a great hole in her side and the roll top had been ripped off. She was a complete mess. All my training, planning, thoughts and determination had led to utter failure. My charity fundraising plan had gone seriously wrong.

I reflected bitterly on my successful paper-boat voyage down the Thames and the depths of despair I now felt. The support boat was carrying me home but I didn't want to see anyone I knew. I had failed. Peering out of the tiny porthole I saw Folkestone bathed in light, the weather beautiful over Kent.

Bernard had sunk down into the depths. My life and priorities became very warped as I sat below the deck and wept for a rubber bath toy. I'm not a superstitious man but at that moment I realised it was 13 July.

Bugger.

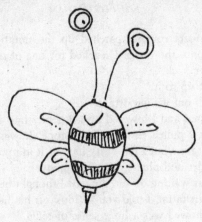

CHAPTER SEVEN

A MONSTROUS CROW

'If not actually disgruntled, he was far from being gruntled.'

P.G. Wodehouse

Getting the bath out of the water was going to be impossible. She had turtled under and was clinging on to the support boat by just one line. Upside down and water heavy we'd need a crane to lift her out. We were about a mile off Folkestone Harbour when a gaggle of Dutch voices cut the air. People were gathering on the deck of a massive salvage boat floating outside the harbour arm.

A Dutch voice shouted over, 'Is that the bath we've all heard so much about?'

Very soon the salvage crane on board whirred into action. Kindly, they plucked the bath from the water like a bedraggled sock and plonked it on their deck. She was a mess. Water poured out of the hole in the flotation tank. The rim of the copper bath had been viciously ripped off and much of the bath itself was totally bent out of shape. Already having lost her showerhead, *Lilibet II* looked very sorry for herself. She'd be insulted but it was entirely right she'd finished her attempt on a salvage boat.

The Hollanders roughly patched up the flotation tank before lowering her into the water. I reached for one of the spare oars.

'I'll row her back.'

'You're not up to it.'

'I know . . . but it's important.'

Andy relented and I lowered myself gently into the bath. In unbearable pain I pulled towards Folkestone. It was probably only half a mile by now but I felt every inch of it in my back, buttocks, hands, shoulder and plums. I was in agony.

Duncan was waiting on the slipway. I thought he'd have a cross, angry or an irritating I-told-you-so look on his face but the only emotion he showed was a huge sense of relief.

We tied off the bath. It was a sunny day on the quayside in Kent. I stood looking at the total wreck before me. The bath had a huge hole in it. I had a fairly big hole in me and the crew had all decided to take up jobs in landlocked places like Derbyshire.

Although the sun was out, the sea was still angry as we found when trying to put the bath back onto the trailer. With me very disabled, it was tricky but we managed it.

Eventually, we sat down to a pint. It had gone very badly. Duncan was the first to take up the conversation.

'I've said this before. It's just not possible.'

'I was just four-and-a-half miles off. Without the faffing about and the weather problem, I might have made it.'

'I think there's something in that . . .' Andy mused, more to his beer than anyone.

We'd all had a very lucky escape. It was a great bit of captaincy from Andy that had got us through.

We all left the pub after just one pint and Gavin and I made for home. As darkness fell we left Folkestone. As darkness fell further we arrived back in Folkestone. I wailed. The satanic one-way system had deceived us into a two-hour round trip. In darkness Gavin and I left Folkestone again. It was then that the trailer lights chose to break. At the same moment the engine started to make an odd noise, wisps of grey steamy fog emerged from behind the bonnet. We pulled over and with the engine running I popped the bonnet. It was so dark but in the dimness I could smell fumes and see there was oil and petrol all over the engine.

'Need a light?'

Gavin helpfully leant over with a lighted candle. We both paused for a moment, surveying the petrol, oil, fumes and proximity of the lighted flame to all three.

'Gav . . . I think perhaps we should look for the torch, don't you?'

'Good idea.'

By a flickering torch I attempted to rewire the electrics and patch up the engine. I was so tired and recovering from inadvertently nearly being blown up, I decided to check us into the first hotel we came to and sort out my shoulder and all other problems the next day.

'Do you have a room for two please?'

'No sorry, sir, we're fully booked – let me check the other hotels in the area.'

I must have looked terrifying in that hotel lobby caked in blood, mud and oil. Gavin didn't look too marvellous either. He had the nervous air of a man who'd glimpsed death twice that day and wasn't yet sure he'd genuinely escaped it.

'I can't explain it, sir, but all the hotels between here and the M25 are fully booked tonight.'

'Brilliant, thank you, goodnight.'

'Has it been a long day?'

'You could say that . . .'

I'd failed in the Channel, narrowly avoided war with France, survived death by exploding engine and now I couldn't even check into a hotel successfully. I'd had finer days.

Gavin and I struck for home.

The next few nights were horrible. I was so tired I could cry, but each time I shut my eyes, images of storms, waves, blood and the spectre of my Uncle Tony shone out of the darkness at me. I'd tried to use his nemesis for something stupidly comic. Now it consumed my dreams to tell me off.

After getting my shoulder strapped up and more general medical attention for the rest of me, there was lots of thinking to do. Where was I supposed to go from here? Was there enough money to pay for another attempt? Would the team want to be involved in another attempt? Could we fix the bath? Could I get fit for it? Had I just proved what Duncan had feared all along, that rowing the Channel wasn't possible in a tub? It basically all boiled down to one question: should I try again or throw in the bath towel?

I'm not good at giving in. For as long as I can remember, I've never given in, and hate watching others do so. My determination verges on the insane. Yet my determination was sorely tested now.

Spending time away from the bath was nice. I got to spend time with my friends, the girl I loved and my family. What was the point of it all? Sport Relief didn't seem remotely bothered at the failure of the bath trip. I'm not sure they thought it was possible anyway. I was still badly bashed up and was enjoying having time to rest. My body enjoyed not training so hard that it took up every second of my day. Now it was focusing on dealing with the pain caused by basic day-to-day issues like sitting down.

When I was small I fell off my skateboard coming down a hill and ripped all the skin off my backside. I had to sit on a cushion for weeks. This was worse. The pain caused by the lack of skin on my buttocks was excruciating. I found any excuse possible not to sit down in company. The few times I went out to dinner in this period always led to the inevitable moment: 'Shall we sit down?' I came up with a variety of excuses, none of which really worked. 'No thanks, I've just joined that religion where you have to eat standing up during July . . .' 'No thanks, I prefer to eat mine pacing up and down, it's part of a diet thing I'm trying . . .' 'Do you mind if I eat mine kneeling? It's in memory of St Joseph?' You'll no doubt be surprised to learn, none of these worked and I spent evenings almost passing out with pain, and not, for a change, at the conversation.

Kneeling at my study desk, my computer flashed and made an irritating noise. An email. It was from someone I've known almost longer than anyone else and yet now hardly ever get to see. Some friends you don't need to see to feel close to or simply be inspired by. We were tiny together in Derbyshire and in the same class at our little school. We played together at break times and at one point even had shoes that matched. I'm sure they were called 'Pods' and we thought they were great, semi-magical in fact. Everyone else thought they were silly.

We raced up and down the tarmac playground together. In summer we were let out into the field to run around and in our final year we were even allowed near the school pond to watch the water boatmen. When I was small she was my close friend. I still remember waking up in the morning, pulling on my socks and looking forward to going to school, not for the lessons, but because I knew we'd get to play together in the breaks.

Now she's a professional sailor and her determination is legendary. The email inspired me and made me curse my lack of determination. The writer of the email: Ellen MacArthur. I read it, replied and determined to make another attempt.

I phoned Simon to tell him.

'Simon? I want to have another crack across the Channel . . .'

'What? It's an insane plan, you might die properly this time . . . I'm in.'

Somewhere south of Wapping, the phone rang: 'Kenny? I want to try and give it another go . . .'

'How much is it going to cost me this time?'

I'd done a rough budget. I'd learnt from the failed attempt, budgeting was something I simply had to get better at. I could hear Kenny smiling.

'Sure. We'll put the money in place to help you try to kill yourself again . . . gladly.'

With sponsors like these, who needs enemies?

My shoulder healed slightly so I joined Mark and the lads in trying to put the bath back together. It really was a mess.

There was a silver lining to the dark cloud of my failure. Simon phoned from Thomas Crapper & Co.

'Tim, you may have fail . . .' he coughed and began again. 'Tim, you may have . . . not quite made it across the Channel in your bath but don't forget your main aim was to raise money for charity. You can still raise money for charity. In one of the sheds at Thomas Crapper and Co we've still got His Imperial Majesty King George V's travel bath. You could auction that off and raise money for charity that way.'

A masterstroke. I left Mark on the riverbank and drove up to the head office of Thomas Crapper & Co. It was a long journey, as I had to keep pulling over to air my raw buttocks and wipe the seeping goo from the seat of the car. After getting lost and missing the innocuous gate twice again, I turned in and up past the cricket pitch on the left. The sheep went on with the same particularly important piece of eating as before and the stream continued to babble happily on the right. I brought the car to a standstill in the bath park, opened the door and bounded out to weave my way deftly through the bath labyrinth. Not finding the Minotaur, I met Simon standing in between the massive Victorian urinals (rampant) beaming in his Edwardian beard.

'What stunning urinals you have.'

He smiled, making his moustaches rise at the corners.

'I've been meaning to tell you this for ages and now's the perfect time . . .' He pointed to the design of a bee stunningly inlaid in the porcelain of the urinals. 'This is a Victorian joke, a sort of a pun.'

My brain started to bombinate. I love puns. 'A bee?'

'Think, Tim, what's Latin for bee?'

'Erm . . . flower bee is *Apis floris* . . . oh Apis . . . "A piss" on a urinal – brilliant.'[12]

'Now come and see the travel bath.'

The silver lining to my dark cloud came with solid silver taps.

'The taps, plug and all the plumbing is solid silver. He was a man of style, George V.'

Simon explained that during Britain's first darkest hour – the First World War[13] – the government asked the King to go round the country and rally the people. The King agreed immediately but had one condition. He must have a bathroom installed on the Royal Train. So Thomas Crapper & Co installed the iron masterpiece and all the solid silver plumbing onto the Royal Train. This was paid for by the War Office. Why have more ammunition when you can have plumbing like that? I'm not an expert on the history of sanitaryware but if there is a greater plumbing masterpiece than this, I'd like to see it. When it was removed and a new one put in its place for the current Queen, Crappers couldn't bare to see their great work destroyed, so kept it.

---

[12] The bee transfer was placed on the urinal as a target – the Victorians knew men liked something to aim at. Cleverly, the bee was even positioned in the ideal place to minimise splash back. Two lesser European bathroom companies have produced a range like this but substituting a fly for the bee (Latin for fly: *Musca Domestica*; not amusing at all) and have put the target in the wrong place, leading to many splashed trousers at hotels in County Cork.

[13] When I was small it was always known at home as the 'First Local Difficulty'. My great-grandfather was the only pacifist my family has ever managed to produce. It says a lot about him that he was a pacifist in World War I who won the Military Medal. This is the 'highest' medal you can win if you're not an officer. Another member of the family (an uncle or cousin, Albert) won the Victoria Cross in the same war. This is the British Army's highest award for gallantry.

'I'll have it polished up and get the enamel looked at, as it would be good if it left here as we intended when it first went out.'

I left Crappers that afternoon and phoned my girlfriend.

'What do you know about charity auctions? I've got a bath . . .'

She had loads of experience at that sort of thing so we worked happily together setting it all up. I went out to the boatyard in the day and worked hard with Mark, then when I'd finished, we'd meet up in the sunshine and plan the auction together. This was a lovely period of my life and of the bath project.

There'd been some press about my failure to cross the Channel. Cynics would suggest that there would have been less press had I made it. One day I got a call from an events company asking if there was anything they could do to help. They'd read about the bath project in the paper and heard that I was going to try again.

I explained that although I was going to try again, I was currently focused on organising an auction to raise money for the charity the trip was in aid of. The man on the end of the phone, Andre, sounded really excited, 'I'd love to help. Where are you at the moment?'

'At the boatyard by the river.'

'I'll come.'

He arrived on the riverbank in a shining open-topped silver Mercedes. The man who stepped out of it would have looked more at home in Monaco or Capri than Richmond. With noticeable incongruity he arrived among the oil-stained overalls of the boatyard. One of London's top party tsars had joined the bath team.

Over the next few days Andre and his team put together all the ingredients of a top night. They found me a huge house to hold the auction in, right in the centre of London. It was stunning, had a huge drawing room, was empty and, better than anything, the owners said we could use it for free.

They opened a charity bank account for the money we hoped to make from the auction. Andre had the great plan of getting a drinks sponsor on board. He thought up ways of lighting the event, staffing the bar, making the place look good and generally did everything that events companies do best. One day he phoned.

'Tim, we can't just auction off the bath thing—'

'It's the Royal travel bath.'

'Yeah . . . we need something more. I can use some contacts and get us some other stuff to go with it. How does that sound?'

'Great.'

He sorted out a Cartier diamond, Rolex wristwatch, some other gems, jewels and even furniture to go with the bath. Brilliant. This was going to be a very special night. It all moved so fast. It's amazing to watch the London party maestros when they get going. They have address books to rival the Delphic Oracle and are not afraid to unleash them.

'I'll sort the press and shall we have some VIP guests too?'

Very soon he'd invited more press than I knew existed. Comic Relief and I couldn't believe the effort that was going into this. He even showed me the RSVP from Tom Cruise's office saying Tom was in town for a movie premiere that week and would love to come and help such a good cause. Things were getting out of hand. My tiny charity auction had taken on massive proportions. The travel bath was so pretty and had obviously generated a huge interest. The whole thing was wonderful. As I continued working hard on *Lilibet II*, I began to look forward to what would be the night of the year.

I forget exactly what it was that made me question him about it, but innocently one day I tried to be helpful. 'If you give me the cheque book I can go and pick up—'

'There's no need . . .' Andre looked stressed, but then he had a lot on his mind.

Eventually he signed one of the cheques from the bank account we'd opened and I went off to pick up whatever it was. It seemed odd to me that I couldn't sign cheques on a charity bank account that had been set up in my name. Not being the brightest bear in the toy box I asked my girlfriend about it.

'I'm sure that's normal, darling . . . He's probably just forgotten to put you on the account.'

'Are you on the account?'

'No sweet-pea but why should I be?'

I looked at the cheque and saw that the bank holding the account was offshore: again, merely slightly unusual but enough to get me thinking. It seemed an awful lot of effort to open an offshore account simply for my charity auction. He'd become a very good friend, particularly with my girlfriend, so I thought I'd just politely ask him about it.

'I see the bank's offshore.'

'Yes, it's the best way of doing these things for tax.'

'Right.'

I don't understand tax so didn't question that, but it led to anther question that then bugged me. 'At the auction, as well as the credit card thing that you've sorted, people often want to give cash – you know in buckets – for the charity . . .'

'Yes.'

'Well, how do we pay that in at the bank?'

He then made a mistake. If he'd thought fast, he could have come up with something better than what he actually said. He might have been tired, or he may have thought I'd support him in it. He looked at me oddly, and a cold tone entered his voice.

'Here's the thing. If we bank it here, we have to pay tax on it, so the best way to deal with it is to put the cash in suitcases and take it over to the offshore bank ourselves.'

'Right . . .'

'That way we don't pay tax . . .' He looked deep into my eyes for a reaction before adding hastily, 'Oh and the charity gets more money out of it.'

I may not understand tax but I knew that being asked to carry suitcase-fulls of cash through airports by conspiratorial-sounding men was a bad plan. I carried on listening to him talking and as I did, realised I didn't know anything about this man at all. I'd met him through the newspaper. I'd checked out his website and it all looked square, but he could have just made it up.

I decided to let him run with things. I didn't have any proof of anything other than that he had a very relaxed attitude to tax. I thought that by giving him more rope, and making him trust me more, if he was up to anything bad, I stood a better chance of seeing what it was. I decided to keep my girlfriend in the dark on what he'd said. I didn't want to worry her. I think perhaps he was gambling on the fact that I'd look very silly if I pulled the event at this late stage so thought I'd join him rather than cancel.

Something happened by chance. An elderly lady sent me a cheque. Not having my address, she posted it to the building the auction was due to be held in. In being re-routed, it somehow missed Andre and ended up on the desk of the man that brokered a deal involving the building. With the cheque was a letter in her spidery handwriting and not knowing what it was, the broker put my surname into Google and phoned me up.

'Why am I sitting here with a cheque for you?'

I explained to him in total innocence about Andre and the events company and the charity auction. The voice that came back was measured and I felt sure could be slightly sinister in the wrong situation.

'I'd be very careful if I were you. Andre has been doing some things recently that have not gone well for him. He's done some things for me in the past, which were good, but I wouldn't touch him now. He's not doing well, if you understand me. Do you know for a fact that he's even still working with that events company?'

Then he said something I could not ignore.

'I thought he'd left the country . . .'

Suddenly the candle burnt a tiny hole in the sack and a chink of light was opened.

'. . . Now, where shall I send this cheque?'

I now know something of the fringes of what I'd become involved in. You may think I'm overpainting the situation. I will try and explain as much as I can. I'm not able to say where I think the broker stood in all this but suffice to say that Andre was a very desperate man indeed. He'd done some 'work' for some people involving very large sums of money – let's call them collectively 'Gangland Inc'. This had gone badly and the money had disappeared. Andre then took up the cutting-edge style of entrepreneurialism pioneered by the Krays, and robbed a few houses to try to make some of the money back.

I didn't want to go to Andre with what I knew. I couldn't produce the paper proofs I'd been shown and my girlfriend was becoming very protective of him.

Finally, a few nights later, she sat in tears on the sofa and told me why. 'He told me not to tell anyone as he's embarrassed about it, so please don't say anything darling, but he's got testicular cancer and may only have a few months left.'

As I wrapped her in my arms and hugged her till she cheered up, I felt awful. What if she was right? What if I was judging a dying man harshly? Feeling two-faced and horrible I began to subtly check on the things he'd set up. My newfound budgeting skill came in useful. I checked with the suppliers on the things he said he'd got us for free due to their generosity: the flowers, lighting, lighting designer, doormen and carpets. The suppliers painted a very different picture. They all expected to be paid: some of them upwards of £10,000.

The budget for the auction was staggering. We couldn't make any money for the charity with such massive expenditure. I poked around further. I hated doing this but felt I'd been left with no choice. The drinks sponsorship turned out to be genuine, and initially I thought this might offset the massive bills he was running up all over London but when it was confirmed that their sponsorship merely came in the form of free alcohol, I realised I was in big trouble. Everything else he'd told me was a tissue of lies.

The house he'd got to hold the auction in was the subject of an ongoing wrangle between a third-world government and some sharp-practising businessmen. The developing nation alleged that the businessmen swindled the house from their country in the late nineties. Whatever the truth of the allegation, to use that building to host a charity auction to raise money for a charity that funds projects in the very country who allege the house was stolen from them is a nonsense.

The offshore bank account was being used to funnel money from three other offshore accounts that were the subject of a fraud investigation. I wasn't even a signatory to my own charity account.

The Cartier diamond, Rolex watch, furniture and other stuff that Andre wanted to auction off under the nose of the entire press corp turned out to be stolen goods: the product of his descent into petty thiefdom. He was intending to use my charity auction as a fence to sell stolen goods to the likes of Tom Cruise.

How had I gone from trying to raise money for a charity to living on the fringes of international celebrity fraud?

Andre, meanwhile, was staying with my girlfriend in a house in the middle of nowhere in Scotland. I had to spend an agonising weekend, knowing that he was at best a crook and fearing that at worst he could be much more. Also he was with the woman I loved in an isolated location.

Standing up to my neck in this horribly murky water, I baited my hook and picked up the phone: 'Andre, hi, the beer delivery is coming in early. I'm away training, shall I send a mate of mine to pick it up?'

There was a pause. I thought I heard dropping spoons in the background. It was a big gamble, he could have just said 'yes' but I reasoned he was so in need of the cash he'd want to get the beer for himself. Also, as far as he was concerned, the auction was still going ahead so we needed that beer.

'No, I'll come down from Scotland early.'

'That's great, thanks so much . . .' I hung up.

The next half a day I spent in London waiting for my girlfriend to get back to the flat. I didn't want to call her, as I knew she'd realise from the tone of my voice that something was up.

Finally, I couldn't wait any longer. 'Where are you now?'

'On the way back, darling.'

'Is Andre still with you?'

'No, he left before me to get the beer delivery.'

Horrible hours later she arrived through the front door. I pulled her into my arms. 'How was Scotland?'

'Fine, we played cards . . .'

'Did you win much?'

'I won the first few hands but in the end Andre cleaned up.'

'Baby, we need to talk . . .'

I unburdened the whole thing to her. Showed her the paperwork and very gently let her know that a man she'd trusted had let her down.

With good spirit she recovered quickly. 'But he's on his way to get the beer delivery. How will we . . . ?'

'I'm not sure that's a problem.'

At the same time, Andre was eagerly closing the door of his Mercedes to pick up the beer in central London; somewhere in a warehouse in west London, the beer sat safely in crates. As soon as I knew he'd left her alone in Scotland, I cancelled the order.

'If you have any doubt left about any of this, please phone him . . .'

'I'll meet with him.' Still she believed in the fundamental goodness of people.

She left a message; he left the scene. Where he went, I don't know. When the beer delivery didn't arrive he left an abusive message on my phone. It said he hated me for having not joined him in his fraud. Before he hung up he swore vengeance on me, then ran away.

In a couple of hours I'd dismantled the whole auction and saved myself, and more importantly Comic Relief, from a terrible situation. I cancelled all the suppliers across London, who shocked me with their kindness. Many even thanked me for having saved them the expense of not being paid. I also had to email all the people who had been invited. I felt terrible about this but, at the time, there was still a chance that Andre might be caught so I agreed not to let people know the real reason why the event had been cancelled. I think I blamed a cold in the end, which was a very lame excuse. I hate any whiff of things that aren't true, and kindly, people didn't push me on it.

The best thing about the situation is that I'd realised what was going on quickly enough to stop everything and no one had lost money. But the silver lining to my dark cloud turned out to be made of lead. My cloud crashed swifter than the Hindenburg and I was left sifting through the wreckage for some debris of hope. The charity auction debacle had really shaken my grip on reality. I'd always thought the world was a generally sunny place but coming across people ready to abuse my optimistic outlook for bad purposes really shocked me to the core.

Subsequently I found out that Andre had been cleverly booking airline tickets on my girlfriend's credit card and had also taken money from her. It was a real lesson to learn: some people can be very cruel. I felt like everything I held close was shifting. Morally, I was a man trying to run up a hill that I'd just found out was made of sand.

I'd failed in the Channel, I'd let down everyone who'd believed in the bath plan and now the sparkling charity auction had turned into a near miss with the fraud squad. My only current hope was that the weather would improve, Mark would get the bath finished and I might be able to make another attempt as soon as possible.

The weather now became awful again. By this point, I'd spent months training, rowing and battling the Channel which meant I'd not been doing anything that made money. I was chronically short of funds, so needed to do something to make some cash.

Leaving university, I'd moved abroad and ended up farming. On my return, I didn't know what I wanted to do. I spent some time with various tutors at RADA before moving on to balance various unsuccessful day jobs with a bit of comedy and acting. Through a series of lovely flukes it was, oddly, comedy that had become the mainstay of my life since I gave up farming. I'd even been nominated for the prestigious Perrier Best Newcomer Award at Edinburgh and since then consistently and joyously failed to live up to my own early promise. With my confidence in the world at an all-time low, I headed for the only place no one would notice a lunatic – the Edinburgh Festival Fringe.

In 2003, I'd turned up at Edinburgh and told the story of the paper-boat trip. I wouldn't call it a stand-up routine, more a story that made people laugh – an enterlecture, or my version of raconteurism. As I'm sure Dr Johnson would have said in later life, trying to define things takes the fun out of them. Whatever that hour of me wittering on was defined as, the show *Paper Boat* became a surprise, if modest, hit of the Festival that year. My tiny venue was totally sold out for three weeks and many of the papers kindly made it their pick of the Festival.

I'd never intended to do a show based on the paper-boat journey, but as a comic, I'd always talked about the things I'd seen and that was just one of them. I thought I'd try a similar hour based on the bath trip to date. Life had got me down, things were not going well and that's often the source of great comedy. While many comics have written well when they've been depressed, I was not one of them. Every time I thought about the bath, the trip, the hilariousness of the ruse – I found myself in bed, lying in a darkened room.

Needless to say, my 2004 bath show was the comic equivalent of a train crash. The audiences, most of whom had come in 2003, were courteous but it was nowhere near my best work. Newspaper critics swarmed in to rip the show and my life to shreds. One reviewer decided that the entire reason the show was rubbish was my choice in shirts.

I'd always tried to take a fairly level-headed view of reviews but already shaken by the total lack of cheerfulness in the bath project, I started to spiral. I was a man swimming hopelessly against a tide of sadness that wanted to engulf me. I gasped brief mouthfuls of hopefulness but in the main, the waves took me. They were relentless.

The only glimpses of light were: my shoulder was better, the bath had been fixed and I might get a weather window in September and finally finish this.

At the end of the first week in September, I got the flu. Long-distance rowing with the flu is not advisable; it also makes your job much harder at sea.

Mid-September, I got a phone call from Duncan. 'Tim, there's a weather window tomorrow . . . I think we can try the crossing again.'

'I'll be there . . .'

'You sound terrible.'

The one good day of September weather coincided directly with the worst day of my illness. I couldn't go: I wasn't the first to be thwarted by it, but man flu had won again.

My last chance to turn things around in 2004 had disappeared. What I'd planned as a hilarious two-week jaunt over the summer would now have to be abandoned or become an obsession that would live on for another year. And for at least another year, at every party, every introduction and most of all, always in my head, I'd be 'the man who failed to row the Channel in a bath'.

I was not in control of my own life. I'd set myself up as a total failure. Just as Dave Gorman predicted[14], my life had become a waking nightmare based on a P.G. Wodehouse plot. Sadly for me there was no Jeeves on hand to pull me out of the onion soup.

There's nothing better when you've had a really tough summer than knowing you have winter ahead, with dark early nights, a roaring fire and the woman you love. My girlfriend and I were getting on like a house on fire, in fact so well it was more like a city on fire. I'd kept a lot of my inner thoughts to myself and concentrated on being there for her. This stopped me thinking too hard about my own gloom and let her know that she was my top priority. Due to work commitments she'd had to move countries, so after missing the last weather window I went to be with her.

Things were going great, although we were living apart. I've always thought that you should never trap the people you love and I felt we were trapping each other by trying to be together while being forced to live apart. Both of our lives found it hard to cope

---

[14] Dave and I had become friends playing in Edinburgh years before. It was during one of those boozy nights he first said, 'Tim, you only exist because P.G. Wodehouse didn't invent you first.' We've been good friends ever since. When he heard about the bath project, he left the same line as a message on my phone. Everyone involved in this book thought it was such a good summary of me that they put it on the cover.

with us taking a week or two off a month to see each other and do nothing much else. That winter, we were away and went to watch a cricket match together. We sat curled up on the boundary, talked, laughed and hugged. She'd been the lantern of my world ever since I first saw her as a girl at college but I felt very clearly now that our relationship was holding her back. We kissed goodbye at the airport and have never seen each other since. Love, like happiness, is an instant, an unforgettable moment in time, and trying to freeze love or keep it in the jar of a relationship kills it.

It was the right decision. At the time it hurt me more than rowing the Channel had done. I stopped swimming against it and gave in to the sea of sorrow. Mentally, I hit the floor.

I'd sunk both my bath and relationship. The charity auction was a farce and I was now trapped in a limbo of bad weather over winter. I was embroiled in a tragedy entirely of my own making. At Edinburgh I'd even died on stage in a bath. My nightmares returned and my sleep became violent again. I spent the winter in a very deep cliché, writing terrible not-quite poetry, drinking more than a bitter, cynical cop in an American B-movie and wondering if I'd make it to spring. I didn't want to see spring. I didn't return calls and did my best to isolate myself from everyone who knew me.

I joined the illustrious list of people who've died in baths to become a downmarket version of Agamemnon: except obviously he was Greek and probably wore a sheet at the time. That winter, all was darkness.

NUNQUAM TE CONFUNDANT ILLEGITIMI

Chapter Eight

PRUNING THE PLUMS

'Stop dying at once, and when you get up, get your bloody hair cut.'

Lieutenant Colonel A.D. Wintle
to his critically ill batman Cedric Mays, who obeyed the order

My blithe plumbing-based ruse had become an albatross. I was a conceited comic trapped by my own comic conceit; living proof that the English love eccentrics – just not as close friends. Every time I thought about the bath I found myself lying in bed with the curtains closed.

Finally I got myself together. I realised how childish, selfish and whiny I'd become. I'd been under a lot of pressure, things hadn't gone well, but it's how you deal with problems that defines you. Self-pity is something no one in my family had ever done and I couldn't fathom how I'd ended up doing it now. My behaviour was shameful. Finally a line from my grandfather appeared in my head: *'nunquam te confundant illegitimi'* which I think roughly translates as 'never let the bastards grind you down'. My grandfather was Victorian when it came to swear words: swearing is fine as long as it's in Latin. It was like someone shining had just grabbed me by the throat and showed me myself. I stopped moping. Simply (perhaps tritely) put, it's better to have tried and died than never to have tried at all.

By March, I was back to reading books on training. I wanted to ease into things gently, didn't want to pull anything. April saw me actually training. Betty and I undertook gruelling sessions together. My avenging angel battered me again, just as she had the year before. I had to fight consistent battles on that Ergo. When things were hurting and I wanted to pass out from the pain, a new voice appeared in my head and said with a silvery tongue, 'Don't bother finishing it, you won't make it anyway, remember what happened last time . . .' Every time it whispered, I dug deeper, found something extra and kept on rowing.

I made calls and began putting the team back together. It was April and a weather window could happen in May.

I'd been trying to contact Duncan Taylor on his mobile and house phone for most of March with no luck. I couldn't work it out. He was normally so reliable. Perhaps he was away on holiday. He knew we'd need to start planning. Finally, in mid-April, his wife picked up the phone at the house. I was really relieved to hear her voice.

'Tim, thank goodness, I've been trying to get hold of you but didn't have your mobile number . . .'

'Duncan's got it.'

'Tim, Duncan's dead.'

Something had just hit me in the forehead. My head hurt.

'What?'

'I know how close you'd become and I'm sorry. I wanted to let you know sooner. He loved planning with you and was so looking forward to . . .' Her voice trailed off and she cried the tears of a woman who's loved the same man her whole life. It was gut wrenching to hear down the end of the phone, and I felt powerless to help her with her grief.

That winter, Duncan had gone to see his doctor with a pain in his chest. He thought it was just a cold or the flu. It was cancer and he died within weeks. Cruelly snatched from his wife and family who didn't really have time to say goodbye. A huge, strong man, seemingly in the best of health with a tremendous energy and sunny outlook had been snatched from the people he touched. I was one of them and it hit me really hard.

While he was seriously ill, Duncan had instructed his wife to tell

Andy to take me across the Channel. I put down the phone to Mrs Taylor and sat deep in thought. More than anything so far, this made me think about giving the whole project up. Then I thought of Duncan and his belief, even when he was ill, that the bath crossing should go ahead.

I picked up the phone and soon heard, 'I wondered when you'd be calling, trying to get us both killed again . . . you mad, mad . . .' Andy was back in the bath.

April passed in a pained and horrible sweat of swearing at Betty, running for hours and doing weights until my arms burnt.

One evening I was eating a baked potato in a flat in London with a friend of mine called Charlotte. Her flatmate breezed through the door.

'Phil, this is Tim.'

'Hi, Tim. What are you up at the moment?'

'I'm training to row the English Channel in a bath.'

Setting off the top of Phil's very tall, former cavalry officer frame was a look of total bafflement. Charlotte smiled as Phil's lips parted to speak again.

'What?'

I told Phil about the bath trip and how far we'd got. He gave me his card.

'I make travel documentaries. I'm sure there are loads of people interested in this bath trip but if you'd like I could come along to try to record it.'

I liked Phil. He was straightforward and believed in things with a great passion. We talked further over the next few days and agreed he would follow the bath trip and we'd try to make a documentary out of it.

Over a celebratory beer, he smiled and said, 'So where is this bath? Perhaps I'd better go and see it. It would be good to get some film of it.'

That was a good point. While I was concentrating hard on my nervous collapse, Mark had carefully put the bath into storage over winter.

'Hi, Mark, where is she?'

'I've rented you a field near the river. She's there, being looked after.'

Mark, Phil and I arrived in a place called Upper Halliford,

somewhere near the Thames, west of Richmond. I brought the car to a stop outside a white cottage on the road adjoining a large iron gate. Behind it were buildings that looked unmistakably equestrian. Phil jumped out and pushed the gates open. I drove into the stable yard. A man appeared from behind one of the barn doors. Mark got out of the car.

'He's here for the bath.'

The drive snaked round the stables to two more sets of gates. The one on the left went into an empty, overgrown and rambling field of nettles. The one on the right led to a graveyard for dead mechanical stuff. I gasped with shock. If the bath was buried in there, we'd never get it out in one piece. The 'caretaker' opened the one on the right. I looked nervously at Phil.

'Oh my mistake . . . she's in here.'

I let out a sigh. He opened the one on the left.

'But that field is empty.'

'Nah . . . you take this and follow me.'

He handed me a sickle and began chopping his way through nettles with a scythe. After 90 minutes of chopping, slashing and being stung we made it to the familiar black-and-white Victorian tiles of *Lilibet II*. She had been totally safe all winter to everyone except sickle owners, people with dock leaves and the supernatural spectre of Death. Safe she might have been; fixed up and in a state to row she was not. Mark had very crudely patched up the storm damage from the last attempt but she certainly wasn't seaworthy and it appeared, looking at the wreck in the nettle patch, that even if I hadn't been felled with man flu, rowing her the previous September would have been almost impossible. I regarded her battered form and stroked her with an affection I'd only felt before for my dog. Like my dog there was a feeling that the bath had never let me down and had tried her best. Unlike my dog, for her loyalty I'd rewarded her with languishing in a nettle patch through a really bad winter.

We found several willing villagers and manhandled the bath onto the trailer to take her back to Richmond and the boatyard.

May passed in a welter of more weights, more swearing at Betty the Ergo, more running, and working on the bath to try to fix the problems of the year before.

In London all was total smiling, sunny bliss. In accordance with my earlier thoughts about weather, the weather in the Channel was awful. With a horrible sense of déjà vu, I could see that this year's attempt was going exactly the same way as the one the year before. So it was with some relief I picked up my phone on 8 June.

'Tim, it's Andy. I think we've got a chance tomorrow. Can you get the bath down here?'

I phoned the Admiral (ret.). He'd been away a lot more than I expected but amazingly picked up the phone. I put it to him that I wanted to go tomorrow.

'Don't attempt the Channel again unless it's flatter than the top of my gin.'

'Thank you, sir.'

Mark, the apprentices and I loaded the bath. A wailing penetrated the air.

'One love! One heart! Let's get together and feel all right . . .' Kenroy swayed drunkenly at the top of the ramp.

Gavin, my number two from the first attempt, had moved to Canada during the winter. He'd flown there to avoid the sea and moved to the most landlocked town he could find. This left me slightly stuck. Without a friend to help me run things on the shore, the bath project would basically be untenable.

Luckily one of my oldest friends had decided to quit work for a bit. Unlike my sketchy employment record since college, Chris had held down the same brilliant, corporate, grown-up job since university. He didn't take a gap year or run off to farm pigs and nutmeg in the West Indies like me. He'd been steadily funnelling cash away while working for a big company. My grasp of what his job actually entailed was vague. What I did know was that he'd done it for a long time and so now had decided to take a break to have a think about what he wanted to do next.

'Chris, it's Tim.'

'Hi, mate.'

'You know how you aren't sure what to do next . . .'

'Yes.'

'How about crossing the Channel with me, in the bath support boat?'

'I didn't see that coming . . . but all right I'm in. When?'

'Tomorrow? We'd be going down tonight.'

'I'll pack and be ready.'

Chris Gilmartin had entered the foam. I've known Chris almost as

long as I've known Ellen MacArthur. He has an eternally sunny outlook
on life. His positive attitude and my relative fear of danger have
combined in the past to lead us to attempt some very silly plans. We
were at school together for a few years too, during which time we
invented some pioneering roof-climbing escapades and fished each other
out of trouble most of the time. Now I needed him more than ever.

With the bath on the trailer, I said goodbye to Mark and the
apprentices and turned down a very kind offer of some medicinal
incense from Kenroy, just as Chris arrived with a rucksack.

'Brilliant. So this is the bath . . . I know I've said this before, but
you are a nutter.'

We jumped in the car and sped off.

'How will I communicate with you in the bath?'

Drat. I'd failed to plan a new communication system for the bath. I
didn't want to own up to incompetence to Chris this early in the project.

'Semaphore?'

'I'm not sure I know any.'

There was silence then Chris had a master plan. 'Mobile phones?'

'Good idea . . .' I thought it through thoroughly. 'Wait. It's not
great as people keep calling my mobile with irrelevant stuff. I don't
know that it's irrelevant till I've taken the call and by then I've
wasted valuable rowing time.'

Chris thought for a moment. 'Stop the car!'

'What?'

'There's a mobile shop. Let's get you a second mobile that only
I'll have the number to. Then if it rings, you know it's me.'

'Brilliant plan.'

The bell rang at the top of the door in the mobile-phone shop
in Richmond. The assistant slouched over.

'Yeah?'

Chris kicked off. 'Hi, we'd like a phone.'

'Any sort?'

'We just need it to work for 24 hours, then we're going to throw
it away.'

He looked a little startled. People probably normally want them
for longer. 'Well there's this one . . .'

I chipped in, 'Nope, doesn't seem sturdy enough for me. It needs
to be very tough . . . The sort where it doesn't matter if someone
stamps on it.'

'I've got just the thing.' He found us a cheap, brick of a phone.

'This looks like it would survive a gunfight.'

Startled the shop assistant changed into Nervous the shop assistant. 'Do you need it to make outgoing calls or just accept incoming?'

'It's not going to be making any outgoing calls.'

'Unless there's a real disaster.'

We both laughed. Nervous's eyes bulged as he filled out the paperwork.

'Can we pay cash?'

By this time, there was an odd dreamlike quality to Nervous. It could just be that he always floated in this semi-chimerical state. I've known people who've worked in shops who swear that the only way to deal with the boredom is to smoke what Kenroy would term a massive religious experiment. But I got the feeling it might be something else. I signed my name on the paperwork as Nervous summed up.

'One throw-away phone, able to withstand a gunfight, with one outgoing call on credit . . . and you're paying cash.'

'Thank you.'

As we left the shop, Chris was in buoyant mood and, expecting the bath crossing to succeed, he turned to Nervous and said, 'Watch the news tonight.'

Nervous whimpered as the door slammed. It was a very odd reaction. As we drove away I thought about it. Chris was obviously thinking about it too. We sat there thinking in silence: him in his woollen bobble-less hat and dark glasses, and me in dark glasses, a massive coat crammed full of stuff I thought I might need, and cap pulled firmly down over my head.

Chris got there first and turned to me. 'Do you think he thought we were dealing drugs?'

'Yep . . . I think he probably did. Or robbing a bank . . .'

'Oh good . . .'

'Should we turn around and go back to tell him we're not?'

'I'm not sure we've got time.'

Somewhere in Richmond, Nervous reached for the phone, thought about phoning the drug squad, and phoned his best mate instead.

After hitting a top speed of 10 mph on the M25, 17 mph on the M3, taking various side roads, getting lost several times and turning back onto roads we'd just left, we finally arrived in Folkestone. As I missed the Holy Grail Arch for the third time, everywhere in Folkestone phones went off and people began to gather at the pub next to the slipway. When we arrived, I'd never seen it so full. I tried and failed to get the bath trailer down the ramp. Chris had never been part of the unloading the bath symphony for two men, a trailer, car and tub played on the slipway, to an audience of be-fuddled pub patrons and lobster pots before, so he sat cringing, hiding behind his hand.

As he was entering his fifth separate hand puppet of embarrass-ment, he said, 'Do you want me to have a go?'

He made it down the ramp first time. Genius. We unloaded the bath as the shadow of a bear cast down on us from the quayside.

'Right – let's get this sorted this time. No more trying to die on me,' Andy smiled. 'We'll leave with the second tide . . .'

Dom and I had talked about this and I knew I had to be firm. Leaving on the second tide was risky as it meant I'd still be rowing when the day breezes started. The bath didn't perform well above the water in any sort of wind. The day breeze would also make the sea choppier. These two things combined would make things very tricky for me. Leaving on the first tide was even more risky as it meant having to get Andy up early in the morning.

'I think we should leave with the first tide . . .'

'That's at four in the morning!'

'Yes, it's early but . . .'

'It'll still be dark. Are you mad?'

'Yes.'

'I'm really not happy about this.'

A short, sharp conversation later, Chris and I checked into the hotel in Folkestone and booked an alarm call for 3.30 a.m.

'Here's your key, sir. Will you want supper?'

'Yes, please.'

'There's an evening of line dancing going on if you fancy it after supper?'

No gentleman has ever line-danced. We went up to our room to drop off kit. Back downstairs we soldiered through cremated remains in the restaurant. The geriatric cowboys and girls of Kent line-danced across the hallway. Falling prey to the elevator music again we arrived back in our room. My phone rang.

'Hello?'

'Hi, mate, it's Grillo. Just wondering if you're going to make it to my birthday?'

Damn and bother. Another thing I'd forgotten. It was his birthday in a few days.

'Erm . . . I'm not sure how to put this. I'm having another go at crossing the Channel in a bath . . . and I'm not sure how long it's going to take, or if I'll make it this time, or if I'll get sick again, or stuck in another storm, or if I do make it, how long it takes to row to London, or if rowing to London is even possible . . .'

He laughed.

'You're obsessed. No problem. Of all the excuses anyone could have, that's a great one – good luck.'

I put the phone down. Chris looked at me.

'Not nervous are you?'

'A bit.'

It was probably only about 10.30 p.m. when we turned out the lamp and tried to sleep with the gentle strains of nightclub bouncers pounding various heads onto the pavements of Folkestone ringing in our ears.

At 3.30 a.m. Chris started to force-feed me Weetabix. 'You're going to need the fibre.'

'Mate, we don't even have a bowl.'

'I know, that's why I've filled this mug with milk, I thought you could dunk them.'

'How many do you think I should have?'

'As many as you can. You're going to need the fibre.'

With the enthusiasm of a man trying to make another man sick, he dunked 12 Weetabix into the mug, opening and pouring hotel sugar sachets over each of them.

'Go on have one more . . .'

'Mate, if I have one more, I'll throw the lot up.'

'OK, that's probably enough.'

While Chris dunked a further two Weetabix for himself, I went to the bathroom and retched at the mere smell of them. Luckily I managed not to throw up. I used to like Weetabix but now just seeing an advert for them on the TV is enough to trigger the memory of that morning and induce emesis. Even before the happy face at the end of the commercial I'm to be found blowing chunks in an adjoining room. We left the hotel and went down to the water's edge.

The French again invoked emergency powers and decided that on that specific day of the year it was again illegal to row anything from Calais to Dover and Dover to Calais but not to row from Folkestone to Calais. Why this was the case was not clear but I took the chance and at exactly 4 a.m. pulled out of Folkestone Harbour. It was pitch black. Only the searchlights of Andy's boat and the lights along the harbour arm illuminated me.

The harbour we left was deserted except for a few battered drunks swaying gently in the breeze. On the support boat was Andy and his crewmate, Chris, Phil's mate who'd come with a camera, a reporter called Ollie who, following the last attempt, was the only one Kenny could persuade to come on the trip and a photographer called Jamie who'd been in the support boat the last time and had come again to see how it would all turn out.

'Keep an eye on the GPS system.'

I couldn't see anything so would have to rely on the GPS to avoid hitting something in the world's busiest shipping lane. It didn't seem to be working. Great. Things had started well.

As the sun began to break through the early morning sky I pulled hard and tried to keep to my course. The sheer weight and drag of the bath was enormous but the plan of leaving really early was working in that there was currently very little wind. In the emerging sun, the water was beautifully flat. I took full advantage and stroked out of the harbour in a lovely rhythm.

I shouted over to Andy, 'It seems busier than last time!'

'Yes, there's a naval exercise going on.'

Brilliant. Of all the days to choose to hold a naval exercise they had to pick the one day I was rowing. So now, as well as the masses of tankers that loomed out of the dawn light at me, frigates dashed up and down the shipping lanes. This was going to be tricky.

I kept rowing and made calculated guesses, going in front of some tankers and behind others, as I slalomed my way across the Channel. All the time the wind stayed low and the water, although not flat, was certainly nothing like as bad as it had been the last time. I made it across the first shipping channel and into the calm of the central reservation.

Each stroke necessitated a different battle with the sea as she shifted around and tried to avoid the oars. My wrists began to hurt, a dull ache started in my back and I began to notice the odd pain due to broken skin caused by the constant chaffing all over my body. On the plus side, I had an indomitable belief that with each stroke I was a tiny bit closer to finishing the ordeal.

About half an hour later, a tiny row began in my head between this formerly indomitable belief that I could make it and a new legion of doubt plaguing me that I'd fail again.

You can't stop for breaks when you're rowing the Channel as the current takes you off course. This meant there was no time to stop for food. Between strokes, I grabbed the occasional bite of banana and gulped down some of the special mix I'd created involving cranberry juice. Staying hydrated was the key to the whole thing. You're also always at risk from sunburn at sea due to the reflection of the sun on the water. I was sitting in the sea surrounded by a ring of copper. The sun's rays were intense and bounced unflinching off the copper and up at me. I had to work really hard to make sure I kept my fluid levels up. Dehydration would lead to a hopeless loss of direction and inability to function properly. I had to avoid this.

At 10 a.m. I realised I'd been rowing for six hours. Six hours into the journey was when the last attempt failed. This time I was still rowing and the thought that now I was in uncharted waters spurred me on. I was tired though, and my body had started to do strange things. My wrists began to hurt even more: my fingers seemed to respond less well, leading me to suspect that the tendons inside my wrists were starting to swell up. The blisters on my hands had got so big that many of them had burst. The result: my hands bled. Every stroke whipped my back.

My buttocks were becoming horrid. At first it felt like sweat running down onto the floor of the bath. Now, I looked down and realised I was sitting in small pools of my own blood and wet, seeping goo. The skin from my buttocks had gone again.

My mind started to wander. I tried to conjugate foreign and Latin verbs to keep it focused and working. I succeeded for a while but in the end my beleaguered brain packed its bags, hailed a cab, got in with a couple of buxom blondes and went off for a boozy lunch in Soho.

My eyes were fixed on the flagpole, which I was using as a sighter. I realised that if I kept the flagpole and showerhead in line with a fixed point on the horizon and kept the three of them aligned, it meant I was going in a roughly straight line. Very occasionally my eyes darted down to the compass to check this but it was always basically correct. On this attempt the compass seemed to be working; at least for now. I looked back up at the flagpole. Due to my treatment by the French on the last trip, this time I'd refused to fly the French courtesy flag. The Red Ensign hung alone on the flagpole.

At 10.35 a.m. I whimpered. The Red Ensign that had hung so beautifully limp on the flagpole suddenly kicked up and puffed away from it. Instantly I knew what this meant. The wind was coming. A single tear rolled down my face. I was feeling quite physically tired and now had the wind to deal with.

By this stage my wrists were being pulled apart with every stroke. Normally, rowing boats are made as light as possible to avoid this problem but the bath weighed a third of a tonne. This coupled with the very awkward angle that I was forced to use to finish the catch, due to the height of the sides of the bath, meant that they had swollen up and were in a terrible state. I looked down at them and realised that they were the width of my hands at their widest point. The pain was intense. Now the tendons were so swollen, I couldn't straighten my fingers. As I just needed them to curl round the oars, this was not a problem. When the sea was behaving so stunningly I'd just gritted my teeth and pulled on but now the wind was a factor, things would get bad. My morale sank.

Soon, the sea began to be commanded by the wind. First the chop got marginally worse. Then small dancing white horses, more dancing white foals, began to appear on the tops of the chop. I whimpered again. This attempt would end like the first. What would happen to me then?

At this point the current kicked in with a vengeance. I wrapped my bleeding claws around the oars and pulled hard. Somewhere deep within me a dark part of my mind woke up and began to drive me on. With a Herculean effort I rowed for the next 20 minutes only to remain absolutely still. I saw a marker buoy that I had passed a few miles away that, if anything, seemed to get closer, meaning that I was being swept back to England. I increased my pace. Being taken in the grip of the current back towards the UK meant the end of the attempt. As I tried so hard to pull forward, the current succeeded in pushing me back. It was a battle I knew I couldn't win.

I thought hard. I may not have been able to beat the tide in the long run but I could hold off her victory for as long as I could breathe. I kept rowing at between 28 and 30 strokes per minute, which, after six and a half hours rowing, was simply the very best I could manage. Ten more crucial minutes went by and I continued to row at the height of my ability and strength to stay absolutely still. The marker buoy just was not getting any further away.

Andy shouted over from the support boat, 'It's no good, Tim, we're going to have to call this off. We're going nowhere.'

Gasping for air, I couldn't speak but words ripped viscerally from the pit of my stomach.

'No! Ten minutes more!'

I was not going to give in. Either the tide would give in or I would not be coming back. That was the decision I made. I increased my stroke rate and gasped for breath. I was in a lot of trouble.

Chris yelled from the boat, 'Come on, Tim!'

Tears ran down my face. The pain was unbearable. My thighs burnt as, totally exhausted, they powered me up and down the slide. Blood, tears and goo mingled in the bath. I thought bitterly of how hilarious rowing the Channel in a bath had seemed, cursed myself, and kept rowing. Simply put, my body was at breaking point; my heart raced blood and oxygen around my veins, trying to keep my exhausted frame in the race against the tide. My mind became important and cruel. It would not let me stop. Something very frightening was happening. I found the truest expression of mind over matter I've ever known.

Again, Andy's voice cut through the air, 'Come on, Tim, that's over ten more minutes! Let's call this a day.'

'Ten more!'

I pulled as though my life depended on it. I just would not give in: all this gut-wrenching effort to sit totally still. Then through the tears, I realised the buoy that I'd been sighting off appeared to have moved further away. I kept pulling like a maniac and checked again and sure enough, the buoy had moved. I was going forward. The current had given me a chance. I continued to row at the same intense pace, not sure how long the current would give me to get somewhere. I pulled on, got a chance for some rhythm and took it.

Andy leant over the side. 'That's it! You're moving forward now!'

Tears ran down my face into the bath. I looked up to the sky, 'Thank you, God.'

Now I inched forwards. After just over 40 minutes of sitting still, now each stroke took me closer to France.

Beating the tide had exhausted me. It was a peak in the trip I hadn't expected to have to conquer. I hadn't planned for it. I was quite prepared to row for 12 hours if necessary to get the crossing done. I'd trained hard to be able to do that. However, I hadn't factored in this sudden burst of energy that would be needed between the sixth and seventh hours. I'd often seen marathon runners who'd had to run one lap faster than they planned forced to pull out of the race, because they'd exhausted themselves and this was the same result that beating the tide seemed likely to inflict on me.

My body had taken a serious hammering over the last seven hours and that was a factor too. But my brain, or whatever it is within humans that drives us, was fast becoming unstoppable. It sought the coastline of Gaul with the feverish desperation of a drug addict.

'Please let me stop!' I wailed, not at the support boat, or the people on it but at the thing in my head that drove me on. I screamed, I cried, I prayed for death as a blessed relief. The dark place in my mind that forced me on began to conspire with my internal organs. The exterior of my body was shot to pieces. It was in a lot of pain but internally the FitzHigham organs were intent on never stopping. Air came into the lungs. My heart ran like a well-oiled engine. Blood coursed through my veins and out of all the various cuts. I felt like a massive industrial machine. Fuel came in, was converted to energy, and powered me forward. All the lightness in my psyche wailed against the primeval maniac now in control both of my brain and this indomitable factory.

I entered hour eight. I turned round and could finally see France. She had sneaked up on me again like a ninja. My left shoulder, that had been so badly damaged in the last attempt, now began to throb again. I kept going but was in a lot of pain.

Andy shouted over from the support boat, 'Tim, you're rowing back towards England – turn round!'

I checked the compass. He was right. Probably by straining to look at France or due to the pain in my shoulder, I'd somehow managed to turn the boat away from France. I wasn't actually rowing directly back towards England, more in the direction of Portugal. But either of them is the wrong direction when you're aiming for France. I corrected my heading but my left arm was beginning to be a little less than useful.

'Guide Me O Thou Great Jehovah' flooded round my head. I thought I might die to John Wesley. My mind battled itself. My body battled my mind and itself. The church choir singing John Wesley battled with Kurt Cobain and the crashing chords of Nirvana. My head swam: what had started as a mere slight argument in my mind now escalated into a near-schizophrenic war zone. I looked over the side of the bath at the cool of the water and thought, 'I could swim the last bit . . . that would make it all stop.' Suddenly the face in the photos at my grandmother's house flashed out of the water at me. Finally perhaps I understood something more of what had happened that day in the Second World War.

Chris Gilmartin's voice cut through the air and hit my mind like a life preserver. 'Tim, four miles to go – pull hard!'

The current around the point of Cap Gris Nez is very strong. It got up now as the wind got worse. Many people make it this far and still fail. My arm finally gave in. I was left with just one decent functioning arm – my right one. My fingers had become so caked in blood and the tendons so buggered that I couldn't stretch them out. I wrapped the claw on the end of my good arm around the oar on my left and kept pulling. Normally this would have made me go in a massive circle. Luckily for me, the current was so strong in the opposite direction, that by pulling on one oar against it, the net effect was that I was going straight. My head hit the oar and I came round. I realised I'd momentarily passed out.

Gilly's voice cut through the air again. 'Tim – only three miles to go – row like a bastard!'

Something within me snapped. I entered a very dark place. Although the sun was streaming down on me, all I could see were shadows and darkness. I pulled and pulled and pulled. Up to the top of the seat, put the oar in, power back down to the bottom of the seat. The monotony of the action did nothing to numb the pain. Periodically if the current dropped slightly I'd have to swap my good arm to the other oar but for the main I kept with the one blade and used the current instead of the other oar.

I was broken. I felt like a small girl out there on the mighty sea. I thought I could see all the people I saw on my training rows at Richmond floating alongside me out at sea. I waved at them. I looked over my shoulder. There was the watchtower of the Navy base at Cap Gris Nez. Would the Navy come out? I retreated back into the hallucinogenic haze of my thoughts. My body was shattered, I hit my head on an oar and realised I'd briefly passed out again.

Gilly shouted from the boat, 'Two miles to go: keep going!'

The words 'never give in' kept thudding round my head. It was a terrifying place to be in mentally. You realise how people are able to become killers. Nothing seems to matter any more but finding a way to ease your pain. All this for a hilarious plumbing-based ruse.

'Ah! Le bain! Le bain! Bonjour! Bonjour!'

I looked up; again, I may have passed out – it was difficult to tell what was reality. There was a roar of engines and boats around me. Had the French Navy come to arrest me?

I focused on the boat nearest to me. In it was a sturdy French fisherman in a hat with as much oil on him as Andy. Suddenly there was a small flotilla of French fishing vessels around me, who all cheered me on and surrounded me as I rowed towards the coast. The last mile and a half was the moving celebration of the Entente Cordial I always knew was possible. The French government and Navy may have made things impossible for me, but the fishermen of France had come out to show their support.

I rallied. Something ancient in me stirred. Broken I may have been but I would not let the French see that.

The beach at Cap Gris Nez is stony and many ships get wrecked on it. The stony beach shelves nastily. Above it is an incline to a ridge at the top. On this ridge is the naval watchtower. Arriving at the beach I looked around. I thought someone would come and welcome me. I would even have been happy if there'd just been a sailor with a pair of handcuffs (in Soho, that constitutes a good night out). But there was no one on that beach. I was very down. Then I looked up to the ridge at the top. It was lined with little groups of French people, cheering and waving. The true Entente Cordial spirit was at work again, brightening up the barren and rocky headland. These people had broken into their own naval base to come and say well done. It proved one vital thing to me: the people who really hate the French government are the French.

I looked up to the ridge, a tear welling up in my eye, and tried to think of a way to express this love. I thought of my GCSE French and how little it had prepared me to deal with this situation. I looked at the boats floating next to me then faced uphill again. I addressed the crowd.

'Merci . . . merci . . .'

There was a huge cheer.

'. . . Où est la gare?'

There was silence. I heard muttering. Then laughter: then another huge cheer.

I heard Chris and Andy on the support boat, 'What's he said?'

'He's just asked the way to the station.'

'Looks like he could use a train on the way back!'

The French Navy did not arrive on the beach that afternoon. The French people lining the cliff top and in the small fishing boat flotilla around me had shown the true spirit of their nation: finally, fraternité won out in the end.

I had made it. I'd made the first successful crossing of the English Channel in a bath. A phone rang.

Chris picked it up. 'Tim, it's Dom . . .'

I rowed out to the support boat. Gilly handed me the phone over the side.

'Dom . . .'

'Chris . . .'

'No, it's me, Tim . . .'

'What . . . has it failed again?'

I burst into tears.

'No, I've made it . . . I've made it . . .'

'Wait . . .' He turned to the people around him. 'He's made it!'

I heard another huge cheer down the phone. I just kept repeating, 'I've made it . . . I've made it.'

Chris leant over the side of the support boat and took the phone back. 'He's a bit tired and emotional . . . Sure, I'll tell him.'

I waved at the French again. I'd made it across the Channel in nine hours and six minutes to join Bleriot, Captain Webb and Dr Blanchard in the history of that illustrious waterway.

Andy appeared on deck. He didn't seem that comfortable with

the enormous display of emotion going on so rubbed his hands on his overalls, looked down and said, 'Well done! I didn't think I'd ever see that! Now, you should probably check the safety hatches.'

I opened up the first one. 'This one is all fine.'

Just the small amount of water in it you'd expect for a boat that had been out at sea for most of the day. I opened the second to see water sloshing everywhere. 'This one is about 80% full!'

Andy appeared back on deck looking shocked. 'What!'

He looked down over my shoulder through the hatch. 'Bloody hell! No wonder she was heavy. With that amount of water in one of them, it's lucky you made it when you did or she would have capsized again! Let's make for home.'

I slumped on the deck of the support boat lying on my front looking out to sea. I looked down at my hands and wrists. My tendons were so swollen it would be two days before I would be able to use a knife and fork again or even curl my fingers round a pen. I couldn't sit down, as my buttocks were lamentable. After over nine hours on a tiny wooden seat, my arse was bleeding. My scrotum was more slit than a pair of 1980s jeans. It was horribly swollen. Men don't normally declare, 'I was gutted my balls had got larger', but I simply couldn't close my legs. I moved more bow-leggedly than John Wayne. I tried to be polite to the journalist and cameraman on the support boat but at the same time, every time the inside of my thigh brushed against one of my swollen raw testicles, I wanted to scream.

I tried to phone the various people who were closest to me. I wanted to let them know what had happened but I was totally unable to use the phone. In the end, Gilly dialled numbers and held the phone to my ear, as it was too small for me to grasp properly.

'Kenny?'

'Yes, Chris. Please say he's not dead.'

'No, it's me – I've made it!'

'You legend! You're a complete nutter but well done!'

Many other conversations like this happened as I shouted into the tiny phone over the roar of Andy's engines. Giving up on yelling as a plan I dictated more texts to Chris.

Somewhere in the Yangtze Valley, China, a phone buzzed. Up to his knees in mud, carrying a camera, Phil Carr punched the air. 'He's made it!' Phil would hopefully be back before I got to London but for now his number two had got the shots.

I went into the cabin. I couldn't hear too well as both of my ears had a combination of chilblains from the wind across the sea and sunburn from the intense sunshine. This had led to pus getting into my ears and causing them to be slightly blocked.

Andy looked round. 'Great job . . . really proud of you . . . oh my knees . . .'

'You should get them looked at, mate . . . and again, thank you. I couldn't have made it without you.'

I went below deck and closed the hatch. I tried to take off the rowing lycra gently but ended up ripping off even more skin. I took the surgical spirit out of my backpack and rubbed it into my inflamed, lacerated scrotum. Having had some small experience of this before, I knew I had exactly two seconds before the unbearable pain hit. I used them to pull the lycra up again. Then pain. The last nine hours were put into their proper context by the agony. I looked at the porthole and passed out.

When I came round we were just outside the harbour arm at Folkestone. The sun was streaming down. Like John Wayne in *The Searchers* I waddled out on deck and looked back across the Channel at where France probably still was. After a really tough year and a half I'd finally laid to rest my Channel ghost. As I looked at the sun bouncing off the water I felt satisfied. If my great-uncle had known I'd made it across – even in such a stupid way – I think he would have smiled. A warm, happy feeling seeped through the pain.

Now there was just the small matter of the 170 miles between Tower Bridge and me.

CHAPTER NINE

HUMPTY DUMPTY HAD
A GREAT FALL

'He'll never sell ice creams going at that speed.'

Eric Morecambe

Andy pulled his boat into Folkestone Harbour as I rowed the battered bath behind. People gathered on the quay shouted out to us, 'What happened?'

Andy looked down at me then shouted up, 'I thought I'd let him make it this time!'

A cheer went up. Many of them I recognised as line dancers. They began to disperse. I'm not sure if they were there to welcome me or if they were just there walking off the effects of the previous night's country-and-western-based overexertion. Either way, it was good to feel they might have turned up to welcome the bath home. The general happiness was mixed with tension. The tide had definitely turned and the water was going out: we had to get the boat and bath moored before we lost the water in the harbour.

We moored the bath at the inner slipway. Andy moored up slightly further out towards the outer harbour, near the low swing bridge that had claimed the showerhead a year before. I went aboard his boat.

'What now? How's the weather for an attempt to make it up to Dover in the morning?'

I could see the shock in Andy's face mirrored in Chris's sunglasses. He took them off and revealed that Andy's shock was nothing compared to his own. They could both see the terrible state my body was in. I knew it too but was buzzing with the fact that I'd achieved what everyone thought was impossible and crossed the Channel.

'Let's have a look at the charts.'

Andy took out the charts of Folkestone and the stretch of the coast up to Dover and then on to Sandwich. I followed the line of the coast northwards.

'Where's London?'

In my head London wasn't that much further than Folkestone by sea. As I looked at the charts it became apparent that London wasn't even on the same charts as Folkestone. London turned out not to be on any of the charts Andy had on the boat. I looked at Andy. 'I'll get the atlas from the car.'

Andy laughed. 'It's not what we normally do at sea, but then we don't normally row baths.'

I knew where London was of course and I knew where Folkestone was, but I think I'd been in denial and wanted them to be closer to each other. By ignoring their positions I think I thought they might move a bit nearer to each other to help me out.

We left the boat and headed to shore. Some of the remaining line dancers went to shake my hand. I smiled and showed them my hands apologetically. They winced, much as I'd have done if they'd shaken my hand. They congratulated me verbally and let me waddle off towards the car.

I overheard one lady turn to the man next to her as they wandered off towards the hotel, 'So he's come from Wales?'

'No, France.'

'Oh, that's all right then – that's much closer than Wales.'

Chris, Andy and I gathered around the atlas on the bonnet of the car. I opened the page at London and Kent. Thinking aloud, I said, 'London really is quite far away . . .'

I'm not sure Chris thought I was serious about the London leg of the journey but he measured things nevertheless. 'It's about 160-odd miles, give or take, especially the way you're going to have to do it.'

'Brilliant.'

Dom and I had come up with a plan and divided the journey round Kent to London up into sections; distances we felt I could row in a day taking into account the important tide and current issues. The next leg on our plan was to have been Dover to Ramsgate. Due to not being able to row from France to Dover, I'd now have to insert a new leg into the plan, which would have to be Folkestone to Dover, then Dover to Ramsgate. Looking down at the atlas the enormity of it all hit me. London was a very long way away.

Why had I said I'd row to Tower Bridge? My body was in a terrible state. All I really wanted to do was sleep. No one had ever gone to these lengths to win one pint of beer before. But I was committed to it and wanted to get started straight away.

Andy's phone rang; he picked it up and listened intently, 'Right . . . Yes, I'll tell him . . .'

He turned, in what was a rapidly fading light. 'The weather's turned again, you'll need to wait at least a day to get up the next bit to Dover. Also I'd suggest you find that leak in the flotation device and fix it . . .'

'Has anyone ever rowed to London from here before?'

Andy thought. 'Not as far as I know. I'm not even sure how possible it is . . . but then I've said that before.'

Fleet Street's Finest, well, more Bermondsey's Finest – Jamie the photographer and Ollie the journalist – had gone to a hotel room to 'file copy'. My phone rang: it was Ollie. 'Tim, I'm up in the room, can you come and just check a couple of things before I send this off?'

I hung up as Andy said, 'I've got to get home. My knees have taken a battering, I've really got to get them sorted out.'

'Thanks, mate, I know it's been tough but we've done it. Keep me posted on the weather and I'll find that leak.'

Chris took me, tired, and in a lot of pain, to the hotel room to see Ollie. Jamie the photographer opened the door.

'I've got some great shots, I've filed and really should leave soon. I've got to photograph some party girls in the West End tonight.'

He must lead a very surreal life. I stood with bleeding buttocks and answered Ollie's questions before he and Jamie left for London having filed the story using a laptop and the hotel's sporadic Internet connection.

As they were leaving, Ollie turned. 'The room's booked all night if you fancy a lie down – I won't be using it from London.' I heard the latch go on the door. Next thing I remember was Chris saying, 'Sorry to have to wake you, mate. We could have a problem.'

I'd been asleep for a few hours. As I'd slept, the tide had gone out of the harbour.

Chris and I stood alone on the pavement outside the hotel, looking down at the bath on a mud flat in the empty harbour.

'Andy wasn't sure the bath should stay in the water with the bad weather tonight but how do we get it out with no way of floating it onto the trailer. There's no water – we definitely can't carry it with just two of us.'

'Hmmm . . . I'm not sure sleep was my best plan.'

'Also, that mud has got really sticky. I'm not sure we're going to be able to stand up in that for long.'

I could see his point. I looked at the bath, the mud flat and the conspicuous lack of water. The bath couldn't stay there, as it might not survive the predicted storm. I needed a plan.

'Right, let's go to the pub and think this one out . . .'

'Uh oh . . . Isn't that how we got into this mess in the first place?'

We pushed open the door and entered one of Folkestone's feistiest pubs, full of very big, loud men. It was the sort of place that even Andy would befriend an undertaker before going into. Chris, who is smaller than me, looked like a lost five-year-old among the hulking masses that surrounded the bar. At just over six foot I might have passed for aged 12. It went dark. We stared up at the grimacing face of the barman. He could have been the landlord and it might have been his attempt at a smile. It was difficult to tell. I became aware I was wearing pink socks.

'What can I do for you?'

Never before have I been more aware of my pink socks. He blew smoke over the bar.

'Funny sort of outfit . . .'

Never before have I been more aware of lycra, which I was still wearing. I may have conquered the Channel but right now could have been just seconds away from death or an entirely new set of sexual choices induced by a misunderstanding over my attire. Chris coughed nervously and his eyes widened. He'd just noticed the pink socks.

I looked the barman directly in the eye, 'I've just rowed the Channel in a bath and I need some help lifting the bath off the mud in the harbour. I'd like to buy a drink for anyone who would like to help, and one for you, landlord.'

The pub went silent. This was dangerous. In my head when Nelson said things like this, people cheered. The silence continued as the words bounced around the inside of the landlord's head. He chewed his cigarette.

'It was you in that bath?'

'Yes, and I've got it stuck on the mud.'

There was a further grim silence. All eyes in the pub (and there were an odd number of eyes I noted) were fixed on a small lycra apparition and his sidekick who might have passed for a football.

'All right, lads, who's going to help this nutter lift his bath out of the water?'

Then there was a cheer. Chris was in total disbelief. Nothing in our various adventures had prepared him for this. We led the pub out into what was now starlight and down the inner harbour slipway. Between 10 to 14 massive men lifted the bath out of the mud and carried it up. We were all caked in mud. If I'd flicked mud at these men in any other context I'd have been dead before it left the spoon. But lifting the bath, they could not have been happier. Chris ran off to get the car and trailer. He arrived back to find the rugby team of men and me, having enjoyed a mud bath, standing smiling at the top of the inner slipway holding aloft the copper one ready to deposit it on the trailer. He pulled the trailer over and we gently loaded the bath. It had never been that easy to load the bath in the whole history of the project so far.

Tightening the last ropes I shouted in triumph, 'To the pub – thank you so much! Drinks are on me!' I sounded more like the Milky Bar Kid than Nelson, but a cheer went up and we went back to the pub. On the way, I went white. Chris noticed.

'What's up, mate? That's gone well.'

'There are no pockets in a rowing lycra.'

'Good job I've got my wallet then.'

In the pub our new friends wanted to know all about the Channel crossing in the bath and we told them the stories. The things we'd seen, the failed attempt. Chris was far better at putting things into words than me. I was still so sore that my focus was more on basic things like not fainting. The landlord brought us both drinks: very kind of him.

I had originally planned to stay in the bath that night but the predicted storm, the problems with the bath's flotation tank and my battered body changed that plan. Chris and I left the pub and walked back to the hotel. Back in the room, I phoned Kenny.

'Well done. That really is super.'

'Thanks, mate – I'm pretty shot to pieces and we're stuck here for at least a day.'

'But you made it. Now we just have to get you round Kent and up to here.'

'Yes, it's a bit further than I . . .'

'Where are you? It's a very odd echo.'

'Erm . . . in the hotel.'

'I know that but . . . are you in the bath?'

'Erm . . . yes.'

'I would have thought you'd had enough of them for one day!'

'I think I'm addicted.'

'Have a great night and well done.'

I sunk back into the bath and let out a scream as the water hit my cuts. Chris shouted through from the next room. 'You all right, mate?'

'Yes, fine thanks.'

And in a way I was. My body was in a very bad way but I'd made it across. With the Channel vanquished my journey could really begin. Finally, after a year of the sponsored bath project, people at last had something to sponsor.

The predicted storm was not as bad as everyone thought it would be. Again, that's the thing with trying to predict weather. The leak, however, was much worse than everyone thought. Mark sent down advice as we worked hard to fix the problem and dry out the bath. My plan to carry straight on with rowing round to London had been immediately thwarted.

Eventually, after trying to fix it near the water in great weather, we had to admit defeat. I found doing anything dextrous almost impossible as the tendons in my wrists were still so swollen I couldn't clench my hands. There was only so much Chris could manage on his own so we took the bath back up to Mark in Richmond to get it sorted. I folded a bath towel and put it on the passenger seat. There was no way I could drive with my hands in the state they were. I bled onto the towel as Chris drove us towards Richmond.

Under cover of darkness Chris and I dropped the bath off in Richmond for Mark. There was no great arrival there. The only person around was the restaurateur who owned the floating restaurant next to the boatyard.

'So you made it across the Channel then?'

'Yes.'

'What now?'

'I'm going to get this fixed and row up to London.'

He looked at me waddling like a hampered crab, smiled and said, 'You make it up to London and there's a bottle of champagne in my restaurant for you.'

We unhitched the bath and trailer at the boatyard and Chris dropped me off in Chelsea. After telling Grillo I wouldn't make it to his birthday I thought it might be nice to surprise him. We stopped off to get a card. Chris wrote in it for me, as I still couldn't hold a pen.

The pub door swung open. Grillo turned. 'What the . . .'

'Hi, I'd shake your hand but it's probably not the best idea. Happy birthday.'

It was a very special night. I basked in the very warm glow of being around my friends and enjoyed them enjoying the fact I'd finally succeeded.

'We're eating in the room upstairs . . .'

We all filed up the stairs behind the birthday boy. My heart sank as we entered the upstairs room, and saw a collection of wooden seats. The landlord had clearly got a job lot of them from a condemned Methodist chapel. I whimpered and grimaced as I sat. It is impossible to get comfortable on a former non-conformist chapel chair when you have no skin on your buttocks. I didn't mention this to anyone. However, there was one thing I couldn't disguise: the state of my hands. Everyone was so kind in not making a fuss. It was the sort of evening that would have been known in

Victorian literature as a hero's welcome. Girls' eyes sparkled and men patted me on the back. It was lovely. But any pompous thoughts of heroism were soon as burst as the blisters on my plums. My hands were still so butchered I couldn't pick up a knife and fork and the kind girl sitting next to me had to cut up my food for me. A man meekly having to be fed by a girl as his buttocks gently bled is not the image of Victorian heroism that would inspire Tennyson.

The next day I spent at the boatyard with Mark. There was very little I could do practically but at least I could tell him the problems I'd faced and how the bath had held up in the water. One thing was uppermost in my mind: how to stop the problems with my wrists that I'd had rowing the Channel. After talking to various people and thinking about the problem, it seemed that it was the angle at which I was pulling through the stroke that was causing the trouble. I left the boatyard that night with the question of how to fix it rattling round my head.

That night I arrived in Pimlico. Gliding down the street towards me was a friend of mine, Laura.

'Darling, I'm so super-proud of you,' she smiled.

We hugged and went off to find some food. I chose the restaurant.

'Are you sure you want to eat here, darling? That one we passed up the street looked much nicer . . .'

My mind was set. Nothing would change it. This one had soft chairs.

Over food, I told her all about the bath trip so far. The other advantage of the place we entered was that it was food you could just about get away with eating with your hands. Phew. At least I'd avoided having to ask her to feed me like the poor girl from the night before. She laughed and smiled as I rolled out the full story of the crossing. The meal passed so fast that had the gentle cough of the proprietor not brought it to our attention, neither of us would have noticed we were the only ones left in the place. At first I thought me eating with my hands had cleared the restaurant but it was late: although I left the proprietor an extra tip just in case.

The next morning the weather was still terrible in Folkestone. I arrived at the boatyard in Richmond to help Mark. Again, there wasn't much I could do but submit to the teasing of the apprentices. They were proud that the bath had made it but still couldn't resist the jokes at the expense of my hands. A knife, fork or normal-sized pen was too small for my battered hands but Mark had an oversized thick pencil. I could hold this in very short bursts before the tendons in my hands and wrists went funny again. I had come up with a thought in the restaurant the night before of how to solve the angle problem. I handed my drawing on an envelope to Mark.

'What's this?'

'I've had an idea for some new oars to help me avoid getting swollen wrists.'

Mark held the envelope in his hand and said nothing. The apprentices stopped. I'd not designed anything since Douglas and I had come up with the bath design over a year before.

Mark sighed. 'I'll see what I can find.'

I went to put the kettle on; at least this was a job that my hands could manage.

Over the next couple of days, Mark managed to get the bath fixed. Finally, the leak seemed under control. We then spent two days, while the weather was still horrible in Folkestone, testing and refining my new ideas for oars. The thing with new blades is that it's all in the gearing. The width of the blades versus the overall length of the oar gives you the difficulty you will experience in pulling it through the water. A very long oar with a very thick blade will be almost impossible to pull through the water. I needed very long oars as this would make the angle I pulled through the stroke at less painful, so we had to take the width of the blade down. However, you don't want to take the blade too thin, as then you can't get the purchase on the water you need to power through it. It's a question of trial and error. How wide could the blade be and still allow me to pull it through the water successfully?

For two days we faffed around trying to get this right. There was nothing else we could have done as the prevailing wind at Folkestone was in totally the wrong direction. Learning to row with totally new oars is like learning to row again. It all feels funny and wrong. Especially if they are as different from the pair you've been used to as my new ones were. I arrived back from one testing row.

Mark looked down from the slipway. 'Who'd have thought when you first started . . .' He turned to someone on the bank. 'Didn't know anything about rowing and now he's designing his own blades . . .'

I got out and peeled the lycra from the still-bleeding cuts on my bottom.

'The oars feel much better. I'd say we're there.'

Silently I wondered if my bottom would ever stop bleeding. My phone flashed in the bath, it was Andy: 'Tim, I've got to see someone about my knees but Eric says he'll be your support boat up to Dover.'

Testing the new blades had been useful. Not only had we tested the new blades but also seen how painful it was for me to row. My body was not holding up well. My buttocks were healing very slowly and I was still walking like John Wayne due to swollen plums. My wrists were also in a very bad way. There was a dull, thudding ache in them. On the plus side, I was now able to use a knife and fork. Mark told the apprentices I was now going to try to make it back to London. They took one look at me and laughed. My ravaged body enabled me to move with the graceful alacrity of a near-dead man of 97. I didn't look like I could make it up to Richmond High Street let alone row the 160 or so miles I was suggesting.

The bath was ready again. Now, the weather in Folkestone turned vile. I waited in Richmond, rubbing cream into cuts and surgical spirit onto my plums.

'Tim, it's Eric, can you get the bath down here? We've got a chance of making it to Dover.'

Mark, the apprentices, Kenroy and I loaded the bath. Chris arrived and we sped off down to Folkestone. Arriving, Chris turned the car to the left.

'What are you doing? It's not here we turn, it's . . .'

My words trailed off. We'd found the Holy Grail Arch on the first attempt. Remarkable!

We unloaded the bath using the third movement of the unloading the bath symphony for two men, a trailer, car and tub on the slipway. By now I was even looking forward to the drum solo played on the tables. I pre-emptively bought drinks for the packed pub as Chris reversed into lobster pots.

We floated the bath and Chris and I met Eric. He was a tanned, grey-haired fisherman with a moustache. He was slightly softer spoken than Andy and seemed slightly older.

'So this is the bath . . .'

'Yes.'

'Right, let's get going to Dover then.'

Chris decided to stay on land that day. We'd realised on the way down that if both of us went on the water, leaving the car in Folkestone, how would we get back from Dover to Folkestone?

Eric took his boat out into the outer harbour. I did up the shoes that are fixed to the footplate in the bath, put the new oars in the gate, fastened the catches and we left.

The weather was stunning, if a little windy, but Dom was right in that the wind had been significantly less than on previous days and was in vaguely the right direction for me to row.

I left the outer harbour arm at Folkestone. It was a relief. The tidal nature of Folkestone had been a constant battle throughout the whole project so far. Dover was not tidal, I'd been told, so I couldn't wait to see it. Only being able to get the bath out of Folkestone in two very specific windows of time each day was something which had made dealing with the weather even trickier. When we'd got a snatch of good weather there had been no water in the harbour and vice versa. It had been a case of incompatibility worse than a flamenco dancer dancing the tango with a man who could only reel to the strains of a band playing the waltz. Yet, with every stroke, as I left her, I began to miss Folkestone. She'd been consistently annoying but I'd grown very fond of her. Without this deep-rooted illogical impulse, divorce lawyers would have much more work.

The first part of the row was very good. The current did what we thought it would and there was very little wind. Always on my right-hand side were the massive white cliffs. They'd seemed impressive when I saw them from halfway across the Channel but now, creeping along the base of them, they were simply awesome. As I looked up at them, their sheer angle seemed implausible and the thought that they might at any moment collapse on top of me gave me an extra boost to go faster. I was focusing in my head when Eric shouted, 'Tim! Look out!'

I looked behind me to see that the white cliffs and I were not running parallel as I thought but that they had crept up behind me to form an impenetrable headland. The sea whipped up. When you get too close to the shore, all the sea wants to do is take you in to the shore and smash you up.

'Come out to sea!'

Eric was yelling for all he was worth. I pulled hard but the current was now very much in control. A frantic 15 minutes ensued. Eric couldn't get me as his boat could not get into that shallow depth of water. I was on my own, facing the white cliffs of Dover. Like David and Goliath, only with less-convincing odds. I diverted all my strength into pulling on one oar. This wouldn't be the most beautiful or efficient bit of rowing but with luck it would save me from being smashed on the rocks.

I looked behind me and saw with relief that I'd managed it. I'd cheated my way out of the clutches of the white cliffs and learnt a very important lesson. If I got too close to the shore, I wasn't really able to fight the current.

An hour later Eric shouted again, 'Stop rowing for a bit, Tim . . .'

'What?'

'We're at Dover, you've made it! We've got to wait for a passenger boat to leave before we can get into the harbour.'

I couldn't quite believe it. I'd made it to Dover. I looked behind me at the mighty harbour and castle perched on top. Somewhere up there was the Coastguard station where I'd had a meeting with Mr Merryweather a year before. I waved, just in case he was looking out of a very powerful telescope. Wash from the wake of the harbour arm or a boat jolted me back into focus. I checked the time and looked at the charts – I say charts, it was actually a photocopy of the road atlas – I was using to navigate. I sat in the bath, thought through what Dom and I had discussed about what he thought the sea, wind and tides might do and measured things on the road atlas. After a few moments Eric shouted over, 'Shall we go into Dover then?'

'I want to have a crack at making it to Ramsgate . . . What do you think?'

'It's not a bad idea while you've got the weather . . . I'm up for it.'

'Great. I'll phone Chris.'

Getting reception is not easy, especially when a massive passenger boat is trying its best to scuttle you, but I managed it.

'Mate, we're going to try for Ramsgate.'

'Is that wise?'

It was a fair question. There's not a suitable harbour between Dover and Ramsgate and if the weather turned, I'd be very stuck. Trying to get to Ramsgate was a very risky business and if I didn't make it, I'd have to turn back and seek shelter in Dover.

'I know the risks and just want to take advantage of the weather.'

'I'll phone Dom and let him know.'

I passed Dover and went on up the coast past St Margaret's Bay. The light wasn't great due to cloud cover and the wind wasn't being very helpful but I'd come up with a plan to deal with it. The good news was that the wind was coming in from an angle behind me. When this happened I'd turn the bath so that the wind came directly behind me and used the wind hitting the roll top of the bath, as you would use a sail. This meant that while I was doing this I was technically rowing in slightly the wrong direction but I had the advantage of being able to use the wind. When the wind changed or I'd rowed so far off course that I had to alter direction, I'd row almost at right angles to the wind. When I was slightly the other side of the course I wanted to be on, I'd turn the bath so that I could use the wind hitting the roll top from behind again and row on. The net effect when seen from above was that I was rowing in a massive zigzag. I'm not sure what made me think of doing this, it just seemed the easiest way of getting further and harnessing the wind.

By Deal, I'd really got this zigzag technique sorted and raced past the pier there at some speed. People waved and I saw a figure that looked suspiciously like Chris racing furtively down the pier towards them. I wasn't close enough to see clearly, so it could just have been an elderly man pursued by bees.

I arrived at the southern tip of Sandwich Bay. Dom and I had come up with two plans for this part of the journey. If the weather was bad or the wind was against me I was to hug the coastline and struggle as best I could around the bay. If the weather was with me I could take a risk and go in a straight line across the bay. But if the weather turned or current frisked me the wrong way then it would make everything very difficult. If I got it right it would save me a lot of time.

The other problem was that due to the sandbanks and very shallow water, once my decision was made I couldn't change it. This was one of those times where I was totally responsible for my own choices. I looked across the bay and shouted to Eric, 'What does the weather look like it's going to do in a couple of hours?'

'There's something nasty coming in, in a couple of hours, I think . . . but it's tricky to tell exactly how long.'

This was a gamble. Could I get across the bay in a couple of hours before the weather came in? I thought hard. I've always loved risk. I altered course and headed for the straight line across the bay. None of the hugging the coast nonsense for me, I thought.

As if to vindicate me, the wind changed in my favour. I turned the bath in line with the wind to take full advantage of this. Using my new-found sail technique to help me, it felt we were going along at race speed.

Eric shouted across, 'You're doing eight knots!'

Sandwich Bay is stunning. It's such a gorgeous place that, in order not to make the rest of Kent jealous at its beauty, the government put a massive power station there to attempt to spoil the view. A testament to its loveliness is that even with that monstrosity there, it's still stunning. A Kent councillor told me that, having realised putting an ill-designed power station in such an area of outstanding natural beauty was a mistake, the council passed an emergency resolution to pull it down immediately at a council meeting 15 years ago.

As I pulled hard, glided along at eight knots and basked in the sunshine, I smiled. Bathtub rowing had never been this much fun. This was how the entire trip should have been in my head. This was great. I'd almost got across the bay when the wind turned and I realised the bath was much heavier on one side. The leak was back. I downed oars and pulled gaffer tape out of the washstand. When things go wrong at sea, they do so fast. In and out of the water, I improvised a patch, got back into the sliding seat and rowed hard. We'd need to make it to Ramsgate fast. The water that had again got into one of the flotation tanks kept conspiring with the wind to drag me off course.

The mist started to come in. I'd failed; the weather had got me again. I was crushed; I knew Eric would soon be pushing to tow me back to Dover. I cursed, dug in and pulled harder. I took hundreds of strokes, swore, corrected for the heavy tank and now unhelpful wind, and gave everything to try and make Ramsgate. I didn't want to have to go back to Dover.

The mist cleared. There was a momentary respite from the wind. I turned. There was the harbour arm: there was the torch at Ramsgate, I felt like a conquering Roman. I'd made it.

I crossed into the main harbour for grown-up ships, then turned starboard (bath right, or my left as I was facing backwards) for the smaller harbour. Chris was waiting for me.

'Well done, mate: from Folkestone to Ramsgate in under five and a half hours. That's better than you thought it would be.'

My old phone (the one that was with Chris as opposed to my new gangsta one that was being hunted down by the constabulary) rang. Chris went to pick it up, then handed it down from the quayside to me. It was Dom.

'Hi, Chris, it's me, how's Tim, where is he now?'

'Dom, it's me, I'm sitting in the bath in Ramsgate.'

'What? What happened? You've not crashed, have you? Did the weather turn? I thought it looked pretty good . . .'

'No, I've made to Ramsgate.'

'That's under five and a half hours!'

'I know. The wind helped. I used the top of the roll top of the bath to channel it.'

I explained the zigzag manoeuvre that I'd come up with. Dom listened, sighed and said, 'In sailing, Tim, we'd call that tacking.'

'It's an official thing?' I couldn't believe anyone had thought of it before.

'Tim, you've just achieved your first sailing manoeuvre. I'm quite proud.'

I handed the phone back up to Chris. Eric shouted over, 'Come on, let's get you moored up.'

The sun came out. This was exactly how the bath trip should be: stunning weather, outstanding times and everyone smiling. I pulled further into the harbour and moored next to a grey boat. A man in uniform appeared on the jetty as I was tying the bath to it.

'Ah, we thought it was you. You're the bath man . . .'

'Er . . . yes . . . I am . . .'

I was a bit shocked. Who was this man who knew all about me? Quickly my brain marshalled my mouth.

'And you are?'

'Oh sorry, I'm the officer commanding this lot.' He gestured vaguely behind him. I realised the grey boat was a Royal Navy vessel, the man in front of me her commanding officer and the flag flapping the breeze the coveted White Ensign.

'Been really hoping we'd come across you. Super effort rowing the Channel. We've been keeping up with your progress on the radio channel.'

We shook hands. It was painful for me but some things are important.

'Fancy a cup of tea? I've just boiled the kettle.'

As you may remember, I have a very strict rule: never refuse a cup of tea. If everyone did this, world peace would be just round the corner. Soon the officer, some of his men and I stood on the jetty and drank tea out of mugs. They all asked questions about the bath and journey so far before the officer said, 'Hope you don't think me rude but it does look such a state . . . Would you mind if we gave the bath a bit of a polish?'

Even staunch critics of the Royal Navy will find it impossible to fault them on politeness. Did I mind? I was over the moon. Before I'd finished my tea, the bath was enjoying several members of Her Majesty's senior service giving her a Rolls-Royce of a polish. The officer, other members of the ship's company and I watched the team expertly buffing the bath. As a taxpayer I'd really got value for money. Eric shouted over, 'Tim, we've got to get some paper-work sorted and find you a smaller mooring.'

I thanked the RN for their great kindness and pulled away from the outer jetty. Eric escorted me and the now-gleaming bath round to the small-boats part of Ramsgate Harbour. Now we'd made it this far up, I'd need another support boat to take me further. Getting Eric to come up from Folkestone every day was not an option I wanted to consider, as it would place me back in the hands of that inconsistent tidal mistress again.

Chris and I waved Eric off and walked up the gangplank to check if we could leave the bath in Ramsgate Harbour overnight. We arrived in the offices of the Royal Harbour of Ramsgate. A man was behind the desk. At first he didn't look up. When he did, I was confronted with two eyes looking in totally different directions. I didn't know which eye to meet so took an average and stared down the middle. This had the net effect that, of the four eyes in the conversation, none of them were looking at each other.

'Hello, I've just arrived from France via Folkestone in a bath . . .'

Perhaps Chris and I had just walked into a Marty Feldman sketch. Without missing a beat he said, 'Of course . . .'

'Here's the paperwork. It's laminated.'

'Of course it is. I'll get you a form . . .' He went over to a filing cabinet at the back of the room in front of a window. 'Bloody hell – there's a bath out there . . .' He turned to me with a face that suggested I'd killed his son.

Apologetically, I offered, 'I did say it was a bath . . .'

'What do you want to do with it?'

'I'd really like to leave it here overnight – I should be gone in the morning – I've got a few repairs to do but then I should be off.'

'Where did you say you'd come from?'

'France.'

'Via Folkestone,' Chris added helpfully.

'Why?'

'I'm trying to raise a bit of money for a charity called Comic Relief . . .'

'Look, leave it here overnight. I'll make a note – we've not got a form for baths, and it's in a good cause. I love that guy who does Comic Relief . . . what's his name?'

Everybody loves Lenny.

'That's it . . . Jonathan Ross.'

Chris and I wandered out and stood beneath the clock at Ramsgate. I looked up at the face.

'That's not the right time is it?'

'It's Ramsgate Mean Time, I've been reading quite a bit today – Ramsgate's in its own time zone.'

I looked at the stunning, sleepy harbour.

'Three hundred years behind Greenwich?'

'It's actually five minutes 41 seconds ahead . . .'

There was a pause then Chris said, 'Tim, I've got to leave too.'

I knew this was coming but I'd really miss having Chris around.

'I've got to catch the train. I really can't miss it.'

'The train to London?'

'Nope. The one to China.'

'Seriously, where are you going?'

Ages ago Chris had booked to go on the Orient Express and it was leaving soon. I'd said goodbye to Eric and now Chris too. This was a day of change in the project. I was sad to lose him from the bath journey but also sad as one of my best friends would be gone for a whole year.

'Send me a postcard. And thanks, mate – I couldn't have got this far without you.'

'Sure you would have done!'

With Chris gone I wandered up the hill to the prestigious Royal Temple Yacht Club. This is a very old club for sailors. The bath is a rowing vessel. Normally there is no love lost between sailors and rowers. They don't get on. The reasons are obvious: one is totally reliant on the whim of the wind, the other faces away from the direction they're going in. Both accuse the other of not looking where they're going. One writes with cheese and the other eats truckles of chalk. This could go very badly for me. I pushed the old timber door into the hall. How would they take to me? I stood daunted in the hall. The Royal Temple is an old-fashioned place, with myriad rules and regulations, many of which are designed to baffle the uniniti-ated and some of which are printed in the front hall. The father of a friend of mine is a member and had suggested I eat there when I was in Ramsgate. As if to emphasise its credentials, the Royal Temple is the yacht club to which Sir Ted Heath used to belong. Unfortunately, he'd died just before I arrived and many of the members had just been to his funeral. It was a sad atmosphere in the club as I entered.

I wandered over to the front desk, gave the name of my friend's father and asked where I could eat.

'Not upstairs.'

The reply came with starch.

'Can I eat in the dining room?'

'You can't eat in the dining room.'

'What about that room there?'

'No.'

'Can I go in the bar?'

He thought for a moment. I could see rules and regulations flashing through his mind.

'Yes.'

'Thank you.'

He watched me go towards the bar door.

'Welcome to the club,' he said without the slightest sense of irony. In his mind, I was honoured to be allowed into the bar. So far the old maxim about sailors and rowers not getting on was holding good. I entered the bar.

'Do you serve food?'

'No.'

Things were not going well.

'Not even crisps?'

'We have crisps. Are you the guest of a member?'

'Yes.'

'Is the member with you as I can't serve you without them being here.'

This was getting silly.

'I've just rowed from France to here via Folkestone in a bath and I just wanted a sandwich . . .'

A man at the bar I'd never seen before smiled across at me and turned to the bar lady.

'He's my guest. I'm sure we can make him some sort of sandwich. Come and sit down . . . How have things been going . . . ?'

'Oh, sorry, I'm Tim.'

'Yes, how have things been going, Tim?' He turned to the lady at the bar. 'This is my old friend Tim.'

This kind sailor explained his boat was stuck in Ramsgate. It seemed it had been stuck there intermittently for many years and he was a regular at the yacht club. As I tucked into a delicious sandwich and a Coke he introduced me to various other people in the bar. We talked for a while before the bath story was introduced. They checked the floating apparition in the harbour with the club telescope before they'd believe a word. Then I went through the story so far and as it ended I thought it might be time to take my leave of them. As I went to leave the bar one of the men who had been laughing at the story waved in my direction.

'Wait, I think I've got something for you. How many committee members are in the room?'

Various people raised their hands.

'I think this lad deserves a burgee, what do you think?'

They all nodded and made the gentle hum of approving noises that occur in well-rehearsed committees. In my head the main question was: what's a burgee? I thought this would be a bad thing to admit to so gently hummed too. Various people in the room raised their hands again.

'Nip and fetch him one, would you?'

The bar lady arrived back with a small triangular flag. It was predictably navy blue and had a gold anchor, white horse and crown on it. The committee man presented it to me as the bar laughed and cheered.

'Well done. It's not every day we meet a bathtub rower. A great effort, good luck on your way round. Remember, wherever you are in the world, if you find another Royal Yacht club, fly this flag and they'll let you in ... and probably give you a drink. Always fly it from your masthead.'

'Thank you, I'll fly it from my showerhead.'

I left the bar to the sounds of more laughter. As I walked down the hill I thought what a great arrangement this was. In my hand was an internationally recognised sign of reciprocal drinking; in a flash an elite fellowship of cross-boundary liver damage had been opened to me. I'd discovered another truly global peace initiative to go with my rules about accepting tea.

The next morning the weather was again terrible. The bath racketed around her berth in the harbour. This would not help the leak. With help I pulled her out of the water, dried her off and fixed the leak again. The weather continued to be terrible as I popped her back in the water.

The next stretch of the journey was a really nasty one. It would take me around the North Foreland – it's the pointy end of Kent. The currents around it are really difficult and just a slight change in the wind can guarantee you wrecked on the rocks. I spent the bad weather walking around the cliff tops looking at the dangers and taking notes on the wind as well as bailing out the bath. I looked out over the dark brooding clouds, driving rain and smashing waves. Water poured onto my face. I was the only captain of an ablution equipment ever to take on this tricky stretch of inland coastal water; I felt like a sailor nervously watching the mighty breakers, waiting to round Cape Horn.

I returned to the bath and bailed out again. Baths keep water in, no matter what: again this proved a fundamental flaw in my plan. I stumped up to the office of the Royal Harbour of Ramsgate again to check I could leave the bath there for another frustrating day. They had been very kind in letting the bath sit there for the last couple of days while I tried to get some decent weather.

The door opened. This time I was met with four eyes: the two that faced in opposite directions and a new pair behind some spectacles that stared at me with the perception of a gimlet.

'Hi, I'm not going to be able to get out of the harbour again today . . .'

The gimlet eyes met mine.

'You're in the bath . . .'

'Yes . . . so sorry it's just that the weather . . .'

'I've been hoping to see you before I have to take things further . . .'

'What?'

'I don't like having your bath here.' Of the many things I would come to criticise in this man, directness was not one of them. 'And I understand you're refusing to pay the harbour fees.'

'I was told they'd been waived.'

'There's only two people who can waive your fees – that's me and him – and we haven't.'

He gestured to the man who had kindly waived my fees. The man looked back at me pleadingly in two directions. It's a look that people around Hitler probably saw a lot. I turned back to the gimlet-eyed Nazi.

'There must have been a misunderstanding.'

'I should say so. So not only do you have to pay the charge for today, but all charges up until this point and there are a few fines to pay too, for paying the charges late.'

This was too much. I was happy to defend the clearly weak man who had obviously suffered years at the hands of Ramsgate's Führer but this was unjust.

'Who is in charge of the port?'

'Captain White.'

'Where's his office?'

'Right over the other side of the quay – over there – and it closes in exactly one minute.'

He smiled.

'Right – I'll be back.'

Breathless I bumped into the man pulling the door shut at the office.

'I'm looking for Captain White.'

'Why?'

'I'm in the bath and they're trying to fine me. It doesn't seem right . . .'

'I'm Captain White – let's go inside.'

In an immediately relaxing office I explained what had happened and why I was rowing.

'You're the man who came from France. I heard you were up at the yacht club the other night.'

'They gave me a burgee.'

'Are you flying it from your masthead?'

'Showerhead.'

'Of course. Let's sort this out.'

The captain barked orders down the phone. For every evil Führer, there's always a Captain White prepared to save the day. Not only was I granted a free mooring for as long as I needed it but also given a place to park the trailer should I need it. This was very kind of him.

With a sense of justice I returned to the office and picked up the passes from the hand of the Nazi who had earlier refused them. The man with the Marty Feldman eyes smiled at me as though, just for once, something positive had happened in his office.

I was stuck in Ramsgate. The weather turned to murder, my heart turned to stone. I wouldn't stand a chance attempting the North Foreland in this. After spending more days in abysmal weather, waist-deep in harbour water, bailing out the bath, I was fed up with life, the universe and Ramsgate. One night my phone rang. It was an old friend of mine called Ollie.

'How are you getting on?'

'Not good – this is not the weather for bathtub rowing.'

'How do you fancy a game of cricket?'

For years I've played for a side called the Mumblers Cricket Club (it's the less well known of the MCCs and is named after Ollie who used to mumble). We only play once a year, when we host a tournament, but it's one of my favourite days.

'How's the weather on the wicket?'

'Dark, windy but at least there's no rain. Are you in?'

Playing cricket in the midst of terrible adversity is more stereotypically British than rain at the Grand National. I sighed at the cliché, smiled, reached into the car and pulled out my whites.

'I'll be there.'

Arriving at the hallowed ground, I was greeted with the familiar sights. Tents dotted around the boundary, people standing near the

pavilion drinking and laughing, and a general feeling that something epic might occur – today could be the year we won a game.

I turned out on a murky, overcast day to thrash at a small, barely
discernible red-leather ball. Swatting hopelessly, I realised that today
was the longest time I'd spent away from the bath. When I was in
the bath in Ramsgate, I couldn't wait to leave. As the ball almost
took out my off-stump for the second time in the over, I realised
that the ball was not the only thing I'd missed. I couldn't wait to
get back to the bath.

Later, I was fielding. The ball whizzed high to my right. It was
uncatchable. I dived towards it, fully waiting to land after a heroic
miss. Somehow, totally outstretched and horizontal as I was, I
realised that in my hand was the ball. I had caught the uncatchable. I held the ball and fell towards the ground using the medium
of gravity. I hit the ground and lost my shoulder. As my arm swung
gently by my side I could see that the ball had stayed lodged in my
hand. I may have lost my shoulder but the batsman was dismissed:
a truly heroic cricketing injury. As I looked at my face in the reflection of the polished leather, I realised the truth of what had occurred.
I snapped back from the rose-tinted version of events to the stark
truth. The ball had whizzed high to my right. It was indeed an
impossible-looking catch; I dived fully outstretched, caught the ball,
hit the ground and lost my shoulder – just as I had in my reverie.
The batsman was dismissed. All that was true. Also true was that,
if the batsman hadn't been dismissed, it was about time for her nap
anyway. I had dislocated my shoulder to dismiss a five-year-old girl.

While the Mumblers batted on in the main match, I'd become
involved in a side match on the boundary with a toddler. My head
was clearly so insanely competitive that I'd broken myself to
dismiss her.

My pain thresholds were very messed up by this stage in my life.
I'd got very used to pain. With a constantly bleeding set of buttocks
and massively oversized plums, a small shoulder injury was nothing.
With a click and a crunch I pushed the shoulder. After the click-
crunch, it was less floppy and seemed to hurt less. The girl gave up
her nap, so I continued playing cricket with her, having got myself
out in the main game for a swashbuckling 25.

Other than always accepting tea, I have another cardinal rule in
life. If you can't lift a champagne bottle, go to casualty. By the close

of play, my shoulder had really swollen up and I couldn't even lift a teacup, which broke my first rule in life. I didn't let on to the members of the team what I'd done and slipped away quietly.

Following my second rule to the letter, I arrived at casualty. Interminable waiting, various exams and an X-ray later I was thrust in front of a less-than-encouraging casualty doctor.

'It's dislocated but is back in place now.' He then went on to explain that I'd stretched either the ligaments or tendons above the shoulder (I forget which, it could have been both, I wasn't paying a massive amount of attention at that point). 'Oh and you've chipped your rotor cuff too.'

'What's that?'

'The shoulder is not a well-engineered joint. At some point it was probably more usefully engineered but since we've left the savannahs of Africa . . .'

I won't record the full explanation here, suffice to say, I'm not a medical man but even I could see that rowing the 130-odd miles left between Tower Bridge and me would not be easy with this. It was the sort of thing that one of my old Phys Ed masters (a man who made us run till we could taste blood) would have called 'challenging'. How had a gentle game of cricket turned out like this? I vowed in future to take up less threatening sports like Cumberlandshire Wrestling.

My descent into Greek tragedy was finally complete. With the first of his mighty tasks achieved, the bearded Hellenic hero had fallen prey to his own fatal flaws: his competitiveness and overly aggressive gamesmanship in the face of five-year-old opposition. I was forced to return home to landlocked Hertfordshire and sit with a strapped-up shoulder. Naturally, the minute the strapping was on, the weather turned really good.

The bath project was as smashed as my rotor cuff. It was over.

CHAPTER TEN

SPOILED HIS NICE NEW RATTLE

'This bowler is like my dog: three short legs and balls that swing each way.'

Brian Johnston

Anyone who has dislocated a shoulder will know the thudding pain that pulses with every beat of your heart. Added to this general pain is a very specific pain that feels like someone has a needle in your shoulder and is pushing it in and out, as though their eternal amusement depends on the grimacing this causes you.

This pain is nothing compared to the unbearable agony of having that shoulder twisted, pummelled and pulled about by a physiotherapist exhibiting more zeal for his task than a religious fanatic. His fake tan parted at the mouth to reveal a whiter than plausible smile.

'Yep. It's been quite badly dislocated.'

He grasped my arm and pushed. Something snapped. I screamed and tried to leave the room. My arm stayed in his firm grip.

'It's really back in now. The X-ray was right, it's quite a bad dislocation and there does seem to be a chip in the rotor cuff. You've also damaged the ligaments and tendons at the top of the shoulder.'

'Can I row?'

'Very funny.'

'Seriously . . . can I row?'

'Not a chance. There are two outcomes if you row. The first is that the shoulder will simply pop out again and the second is that you will do irreparable long-term damage to the shoulder . . . just look at the size of it in the mirror. Can you lift your arm up? Go on, try . . .'

I tried lifting my arm up. I got it up a bit but it wouldn't respond beyond a certain height. I tried rolling my shoulder. That didn't work either.

'See, you're not going to be doing anything with that for a while.'

I left the physio feeling very down. I had scuppered my own chances of success. I'd always thought it would be the weather that would finish off the bath project, not my own stupidity. Now the same stupidity that had started the bath project had finished it.

I stood in Hertfordshire with my arm strapped up like Nelson, looking out of the window over the countryside. My shoulder was very swollen. Finally, if only the local village infant school chose the right play – I was a dead cert for the role of either Quasimodo or Richard the Third – my shot at stardom was at hand. The weather outside was blissful. This would be perfect to row the bath. My phone rang. It was Dom. I'd not owned up to him about the cricketing injury mainly as I felt so very stupid.

'This is great weather, Tim, go, go, go. You'll easily make London in this . . .'

'There's been a slight hitch.'

I'd conquered the Channel and felt invincible. Now, I felt weak, old, battered and frail but mostly very stupid. He listened patiently as I explained the situation.

'Well, that could be the end of it.'

'I've got to see a physio again, but it's quite painful.'

I put down the phone and sat thinking. This was a vital time in the bath challenge. The bath sat bobbing up and down in the sun at Ramsgate Harbour under the watchful eye of Captain White. We had done roughly 60 miles of the challenge and still had roughly 120 left to make it to Tower. I sat broken in Hertfordshire. I knew I had to keep my overall body fitness up. I didn't think it was over and that was the main thing in my favour. But how could I exercise? Time spent on Betty the Ergo was not an option as my shoulder was wrecked.

I balanced on a stool and fetched down my favourite book on Nelson. I held the big tome on my knees and opened the cover with my good arm. What had the great man done when he'd been unable to go out to sea? Long walks. Of course: that was the answer. I thought I'd better check it with the physio. I shuddered as his lascivious tone penetrated my ear.

'I want to go on long country walks to try and keep fit,' I said.

'I'm not sure that's a good plan. If you fall over you might damage the shoulder even more . . .'

'Oh. Thank you for the advice. I'll see you for my appointment.'

I checked the strapping around my arm. Found my coat and deerstalker hat and put on my wellies. Putting on wellies is not easy with a broken shoulder. An hour later I was outside, striding across the fields of Hertfordshire and feeling much better. I took great care over stiles and through gates so as not to hurt my precious shoulder. I walked at a brisk pace, from my village, through the woods, past the golf course and into the next village. I didn't see Mr Darcy or Elizabeth Bennet but I'm sure they were out having a similar walk somewhere. I crossed through the next village and out the other side into more woods and fields. Damn the medical establishment and their advice. This walk was just what I needed to sort myself out. I caught my foot on a tree root, tripped and fell over.

Instinct is a very clever thing. Somehow I contrived to take the weight of the fall on my left shoulder and arm. My damaged right arm didn't touch the ground. It still hurt as I'd jolted it but it certainly would have hurt more if it had hit the ground.

I got up and cursed myself for cursing the medical establishment. Somewhere in a physiotherapy office a perma-tanned hand put a pin and a small voodoo doll of me back into a cupboard; a mouthful of whiter-than-white teeth let out a nefarious laugh.

I got up, my other shoulder hurting a bit, but I was more shocked than anything. I struck out once more and about an hour later arrived back at home feeling much better.

The days passed in blissful sunshine. I walked, read and cursed myself. On the Wednesday I was to give a speech to the Company of Watermen and Lightermen of the River Thames at their hall in London. It was to have been, for me at least, a celebratory dinner for the finish of the bath project but bad weather and my arm injury put paid to that. However, the meal still went ahead and I arrived with my arm heavily strapped up.

Very kindly, they cut up my food for me and all made jokes about Nelson. I was able to eat the meal with just a fork. I gave the speech on how the bath trip had been so far and that went well. I also had to take an oath of allegiance to the Queen. I was being officially inaugurated as a Freeman of the Company that afternoon too and this was part of the ceremony that dates back hundreds of years. The Master sat on his chair in the stunning courtroom at Waterman's Hall and the massive Company Bible was brought out. I knew there was no way I could hold it. The Clerk smiled.

'You could hold it with your wrong hand.'

I wasn't sure if that was legally dubious so decided not to take any chances.

'Put it in the sling, if that's OK?'

The Bible was balanced in my sling and I entered the Waterman's Company, to laughter and more jokes about Nelson.

Back at home after the dinner I resolved to fight my predicament. I simply had to get my shoulder better quickly.

I drank quite a large glass of whiskey and took my arm out of its strapping. Many years before I'd broken my shoulder falling off a horse and that time a nice Indian doctor had suggested many exercises to help me get better faster than usual. He'd based his plan on his knowledge of medicine and yoga. This routine of stretching I now did obsessively. I also got some tiny weights out and started trying to do repetitions with them. It was a very, very painful process but I knew I had to get back to the bath and finish what I'd started.

I saw the physiotherapist again and also a second one. I lied to both of them and didn't mention the weights or stretching but both were amazed at the progress I was making. I hated lying but thought that the torturous system of weights and stretches I'd created was probably not going to make the medical profession very happy. All the time uppermost in my mind was the drive to get back in the bath.

My phone rang. It was Pimlico Laura.

'Why don't you come down with me for the weekend?'

This was great. Firstly, it would be lovely to see her. Secondly, she lived in Kent and it would take me closer to the bath.

She had stuff to do on the Saturday afternoon so would drop

me off in Margate. I was aiming to get to Margate when the bath was able to leave Ramsgate so thought it might be good to have a wander around the place, make friends and see what the mooring situation was like.

I've always had an ingrained distrust of Margate. It could be stories I overheard my godfather telling of Mods and Rockers clashing on the beaches there or the endemic sadness that hangs over towns that only sparkle for a season. Laura dropped me off. She waved brightly, screeched tyres and as pedestrians dived for safety, yelled, 'I'll pick you up later . . .'

I was shocked. There was a carnival atmosphere in the air. The bunting was out and the streets were crammed with people. I had no idea what was going on but it seemed all my visions of Margate were immediately proved wrong. This was a vibrant place full of colour. I tried not to let people jostle my shoulder as I made my way through the crowd. On the way to the water's edge I spotted a sign that said 'Margate Yacht Club: Members Only'. The door was open. Very welcoming I thought, so I went in. I'd been accepted in the Royal Temple so yacht clubs were my new favourite places in the world. If only I'd brought my new burgee with me.

The Margate Yacht Club was less polished than the Royal Temple. Having said that, there are several regiments of soldiers whose boots are less polished than the Royal Temple. In Margate YC there also seemed to be less people. Those people there were crowded around the windows and looked down on something. A lady with bleached blonde hair turned towards me as I entered and smiled. I smiled back: 'What's going on?'

'It's the Margate Raft Race . . .'

'Oh. Can I have a look?'

'Of course.'

From the window I could see the whole of Margate out and playing. They were all massed around the harbour, watching people row old oil drums strapped together. The start seemed to be over the other side of the bay where I couldn't quite see, but the finish was at the coastal end of the harbour arm just below us. The great train robber Ronnie Biggs said he wanted to 'Come home (from Brazil), see Margate and go to prison.' On a day like today, basked in sunshine with everyone out and having fun, I could really see why. Today Margate was Xanadu. The contents of the yacht club were totally focused on the race so I decided the best thing to do was wander down to the harbour and see if I could buy a programme to tell me what was going on.

After carefully guarding my shoulder through the crowds, I made it to the top of the slipway. I turned to the man next to me.

'What's going on?'

'It's the annual raft race ... How do you not know that? Are you a visitor?'

Not knowing if this was a good thing I answered tentatively, 'Yes ...'

'Well you've come to the right place. This is the Town Mayor.'

There's a drill when you meet a Mayor. Luckily, I've met Mayors before. Once when I was on tour, I tried to meet a Mayor in every place I played. I didn't quite manage it (some of them didn't want to play) but in three months I notched up 13 Mayors, three Headmasters, a cathedral Dean and a Duchess.

I rolled out the drill and chatted to the Mayor. He introduced me to the Town Sergeant whose job is to follow the Mayor of Margate around.

'... But what does he do?'

'Makes sure no one nicks his chain.'

We all laughed. It was probably important in times gone by but today, with the sun out, this was such a happy place that I couldn't imagine anything like that happening. Then I explained about the bath, the trip, the aims and that I'd like to moor up in Margate when I made it round from Ramsgate. The Mayor said, 'Of course we'll find you a place to moor up. It'll be nice to have you. You can either use the harbour, or, if it's finished, the replacement pier. We lost the last one in a storm a while back but we're re-building it.'

After a lovely couple of hours in Margate, I saw people jumping and nervously clinging to buildings. Laura had arrived in her car. Other than the throbbing pain in my shoulder, this was a very happy day.

'I've finished all my jobs. Shall we go for a walk?'

I uttered a short prayer and we sped off. Laura drives with a recklessness that even the most bloodthirsty Viking would find unnerving. We arrived at her parents' house. She got out to kiss her mum hello and while she wasn't looking, I fell out of the passenger seat and kissed the ground in thanks for my deliverance. For the rest of the afternoon we walked through the cornfields to the south of Margate. I took my arm out of its strapping and ran my hands through the ears at the top of the corn. My hands were not quite healed but this was a divine experience. Like a Roman soldier in the poems of Catullus I'd found the couch I'd longed for. I spent the next hour picking corn ears out of the goo patches that still littered my hands. Catullus never mentions this.

The next day Laura dropped me off back in Hertfordshire. I took my arm out of the strapping and, sweating heavily, went back to doing my weights. The events of yesterday had only made me more determined to get back to the bath. I wanted to get to Margate: playground in the sun. My phone rang. It was Dom.

'Tim, I'm not sure how your shoulder is but I thought you should know, there's a really good weather window coming but after that I don't see a weather window for about eight days. I think if you can, you should try and make it round the Foreland.'

'Right . . . I'll give it a go . . .'

I started to make arrangements. With Eric gone, I needed a new support-boat skipper.

Finding a support-boat skipper was turning up an interlocking medieval-style network of connections. Andy and Eric couldn't help as they were in Folkestone. They knew people in Dover but not Ramsgate. By not stopping in Dover I'd missed out a vital link in the chain. The support-boat skipper is an odd thing. If things go well, you shouldn't need one at all. If things go badly, like on the first attempt, your life can depend on them. All they have to recommend them is the fact that they're still alive. It's tricky finding one in a place where you know no one and when you're rowing a bath. Still, I started with Eric and Andy's list of Dover fishermen to find a list of Ramsgate-based fishermen. Most of my conversations that day consisted of:

'Hello, I need a support-boat skipper . . .'

'Sorry, I don't do that – got to go.'

With some I made it as far as:

'Hello, I need a support-boat skipper . . .'

'Where from?'

'Ramsgate.'

'Sorry, I'm not there at the moment.'

'When will you be back?'

'Not for a week or so . . .'

Finally, I got some really good leads that led to:

'Hello, I need a support-boat skipper . . .'

'Where from?'

'Ramsgate.'

'Right – what are you up to?'

'I'm rowing a bath . . .'

'I've got to go – bye.'

Things were not going well. I was again stumped by how unavailable the fishing fraternity could be. I tried another number.

'Hello, I need a support-boat skipper . . .'

'I'm really a cockle fisherman . . . I do fish for other stuff.'

'Good . . . I just need a support-boat skipper to get me and my bath out of Ramsgate . . .'

'You're in a bath?'

'Yes – don't hang up . . .'

'I thought I was seeing things in the harbour – where have you come from?'

'Well France, sort of . . . via Folkestone . . .'

'Now it all makes sense – I heard people talking about you on the radio and in the pub – it's for some charity isn't it?'

'Yes.'

We met on the harbour at Ramsgate one morning. I'm not sure what my image of the traditional Kentish cockle fisherman was, but it was not the beach surfer dude who got out of the silver convertible Mercedes that stood in front of me.

'Hi, I'm Dave.'

Behind me, he saw the bath.

'Ah, there she is – you'll have to do a bit of bailing out before we give this a try. This beats winkles.'

I had realised my place in the world – somewhere slightly higher than a winkle.

Chris had left to catch the train to China. Luckily for me Phillip Carr had just arrived back from China. Obviously China has a strict one-in one-out policy, like all the best Soho nightclubs. Phil stood next to me on the docks as we both looked at Dave. Another man in a T-shirt with 'Whitstable' written on it wandered over.

'What are you up to?'

'I'm trying to row my bath round to Margate.'

'Oh, you're the guy in the bath . . . Mind if I come too – I'm not up to much today.'

Whitstable was one of the places I was trying to get to after Margate so I took his arrival as a sign. I viewed his T-shirt with the same prophetic awe that people applied to John the Baptist and invited him to ride on the support boat.

I stood by the bath making my final preparations. Captain White arrived.

'You're off, are you?'

'Yes. Thank you so much for all your help.'

'I just came to warn you – it's my last day today. I can't stay on any further, I was really meant to leave last week. Lucky you've got the weather as I'm not sure how my successor would react.'

I took from his look that his successor might have been either the Nazi gimlet man or some close member of the Führer's family. It seemed from his tone that he'd stayed on to shield me. I never got to the bottom of this but if he did, it was an even greater act of kindness than I was aware of. I shook his hand firmly, winced and thanked him again before he wandered off to his office.

I got into my bath and locked down the oars. My shoulder was still in a lot of pain. All the advice had been not to row with a broken shoulder. Phil was loading the myriad kit bags containing his camera equipment onto the support boat. He glanced over just as I was taking some of the world's strongest painkillers.

'How is the shoulder?'

'It's either going to pop out immediately, which will mean this is a very short day of rowing, or it'll hold in place.'

'What are those pills?'

'Something they give to horses I think . . .'

'Dave says off you go, he's got to do some final checks – we'll be right behind you.'

'Great. Meet me in Margate and bring a vet.'

'What?'

'I'll need more painkillers.'

Nervously, I put the oars into the water and, so carefully it was like I'd wrapped my shoulder in velvet, took a slow pull through the stroke. My shoulder stayed in. I took another very gentle stroke and again my shoulder stayed in. I rowed off past Dave doing final checks and out towards the outer harbour wall.

I was leaving Ramsgate. It was 18 July, over a month since I'd made it across the Channel. The only danger I now faced for my shoulder was if the sea jerked it out of its socket. Knowing that my row could be a short one if the weather turned I tentatively pulled on past the harbour arm and out into the chop. Ramsgate had held me for much longer than planned and almost been the end of the project but finally it seemed I was free. The legendary theme to *The Great Escape* mingled with the wind and whistled round my ears.

I pulled up through an increasing wind and swelling sea past Broadstairs. I saw a couple of wrecks on the rocks that stuck up through the spray. I decided to row round the point as far out at sea as possible without getting involved in the shipping lanes. This plan did not work as brilliantly as I'd hoped. The current seemed intent on pushing me back in towards the rocks. After much straining and grunting we achieved a draw and I stayed away from the rocks at what I judged to be a safe distance. Through the sound of the waves breaking on the shore Dave shouted desperately, 'Tim! Below you!'

I looked overboard at the jagged rocks just a few inches below the surface. It was horrible. The bath needed a draught of ten inches and just one of those rocks could wreck her. I'd accounted for rocks above the waves but not the more damaging ones below.

I saw an area with no rocks directly to my left. I pulled at right angles to my current position using just one oar and took myself out in a north-north-easterly direction. I had to keep my attention focused on where the rocks were not. This was fine when the water was clear. When the water was too foggy to see rocks, I got my knife, attached it to a bit of string and dropped it overboard. Using this method I navigated my way out through the lethal labyrinth. I'd escaped, but this time it really was a case of only just. Dave's boat was equipped with up-to-date sonar equipment to help him gauge heights; I'd been forced to make do with an improvised system, probably last used by Nelson as a midshipman. The main thing of course is that it had worked.

Out at sea near the tip of North Foreland in a bath, the wind began to get worse and my shoulder was not really on very good form. However, against increased odds I made it to Margate and triumphantly pulled in to lie next to the harbour arm. I moored up, ran up the steps and across the street to the sign saying 'Margate Yacht Club'. Brilliant. This was going well. I may have a shoulder that felt like it was about to be pulled off by wild horses but I'd made it to Margate and there was the familiar oasis of the Yacht Club. I smiled, as this time I'd remembered my burgee from the Royal Temple. Surely having it would ensure me an even warmer welcome. This was going to be great. This time the door wasn't open. I rang the bell on the buzzer. A female voice answered. Even better.

'Yes?'

'Can I come in?'

'No.'

'I've just rowed into the harbour and wondered if you could help me finding moorings?'

'No.'

If I hadn't known better I would have suspected this was an automated message. I really needed their help. I knew no one in Margate except the Mayor.

'I really need some help . . .'

'So?'

This was not going well. Where was the cheery welcome that Kubla Khan gave the visitors to his pleasure dome? This woman was so chilly she was at threat from global warming.

'What do you suggest I do?'

'Go?'

Desperate times called for the desperate and thoroughly un-British measure of using my new-found honour.

'I've got a burgee from the Royal Temple . . .'

'So what?'

'I met a blonde lady in here the other day . . .'

'Really!'

'Could you at least tell me somewhere that might be able to help?'

There was a pause. I may have imagined it but I was sure I heard cruel sniggering.

'The Mayor suggested I . . .'

There was a sigh.

'Try the office across the road.'

I entered the office across the street.

'Hi – I've spoken to the Mayor and he said I could moor the bath on the harbour.'

'I wouldn't do that – it'll stick in the mud and you'll not get it out again.' Great, another tidal harbour: I remembered the fun I'd had at Folkestone. This was the difference between a kind invitation from a Mayor who knew nothing about maritime affairs and the informed word of the experienced harbour staff.

'He mentioned a pier?'

'Oh, that blew up to Clacton in a storm – he probably told you – we're rebuilding it.'

'Yes, where's the rebuilding?'

Perhaps I could have moored there, even though it wasn't totally finished.

'We've not started it yet.'

'When did you lose the last one?'

'1978.'

'So how can I moor here now?'

'You want to moor here now?'

'Yes.'

'That's not going to be possible.'

I sat on the harbour arm not quite knowing what to do. I could leave the bath moored on the outside of it. That was a very risky strategy as, if the weather turned bad, it could get smashed. I could leave the bath moored on the inside of it but the informed advice was that I'd end up stuck in the mud and never be able to get out. Perhaps he wasn't telling the truth. I didn't know whether to believe him or not. My time outside the Yacht Club had tarnished Margate a bit for me.

'What's up?'

I looked up and saw the familiar jovial figure of the Mayor. One of only two cheerful people in Margate as it now turned out.

'I wanted to moor up here.'

'Yes – no – you can't do that . . . I thought you meant next year – what with your arm being in a sling and all that . . .'

I suppose it was fair enough.

'Perhaps I could leave the bath here somehow?'

'I wouldn't leave that here – that copper will be stripped down and sold for scrap before you can say "murder".'

An odd choice of phrase but one I'll never forget.

'By smugglers?'

'No, school kids.'

'Shouldn't they be in school?'

'Nah, this is Margate mate . . .'

For a Mayor to admit the ruination of the entire town education system in this way, things must have been pretty serious. We talked further and a less positive picture of Margate began to appear. A man came running down the harbour arm.

'Here, mate! Don't linger here, you'll get stuck in the mud.'

I didn't seem to have a choice. I made up my mind. Shook hands with the Mayor and thanked him for coming down to see me before shaking the dust of Margate from my feet and pulling out of the 'harbour'.

With no moorings in Margate as promised, if the weather became bad, I was in trouble. The tide was turning, hence the 'harbour' emptying. I came up with a plan. Finally, I'd found a use for my hitherto totally pointless and weighty anchor. I could throw it down and wait the seven or so hours till the tide turned again. When the tide came back in my direction I could catch it westbound, just like a bus, and hop off at the next place I knew I could moor: Whitstable. If the weather turned against me, Margate not having moorings could be fatal.

Margate had become clear. All the surface joy in the place had faded. I looked at the town and her empty streets: a consistent and bitter reminder that once they'd been full. The raft race was exposed simply as a constructive way for the local hoards of delinquent brigands and still resident Mods and Rockers to use up the oil drums they had left over from setting fire to things. I remembered Ronnie Biggs's wish – 'See Margate and go to prison' – and realised this was the town motto. With the hinges off and me in potentially a very tricky situation: 'Gateway to the sea, gateway to health' had been exposed as a lie. Now it all made sense. That was why the Town Sergeant was such a burly man. He'd been the only person not to laugh when he said he was there to stop people nicking the mayoral chain. He meant it. If only I'd got a sergeant to guard the bath.

Evidence would suggest that, with no moorings and an automated door message, members of the Margate Yacht Club outside the annual raft race are rarer than the Yeti. I did not fly their burgee from the showerhead of the bath.

* * *

Weather is the single biggest factor in determining events in history. Would Agincourt have turned out the same in the sunshine on hard ground?

I phoned Dave who, thinking I was safe in Margate, had set off back round to Ramsgate.

'There's been a slight change of plan.'

'What?'

'There's a problem.'

'Good, we've got a slight one here too.' As it turned out, Dave was a master of understatement. 'I'll get Phil to call you in a bit – what's your news?'

'The moorings in Margate don't exist.'

'What about the harbour?'

'It's not possible. Long story but believe me if it was at all possible I would have been there now.'

'Oh dear . . . what are you going to do?'

'Row against the tide for as long as I can then anchor down and wait it out.'

'That might be tricky. There's some weather on the way. I'm coming to get near you. Get in to near the coast until we find each other.'

I don't like it when fishermen use the word 'weather' in that way. They don't say 'bad weather', just 'weather'. Weather is all bad to fishermen. To fishermen, weather is defined as a change from perfect conditions.

I rowed as much as I could against the tide. Luckily I saw a buoy, rowed towards it and phoned Dave. The paintings (numbers, letters, colours and shapes) on it seemed to mean something to Dave. I tied the bath off to it. Drat. I still hadn't got to use my anchor. Luckily the weather was still fair if a little choppy but the tide was beginning to race. I phoned Phil.

'Hi Tim, great you've called . . .' There was something in Phil's voice I couldn't place. 'Let me just put you on to Peter.'

'Peter?'

'Your team mate in the T-shirt . . .' I could hear Phil shouting to Peter. 'You'd better come and tell Tim – he could be in trouble if he doesn't know too . . .'

'Hi, Tim?'

'Yes.'

'It's important that you know this. I'm on the run from the American Secret Service. The President is aware of the situation.'

Oh great. Me and my prophetic hunches.

'How? Why?'

'I can't tell you but this is why it's important that we don't go back to Ramsgate – I've told Dave – I might have to take over the ship . . .'

'Don't panic, Peter – I now understand – Dave understands too and is turning the ship around to get you away from Ramsgate.'

'Good, the FBI will be waiting there.'

'Put me back on to Phil.'

'OK.'

Phil came back on the line.

'Great work, Tim.'

I think he may have been being sarcastic or suppressing a laugh at the whole craziness of the situation but I decided not to press it.

'Thanks, mate. All good. See you when you all get back here.'

You may think I'm making this up. Of all the people I could have picked to accompany Dave and Phil I managed to find a man who genuinely believed he was on the run from the FBI and was prepared to take over my support boat to escape.

One question was uppermost in my mind. In this situation, who supports the support boat? I cursed myself for not booking a support-support boat.

Dave arrived with a very stressed-looking Phil and an increasingly paranoid-seeming Peter. I remembered from my Nelson book that just one paranoid or insane crew member had been known to upset the balance of an entire frigate. In another book I'd read that there was one North-West Passage expedition where one officer ended up howling at the moon. This was a very delicate balance. Then the weather turned nasty. After sitting in a terrible storm off Margate for half a day waiting for the weather to give in and the tide to turn, Dave and I had to accept the inevitable. The electronic devices on his boat did not lie, nor did the shipping forecast, nor did the Met Office. This storm was not going to go away.

After half a day of storm the sky went black. It was night. Concern swept the boat and lashed us even harder than the waves. Dave was increasingly worried about getting back round the lethal North Foreland to Ramsgate in the dark. Peter was increasingly concerned as he said the FBI mainly came out at night. And Phil was concerned about being in a confined environment with Peter after dark. There was always the option that had been raised earlier. I could be towed to Whitstable and released near the harbour. It would seem like I'd heroically made it through the storm in the bath. This was tempting on many levels: first, it got me closer to Tower; second, I'd get to look like a hero; and third, I'd get a warm bed in Whitstable and a safe harbour. On the other side of the argument: it was cheating and that was unthinkable.

There are some points on a journey where you have to take a call that is tough on you personally but good for the team. I went to talk to Dave.

'What do you think?'

'We can't stay out in this.'

'We can't get into Margate.'

'You won't be towed to Whitstable.'

'Can we make it to Ramsgate?'

'It's going to be really hard going round the North Foreland in the dark in this storm and with your bath off the back.'

'What?'

'We can't leave it here, Tim.'

'Good point.'

'The other problem is how to persuade Peter not to do anything silly if we go back to Ramsgate – he's been on about this all day – he's in some kind of programme too for rehabilitation. He really does think if we go back to Ramsgate he's going to face charges in the US.'

Phil appeared in the doorway just long enough to hear the last bit.

'So over to you, Tim.'

This was going to be a tough conversation. If he believed he would be arrested by the FBI in Ramsgate, I just had to believe that too, and all could be fine. The boat jumped up and down in the water violently as I rolled over to Peter and looked him straight in the eye.

'Peter. I've been thinking. The FBI must have seen us leave Ramsgate this morning.'

'Yes, but they wouldn't know where we were going.'

'True but they'll be scouring the coast for you by now and are sure to have made it to Margate and asked questions. The bath is not very inconspicuous.'

'What?'

'They'll know I've been to Margate.'

He snapped and got very angry immediately. I understood Phil's worry. He shouted, 'Damn! They might take my businesses away.'

'Businesses?'

'Oh, I'm a millionaire. I'm a millionaire.'

'Of course. But wait. Them seeing me in Margate might have helped us.'

'How? How?'

My godfather's wife used to work with people like Peter a lot. I began to remember how I'd seen her handle them when I was small.

'They will think that I've been through Margate. I told the Mayor that I was heading to Whitstable.'

'So?'

'Well, you're even wearing a Whitstable T-shirt.'

'So?'

'So they'll think we've gone to Whitstable and go to Whitstable. Meanwhile we go to Ramsgate and drop you off. You disappear and don't go to Whitstable for a bit and everything will be fine.'

'Let's go to Ramsgate. How long have you been a spy, been a spy, too?'

'I've never been a spy.' I winked like I'd just said something in code. It seemed to do the trick. 'Dave! Turn this boat around!' I attached the bath to the back and we headed off.

The way back to Ramsgate was a horrid journey in the dark. I heard Dave on the phone to his wife saying, '. . . we might not make this, I love you . . .'

That's never an encouraging thing to hear from a skipper. Out on deck I'd rallied Peter. He could not have been more stoic in the situation. He began to repeat himself a lot more. Possibly as his meds were wearing off – it was difficult to tell in the dark at sea. However, despite this, he helped me secure the bath on countless occasions and often only Peter diving and holding on to a line stopped us from losing it. Phil meanwhile was filming waves, generally being David Lean and only on occasion looking nervously at Peter.

This was undoubtedly a very tough and supremely dangerous situation. North Foreland is really dangerous in a storm. Although things were bad, I'd been through bad storms before, recently with Andy in the Channel, and this didn't seem so terrifying. I think I thought we were safer being close to the shore. If that was the case it wasn't true, as I certainly couldn't have swum the distance in the storm we were in. Oddly, I think I felt safe knowing that I had three good men around me. One may have been focused on filming waves, another ruminating on his own mortality and the one third clinically mad; but together we were a pretty good team as it turned out.

I understand we were the last boat that made it into Ramsgate Harbour that night. A testament to Dave's good seamanship and the general teamwork in keeping together.

I finished the day exactly as I'd started, with a shoulder in agony, bailing out the bath in Ramsgate. I looked up at the storm. Things were not going well and as I sat bailing in the rain was reminded of the words of the prophet Paula Abdul.

CHAPTER ELEVEN

FOUR YOUNG OYSTERS HURRIED UP

'Interests in life: balls, riding, dining and making a fool of myself.'

George Francis Lyon RN

The day had not gone well. My phone rang. It was Janette. There's a very fine line between agent and psychiatric nurse but most days Janette errs on the side of agent.

'Look at you, getting letters from the Palace.'

I was shocked. I'd received a letter from Buckingham Palace the week before when I was in Hertfordshire healing my shoulder. It was a very generous and kind letter from the Queen via Her Private Secretary congratulating me on crossing the Channel in the bath. Not wanting to be brash, I'd kept this letter secret from everyone. Even Janette.

'What? How do you know about it?'

'Know what?'

'About my letter.'

'How did *you* know about it?'

'About what?'

I'd had a hard day and like every brilliant nurse in a jim-jam clinic, she sensed this and said, 'Hang on, let's start again shall we?'

'Good.'

'I am talking about a letter you've received from the Palace, what are you talking about?'

'My letter from the Palace . . .'

Eventually, after enough confusing dialogue to fill a moderately successful Jim Carrey movie, one of us (and my money would be on it being Janette) twigged that there were in fact two letters from Buckingham Palace.

The first letter, to me at home, was the letter congratulating me on making it across the Channel in the bath. Like a Shakespearian plot, there was also a second letter from the Palace. This had gone to Janette as my agent.

'Shall I open it?'

Perhaps it was just a copy of the first letter? Or it could be something else. Suddenly, I was really excited.

'Yes please . . .'

'Hang on, let me get the scissors.'

With full gravitas, Janette read out the embossed writing like a great actor reciting a speech. Some Soho agents may get invitations from the Palace daily, but for the two of us, this was a first.

'The Master of the Household has received Her Majesty's command to invite Mr Tim FitzHigham to a Maritime Reception to be given at St James's Palace by the Queen and the Duke of Edinburgh . . .'

That night the Royal Ramsgate Harbour seemed to shine. I may have been as stuck in Ramsgate as I had been in Folkestone but I was going to visit the Palace for rowing the Channel in the bath. Brilliant.

To celebrate I decided to sleep in a hotel that night. As I lay down to shut my eyes I determined I would make it to Buckingham Palace in time to hobble around awkwardly as the Queen moved seamlessly away from me down a line up.

Finally, we got the weather. Again.

This time I left Ramsgate with just Dave and Phil in the support boat. We made it round the rocks at North Foreland to Margate. It turns out that this is a very difficult stretch of water no matter how many times you attempt it.

It's true (also fortuitous in terms of keeping the story moving along) to report that this was a very uneventful leg of the journey.

After the sea had done its best to drown me and smash me on rocks again, I finally drew level with the buoy I'd tied off to the last time. Dave shouted over, 'Right now we can row again! Now we're on a new bit. Will we make Whitstable?'

As I dipped the oars in, I knew that we really had to make it to Whitstable. It was the next safe harbour towards London. The other harbours couldn't shelter the bath if the weather turned bad. In other words, if I didn't make it to Whitstable, I'd end up back in Ramsgate again. For the morale and sanity of the troop in the bath, that was unthinkable.

The other significant factor was the tide. Not only did I have to make it to Whitstable, but also I had to make it to Whitstable before the tide turned. The tide had been a factor in Folkestone as the water disappeared from the harbour twice a day. Now, tidally, I was at the place where the Thames met the Swale. At this point both rivers empty twice daily into the North Sea. So twice a day it would become impossible to row against that tide as it flowed east. There were just two specific time windows per day where I could row west towards London. Each window was about seven hours long. If I didn't make it to Whitstable in this seven-hour chance, I would end up either back Ramsgate, moored next to a shipping buoy in Margate or learning to cook pickled herrings in Reykjavik. The clock was ticking. The stakes were high.

It was an evil row from Margate westwards. I passed lots of houses, which on inspecting my road atlas I could only think was Westgate-on-Sea. The wind that had been so useful earlier in the day now tried to take me back towards Broadstairs. My trick of using the roll top of the bath as a sort of sail was utterly useless as the wind was coming straight at me the wrong way. I hit a sandbank. Dave and Phil were powerless to get to me. The water was too shallow for the bath so Dave's boat didn't stand a chance. What could I do? This was an entirely new problem. I'd never hit a sandbank before. The bath gently nestled there as I poked around in the water with the oars trying to free myself.

Eventually, the wind and tide wrenched me off the sandbank. This was the first time since that glorious row from Folkestone to Ramsgate that I could honestly say the weather helped me. I think it only did so by mistake. Cursing its kindness the weather rounded on me with vengeance, making the sea really short and choppy. It was almost impossible to take any sort of strokes at all. The wind wanted me to go back to Ramsgate and was attempting to force the issue. I tried to use another trick I'd learnt: hiding in behind any headland in front of me and using it as a windbreak. I realised there was no headland and became marooned on a second sandbank. This one I shared with a seal.

It was all very frustrating. The seal looked at me. I looked at the seal. We exchanged a few pleasantries. I assume they were pleasant; she (I think she was a she but unfortunately didn't get to know him/her well enough to ask) didn't attack me so that seemed to indicate the native was friendly. My attempts to try and row the bath off the sandbank failed. The wind and waves didn't help this time. Eventually, I attached the oars to the bath and got out onto the sandbank. Knee-deep in the surf I pushed the bath off, jumped back on and rowed away in a wobbly line.

Finally I glimpsed the twin towers of the Roman fortress at Reculver. This threw me deep into thought. This was obviously where the Romans had stopped to deal with the tide of the Thames. If only Roman moorings were still as well built as their fortresses I could have moored up there. As I was thinking this, I heard the familiar gentle swishing sound. I was marooned on another sandbank. Bother.

I'd like to write that things got easier. They didn't. This was a very tough stretch of rowing. A short choppy sea, wind in the wrong direction and a multiplicity of sandbanks all conspired to give me the feeling not of rowing the bath but of dragging her onwards. Eventually I saw houses again and let out a yelp of joy: it must be Whitstable. I checked the atlas. It was Herne Bay: still miles to Whitstable. I let out a yelp (less joyful), dug the oars into the water again and rowed on.

However, just past Herne Bay the wind let up. For the first time that day it stopped going against me. After fighting it for so long I now felt less hampered than the relevant Fortnum's department on Boxing Day. With no resistance, it seemed I could now go superhumanly fast; I whipped along the coast towards Whitstable.

Dave and I had come up with a plan. Whitstable sits on the east side of an estuary. On the west side of it is the Isle of Sheppey. If I arrived at the estuary and the tide had not turned then we thought I should have a go at crossing it to reach the Isle of Sheppey. There's no decent bathroom mooring on the east of Sheppey but if we had the tide I could take a chance and go north round the island to try and reach Queenborough on its west coast by the time the tide turned.

On the other hand, if I arrived at the estuary and the wind or tide was against me, I should take the safer option and pull for Whitstable where I had safe moorings. Earlier in the day when I was marooned and writing poetry with the seals near Reculver neither of these plans looked likely. However now, as I checked the road atlas and confirmed that what I could see was definitely Whitstable, either seemed possible. I called to Dave, 'Mate, we've made it – I didn't see that coming . . .'

'Neither did I. You've got the tide – the wind might get a bit changeable but there's a good chance we can make it round the north of Sheppey . . . What do you want to do?'

'Let's go for Queenborough.'

I've always loved a gamble. I started rowing across the estuary. It was unbearably hard and put my newly healed shoulder to the harshest test. The current of the Swale wanted to take me one way, the Thames was intent on driving me another. All the time both of them seemed to want to take me away from the direction I wanted. Still, I battled on and eventually after much straining, made it to the relative shelter of the north coast of Sheppey. I passed a settlement and glancing at the road atlas judged this to be Leysdown-on-Sea. It could have been Warden – due to the spray of the sea the ink on the photocopied atlas had run a bit at that point.

Then, the wind turned, the chop got noticeably worse and the gangsta phone rang. It was Dave.

'Mate, there's some weather coming in here, it's going to be frisky. What do you want to do?'

'I'll have a go at making it to Queenborough and failing that Sheerness.' (It was moderately closer.)

'OK, but you're going to have to pull hard.'

I hung up, dug in and pulled hard. I'd been rowing all day and was shattered but I knew I could make a significant dent in getting to London if I could make Queenborough. I rowed on and just as I sighted what I judged to be the outskirts of Minster or something between there and Warden (the road atlas was becoming more smudged by the stroke) the mist came in. Then the tide turned to race away from London. The wind changed direction and was trying to push the sea back to London. The result for me was very big waves and a lot of problems. It was like being in an epic painting by Turner. Dave's boat bobbed around me. The bath was simply not able to cope with this sort of weather. Then the light faded as the cloud cover thickened. I'm not sure of the sea state that day but it seemed close to as bad as the one I faced in the Channel on the first attempt. White wave tops crashed down on me in the dark mist as I lurched around and tried to take strokes.

I felt I could have carried on fighting through all the other problems that now faced me except the lack of visibility. Somewhere off the port of Sheerness lies a monster in the form of the SS *Richard Montgomery*. This is a semi-sunken World War II American munitions ship. In August 1944, she dragged her anchor in the shallow water and grounded on a sandbank. Now she lies in two sections and conservative estimates suggest there's in excess of 1,400 tonnes of unexploded ammunition still in her hull. You can see where she is due to a series of buoys that mark the exclusion zone around her. She's 'semi-sunken' as you can clearly see her masts poking out of the water at all states of the tide. However, fighting to get past that danger in very restricted visibility was not the best plan I'd come up with. Dave was afraid too; my phone rang.

'There's that explosive ship not too far from us.'

'I know ... I'm not sure it's a good idea going near it in this storm.'

'What do you want to do? I'm losing sight of you ...'

'I'm going to turn and make for Whitstable – we can pick this up in the morning. We're not going to make Sheerness in this.'

'Good choice.'

In some ways it was a good choice. In others it was a very bad one. Just as I'd had to battle the tide to get to my current position I now had to battle even more ferocious conditions to get to Whitstable. I was stuck in a howler of a storm. I battled chop, spray, wind, current in the wrong direction and a road atlas that was now just a mass of soggy papier mâché. I'd taken a gamble and tried to beat the weather: again, it had beaten me. It took me over two hours to complete what should have been a half-hour row to Whitstable.

The cloud cover cleared and the rain stopped. The light got slightly better. It was dusk but not black and misty as it had been out off the north coast of Sheppey. There was still mist but the visibility was much better here. A RIB arrived containing the Vice-Commodore of the Whitstable Yacht Club. She shouted over as she drew circles around me in her powerful boat.

'Wondered when you'd get here. What weather you've brought with you. Amazed you made it.'

'Am I glad to see you . . .'

The Vice-Commodore and I had spoken on the phone lots. She was called Wendy and could not have been more helpful.

'You must be shattered but we saw you through the telescope and there's a few people that want to say hello – can you bear it?'

Being stuck between two ports, not making one and having to pull back to the other was exhausting. It was exhausting battling the storm. However, if people had turned up to say hello, it would be rude not to go and see them.

'Of course.'

I pulled towards the jetty at the yacht club. On the jetty was quite a crowd of people. There were children, members of the yacht club, even a press photographer and a reporter. They were all so kind. Wendy had obviously extended a brilliant hand in organising this. It really cheered me up. They presented me with a Whitstable Yacht Club burgee to fly from the masthead: again, navy blue with a red cross on a white shield. By the end of the day my mood had totally reversed and I was thinking, thank goodness I hadn't made it to Queenborough or I would have missed this.

Wendy and I moored the bath up on one of the Whitstable Yacht Club moorings and she took me into land. The yacht club offered me a room for the night and a shower. I went in under the jet, water hit my cuts and pain coursed through me. I went to scream but managed to bite my hand instead. I'd obviously developed new cuts between here and Margate and reopened older cuts too. I did my best not to curse while trying to wash myself as well as I could.

Bedraggled but clean I went out of the yacht club to find some food. After foraging, shattered and in pain, I went to bed. Oddly enough the cuts and dull thudding pains didn't seem as bad. I'd made it this far and had a warm bed and new friends around me. I liked Whitstable.

The pressure really had taken hold of me. I must make it to Tower Bridge. The bath trip was intended as a charity fundraising project that was supposed to last a month, a year and a half ago. Not only did I want to end it but also there were some other pressing concerns. Firstly, their bosses were beginning to ask my various sponsors exactly where the money they'd been giving me was going. In other words, without the shots of me coming under Tower Bridge they were getting nervous. This was fair enough, they'd kept faith with me for an extra year; it was time to prove them right. Secondly, rather rashly as it turned out, I'd booked a slot to do a show in the wonderful Pleasance Theatre at the Edinburgh Festival. Fifteen missed calls from the lovely (if put upon) artistic director of the Pleasance told me that the previews for that show kicked off in Edinburgh in just a few days. There was no way from my present position I'd make it to Edinburgh for that. Janette had been working hard and had managed to get them to scratch the previews. However, this meant refunding tickets, disgruntling audience members (I've put 'members' as amazingly there was more than one) and leaving an empty venue in the world's most over-subscribed arts festival. More depressing than that, scratching the previews only bought me an extra three days. Serious questions were being asked about my commitment to my day job. When your day job is making people laugh, serious questions are a bad thing. I currently had just seven days to get to the Festival on time.

All these thoughts vanished as a knock at the door woke me up. It was Wendy's husband with a cup of tea. I looked down with guilt at the milk and two-sugared marvel. As I sipped it, I couldn't quite work out why, in my dream, the artistic director of the Pleasance had been played by a giant bee; I wasn't sure why this was scary as, when awake, I quite like bees. He smiled and handed me a biscuit: I like Whitstable.

'Thought you might like this, you'll not be getting anywhere today.'

'What?'

'Look out of the window.'

I looked and saw nothing but a wall of mist.

'Where's the bath?'

'Exactly, there's no visibility, you'll not get away today. This happens here.'

'Come to that, where's the sea?'

'The support-boat skipper's radioed in, he's on his way back to Ramsgate.'

I got dressed and stumped off down to the yacht club bar. Nothing ever seems as bad when viewed through a pint glass in a bar.

I got talking to the barman. He'd been pulling pints in the bar for years. While we were nattering I noticed a chart on the wall. It was the most relevant one for Whitstable and also had on it the Isle of Sheppey. I looked at it and suddenly all the stuff Dom had been desperately trying to drum into me for weeks began to clear. I turned to the barman.

'Excuse me, but, from this, it looks like the tide comes in from both sides of the island and meets in the middle at the southern-most point of the Isle of Sheppey?'

'Yes, it's an odd thing that. You'd expect it to run in west to east and out east to west, but it doesn't. It's cos of the Medway meeting the Swale.'

'So hang on, I could row to the southern point of the island with the Swale tide coming in, put the anchor down, wait for the tide to turn and then row out the other side with the Medway tide going out.'

'Erm . . . yeah, I suppose you could. I've not seen it done but it must be possible.'

Straight away, I phoned Dom and explained my plan. He was at work and didn't have the charts in front of him but still responded.

'I'm not sure exactly how the currents work down there but just follow what we discussed about charts and I'm sure you're right. Sorry not to be more helpful but, on the plus side, if it works this is your first naval plan and it will have been a success. The responsibility for this is with you . . . good luck.'

I checked the charts again. People had started to gather in the bar. Word had got around that this was my thinking. The bar marshalled itself and managed to become several voices all saying the same thing: 'I'm not sure it'll work.'

'You'll have to get the currents just right.'

'If the anchor slips or if you get the tide wrong you'll end up in Herne Bay.'

'. . . Or Margate.'

I checked the charts and all the various voices agreed that my theory was technically possible, although they thought it mad and unworkable practically. In my head I substituted the words 'radical' and 'bold' for 'mad' and 'unworkable' and picked up the phone.

Until now I'd been taking guidance from the MCA (Maritime Coastguard Agency) and the Port of London (the PLA, who look after the Thames from Margate westwards). At no point did I think I'd need to contact the Head of the Medway Ports. However, I couldn't row on the Swale or the Medway without his permission. This was a very important phone call.

The man who runs the Port of London is a Rear Admiral and very senior. You don't get to speak to him, only the people way below him. It takes a few days for anything to get done, as there is a complex chain of command. A bit like a god or a djinn, the only way you know he actually exists is that the Port of London runs smoother than a lube factory.

I picked up the phone in the bar and phoned the Medway Port Authority. I'd have to talk to the person at the top, as I needed to get emergency permission to row today. I put on my very grown-up voice, as I'd need to circumvent the massive wall of bureaucracy fast. The receptionist picked up.

'Hello, Medway Ports?'

'Good morning, I'd like to speak to the person in charge. It's quite important.'

'Is it a maritime matter?'

'Yes.'

'You'll want the Harbourmaster. I'll put you straight through.'

'What? I mean . . . thank you.'

In all my long dealings with the Port of London this had never happened. My shock was compounded when on the other end of the line was the world's most affable man.

'Hello, I'm Steve. How can I help?'

'Erm . . . I need permission to row on the River Swale, around the south side of Sheppey.'

'Right, what sort of vessel is it?'

I took a breath. I really needed Steve's help. Without it I couldn't go round the south of Sheppey. More than that, if he chose to, he could delay his permission until I'd lost the tides and my chance of progressing. It wouldn't mean the end of the trip but it would mean I couldn't row any further today. Potentially, if the weather stayed bad, not having Steve's permission could hold me at Whitstable just as long as I'd been stuck in Ramsgate.

'It's a bath, well . . . more a sort of bathroom . . .'

'You've rowed it from France? I wondered when you'd call. When do you need to row round Sheppey?'

'Today?'

'No problem . . . where are you mooring for the night?'

I'd planned this. Sheerness is a really busy port so I knew I couldn't moor there. Previously, I contacted the Harbourmaster at Queenborough and got a mooring from him.

'Queenborough. I've got permission.'

'That's great, I'll look out for you when you come past me at Sheerness.'

I thanked Steve, put the phone down and turned to the bar.

'Right, we're on. What time does the tide turn today?'

Someone checked a tide table.

'It'll be starting about now.'

'Crikey. Right. We're going to have to move a bit.'

Auditioning to be head of the Port of London, I issued instructions. Everything had to be done fast. First, Dave and Phil were recalled from somewhere near Margate. Then I packed quickly and a RIB was made ready to take me out to the bath. The mist was still like a pea-souper and we couldn't see the bath till we were almost on it. I'd missed the start of the tide but if I didn't make best use of the rest of it, my plan would definitely fail.

I jumped into the bath, thanked Wendy, put the oars in the gate and locked them in. Taking out a compass and a chart I'd been given in the yacht club, I untied the bath, waved at where Wendy had been in the mist and pulled off.

I sculled as hard as I could up the estuary, very aware that I had to get over halfway round the south of the island for my plan to work. A motley assortment of vessels appeared out of the mist at me. People on board nervously dived toward drinks cabinets as they saw the bathroom looming out of the mist.

Rowing through the mist in the marshes south of the Isle of Sheppey reminded me of Magwitch and Pip in David Lean's *Great Expectations*. It was a very haunting and Dickensian morning on the river. I was all alone. Dave knew my plan and he and Phil were trying to catch me up, but both of us became aware that if I hadn't set off without him and kept with the tide, all would be lost.

People are unkind about Sheppey. They call the inhabitants of the island 'Swampies'. This is not a term of endearment, although like many previously derogatory terms some islanders are trying to reclaim it as cool. The guidebooks on Sheppey are equally uninspiring. One says: 'If Kent is the Garden of England, then Sheppey is the diseased cabbage in that garden.' Another: 'The economy of the Isle of Sheppey has been in consistent decline since the Viking invasion.'

As I rowed this stretch of water totally alone in the marshes, with only memories of the convict Magwitch to keep me company, I began to feel as though someone was watching me. It's not difficult to get paranoid, alone, rowing through a mist-filled marsh.

Suddenly a head popped out of the water just five feet from the bath. I missed a stroke. Perhaps it was the dead body of the man who'd written the guidebook? I looked again. Through the mist it was difficult to see but it seemed too hairy. Was it a Labrador? Again, through the mist, it was difficult to tell and if it was a Labrador, where was its owner? Another similar head popped out of the water nearer to the bath. It looked like a frogman. Would the world's longest bath trip end in murder? My breath stopped and I looked the frogman square in the eyes. He came towards me in the mist and as he got closer, turned into a seal.

More heads then joined the first two and swam playfully alongside the bath. I was entirely alone on a river by a marsh with only a seal colony for comfort. Sheppey was being stunning to me. One of the seals looked very like my flatmate from the sandbank yesterday: although it's quite hard to tell with seals as they all wear similar coats.

After an hour, Dave and Phil arrived to find the seal colony swimming entirely unabashed around the bath. Barking and frolicking, they were really beautiful. This was an incredible emotional experience: a sort of lower-budget chav version of swimming with dolphins.

Now with Dave, Phil and seal cheerleading-squad, my morale rocketed and I pulled as hard as I could round the south of the island to reach the magic halfway point. The main problem with the magic halfway point is that there's nothing there to tell you that you've reached it. How could I tell where the 'right' place to stop was to make the plan work? I had a vague idea but it was only vague.

I rounded a corner on the right side of the river; by that I mean the right side according to the guidelines. By coincidence, it is on the right side of the river, although as I faced it backwards it felt more like my left. Having rowed up and down the Thames training countless times I was well drilled on river etiquette. Rowers have to follow this more than most, as they can't often see what's ahead of them. Dave and Phil were a little way behind me at this stage. They couldn't see round the corner but saw me pull out of view around the bend and heard a massive ship's horn.

I heard the horn and saw Dave appear round the corner at some speed. I looked over my shoulder and saw the owner of the horn bearing down on me on the wrong side of the river. It was an implausibly large boat to be on that stretch of the river. A polite discussion about rights of way didn't seem possible. This was a very dangerous situation. The river was narrow, he was vast and on the wrong side of it (according to river etiquette) and I was in a bath. With all the misplaced confidence of a drunk major blowing off in a golf club, he sounded his horn again. My seal escort disappeared fast. Like the crew on the *Titanic*, they'd seen the iceberg. The horn noise echoed around the marshes of Sheppey and even the birds left.

Dom had taken me through horn signals we thought I might have needed in the Channel. Of course they'd proved to be pointless in the Channel as everyone uses GPS and radio. I racked every hole in the Swiss cheese of my brain. What did one blast mean? I sat there stunned. It definitely meant he was going to turn to port. Or perhaps it meant he was going to turn to starboard? Bother and one blast. As the ship continued to plough straight at me, I searched the washstand for the almanac. It had obviously gone overboard in the night. The ship sounded again, a single sharp indignant blast. Things were happening very fast. Then the ship sounded his horn five times.

Something clicked in my brain: five blasts definitely meant, 'I am doubtful you are taking sufficient avoiding action.'

The captain of that ship was very cross. Having remembered the meaning of five blasts, suddenly I was sure one blast meant he was going starboard. It made no sense in terms of his position on the river at all but I thought I just had to trust him and my own memory.

I swerved to my starboard and headed into the bank. This was all wrong, I'd been in the right all the way through this but he seemed so confident and had roughly 1,200 tons to back his opinion.

The tanker turned off into an unloading-type harbour to starboard. It was totally hidden from me and suddenly made sense of him wanting to go to starboard. His wash on the turn almost landed me in the middle of the field. As I bobbed violently next to the bank I saw a tiny sign covered in foliage. It explained how I had been totally right in my actions on every other stretch of river in the country; however, in this particular part of Sheppey, to accommodate the secret unloading-type harbour, the river regulations were reversed.

A breathless Dave and Phil caught up with me at the bank. Dave leant over.

'That was a close one. Weird he was on the wrong side . . .'

'Have you seen the thing covered in a bush?'

'Oh . . . they've reversed everything . . . right . . .'

I tried to row on away from the bank. It could have been the shock of nearly being scuttled but rowing here was like trying to run through concrete. I took a few strokes and seemed to get nowhere. Dave shouted again, 'I think the tide is turning! Best just put an anchor down and wait.'

'Are we halfway?'

'I'm not really sure . . . it's a bit tricky to tell . . .'

I'd travelled over 100 miles and never used the very heavy anchor; now, finally, I unclipped it from the bathroom floor and dropped it overboard. Dave shouted, 'You could have just tied off to me.'

'That's not the point.'

We all sat there waiting for hours. Dave and Phil on the support boat, me in the bath and the now-returned seal escort in the water. All was very calm. Despite the unflattering comments in the guidebooks Sheppey has some very pretty parts. Dave made cups of tea and even bacon butties, which Phil and I tucked into and the seals politely declined. We waited on. It was agonising, sitting there bobbing up and down, whistling, humming and waiting. Most agonising of all was not knowing if my plan had worked or failed. Had we made it halfway?

I was looking out over the water ruminating on all these things when I saw a reed turn in the water. The reed changed direction. I shouted to Dave.

'Mate, it's turned, the reed has turned!'

'What?'

'I think the tide has turned, I think we've done it! I think it's worked!'

Sometimes the tiniest thing can signal the mightiest change. After dropping a line in the water and trying some other tests, we both weighed anchor. I put the oars in the gate, screwed them down and pulled off.

We rounded a bend to see the tiny Kingsferry Bridge: the only thing that links Sheppey to the mainland. The showerhead cleared the underside of the bridge but there was no way Dave's boat would make it. The bridge keeper agreed to raise the bridge for Dave, which was kind, but said that it would take some time.

'Dave, I'm going to keep going as I don't want to lose this light and the current.'

With that, I sped off. In the deteriorating light I saw the Kingsferry Bridge being slowly raised and Sheppey once again being cut off from the mainland. The tide was being so helpful now. I'd obviously left the River Swale and was now on the mighty Medway.

I'd planned to get moorings at Queenborough. Dave and Phil caught up with me just upstream of the town.

'Where do you want to moor up?'

'I've still got some light and amazing current – I want to try and get to Sheerness so we don't have any current problems in the morning.'

'The light really is going but you've certainly got the current. Can you moor at Sheerness?'

Sheerness is one of the busiest ports in the country. It's a major centre for importing cars among other things. How or where we'd put a bath in there was anyone's guess.

'I'll phone someone.'

I picked up the gangsta phone and dialled Steve.

'Steve, hi, it's Tim. I've got light and wondered if there was anywhere I could moor in Sheerness?'

'You've made it round today?'

'Yes.'

'Good work. It's not been the best of days ... erm ... there's the inner harbour, I'll clear a berth for you ...'

What a great man. Steve described where I needed to go as I narrowly avoided a buoy and its associated sailing ship upstream of Queenborough.

'Dave, we can moor in the inner harbour with the police boats.'
'I'm impressed.'

The tide picked up and I shot through Queenborough like Gonzo out of a cannon. As I came out downstream of Queenborough, darkness fell on the Thames. Dave flicked a switch and a bank of spotlights came on over the top of his cabin. I flicked a switch and two small and rather inadequate-looking lights sprang into action on the bath. It really was dark. The tide kept forcing me on, down towards Sheerness; soon vast shapes began to appear out of the darkness. Huge big ships, leviathans to the bath, loomed out of the dark, their mighty prows completely dominating me. They towered over me so utterly that they seemed to defy the basic laws of physics. Ranks of them appeared out of the night, all with names that sounded like a new and interesting sexual disease from ports with names like euphemisms for farting.

I saw a flash in the water, stopped and went cold.

'Dave! Get over here quick. I thought I saw a hand.'

Dave shone the light where I thought I saw the hand and we searched in the water. It was all so black.

'If you're sure we'll have to report it, Tim, but you'd better be sure, as searching for it in this will be a heck of a job . . .'

'I'm not, I couldn't say, it could have been a fish . . .'

Everything was so dark. Sheppey's busiest port was in total silence other than the gentle splosh of my oars in the water and the hum of Dave's engine on low revs. I rowed on past the *Gonnesyphilis* and found the tiny aperture that led to the inner harbour.

By now it was totally black and I pulled in through the massive thick walls of the inner harbour like a clandestine Napoleonic invader. Piratical-looking sailors crowed around the quayside above me. All eyes were trained at the new shiny thing that was coming in to dock alongside one of the Harbourmaster's boats.

One of the buccaneers on the quayside above shouted down in broken English, with an accent that would not have been out of place on a Bond baddie's henchman of the mid-1970s, 'Where you come from in bath?'

I stood in the bath and stared up at the faces illuminated in the harbour lights. 'France!' My shout echoed off the thick walls of the harbour.

'I tell you! It him!'

The regiment of corsairs cheered and waved. I was really shocked. Dave shouted over, 'They've heard about the bath!'

I pulled the oars from the gate, scrambled out of the bath and onto the quayside to have my hair ruffled and back patted by men who I'd never met and would probably never see again. That night, we all shared a common smile at the stupidness of the bath. As the men dispersed back to their various ships, I went back down to the bath, Dave, Phil and the support boat.

I was flushed with the happiness of the quayside above; Dave and Phil looked grave. Dave spoke first.

'Tim, I'm not sure I can come any further up. I have to keep going back down to Kent to refuel and I'm just aware that every time I do that, I slow you down. I know it's all tidal from here and I don't want to stuff it up for you. It's just that Ramsgate or even Herne Bay is miles from here and it takes me so long to get back . . . then you might have missed the tides . . .'

Dave had been through so much with us. He'd got me from seeming defeat in Ramsgate through the tricky waters of Margate and all the way to the western tip of the Isle of Sheppey. I didn't want to lose him. It had become as much his story as mine and I wanted him to finish it with me. I looked at him, much as Scott probably looked at Captain Oates: Dave was right, his need to refuel and the fact all his contacts and knowledge were in Ramsgate would slow me down. I'd assured the Port of London that I wouldn't come up the Thames without a support boat and with the very tidal nature of the rest of the journey a 'Dave refuelling' stop might cost me a tide, day's rowing or with added bad weather even longer. There was serious pressure mounting for me to get the trip finished and even a day now would make the pressure much worse.

'Dave, thank you . . . I . . .'

He smiled. 'Good luck, mate, it's been great being with you . . .'

He turned the key and his boat engines roared. He saw us looking down at him, smiled mischievously and said, 'I'm just going out . . . I may be some time . . .'

With that, Dave the remarkable cockle fisherman glided out of the inner harbour at Sheerness. Phil and I waved him off into the blackness. Phil turned to me.

'So, where are we going to stay tonight?'

Bugger. I hadn't really planned that. I took out the gangsta phone and dialled directories. 'No bother, I've got a plan.'

I arranged taxis and somewhere to store Phil and his plethora of kit. The main problem on my mind was my promise to the Port of London. The Thames from here up is a very busy, commercial stretch of water and they'd insisted I have a properly aware Thames support boat. Dave's decision was the right one but it did leave me unable to go any further without someone to take his place.

Without a support boat, I was stuck.

CHAPTER TWELVE

MONKEY STOPPED TO PULL UP HIS SOCK

'They had brought a large map representing the sea
Without the least vestige of land:
And the crew was much pleased when they found it to be
A map they could all understand.'

Edward Lear: 'The Hunting of the Snark'

I woke early the next morning. The way the tide was that day, if I could find a support-boat skipper I could still go on the late-morning tide.

'Hello, I need a support-boat skipper . . .'
'Sorry, I don't do that – got to go.'
The familiar tale started again . . .
'Hello, I need a support-boat skipper . . .'
'Where from?'
'Sheerness . . .'
'Sorry, I'm not there at the moment . . .'
'When will you be back?'
'No.'
'What? Hello?'

I was greeted with the blank dial tone. By phone I scoured Sheerness, Allhallows-on-Sea and even St Mary Hoo with no luck. I spread the field up to Tilbury with equal lack of success. I even tried Essex in the hope of finding someone but Southend, Shoeburyness and Canvey all turned out to be fruitless. It was clearly the closed season on lesser-spotted support-boat skippers.

I sat on the quay of the inner harbour at Sheerness, more stumped than the man standing in front of Adam Gilchrist. I was stuck.

A worm of thought popped its head out of a hole in my Swiss-cheese brain. The oath I'd taken with one arm at the Company of Watermen and Lightermen. I picked up the phone again.

'Hello, can I speak to the Clerk of the Watermen?'

'I'll put you through.'

'Hi, Colin, it's Tim. I need a support boat going from Sheerness to somewhere like Gravesend. Can you suggest anyone?'

'You'll want to finish at Gravesend . . . you'll be looking at someone like Mr Palmer, he's got a firm down there. I'll get you the number.'

Being a Waterman turned out to be great. I thanked Colin and hung up.

'Hello, is that Mr Palmer . . .'

I employed the technique I'd found the most helpful in the past. I explained the serious nature of the bath trip first: about Colin, my link to the Watermen and that I was trying to raise money for a charity. Then I took a deep breath and broke him into the full truth.

'It's a bath . . .'

'Oh, you're the nutter in the bath – have you really rowed from France?'

'Well, yes . . . sort of . . .'

'I wondered when you'd get this far.'

It was strange but the bath seemed to have become well known, at least among river people. I'd become 'the nutter in the bath', a mere sidekick to the star that I'd created. I felt like Ernie Wise.

'I need a support boat to get me from Sheerness to up near you.'

'It's quite a choppy day on the water. Are you sure the bath can take it?'

Now it seemed the bath was the one in charge. I felt like saying, 'I'll have to ask her,' but managed, 'I'm sure we'll be fine.'

'I'm not at Sheerness today but my brother's there as it turns out, running something up for me. I'll give him a shout and call you back.'

I pulled out of the sheltered inner harbour of Sheerness, past the vast prow of the *Herpemdyia* (Registered Port: Tundervelt) and out into wind swirling round my ears, dark sky and a very choppy wash. In increasingly bad visibility I saw the red-on-white lettering of Palmers' Marine. Mr Palmer's brother eyed me sceptically.

'You'd better keep up, I can't slow down too much cos of the freight.'

Ahead of me across the Medway Estuary was the dreamily titled Isle of Grain, which sounds like it plays host mellifluously to a stunning medieval farming community. A place where simple rural types take nature's finest and create bread that tastes like clouds. It doesn't. It is a single, massive, ugly power plant or at least that's what it appeared to be in the glimpses I caught of it through the mist: a mass of huge chimneys that probably, on a clearer day, would have belched smoke out into the sky. In a sky filled with mist, it was difficult to tell; I took the smoke belching as read and tried to battle on through the chop.

In the shadow of the dark satanic mills of Grain, the Medway Estuary had me in its power. Several problems were at work. Here, the Medway hits the Thames at right angles, which creates a chop. The prevailing winds can come from any number of angles and change at a second's notice. That meant that from having a following wind with the tide, I suddenly found myself the wrong way round with a wind going against the tide, creating more chop. There were also massive tankers coming in and out of Sheerness, Tilbury and all the other loading stations up the Thames. These things are huge: the friends and relations of, if not the actual ones, I met in the Channel over a month before. Their stopping distances are terrifying and in such a relatively confined area of water, any collision with them would end very badly. The other problem they created for me was throwing up huge amounts of wash, which only added to the chop. This leg of the row was not the stroll in the sunshine I'd been planning but turned out to be very difficult.

'It should get a bit easier once we get level with Grain.'

Mr Palmer was the first support-boat skipper I'd had who was involved in freight. All the others had been fishermen. I couldn't put my finger on what that difference meant but somehow it made a difference. He seemed somehow more urban and industrial. He also seemed fairly sure that I was a total waste of time.

I pulled hard and bailed out alternately as he shouted things at his son. His son also eyed me with suspicion. The dynamic between support-boat skipper and bath had found a new expression. From the uncontrolled excitement of Dave, the bath had moved to the hassled, inconvenienced monosyllabic responses of Mr Palmer's brother (also, of course, called Mr Palmer).

My seal escort reappeared just in time to maroon me on a sandbank. I saw Mr Palmer sigh and his son stifle a laugh. As an ablution mariner trying to impress a new support-boat skipper, there are better ways to show off than becoming marooned on a sandbank. A combination of wind and desperate flailing from me finally dislodged the bath. Mr Palmer's brother, Mr Palmer, sighed again, although the seals clapped.

I put in a supreme effort. I bailed out the bath, rowed on through the chop and spray and tried hard not to be capsized. It was a terrible day and I seriously considered giving up and pulling back towards Sheerness. The conditions in the water were very dangerous, especially in a bath. I'd not been out in anything like this since the first time I tried to cross the Channel. The bath pitched and rolled like I'd not seen her do in a year. Spray was everywhere but I determined not to give in. I paused in the rowing and fumbled for the road atlas. There didn't seem to be anything useful in terms of moorings near me; I'd just have to keep rowing. The waves tried to steal the oars from the gates and snatch them away from me several times. I simply pulled hard, bailed when needed and tried to keep the bath afloat. A year ago I would probably have gone under in this. Now, I'd had a year to practise.

I began to notice that the chop was getting better. The mist hadn't lifted exactly but it had improved. Mr Palmer's brother's son came out on deck.

'Dad says would you like a cup of tea?'

'Yes please.'

'Sugar?'

'Two.'

He disappeared again. I rowed through increasingly better-looking water. Clearly I'd made it through the worst.

The son reappeared and leant over the side of the boat.

'Here you go. That was quite rough.'

Then his dad appeared behind him and leaning over the side he cracked the first smile I'd seen from him all day.

'That's a great bit of rowing, I thought you'd go under . . . do you want a bacon sarnie?'

I would have pawned the Koh-I-Noor for a bacon sarnie right then and reached up to take it.

'You must have rowed quite a bit . . . did you ever do Doggets?'

'No, I'd never rowed before the bath trip, but it's taught me a bit . . .'

'I'll say . . . that was good work. It should get a bit easier for a bit now, you're out of the main chop.'

The seals shouted that they thought we should get a move on. I finished the sarnie and fumbled for the oars again. The strange dynamic of support-boat skipper and bath had entered another chapter. It seemed that through the tough water and near capsizing I'd earned their respect. Now they wanted the bath to succeed just as much as I did. I finished the dregs that proved it and handed back the mug before digging in and rowing off again.

The river was kind as I rowed past what the atlas told me was St Mary Hoo. My shoulder was painful. I'd been taking the very strong painkillers every day I'd been on the water and they seemed to be working but every now and then, usually shortly before I was meant to take the next dose, the pain would thud back through the happy numbness.

Large tankers passed me on the way out to sea and hooted their horns. I shouted up to Mr Palmer, 'I'm nowhere near in their way.'

'They're not cross with you, they're hooting to support you.'

'What?'

'The Port of London have enforced a slowdown on the river to try and help you.'

'What?'

I paused rowing to listen as Mr Palmer explained that someone from the Port of London had come on the radio earlier in the day and enforced a temporary slower speed limit on the Thames between Gravesend and Sheerness to help me with the bad weather. This meant that all the big tankers had to go at a maximum speed of five knots. Totally shocked by the enormity of the kindness, I pulled on the oars again and as the next tanker hooted at me I found I was crying. I looked over at the massive ship gliding majestically towards the sea at under five knots and waved. I was choked up; someone at the Port of London really wanted me to make it.

The river bent south as another tanker hooted. I turned to my right with the bend. The weather turned bloody again. The wind got up. The rain came back and the mist swept in again. I squeezed on the oars as hard as I could and begged the rain and wind to stop. This leg of the journey had just got hard again. Blood dripped off me and into the bath as all my cuts stung in the rain. The raindrops got larger as I rowed on. Finally they became hailstones: this was a classic British summertime. My shoulder felt even worse in the cold and hail and my back was in agony. Pulling something a third of a tonne is not easy at the best of times but in a hailstorm it was hideous.

I swore vigorously and rowed on. Eventually, after more Anglo-Saxon language than appears in the Chronicle, I saw a sign sticking out of the water on a pole. It simply read 'Higham Blight'. Through the tears, water, spray and hail, I laughed. I was a very Blighted Higham and the river had been waiting for me to turn up for hundreds of years. I rowed, swore, bled and bailed out as I crawled on upstream, desperate to reach Gravesend. It was a very tough time. All the while Mr Palmer and his son shouted encouragement from their boat as more tankers tooted on their way out to sea. I just had to make it to Gravesend.

Finally, the river bent west and I looked over my shoulder to see Gravesend. I rowed on, desperate to get to it. It was certainly not a very pretty bit of rowing but with every other stroke I moved closer towards it. The sun appeared briefly, warming the hail into rain and after a few moments a rainbow bent over Gravesend. It was stunning. Somewhere in the town centre, a leprechaun cartel plotted a bank heist.

Apparently, not much epic poetry has been written about Gravesend but as I looked at the town bathed in a rainbow I would gladly have written several sonnets, probably involving the rhymes 'river penned' 'rainbow's bend' and 'shelter lend'. Luckily for the poetic reputation of Britain, just as I was searching for a pen, the weather became appalling again. I shelved all thought of becoming the new Byron and had to concentrate on the more pressing issue of not capsizing. The waves, wind and stone-like hail were clearly on the side of poetry and set against me surviving long enough to murder any on to paper.

'Head for the pontoon!'

'But it's the Port of London one . . .'

Our conversation was made difficult through the spray.

'It's fine, you've got permission. Tie off and we'll see you in the pub.'

I tied off at the PLA pontoon in simply horrid weather. Mr Palmer and his son berthed slightly further upstream on another pontoon. My phone rang.

'Tim, it's Joe . . .'

I've known Joe since I was three and a half. He's now in IT and had kindly been running a website dedicated to the trip. On www.timstub.com were pages about the various legs of the journey and a link to the Comic Relief website where people could give money to support the trip.

'Tim, you're not going to believe this but the website has had over 50,000 hits.'

'What? So over 50,000 people have visited it?'

'Yeah. Well, it could just be one person who's a bit obsessive and has visited it 50,000 times, it's tricky to tell . . .'

'Crikey . . .'

'We've had emails from all over the world, from exotic places like Swaziland, Australia, even Cornwall saying that if you make it to Tower Bridge people are going to hold bath parties to try and raise even more money . . .'

'Wow – that's incredible . . .'

I sheltered under the roof of the PLA office on top of the pontoon as the hail died off to torrential rain again.

'You've even got the ultimate Internet accolade.'

'What?'

'Someone has created a website devoted to hating you.'

'Great news, mate . . .'

I'd had no news of how people were taking the bath trip and couldn't have cared if there was an army of sites dedicated to hating me. People were interested. We must have been raising money. That was great. Also, I'd made it to Gravesend and was safely moored on a PLA pontoon for the night.

I'd spoken to various experts on rowing and all of them had said it would definitely take at least five days to make it from Margate to Gravesend. However, as no one knew anyone who had actually rowed it, they couldn't be sure. In a third-of-a-tonne criminally heavy bath full of water, with a badly damaged shoulder and in less than great weather, I'd made it in just three.

I hung up the phone and, buoyed up by all the positives that now littered the project, returned to the bath. It was sinking. I jumped on board, pulled gaffer tape out of the washstand and did the best I could in the driving rain. If the bath would just hold up for a few more days I might just actually make it.

After liberally applying gaffer tape to the flotation tanks I headed up to join the Palmers at the Ship & Lobster. The room erupted into applause as I entered, then peals of laughter at my appearance – something like a drowned rat in lycra. Stories flooded out and very soon I discovered that my support-boat skipper had been born in the flat above the bar. The pub and pontoon had been his parents' business before he and his brother had taken it over. I relaxed and had a beer with them all. I'd not had an evening 'off' for ages. The bath was safe at the pontoon. The stories floated on and eventually flowed into the tale of our day rowing through the horrible weather. By the time Mr Palmer had started telling it, I was slumped soporifically in a chair near the window. The more he told the tale, the worse the storm of the day became and by the end we were all sure there was a whale somewhere near Higham Blight.

I slept really well that night. I was content, not just after a lovely evening in the pub, but also safe in the knowledge that although the weather could now slow me down, it could not stop me for a single day longer. Now, the weather would be dictated to by me and not the other way round. The Thames was narrow enough from this point westwards that I could row even if the weather was bad. The weather couldn't stop me . . . unless of course it was really fierce.

The next morning the weather was really fierce; like a vicious pride of lions it tore at the pontoon. For two days a thick Victorian fog descended on the Thames accompanied by dreadful rain and a lethal wind in totally the wrong direction. Every morning I'd turn on the radio in a deep funk, fully expecting to hear '. . . and now the weather forecast with Little Dorrit, before the breakfast news with Bill Sykes . . .'. This was weather straight out of Dickens. There was no way I could go out in that sort of storm. Mr Palmer wasn't even letting his own larger boats out. Lashed by rain, wind and in a huge fog, the Palmers and I manoeuvred the bath to the safer side of the pontoon. Water poured into my now-useless flotation devices as the gaffer tape came loose. The enormous difficulty we had in manhandling the bath round from one side of the pontoon to the other simply underlined the utter futility of any attempt to get out on the river that day.

Stuck in Gravesend, Phil arrived down with some post for me. Among the various things was another burgee: this time from Denmark. From the letter, it seemed that someone over there had read about the bath on the website and decided to send me a flag to fly. Drinking a Coke in the bar at the Ship & Lobster, I unfolded the small Danish flag and tied it to the Royal Temple and Whitstable Yacht Club ones. When the weather improved, it would fly proudly from my showerhead and we'd enter London, a terrifying Viking sanitary invasion force of one.

The next morning the weather improved. I missed the first tide in trying to get everyone organised. We left on the second. Joe, who'd been designing the website, and another mate of ours from Cambridge boarded the Palmers' support boat with Phil and the skipper.

I applied more gaffer tape, bailed out the flotation tanks and undertook the now-familiar routine of getting safety equipment, oars, attaching the showerhead, forgetting something (usually my compass or the atlas) before getting in the bath, attaching my shoes and rowing off. Gravesend still looked stunning in the light but I was glad to see the back of her. The day before in the horrid weather I'd begun to sense another Ramsgate.

Pulling out of Gravesend, various tankers streamed past on their way out to sea. Just as with the last leg, the Port of London had enforced a speed-limit slow down on the river to make it easier for me to continue and the tankers all hooted their horns in support. They could have been hooting in angry frustration at the slow down; it was impossible to tell complex emotions from hooting. Some tankers could even have been hooting in protest at the ambiguity of hoots as a method of communication.

To my shock, boats came out full of people cheering and waving.

I'm not sure if they had come specifically to see the bath or if they were just out on the river and happened to bump into us. Although the people who had signs with 'Tim' and 'Bath' written on them had either come to find us or were having a very surreal day out: 'I've been coming out on this river for the last 30 years with this sign, Enid . . .'

'The "Tim Bath" one . . . yeah . . .'

'And every week – nothing. Now some bloke has gone and rowed out in a bath from Gravesend just to support my sign.'

'Amazing what people will do when you make a sign.'

'Best give him a wave or he'll think I don't appreciate his effort.'

'How do you know he's called Tim?'

'Just a hunch.'

'Could be a sign . . . tea?'

As I left the boat full of people waving, the river narrowed radically. This was the narrowest point I'd seen so far. It also turned out to be one of the busiest. There was a huge number of ships coming from somewhere on the north bank. Checking the atlas I realised it was Tilbury Docks. Avoiding the tankers, I followed the river as it bent first north, then south. As I rounded the third bend to see it straighten up, I saw a truly majestic sight: the Queen Elizabeth II Bridge.

It is the most incredible piece of engineering. As I went under the massive arch I whistled up into the air. In the paper boat I'd rowed under every other bridge on the Thames and under all of them I'd whistled a bugle call my grandfather taught me. The QE II Bridge was the one I'd never been under and finally I'd managed it. On top of the bridge I could see people waving. It's a very busy stretch of road and how they'd managed to be there to wave I'm not sure, but it spurred me on once again to know that I must make it to Tower Bridge.

It was a difficult row, not as bad as others I'd faced but still very tricky. This was mainly due to the wind, which conspired all day with unerring accuracy to come from totally unhelpful directions. Also, oddly, my body felt worse having had a day off. I think perhaps it thought the ordeal was over and so had relaxed a bit only to be dragged kicking and bleeding back into the bath. The painkillers had my shoulder under control but the biting wind was unkind to my various cuts.

I rowed on in pain and looked back. Having gone under the QE II Bridge an odd feeling hit me that I was home. I'd not felt this quite so strongly before. All my focus had been on getting to London. When I'd crossed the Channel I'd not felt home as I'd been forced to row *to* France rather than to Folkestone. Folkestone, Ramsgate, Margate, Whitstable and Sheerness had all been temporary homes to me and the bath; like homes, I'd loved and hated them variously but never felt as I did now. The QE II carries the M25 and the M25 has always seemed to me like the boundary to Greater London. The bath had passed the outer marker and was preparing for the final approach.

My initial plan for the day was to make it to Erith Yacht Club by nightfall. The PLA were not keen on having the bath out on the river after dark and, having seen the size of the tankers and container ships around me, I agreed with them. Erith YC seemed very accommodating and said they'd love to have the bath moored up for the night, although there did seem to be some unclear issue relating to a gate and a key. The new support-boat skipper from Palmers', Mick, shouted down, 'You're never going to make Erith at this speed ... we're going to have to look for some other mooring tonight.'

The wind had buffeted me more than a Women's Institute gathering. My progress had been radically slowed as a result and Mick was right. I scrambled for the atlas. I just couldn't find anywhere that seemed useful. Things were looking bleak. A return to Gravesend seemed the plan we'd have to adopt.

I rowed on a little despondently but began to realise that the wind was dropping. I still stood a chance. I speeded up and in a short time rounded a bend to my right. From the hanging glow of the evening sprang one of the most romantic, eccentric-looking sights on the river. A ship perched lightly on the muddy bank at a jaunty angle with a small flotilla of yachts at anchor bobbing around just yards from it. A red flag with a white crest and blue cross fluttered happily in the breeze. Mick shouted over, 'That's the yacht club. I don't believe it.'

At higher tide the boat probably floated impressively but sitting coquettishly on the silt there was something unbearably attractive about it. I pulled in, the Royal Temple, Whitstable and Danish flags fluttering from the showerhead, and hailed the yacht club in the traditional way. What was the point of Dom teaching me all that etiquette stuff if I never used it?

'Ahoy, Erith Yacht Club? Permission to come aboard?'

'You must be Tim. You're very welcome.'

A man appeared and finally answered the age-old question of where Santa lives in summer. A more mirthful, jocund, white-bearded man would be hard to find.

'Fancy a pint? We've a bar upstairs.'

Did I fancy a pint? Somewhere in a wood the Pope pulled down his pants and opened a newspaper, while in a church in Hornsey a bear took his first communion. I tied off the bath and bounded up the stairs. The gangsta phone rang.

'Hello, is that Tim?'

'Yes . . .'

'Good. This is President . . .'

'Pardon?' Something metaphysical punched me in the face; I reeled and almost fell down the steps I'd just bounded up. 'The President?'

'Yes.'

Thoughts mounted cars and drove a Formula One track in my head. The President of the United States was on my phone. This was unbelievable. I steadied myself and tried to make sense of things. If this was the President, why did he have an accent plummier than a jam factory?

'I'm phoning about an escort for a bath. This is HMS *President*.'

'Pardon?'

Just as the mist cleared and I realised it was not the President of the United States on the phone, smog billowed in. On the phone instead was the Royal Navy about providing an escort for the bath. I wasn't sure which was more surreal. I listened in awe as the officer explained what would be happening when I reached Tower Bridge. Some wondrous plotters had been very busy. There were plans afoot that I must start off on the right foot and not put the other one wrong.

Having pulled myself up the stairs, I was greeted by the not-very-cunningly disguised off-duty St Nick who'd just pulled me a pint. There were a few very merry people in the yacht club bar. When you've got Santa behind the bar everyone is happy; except on Christmas Eve: when he doesn't show up till late and getting a pint takes ages. We laughed a lot before they presented me with an Erith Yacht Club burgee. The gangsta phone rang; it was Phil.

'Mate, Mick wants to get you further up the river, he says he knows of a great mooring up a bit . . .'

I left the bar, got on the bath and rowed off upriver to find Mick, Phil and the support boat. As I rowed up with a pint of strong ale inside me I reflected that things were going well. Mine was a pot of ointment half full with just two small flies spoiling the picture by copulating in it.

The first fly was that I was due at the Palace soon and I only had one suit with me. The suit in question had been one of England's finer bits of tailoring when I'd inherited it but after a couple of outings with me it had somehow inexplicably become covered in a resolute mixture of chocolate, horse manure and car oil. I wasn't sure if Erith would have a dry cleaner and if it did, I'd only be here overnight (weather permitting) so how was I to collect the suit after the usual three days of cleaning?

The fly's girlfriend was that I simply could not find a mooring near Greenwich for the following night. I'd chosen Greenwich as it was controllably close to the Tower, so there was no chance I wouldn't make it under the Bridge the day after.

Up to that point in the journey people had been really kind with moorings. Vanquished Ramsgate fascist and disaster at Margate aside, everyone had offered me moorings for free to help keep the cost of the project down. London was sadly a very different story. I'd battled so hard to make it to London and was met with nothing but unhelpfulness. No one would give me a mooring. By that I mean no one would *allow* me to have a mooring even if I paid for it. Contrary to what I'd thought, most moorings and pontoons in London are privately owned and the owners did not seem friendly or helpful.

There'd been one exception to this in a lovely family-owned marina near Tower Bridge who kindly offered me a berth. Sadly their harbour was tidal so I couldn't take advantage of the offer. Due to the way the tide works, and the mechanism they use to keep water in the harbour at low tide, I would have been trapped there until very high tide. By the time I could have got out, I would have found it really quite tricky to battle up to Tower Bridge before the tide turned against me.

I'd been making dozens of frantic calls to anyone I could think of about this and none of them had turned up anything positive. I rowed on as my ointment looked a little less than half full and one of the flies rolled off the other and lit a cigarette.

I checked the atlas and realised I'd now made it level with the centre of Erith. I turned and up ahead, floating near some barges, was the support boat. I could see what Mick meant. Mooring up to one of the massive Thames barges was an inspired idea. Attached to one of these safe, sturdy, dependable Thames giants, the bath would be totally out of harm's way for the night.

'Here's your mooring, Tim.' He gestured behind him to the mighty Thames barge, in front of which was a small derelict sinking boat attached to an equally uninspiring precarious-looking buoy.

'You think I should moor up on the sinking ... I mean ... powder-blue boat?'

'It'll be fine, no one has moved this thing for years.'

'You don't say ...'

Mick was an experienced man of the river. He was a Thames-approved skipper; I was a man in a bath so I took his advice. It didn't seem the best mooring I'd ever seen but perhaps I'd been spoilt with moorings in the past. The Royal Harbour of Ramsgate this was certainly not. What was certain, however, was that the bath would not get stolen from this mooring as it was right out in the middle of the river. Also, as long as my knots held up, the bath would not get loose. The proof of this was the gently rotting powder-blue spectre that floated alongside me. Clearly that hadn't been loosened from the buoy for several years.

I boarded the support boat and as Mick steered us towards the pier, checked the tide tables and did the various calculations that we'd need to make the journey tomorrow. Even up to a month and a half ago these various calculations had totally baffled me; I stood more chance of passing medical exams in Swahili than getting them right. Now they came as second nature. As I was doing them, I realised I hadn't phoned Dom for days. I had become the self-sufficient thing in the water that Dom had tried so very hard to create. I may not have become a salmon but I certainly felt I could pass for a newt.

I discussed the morning plan with Mick before saying goodbye to the others. Joe, Phil and the rest were going back with Mick in the full hope their cars would still be in Gravesend. I got all the kit I needed out of the support boat and jumped up onto the pier. I had the pressing issue of a couple of flies to deal with.

As I hit bed that night, my head was unbearably heavy. I was exhausted and had to lie in a specific position so as to stand any chance of sleeping without lying on or opening myself up to the pain of my various cuts. On the plus side, things were going well. Before bed I'd been kneeling (I still couldn't sit that well) and realised that finally after over a month of rowing I'd just entered the London *A to Z* on page 85. The bath had passed the middle marker; surely even a drunk pilot could land her from here. After months in the bath with it, I could finally put down the atlas. To celebrate I had a large glass of Irish whiskey and after all the rowing of the day, passed out as pissed as the best of the genus Salamandridae I now truly was.

Six hours later I was woken up by the sound of a castrated bee. I grabbed my phone.

'Hello?'

'What the fuck is that thing tied to my boat?'

Oh good, another day had started well.

Chapter Fourteen
[There is no Deck Thirteen on a Ship]

A POPOMASTICK SCULLER

'History will vindicate me: I shall write it myself.'

Winston S. Churchill

The earliness of the morning, coupled with the large intake of Ireland's finest the night before conspired to make me slower than a 20-stone sprinter.

'What?'

'There's some fucking thing tied to my boat. I phoned the Port of London to ask what the fuck is going on, and they give me your number.'

'What . . . it's half past . . . you're up early . . .'

'I work with my hands.'

I try charm. 'Are you a carpenter?'

'No, I'm a fucking boxer!' An already bad situation just got worse. 'What are you going to do about this?'

'Just give me one second . . .' On the other end of the phone was a very deep, gravelly voice belonging to an obviously furious sweary man. I had to think fast. 'Firstly, what's your name?'

'Let's say it's Mr Green – now what are you going to do about this?'

'Have you been boxing all night?'

'No, I've just got back from splitting up fights at the local night club – now what are you going to do about this problem?'

My pacifying charm offensive was not going well. How could I politely let the presumably enormous Mr Green know that we'd tied the bath to his powder-blue pride and joy as we'd assumed it was more deserted than the *Marie Celeste*?

'We thought it was scrap . . .'

At the school of politeness and charm my teacher had just handed in her notice before scouring the pages of *Stupidity Weekly* for a new job.

'What the fuck! Does it look like scrap to you?'

My mind raced. This was a crucial moment. 'Well . . . it could do with a bit of spring clean.'

'I'm down here now on the shore looking out at my boat and your thing tied to it!'

I stopped listening midway through that line. 'You're on the shore?'

'Yes.'

The already worse situation just got horrendous. He was within eyesight of the bath. Now, there was no way I could sneak down there, swim out and loosen it from the mooring without a bellicose pugilist using me as an innovative new way to measure up for opera gloves.

'How much money are you going to pay me to make this go away?'

'What?' The question startled me in its frankness.

'How much money are you going to give me to make me happy about this?'

'It's a project to raise money for a charity. There isn't any money to give to you . . .'

'I'm a charity. Now, again, I'm asking, how much money are you going to give me?'

There was something else trying to break through into my mind. Something he'd already said that I should have seen was important. As I thought of how to get out of this new hole, I re-ran the conversation in my mind. 'How did you say you got my number?'

'I phoned the Port of London, described your bath and they gave it to me.'

Brilliant. So now the Port of London were involved. Mike's fabulous mooring could not have turned out any worse.

'Look, I'll phone the Port of London and give you a call straight back.'

He protested for a while about me hanging up and made me write his number down twice, even though it had appeared on the window of my phone, before ending the conversation with, 'I want my money so make sure you call me back, or else . . .'

It was very early in the morning for this. I phoned the PLA.

'Hello, it's Tim, I need to speak to someone about a bath and a buoy near Erith.'

'It's been á morning for it. Someone else phoned up with those exact words earlier. Is it some kind of code?'

'Not exactly.'

'Oh I see . . .' she said conspiratorially. She clearly thought I was James Bond and there was a major operation going on that day code-named 'Bath, buoy, Erith'. 'I'll put you through to the man I put him, before you, through to.'

'Hello?'

'Hi, this is Tim FitzHigham, I'm phoning to apologise for any trouble I've caused with the bath.'

'Ah, I wondered when you'd call.'

'I really thought that boat was derelict and so . . .'

'Let me stop you there.' Uh-oh, this sounded a bit ominous. 'This sort of thing happens all the time on the river, skippers tying off on things they shouldn't. I would be surprised if the man who called you even owned that mooring himself . . .'

'So I shouldn't pay him for tying off there by mistake?'

He burst out laughing.

'I'll take that as a no . . .'

'Absolutely not. He sounded pretty aggressive but there's no way you should give him any money.'

'Right.'

'If you can get down there soon and sort it out I'd appreciate it as I don't really want to have him on the phone again this morning but other than that, really, think no more about it. We're all looking forward to seeing you go under that bridge. Best of luck.'

'Erm . . . thanks.'

I hung up. That had gone much better than expected. I'd gone from expecting to pay fines and a mooring fee to Mr Green to having a pat on the back and no extra cost. I phoned Mr Green. I'd had one of the shortest careers on record at the Foreign Office so this was not going to be easy. The smart money was on it going really, really badly. After a long and tricky chat with the husky, sweary, nightclub bouncer he gave up pressing me for money and our conversation turned to his new favourite preoccupation.

'OK, fine, you can have the mooring for free, but if you do any interviews you must make sure you thank me for having generously given it to you.'

'Right . . .'

'You tell anyone on the radio or whatever that you couldn't have made it to London without me . . . or else!'

'Well, thank you for being so understanding about the whole thing, Mr Green.'

'That's OK.'

'And good luck with the boxing.'

'I only do it to keep in training for the bouncer work.'

I hung up. I'd like to think I'd made a new friend but I couldn't be absolutely sure. On a radio station in Erith later that afternoon I thanked Mr Green and they played 'A Hard Day's Night', dedicated to him.

I'd missed the first tide of the day, so had to wait for the second. While Mike went out and shifted freight around, I made more phone calls to try and sort out a mooring near Greenwich.

No one was going to budge on the issue. It was becoming pretty desperate. Bizarrely I seemed to have come up against the Department of London Transport. They were *so* charming; I now know who trains traffic wardens in tact. Caesar would never have crossed the Rubicon if he'd had to deal with anyone at Ken Livingstone's office. There was simply no reasoning with them. The conversation can be summed up in two lines:

'Can I moor on the pontoon near the National Maritime Museum?'

'No.'

It took 20 minutes to exhaust all the possible ways of saying this. The obnoxious man on the phone said he could not have cared if I'd rowed from Cape Horn to Greenwich. He said he hated charity; except his own, devoted to the care of pontoon managers in the Greenwich area. Nothing I could say would change his mind. I hung up totally frustrated. His was the only pontoon I could realistically use and he was not going to budge.

My phone flashed and the friendly voice of the Clerk of the Watermen graced my ear.

'Hello Tim, how's it going? I'm really looking forward to seeing you come under Tower Bridge.'

'Rowing is going great. I'm having trouble with getting a mooring near Greenwich.'

'Who have you tried?'

I took him through all the options I'd exhausted.

'My, you have been busy. Why don't you give him half an hour and call him back?'

We talked a bit more about the various things that had been going on. People on the river, my issues with Mr Green and the fact I was trying to leave with the second tide that day before I hung up.

Half an hour later my phone rang. It was the obnoxious man from Greenwich Pier.

'I'm sorry not to have got this sorted earlier but of course you can come and moor here.'

I couldn't quite believe what I was hearing. Perhaps this was some sort of cruel trick.

'What? Er . . . thank you. That's very kind of you. I'll only be there overnight and be gone in the morning.'

'Apparently you can stay as long as you like. I've had the Royal Navy, Port of London and the Watermen on the phone. You've got some friends, you have. I've never heard my boss use language like that to me. It seems I owe you an apology.'

'Think nothing of it. I'm sure you were just doing your job. I look forward to seeing you later.'

With that, the former mooring moron turned into a friend. One fly had finally bitten the dust. Now there was just a suit to deal with.

Mike arrived with his usual bluster. He was really pleased we were on the second tide as he'd been able to move freight around all morning. On such good form he was almost ready to burst he shouted over, 'I hear you got into trouble for choosing that mooring! I did warn you!' He smiled mischievously. 'Your name'll be mud on the river if you're not careful! You know . . . like the banks . . .

get it?' He let out a laugh stained with years of cigarettes and early frosty mornings. I smiled and loaded kit onto the support boat ready for the off. Phil arrived and loaded his masses of kit bags containing all sorts of cameras, lenses, tripods etc. Mike upped the revs and we chugged off into the middle of the Thames to arrive at the powder-blue *Marie Celeste* and the bathroom that floated next to it.

I jumped aboard. Mike handed down the kit. I strapped myself into the shoes, popped the oars into their gates and we headed off upstream with the tide. It was not a long row up to Greenwich and the river was much narrower which made things easier for me.

I rowed on up through what was and sort of still is London's industrial heart: lots of factories making stuff, supplying something somebody needs to somewhere. The river winds basically north-west at this stretch so the wind blowing south-east was less than helpful but luckily it was not as ferocious as it had been in the past. The river straightened and I found I was rowing more or less due west before it wound and meandered again, taking me south-west. The Romans certainly hadn't designed the River Thames, or if they had, the normally sober architect of the straight roads had drawn up the plans while spending the afternoon in a taverna after winning heavily, betting on the lions versus the Christians cup match. The river wiggled on and finally I saw the Woolwich Arsenal Ferry as it narrowly missed me.

I'd actually made it to Woolwich. When I'd been sitting in Ramsgate, bailing out water, Woolwich had seemed a distant dream. Now I was there, I knew how the Spanish felt having dreamt for so long of finding gold-filled El Dorado only to arrive and discover it looking less like the bullion vault of fable and more like the rough end of, well, Woolwich.

You don't realise how close to the Woolwich Ferry the Thames Barrier is until you've rowed it by river. In under 300 strokes I'd almost crashed into it. It is some piece of engineering; like a very small Sydney Opera House. This polite-looking piece of architecture serves a mighty purpose. Finally, I understood it fully; it protects London from the power of the elements and mighty sea I'd just rowed through and also regulates the flow of water going east out to sea. Without it, Gravesend and Erith would be distant flooded memories, or towns inhabited by people wading through their daily lives on stilts.

Again, it's shocking how close the Millennium Dome is to the Thames Barrier. For the first time on the trip I wanted the elements to slow me down. I'd been looking forward to this part of the trip since I'd made it to France. In my head (not having checked the charts of course), I thought I'd see the Woolwich Arsenal Ferry one day and Thames Barrier the next, before setting out on the third to pass the Dome in a blaze of sunshine. Now we were rushing past them all so fast. I had become a sightseeing glutton. As I reached the Dome finally I got perfect weather. It was the first time since before Ramsgate. The sun came out, filling the sky with a massive orange orb. It was like rowing home. Suddenly things seemed tropical. In my head, a tune reappeared that used to wake me up every morning when I lived abroad. I looked over my shoulder at the sun-filled sky, the Dome in the foreground and smiled; the familiar drum roll started in my mind and the first line kicked off, 'Hail Grenada, land of ours we pledge ourselves to thee . . .'

The Dome is on a promontory. I rounded it beneath a perfect peach sky and saw the pyramid roof of Canary Wharf. I was finally in London. People waved and shouted down from windows on the Thames. As I went past Nelson Docks, sailing boats and kayaks came out and followed me as I rowed on.

Finally, as the sun entered its final stages of setting in the sky I arrived at the jetty next to the Royal Naval College at Greenwich. A man in more uniform than an admiral came out onto the pontoon and shouted over, 'We spoke on the phone. Can you moor on the inside as that would be more helpful to us?'

Oh good, the initially unhelpful man was there to watch me moor up.

I pulled the bath round to the inside of the pontoon. The tide was really racing on that side. It was funnelled like wind in a test tunnel. Trying to moor the bath in that was as tricky as navigating rapids in a bin bag, wearing clown shoes made of boulders. I had to pull really hard to get up to the mooring position and when there, the bath wanted to slip out again and go with the current, away from the pontoon. Once, when I got up to it successfully, I threw the line over to the ostentatiously dressed man only for him to shout back, 'I'm not really sure how to tie you off . . .'

The line slipped gently off the pontoon and back into the water. Finally I came up with what seemed to be the only viable plan. I pulled hard and got the bath into position. Then, holding the line, I jumped from the bath onto the deck of the jetty and looped the line around a fixing as the bath jerked off and tried to leave me to go off downstream. Via some jostling of the line around the fixing I finally got the bath to a position where I could jump back onto her and get another line. Jumping back with that one, I tied it to another fixed point of the pontoon. It was possibly the worst plan I'd come up with to tie off. Dangerous and incredibly risky but it had worked.

Mike was having similar problems with the support boat as he thrashed the engine to try and get it into the pontoon. At one point he reversed and trapped the bath between the metal hull of his boat and the metal of the pontoon. This was very dangerous. In this position the bath would be snapped in an instant. Desperate and worried I shouted, 'Move out! Go forward!'

'What?'

Under the sound of his thrashing engines, there was a crack from the bath.

'You're crushing the bath! Move!'

He thrashed the throttle and the support boat jolted forward away from the bath. I looked at the bath, waiting to see her go under. I exhaled all the breath in my lungs. To have dragged a third-of-a-tonne piece of plumbing all the way from France only to have it crushed by the very boat that was meant to be supporting it less than five miles from target would have been utterly heart breaking. Tentatively I stepped onto the bathroom floor and began checking the hulls. Luckily, it seemed it was just a tiny crack above the waterline. Less than ideal but a lot better than it could have been.

I stepped back up on to the pontoon deck to see a fast orange boat mooring alongside it on the other side. As it pulled level one of the men removed his helmet.

'Which tide are you going to go with for Tower Bridge tomorrow?'

'Erm . . . I think the second one.'

'OK, thanks and we'll see you there. Sorry, must go, we've got to be further downriver . . .'

With that, he re-helmeted and the RNLI speedboat hacked off downriver leaving me bemused on the pontoon.

The sun had really gone now. As I stood on the bath watching the lights dancing off the river I tried to analyse why I was suddenly taking so long. I could have gone on the first tide tomorrow, I could have probably made it under Tower Bridge today, if Mike had arrived on time and I'd rowed faster. I followed the line of the green laser marking the Greenwich Meridian up into the sky. If anywhere was the place to reflect on time, this was it. Weirdly, now I was so very close to Tower Bridge, I wanted it to be further away. Very often we have so little purpose in life and for so long getting the bath to the Tower had been mine. Now it was nearly over, I wanted it to last for ever.

The sun came up the next morning. It was a glorious English summer day as I walked across the lawn amid Wren's magical buildings. Feeling like a mid-18th-century midshipman I pushed the massive doors and came to a halt at the reception desk of the National Maritime Museum. Heroic naval scenes and ships in cases surrounded the reception desk; behind it, a woman sat talking on the phone. She finished.

'Can I help you?'

'I was told to ask for Deirdre.'

'I'll phone her. You can take a seat.'

Deirdre was someone I'd been speaking to on the phone for a while. She was running a campaign based in the Maritime Museum and had kindly said I should call in on my way through that part of London.

'Ah, Tim, there you are. Do come upstairs.'

I followed Deirdre through passages and corridors, up staircases and under atriums until we ended up in a tiny office at the end of a long corridor. On the way I realised my phone was running low on power. There were calls I needed to make, things that had to be organised.

'Does anyone in your office have a phone charger for this?'

'Yes, I've got one and better still, I've got to pop out for a bit. Why don't you have a seat at my desk and make calls. I'm sure you've got a lot to organise.'

The view from the desk was stunning. I stared out over the sun-drenched lawns I'd just walked across. There was little time for wistful romantic glazing over; there was a lot to organise. I picked up the phone and began to deal with all the various things that needed to come together later that day like some admiral planning a battle. I worked on from the now-empty, tiny broom cupboard feeling increasingly like a cross between Nelson and Gordon the Gopher. Deirdre arrived back.

'Right, let's go to the bath. There's some people who want to take pictures.'

As we wandered back out to the lawns past the portraits of the great mariners of the past, I was sure they seemed to smirk. Quite what men like Hardy, St Vincent and Collingwood would have made of the bath would be anyone's guess. Deirdre's pace was vigorous but on the way back to the bath she still had me giggling as I trotted alongside her at stories of polo matches in Ulan Bator when she was younger.

We arrived at the bath and did photos before going back up to the broom-cupboard office. Surrounded by Deirdre and her stunning team, I made more calls.

Before leaving the NMM I went down to the lavatory and gaffer-taped up my hands again before applying more surgical spirit to my still-lacerated swollen plums. When I'd first applied it after crossing the Channel, I'd passed out with the pain. Later in the trip around Margate, I'd applied it to my nethers and it felt very painful but I'd at least managed to stay conscious. Around Gravesend, when applying it, it burnt and I felt vaguely morally dirty. Now when I applied it, it felt warm and oddly comfortable. I made a mental note to go through surgical spirit plum cold turkey the moment today was over or seek help. Whimpering, I pulled up my rowing lycra and waddled gingerly out of the lavatory.

The last tide of the day did not obey Naval time. Contrary to everything the Navy and I wanted and expected of it, the tide was late. I paced up and down on the tiled bathroom floor waiting for it to turn.

We all waited for the tide. Once again nature had stopped me. A grey launch arrived at the pontoon with two sailors on top and a White Ensign flapping in the breeze. One shouted over, 'We thought we'd meet you on the way down, you still here?'

'The tide's being slow today . . .'

The grey launch pulled into the pontoon. I started.

'Andy?' A boyish-looking sailor grinned in a way that would have made Just William justifiably proud. 'I thought you wouldn't remember . . .'

Andy had been the Navy coxswain who'd escorted me down the Thames in the paper boat two years previously.

'I wouldn't have missed this. I asked to change shifts to be here.'

I grinned in a way that would have made an idiot justifiably proud. I was very touched.

More boats arrived. The RNLI, the Port of London, various marine companies and Thames Watermen all sent boats. Everything was going really well. Boats were assembling for the off. This was going to be a top evening. Finally, a gorgeous wooden launch built by 'Uncle Bill' who has the boathouse next to Mark's came bombing down the river. At its helm was Uncle Bill himself.

'Thank goodness, I thought I'd missed you!'

'Is Mark coming?'

'No, he's had to go up to Henley today. There's been some sort of emergency. He told me to say well done.'

I felt a bit down that Mark couldn't be there to see the completion of everything we'd worked so hard for. Still, at least Uncle Bill was there so someone from the boathouse would get to see it. Phil handed me my phone.

'It's Comic Relief, mate, I think you'd better take this . . .'

My sadness at Mark's unavailability was compounded by the following conversation. Comic Relief couldn't send anyone down to the river either. This was a blow. I understood how busy everyone in the organisation must have been but it was a real shame. They'd promised that someone would be there to give me my other sock. Silly as it may sound, I really wanted to get it. I'd been trying so hard to reach London and raise money for them and the thought of eventually making a pair of Sport Relief socks (albeit a year late) had kept me going at times. Eventually they agreed to send someone down to pick up any money that might be donated that evening but as for anyone officially coming down to present me with a sock, no one could make it.

I hung up feeling a bit glum. Perhaps no one would be turning up. Maybe there would just be me and a bunch of boats?

A photographer and reporter arrived from Kenny. The reporter was the same one who had crossed the Channel with me.

'Hope the journey is a bit less painful for you today . . .' He grinned. 'Kenny can't be here, he's got to make sure tomorrow's paper goes out, but he sent you this . . .' He handed me a large bottle of champagne and an envelope. Inside the envelope was a sticker with 'Well done, you made it, Kenny'. I peeled the back off the sticker and stuck it to the roll top. At least Kenny would sort of be there when I went under the bridge.

I had a huge moment of doubt. I'd always thought that people would turn up to welcome the bath but these key members of the team not being there gave me a real pause for thought. People had been going on with their lives while I'd been faffing around on the river. Would anyone bother to show up? I could have set up one of the most embarrassing moments of my life: to arrive in London and be greeted by no one. Perhaps it would have been better not to have bothered coming round Kent at all. I was suddenly struck with fear. I'd not been afraid at any point in the trip before but suddenly it was a fear of rejection by a city I love that made me stop. I stared into the water. Mike broke me out of it.

'Tim! The tide's turned!'

There was no time to dwell any more on this rather depressing series of thoughts. I'd set this up. I had to go through with it.

This stretch of the river is familiar to anyone who watches *EastEnders*. In the official technical maritime description: it's the really wiggly looking bit you see on the credits just after they kick off. I leant over the side and checked the gaffer tape on the flotation tanks. If it could just hold up for another few hours I would get to see the Tower.

I lowered my skinless bottom into the sliding seat of the bath and winced a little as the cheeks hit the wood. On the plus side, however, finally, it was nearly all over.

The sun was turning to set as I pulled off from the pontoon at Greenwich. Its rays glinted off the Victorian showerhead. The plumbing below was shot to pieces and it couldn't suck water up any more but it still looked splendid in the half-light. Flying from the showerhead of the bath were all the yacht club burgees and the one Danish one that I'd been presented with. Behind them, towards the stern, on its own masthead, flew the Red Ensign that had been with me since the start.

As I pulled on the oars with gaffer-taped hands, I looked around me. The bath, in the half-light, with her escort boats and the sun setting behind was like some haunting sanitaryware parody of

Turner's *The Fighting Temeraire*. I smiled at the wonderful ridiculousness of the scene. The bath was as battered as the pictures of the *Suhaili* when Robin Knox-Johnston pulled her into Falmouth. A craft, ill-designed for her purpose which had held up against the odds to make it. I was shot to pieces, with gaffer-taped hands, surgical-spirit-numbed plums and a still-broken shoulder, but if both of us just held together for the next hour or so, we would make it.

As I rowed up the last short hop to Tower Bridge I noticed that people began to appear on the riverbank taking pictures, shouting and waving. Sailing boats and kayaks again came alongside the bath: as well as the support boats that had already joined us, a small flotilla was gradually gathering, splayed out behind a Thomas Crapper bath.

I relaxed into the row. Never had the conditions been this good. It seemed finally even the weather conceded that I stood a chance of making it. Yet as I took the curve around Rotherhithe something took hold of me. True, I was in pain but I wanted to make this. A focus suddenly clicked in. I increased the stroke rate. I'd become a man in command of rowing, rather than the useless master of capsize that had started this project.

I rounded the final bend near Wapping and looked over my shoulder. There it was, in front of me: Tower Bridge.

I turned back to face the taps, dug in and increased the pace again. Nothing would stop me now. I heard various voices screaming into the darkening sky: 'Come on Tim!' I pulled as though nothing else in my life had ever mattered before. I was going to make this.

Upriver of me, aboard HMS *President*, sailors stood to attention on deck, flags flapping in the breeze. People crowded the bank under Tower Bridge cheering and shouting; people lined up on top of the bridge and leant over the side craning to see what was happening.

The noise told me all I wanted to hear: London had turned up. A lump welled up in my throat. The gaffer tape had started to come loose; I wrapped blood-drenched hands around the oars, looked into the reflection in the taps and pulled on, getting faster and faster as I sensed the end was near. The bath voyage would end with a racing finish.

For a year and a half of my life I'd been a man in ill-fitting, blood-stained lycra, defined by my total failure to get here. It had obsessed me, hospitalised me twice and almost killed me, but now I could see Tower Bridge.

People shouted and cheered. I pulled on. To the lasting shame of all my antecedents my stiff upper lip collapsed altogether and as I pulled, tears rolled down my cheeks. I wasn't crying at the pain, although it was intense, but at the fact that people cared. It seemed that for once a random lot of people had come together, forgotten all the aggravating things in their lives and united to celebrate something very silly. In the final strokes of the bath, I cried with a sheer unadulterated sense of joy.

Before I realised it, I was under Tower Bridge. Horns on all the escort boats around me sounded off. One of the mighty Thames Fire Ships, an updated version of those that had been used for Winston Churchill's funeral, sucked up water from the Thames and spewed it out in a massive victory arch. Even people on the bridge were soaked. Everything seemed to slow down. I pulled under Tower Bridge and sank back into the roll top of the bath. All I could manage was to gasp between breaths, 'Yes, yes . . .'

I removed the remainder of the gaffer tape from my hands – most of it had already come off – and raised my exhausted arms up in the sky. Still breathless, I shouted again, 'Yes! Yes!'

I'd done it. Boats criss-crossed around me as the Navy escort tried to help keep the flotilla in order. I pulled a couple of extra strokes just to check I really had made it under the bridge. The Thames Fire Ship carried on spewing water everywhere, boats sounded their horns and I undid my fixed shoes in the bath. Within seconds I had the Red Ensign flag and its masthead in my battered hands, held it aloft and waved it victorious at the people on the bank, those on the bridge and to anyone who might have been watching from outer space. The first person to row the Channel in a bathroom was indefatigably British.

Putting the flag down for a second, I remembered the champagne from Kenny in the washstand. Very soon, to cheering from the bridge and bank, I'd sprayed *Lilibet II*, myself and the Navy, before feeding some to the river and drinking the few mouthfuls that remained.

The moment of victory is so short compared to the length of time an achievement has taken. With the last drop of champagne gone, I flourished the Red Ensign again before turning the bath towards the Tower of London and rowing back under the bridge to the mooring I had at HMS *President*. In all of its grizzly history, no one had ever been as pleased to see the Tower of London as I was that evening. As I rowed back, now against the tide, towards *President*, the Fire Ship went off again. The shower of the bath looked on impotent and jealous at the massive power shower being given to the people on the bridge.

I stepped off the bath. This is a crucial moment for anyone involved in maritime. The journey was over and leaving the bath filled me with an overwhelming sadness. Simply put: I did not want to leave her. She had been my home for a month and a half and, more than that, she'd been the focus of my life for nearly two years, and now our journey was at an end.

Stepping up onto the pontoon, I was greeted by the second-in-command of *President*. He saluted very smartly, shook me by the hand and broke into a huge grin.

'Welcome aboard, Tim, well done. There are some people to see you.'

Coming down the gangplank to the pontoon was the Alderman of Tower Ward. He's called Richard and is a very kind man indeed. Aldermen are the next rank down from the Lord Mayor of London (in fact all Lord Mayors must be Aldermen first), so he's also quite senior. He looked splendid in the traditional full regalia of the Alderman: a red fur-lined gown, black bicorn fur-lined hat and white gloves. He grinned.

'I understand there's no one else to give you this.' He pulled out the Sport Relief sock that would make my pair. 'You've very richly deserved it. Well done.'

I shook him by the hand and felt very special. Someone from Comic Relief had obviously been thinking of me after all. Finally, a year and a half after getting the first one, I now had a second Sport Relief sock.

'Where are Mum and Dad?'

Richard smiled. 'Your parents are probably drenched, they're on that Fire Ship.'

Dom appeared on the pontoon and, much to his old-style British embarrassment, had to suffer me flinging my arms around him. Then Simon, Managing Director of Thomas Crapper & Company, arrived next to us on the pontoon. It was genuinely a treat to have them next to me in the moment of triumph. Simon grinned.

'Tim, you should be Grade Two Listed and preserved for the nation.'

Richard the Alderman turned to him and smiling said, 'Surely you mean Grade One, with a star!'

The Fire Ship arrived at the other side of the pontoon and the smart sailor who had greeted me helped my mum, dad, sister, brother-in-law and three friends off it. Hugging my family was one of the greatest moments of the bath journey. The smart sailor said to Mum, 'You must be very proud of him.'

Dad grinned as water dripped off him. Mum simply smiled quietly. 'More relieved he's made it back safely . . .'

My three friends Clare, Charlotte and Jane formed a collective, beaming from ear to ear; they'd become very giggly with hoards of buff firemen to play with and, although wearing their kit, had somehow still managed to get soaking wet. The newly formed trio of the women's auxiliary fire service gave me a big excited hug. If A.A. Milne had bumped into them, there would have been three Tiggers in *Winnie the Pooh* instead of just the one.

'We got to use the hoses, we got to use the hoses! Did you see us soaking the bridge?'

Finally, with my family, friends and the second-in-command in tow, I walked up the gangplank of *President* and onto the deck. I was totally blown away; the deck was crammed with people. So many friends had turned up. It was very moving. Coming forward from the crowd was the Officer Commanding of *President*. The smart second-in-command stiffened, saluted and introduced me. At first she looked very grave and serious. I wasn't sure she liked having all this nonsense on her command. Then, there was a twinkle in her eye, she burst into a smile and shook me by the hand.

'Welcome to *President*, very well done. I'd like to offer you the Ward Room to celebrate with your friends. You deserve it, rowing all that way is a heck of an effort . . . and in a bath. Come in.'

I took to her immediately. I'd never been allowed in the Ward Room before. This was an honour and to have it for the night to celebrate was very kind.

It was a truly great evening, with people from all stages of the bath trip now colliding, reunited over drinks and laughter. I introduced Wendy and her husband to my mum and dad, met the people who'd been with my friend Rich on the QE II Bridge in Kent before finally owning up to Ollie and the Mumblers why I'd had to leave the field so fast that afternoon after the match.

With horns sounding, people shouting and cheering, Fire Ships going off, flags flying and Royal Navy saluting, the bath had come home to a most beautiful and peculiarly British celebration of the epic absurd. All the threads of my plumbing odyssey had come together as London celebrated one of the most eccentric happenings on the Thames in years. The bath had finally reached the finish.

The Master of the Household

has received Her Majesty's command to invite

Mr. Tim FitzHigham

to a Maritime Reception to be given at St. James's Palace

by The Queen and The Duke of Edinburgh

20th July, 2005 at 6.00 p.m.

Dress: Lounge Suit | Day Dress
Uniform

WRAPPED UP WARM IN THE ODCOMBIAN BLANKET

'It is the duty of everyone to protect those less fortunate than themselves.'

David Kent Anns

It is easier to teach piano to a swarm of bees than to attempt to Windsor-knot a tie while sprinting down Pall Mall. Running as fast as I could, one of England's formerly decent pieces of tailoring became a blur to onlookers as an errant tie flapped in the breeze behind me. I finally managed to get the short bit of my tie through the hole just as my phone rang. It was a cousin of mine.

'Hi Tim?'

'Yes.'

'It's me.'

'Hi, I can't talk for long, I'm late for the Palace thing . . .'

'I heard it was today. You're always late for everything. Could you not have made sure you were on time today for once? She is the Queen, you know.'

'I'm nearly there . . .'

I broke into a trot – the Aethaneum up ahead.

'Right ho, thought you should know, you're in the newspaper, there's a cartoon and everything . . .'

I stopped. 'What?'

'I'll read it, if you like. I'm not sure you've got time for all of it, so I'll just give you the best bits. It's under the headline "Bath-time at Buckingham Palace". "The Queen champions British explorers, no matter what frontier they push. Tomorrow, Tim FitzHigham will dine at Buckingham Palace . . ."'

'It's actually St James's and I'm not really dining as such, just sort of nibbling, really . . .'

'That's the least of your worries. You've obviously spoken to them as they quote you.'

'Yes, I remember talking to him when I was around Margate stuck in a storm. We talked about lots of stuff, the letter from the Queen, the paper boat, all sorts, he was a nice guy.'

'That bit's all fine . . .'

'What's the problem then?'

'Let me finish. "Tim's panicking as the only suit he owns is covered in horse manure."'

'D'oh! Me and my big mouth . . .'

'Great work, cuz.'

'What if the Palace have seen it? That could make it a tricky afternoon.'

'Have you had the suit cleaned?'

'Of course.'

'I shouldn't worry about the Palace, it's the *Independent*, I'd bet you five quid the Palace staff all read the *Telegraph*, except the socialists among them – they'll read the *Mail*! So no one will have seen it. Just thought you should know in case.'

'More alarmingly, what happens if my mother's seen it?'

'That's more of a worry.'

'Thanks for the heads-up, mate – what's the cartoon like?'

'Hilarious. It's you in a suit made of dung.'

'Oh good . . . hang on, why are you reading the *Independent*?'

'Remember why your grandfather always took the *Mirror*?'

'Erm . . .'

'It's always good to know what the other side are up to!'

'Oh . . . er . . . right . . . I'd better . . .'

'Yes, sure, off you go . . . have a great time.'

What other side? I left confusion aside and concentrated on other matters. I never thought there'd be a cartoon of me in a newspaper. I suspect like everyone who's ever had a cartoon of themselves in a paper, I couldn't wait to see it. However, before I could get to the newsstand there was the not-insignificant matter of the Royal reception I was late for. Cantering now, I finally completed my tie as I passed the Reform. Moments later I drew level with Crown Passage and rounded the corner into Marlborough Road. In a whirl, I pulled out my invite and cleared security, trotted along a few corridors, bounded up a gilded stairway and finally found myself in a red gilt-trimmed room across a large table from a member of the Palace staff.

Even though I must have looked smart, facing the gimlet-eyed gaze of a member of Her Majesty's finest, I felt scruffier than my old dog. There was a list of the people that were allowed into the Palace that day; I froze. I've hated lists since I first heard of them behind a desk in a small classroom in Derbyshire. Suddenly I was paralysed by not knowing which letter I'd be under. Stentorian tones emerged from the mouth beneath the gimlet eyes.

'Name?'

'Erm . . . I'm not really sure . . .'

'What?'

'Well, I could be under T for Tim or F or C for Channel, or something else.'

A cheerful-looking member of staff then emerged.

'You must be Tim FitzHigham, suit's looking good – you can't even smell the dung!'

My heart sank. 'Oh good, you've seen it . . .'

'Yes, very funny, this way.'

With a smile that brightened the room she pushed open a door at the end of the one we were in and suddenly in front of me was a room of people looking as nervous and excited as I felt.

'The boss will be along in a mo, someone will find you with refreshments . . .'

With that she handed me a very smart badge with my name on it and left the room. I looked around and, like an experienced croupier, shuffled my feet. I was in the first of three interconnecting rooms. All of them were exquisitely decorated in the same red and gilt colourings of the room before. Candelabras larger than small children sat near the windows and everything glistened beneath the enormous sparkling chandeliers. The furthest room from me contained a throne. It was obvious to even the dimmest intellect that if it was a palace you were searching for, this was a pretty good place to look. I whispered to myself, 'We're not in Kansas now, Toto . . .'

A naval officer in uniform spun round. 'What?'

'Oh . . . er . . . nothing, I was just . . . er . . .'

Not sure how to explain I was momentarily playing a small girl called Dorothy, I thought I'd better try something else. 'Sorry, hi, I'm Tim . . .'

We started chatting away about the Navy, how long he'd been in and what ships he'd been on. While we were doing this I caught sight of the Queen across the room. The good thing about being a rower in a room of sailors was that I was by far the tallest man there. I'm not freakishly tall; it's just that sailors are traditionally quite short. My eye halted and sprung to attention: gazing at Her Majesty, all other noise became a blur. It was a lot to take in. Just across the room from me was a person I'd sincerely admired since I was tiny. Not only had I admired Her, my entire family admired Her and had been trying for years to die for Her in a variety of imaginative ways. Before Her they'd been trying to die for Her father, grandfather etc., and the ideals they believed in.

I became predictably nervous but also, and this was baffling, a huge feeling of protectiveness swept over me. I was sure that the room was teeming with Royal Protection Officers filling every crack in every door, lurking behind every curtain, banging their heads beneath every tablecloth but a strange feeling appeared in my stomach: I felt protective of the Queen. I've had the feeling before around my grandmother, sister (when she's sick), mother and also when friends of mine have been pregnant, but quite why it hit me then was weird. Across the room, above the heads of the others, the Queen saw me and seemed to smile at me. I could just have projected that on to Her in my own mind; she could just have been smiling at the room decoration in general; not knowing Her well, it was impossible to tell. Instinctively, I bowed my head in Her direction. Looking back up from bowing my head I saw Her smile again. The first piece of instinctive pre-decimal etiquette I'd knee-jerked into had seemingly been correct. I turned my gaze back down to the officer in uniform; he'd obviously just asked me a question that I'd missed.

'I'm sorry?'

'It says "cross-Channel rower" on your badge, what did you do? Other than the obvious of course . . .'

This was a question I'd been trying really hard to avoid. In the room waiting patiently to meet the Queen were the truly great heroes of current British Maritime. Men like the First Sea Lord, the Second Sea Lord, round the world yachtsmen and -women and the heads of various illustrious maritime bodies, the Coastguard, RNLI and other senior organisations. I had rowed the Channel in a piece of ablution equipment. The longer I could keep that secret, the better.

'Erm . . .' My mind floundered around desperate for something to say other than mention the bath, 'Erm . . .' This was getting awkward. '. . . I sort of rowed the Channel in a bath . . .'

The officer looked stunned. 'What?'

'I sort of took a bath and rowed the Channel . . .'

'That was you?'

'Er . . . yes . . .'

'You'd better come with me, She wants to see you.'

'What?'

It turned out that the smartly dressed naval man was an equerry at the Palace. Equerries are serving military officers who attend on the members of the Royal Family.

Suddenly, from loitering near a curtain at the back, I found myself at the front of the queue to be presented to the Queen. The equerry handed a card with my name on to one of the stunning ladies-in-waiting who surrounded the Queen and whispered something in Her ear before withdrawing to stand smartly beside me.

One of the many things my grandfather decided I needed to grasp at the age of five was a total command of absolutely correct royal etiquette. We would spend many happy hours in one of his enormous greenhouses with him drilling me in the correct way to greet and address various members of the Royal Family, Ducal lines and all aristocratic stations south. As the Queen was often unavailable for these important tutorials, she would normally be played by one of his prize marrows or a large pumpkin.

During the second local difficulty, as my grandfather called it, or, as it's more commonly known by history, World War II, my grandfather was running back to barracks after some military exercise or other. He was running alone; the ability to act as an individual was one of the hallmarks of the regiment he was in. A large black car, a Rolls-Royce or something similar, glided past him before coming to a stop up ahead of him in the road. The driver's door opened and a man in a smart uniform got out, approached him and demanded to see his papers. My grandfather presented them. The man inspected them and went to the back window of the car. The man in the smart uniform opened the back door of the car and out stepped Queen Mary (wife of George V[15], grandmother of Elizabeth II). Shocked, Grandfather followed the rigid codes of etiquette that had been taught to him and the Queen-Empress was kind enough to offer him a lift back to barracks in Her car. Sitting in the back of the Royal car the first thing She asked him was, 'How is the war going?'

---

[15]By an odd coincidence, the man whose travel bath I'd tried to auction the previous year.

He looked at Her and always said his eyes widened. He felt that in one question She had taken the entire fate of civilised Europe and rested it on his shoulders. At the time my grandfather was just a young soldier and his grasp of high command policy would have been sketchy but he did his best to enlighten Her Majesty as to the things he knew and the morale of the regiment. He was a great storyteller and the bit at the end was my favourite. He got on well with Queen Mary and they chatted for quite some time. Before the car stopped he'd been ahead in the exercise but due to his delightful conversation with the Queen-Empress he arrived back at barracks much later than the rest of the regiment. When questioned by his senior officer as to why he was so late, he replied that he'd been unavoidably delayed as he'd got a lift with Queen Mary in Her Rolls-Royce. The senior officer looked him squarely in the eye and said, 'Come on David, if you're going to make excuses at least make them believable.'

The moral of this story, he felt, was that you never knew when absolutely correct Royal etiquette would be needed. He clearly resolved then that his grandson would never be found wanting, as the marrows and I later found out.

Now faced with the Queen and not a marrow, suddenly my lessons in the greenhouses came good. Never speak to the Queen until She speaks to you. Never ask Her questions. The first time you speak to Her, call Her 'Your Majesty', after that always 'Ma'am'. Never say, 'It's a pleasure to meet you,' it is taken as read that it's a pleasure to meet the Queen. Never shake hands with the Queen; that could be correct or could just have been as the marrow had no arms. If She offers you Her hand, touch it only briefly. Never turn your back on Her for a second and bow from the chest or, if you have a bad back, the neck. Of course, like any good set of rules there are hundreds of exceptions, for example, as a Waterman, you *are* allowed to touch the arm of the sovereign in a special tradition going back centuries. There were a whole lot of rules and exceptions like this that I'd been taken through day after long happy summer day in the greenhouses and that's why grandparents are great. I bowed at the chest. The Queen offered me Her hand.

'So you rowed the Channel did you?'

'Your Majesty, how kind of you to ask, yes I did . . . in a bathtub.'

The Queen has very stunning blue eyes and on hearing this they distinctly twinkled and She broke into a smile. For the next ten to 20 minutes we giggled with each other. She is a very funny lady.

One moment the conversation was straight out of a Bond film.

'A copper bath, with a floor, it must have weighed half a tonne.'

I smoothed my hair slightly, not wishing to miss the chance. 'It was actually only a third of a tonne, Ma'am, but it was still really rather heavy.'

The next minute it was out of the *Goon Show*.

'Did you not think of putting a sail on the bath and sailing it?'

'I did consider a shower curtain, Ma'am, but I couldn't decide on the colour . . .'

Towards the end of our time together I thanked Her for Her constant support in my attempts to raise money for charity. She smiled and modestly mumbled something about how She wasn't sure exactly why Her support had helped but if it had, She was pleased. Very kindly, She thanked me for coming before She moved on to talk to the Head of the Coastguard and I was left with a stunning lady-in-waiting wearing a beautifully cut pink dress.

'Thanks for coming, Tim.'

'Erm . . . I was just very shocked to be asked.'

'We don't often get to see the boss laugh like that.'

'Erm . . . my pleasure.'

'And may I say, very well done.'

Then she was gone too and I was left, feeling just a little shaken (and not unstirred) with only a glass of Bollinger for company. It's not every day you get to see the most easily recognisable face in the world looking directly into your own. The face I'd just been looking at is on the stamps, I reflected as I admired the taste of whoever had chosen the Bollinger. All the marrows in Berkshire hadn't prepared me for this. I tried to get out of the limelight that surrounded the Queen only to find I'd been expertly guided by the officer equerry into the company of the Duke of Edinburgh.

His Royal Highness initially appeared to be under the impression that I was some sort of war hero. Initially, I put this down to vagueness but then realised it was actually due to some very shrewd observation by the Duke. I was wearing an old family tie of some long-disbanded regiment, which my great-grandfather had worn throughout the First World War. The Duke recognised the tie instantly and was clearly wondering why I was wearing it. Sheepishly I explained that I had been asked to attend the event not for being a war hero but for rowing the English Channel in a bath. The Duke looked stunned and thundered, 'What?'

'I rowed the English Channel in a bath ... well, more a sort of bathroom ...'

'What?'

I could see he thought I was teasing him. Behind his eyes I perceived he was trying to work out how best to deal with me. Any minute I feared the cantankerous, irascible spirit for which the Duke is so famous would obliterate me more completely than fast-flowing lava. Like an Exocet missile his eyes locked on to mine. I gulped like a compromised ship about to take the final hit. Luckily for me just as he was about to bury me, the First Sea Lord appeared at his arm.

'The tragic thing is – it's actually true; he did row the Channel in a bath.'

The Duke smiled, then chuckled, and then he laughed before swinging into the conversation with gusto. He asked lots of questions about the weather, journey round Kent, speed of the bath, type of oars etc. Somewhere on the other side of London, Dom must have been beaming with pride as I trotted out all the information the Duke requested, none of which I'd have known without Dom. The Duke turned out to be a very funny, clever and knowledgeable man. It's impossible on meeting him to reconcile the dynamic, polite, kind and hilarious man with the image of him I'd read about in the press.

After a while, the Duke and Sea Lord left me to resume my post near the curtain and practice foot shuffling. I took another sip of Bollinger and mused that it was a very surreal day. A youngish man standing next to me said hello and we got into conversation. It wasn't until we'd exchanged a few stories and made each other laugh a few times that I realised the funny, charming, mischievous man in front of me was Prince Edward. Either he was on the best form of his life that day or has been as much abused in the popular imagination as his father. He was so very funny.

The Queen was joined by Prince Philip and they left the room. After they'd left I made to leave too but on my way out a man approached me.

'Hello Tim, I'm Brigadier Black, one of the equerries . . .'

His name wasn't Black but I can't remember what it was, also he may not have said equerry but some other Palace posting. I would blame discretion but probably a more likely explanation is the excellent Bollinger. What was certain was that he was a senior member of Palace staff and a brigadier.

'. . . just thought you'd like to know: when the boss left the room, She turned to Prince Philip and said She thought She'd just met the maddest man in Her Kingdom. Well done, and thanks again for making Her smile.'

As I finished the day barside at a hotel in St James's (predictably, after having had to spend part of the day as Bond, sipping one of London's finest Martinis) I knew what line would replace James Cracknell's to be written on my tomb.

In the days that followed the bath trip various letters arrived including one from Number Ten signed 'with best wishes' and 'yours sincerely Tony Blair'. I also had a very kind letter from the chairman of Comic Relief. It seemed that a single blood-inducing piece of stupidity I'd thought up in the bath had made a lot more people smile than I thought it would. The bath had completed around 200 miles from France to Tower Bridge and the timstub.com website had received in excess of 50,000 hits.

Matthew Pinsent, James Cracknell and Steve Williams did treat the rest of the world as they had treated the bath and won gold in the Olympics at Athens. The margin was much closer and there was no time for pitch and putt.

A mere six days after stepping off the bath under Tower Bridge in London I stepped onto the stage at the Pleasance Theatre in Edinburgh. Would the audiences be as relieved as the Pleasance artistic director that I'd finally turned up?

I'd had no time to prepare the show or try it out. Most comics like to start trying out material in March, before beginning the process of honing it until the Festival in August. I'd had four days to recover and tend to my wounds, one day to pack my stuff and another to drive north to Scotland. During this, there had not been much time to think of something to say.

I walked out on stage with no clue what to say other than a

vague idea I should tell the bath story in my own way as truthfully as possible. In my undecided mind, the show would be an acoustic stand-up storytelling hour called *In the Bath: Unplugged*, as I hate show titles with puns in them. Still haunted by the critical mauling I'd taken the year before I was very apprehensive about doing anything but the slot had been booked and it would have been very bad manners of me to have wasted it.

The first show was a very curious experience. I arrived on stage with a couple of sheets of paper to help me remember the thread of the story and started to talk. I finished telling the stupidity of the truth before the audience sat totally silent at the end. The CD of music that was meant to kick in had failed. The lights went down and I realised a tear had rolled down my face. That doesn't normally happen to me in shows that are meant to be funny. I stood silent on stage not really sure exactly what I'd just said before one person started to clap. Almost immediately the whole audience started to clap, before standing up. I stood frozen and faced a standing ovation. People on the front row even got on stage and gathered around me in a big group hug. It was a comedy show that made people happy to cry at the end. Before I knew what had happened the bath show had kindly become critics' choice in the *Evening Standard,* the *Guardian, London Metro* and *Edinburgh Three Weeks* and sold out for the rest of the run at Edinburgh. The show was not eligible for most of the awards, as I fell foul of various eligibility rules because I'd been stuck out at sea and missed bits of the Festival, but amazingly in the final week it won the *Three Weeks* Editor's Award. *In the Bath: Unplugged* has now played in hundreds of theatres, barns, places and palaces all over the UK and abroad. From the first day, there's not been a music CD at the end. Some mistakes work better than the plans they destroy.

What about the bath herself? After the incredible reception at Tower Bridge, Uncle Bill Colley arrived the next morning to tow the bath back up to Mark in Richmond. I wanted somewhere for the bath to go that would be warm and comfortable for her but after phone calls to every museum or gallery I could think of, it was obvious that no one had the room or inclination to take in the star of our double act. The bath spent a year falling into disrepair on a mooring near Richmond, of interest to only the most dedicated sailors, rowers and people that came to the bath shows. Throughout all of that time I kept trying to find someone to take the bath. Despite all my efforts nothing seemed to be possible. Then one day my phone rang.

'Tim, it's Ben at the National Maritime Museum in Cornwall.'

The National Maritime Museum in Cornwall is one of my favourites. From 2003 to 2007 it was home to the paper boat, so I'd got to know the staff quite well.

'We're staging a new exhibition called "Mad Dogs and Englishmen" and we were wondering if we could have the bath.'

From a dilapidated state at her mooring in Richmond, *Lilibet II* was plucked for stardom. Many people: Mark, the apprentices, the restoration team at the National Maritime Museum and I, worked really hard to clean up and restore her to the shining state she was when she first floated off the boat ramp in 2004. After all the hard work, in late 2006, *Lilibet II* took her place as the centrepiece of the new exhibition. It was a lovely moment to pan around the main gallery of the National Maritime Museum, Cornwall, looking at all the famous mastheads and see, sparkling in the middle of them, a Thomas Crapper showerhead.

It is difficult to say exactly how much money the bath project raised for Comic Relief as, incredibly, in the years since I stepped off the bath money has still been coming into the fund, but the last time anyone checked it was in excess of £30,000. Wherever the bath is, there is normally a Comic Relief collecting bucket not too far away.

After its narrow scrape with international fraud Simon and I decided not to auction off George V's travel bath. We were both uneasy about it even before the attempted fraud as we felt something that stunning should be enjoyed by as many people as possible. We took the decision to make it available for everyone to see and so it's now on display at the small ablution museum near the head offices of Thomas Crapper & Company.

Just as Shackleton had been knighted and Nelson made a viscount for their heroic deeds, I was made Waterman to the Mayor and Unitary Authority of Swindon. Other honours and laurels followed swiftly after that. I was made Commodore of Sudbury Town Quay in the County of Suffolk. Normally the Commodore of a Quayside is responsible for the safe landing of large ocean-going vessels; since Sudbury is 25 miles inland, my main problem is the car parking. Although I do get a rather natty pennant (flag) that I can fly from any ship or boat I happen to be on, and a big hat. If something is worth doing, it's worth doing wearing a very big hat.

In Selby, a stunning market town in Yorkshire, I was given a title first used in the time of William Rufus (son of William the Conqueror): Pittancer of Selby in the Ridings (which sounds like something out of Tolkien). The title of Pittancer gives me various medieval rights and privileges. On Maundy Thursday every year I attend the Pittancer's service in the Abbey in Selby. After it, I am obliged to give the Prebandry of the Abbey (the priest who runs the place) one pound in order to help him maintain himself throughout the year. In addition to this, if there are any stray Benedictine monks found wandering in the Abbey grounds on that day, I am obliged to give them the medieval measurement of a pittance of eggs and cheese to feed themselves. My main concern every year is that a coach trip of Benedictine monks will randomly happen to be passing through Selby that day and I'll have to cook up the world's largest cheesy omelette in the market place.

In 2006 I was asked by the UK Environment Agency to team up with the TV impressionist Alistair McGowan. We were both made spokespeople for the United Nations World Environment Day. My part of this was to try and get people to spend less time in the bath and take a shower instead.

I was really overwhelmed by the kindness of the various Mayors, Town Councils and Boroughs that wanted to show their support for the bath project. To be a spokesperson with the UN and Environment Agency was something I never thought possible but still there was one even greater honour in store.

Simon phoned up from Thomas Crapper & Company.

'Tim, in honour of the Channel crossing by bath, we at Thomas Crapper and Company are going to release a commemorative lavatory named after you: *The FitzHigham*.'

Finally, my family seat: I was flushed with pride, couldn't get it out of my *cistern*; this was the zenith of toilet humour. A loo named after a fool, Simon had created genuine Comic Relief.

'It will have a little picture of you rowing the Channel in the bath, inlaid into the porcelain for people to aim at . . .'

Simon believes that *The FitzHigham* is only the second commemorative lavatory issued in the entire history of sanitaryware and he's a relentlessly enthusiastic sanarack.

'The first commemorative lavatory was produced in celebration of Queen Victoria's Jubilee . . .'

The FitzHigham turned out to look as stunning as it was eccentric. When people buy them, some of the money goes to Comic Relief. All Thomas Crapper loos have the company seal on them with 'Made in Great Britain' written round the edges of it. All except *The FitzHigham*; Simon left an 'e' off, so it reads 'Mad in Great Britain' instead. A few weeks after the first one was made I got a call from Simon.

'You've got a very strange bunch of friends. They all appear to want to go to the loo on you. I've got a waiting list for them now . . .'

The official position of the French government has never changed. Their position is very clear: to them, officially, the bath crossing of the English Channel never took place. The logic they use to justify this staggeringly silly position is that if it had happened, the French Navy would have been duty-bound to arrest me. Gallic logic dictates that as I was not arrested, the bath crossing must not have taken place.

It is a customary courtesy to any foreign nation in whose waters you find yourself to fly a small national flag of that country next to the larger one of your own. For the first failed attempt to cross the English Channel in the bath I happily flew a small courtesy *Tricolore* with my larger Red Ensign when in French waters. That *Tricolore* was lost in the storm during the first attempt. Due to the very unhelpful behaviour of the French government, with sadness at the death of *fraternité*, I refused to fly the *Tricolore* again. The successful crossing and subsequent trip round Kent to Tower Bridge was made with no French courtesy flag.

My time in the bath taught me something that I have been trying hard to share: we live in a nation where you can say, 'I'm going to do something really, really hard – like climb Everest, row the English Channel or run to Timbuktu.' Rather than being encouraging, the great British people will stoically stare you in the eye and say, 'It's not that hard.'

Or, 'What are you complaining about?'

Or, 'Get a hair cut.'

Perhaps the last one is just what they say to me. These discussions often carry on even after people have completed their achievements and fulfilled their dreams. There seems to be a tendency to look to discredit rather than support. But, if you say to those same stoic, staring-eyed Britons, 'I'm going to do something really, really hard – like climb Everest, row the English Channel or run to Timbuktu . . . *dressed up as a badger, wearing a diving outfit, or in a bathtub*', then they'll back you to the hilt. I'm not sure what it says about us as a nation in the 21st century but I offer it up as something I've found to be undeniably true. However, what this wonderful trait in our national character does mean is that if a Briton attempts something absurdly stupid with the unerring enthusiasm of a manic five-year-old they will be supported, encouraged and given every assistance the country has to offer.

It was September after the Edinburgh Festival had finished and somewhere in a pub in Hertfordshire I sat down. In front of me was the pint I'd rowed 170 extra miles to win.

'There you go, mate. Well earned.'

'Thanks.'

As I wrapped my lips around the cool glass and the delicious brown liquid hit the back of my throat I closed my eyes. Sometimes attempting the absurdly stupid can help achieve the impossible.

AFTERWORD

By Simon Kirby
Managing Director of
Thomas Crapper & Company

When Tim telephoned to explain his ridiculous idea, we assumed that my friend Ronnie Wootton was on the line. Ronnie is a well-known character in the architectural salvage trade who delights in making spoof telephone calls. My long-suffering secretary, a Czech girl called Radka, has dealt with many of his ludicrous enquiries, each delivered in one of a variety of accents. In addition he normally gives an 'interesting' name, for example: 'Edward Heath'; 'Rhett Butler'; 'Harry Lime' or 'Don Keebles'. (Say the latter out loud.)

Therefore when she heard the moniker 'Tim FitzHigham', she perhaps assumed it was another example of British humour. Crapper & Co seems to attract eccentrics like an antiques shop attracts VAT inspectors, so I expect it was inevitable that Tim would pitch up here one day. Warrick (our General Manager) and I decided instantly to support Tim in his heroic and very British endeavour, so we did what we could, having explained that we were rather financially over-committed.

We are based as far from the coast as it is possible to be within

241

these islands, and none of us has any maritime experience. Hence we had no idea how terribly dangerous was his plan; had we known, we would have tried to dissuade him!

Not that we could have succeeded. Even during the grim period after his first attempt, it was clear to us that he would try again. This despite his having been confounded (and nearly killed) by violent storms and the spite of bureaucrats. I am sure I would not survive even the training so I cannot begin to comprehend spending two years on such a project, including the performance of TWO Herculean rowing feats in hostile conditions. Whenever I see film of the first storm, I have to look away. Then I take two aspirin, and having prostrated myself, grasp the floorboards until the giddiness subsides.

The eccentric Tim FitzHigham is an inspiration: he accepts daunting challenges, he stands up for his beliefs and principles, he entertains everyone around him (as well as the paying public) and he raises huge sums for charities. For us, it was an honour to be of some assistance. Thank heaven there are still folk like him.

I am concerned that there are simply not enough of these people, so I decided to develop the impromptu declaration I made upon Tim's victorious embarkation of HMS *President*. Crapper & Co have been holding discussions with the Art Fund, the Tate Modern and English Heritage. Our joint proposal is that after he has been formally listed (Grade One, definitely) then that nice Mr Hirst will be commissioned to mount him in a Victorian bath full of aspic, and thus he will be preserved for posterity.

Sorry, Tim. I am aware that this is a little hard on you. But remember: once again, you are doing it for Britain!

THE APPENDICES

You've made it. Hope you enjoyed the book. I thought I'd include a few appendices – think of them as DVD extras for a book. So you can either read them or just turn off now ... up to you, but if you are going to turn off, may I take this moment to thank you for reading my story. Thank you.

Appendix A

A WORD FROM CHRIS GILMARTIN

Chris was on the support boat for the successful attempt and has kindly written this so it's over to him for his bit . . .

'Here's how I remember the bath affair. I was having an entertaining year off work, meeting up with Tim. During one long inebriated afternoon I agreed to help. I have a vague recollection of a few false starts, with Tim explaining the various weather, tide, crew issues . . . there seemed to be quite a few issues . . . but then there was a call where Tim said it all looked good.

'In Richmond I was introduced to a most important activity in boatyards: that of confused waiting. Eventually Tim backed the battered diesel estate car and trailer down the slip ramp and rowed the bath over to it, where the boatyard chaps manhandled it onto the trailer. I had to drive the car back up the ramp. Doing a hill start in an unfamiliar car with a third-of-a-tonne bath trying to pull you backwards into the Thames isn't recommended, but we got away with it, and a scant three hours late we were away. Stopping only to buy a mobile phone (previous one "got wet" which seemed a bit ominous) we headed down to Kent.

'We arrived in Folkestone, put the bath in the water and checked into the Hotel of Doom. The clientele looked like zombies, and the whole place had a faintly bizarre air about it, as if nobody actually expected paying guests to turn up. We were running very late though; I think we got to sleep about midnight, after setting alarms for 3 a.m.

'The morning started with Tim wolfing Weetabix as I prepped a bag for the support boat. The part where sunrise started was beautiful. Following this, things on the support boat settled into a routine. Essentially: have a cup of tea, chat, have another cup of tea, chat, and every now and then a gingernut biscuit (good for seasickness, Tim said) to break things up a bit.

'There were times when the sea was glassy smooth, and times we were getting bounced up and down so much that people got seasick. First it was cold, later everyone got sunburnt. Conditions were changeable, and at one point it looked like Tim was caught by the tide and would be swept too far south.

'Towards the end, I shouted "row like a bastard!" Clearly motivated by my exceptional coaching, he pulled through and all of a sudden it looked possible, probable, that he would make it. The shouts of support grew more strident. We'd helped him get this far, we weren't going to quit now, and neither was he.

'After about nine hours, he made it to the French coast. Unfortunately for him I think everyone shook Tim's hands, which probably hurt a bit. I recall he was unable to hold a phone, he seemed slightly delirious and rambling (yes, more than normal), and obviously overjoyed. Back in Folkestone we'd missed high tide so were unable to get the bath out of the water so Tim and I dropped into a local pub for a few well-earned beers.

'Tim hadn't changed out of his rowing outfit and it's fair to say this attracted attention. Attention turned into a rapt audience as Tim explained what he'd been doing that day. The locals turned out to be impressed, and Tim promptly recruited them to assist getting the bath out of the water at closing time. How Tim thought we'd have managed if we'd not chanced on a pub, I've no idea. I'm not entirely convinced he does either! Lashing it to the trailer was much harder than before as, due to a leak, the pontoons were half full of water.

'A short time later the phone call came: we were good to go again. I elected not to spend another day confined in the support boat, but instead drive the car and trailer up the coast taking pictures and videoing on the way.

'I was drinking tea then figured I should check out Deal before Tim arrived. As I got to the shore, there was Tim and the support boat, making great headway. Too much headway in fact, he was really moving. I ran shouting for people to get out of the way. I thundered down to the end of the pier, nearly fumbled the camcorder into the water, and caught the sight of Tim majestically sweeping past to a smattering of applause from some little old ladies.

'At Ramsgate there was some further slipway fun: this one really was slippery. I proudly donned my Wellingtons and waded in to assist. My Wellingtons leaked. We then went to the pub for a pint.

'I went back to my year off as whenever I was free Tim couldn't row, and when he could I wasn't around. In the end I had to head off before Tim made it to Tower Bridge. Tim finally finished his epic journey just after I'd started mine, albeit with more traditional transports . . . and much drier feet.'

APPENDIX B

THE BATH AND HISTORY

When I started rowing my bath I wasn't aware of the unsung but pivotal role in human history of that lowly piece of plumbing. While lowering our buttocks, how many of us have realised the bath or associated sanitaryware below us has been used variously as a grizzly weapon of death, kingmaker and even the hand of God. Things nearly ended badly for me. I believe the reason I survived is to put the record straight. Here are some of the most important times that humble ablution equipment has shaped the course of human history.

Eglon
The first time the lavatory was definitely used as an instrument of death is not recorded. Perhaps two cavemen got into a fight over which was the softest loo roll. However, the really brutal bit of the Bible (Judges 3:12–30), before God invented political correctness and mercy came to Him, has the lurid tale of Eglon, the very fat King of Moab who conquered Israel and went to the lavatory there for 18 years.

The Israelites wore out handkerchiefs crying to God for a deliverer.

God said the deliverer must be left-handed. Ehud was the son of Gera the Benjamite (isn't that a type of yeast-based sandwich spread?), a flourishing lefthander and the school lazy-rounders champion.

The Israelites sent Ehud to Eglon with a nice pressie to say how much they enjoyed him ruling them despotically. It was a double-edged sword a foot-and-a-half long. Eglon was not suspicious at this. Ehud said he had a message from God. Eglon was bursting to defecate so Eglon and Ehud went to the loo together. The last time anyone even mentioned double-edged swords and coming to the loo with me I discovered he'd also been putting Rohypnol in my Guinness for the previous two hours. But again Eglon was not suspicious. Eglon sat to evacuate his bowels and Ehud stabbed him so deep the handle went in after the blade and Eglon's blubber closed around it. Ehud scarpered out of the window.

By the time Eglon's servants crashed the door in, Ehud had taken up the trumpet in Seirah. After playing solos in a Dixieland jazz combo he led the armies of Israel against the people of Moab and murdered about 10,000 of them. Israel then took control of Moab and the bathroom had altered history's epic ebb for ever.

Agamemnon

Greek history was changed by one bath. Agamemnon was a classic Greek classical hero from one of the most distinguished families in Greece: notable ancestors included a murderer, a rapist, several cousin marriages and at least three raging pederasts. He became King of Mycenae and possibly Argos too. He'd ordered the Kingship of Mycenae from a catalogue but the one from Argos came by mistake. He wasn't sure if the mix up had occurred at the post office or in dispatch so ruled them both just in case.

He married Clytemnestra who was, in ancient Greek terms, a bit of a hottie (she does look quite stunning on the vases). Things were going well before Agamemnon said, 'Someone has to work in this relationship, darling,' and left to lead the Greeks in the Trojan War. It took a while and he missed his wife, so saying to himself 'what happens in war, stays in war' took a doomed prophetess called Cassandra for a bit of fun on the dark nights.

Eventually the war finished and he and Cassandra returned home to find Clytemnestra had also been a bit lonesome so had been ravaging Aegisthus.

Aegisthus was a sort of a cousin of Agamemnon's – with that much incest, bigamy, rape, murder and pederasty in the family, most people were. Aegisthus thought the best way to sort it out was to have Agamemnon round for tea. Nothing is ever so bad after a nice cup of tea. It was a long journey to Aegisthus's and Agamemnon fancied a bath. Clytemnestra fancied Aegisthus so went to the bathroom, seductively popped a blanket on Agamemnon as he dozed in the bath and brutally murdered him with an axe.

Cassandra the doomed prophetess waited for Agamemnon to finish in the bath, again cursing the mix up at the labour exchange. She'd actually applied to be a normal prophetess but they'd ticked the wrong box and she ended up a doomed one instead. Clytemnestra came out of the bathroom and killed Cassandra. 'The lives of doomed prophetesses never end well,' thought Clytemnestra as she and Aegisthus ruled Mycenae until family tradition got out of control in a party game and her son Orestes savagely murdered them both.

Seneca the Younger

Son of Seneca the Elder, Seneca the Younger was one of the greatest orators, statesman and stoic philosophers of Rome.

In his writings Seneca the Younger emphasised the need to live a moral life. In his life he slept with anything that moved: women, men, livestock and the wives of his friends being his favourites.

Eventually after a life of chronic excess he got caught up in the Pisonian Conspiracy – a plot to kill Nero who'd gone a bit far even for a Roman Emperor. Nero caught the conspirators and ordered his loyal friend Seneca to do the decent thing and slit his wrists.

Seneca had led such a life of excess that slitting his wrists didn't kill him; the blood (mainly alcohol) came out too slowly which only caused him minor irritation. With wrists bleeding Seneca then drank poison, which didn't work either, as it tasted better than the home brew at his local. He then jumped into a hot bath in an attempt to scald himself to death. That failed so he used the hot water to try and make the blood flow faster. This didn't work. Seneca next tried drowning himself. Even that didn't work. Slitting his wrists, downing poison, burning himself to death and drowning himself had failed. Finally he accidentally suffocated on the steam rising from the hot bath while trying to drown himself again.

Commodus

Lucius Aelius Aurelius Commodus Augustus Herculeus Romanus Exsuperatorius Amazonius Invictus Felix Pius (or Commodus as he was known to his cousin-mum) was the last of the Nervan-Antonian dynasty of Roman Emperors. Like all great Emperors, instead of eight great-grandparents he made do with six. He's the one played by Joaquin Phoenix in the film *Gladiator* with Russell Crowe. There's a few things in the film that don't totally reflect history but one major one that we must correct here.

Previous Roman Emperors had married horses but in 192 AD Commodus went madder than the rest. He re-named Rome the 'Colonia Lucia Annia Commodiana' and put defenceless wounded soldiers and people with no feet in the arena and clubbed them to death believing they were giants.

The Romans had had enough. Marrying horses was encouraged in Emperors, changing the name of Rome and beating unarmed amputees was not. As if to prove the Romans right, the Temple of Vesta burnt down. No one was anywhere near it with the matches, all of them said so. Commodus held Plebian games and had a Swan Vesta amnesty. He fought as a gladiator every afternoon. It was a bad year for the bookies as it was impossible for him to lose and treason for them not to give odds on him.

Eventually the bookies plotted to get rid of him. They poisoned his food but Commodus simply threw it up. The Romans remembered the trouble they'd had with Seneca Jr so decided to rely on the old failsafe.

In a tradition still alive and well in certain hotels in Rome, Commodus was sharing a bath with a nude wrestler called Narcissus, who was in the pay of the bookies. Commodus and Narcissus were on the third round of 'hunt the soap' when Narcissus strangled him to death.

All statues of him were toppled and Rome became Rome again thanks to two naked men wrestling in the bath. This didn't make the final cut of the film and they went with the slushy historically inaccurate stuff in the arena instead.

Elagabalus

Following the 'if it ain't broke . . .' school of politics, Elagabalus was another Roman Emperor who died in the bathroom. He was as bad and as mad as Commodus. Whereas Commodus offended Rome as a gladiator in the ring, Elagabalus offended Rome with an entirely different ring, working as a prostitute in the temples of Rome, taking all comers. His granny eventually had enough of this and had him murdered in the loo with his mum Julia Soaemias before replacing him as Emperor with another of his cousins less inclined to prostitution.

James the First

James I was King of Scotland from 1406-ish to 1437 (not officially crowned in 1406 but 1424. Easter was late that year). In 1437, on a routine trip to the bathroom while staying with some monks, Sir Robert Graham and a bunch of people battered on the loo door to kill him. A lady-in-waiting bravely stuck her arm through the clasps where the door bolt should have been and the King jumped into the loo to escape through the sewer. Loos didn't have U-bends in those days. Unfortunately for James he was a big fan of tennis.

He kept losing tennis balls down a drain near the tennis court so had the drain outlet blocked up. To his horror it turned out to be the outlet of the very drain he was trying to escape in. Stuck down the loo in the sewer, Robert Graham and the others brought his life to a very messy end.

Marat

Perhaps the most famous of all bath-based deaths. Jean-Paul Marat was born in Switzerland but became a great mate of Robespierre and gamely joined in with the French Revolution. Marat had to spend hours each day when he wasn't running France in the bath due to a mysterious skin complaint.

At that time things were more confused in Paris than usual and trying to simplify anyone's belief was impossible. The young Charlotte Corday, a Girondin (in favour of democratic revolution) with Royalist sympathies, used the old rouse from Ehud in the Bible and arrived at Marat's house with a message for him. She knew it wouldn't work if she said it was from God as the Revolutionaries weren't keen on Him. Cunningly she said it was from the townspeople of Caen. Marat never stopped thinking about politics or tottie so let her into the bathroom. She stabbed him to death. The French have been wary of baths ever since. Luckily the very famous artist Jacques-Louis David happened to be in Marat's bathroom at the time too and painted the most famous picture of a bath-based death in history.

Other important historical events involving baths.

Show-business people have had an even worse time with bathrooms than Roman Emperors.

The great comedian Lenny Bruce was found dead in the bathroom of an overdose. Charlie Chaplin's son, imaginatively called Charlie Chaplin Jr, also an actor, died in his grandma's bathroom. Judy Garland died in the bath of an overdose. Jim Morrison, the Doors singer, died in a bath in Paris of unknown causes. Elvis Presley died in the bathroom of Graceland of a heart attack: although he's been sighted and cited as a bathroom attendant many times since.

That bath ...

As the world's leading bathtub mariner, there's one bath that people always mention: history's most positive event involving plumbing.

King Hiero II of Syracuse had a new crown made in the shape of a laurel wreath. He wanted to know if it was made of solid gold or if the goldsmith had tricked him. At the time people could only measure the density of things if they were cube-shaped. The King didn't want to melt his new crown into a cube but was troubled by the shifty-looking goldsmith. Luckily the King was related to the greatest mathematician of all time: Archimedes.

Archimedes was taking a bath at the time and had realised, as he got in, that the water rose relative to his mass, discovering displacement. This effect could be used to determine the volume of the crown and therefore its density after it had been weighed. The more cheap metals had been added to the gold, the lower the density of the crown. Keen to tell his cousin, he jumped out of the bath and ran through the streets shouting 'Eureka' or 'εὑρηκα!' in Greek. Being a maths genius he was tolerated by the King, dripping wet and stark-naked in the throne room. The goldsmith had been cheating and Archimedes was given a towel. Archimedes is quiet on what happened to the goldsmith but the fairly smart money is on his business not going awfully well after that. The very smart money is always on a horse called Flirty Jill.

Appendix C

A COCKTAIL LIST ...

BIBO ERGO SUM

It's drinking things like these that led to the messy trip you've just read about. I'm not an alcoholic, I drink less than my doctor; but seeing his corpulent, heart-attack-primed form rolling around the surgery leads me to think that drinking in moderation is probably the best way to be. However, that said, here are a couple of belters for you to enjoy if you want to end up like my doctor. If I had a dream job it would be being a booze chef.

Shandy
I like ginger a lot. Between capsizing at university, losing the myriad temp jobs mentioned earlier and attempting to float in a paper boat, I lived abroad. A lot of my time there was spent farming. Ginger was one of the things that grew on the farm. It's also good for seasickness.

Before the Second World War if you ordered a shandy in a pub it would be made of beer and ginger ale. Then war came and ginger was scarce so they went over to making it with lemonade. That's why if you order it in a pub now, they will instinctively make it using lemonade, spilling it everywhere, as no barperson ever seems to have been taught to let it settle first.

My recipe for a really good shandy is to take three quarters of a pint of bitter and top the rest up with Stone's or Crabbie's Green Ginger Wine. I'd recommend not drinking more than a few of these as it turns out to be fairly potent.

When tucked up next to a fire on a cold winter night, this drink is great for two as you can have half pints each.

If it's the hot day in summer then you can apply it to lager too. Three quarters of a pint of lager and a quarter green ginger wine.

The Stir and Drink

I found this one when I was living abroad, too. I lived in a shed on stilts down a track cut into the hillside by goats running along it over the years. A little further up the track, where it hit the bigger track, was a rum shop run by a lovely lady called Miss Louie. I'd go there most nights after work. We'd tell stories, make each other laugh and play dominoes. Together we created a variant of something they used to drink in that village a long time before I arrived. It involves very strong dark rum: something around the 80% volume (160% proof) mark. Put a generous measure of dark rum into a glass. Add twice as much milk as the rum and enough Angostura Bitters to make the liquid go a chocolate colour. Just before the milk congeals, starts to turn to cheese or begins to look like a weather front in the glass stir briskly and drink. Do not drink this if you are lactose intolerant.

Another tip I got while I was abroad was from my grandfather. If you're ever worried about impure water, just add a spot of whiskey (or whisky), swill it round and that will kill most bugs.

The Polish

The Edinburgh Festival Fringe has changed quite a bit over the last few years from being one big fire-juggling party where people went to try new things out to becoming much more of a corporate trade fair for jokes.

Before the change there was a big party every night. Many of them were parties where no one knew who they knew, where they were or why they were partying. Edinburgh used to be like Lent but with the focus on taking up everything and creating excess for 40 nights rather than giving it up. It was the ultimate hedonists' playpen.

At one of these parties we realised that the bar was free and to celebrate I invented a new cocktail. The result was The Polish, named after the nice lady who was pouring the drinks. Again, it's got a touch of the ginger about it as one of the people I was with had flaming red hair.

I'm going to give you the amounts that make up a pint as that's the best thing to mix it in. Take half a pint of whisky (Scottish), add a quarter of a pint of green ginger wine and a quarter of a pint of ginger vodka. This is a drink designed for the professional debauchee and anyone wanting to invest in a serious hangover, guilt, remorse and denial the next morning.

Pimm's Casino Royal

This is a lovely drink for the summer but not mid- or high-afternoon. It is the late-afternoon sister of the Pimm's Royal. Simply put. Make all the loveliness of a Pimm's Royal with Pimm's, champagne and lashings of fruit then simply add sherry to taste. When people are falling away after a hot afternoon of playing, the introduction of something new to the taste buds will perk them up or lead them happily to a disco nap before the evening.

The Lancaster Bomber

This was an old naval favourite and was taught to me by my favourite Commander (now retired). It's called the Lancaster Bomber because it writes you off. The instructions were handed to me as follows. 'First find a large fermenting bucket or vat of some sort: empty into it one bottle of vodka, one bottle of Cointreau, one bottle of Grand Marnier. Add three litres of orange juice and four litres of lemonade. Gather team, finish vat and then you're ready for the Mess Dinner.' You don't have to be in the Navy to attempt this but I'd suggest any dinner after this will be messy.

APPENDIX D

MORE BATH-BASED SKULDUGGERY

Having rowed a bath people often ask about other bath-related things. This is another of those. It's on a par with Marat's death as another infamous episode in the history of sanitaryware. I've lifted the details on this from the Scotland Yard files. This is the case of the Bride of Bath Murders.

On 13 July 1912, Bessie Williams was found dead in her bath at 80 High Street, Herne Bay. Five days beforehand she'd made a new will in favour of her husband, Henry Williams. The doctor who examined Bessie convinced the inquest jury it was epilepsy and the cause of death was asphyxia brought about by drowning. The jury returned the verdict: 'Death by misadventure'.

Meanwhile George Joseph Smith was trying hard to please his future parents-in-law. Alice's father Mr Burnham said George was of a 'very evil appearance' so totally suitable to marry his daughter. On 12 December 1913 Alice went for a bath at the apartments she shared with her husband in Blackpool. She never returned. Her body was found much later. Her kindly landlord, Mr Crossley, noted that her head, unusually, was, at the foot of the bath. Alice had insured herself for £500; the beneficiary was her new husband. The inquest jury's verdict was that Alice had 'Accidentally drowned through heart failure when in the bath.'

On 18 December 1914, Margaret Elizabeth Lloyd (nee Lofty) was found dead in the bath at 14 Bismark Road, Highgate, London. Earlier that afternoon Margaret had made a will in favour of her husband John Lloyd. The verdict of the inquest jury was accidental death.

No one saw a pattern, until on 3 January 1915, Alice Smith's former landlord Mr Crossley wrote to the Metropolitan Police. He enclosed a newspaper cutting about the death of Margaret Lloyd, and remarked how similar it was to the death of Alice.

The Yard's finest sprang into action. Divisional Detective Inspector Neil went back to Herne Bay, Blackpool and Highgate and inspected the baths with pathologist Dr Sir Bernard H. Spilsbury (of the Crippen Case) who concluded all three baths were too small to allow grown women the space to drown.

Det. Insp. Neil was beginning to suspect that this was one of his most intricate cases yet. He came to the groundbreaking conclusion that Henry Williams, George Joseph Smith and John Lloyd might be the same person. He investigated Williams-Smith-Lloyd and found that he'd been born George Joseph Smith in Bethnal Green on 11 January 1872. In 1898 he married Caroline Beatrice Thornhill. Thornhill had been the Bonnie to his Clyde but got scared of him and fled to Canada in 1903. He then simultaneously married a widow Florence Wilson, Edith Peglar (under the name Oliver George Love), Sarah Freeman (under the name George Rose Smith) and Alice Reid (under the name Charles Oliver James). He cleaned out their savings and left them before marrying the first of his ill-fated brides: Bessie. How anyone at the Yard or more importantly Williams-Smith-Lloyd-Love-Smith-James was able to keep track of this is remarkable.

Det. Insp. Neil stopped Williams-Smith-Lloyd-Love-Smith-James on 1 February 1915 in Uxbridge Road. He appeared at Bow Street and was charged with 'causing a false entry to [be] made in a marriage register'.

But Williams-Smith-Lloyd-Love-Smith-James had more to worry about than bigamy. Although under British law at the time he could only be tried for the first murder, the court was informed of the other two to establish a pattern. The clinching evidence came from the 1915 Highgate funeral. The undertaker H.F. Beckett told the court he distinctly heard Williams-Smith-Lloyd-Love-Smith-James say to him, 'Get it over as quick as you can,' and after the funeral, 'Thank goodness that's all over.' Punctual or devious? The court went for the latter. He was found guilty of the murder of Bessie Williams, found dead in a bath, with Alice Burnham and Margaret Elizabeth Lofty taken into account. He was sentenced to death and executed at Maidstone Gaol on 13 August 1915.

Divisional Det. Insp. Neil, the Yard's finest, had won the day.

Appendix E

SOME POEMS . . .

Not sure including a poem by me is the best way to finish this off (see chapter 12 for details). Thankfully neither does Trevor the publisher.